Newport Library and Information
Ser

Z36

D1150278

TAUN HOUSE Libraries
newydd

Death Day

Renegades

Also by Shaun Hutson

SHAUN HUTSON OMNIBUS

Death Day
Renegades

SHAN HUTSON

A *Time Warner* Paperback

This omnibus edition first published in Great Britain by
Time Warner Paperbacks in 2003
Shaun Hutson Omnibus Copyright © Shaun Hutson 2003

Previously published separately:
Death Day first published in Great Britain in 1987 by
Star Books, A Division of W. H. Allen & Co plc
Published by Sphere Books Ltd in 1990
Reprinted 1990
Published by Warner Books in 1992
Reprinted 1993, 1994, 1995, 1996, 1997, 1998, 1999, 2001
Reprinted by Time Warner Paperbacks in 2002
Copyright © Shaun Hutson 1986

Renegades first published in Great Britain in 1991 by
Macdonald & Co (Publishers) Ltd
Published by Sphere Books Ltd in 1991
Reprinted 1991
Published by Warner Books in 1997
Reprinted 1999, 2001
Reprinted by Time Warner Paperbacks in 2002
Copyright © Shaun Hutson 1991

The moral right of the author has been asserted.

*All characters in this publication are fictitious and any
resemblance to real persons, living or dead, is purely coincidental.*

All rights reserved.
No part of this publication may be reproduced, stored in a retrieval
system, or transmitted, in any form or by any means, without the prior
permission in writing of the publisher, nor be otherwise circulated in any
form of binding or cover other than that in which it is published and
without a similar condition including this condition being imposed on
the subsequent purchaser.

A CIP catalogue record for this book is available from the British Library.

ISBN 0 7515 3500 1

Printed and bound in Great Britain by
Mackays of Chatham plc, Chatham, Kent

Time Warner Paperbacks
An imprint of
Time Warner Books UK
Brettenham House
Lancaster Place
London WC2E 7EN

www.TimeWarnerBooks.co.uk

Death Day

AUTHOR'S NOTE

I always think that this kind of message at the beginning of a book should be more aptly called 'Author's Intrusion'. Those of you who agree with me will doubtless already be well immersed in chapter one. For those of you who remain with me, please excuse this brief moment of pretension and accept a word of explanation.

Death Day was originally written when I was nineteen, one of many manuscripts with which, at the time, I was bombarding publishers in the hope of getting accepted. Don't worry, this isn't going to turn into a 'How I made it after years of struggling' congratulatory introduction. I just want to say that there are ideas and themes in *Death Day* which were developed in my later books so, if you happen to find a scene that seems slightly familiar to some of my other stuff, don't think you're being ripped off. You're not. I leave *that* to certain other authors. Nevertheless, apologies for any feelings of déjà vu in my regular readers. To those of you reading *Death Day* without having read my other work I have just one question: where have you been for the last six years?

Right, this is starting to become too self-indulgent. The novel beckons. But first, some people who deserve thanks for what they've done during the past few years. This list could be longer than the book so I'll be brief this time. Many thanks to Nicola Davies, who first wondered if there might be *something* about this novel. To Bob Tanner (—blame him, he launched me). Special thanks to Sheelagh 'Smoke on the Water' Thomas for her continuing work with my efforts. To Ray Mudie and 'The Wild Bunch' (otherwise known as W. H. Allen's sales team). In fact, to everyone at W. H. Allen I extend my thanks. And, most important of all, to my parents and to Belinda.

To those named and dozens more who've given me friendship, love, inspiration and support (and who'll doubtless be mentioned in the acknowledgements of the *next* book . . .), thank you.

Shaun Hutson

> *'Hell hath no limits,*
> *nor is circumscribed in one self place;*
> *for*
> *where we are is Hell,*
> *And*
> *where Hell is must we ever be . . .'*

—Christopher Marlowe

PROLOGUE

The woman was thrown to the floor of the tiny cell, her face ground into the reeking straw which covered the stone. She made few sounds, even as a heavy boot was driven into her ribs. She felt bone splinter and the air was torn from her. Powerful hands dragged her to her feet, pinning her against the cold wall. Her head was wrenched up by her long hair until she was face to face with the tallest of the three men.

His face was shrouded by deep shadows, some caused by the gloom inside the cell, but most by the wide brim of his hat. He stood in silence, watching her through heavily lidded eyes. She met his stare, the merest trace of a smile on her lips.

The two men on either side of her suddenly released their grip on her wrists and began tearing her clothes from her. Her full breasts swung into view, already marked with numerous scratches and red welts. She did little to resist as they tore the last clothing from her and then slammed her, naked, back against the wall.

The tall man reached into his pocket and pulled something out. It looked like a piece of wood, as thick as a man's finger but it bore a needle like point of steel. He touched the point to a place close by her right nipple and pushed.

Now she broke her silence and screamed as the steel punctured her flesh. Blood welled up and dripped from her wound.

He repeated the procedure until her chest was reduced to a bleeding ruin. He reached lower, pushing it into her belly.

Pain lanced through her and she felt as if she would pass out but rough hands tugged at her hair and face, slapping hard until she found her vision clearing.

The tall man stepped back, pocketing the pointed implement.

'Speak,' he said, quietly. 'Where is your master?'

The woman met his gaze but did not answer. She felt one of her arms being forced up her back, the strain on the joint becoming intolerable.

'Where is your master?' the tall man repeated.

Her shoulder felt as though it were burning as yet more pressure was exerted on her twisted limb.

She opened her mouth in silent agony.

There was a loud crack as the arm broke, unable to withstand any more such pressure. The bone snapped above the elbow, the power exerted on it so great that the shoulder was dislocated too.

The woman screamed loudly.

'You think he would hesitate to speak your name where he in *your* position now?' the man asked her.

Her head sagged forward for a moment and

the tall man nodded towards his companions who immediately took a firmer hold on the woman's arms and began dragging her from the cell. Along a narrow dripping corridor they took her until they reached a larger room. There they secured her to the stone wall with shackles and one of them hurled some water at her. It revived her, the clear liquid dripping from her body, mingling with the blood which had congealed there.

She saw the tall man reach for the branding iron, its tip white hot as he pulled it from the brazier. A flicker of fear passed behind her eyes as he approached her with it, the glowing end mere inches from her face.

'What is the secret of the circlet?' he asked.

She gritted her teeth and shook her head.

The iron came closer until she could feel the heat then, in a moment of mind numbing agony, she felt it touch her cheek. Her scream rose mightily within the room as the burning metal seared her flesh, a great raw welt rising beneath the brand. The acrid stench of her burnt skin filled her nostrils and she passed out.

More water was flung at her, hands slapped hard at her cheeks until she regained consciousness.

The tall man remained before her, the branding iron still burning hot.

She closed her eyes, tears spilling down her cheeks.

'Why prolong the pain?' the tall man asked her. 'Speak now. Is it true that the circlet only afflicts those who are first to touch it?' He moved the glowing iron closer. 'Only those who are first to touch the amulet are tainted. Is that true?'

She didn't answer.

He snarled and pressed the red hot rod to her breast.

It took much longer to revive the woman this time but when she did eventually come round she felt heat between her spread legs. The iron had been re-heated and now, the probing brand, white hot, hovered precious inches from that most sensitive area.

'Is it true about the amulet?' the tall man asked her, the rod like some burning, agonizingly hot penis. It quivered between her legs.

'Yes,' she shrieked. 'The first to touch the amulet is tainted but none thereafter until my Master has held it again.'

The tall man smiled and turned away from her. He replaced the branding iron in the coals and turned back to face the woman. She felt sick, the pain which racked her body gripping her like a fist. The other two men unshackled her and dragged her from the room, back along the corridor but this time up into the daylight.

There were hundreds of people standing outside the building. They shouted things at her as she was thrown to the ground amongst them. Some spat at her. But the babble died down as the tall man emerged into the light.

'Let all know that in this, the year of Our Lord 1596,' he began. 'This woman has confessed to the sins of which she was accused. She knows the secret of the amulet and he who holds it.'

He pointed an accusing finger at her.

'There is but one punishment for this blasphemy.'

It took but a moment for them to find a rope and secure a stout knot. Two of them looped it round her neck and dragged her to the nearest tree, where they took hold of the end and tugged her up into the air. She kicked and struggled for what seemed like an eternity, spittle and blood dribbling over her cracked lips but, eventually, her movements ceased and only the wind stirred her motionless form.

'We have dealt with the disciple,' said the tall man. 'Let us destroy the Master.'

There was a roar of approval from the crowd, many brandishing pitchforks and clubs above their heads.

'Let us rid ourselves of this pestilence forever,' the tall man said. 'We know where its source lies, let us erase it from God's earth.'

He set off, followed by the maddened crowd. They knew their destination and there was a firm determination about them.

However, many shuddered as, overhead, dark clouds began to gather and the first soundless fork of lightning rent the air.

'Be not afraid, God is with us,' the tall man called.

The storm clouds gathered in huge black masses. Like dark warnings.

PART
ONE

1

There was a dampness in the morning air which promised rain.

The sky was heavy with clouds, great, grey, washed out billows which scudded across the heavens, pushed by the strong breeze. The same breeze which stirred the naked branches of trees. They stood defiantly against the wind, shaking skeletal fingers at an invisible defiler which rocked and battered their flimsy forms. Birds huddled in the branches, feathers stirred and ruffled by the strengthening gusts.

Rain-soaked piles of leaves lay in tightly packed masses about the tree bases.

Seasonal transition had nature in limbo. The time when winter has passed but the earth has not yet erupted into that frenzy of greenery which is spring. That time was still to come.

There had been more rain during the night. Enough to darken the concrete paths of Medworth. The town had its fair share of rain, standing, as it did, in the rolling hills of Derbyshire. The nearest town of any size lay twenty miles away to the west, but the people of Medworth were content with their own patch of miniature metropolis. The town was small, a population which struggled to reach nine thousand, but there was plenty of work within the town itself. It was built around a large shopping centre. The shops themselves employed more than a third of the total labour force, many of the rest being accounted for by the town's small industrial estate built a mile or so out. It consisted of a small iron foundry and brewery as well as a number of smaller factories.

The few farms which were scattered on the hills nearby were concerned mainly with arable crops, the odd scatterings of livestock kept for the benefit of the individual farmers rather than for any serious commercial purposes.

To call Medworth a thriving community would have been an overstatement, but it ticked along comfortably, satisfied with its own seclusion.

There was little entertainment to be found. The old cinema had closed down two years earlier and now remained nothing more than an eyesore in the centre of town. A large building, almost imposing in its obsolescence, it stood at the top of the main street, now just a darkened shell.

Its presence represented a reminder of the past, of a time when life was lived at a slower pace. Progress had come slowly and almost resentfully to Medworth.

By eight o'clock that morning there were people in the streets, and, an hour later, another working day had begun.

2

Tom Lambert brought the Capri to a halt and switched off the engine. He looked out of the side window and read the sign which spanned the iron gates.

'Two Meadows.'

In ordinary circumstances he would have smiled. The name of the cemetery always amused him. After all, it was built on a hillside two miles outside of town. Not a meadow in sight.

Lambert sighed and ran a hand through his short brown hair, catching sight of his own pale face in the rearview mirror as he did so. He readjusted it, as though not wanting to see his reflection. The wind rustled quietly around the car, somehow far away. It seemed to him as though, here inside, he was insulated against all sound and sensations.

He wished it was an insulation against his own emotions.

As he climbed out of the car, Lambert realized just how cold the wind was. He shook himself and pulled up the collar of his leather jacket before reaching onto the back seat to retrieve a bunch of carnations. He sniffed them. No scent.

Greenhouse variety. He locked the door and pocketed the keys.

His feet clattered noisily on the pebble driveway of the cemetery. He wondered why they had never bothered to pave the path. It wound right through the cemetery before disappearing out of another gate a mile and a half further on. That was one of the things which always amazed Lambert. The sheer size of the place. There seemed enough plot acreage to bury half the population of Britain, never mind the occupants of Medworth.

He continued up the path, passing the first rows of gravestones. The plots were in various states of disrepair according to their age or the consciences of those who had buried someone there. Few of the older graves bore flowers. An urn might sport a few withered blooms but most were bare.

To Lambert's right, along a broken path, stood the church. Its great steel-braced oak doors were closed. The bell tower, topped by the twisted black spire, dominated the bleak skyline and as he looked up, he could see the battered weather vane twisting in the wind.

Almost thankfully, he reached the footpath which led off from the main drive. The noise of the crackling pebbles was beginning to grate on his nerves and as he walked along the muddy path between the rows of gravestones he was pleased by the silence. It was broken only by the mournful sighing of the wind in the nearby trees. They stood like sentries, watching him pick his way through the maze of stone memories, and if they could have spoken they would have known

18

this young man. Lambert had been coming here at the same time for the last two weeks and he wondered how much longer he would continue to do so. Perhaps his entire life would be spent edging his way between marked and unmarked graves, looking for one in particular. The same one he came to every morning at nine o'clock.

Beneath the shade of a huge oak tree, he found it.

Amidst the brown and grey of the cemetery, the plot stood out with an almost unnatural blaze of radiance. Flowers of every kind were laid across it, some still wrapped with the cellophane in which they'd been brought. He bent and picked off two fallen leaves which had found their way from the low tree branch onto the grave. Lambert lowered his head. He didn't need to read the inscription for he had it burned into his mind. It was there constantly, gnawing away at him like some kind of parasite.

'Michael Lambert—Died January 5th 1984'

He had been twenty.

Lambert thought that most of his emotion was spent but, as he bent to lay the bunch of carnations on the grave, a single tear slipped from his eye corner and rolled down his cheek. He straightened up, wiping it away. He stared down at the grave. His brother's grave. He gritted his teeth until his jaws ached. He wanted to shout, to scream at the top of his voice. Why? Why did it have to be Mike?

He spun round in a paroxysm of helpless rage, driving one fist as hard as he could into the solid bark of the oak. Pain shot up his arm but he ignored it, his back now turned to the grave as if he could feel his brother's eyes staring out reproachfully at him. Images flashed into his mind.

The car. The screaming of brakes. The explosion.

Oh Jesus Christ, he wanted to scream again.

Lambert felt the tears running more swiftly down his cheeks now as the thoughts returned with a clarity which sickened him. Living with the memory was bad enough, if only it weren't so vivid . . .

They had gone out that night, ten of them including Mike and himself. What was it blokes liked to call it, the last fling? Stag night, booze up, piss party, call it what you like. It had been the night before Mike was due to get married. A right little cracker he was landing too. Sally. He couldn't remember her last name, but he realized what a lucky man Mike was. Lambert himself was to have been the best man. He was going to drive Mike home that night, *he* was going to be the one who kept his eye on his baby brother. (There was three years between them, Mike was twenty, Lambert had just turned twenty-three.) *He* was the one who was going to stay sober, let Mike get boozed up, let him enjoy his last night.

Now, as he remembered how prophetic that statement turned out to be, Lambert hated himself even more.

They had carried on drinking late into the night but it had been Mike who had remained sober, Lambert himself who had got pissed. So pissed he asked Mike to drive them home. So pissed he had not closed his car door properly (the thing that probably saved his own life). So pissed he'd forgotten Mike had only passed his driving test a few weeks earlier and had no experience at night driving.

And now he remembered, how the car went out of control as it hit the patch of black ice. How the car swerved and *he* was thrown clear while Mike struggled with the wheel, trying to avoid the lamp post.

Drunk and in pain, Lambert had seen the car smash into the lamp post. Seen Mike catapulted through the windscreen, heard his scream of agony as the jagged glass shredded his face and upper body. Then Lambert had crawled across to his brother's body and sat with him, ignoring the blood which had splashed for fifteen feet across the pavement, ignoring the pieces of glass embedded in Mike's face and neck, the final spoutings of his blood jetting darkly into the night.

When the ambulance arrived, Lambert had been sitting on the pavement holding his dead brother's hand. At that precise moment of course he didn't know that Mike was dead. He only realized that when the two ambulance men lifted the shattered body. There was a dull thud and the head dropped to the ground, the neck severed by the savage cuts.

At that point, Lambert had collapsed.

And now, he found the courage to look back at his brother's grave. He wiped the tears away, suddenly becoming aware of just how cold the wind was getting. He shivered, cold in spirit as well as body.

'Shit,' he said aloud, shaking his head. He

inhaled, held the breath then let it out very slowly.

The family had been very understanding about it. God, how fucking ironic, how bloody magnanimous of them, he thought. Never mind about your brother, it wasn't your fault. He felt suddenly angry. So, maybe it wasn't his fault, but, he told himself, what good were consolations when you had to live with the thought for the rest of your life?

He'd woken screaming for nights afterwards. Debbie understood, she always understood. He thanked God he had her. They'd been married two years but already he wondered what the hell he'd have done without her. If he hadn't had her with him during the last couple of weeks he'd have gone up the wall. Everyone had been very understanding but it had done nothing to ease the guilt. He wondered what would.

There had been nothing about it in the newspapers. Lambert knew Charles Burton, the man who ran *The Medworth Chronicle*. The two men disliked one another but Lambert had managed to persuade him not to mention his name in the local rag. It wouldn't have done his reputation much good either. He'd been surprised that he hadn't heard more from Divisional HQ in Nottingham. Lambert, as head of Medworth's small police force, could do without the kind of publicity which the crash might have brought. He was surprised he hadn't been asked to resign or some such drastic measure, but, as Debbie had said to him at the time, he hadn't killed his own brother. He had only been involved in the accident which had taken his life.

Lambert was the only one who felt like a murderer.

He lingered a moment longer, then, almost reluctantly, he turned and made his way back along the path between the graves until he reached the gravel drive.

It was after nine but he was in no hurry. He'd been told to take a month off. Get his thoughts back into one piece. The men under him were all capable. Capable enough at least to run things until he returned.

He walked, head bowed, collar turned up against the wind. Lost in his own thoughts, he almost bumped into the tall man coming through the cemetery gates.

The man was carrying a pick over his shoulder and there was a younger man behind wearing a pair of bright orange overalls.

Lambert sidestepped the pair who continued up the gravel drive, their mud-caked boots making it sound as if they were walking on cornflakes. Lambert saw their council van parked across the road outside the vicarage. There was movement in the bay window of the building and Lambert saw Father Ridley standing inside. He waved cheerfully to the young man who raised a hand in weary acknowledgement. He fumbled in his pocket for his keys and unlocked the car door. He slid behind the wheel, started the engine and swung the car round, pointing it down the hill in the direction of the town. Lambert flicked on the radio but, after a moment or two found that he didn't feel like listening to music. He switched the set off.

He drove the rest of the way in silence.

'It'll take until next Christmas to clear this lot,' said Ray Mackenzie, dropping his pick dejectedly.

He was looking at a patch of ground about half the size of a football pitch, surrounded on three sides by densely planted trees. Some had even encroached into the heavily overgrown area itself. The grass and weeds were waist high in places and, as Mackenzie stepped forward, he snagged his arm on a particularly tall gorse bush. He muttered something to himself and kicked at it.

The area was beyond the main part of the cemetery, two hundred yards or more from the central driveway along which they had just come. Situated in a slight hollow, it was effectively masked from the rest of the area. Only the fact that the top halves of the trees poked up above the rim of the crest testified to its existence. The grass was neatly cut only up to the very edge of the crest then it sloped down into the area where the two men stood. Nature run riot.

'Fancy letting it get in this state in the first place,' complained the younger of the two men. Steve Pike had quite fancied the idea of working for the council at first. Weeding the flower beds in the town gardens, cutting the grass in the park? It had seemed like a good idea. As he surveyed the expanse of twisted gorse, bracken, heather and waist high grass he began to have second thoughts.

Father Ridley had called the council offices and asked if they could send some men to clear a patch of ground for him.

'Well,' said Mackenzie. 'Standing here looking at it isn't going to make it go away.'

With that he drove his pick into the ground, turning a large clod. He grimaced as he saw the size of the worm which clung to it. He broke the clod with his pick and continued digging. Steve stood watching him.

'Come on,' snapped Mackenzie. 'Get the sickle and cut some of that stuff down.' He pointed to a dense growth of ragweed which was fully two feet high. Steve went to the canvas bag they had brought with them and pulled out the sickle, then he set to work, hacking away at the recalcitrant plants. Mackenzie swapped his pick for a shovel and was soon turning the earth. But it was quite a battle.

Steve too found that the roots of the bramble and gorse bushes went deeper than he thought. Great thick tendrils of root clung to the earth like bony fingers.

They worked on. Yet despite the fury of their exertions, both men began to notice something odd. Both were soaked in sweat but both could feel their bodies trembling from the cold. A cold the like of which neither had experienced before. A deep, penetrating cold which was almost oppressive. Mackenzie stopped digging and looked up.

Another thirty minutes and the men decided that it was time they stopped for a while. Steve looked around. They had done quite well considering the size of the problem. At least a quarter of the overgrown area had been cleared, the earth now dark beneath their feet. Mackenzie looked at his watch. The second hand was frozen. It had stopped, the hands pointing to 9:30. He shook it and grunted.

'What's up?' asked Steve, taking the fag he was offered.

'My bloody watch has stopped,' Mackenzie told him.

Steve rolled up his sleeve, his forehead creasing. He tapped the face of his own time-piece.

'So has mine,' he exclaimed, extending his arm so that Mackenzie could see. The twin hands were immobile.

Stuck at 9:30.

Lambert parked the Capri in the small driveway beside the house and got out. The next door cat scampered across the front lawn as he walked up the path to the back door and he hissed at it. The startled animal spun round and fled off through a hole in the fence. Lambert smiled thinly to himself.

He found his back door key and let himself in. It was after nine-thirty so he knew that Debbie would be gone. She always left well before nine, sometimes before he even drove for the cemetery. The kitchen smelt of pine and new

26

wood, and Lambert inhaled deeply. He crossed to the kitchen table and sat down, noting that two letters were propped up against the tea pot. He smiled again. Although the letters were addressed to Mr and Mrs T. Lambert, Debbie had left them for him to open. She always did. He considered the envelopes for a moment then dropped them back onto the table and crossed to the sink to fill the kettle. He stood for a moment, looking out of the back window, thinking how badly the grass needed cutting. The gardens on either side were in a worse state and that, at least, comforted him somewhat.

Their house was roomy, semi-detached, with three bedrooms, a dining room, kitchen and spacious living room. The third bedroom was to be used as a nursery when, and if, the need ever arose. Lambert looked down into the aluminum bottom of the sink and saw his own distorted image staring back at him. At the present time, there was no talk of children. Both he and Debbie had promising careers: he was one of the youngest Inspectors in the Midlands force and Debbie was chief librarian at the large Victorian looking building in the centre of Medworth. Lambert shook his head. An Inspector in charge of a force of less than twelve. That was police logic for you.

The shrill whistling of the kettle interrupted his thoughts. He made the tea, poured himself a cup and carried it into the living room where the daily paper was waiting on the arm of his chair. Debbie again. God how he loved that girl. He suddenly began to feel warmer, the incidents of the morning gradually subsiding. Diminishing but never fading.

He flicked through the paper, hardly seeing the words, then he folded it up and stuck it in the paper rack. Lambert gazed across at the bay window.

It was the inactivity more than anything which wore him down. The same routine every day, stuck in the house trying to find jobs that he'd already done two days before. The doctor had told him to rest for a month after the accident, but the time was dragging into an eternity. He glanced down at the phone on the table beside his chair and rubbed his chin contemplatively. Should he ring the station? Just to find out if they needed him for anything?

He grunted and turned away, warming his hands around the mug of steaming tea. He eyed the phone again but, instead, went and retrieved the letters from the kitchen. He tore the first of them open, knowing from the 'Private' stamp on the top left hand corner that it was a bill of some sort. Electricity. He muttered something to himself and re-folded it then tore open the second.

It was from his mother. He read it briefly, not really seeing the words on the blue tinted pages. Everything was all right, his father was fine. Hope he was feeling better. Etc., etc., etc. Tactfully no mention of Mike. He pushed the letter to one side and finished his tea. The same old crap every time. Debbie usually replied to them. Lambert picked up the letter once more and read the line which never failed to annoy him.

'Your father is fine.'

He threw it down. Father. Fucking stepfather. His own father had been dead for ten years. Lambert had watched him die, day by day. A little at a time. He remembered coming home from school every dinner time when he was twelve and finding his father sitting at the table, the bottle of whisky gripped in his palsied hand. Lambert hated him for his drinking, he hated him for what it had made him. But most of all, he hated his mother because she was the reason his father had begun drinking in the first place. Her and her fancy man. Mr Ted bloody Grover. 'Your father.' His new father, his fucking stepfather.

He tore the letter up savagely, hurling the pieces away from him in rage, his breath coming in short gasps.

Cirrhosis of the liver had caused his real father's death. Or precipitated it anyway. Lambert remembered finding him that day. His head thrown back, his eyes open. The yellow blobs of vomit still on his lips, the empty bottle gripped in his rigid fingers. Choked on his own puke.

Why was it, Lambert thought, that the painful memories always stayed more vivid than the pleasant ones? To him at any rate.

He reached for the phone and dialled Medworth police station. The phone rang a couple of times, then was picked up.

'Medworth Police Station,' the voice said.

Lambert smiled, recognizing the voice as sergeant Vic Hayes.

'Morning, Vic,' he said.

'How you keeping, sir?'

'Not bad. What's doing?'

There was a pause at the other end as Hayes tried to think of something he could tell his superior. His tone sounded almost apologetic, 'Nothing really. Mrs Short lost her purse in the Bingo hall, she thinks it was nicked. Two kids took a bike from outside old man Sudbury's shop and I've got bloody flu, that's all I can tell you.' The sentence was finished off with an almighty sneeze.

Lambert nodded, 'So there's nothing worth me coming in for?'

'No, sir. Anyway, aren't you supposed to be resting? I heard that the doctor gave you a month off.'

'How the hell do you know that?' asked Lambert, good naturedly.

'I bumped into your wife the other day,' Hayes explained. There was silence for a moment, then the sergeant said, 'By the way, sir, we were all very sorry about what happened.'

Lambert cut him short, 'Thanks.' He moved hurriedly on. 'Look, Vic, if anything does turn up, let me know, will you? Sitting at home here is driving me up the bloody wall.'

'Will do, sir.'

They said their goodbyes and Lambert hung up, plunged once more into the silence of the room. He clapped his hands together as if trying to shake himself free of the lethargy which gripped him. He got up, tired of the silence, and crossed to the record player. He selected the loudest recording that they had in their collection and dropped it onto the turntable.

Someone thundered out 'Long Live Rock &

Roll' and Lambert went back into the kitchen to make himself some breakfast.

Already, the emotions were slipping to the back of his mind, waiting to be stirred perhaps the next day, but, for now, he began to feel brighter.

'Long Live Rock & Roll' blasted on.

Debbie Lambert looked at her watch and noted with delight that it was nearly one o'clock. She took off her glasses and massaged the bridge of her nose between thumb and forefinger. There was a nagging ache behind her eyes and she closed them for a moment. The ledgers lay before her as if defying her to carry on work. This was the only part of her job she hated. Cataloguing. She was thankful it only happened once a year. Every book in the library, all 35,624 of them, had to be listed by author, publisher and serial number. She'd been working at it now for more than a week and hadn't even got half way. She resolved to take some of it home with her that night.

Mondays were usually quiet, but today there were agitated babblings from the direction of the children's section. A party of twenty kids from the local infants school had been brought in with the idea of introducing them to the delights of a library. Debbie could see two of the little darlings giggling uncontrollably as they pawed through a book on early erotic art. She barely suppressed a grin herself, especially when the kids looked up and saw her watching them. They both turned the colour of a pillar box and hurriedly replaced the book.

'Don't you just love kids?' said Susan Howard, struggling past with an armful of books.

Debbie raised one eyebrow questioningly and Susan laughed. Nice girl, thought Debbie, about twenty, a year or so younger than herself. They got on well together. All the staff in the building did. There were just four of them: herself, Susan, Mrs Grady and Miss Baxter (who took care of the research section, or reference library as everyone else liked to call it). Debbie had wondered whether Miss Baxter would resent being under a woman more than thirty years younger than herself, but there had been no animosity shown. The previous head librarian had died three years before and few people suspected that the job would go to someone as young as Debbie, but her aptitude for the job was undeniable. She had, since she took over, tried to change the image of the building somewhat. She disliked the staid, Victorian picture of libraries which most people had. Of old spinsters in long skirts and horn-rimmed glasses hobbling about the corridors, and endless leather-bound dusty volumes which no one ever read. Since she had taken over, more youngsters had joined. Attracted no doubt by the presence of Susan, and, she hoped, herself. More men were members now than ever before.

She dropped her glasses into her handbag and stood up, shaking her legs to restore the circulation. She'd been sitting in more or less the same position for nearly four hours, bent over the ledgers and her shoulders and legs felt as if someone had been kicking her. She exhaled deeply and swept a hand through her shoulder-length blonde hair.

'Sue,' she called quietly, 'I'm just popping out for lunch.'

The other girl nodded and struggled on with her armful of books.

Debbie walked out, the noise of her high heels clicking conspicuously on the polished wooden floor. As she reached the exit door she eyed her reflection in the glass and smiled. She had a good figure, slim hipped, the small curve of her bottom accentuated by the tight jeans which she wore. The thick jumper which covered her upper body concealed her pert breasts and made her look shapeless, but she dressed for comfort, not show.

As she stepped out into the street, an arm enfolded her waist and she spun round anxiously.

It was Lambert.

Debbie smiled broadly and kissed him.

'I thought you were at home,' she said happily.

He shrugged, 'I ran out of things to do. You were the last resort.' He smiled as she punched him on the arm.

'Cheeky sod,' she giggled. 'I was just going for lunch.'

'I know.'

'My God, you're not a policeman for nothing, are you?' she said sarcastically, trying not to smile.

He slapped her hard across the backside. 'Come on, Miss Librarian, let me buy you some lunch.'

The nearest cafe was busy but they found a seat near the window and Debbie sat down while

33

Lambert fetched the lunch, picking food out from beneath the plastic fronted cabinets. He returned with a laden tray and began unloading it onto the table.

As they ate, she told him about her morning's work and about the kids. He smiled a lot. A little too much perhaps. She reached across the table to clutch his hand.

'You all right?' she asked.

He nodded, 'I walked down here to meet you,' he told her, 'I needed the air.'

She smiled, then trying to sound brighter, 'Were those letters anything important this morning?'

He told her about the bill. 'The other one was from my mother.'

'What did she have to say? Or do you want me to read it when I get home?'

'I tore the fucking thing up,' snapped Lambert.

Two women on the table next to them looked round, and the policeman met their stare. They returned quickly to their tea, and gossip.

'What did it say?' asked Debbie, squeezing his hand tighter.

He shrugged and took a sip of his tea before answering, 'The same old shit. Same as always. I don't know why the hell she can't just leave me alone. I never asked her to start writing in the first place.' He slammed his cup down with a little bit too much force, making a loud crack.

The two women looked round again and this time Lambert thought about saying something. But he returned his gaze to Debbie. Her eyes were wide, searching his own, trying to find something that lay beneath his visible feelings.

There was a long silence between them. The only sound was that of many voices talking at once, each lost in their own world, making sense alone but, combined, becoming a noisy babble of nonsense. People around them chatted about the weather, their families, their jobs. The everyday monotony of life.

'I phoned the station,' said Lambert, at last.

'Why?' asked Debbie.

'I wondered if there was anything I could do, or if they needed me.'

Debbie looked at him reproachfully, 'Tom, the doctor told you to rest. You're not supposed to be at work. Sod the bloody station. They can run things without you.'

'I can't sit at home all day doing nothing,' he protested, 'it's driving me crazy.'

'Well, going back to the station isn't going to help either.'

'At least it might give me something else to think about. That's what I need, something to take my mind off what's been happening. You don't understand what it's like, Debbie,' he gripped her hand. 'I relive that bloody accident, that night, every time I visit Mike's grave. Even when I'm not there, it's still with me, you don't forget something like that easily.'

'No one expects you to. Just stop blaming yourself.' She didn't know whether to be angry with him, or feel pity.

'Shit,' he said it through clenched teeth, his head bowed.

She watched him for long seconds, a feeling

of total helplessness slowly enveloping her. Finally he looked up and swallowed hard, 'I'm sorry,' he whispered.

'Don't be,' she told him.

He shook his head, moisture brimming in his eyes. He exhaled deeply, 'I asked Hayes to get in touch with me if they need me anytime.'

She opened her mouth to speak but he raised his hand, 'It's the only way, Debbie. I'll go off my head otherwise.'

They finished eating. He looked across the table at her and smiled. She glanced up at the clock on the wall of the cafe and saw that it was approaching two o'clock.

'I've got to be getting back,' she said, reluctantly.

'I'll walk you,' he said, standing up.

The town was busier as they walked back to the library. People were looking in shop windows and talking on street corners. A number spoke to the young couple as they walked, as both were well known within the town.

When they reached the steps of the building, Lambert put his arms around his wife's waist and kissed her.

'What will you do this afternoon?' she asked.

'Never mind me,' he said, smiling. 'You get back to your cataloguing.'

He turned to leave but she caught his arm and pulled him to her, her lips seeking his. He felt her moist tongue flick over the hard edges of his teeth before plunging further into the warm wetness of his mouth. He responded almost ferociously, pressing her close to him, anxious to feel her body against his own. Finally she pulled back. He ran an index finger across her soft cheek and smiled.

'See you later,' he said.

As he turned, she called after him and he stopped, listening.

'Tom,' she said, 'I love you.'

He smiled, 'I know.' And he walked off.

4

Steve Pike poured himself another cup of tomato soup from the thermos and watched the steam rising from the thick red liquid. He took a sip, wincing at the plastic taste, but he persevered, taking a draw on his fag to deaden the flavour.

'Want some?' he asked, pushing the cup towards Mackenzie.

The other man shook his head, and after stuffing the remains of a sandwich into his mouth, pulled a small metal flask from the pocket of his parka.

He took a hefty swing and smacked his lips, 'Stuff your soup,' he said, 'I'll stick to this.'

From where he sat, ignoring the dampness which was seeping through the seat of his trousers, Mackenzie could see the church clock. Its metal hands were at three-twenty. He glanced down at his own watch once more. Despite winding, it still wasn't working. Bloody Russian crap. Next time he'd get a Timex.

Squatting on the dark earth, Steve looked around. They were well across the clearing, almost halfway. The high grass and weeds had been cut down behind them; tomorrow they would cut down the remaining vegetation and, after that, dig it all into the soil.

'We'll go as far as that tree stump today,' said Mackenzie, pointing to a gnarled knob of wood which jutted out of the climbing grass like a beacon. It stood about two feet high but was nearly that width across the neatly cut base. Someone, many years ago, had chopped it down and, what was more, they had done it with amazing precision. The severed trunk was as smooth as formica on its darkened diameter. It reminded Steve of a table, as if it had grown in that shape for some purpose.

'That's going to take some shifting,' said Mackenzie, taking another pull from his hip flask, 'I bet the bloody roots go down for yards.'

Steve looked around the clearing: the darkened area of earth strewn with chopped down grass, and that which lay beyond, rampant with clotted outcrops of weed. Not a wild flower in sight.

'I wonder why they wanted it cleared?' he said.

'Well,' said Mackenzie, 'it is a bloody eyesore. Christ, I shouldn't think it's been seen to since the fucking cemetery was opened.'

Steve wasn't satisfied. 'But it's out of sight of the rest of the place, you can't even see it from the driveway.'

Mackenzie turned on him irritably, 'What the bloody hell does it matter why they want it cleared? Perhaps they're expecting lots of people to peg out and they want somewhere to put them. How the bleeding hell should I know why they want it cleared?'

'All right, keep your shirt on. I was just curious.'

39

Mackenzie grunted. 'Why bother about it? As long as we get paid for doing it I couldn't give a bugger what they want it for.' He drained the last drops of brandy from his flask. He shook the flask and dropped it back into his pocket.

'I'll tell you what,' he said, 'it's getting colder. I reckon we'll have a frost tonight.'

'It is bloody cold,' said Steve, softly, almost to himself.

He threw what was left of his soup onto the ground and pushed his thermos into his lunchbox.

Grumbling, they returned to cutting down the sea of weeds and grass. Mackenzie straightened up sporadically and massaged the small of his back, groaning with the ache that had settled there. He drove his spade down hard and felt it connect with something solid. He pawed away the earth and saw a root as thick as his arm. And the tree stump was more than three feet away. He groaned inwardly. Shifting it was going to be harder than he'd anticipated. He lifted the spade above his head and brought it crashing down on the root, severing it with a powerful blow.

'Steve.'

The youngster turned.

'There's a couple of hatchets in the work bag. Go and get them. We'll chop the bloody thing free.'

Steve nodded and headed off to fetch the tools. Then he heard Mackenzie call again. 'And bring the crow bars too.'

He returned a moment later with the tools to find Mackenzie leaning on the tree stump. He took an axe from Steve and set to work, hacking through the thick roots until the sweat began to soak into his coat. But neither of them removed their jackets because it was getting so cold. Mackenzie could feel the biting iciness catching in his throat and he half expected to see his laboured breath frosting before him in the freezing air. Steve too, slashed away at the tentacles of root, watching as sap oozed, blood-like, into the earth.

It took them nearly half an hour to free the stump.

Panting, Mackenzie picked up the crow bar and motioned for Steve to do the same. They slid the clawed prongs under two sides of the stump and, at a given signal, pressed down on the iron levers as hard as they could. Their faces turned bright red with the effort and veins stood out angrily on both men's foreheads.

'Hold it a minute,' gasped Mackenzie.

Steve was fit to drop. He had never known exertion like this in his life and, if he had his way, he'd never have it again. They tried again but the stump remained stuck fast as if driven into the soil with some gigantic steam hammer. It was like trying to pull a masonry nail from a wall with your fingers.

'Couldn't we both try it from the same side at once?' offered Steve, not really caring now whether they moved the bloody thing or not. He didn't know why they just couldn't have gone round it.

Side by side, they prized the crow bars deep beneath the stump, Mackenzie eventually shouting in angry frustration.

'Fuck the bloody thing.' He threw his bar to

the ground and stood, hands on hips, staring at the recalcitrant stump which seemed to grin back at him as much to say, you might as well forget it.

'Does it matter that much?' Steve asked timidly.

Mackenzie exploded, 'Of course it matters, you stupid little bastard. How the hell are they supposed to turn it into a fucking burial plot with that stuck in the middle?'

He retrieved his bar.

'Come on,' he snarled and they set to work again. To Mackenzie, it had become a matter of pride; he intended moving that stump if he had to stay there all night and do it.

There was a slight creak and it lifted an inch. They pressed down harder and it lifted a little more.

'It's moving,' shouted Mackenzie, triumphantly.

Inch by agonizing inch, the tree stump rose, bringing with it more thick roots which hung like hardened veins from its dirt encrusted base.

It lifted a foot. Then eighteen inches, a great sucking sound filling the air as it began to come free.

Then they noticed the smell. A fetid, choking stench which smelt like excrement and made them gag. Steve felt his muscles contract, the hot bile clawing its way up from his stomach.

'Keep pushing,' shouted Mackenzie, tearing the lump of wood from its earthy home until the many-rooted base was at a ninety degree angle to the ground. Both men put their shoulders to it, preparing to push it over.

It was then that they looked down into the hole.

Mackenzie opened his mouth to scream but no sound would escape. The cry caught in his throat and rasped away. His eyes, riveted to the sight below him, bulged madly, the blood vessels in the whites threatening to burst. Steve made no attempt to stop himself and vomited violently, not quite daring to believe what he saw.

Lying in the hole, its body coated in thick slime, was a slug the size of small dog. Its body was a sickly greyish white colour, covered from head to tail with thick slime. As the horrified men stood transfixed, its twin antennae slowly grew towards them, lengthening like car aerials, until they had reached their full height. The bulbous eyes waved gently at the end of the antenna and the abomination slithered forward.

With a scream of sheer horrified revulsion, Mackenzie snatched up the crowbar and struck the creature. It made a hideous gurgling noise, the antenna retracting swiftly. Mackenzie struck again but, seeing that the blows were having little effect, he grabbed the axe, lying discarded by the tree stump and brought it down with terrifying force on the monstrous thing.

His blow split it in half and, a shower of virulent pus-like blood spouted into the air, some of it spattering him. Screaming like a maniac he brought the axe down again, this time splitting the thing lengthways. A reeking porridge of blackened entrails spilled onto the ground, the stench nearly making Mackenzie faint. Sobbing now, he brought the axe down once more, this time slicing off one of the antenna. He sank to

43

his knees, the slimey mixture of yellow blood and dark viscera covering him. He gripped the axe and screamed.

Steve Pike lay unconscious behind him.

It was a full hour before Mackenzie was able to think clearly, or even to look at what remained of the thing in the hole. God alone knew how long it had been there, what it had fed on. And only now did he see that it had been lying on something. A box of some sort.

Steve had come to about twenty minutes ago, seen the creature's body and thrown up again. Mackenzie didn't blame him. Now both of them sat looking down into the hole left by the torn up tree stump, wondering what was in the box on which the slug had been lying.

'It looks like a coffin,' said Steve, quietly.

Mackenzie nodded and leapt forward, tentatively touching the wooden lid. It was soft to the touch, like mildew. He poked it with the crow bar and a lump fell off. Both men stepped back.

'What if there's another one of those things in there?' said Steve, apprehensively.

Mackenzie ignored him and stepped down into the hole. Christ, it was deep, a good three feet deep, the rim of it level with his waist.

The sky above was growing dark and he had to squint to read what was on the lid.

'It's a name or something,' he said.

Steve swallowed hard and looked around him. The wind had sprung up and the trees were rustling nervously. 'For Christ's sake hurry, Mack,' he said. Night was drawing in fast, clouds gathering like premonitory warnings above the cemetery. Birds, returning to their nests, were black arrowheads against the purple sky.

Mackenzie bent and looked closer. There was a name plate but the name had been scratched out making it unreadable. Only the date was visible, caked over with the mud of four hundred years.

1596.

'Christ, it's old,' said Mackenzie.

He slid his crow bar under one corner of the lid and wrenched it open.

Both men found themselves looking in at a skeleton.

'Jesus,' groaned Steve, noticing that the empty eye sockets had been stuffed with rag. The blackened skeleton lay in what remained of a shroud, now little more than rotted wisps of linen. The mouth was open, drawn wide in a way that made it look as though it were screaming.

But the most striking thing was the medallion.

It hung around the neck of the skeleton, almost dazzling in its brilliance. As if the rigours of time had been unable to make an impression on it.

'Fucking hell,' gasped Steve, 'it must be worth a fortune.'

The medallion consisted of a single flat circle of gold suspended on a thick chain. There was an inscription in the middle, and more jumbled lettering around the rim of the circlet but, as Mackenzie leant forward, he could see that it was no language he recognized. He hazarded a guess at Latin and would have been pleased to know that his theory was right.

'Shouldn't we tell the vicar about this?' Steve wanted to know.

Mackenzie shot him a warning glance, 'You're joking. After what we've been through getting this, I want a souvenir.' Reaching down, he ripped the medallion from around the neck of the corpse. Smiling, he studied it lying in the palm of his hand.

'A fortune,' he said quietly. It was then that he noticed the slight sensation of warmth in his palm. At first he dismissed it as imagination, or the sweat of his exertions. But the heat grew stronger, the skin on the palm of his hand began to sizzle and, as he watched, the medallion began to glow.

He dropped it with a startled grunt. It stared back at him from the damp earth.

'The bloody thing burned me,' he said, looking up at Steve.

The younger man frowned and looked down at the medallion. He reached forward and prodded it with his fingers.

'Seems alright to me,' he said, picking it up.

Mackenzie snatched it from him, holding it for a moment or two. Nothing happened. Perhaps it had been his imagination. He looked down at the palm of his hand. There was a scorch mark the size of a milk bottle top on the flesh of his hand. He dropped the medallion into his pocket and picked up his spade.

'Let's fill it in,' he said.

'I still think we should tell the vicar,' Steve persisted, shovelling earth.

'Shut up and keep digging.'

They buried the coffin and its skeletal occu-

46

pant and the slug then set off back to the cemetery proper. Mackenzie was quiet, staring ahead of him as he walked, and Steve had to hurry to keep up with him.

'What are you going to do with the medallion?' the youngster asked.

'Mind your own fucking business,' rasped Mackenzie.

Steve swallowed hard, disturbed by the tone of the older man's voice. What he had just seen had caused him enough trouble, he didn't want to end his first working day with a fight.

When they reached the van, parked outside the cemetery, they dumped their tools in the back and Mackenzie threw the ignition keys to Steve.

'You drive,' he ordered, 'I've got a blinding headache.'

Steve didn't argue. He got in, started the van and drove off towards Medworth. Mackenzie sat silently beside him, head bowed, his breathing low and guttural.

The youngster put his foot down. He would be pleased to get home.

5

Debbie Lambert turned the big master key in the door of the library and smiled at the three women behind her.

'Another day, another dollar,' she grinned.

The women said their goodnights on the steps of the library then went their separate ways into the chill night. Although it was only six-fifteen, frost was already beginning to speckle the roads and pavements. It would be black ice by ten that night.

Debbie shivered and walked around the side of the building to the car park. She was struggling under the weight of a large plastic carrier bag she held. It was jammed full of ledgers. Reluctantly she had, as expected, been forced to take some work home with her.

After dumping the carrier on the passenger seat she slid behind the wheel and started the engine of the Mini. It spluttered a little then burst into life and she guided the car out into the street in the direction of home.

The journey didn't take her long. Their house stood on a small private estate about ten minutes from the centre of town, in a street with only six houses on each side of the road. As she turned into the street she could see lights blazing from the living room windows of their house. She parked her Mini behind Lambert's Capri and walked around to the back door.

The smell of cooking met her as she entered the kitchen, and she sniffed appreciatively. Lambert, dressed in a plastic apron with a bra and knickers drawn on it, was standing by the cooker stirring the contents of a large saucepan.

Debbie took one look at him and began laughing.

'I bet this never happens to Robert Carrier,' he said, grinning.

She crossed the kitchen and kissed him, peering into the saucepan.

'What is it?' she asked.

'What is it?' he mimicked her. 'It's stew, woman, what does it look like?'

She nipped the end of his nose and retreated into the living room. There, she dumped her carrier bag full of ledgers on the coffee table and called to Lambert that she was going to change her clothes. He shouted something about slaving over a hot stove and she laughed as she bounded up the stairs.

His mood had changed, she thought with relief. But that had been the problem since the accident. His temper and character seemed to fluctuate wildly. One minute he was happy, the next he was plunged back into the abyss of self-reproach and guilt. Debbie removed her clothes and left them in an untidy heap on the end of the bed. She fumbled in the drawer for a t-shirt, stood before the mirror, unhooked her bra and threw it to one side before pulling on the t-shirt.

Her nipples strained darkly against the white material. She slid into a pair of faded jeans, patched so many times she'd lost count, and padded, barefoot, downstairs.

Lambert was ladling out the stew when she walked into the dining room.

They ate slowly, at a leisurely pace, chatting about this and that, feeling the tensions of the day slowly drain away.

He poured her another glass of wine and sat down again, gazing across the table at her as she drank.

'I'm going back to work at the end of the week,' he said quietly.

She paused, her glass midway to her lips and asked why.

'Because I can't sit around like this any longer.'

'You know what the doctor said.'

'Oh, sod the doctor. He doesn't know what it's like. Sitting here every day and night thinking about that bloody accident. I need to go back. I need something to occupy my mind.'

'You said yourself that there was nothing doing.'

'I know,' he took a sip of his wine, 'but at least I wouldn't be shut up here in the house all the time.'

'Just give it a little longer, Tom,' she asked.

'It's been a fortnight now,' he said, his voice growing to a volume which he didn't intend. He looked down at the patterned table cloth and then across to her again. 'I don't think I'll ever be able to face it, so I might as well just keep running.' He drained his glass and poured himself another.

'And what happens when you can't run anymore?' she wanted to know.

He had no answer.

Ray Mackenzie stood on the pavement outside his house as the van drove away and rubbed his eyes. Christ, the bloody headache was getting worse and now his eyes were starting to throb. He felt as if he hadn't slept for a week. He looked up into the dark sky and inhaled deeply. As he walked, the medallion bumped against his thigh, secure in his trouser pocket.

There was a small tricycle lying outside the back door and he bumped his shin against it as he rounded the corner. Snarling, he lashed out at it, sending the tiny object hurtling across the yard.

Inside, June Mackenzie sighed. It looked like one of those nights. She had been expecting him for the last hour and a half. He'd probably been down the pub for a couple of pints. Well, she'd give him a piece of her mind when he came in. Half past seven. What sort of time did he call this? It was the same every day, wondering if he'd be home straight from work or down the bloody pub with his mates. She had put up with it for the ten years they had been married but she sometimes wondered how much more she could stand. If not for Michelle, now nearly five, she would have left him long ago. At thirty-four, she felt that life was somehow passing her by. Even if he'd *offer* to take her out once in a while that would be something. But no, same routine

51

every night. He came home, stinking of booze. Had his dinner, went back down the pub until nine then flopped in front of the TV for the rest of the evening. Christ, what a way to live a life. His idea of a great night out was sitting and watching a darts match down the local. He'd asked her to come with him occasionally but there was no one to look after Michelle and, besides, she didn't fancy sitting with a bunch of boozy men all night, cracking jokes about their wives' frigidity.

June shook her head. There must be more to life than this?

She had thought about trying to get a flat for herself and Michelle but the waiting list was four years long and, with the child just starting school she didn't want to move too far away. Besides, her own measly wage could never support them. She worked part time as a cleaner in a car showroom but there had been talk of cut-backs and she was beginning to wonder how much longer they would keep her on. Ray didn't earn a lot. Just enough to pay the rent and the H.P. They had everything on H.P. If he ever lost *his* job and the payments couldn't be met, half the house would be repossessed. She shuddered at the thought.

The back door flew open and Mackenzie staggered in.

'Who left that fucking thing outside the door?' he shouted, rubbing his bruised shin.

'Do you have to shout?' she demanded, 'do you want the whole street to hear you?'

He walked off into the living room, grunting

at Michelle who was playing on the rug in front of the gas fire.

'Your dinner is ready,' called June, 'and has been for the last hour.'

He ignored her and stormed upstairs, his heavy boots crashing heavily across the landing. She knew that he must have gone into their bedroom. She shook her head angrily.

'What's the matter with Daddy?' asked Michelle.

Mackenzie moved about the bedroom without turning on the lights. His headache had grown steadily worse and he found that bright light aggravated it. Despite the blackness in the room, broken only by the dull glow of the street lamp outside, he moved with assurance. Sitting on one corner of the bed, he pulled the medallion from his pocket and studied it. He guessed by its weight that it must be solid, a good pound and a half. He tried to guess at the value but the persistent buzzing pain which throbbed behind his eyes and in his temples made rational thought impossible. He sighed, disturbed at the intensity of the pain. It felt as if someone were driving red hot nails into his scalp. He stood up, shakily and crossed to a drawer where he pulled out his wife's jewel box. It was wooden, the top carved ornately, making it look more valuable than it actually was. He flipped it open, emptying its meagre contents onto the floor. Then, carefully, he laid the medallion inside. It seemed to wink mockingly at him and, for a moment, a wave of icy air enveloped him. He shut the box lid and it passed. He hid the small box beneath his pillow and walked out of the bedroom.

When he entered the kitchen, his dinner was on the table. It had dried up long ago, the chips looking like mummified fingers.

'I don't want any dinner,' he growled, raising one hand to shield his eyes from the bright glow of the kitchen's fluorescents.

'Look,' said June, 'it's not my fault it's like that. If you'd come home at the right time.'

He cut her short. 'No fucking dinner.' He screamed the words, grabbing the plate and flinging it at the far wall where it shattered, splattering food in all directions. He turned on her, spittle sticking in white blobs to his lips. June was suddenly afraid.

She took a step backward, watching him as he glanced up at the light. He hissed and covered his eyes as if the white glow were causing him pain.

He rushed to the switch and slapped it off, plunging the room into darkness.

'Ray,' said June, her tone softening, wondering just what was happening, 'what's the matter?'

'Light,' he grunted, 'can't stand the light.'

He turned and stalked into the living room, recoiling madly from the shaded hundred and fifty watt that illuminated the room.

'Turn it off,' he screamed and dashed for the switch.

The room was now lit only by the glow of the television screen and Mackenzie growled something as he stood looking at it. Michelle got to her feet and ran to her mother, suddenly frightened by her father's behaviour. He put both

54

hands to his head and moaned, slumping into one corner of the room, head down.

June crossed to the phone and began dialling, 'I'm going to get a doctor,' she said.

Mackenzie leapt to his feet and was across the room in a second, his hand closing around his wife's wrist in a grip which threatened to snap the bone. She gasped and tried to pull away. The phone dropped uselessly from her hand and swung by its cord. His voice almost a whisper, now surprisingly calm, Mackenzie said, 'No doctor.'

She looked down at the hand which gripped her arm and tried to pull away. Mackenzie smiled, his eyes blazing in the reflected glare of the TV. He released his grip and pushed June away. She bumped into a chair and nearly fell.

'What the hell is wrong with you?' she said, becoming angry, 'had too much to drink?'

He snarled and stepped towards her, bringing his arm back then striking forward with the back of his hand. The blow lifted June off her feet and sent her crashing into the metal guard of the gas fire. She rolled forward, blood weeping from her split lip. Still stunned from the force of the blow, she peered up at him. Mackenzie stood, legs astride, glaring down at her, his eyes narrowed to protect himself from the light of the TV.

'You bastard,' she said softly. 'You mad bastard.'

Michelle began to cry. She had been standing in the doorway between kitchen and living room and had seen it all. Now she watched as her father turned and stormed out of the room, his feet slamming up the stairs. She heard the sound of a door being smashed shut. Then she ran to her mother who had managed to drag herself up onto her knees. She caught the little girl and hugged her to her chest, feeling her own blood dripping slowly down her chin.

This time he'd gone *too* far.

June looked up at the clock on the mantelpiece. It said ten thirty-five.

She had put Michelle to bed two hours before and had sat, alone, staring blankly at the television. There had been no sound from Ray. She had gone up there once and tried to open the door but found that he had locked it from the inside. She licked a tongue across the swollen cleft in her lip. The bastard must have fallen asleep. She had called his name but there had been no answer. Not a sound from inside the bedroom. She had then gone to the child's bedroom at the far end of the landing and peeked in. Michelle had been asleep, a ragged old Snoopy clutched between her tiny hands.

Then June had returned to the living room. She had sat there all this time. Wondering what to do. If Ray wouldn't open the door, she'd just have to sleep on the sofa. She gritted her teeth. God, would she give it to him in the morning!

She waited ten more minutes, until the hands of the clock had crawled onto ten forty five, then she moved quickly through the house, locking doors and windows, pulling plugs and prepared to go upstairs. She doublechecked the back door. Burglars had always been one of her biggest fears. Though, God knew, *they* had nothing worth taking. Nevertheless, she pulled the bolts tight, peering out of the small window into the darkness beyond. The street lights still glowed like trapped fireflies and one or two lamps burned in front rooms but apart from that, the street was quiet.

She closed the hall door behind her and walked wearily up the stairs. As she reached the landing, she cautiously opened the door to Michelle's room. The child was still sleeping. June smiled and pulled it shut. Then she padded along to her own bedroom. There was no sound from inside and she put her hand on the knob, expecting to find it twist impotently in her grip.

Instead, the door opened.

She half smiled. The sod must have come to his senses. June went in, closing the door quickly behind her. Mackenzie was lying in bed, his head covered by the blankets, facing away from her. She undressed quickly and slid into bed beside him. He grunted as she did so, a deep guttural sound which made her sit up. His body moved slightly and she saw his hand slowly pull the covers down. June found herself staring at the back of his head.

'Ray,' she whispered, touching his shoulder.

He didn't move.

'Ray.' She shook him harder and this time he rolled over and looked straight at her.

She would have screamed had he not fastened one powerful hand around her throat. He pulled her close and she felt and smelt his fetid breath on her face.

His eyes were gone.

No whites, no pupils. Nothing. Just two blood

red orbs which swelled like crimson blisters from the dark skin which surrounded them. Saliva ran in a crystal river from both corners of his mouth, his red lips flecked with spittle. The nostrils flared as he tightened his grip on her throat and she made a gurgling noise and tried to pull his hand away.

He was on his knees now, above her, bringing more pressure down on her, as if he wanted to force her through the very bed itself. She struck out at him, her long fingernails raking his skin and tearing three bloody furrows but he kept up the pressure, that insane grin still smeared across his face. The rictus which showed his yellowed teeth, dripped mucous. June saw white stars dancing before her eyes and she knew she was blacking out. Then, suddenly, and with a force far beyond that of a normal man, he lifted her in that one hand and threw her across the room.

She slammed into the wall, cracking her head. June slumped down, clinging desperately to consciousness. She had one thought. One rational thought in a world gone mad. She must get to Michelle.

But the creature with the burning red eyes, the creature which had been her husband, rose slowly from the bed and walked purposefully towards her.

She staggered to her feet, wondering if she could make it to the bedroom door. If only she could get past, lock him in. . . .

Dazed, she bolted for safety but Mackenzie caught her arm and, with terrifying force, hurled her backwards. She slammed into the dressing table, her head snapping forward to smash into the mirror which splintered. Shards of glass sprayed out into the room, one of them falling at Mackenzie's feet. He bent and picked it up. Razor sharp, it was the length of a milk bottle. He could see his own vile reflection in it as he advanced on her.

June began sobbing, blood pouring down her face from a cut on her forehead. She tried to scream but it came out as a strangled cough. She raised a hand to ward him off but he brought the shard of mirror sweeping down and it carved off her thumb.

'Ray,' she croaked and he was upon her.

The bedroom door opened slowly and Michelle stood there. The noises from her parents room had woken her. Now she stood quietly, watching as her mother died, bleeding from a dozen savage wounds. The child didn't move, her eyes riveted to the slaughtered body.

There was a movement beside her and she looked up, not quite realizing that the thing with the burning red eyes which stood above her, clutching a length of blood splattered mirror, had once been her father.

6

Debbie yawned and took off her glasses. She shook her head and sighed deeply. The ledgers stared back up at her, defiantly. Her eyes were beginning to grow tired and she could feel the pain gradually gnawing its way from her shoulder to her neck and up the back of her head. She leant back in her chair and stretched, letting out a moan. The room, lit only by the light of the table lamp, seemed to crowd in on her and she promised herself that she would finish in half an hour. She'd been at it solid for three hours.

'Enough.'

Lambert slapped his hand down on the ledger spread out in front of her and she jumped.

'Christ,' she said, 'you frightened me.'

'Wrap your gums round that,' he said, handing her a steaming mug of coffee.

He stood behind her and rested his hands on her shoulders, massaging gently. She purred contentedly.

'Call it a night, Debbie,' he insisted, his fingers working more strongly. She flexed her shoulders, enjoying his expert touch.

'What have you been doing?' she asked him, closing her eyes.

'Watching TV, reading. Nothing much.'

She took a sip of her coffee, squirming as one of his hands slipped down and touched her breast. She reached up and held it, pressing his hand to her bosom. He responded by squeezing it, feeling the nipple grow hard beneath his palm. He ran his free hand through her blonde hair, tracing one finger across her cheek until he reached her mouth. She parted her lips slightly and licked at the end of the probing digit. He pulled it away and allowed his hand to find its way to her other breast. Both hands now clamped firmly on the pert mounds, he gently rubbed them, becoming aroused himself by Debbie's tiny moans of pleasure.

She put down her coffee and swung round on the swivel chair to face him. He smiled down at her, watching as she pulled off her t-shirt, revealing her firm breasts, the hardened nipples now pink buds.

She reached forward and fumbled with his belt, pulling it free and undoing the top button of his jeans, slowly easing the zipper down. She pulled him closer to her, excited by the sight of his erection. She bent low and kissed him and he groaned from the sensations in that most sensitive area. Her lips fastened around his swollen organ and she drew him still closer, bringing her hands round to grip his buttocks. He held her head, not wanting her to stop the motion of her mouth and tongue but also wanting to enjoy her more fully. Gently, he pulled away and knelt before her, helping her to slip out of her own jeans and knickers.

She raised one foot which he caught and

kissed, taking each toe into his mouth in turn before allowing his tongue to flick its way up the inside of her leg towards her own pulsing desire.

She edged forward on the chair, giving him better access and, as his tongue parted her nest of light hair, she gasped. He plunged deeper, allowing his probing tongue to taste her flowing juices and she pressed hard against his face until he put his hands beneath her and lifted her to the floor, impaling her on his erection.

Slowly at first, but then with increasing urgency, Debbie moved back and forth until her gasps became cries, mingled with his own muffled gasps of pleasure as they reached a peak together and he buried his head between her breasts.

As the sensations subsided, they lay beside one another, aware only of the warm glow from the other's body and the plaintive howling of the wind outside.

Debbie leant over him and kissed his chest before looking into his face. He smiled up at her and stroked her cheek with one hand.

'Maybe cataloguing isn't so bad after all,' she said and they both laughed, holding one another tightly. They lay there on the floor, naked, for a little while then Debbie said:

'I wonder what it's like to go through life without someone to love. Without someone who loves you?' She twisted the hairs on his chest into little spirals with her index finger.

Lambert shrugged, 'I've never thought about it.'

She smiled, 'What was it Shakespeare said,

"It's better to have loved and lost, than never to have loved at all." '

'Something like that,' said Lambert, trying to suppress a smile.

'What's so funny?' Debbie wanted to know.

'You're very philosophical.'

'Am I getting boring?' She looked into his eyes.

He tutted and sighed, 'I might have to give that some thought.'

She pinched him.

'Ouch,' he said, sitting up, 'you bitch.'

She giggled.

'Assaulting a police officer is a very serious offence,' said Lambert in an officious voice. 'You have been warned.'

'And what if I do it again?' she asked, teasingly.

'I shall have to consider my verdict carefully.'

Debbie kissed him on the cheek, 'how about an early night?'

He agreed.

Lambert sat up, sweat coating his body. He stared wildly around the room, his breath coming in gasps. Glancing down at the alarm clock he noticed that it was four a.m. The luminous arms of the clock glowed like gangrenous glowworms in the darkness. Beside him, Debbie stirred, murmured something in her sleep, and was silent again.

As carefully as he could, Lambert swung himself out of bed and padded to the bathroom. He turned on the cold tap, filled the basin with water and splashed his face. As he looked up, a haggard face stared back at him from the bathroom mirror. The dark lines under his eyes looked as if someone had drawn them with charcoal. He peered down into the clear water and splashed more onto his face.

When he was sure he had calmed down, he let the clear liquid out of the basin and padded back to the bedroom, pausing on the way to look out into the night. He could see nothing. Not a light anywhere, just the watery moon slowly being smothered by banks of thick cloud. He shivered, realizing that he was still naked, and hurried back into bed.

He closed his eyes and waited for sleep, but it wouldn't come. No peaceful oblivion, just that same stubborn image. The one which had woken him in the first place.

The car careening towards the lamp post, smashing into it. His brother hurtling through the windscreen, while *he* sat in the road watching.

Morning was a long time coming.

7

Maureen Bayliss piled the last of the breakfast dishes in the sink and looked at her watch. She sighed. Time to get the kids off to school. The washing up could wait until she got back.

'Mum. Mum, I can't find my boots,' shouted little Ronnie Bayliss from the living room.

Maureen hurried to the door and pressed a finger to her lips. 'Don't shout,' she rebuked. 'Your Dad's trying to get some sleep.'

She looked up at the ceiling as if fearing that her husband, Jack, had been woken by their son's frenzied howlings. Jack worked nights at Medworths Foundry, and if he was disturbed while trying to sleep, he'd be like a bear with a sore back for the rest of the day. *That* she could do without. She told Ronnie that his football boots were in the kitchen and he pushed past her to find them, eventually stuffing them into the red vinyl bag along with his other games equipment.

'Is Carol ready?' asked Maureen, glancing once more at her watch. 'We're going to be late.'

A moment later, the hall door opened and Carol Bayliss emerged. She was a year younger than Ronnie, about six, and Maureen was pleased that they went to the same school so that the boy could keep his eye on her. Carol was a quiet child, withdrawn. Exactly the opposite of Ronnie. Just the type of child whom other kids seem to find a source of amusement. She herself had been to the school twice to report instances of Carol being bullied by older girls and she didn't intend letting it happen again.

Now she helped the child into her navy blazer and straightened her pig-tails, kissing her lightly on the top of the head.

Maureen peered out of the living room window and saw that the sun was shining, but she put on her leather coat just in case. There were dark clouds gathering to the east and she didn't fancy getting caught in a shower on the way back from the school. She struggled with the buttons, horrified to see that she was indeed putting on weight as Jack had told her. She breathed in and managed to button it, hardly daring to exhale for fear of the buttons flying across the room.

'Everybody ready?' she said, and the kids scurried out of the front door before her.

She followed, closing the door as quietly as possible so as not to wake Jack, and headed up the garden path. As she turned the corner, she couldn't help but notice that the curtains of the Mackenzie house were still drawn. It was unusual for June to be so haphazard, thought Maureen. She was usually a stickler for detail. They had lived next door to one another for the last ten years and had become close friends, both of them having their children about the same time. Now they walked, with the kids, to school every morning, did their shopping together and generally went about their business as one.

Ronnie opened the gate which led down the path to the front door of the Mackenzie house and, as Maureen followed him, she saw that upstairs curtains were drawn as well. They've probably slept in, she thought to herself and reached for the brass knocker, smiling to herself, imagining June's panic when she realized what had happened.

Maureen struck hard, stepping back in surprise as the door swung open. Ronnie was about to dash in when she grabbed him.

'Let's go and wake them up,' he said, leering mischievously.

Maureen suddenly felt uneasy. Why should the front door be open when all the curtains were drawn? Perhaps Ray had gone out early that morning and forgotten to close it behind him. Perhaps they hadn't locked it the night before, there had been a strong wind after all.

Perhaps. . . .

Perhaps what?

Maureen took a step back, pulling Ronnie with her. He looked up at her, 'What is it, Mum?.'

'Come on,' she said, trying not to convey the note of anxiety in her voice. No, why lie to yourself Maureen Bayliss, she thought, for some unknown reason you are scared. There's something wrong here.

She locked the gate behind them and told the kids to stand still while she went and fetched Jack. She fumbled in her purse for the front door key, went in and rushed upstairs. She pushed open the bedroom door, waking Jack immediately. He rolled onto his back, his eyes bleary.

'God, what is it, love?' he said, trying not to sound irritable.

'It's next door,' she told him. 'The curtains are all drawn and there's no answer when I knock.'

'They probably just overslept.'

He tried to roll over again but she pulled him back, 'Jack, for Christ sake, the front door is open.'

'So what?' He was losing control of his temper.

'There might be something wrong,' she persisted.

He snorted, 'Like what?'

'You never know, you read of all sorts of things happening these days, they might all be dead. Burglars or something.'

He waved her away, 'You're going to have to stop reading The News of the World. Things like that don't happen around here, love. This is Medworth, not bloody New York.'

'Then I'm going to phone the police,' she told him, heading for the landing.

He swung himself out of bed and caught her at the bedroom door. She could see that he was angry. 'All right, I'll go and look.' He pulled on his dressing gown and stormed off down the stairs.

'You're not going like that?' she asked.

He turned as he reached the front door, 'Why not? They're going to think I'm off my bloody head when I walk in there and they're all tucked up in bed anyway. I might as well look the part.' Muttering to himself, he headed out into the street.

Ronnie and Carol saw him coming and started to laugh.

'You can shut up too,' he said and headed down the path towards the Mackenzie house.

Maureen ran after him and he paused at the door, still open. 'You'd better wait here,' he said, sarcastically. 'I mean, if they have all been butchered, the killer might still be around.' He shook his head and banged on the open door.

'Ray,' he shouted.

The house greeted him with silence.

Mrs Baldwin from across the road passed by, giving Jack Bayliss a funny look. She turned her nose up and walked on. He bowed mockingly and the old lady hurried past. Ronnie and Carol laughed again.

Jack took a step inside and shouted once more. There was no answer, no sound of movement. Nothing. The hall door to his left was closed, the staircase straight ahead of him. The curtains at the top of the landing were drawn, plunging the house into a kind of murky twilight. He walked into the hall and pushed open the door. Christ, it was dark in there. He swallowed hard, squinting into the gloom, and called again.

Silence.

He took a step into the room, casting a furtive glance around. Jack could feel the tension building within him as he padded towards the closed kitchen door and, he almost hit the roof when he felt a hand on his shoulder.

Scarcely stifling a yell he turned to find Maureen standing there.

'Did you have to do that?' he panted, his heart thudding against his ribs.

'I told you there was something wrong,' she persisted.

He peered into the kitchen and found nothing, discovering his scepticism rapidly draining away. His tone, when he spoke again, had lost its flippancy.

'I'm going to look upstairs,' he told her. 'You wait in the hall.'

As he ascended the stairs he looked around. Nothing had been disturbed; whatever had happened it hadn't been a visitation by burglars.

He reached the landing and looked around. There were four doors facing him, set in a kind of L shape. He leant over the banister and saw Maureen looking up at him. Angry with himself for allowing the atmosphere to affect him, he opened the door nearest to him and looked in.

A child's room, he realized from the scattering of toys on the floor and the flowered bedspread. No sign of anyone. He closed that door and moved to the second. It was an airing cupboard. He tutted and was about to open the third door when something caught his eye.

It was lying outside the door of the fourth room, which was, itself, slightly ajar. He crossed cautiously to the discarded object and picked it up. It was a toy, a stuffed animal. Of course, Carol had one. It was Snoopy.

He dropped it when he noticed the blood which covered its floppy head.

His eyes suddenly darted round the darkened landing, flitting from door to door. Fear and anger vied for control of his emotions. He slowly pushed open the door to the fourth room.

From her position in the hall, Maureen Bayliss

70

heard her husband scream. A sound which was rapidly choked away as he vomited.

She called his name and raced up the stairs taking them two at a time. As she reached the landing, he staggered drunkenly from the room, waving her back. His face was the colour of cream cheese and thick mucous was dribbling down his chin.

'Jack,' she said, terrified.

'Call the police,' he gasped, struggling for breath.

'What is it?'

'Do it,' he roared at her, dropping to his knees, his entire body shaking. He tried to control his heaving stomach but, as the door swung back gently on its hinges once more, he couldn't. For although he had his back to the horror he had discovered, the thought alone was enough to make him throw up again. He reached back and slammed the door shut, listening as his wife dialled 999 and babbled out her message. He heard her put the receiver down and then he fainted.

8

Sergeant Vic Hayes stood in the bathroom of the Mackenzie house and drank down another tumbler full of water. He stood against the sink for a moment, regaining his composure, then, taking one last mouthful of water, he walked back into the bedroom.

At fifty-two, and with more than thirty years experience on the force, he had seen some sights. Road accidents, industrial accidents, baby batterings. But never anything like this and in Medworth, of all places. He'd been a sergeant here for more than fifteen years and there hadn't been anything worse than a bad case of G.B.H. in all that time. The offender was doing five to ten in Strangeways; Hayes had given evidence at the trial. The man had attacked his girlfriend's father with a spanner. Made a right mess of his face too.

But never anything like this today.

He entered the bedroom and saw Doctor John Kirby leaning over the first of the bodies, just as he had been doing when Hayes had left the room. Hayes didn't care for Kirby much. He was good at his job, but a bit of an arrogant little bastard. He'd come straight from medical school to his position as Medworth G.P. and he also doubled as Police doctor. Not that his services had been needed until now.

Two ambulance men stood by the door with a stretcher, their eyes looking at the floor. In fact looking at anything other than at what Kirby had at his feet.

Hayes took a deep breath and leaned over him. 'Whoever did this was a very strong man,' said Kirby, matter of factly. 'It's difficult to tell of course without an autopsy, but, I'd say these cuts are nine or ten inches deep.' He pointed to the throat. 'This particular blow practically severed the head.'

'And the little girl?' asked Hayes, not daring to look behind him. Lying beside the open door was the body of Michelle Mackenzie, her tiny form disfigured by a dozen wounds.

Kirby nodded. 'The injuries are the same, so is the disfigurement.' He stroked his chin thoughtfully. 'Strange.'

Hayes nodded. He knew of which 'disfigurement' Kirby spoke and it was that final touch of horror which had forced him out of the room when he had first seen the two bodies.

Both had had their eyes torn out.

'As I said before,' said Kirby, 'without an autopsy it's difficult to give precise details, but from the scratch marks on both of their faces and . . .'

Hayes cut him short, 'All right, doc. I'll wait for the reports.' He walked out, leaving the ambulancemen to load the bodies onto their stretchers. Kirby followed them out. Hayes watched him leave. He stood on the deserted landing for a moment then wearily made his way down to the living room. Through the open front door he saw the two bodies loaded into the ambulance which, after Kirby had climbed into the back, drove off. Hayes took off his cap and flopped into one of the arm chairs. Where was Ray Mackenzie? Could the husband be the killer?

'Find anything?' he asked, wiping his forehead.

P.C. Gary Briggs nodded and lifted a plastic bag from the coffee table. It contained the jewel box which had belonged to June Mackenzie. Hayes took the box out and opened it.

'We found it upstairs,' Briggs told him, 'under a pillow on the bed.'

Hayes looked into the box and saw the medallion. He studied it a moment then looked up at Briggs. The youngster shrugged. 'It's bloody old, whatever it is.'

Hayes handed it back. 'Take it down to the station. Lock it in the safe.'

Briggs nodded and dropped the medallion back into the jewel box.

'Did anyone talk to the woman who reported this?' asked the sergeant.

'Tony did,' answered Briggs, nodding out of the window, indicating P.C. Walford standing outside the front gate talking to a group of people who were trying to see into the Mackenzie house. 'Her husband found the bodies. She reported it straight away.'

'Poor bastard,' said Hayes, quietly, 'it must have been quite a shock for him.'

Hayes struggled to his feet, feeling more aware

of his ample stomach than usual, and replaced his cap on his balding head.

'What do you want us to do, Sarge?' asked Briggs.

'Just keep this quiet. I don't want word getting about, understand? This is a nice town. The people aren't ready for this sort of thing. If any reporters turn up, tell them to fuck off.' He paused as he reached the door. 'I'm going back to the station, I'm going to get in touch with Inspector Lambert. I think we need him on this one.'

He walked out into the fresh morning air and inhaled deeply, allowing the crisp wind to wash the stench of blood and death from his nostrils.

He nodded to Walford as he passed, on his way to the Panda car parked across the street. Hayes slid behind the wheel and started the engine, picking up the car's two-way radio as he guided it out into the street. He flicked on the transmitter and spoke through the crackle of static, 'Puma One to base.'

The static crackled more fiercely.

'Puma One to base, move your self, Davies.'

There was a buzz as he flicked to receive and a metallic voice came through, 'Sorry, Sarge, the kettle was boiling, I had to turn it off.'

'Well, put mine out, I'll be back in two minutes and Davies, remember, one sugar, I'm trying to slim. Over.'

'About time, Sarge.' A giggle. 'Over'.

'Fuck off. Over and out.'

Lambert heard the phone ringing as he stepped out of the Capri. He hurriedly locked the door and sped towards the house, wondering who was calling and hoping they wouldn't ring off before he got to the phone. He fumbled out his front door key and dashed in, snatching up the receiver in the nick of time.

'Hello,' he said, breathlessly.

'Hello, sir.'

Lambert recognized the voice immediately as Hayes. 'Sergeant. What can I do for you?'

'I've rung twice before, I didn't think you were there.'

'I was at the . . .' Lambert's voice trailed off and Hayes realized that his superior had been to the cemetery. 'What's so important Sergeant?'

'Well, sir, you asked me to tell you if anything happened.'

'Yes.' Lambert suddenly felt excited.

'I'm afraid we've had a double murder.'

'Where, for Christ's sake?'

'Elm Street. Number . . .' Lambert heard the rustling of papers at the other end of the line, then Hayes came back on, 'number twelve. The wife and daughter. The husband is missing. We're treating the husband as prime suspect.'

'What do you make of it?' asked Lambert, scribbling something down on the pad beside his telephone.

'Knifings sir, both of them.'

'Got the weapon?'

'Not yet.'

'What're the names of the victims?'

'Mackenzie. June, that was the wife, and Michelle, the little girl, aged about five we think.'

Lambert wrote the details down on the pad,

the receiver cradled between his shoulder and his ear.

'Do you need me down there?' he asked hopefully.

'Not at the moment, sir. I've got some men out looking for the suspect and Doctor Kirby is doing autopsies on the victims this afternoon.'

'Ring me back the moment you get the results of those,' Lambert told him, 'or if anyone sees this Mackenzie, right?' He hung up, a sudden surge of adrenalin firing his body. He had forgotten about Mike for a moment, had managed to push that thought to the back of his mind. He had his work again. Now nothing would stop him from returning. He sat down, his thoughts jumbled, and read what he had written on the pad.

Double Murder. June and Michelle Mackenzie. Husband chief suspect, disappeared. Knifed. No murder weapon found. Autopsies performed.

What was Debbie going to say? He half smiled.

The phone rang again at four twenty-three that afternoon. The policeman snatched it up. 'Lambert,' he said.

'Hayes here, sir. We've got the results of the autopsy.'

'Go on,' said Lambert, suddenly realizing that he hadn't got a pad or pen. 'Hold it a minute,' he said, retrieving them from the coffee table. 'Right, fire away.'

'Dr Kirby's here, if you want to speak to him, sir,' Hayes told him.

'Put him on,' instructed Lambert, hearing the

murmurings at the other end of the line. A second later, he recognized Kirby's voice. They exchanged pleasantries, then Lambert said, 'What's the verdict, John? And keep it simple, please.'

'Messy ones, Tom, both of them. I found traces of skin under the fingernails of the woman. I would think your suspect is probably walking around with some pretty hefty scratch marks on his cheek. What order do you want them in?'

Lambert was puzzled, 'What do you mean?'

'The mother or the girl first?' Kirby told him.

'It doesn't matter,' said Lambert, impatiently.

There was a pause at the other end and the policeman could hear the sound of papers being rustled, then Kirby again. 'The little girl. I found six separate wounds, mostly around the upper body and neck. The deepest was eight inches, the fatal wound probably, situated just below the larynx. If it's any consolation, I think she was dead before he cut her badly.'

Lambert scribbled details, 'And the woman?'

'Twenty-three separate wounds.'

'Shit,' murmured Lambert, still writing.

Kirby continued, 'Mostly in the abdomen, chest and neck as before. The weapon was double-edged, jagged and tapering, which would explain the width as well as the depth of the wounds.'

'What do you think? Butcher's knife, something like that?'

'No. I know what it was, I've got it in my office right now. It was a piece of glass, or mirror to be more precise and the reason your boys couldn't find any murder weapon was because it was still embedded in June Mackenzie's body. I took a piece of mirror nearly fifteen inches long from behind the rib cage. It had been driven in from above, just behind the right clavicle, collar bone to you, and it had punctured the heart. I'd say that was the death wound.'

'Jesus Christ,' said Lambert.

'One more thing Tom,' added Kirby, as if the catalogue of atrocity hadn't quite been enough, 'the eyes were taken.'

'Taken? What do you mean taken?' It sank home. 'Oh God, he didn't cut those out too did he?'

'Well now, that's the whole point. My examination revealed that they were removed without the use of any external implements.'

Lambert's nauseated anger broke forth, 'What the hell are you trying to say? Did he cut out their eyes or didn't he?'

Kirby's voice was low, controlled, 'From the scratches on the cheeks and bridge of the nose, I'd say he tore them out with his bare hands. The fingerprints matched those of Ray Mackenzie.'

Lambert tried to write down that last piece of information but, as he pressed down on the paper, the point of his pencil splintered.

'Tom?' Kirby's voice called, 'you still there?'

Lambert exhaled deeply, 'Yes, sorry'.

'Did you get all that?'

'I got it. Put Hayes back on, will you?'

The sergeant's voice replaced that of Kirby, 'Yes sir.'

'Get every available man out looking for Mackenzie. I want that fucking maniac caught before this happens again.' He hesitated a moment then said, 'I'll be in touch. If anything happens in the meantime, let me know.'

He put the phone down. For long moments he stood staring at the pad, the scrawled details of the twin deaths.

Eyes torn out.

Lambert threw the pad down and crossed to the cabinet beside the bay window. He pulled it open and took out a bottle of scotch. He poured indiscriminately, filling the tumbler practically to the brim, then he swallowed half its contents, wincing as the amber liquid burned its way to his stomach. He held the glass, considering it in his hand, then he drained it. Rapidly refilling the crystal tumbler, he wondered how many more of them he'd need before Debbie got home.

She found him sitting in the darkness, only the light from the streetlamp outside illuminating his dark outline. He sat still, the glass still clamped in his hand, staring out of the window, scarcely turning when she entered the room and flicked on the table lamp. The room was suddenly alive with subdued light, changing from the drab place of darkness it had been a second ago into a warm grotto.

He smiled at her.

'Tom, what's the matter?' she asked, crossing to him. Immediately she smelt the drink on his breath.

He lifted the glass in salute and swallowed its contents before setting it down gently on the carpet beside his chair.

'Would you like a drink?' he asked. 'There's plenty more where that came from.'

She took hold of his hand. 'What's wrong?' she repeated.

He looked at her, his smile fading. 'Last night, two people were murdered. A woman and a little girl. Do you know how old that little girl was? Five. Only five years old. They were stabbed and then their eyes were torn out. Bodily.'

Debbie shuddered, 'Oh my God.'

'The crazy bastard who did it is still on the loose.'

They looked at each other, their eyes probing, searching the other's for some sign.

'I'm going back, Debbie,' said Lambert, flatly. He reached out and stroked her cheek, noticing the moisture building within her eyes. She gripped his hand and pressed it to her face, kissing it.

'Tom,' she said, a tear running down her cheek, 'I just want you to be all right. This business with Mike, it's torn you apart and now this on top of it. Please, give it a couple more days, they can manage for a couple more days.' Tears were flowing quickly now and he reached out and brushed them aside.

'I'll be all right,' he said. 'They need me. If this bastard did it once, he might do it again. I can't let that happen. I have responsibilities. I'm supposed to be the law here.'

She stood up, suddenly angry, 'Oh, for Christ sake, you make it sound like a bloody Western. The law. Your responsibilities. You don't have to carry the can for *everything*, Tom. Not for every bloody cause going. You don't have to feel guilty about all the things you do. You'll be telling me next it was *your* fault those two people were murdered.' She wiped away the tears, rubbing her eyes when they clouded her vision. 'You know I think you actually enjoy it at times. Being the bloody martyr, shouldering the troubles of the world.'

He watched her, standing before him like some sort of nubile prosecution counsel.

'It's called caring,' he said, softly.

She didn't move, just stood still in the centre of the room shaking gently, tears staining her cheeks. He got up and crossed to her, his arms enfolding her. She tried to push him away at first but, finally, her arms snaked up around his neck and she pulled him closer, tasting the whisky on his breath but not caring. Wanting him near to her, to feel his body next to hers.

They stood there for a long time, locked in passionate embrace, clinging to each other in that twilight room, while outside the dark clouds of night began to invade the sky.

9

The photo on top of the television smiled back its monochrome smile at Emma Reece. It showed a young couple on their wedding day, the bride resplendent in her white dress (though now looking somewhat sepia tinted because of the age of the photo). The young man was kissing her on the cheek. She looked across at her husband, slumped in the chair, and smiled.

'It's hard to believe that was twenty-five years ago,' she said.

'What's that, love?' he said, his eyes not lifting from the topless girl in the newspaper he held.

'The photo.'

Gordon Reece put down the paper and looked up, also seeing the picture. He smiled. 'God, I was a handsome bugger in those days.'

Emma snorted, 'And still as modest.'

He winked at her, 'If you've got it, flaunt it, that's what I always used to say.'

'You used to say a lot of things,' said Emma, running a hand through her hair. 'Do you think I should have it dyed before Saturday?' she asked.

'What?'

'My hair. Do you think I should have it dyed before the party on Saturday?'

He shook his head. 'Women. Why the hell can't you just grow old gracefully? If you're grey, you're grey. Who cares? You never hear me complaining about the colour of my hair.'

'It's different for men,' she told him. 'Besides, I want to look my best for our Vera. If she's flying all the way from Australia just for our twenty-fifth anniversary, the least I can do is look presentable.'

'She's coming to see *you*, not your bloody hair.'

Emma pulled at the greying strands, watched by her husband who smiled benignly and shook his head. He returned to his paper.

'It'll be marvellous to see her again after all these years,' said Emma, wistfully.

'Yes dear,' answered Gordon, his head still buried in the paper.

'I wonder what the little boys will think of England.'

Gordon looked up and grunted. 'They'll probably wonder why it's so bloody cold all the time.'

There was a rustling from behind Emma's chair and their three-year old Labrador bitch, Sherry, emerged wagging her tail frantically. Emma patted the dog and it stretched out in front of the fire. Gordon moved his feet to give the animal more room.

'I think she wants her walk,' said Emma, retrieving the leash from the sideboard. There was a photo of their daughter on it and she paused to study the photo for a moment before handing the leash to Gordon.

'She's all right where she is,' he protested, nudging the dog with his toe. The animal looked round. 'You don't want to go out, do you girl?'

He shook his head vigorously, as if trying to convince the Labrador that he was right.

'She needs it,' persisted Emma.

Gordon grunted and began fitting the leash, glancing up at the clock on the mantlepiece as he did so.

'It's nearly half past ten,' he said.

Emma half smiled, almost knowing what was coming next.

'So?' she said.

'There's a match on after the news. A big game. Arsenal and Liverpool, it's . . .'

She cut him short. 'Oh all right, I can take a hint.'

Emma went into the hall and pulled down her old navy blue duffle coat and fastened the buttons. She held out her hand for the leash, the dog now excitedly waiting. Gordon winked at her.

'I don't know how I've put up with you for twenty-five years,' she said, trying not to smile. She could hold it back now longer when he blew her a kiss. Laughing, she led the dog out into the hall. Gordon heard her say, 'Back in a bit,' and then the front door slammed shut.

He settled down to watch the game.

As Emma stood on the doorstep, fastening the last toggle of her coat, she shivered. She had not realized just how cold the wind was. Now it lashed her face with icy barbs and felt like a portent of frost or even snow. The sky was clear, the full moon suspended on invisible wires like some huge fluorescent ball. It cast its cold glow over the town, guiding Emma as she walked. The dog tripped along nimbly beside her, its breath forming white clouds in the chill atmosphere.

Lights burned in most front rooms as she walked down the street, and their muffled glow made the night seem a little less forbidding. The estate on which they lived was clean, populated by families well known to one another, and there was a feeling of belonging which Emma had never encountered before. She and Gordon had lived in Medworth for over twenty years, London before that. Both of them found the solitude and peacefulness of country life a positive lift after the hustle and bustle of the capital. Her parents had both come from around this area, so she herself was no stranger to their ways.

She had finished work for good when Vera was born. Gordon had had a good job and his wage was more than enough to keep them comfortably. With their own anniversary due on Saturday, just two days away, things looked rosy. They were only having a small get together, family mainly, and a couple of close friends. But what really made the occasion for Emma was the fact that she would be seeing her daughter again after so long. Suddenly she forgot the cold of the night, instead overcome by that familiar warm glow which comes with expectations.

At the bottom of the street, the road curved sharply away to the right and more houses. Straight ahead lay a large expanse of rough ground and thickly planted trees which locals called The Wasteland. Emma laughed to herself. If old Henry Myers, who owned the land, could hear them, he'd go mad. Myers had a small farm right on the edge of the estate. No livestock, just arable crops like the other small holdings dotted around the outskirts of Medworth. Still, he made a living from it. However, with this particular field, he seemed to have given up. Nothing but stumps of grass and a positive jungle of weeds grew there, the whole thing flanked by a string of cedars. A muddied footpath led to a stile over which one had to climb to get into the field; and it was up this path that Emma led the dog.

The animal scrambled beneath the rotted obstacle while Emma struggled over the top, nearly slipping off. Sherry was panting excitedly as Emma unhooked her leash.

'Off you go, girl,' she said, and the dog bounded away into the field, leaping about like a lamb in spring. Emma leant against the stile for a moment watching the dog, then she began to walk around the perimeter of the field.

The trees crowded in on her from one side, kept back to a certain degree by a high fence of rusty barbed wire. The fence was broken in numerous places, the lengths of wire hanging down in the mud.

The wind combed through the branches creating a sound which reminded Emma of sheets blowing on a washing line.

She jumped back as a low branch, propelled by a gust of wind, snatched at her face. She decided to move further away from the trees, perhaps even to join the dog in the centre of the field.

There was a loud snap as a branch broke behind her.

She spun round, her heart thumping. There were scuff marks around the base of the bushes and beneath her lower strands of barbed wire, which she took to be the work of rabbits.

Or rats?

The idea of being in a field with rats made her shudder and she looked across towards the dog, anxious now to get home. Back to the warmth of the fire and the comforting glare of electric light. She looked up at the moon, suddenly covered by a bank of thick cloud. The field was plunged into momentary darkness and Emma felt suddenly, unaccountably, afraid. She rebuked herself as the cloud cleared and cold white light once more flooded the ground. Nevertheless, she pulled the leash from her pocket and prepared to call the dog.

There was more movement in the bushes behind and she turned, convinced that the creator of the disturbance was much too big to be a rabbit or a rat. Perhaps some kids messing about. She tried to fix that idea in her mind, her eyes glued to the source of the disturbance. She stood riveted for long moments then turned slowly back to call Sherry.

The dog was crouching in the centre of the field, its head resting on its front legs, whimpering quietly. Even from as far away as fifty yards, she could see it was quivering, its eyes fixed on something in the bushes behind her.

She turned, the breath catching in her throat.

The thing that had once been Ray Mackenzie hurtled at her from the cover of the bushes, a shower of leaves accompanying his charge.

Emma opened her mouth to scream, her eyes riveted to the contorted face, now lit obscenely by the moonlight. The feral grin showing discoloured teeth, the three deep scratch marks on one cheek but above all, and this was the last thing she saw before he was upon her, the glowing red orbs that were eyes, burning with the fires of hell.

Mackenzie launched himself at her, cleared the fence and slammed into her, knocking her into the soft mud.

Emma screamed, the sound finally choking away as Mackenzie fastened both talon-like hands around her throat and lifted her off the ground. He held her up at arms' length, her legs dangling uselessly, trying to kick him, trying to ease the grip which was killing her. Through eyes clouded by pain, she saw him grinning, those terrible red eyes burning madly. Then he flung her, as an angry child might fling a rag doll. She crashed into the barbed wire fence, the cruel spikes gouging her flesh and ripping her cheek. She tried to rise but he was upon her again, his weight forcing her down, one hand clamped across her face, pushing her head down as if he wished to drive it into the very earth itself. She struggled vainly, striking feebly at him, her tear-filled eyes catching sight of his other hand. A hand which reached for a length of broken barbed wire. Ignoring the barbs which tore open his palm, Mackenzie snapped the wire free as if it had been thin string. He released his grip, momentarily, on Emma's face, holding the two foot length of barbed wire above her. She made one last desperate attempt to get up and did, indeed, manage to stagger a few feet from him. But her legs gave out and Mackenzie caught her, looping the barbed wire around her neck and using it like some kind of spiked garotte. He pulled with all his strength, watching as Emma raised one hand to ward off the attack. It was useless.

The barbs tore her flesh, puncturing the twin carotid arteries sending spouting fountains of blood spraying into the night air. Blood filled her mouth and, mercifully, she blacked out. But Mackenzie kept pulling, those insane red eyes glowing like beacons, yellow spittle dribbling down his chin. He jerked the body up, hardly realizing that she was dead, failing to appreciate that the wire was embedded so deep it had practically severed her head. He dropped the corpse and stared down at it for a moment.

The eyes were still open, glazed and wide with terror and agony.

Mackenzie dropped down and bent over the head.

In the middle of the field, the dog watched silently as its mistress was killed. Fear pinned it down as surely as if six inch nails had been driven through its paws. It had seen the man emerge from the woods, seen the awful struggles of its mistress. Then finally it had seen the man bend over her, his hands groping at the lifeless face with frenzied movements before he disappeared once more into the woods.

Only then did the dog wander slowly over to the lifeless body, its nose twitching at the stench of blood and excrement. It whimpered, nuzzling against the corpse as if trying to stir it into life. It stood there for long moments, howling up at the moon, then it scampered off, leaving the body of Emma Reece alone.

'You stupid sod,' yelled Gordon Reece, shaking his fist at the television screen, 'I could have put the bloody thing in from there.' He flopped back in his chair, watching as Liverpool mounted another attack.

'Five hundred pounds a bloody week and he can't score,' grunted Gordon.

It was approaching half time and the scores were still tied at one all. He hoped Liverpool would win. He had a lot of money riding on it, both in the betting shop and at work. Besides, he'd never live it down with Reg Chambers at work, a bloody Arsenal supporter. He'd really rub it in if Liverpool lost. But more importantly than that, Gordon had a fiver bet with him on the result. He didn't tell Emma about his little flutters at work, it would only worry her. She sometimes asked him how he got through his money so quickly. He couldn't tell her it was because he was fond of using that well worn phrase 'Put your money where your mouth is'. Unfortunately, just lately, Gordon's mouth had got the better of his wallet. He'd been losing a lot recently. Still, never mind. The reds would do it in the second half. He hoped.

Half time came and with it the commercials. He pottered off into the kitchen to make a cup of tea. Emma should be back soon. The least he could do was make her a cup after having been out in that freezing wind. He lit the gas beneath the large whistling kettle and retired to the living room.

It was then that he heard the scratching.

At first he thought it was the beginning of rain against the windows, but as it became more insistent he realized that it was coming from the front door.

Emma, he thought. Forgotten her key probably. He flicked on the hall light and opened the front door.

The labrador stood on the doorstep, its baleful eyes dark with the horror it had witnessed. Silent testimony to a secret beyond death itself.

Gordon looked at it, shivering before him. It was only a second before he noticed that the dog held something between its jaws and a second more until he realized what it was.

A blood splattered leash.

10

Lambert could hear the persistent ringing and, at first, thought that the noise was in his head. He sighed when it didn't fade and opened his eyes.

The ringing continued.

It was the phone in the hall. He glanced across at the alarm clock on his bedside table and then down at his own watch. No discrepancy between them. It was four-thirty a.m.

He rolled onto his back as the ringing continued, persistent and unceasing. Debbie had one hand across his chest, her fingers nestling softly in the hairs. He smiled and traced a pattern on the back of her hand. She moaned in her sleep and rolled over.

The phone kept ringing.

'Shit,' muttered Lambert and swung himself out of bed, shivering slightly. It was still dark outside and he didn't want to put the bedroom light on for fear of waking Debbie. So he tiptoed across the carpet to the door and, closing it behind him, hurried downstairs to silence the phone.

'Lambert', he said, sleepily, rubbing his eyes with his free hand.

'Sir.'

He recognized the voice at the other end as Hayes, equally weary but with an edge to it.

'There's been another one.'

Lambert shook his head, trying to dislodge the last vestiges of sleep which still clouded his brain. 'Another murder?'

'Yes, sir.'

He exhaled deeply, 'Oh God.' A moment's pause. 'Who?'

'We got the name as Emma Reece. Fifty-two years old, lived up the estate near old man Myers' farm.'

'Who found her?'

'Her husband. Apparently she took the dog out for a walk, across some field at the bottom of the road. The dog ran back to the house carrying its own leash. The husband went looking for her and found her lying in the field.'

Lambert yawned and cleared his throat, 'Where's the body now?'

'Doctor Kirby's got it at the morgue,' Hayes told him.

'I'll be right there.' He hung up. Lambert sat staring down at the dead phone for a second, lost in his own thoughts, then he padded quickly upstairs. Moving as quietly as he could, he pulled his clothes from the wardrobe and crept out again. He dressed in the living room, drinking a cup of black coffee while he did so. Then he found a piece of paper and scribbled a note:

Duty Calls, darling.
Love you.

Tom

He propped the note up on the kitchen table and left by the back door.

The drive to the police station took him less than fifteen minutes and, as he parked the car in its usual position, dawn was beginning to claw its way into the sky. The air felt heavy with dew and the smell of cut grass, and Lambert inhaled deeply as he mounted the set of steps which led to the main door.

The small annexe inside the main door was hung with various crime prevention leaflets, some of which were so old they looked like parchment. Lambert smiled to himself. He had almost forgotten what the place looked like. He walked through the double doors which led into the station proper and found Sergeant Hayes propped up behind the desk with a mug of tea in front of him.

'Hello, guv,' he said, smiling.

Lambert smiled back. Just like old times, he thought. He passed his office, a door to his left marked with his name and thought about going in. But he had no reason to, so he lifted the flap of the desk and walked through into the duty room beyond.

It was a large room, its floor covered by a carpet the colour of rotten grapes. There were three or four worn leather armchairs and a couple of hard backed wooden chairs dotted about. The notice board, which covered the entire far wall, was littered with pieces of paper. Duty rosters, areas to be patrolled, who was due for night beat etc. The paraphernalia of normal police work. He recognized P.C. Chris Davies, slumped in one of the chairs and nodded at him. Davies, a big man with ginger hair, raised a hand in acknowledgement and stood up. Lambert waved him back to his seat.

'You were first there?' asked the Inspector.

Davies nodded. 'Whoever it was made a bloody mess of her. I've never seen anything like it.'

The constable looked younger than his forty-three years, but this particular experience had given him the appearance of a man who had been deprived of sleep for a week. He took a sip of his tea, hands still shaking.

Lambert walked out of the room and back to Hayes.

'Where's Kirby?' he asked.

'Downstairs. I don't think he's finished yet.'

Lambert made his way down the corridor which passed his own office, and headed towards a green door marked private. To his left and right were the cells. The green door was the entrance to the police pathology lab and Lambert hesitated before turning the knob.

The smell hit him immediately. The pungent odour of blood and chemicals which always made him heave. He blew out a long breath and descended the five stone steps which led down to the lab itself.

It was, as seemed common to these establishments, green and white in colour, the floor of shiny white ceramic tiles contrasting with the sea green of the walls and ceiling. A bank of fluorescents threw a cold white light across the grisly proceedings below. In the centre of the room was an aluminum table. The work bench, as Kirby liked to call it. There was a body on it, covered at the moment by a thick white piece of rubber sheeting.

The door to the little bathroom at the side opened and Kirby emerged, wiping his hands with a towel. He was chewing something which Lambert took to be a peppermint. The doctor smiled and offered one to Lambert, who declined.

'Finished?' asked the policeman, indicating the corpse.

'I was just about to start,' said Kirby rolling up his sleeves. He crossed to a closet and pulled out a plastic apron which he quickly put on. 'I can tell you without a post mortem that this woman was killed by the same person who killed that little girl and her mother.'

Lambert looked puzzled. 'How, for Christ's sake?'

Kirby pulled back the sheet and Lambert felt his guts turn a somersault.

Emma Reece's eyes had been torn out.

'Jesus,' gasped Lambert, stepping back, unable to look any longer at the mutilated sockets. 'You're sure it's the same killer?'

'The scratches around the cheeks and nose are identical to those on the first two victims. There's no doubt about it. Mackenzie's marks are all over the body.'

The doctor stood beside the corpse, looking at Lambert, whose own gaze was riveted to the deep, savage gashes in the woman's neck.

'How was it done?' he asked.

'He strangled her with barbed wire,' said Kirby flatly.

Lambert pushed past the doctor and pulled the sheet back over the body. 'Forget the autopsy,' he said.

'Are you sure? I mean it's standard procedure . . .'

'Fuck standard procedure,' snarled Lambert, loudly. He bowed his head and leant back against the table. When he spoke again his tone was more subdued, weary even.

'What's the motive, John?'

'You're the policeman,' said Kirby smiling.

Lambert grinned weakly and nodded. 'No motive. The bastard hasn't even left us a motive.' The inspector walked past Kirby. 'I'll be in the office if you want me,' he said and left.

Kirby took off his apron and hung it up again. He looked at the corpse beneath the sheeting for a second then he crossed to his bench and began writing his own report.

Lambert had a pad before him on the desk and, on it, he was trying to make a list, but the words wouldn't go down in coherent order. He read back what he had:

No motive. Injuries identical. Ray Mackenzie.

He circled 'No motive' and got wearily to his feet. The wall clock said six-twenty a.m. Lambert yawned and rubbed his eyes. Debbie would be up by now, she'd have read his note. He wasn't sure what her reaction to it would be. Not that it really mattered.

He thought of Mike.

Should he visit the cemetery today? He sat down on the edge of his desk, reaching for the pad. He reread his notes. Notes. That was a laugh. What bloody notes? A page full of maybes and whys. He read it once more.

No motive.

The words stuck out like compound fracture.

But they carried with them a resonance which Lambert found all the more disturbing. If there had been no motive for the three killings, then Mackenzie could strike anywhere and at anytime. Christ alone knew who was going to be next. The wife and daughter, perhaps he could understand. Maybe Mackenzie had come home in a drunken rage and killed them both in a fit of temper. But Emma Reece. . . .

And the eyes. Why take the eyes? Was there some significance in that particular mutilation?

Lambert threw the pad across the room in a fit of impotent annoyance. They had to catch Mackenzie, and fast.

He tried to imagine what Gordon Reece must have felt like, finding his wife like that. The poor bastard was under sedation at home. The funeral was tomorrow and he had refused to speak to any policemen until after it was over. Lambert had learned that it was to have been the Reeces' silver wedding anniversary the following day. There was nothing to celebrate now. The family were united to see Emma Reece buried, instead of to celebrate a union which had lasted twenty-five years. Lambert suddenly felt very angry. He wondered how he was going to be able to face Gordon Reece on that coming Sunday. Still, he'd learn to live with it. Everybody had to sooner or later.

Lambert thought about Mike again. Should he visit the cemetery?

He could fight the urge no longer. Telling Hayes where he could be reached, he hurried out of the police station and, climbing into the Capri, headed for Two Meadows.

As he drove, he wondered how much longer it would be before the memory faded.

He wondered, in fact, if that day would *ever* come.

11

Debbie heard the car door slam in the driveway, followed a second later by footsteps heading for the back door. She turned expectantly towards it as Lambert entered.

He smiled tiredly at her.

'You look wrecked,' she said, quietly.

'That is the understatement of the year,' he said, kissing her gently on the forehead. He walked into the sitting room and got himself a drink. 'Want one?' he called.

She asked him for a vodka and he poured it. His own tumbler full, he drained it quickly, then poured another before returning to the kitchen where he sat at the table.

'You got my message this morning?' he asked.

She nodded, sipping her drink.

Lambert exhaled deeply and took a large swallow of scotch.

'Was it another murder?' she asked.

'Yes. A woman in her fifties.'

'What was her name?' He smiled at her, 'That's supposed to be police business.' There was a moment's silence then he said: 'Emma Reece.'

'Oh my God,' said Debbie, putting down her

drink. 'I knew her. And her husband. She was a regular at the library. When did it happen?'

'Last night. She was out walking the dog and . . .' he drew an index finger across his throat in a cutting motion.

'Was it the same one who killed the Mackenzies?' she wanted to know.

'Yes.' He would say no more.

'What about Mr Reece?'

'He's sedated, apparently. The funeral's tomorrow. I've got to talk to the poor bastard on Sunday.' He finished his drink. 'You know I can understand how he feels. It's like being punched in the guts when something like that happens to someone close, like having all the wind knocked out of you.'

'You went to the cemetery again today.' It came out more as a statement than a question.

He nodded, prodding his food with his fork as she laid it before him. She too sat and they ate in silence. After a while, she looked across at him.

'Want to talk about it?' she said, smiling.

'About what?'

'Anything, I'm game.' They both laughed.

'I'm sorry, love,' said Lambert, 'it's just that, well, this whole business worries me. I feel so fucking helpless. Do you know that in all the police records of this town there's never been one murder, one rape or one mugging? And now, in the space of three days, I've got three corpses on my hands.'

'You make it sound as if it's your fault.'

He shook his head. 'That's not what I mean. I wanted to get back to work, you know that.

But not under these circumstances. Christ, three bloody murders. I didn't think things like that happened in Medworth.' He fetched them both another drink and sat down again, pushing away the remains of his meal.

He looked up to see her eyes on him, something twinkling behind them, the beginnings of a smile on her lips.

'What's up?' he said, also smiling.

She shook her head. 'My old man. The copper.'

He laughed. 'What sort of day have you had?'

'Don't ask.'

She got up and walked around the table. He pushed his chair back from the table and she sat on his knee. He put both arms around her waist and pulled her towards him. She kissed his forehead.

'What do you want to do tonight?' she asked. 'We could drive into Nottingham, see a film, take in a club.'

He shook his head.

'I just thought it would be a break.'

'I don't think I could concentrate on a film tonight. What's showing anyway?'

She giggled, ' "Psycho".' She leapt to her feet and dashed into the living room.

'That's not funny,' he called after her and set off to catch her.

He grabbed her arm and pulled her down onto the sofa beneath him. She was laughing her throaty laugh as he pinned her arms and glared at her.

'That was not funny,' he repeated. Then suddenly, they were kissing, their mouths pressed urgently together, tongues seeking the other. He pulled away and looked down at her, her blonde hair ruffled, her cheeks flushed, her mouth parted slightly and moist with the kiss. She pulled him to her again her left hand reaching further, fumbling for the zip on his trousers. He slid his hands inside her blouse, causing one button to pop off in the process. He felt the firmness of her breasts, kneading them beneath his hands feeling the nipples grow to tiny hard peaks. She squirmed beneath him, fumbling with the button of her own jeans and easing herself out of them. But, as she rolled over to pull them free, they both overbalanced and toppled off the sofa. They lay there, entwined, laughing uncontrollably.

'This never happens in films,' said Lambert, giggling. 'They always do it right.'

She ran a hand through his hair and licked her lips in an exaggerated action of sexuality. She couldn't sustain the facade and broke up once more into a paroxysm of giggles.

'What about the washing up?' said Lambert in mock seriousness.

'Screw the washing up,' she purred, tugging at his belt.

'There are more interesting alternatives,' he said and, once more, they joined in a bout of laughter. Laughter — something Lambert thought he had forgotten.

At roughly the same time as Lambert and Debbie were eating their meal, Gordon Reece was pouring himself his fifth scotch of the evening. He had begun drinking at four that afternoon, large wine glasses full of the stuff, and now, two hours later, the first effects of drunkenness were beginning to descend upon him. The drink brought a kind of numbness with it. But it gave him no respite from the image of his dead wife. Her eyeless, mutilated corpse lying in that field like some discarded scarecrow.

He filled his glass again and stumbled into the living room which was lit by the light of a table lamp. The labrador was stretched out in front of the open fire and the animal turned and licked his hand as he stroked it. Reece felt a tear well up in his eye. He tried to hold back the flood but it was impossible. He dropped to his knees, the glass falling from his grasp, the brown liquid spilling and sinking into the carpet. Sobs wracked his body and he slammed his fists repeatedly against the carpet until his arms ached.

God, he thought, please let tomorrow pass quickly. The funeral was at ten in the morning. There wouldn't be many there: he had specifically asked that it should be a small affair. He had phoned Vera earlier in the day, told her what had happened. He'd broken down over the phone. The doctor had given him some tranquilizers and he knew that he should not be mixing drink with them, but what the hell did it matter anymore.

He looked up at the photo on top of the TV and the tears came again. Gordon Reece sank to the ground, the dog nuzzling against him as if it too could feel his grief.

12

Saturday came and went. The funeral of Emma Reece went off without incident. Father Ridley did his duty as he always did. Gordon Reece wept again, finding that anger was slowly replacing his grief. He felt as if there was a hole inside where someone had hollowed out his body. No feeling any longer, just a void. A swirling black pit of lost emotions and fading memories of things that once were but would never be again.

It had been a beautiful day: bright sunshine, birds singing in the trees, God, that seemed to make it worse.

The guests had gone now. The hands on the clock on the mantelpiece had crawled on to twelve fifteen a.m. and Gordon Reece lay sprawled in his chair with a glass in his hand and the television screen nothing but a haze of static particles. Its persistent hiss didn't bother him because he couldn't hear it. He just sat, staring at the blank screen and cradling the nearly empty bottle of scotch in his lap. He had taken a handful of the tranquilizers. He didn't know how many precisely, a dozen, perhaps more. Washed down with a full bottle of whisky, that should do the trick nicely, he thought and even managed a smile. It hovered on his lips for a second then faded like a forgotten dream.

The doctor had told him not to drink with the tablets. Well, fuck the doctor, he thought. Fuck everything now. He would have cried but there was no emotion left within him, no tears left. All that remained now was that black hole inside him where his life used to be.

His bleary eyes moved slowly from card to card, all put out on the mantelpiece.

'With Regrets.'

'In Deepest Sympathy.'

He looked away and poured what was left of the scotch into his glass. He flung the bottle across the room where it struck the far wall and exploded in a shower of tiny crystals.

In the kitchen, the dog barked once, then was silent.

Reece watched the stain on the wall, the dark patch slowly dripping rivulets of brown liquid. He finished his drink and gripped the glass tight, staring at the photo of his wife on the TV. He clenched his teeth until his jaws ached, his hand tightening around the glass, squeezing.

He scarcely noticed when it broke, sharp needle points of crystal slicing open his palm. The blood mingling with the whisky as it dripped onto his chest. He felt no pain, just the dull throb as his blood welled out of him. He dropped the remains of the broken tumbler and closed his eyes.

Surely it wouldn't be long now.

He awoke at three that morning, aware of the burning pain in his torn hand. His head felt as if it had been stuffed with cotton wool and there was a band of pain running from temple to temple which gripped tighter than an iron vice. He moaned in the depths of his stupor, the noise coming through vaguely as if from another world.

The television was still on, its black face dotted still with the speckles of white static.

The dog was growling.

But there was something else. A noise louder than the others, the noise which had woken him. He listened for a moment.

There it was again. A persistent rattling and banging.

Reece tried to rise and the pain in his head intensified. He almost sank down again but the rattling continued and he hauled himself up, nearly toppling over again from the effort of standing. His clouded brain tried to locate the source of the sound and he finally realized that it was coming from the back door. He grunted and staggered out into the kitchen.

In the darkness he almost stumbled over the dog. The animal was making no sound now, just lying with its head on its outstretched front paws, whimpering. Its eyes riveted to the back door.

Reece stood still for a second, listening. His own blood roared in his ears and he was more than aware of his laboured breathing.

The rattling began again, louder this time. he squinted through the darkness, trying to clear his head, trying to see what was making the noise. He stepped closer and then, in the dull light which was escaping from the living room into the kitchen, he saw it.

The handle of the back door was being moved up and down.

Reece swallowed hard.

Someone was trying to get in.

If he had been sober, perhaps his reaction would have been different. Perhaps he would have noticed the dog, cowering in one corner, perhaps he would have noticed the deep cold which had filled the room. Perhaps he would even have called the police.

As it was, he reached for the handle, his other hand turning the key in the lock.

The rattling stopped and, through clouded eyes, Gordon Reece saw the handle slowly turn as the door was pushed open. He took a step back, rubbing his eyes, his heart thudding against his ribs.

The door swung back gently on its hinges and the room suddenly became colder.

Reece gasped, not sure whether he was asleep or not. Was he dreaming? Perhaps he was already dead and in hell. His dulled brain had no answer to give him this time.

Standing before him, the dirt of the grave still clogging her empty eye sockets, was his wife.

There was a blur of gold as the labrador bolted through the open door into the night and Gordon opened his mouth, not knowing whether to be sick or scream.

The thing which had once been Emma Reece took a step towards him. Her lips slid back to reveal teeth dripping saliva and Gordon saw the savage wounds on her throat which had killed her, the deep scratches around her eyes. Eyes? There was nothing there. Just the torn sockets, black and empty as night. But there was something more and now Gordon prayed that his mind was playing tricks on him. For in those twin black voids were two pin pricks of red light. Light that glowed like the fires of hell and, in his last moments, Gordon saw that red light fill her empty eyes.

He had no time to scream before she was upon him.

13

Lambert looked at his watch and then up at the clock on the police station wall. It was nine fifteen, Sunday morning.

'Shit,' he said, 'might as well get it over with.'

Hayes nodded.

'What's Reece's address?' asked the Inspector.

Hayes flicked through the files and found it. Lambert wrote it down. He looked around the duty room. There were only three constables on duty this morning. Three at the station at any rate. The other seven were out looking for Mackenzie.

'P.C. Walford, you drive me,' Lambert smiled. 'Why the hell should I use my own petrol?'

Walford followed him out into the car park and unlocked one of the four Panda cars which the force possessed. Both men got in and Walford started the engine.

'It's a beautiful day,' Lambert observed as the Panda moved slowly through the streets of Medworth. 'Too nice to be doing this sort of thing.'

Walford smiled. 'Where do you reckon Mackenzie is, guv?'

Lambert shrugged. 'He's probably left the area by now. I mean, looking at it logically, if he was still around here we'd have found him by now.'

Walford wasn't convinced. 'There's plenty of places to hide in the hills around town. There's caves that run for miles.'

'Maybe. We'll see what turns up.'

'My Mum's scared about all this, guv.'

'You haven't been talking have you, Walford? I don't want too much of this getting out. In a small town like this panic could spread quickly.' He paused, looking out of the car windows. 'I just wish we could find the bastard before he has the chance to do it again. I'd rather people read about this sort of thing in the paper *after* we caught him. If there's too much talk before hand, it won't make *our* job any easier.'

They drove for a little way in silence then Lambert asked, 'You live with your parents then?'

Walford nodded. 'I've been trying to find a place of my own but I can't afford it.'

The Inspector studied his companion's profile for a moment. The lad wasn't much younger than him. He guessed there were three or four years between them.

'I sometimes wonder why I joined the force,' said Walford suddenly, swallowing hard and looking at Lambert as if he had said something he shouldn't. The Inspector was staring straight ahead out of the windscreen. He was silent for a time and the constable wondered if he had heard, then Lambert said:

'It makes me wonder why *anyone* joins.'

'What about you, sir? Why did you join?'

asked Walford, adding quickly, as an after-thought, 'If you don't mind me asking.'

Lambert shook his head. 'Sometimes *I* wonder. At one time I would have said principles.' He laughed mirthlessly. 'But now, I don't know. I thought at one time that, well, I thought I could better myself. Sounds like bullshit doesn't it?' He glanced across at Walford but the P.C. had his eyes on the road. 'I didn't want to end up like my old man. A nothing for the whole of my fucking life.' His voice had taken on an angry edge. 'This job gave me something I never had before. Self respect. A sense of importance, that what I was doing was making some difference to a tiny part of the world.' He grunted indignantly.

Walford brought the car to a halt.

'That's it, sir,' he said, pointing across the road. Lambert flipped open his notebook and checked the address. He nodded.

The house was the end one of a block of three. Two storey dwellings, the standard, council built red brick structures. Identical to all the other houses in the street. In fact, the same as every one on the remainder of the estate. Lambert noted that the curtains, upstairs and down, were drawn. He inhaled deeply, held the breath then let it drain out slowly.

'You stay here,' he said, opening the door and getting out. Walford watched him as he walked across the street and down the path to the front door of the Reece house.

He knocked twice and waited for an answer. When none came, he walked around the side of the house. There was a purple painted gate barring his way into the back yard but he found, to his relief, that it was unlocked. Perhaps Mr Reece was in the garden.

As he walked around the back, Lambert could see that the garden was deserted. At the bottom was the shattered remnants of a greenhouse, the wooden frame now bleached and bare like the bones of some prehistoric creature. The garden was badly overgrown. He knocked on the back door loudly and called Reece's name.

There was no answer.

Lambert tried the door and found, to his joy, that it was open. He stepped into the kitchen, recoiling immediately from the smell. It reminded him of bad eggs. And, Jesus, it was cold. He pulled the back door closed behind him and looked around. Nothing unusual. A dog basket in one corner near the larder. A calendar which was a month behind where someone had forgotten to turn the page. Lambert looked down at the floor. There were scuff marks on the lino. He bent to get a closer look, nothing unusual about them. Traces of dirt around too. He stood up and walked into the living room, which was still in darkness because of the drawn curtains. Lambert noticed the shattered bottle of scotch, the broken glass beside the chair and fragments of it still stained with blood. He rubbed his chin thoughtfully and, using his handkerchief, picked up one of the fragments and dropped it into his jacket pocket.

He crossed to the window and pulled back the curtains. Sunlight flooded the room, particles of dust swirling around in its beams. But, despite the warmth of the sun, the room still felt like a fridge.

Lambert went out into the hall and called up the stairs.

'Mr Reece?'

Silence greeted him. He hurried up the stairs and checked the two bedrooms and bathroom. All were empty.

From the Panda car, Walford saw him emerge from the house and stride down the path of the house next door. He knocked three times, receiving no answer.

'Where the hell is everybody in this bloody street?' said Lambert under his breath.

The front door of the house beside opened and a woman popped her head out. She was in her forties, her hair in curlers and she reminded Lambert of a hedgehog in a dressing gown.

'Do you know Mr and Mrs Reece?' asked Lambert.

'Why?' asked the woman, suspiciously, retreating further behind the half open door until only her head was sticking out.

'I'm a policeman,' Lambert told her. 'I wanted to talk to Mr Reece but there's no one in. Have you seen or heard him around today?'

'Terrible business that,' said the woman, shaking her head. 'And with it only happening down the street too. Makes you scared to go out.'

'Have you seen Mr Reece?' persisted Lambert.

'And what with that other couple being murdered too. I tell you, I don't feel safe, even when my old man's home.'

Lambert was losing his patience. 'Have you seen Mr Reece today?'

'What?'

The Inspector bit his lip. 'Reece. Have you seen him go out, did you hear anything during the night?'

The woman looked horrified. 'He's not dead too, is he?'

Give me strength, thought Lambert. 'No, I just wondered if you'd seen him.'

He turned and set off back up the path, annoyance bubbling within him.

'You'd better hurry up and catch the killer, we could all be murdered in our beds,' called the woman.

'Thank you for your help, madam,' said Lambert and slammed the gate behind him. It was as he looked across the road that he saw Walford climbing out of the Panda.

'Inspector, quick,' he called.

Lambert ran across to the car.

'Message from the station, just come through,' explained the constable.

The Inspector climbed into the car and reached for the two-way radio. He flicked the transmit button.

'Puma Two to base. Lambert here. Come in.'

A hiss of static then Hayes: 'Guv, you'd better come back. We've got Mackenzie.'

There was a grin of satisfied relief on Lambert's face.

'Be right there. Puma Two, out.' He put down the two-way and pointed ahead. 'Let's move.'

With a screech of spinning tyres, the Panda sped off.

Hayes met Lambert at the door of the police

station and, together, they hurried down the corridor towards the cell where Mackenzie was being held.

'Where did they pick him up?' asked the Inspector, excitedly.

'He was run down by a car, outside Two Meadows early this morning,' Hayes told him.

Lambert looked puzzled. 'What the hell was he doing up at the cemetery?'

The question went unanswered.

'Who's with him now?' asked Lambert.

'Dr Kirby and Davies and Bell. They brought him in. The bloke who ran Mackenzie down phoned the station, I got them to pick him up.'

'Well done Vic,' said the Inspector. He suddenly stood still. 'You said he was run down. Is he hurt badly?'

Hayes smiled humourlessly. 'That's the funny thing. There's not a mark on him.'

Lambert pushed open the door to the cell and walked in. Standing on either side of the door were Constables Davies and Bell. Sitting on a chair next to the bed was Kirby and, lying on the bed itself, was the motionless figure of Ray Mackenzie.

'All right, lads,' said Lambert, motioning the two constables from the room. He closed the door behind them and looked at Kirby.

'Well?' he said

Kirby smiled, 'I haven't done a thorough examination yet.'

Lambert walked across to the bed and looked down at the prostrate form, the eyes tightly closed, mouth slightly open. He noted with disgust that a thin trail of saliva was dribbling

117

from it. Kirby got up and crossed to the small wash basin in the cell, spashed his hands and dried them quickly. Then he reached into his black bag for his stethoscope. He pressed it to Mackenzie's chest, hearing at the same time the guttural laboured breathing.

'The heartbeat's strong,' said Kirby.

He checked the blood pressure and found it a little low, but nothing out of the ordinary.

As he rummaged for his pen light, Lambert said, 'Hayes told me a car hit him.'

'Apparently,' said Kirby, still searching.

'Was he unconscious when they brought him in?'

The doctor nodded, finally laying hands on his pen light. He bent closer to Mackenzie and pulled back one closed eyelid.

'Jesus Christ.'

Both men stepped back.

'What the hell is wrong with his eyes?' gasped Lambert.

Kirby, annoyed with himself for having been startled, now leant forward once more and gently pushed back the eyelid. He found himself staring into a glazed orb of blood. No whites, no pupils. Just the fiery red of blood. He exhaled deeply and flicked on the penlight.

'It looks as though there's been some sort of haemorrhage in the vessels of the eye.' He checked the other one and found it was the same. Slowly, he bent forward and shone the tiny beam of light into Mackenzie's right eye.

The man roared a deep, animal bellow of rage and struck out. The powerful fist caught Kirby in the chest and knocked him back against the wall. He coughed, gasping for air.

Mackenzie lay still again.

'You all right?' said Lambert, helping the doctor to his feet.

Kirby coughed again and shook his head. His face was flushed and he rubbed his chest painfully. Only after a minute or so did he find the breath to speak.

'Tom, I want him strapped down before I continue the examination.' He groaned, 'Christ, the bastard nearly broke a rib.' Kirby sucked in air, finding the effort painful but gradually it passed and he retrieved his pen light. Davies and Bell, meantime, had entered and were binding Mackenzie to the bed with thick rope. The Inspector checked that the bonds were secure and looked at Kirby.

'Pull his eyelids up,' instructed the doctor, watching as Lambert moved to the head of the bed. He leant over and gently drew back Mackenzie's thick lids, exposing the red spheres beneath. Kirby, keeping his distance, directed the pen light at them.

Mackenzie roared again and tried to lunge forward but the ropes held him down. Lambert exerted an iron grip on his head giving time for Kirby to get a decent look. Mackenzie's screams of enraged pain echoed around the small cell, nearly deafening the two men. Kirby leaned closer, smelling the fetid breath in his face and nearly wincing away from it. But he kept the beam focused on the red eyes until he was satisfied. Then he flicked it off and Mackenzie's body went limp. The room, silent now, was disturbed only by his guttural breathing.

Kirby shook his head. 'Like I said, I would think it's something to do with the blood vessels in the eye. Possibly a disturbance of the cornea.'

'Would that explain his sensitivity to light?' asked Lambert.

'Not really. If it is corneal haemorrhage then there'd be no sight at all; he wouldn't even have been able to see the light.'

'What do you recommend?' Lambert wanted to know.

Kirby shrugged. 'Leave him for now. I'll come back in the morning and take another look. But Tom, I'd leave those ropes on.'

Lambert nodded and both men walked out, the Inspector being careful to lock the cell behind them. He posted Davies outside, telling the constable to let them know if there was any sign of movement from Mackenzie.

The Inspector looked at his watch. It was ten forty-three. It had been some morning.

'Fancy a drink?' he asked and Kirby nodded.

The snug bar of 'The Blacksmith' was empty when they walked in. The grate, where a coal fire burned at night, was empty. Just a cold black hole and the room itself was chilly but neither of them noticed. Lambert bought the drinks and returned to the table.

'Cheers,' he said, downing a large mouthful of scotch.

Kirby returned the compliment and sipped delicately at his half of lager.

'You realize this is unethical,' said the doctor, smiling.

'What?'

'A doctor *and* and a police Inspector drinking on duty.'

Both men laughed.

'Sod the ethics, John,' said Lambert. 'Right now, I need this.' He took another swig and cradled the glass between his hands.

'I wonder what the local paper would make of this?' pondered Kirby.

Lambert grunted. 'They've got enough to keep them going at the moment without wondering whether you and I are drinking.' He paused for a moment. 'Three murders. Jesus. In a town this size.'

'Just be thankful you've got the killer.'

'I am, don't get me wrong. But there're things about this case that don't add up. And more than that, I've got a missing person on my hands too. Gordon Reece has . . .' struggled for the word, '. . . disappeared. I went to talk to him about his wife's death this morning and there was no sign of him. The neighbours haven't seen or heard him about since yesterday morning and I found *this* in the living room of the house.' He reached into his jacket pocket and pulled out the handkerchief. Unwrapping it carefully he revealed the bloodstained lump of glass.

'Three murders, the victims mutilated, and the husband of the third victim has disappeared without trace. Can *you* tell me what the hell is going on in this town?' He drained his glass and slammed it down on the table.

'I don't see your problem, Tom,' said Kirby,

'you've got the killer. The missing man probably just left town, couldn't face the questioning or whatever. It's probably quite simple.'

Lambert exhaled deeply, his eyes riveted to the lump of blood-stained glass lying on the table in front of him.

14

Four fifty p.m. and the purple hues of approaching night were beginning to colour the skies above Medworth. Dusk hovered expectantly, a portent of the dark hours to come. It was the time when working people began to count the minutes to signal the end of the day's labours. A cold breeze had sprung up during late afternoon and there was a promise of frost for the coming night.

Tom Lambert shivered a little in his office and stared down at the solid gold medallion lying on his blotter. He prodded it with the end of a pencil, reading over and over again the strange inscription on it and around its edges. He had scribbled the words down on the edge of his blotter and he determined to look up their meanings when he got home. Debbie might even know. She knew a little Latin. He looked at the pencilled words:

MORTIS DIEI

Below it, the symbols which ran around the edging of the medallion;

UTCON (scratch mark) XER (scratch) ERATICXE (two scratches)

SIUTROM (scratch) A.

Lambert shook his head. The second set of words didn't even look like Latin.

He'd found the medallion quite by accident that afternoon. Returning from the pub about one, he had gone to deposit the chunk of blood stained glass from Reece's house in the safe where items of evidence were kept. He'd noticed the jewel box which had belonged to June Mackenzie and asked Hayes what it was. The sergeant had explained how they had found the box in the bedroom of the first victim and, upon opening it, Lambert had discovered the medallion.

Now he sat with it before him, wondering how on earth a man like Mackenzie had come to possess an object so obviously valuable. The policeman couldn't begin to guess at the age of the thing but, from the weight of it and the thickness of the chain which supported it, he could at least ponder over its value. It was as he looked closely at it that he noticed the gossamer-like strands clinging to the links of the chain. He bent closer and pulled one free. It felt coarse as he rubbed it between his thumb and forefinger. There was more attached to the other links and something else.

It looked like dried mud.

Lambert exhaled deeply. Perhaps a forensic test would establish exactly where the gold circlet had originated. He pulled a few of the coarse strands free and scraped some mud away with the tip of his pen knife. Then he reached into his desk drawer and took out a tiny plastic bag. Into this, he carefully pushed the fibres and mud. He sealed it with a piece of cellotape and left it on his desk, reminding himself to ring Kirby before he went home, perhaps even run the stuff around to the doctor himself.

Once more he looked down at the medallion, the inscriptions causing his forehead to crease as he tried to make sense of them.

MORTIS DIEI

The words had been engraved across the centre of the circlet but the other inscription . . .

Running around the outside of the medallion, he wasn't sure where the words began and where they ended. He determined to take it home that night, let Debbie take a look at it. The thought of her made him look up at the clock. He smiled when he saw the time and realized that he would set off soon. He was looking forward to getting home. It had been a long day. Every day seemed to be a long one just lately and he told himself it was just a matter of getting back into the swing of things. There was nothing more he could do at the station that night. Mackenzie was still flat out in his cell, tied securely by the ropes. Davies was outside the cell just in case there was any sign of movement from him. The constable had orders to contact Dr Kirby immediately if there was any change.

Lambert pulled another plastic bag from his drawer and slid the medallion into it, then he popped the little package into the pocket of his jacket.

He got to his feet and crossed to the window of his office. Night had descended now, casting its black shadow over the land. Lambert could see the lights of houses in the town twinkling like a thousand stars. The police station was about a mile out of town, built on a hillside which looked over Medworth like a guardian. Far below him, the town lay spread.

Lambert yawned.

The door of his office flew open, slammed against the wall and rocked on its hinges, the impact nearly breaking the frosted glass in it.

Davies stood there panting. 'It's Mackenzie, sir, he's going crazy.'

Lambert dashed past the constable, heading for the cell, aware now of the noise coming from the end of the corridor. Hayes emerged from the duty room and joined the other two men as they reached the cell door. Lambert eased back the sliding flap of the peephole and drew in a quick breath.

Mackenzie had broken his bonds and was throwing himself against the walls frenziedly, every now and then turning towards the open peephole and fixing Lambert in a stare from those blazing red eyes. The Inspector felt the hairs on the nape of his neck rise. Then Mackenzie spun around and hurled himself at the small window at the far end of the cell. It was about half way up the wall. No more than a foot square, it was set at a height which would have made a man of average size stretch to reach it. Wire mesh covered the bars which firmly blocked the narrow opening.

As Lambert watched, Mackenzie leapt at the window, tearing away the wire mesh as if it had been fish netting. Then he fastened his powerful hands around the bars and pulled, roaring in frustration when they wouldn't budge. The darkness outside called him and he would stop at nothing to reach it. Realizing that he could not move the bars, he turned his attention to the cell door. He slammed into it, pressing his face to the peephole and for a split second Lambert found himself staring into those empty crimson eyes. There was nothing there. No emotion registered in them. Nothing. Just the glazed red of two enormous blood blisters. The rage and hatred was registered on Mackenzie's face, the lips drawn back to reveal the yellowed teeth, saliva spattering the room as he spun about in a frenzy.

'How long has he been like this?' Lambert asked Davies, who was white with fear and thankful that a twelve inch thick steel door separated him from the maniac inside.

'A couple of minutes,' he answered, 'as soon as it got dark, he started.'

Lambert looked at Hayes but the sergeant looked blank.

'Get Kirby down here fast,' snapped the Inspector, watching as Hayes scuttled off.

Peering once more into the cell, Lambert said, 'Why isn't the light on in there?' He looked up at the hundred watt bulb, unshaded, in the ceiling of the cell.

'I was just going to do it when I looked in and saw what was going on,' explained Davies.

Lambert stroked his chin thoughtfully, remembering how violently Mackenzie had reacted to light that morning.

'Turn it on,' he said.

Davies flicked a switch and the cell was suddenly bathed in cold white light.

Mackenzie screamed and raised his hands, snatching at the light bulb, trying simultaneously to shield his eyes and to reach the blinding

127

object. His head throbbed as he tried to shield himself from the glare and he backed into a corner like a dog who knows he's about to be beaten. As Lambert watched, Mackenzie slumped to his knees, bowed his head and covered it with his arms. He was growling, the sounds gurgling in his throat. The Inspector watched amazed as Mackenzie slowly raised himself up again, one arm shielding his eyes, and staggered towards the light. Then, with a howl of rage, he leapt and smashed a fist into the bulb, shattering it and ripping the flesh from his knuckles. He seemed not to notice the pain, relieved only that the room was, once more, in darkness. Blood dripped from his lacerated hand but he grunted and raised a dripping fist defiantly towards the peephole.

Lambert slammed it shut and exhaled deeply.

'Jesus,' he breathed, softly.

'What do we do, sir?' said Davies, listening to the sounds coming from inside the cell.

Lambert had no answer for him. He pushed past the constable and headed for his office. Davies squinted through the peephole just in time to see Mackenzie tear the wash basin from its position on the wall. He lifted it above his head and flung it to the ground where it shattered. Large chunks of porcelain flew about the room like white shrapnel. Water from the ruptured pipes jetted into the cell spattering Mackenzie, but he ignored it, turning once more to the tiny window and gripping the bars in a frenzied effort to tear them free.

Davies closed the flap. He swallowed hard and

sat down outside the cell, the noises of destruction from inside ringing in his ears.

While he was waiting for Kirby to arrive, Lambert phoned home to tell Debbie that he'd be late, but he got no answer. She couldn't be home yet, he reasoned. He slammed the receiver down and said to no one in particular, 'Where the hell is Kirby?'

Hayes emerged from the duty room carrying a steaming mug of coffee. He handed it to Lambert who smiled.

'I could do with something stronger, Vic.'

The sergeant grinned and pulled a silver flask from the pocket of his tunic. He unscrewed the cap and poured a small measure of brown liquid into the Inspector's mug. Then he repeated the procedure with his own.

'Purely medicinal, sir,' he said.

Lambert smiled broadly and drank a couple of mouthfuls.

From down the corridor they could still hear the frightful noises coming from Mackenzie's cell.

'He's mad,' said Hayes, flatly.

'I hope so,' said Lambert, enigmatically. 'I really do hope so.' Hayes looked puzzled.

The door leading from the annexe opened and both men looked up. It was only constables Ferman and Jenkins arriving for night duty.

'What's all the noise?' asked Ferman.

'Never mind that,' snapped Hayes. 'Just get on with your job.'

Ferman raised two fingers as he walked past, making sure that he was behind Hayes when he did it. The two men disappeared into the duty room.

Kirby walked in, his black bag clutched firmly in his hand. He nodded curtly.

'About fucking time,' snapped Lambert, impatiently. He hurried out from behind the enquiry counter and led the doctor down towards the cell.

'My receptionist told me you called,' explained Kirby. 'I'd been out on an emergency.'

'Well, we've got an emergency here, right now,' growled Lambert.

Kirby caught him by the arm. 'Look, Tom, my responsibilities are to my patients. I'm a G.P. first and foremost, a bloody police doctor second. Understand?'

The Inspector held his gaze for a moment. 'Listen to that,' he said, inclining his head towards the cell.

Kirby heard the sounds of pandemonium and frowned. He followed Lambert to the cell door and peered through the peephole. Mackenzie was hanging from the bars with his talonlike hands, blood from his injured limb pouring down his arm.

'He broke the light bulb,' explained Lambert, 'the light drives him crazy. It seems to cause him pain.'

'How long has he been like this?' asked Kirby, not taking his eyes from the hole.

'Since it got dark,' said the Inspector, flatly. 'What can you do?'

Kirby let the flap slide back into position, covering the hole. 'Nothing. If I give him a shot of something there's no guarantee it'll knock him out. That's assuming I can get close enough to administer it in the first place.'

'There must be something you can give him,' snapped Lambert.

'I've just told you,' said Kirby, his tone rising slightly. 'I've got Thorazine in here, but there's no way of knowing if it'll work and *I*, for one, don't intend going in there with *him* like that.'

The two men stood silently for a moment, looking at one another. Then Kirby said, more gently, 'Just leave him. I'll look at him in the morning. If he's calmed down.'

'And if he hasn't?'

The doctor peered through the peephole again, 'This will hold him won't it?' He banged on the metal door.

Lambert nodded, 'Yeah.' There was a note of tired resignation in his voice.

'I suggest we both go home, Tom. If anything more happens during the night . . .' The sentence trailed off and he shrugged.

Lambert touched the metal door gently, listening to the bellowing and crashing coming from inside.

'I just hope it *does* hold him,' he said, quietly.

15

Lambert lay on his back in bed, staring at the ceiling. Outside, the wind whispered quietly past the windows. A low, almost soothing whoosh, which occasionally grew in power and rattled the glass in its frame, as if reminding people of its power. But, at the moment, it hissed softly past the dark opening.

The clock on the bedside table ticked its insistent rhythm, sounding louder than usual in the stillness of the night. The luminous hands showed that it was after three in the morning.

Lambert exhaled and closed his eyes. Images and thoughts sped through his mind with dizzying speed.

Mackenzie. The disappearance of Gordon Reece. The medallion.

The medallion.

He had shown it to Debbie earlier on and she had confirmed his own suspicions that the inscriptions were, indeed, Latin. Well, the central one at any rate. The gibberish around the rim of the circlet foxed her too. She said that she would try to find out what the inscriptions meant. There were reference books in the library which might tell them. He had dismissed the idea, telling her that there was probably no significance in it anyway. But something nagged at the back of his mind. Something unseen which had plunged teeth of doubt into his mind and had held on as surely as a stoat holds a rabbit.

He sat up, trying not to disturb Debbie. She was asleep beside him, her breathing low and contented. As regular as the ticking of the clock.

Every minute he expected the phone to ring. To hear Hayes telling him that Mackenzie had broken out. Lambert dismissed the thought. That was impossible. The cell door was a foot thick, the bars of the windows embedded two feet into the concrete. He couldn't possibly get out. Lambert swallowed hard and ran a hand through his hair. He closed his eyes and brought his knees up, resting his head on them.

Again the thoughts came back. Alien thoughts with no answer.

Mackenzie's sensitivity to light. His eyes (if that was the word). The frenzy which overcame him during night-time. The mutilation of the three victims. Why had the eyes been torn out?

'Oh Christ.'

He said it out loud this time, cursing himself as he heard Debbie moan in her sleep. He watched her sleeping form for a moment, worried that he had woken her. When she didn't move he returned to his previous position. Head bowed on his upraised knees.

'What's wrong, Tom?'

Her voice startled him and he turned to see her looking up at him.

'I'm sorry I woke you,' he said, reaching for her hand and squeezing it.

'What is it?' she asked, her voice gentle.

He sighed, 'I can't sleep.'

She snuggled closer to him and he felt the warmth of her body, naked beneath the sheets. 'What were you thinking about?' she wanted to know.

'This and that,' he said, smiling wanly.

'Don't give me that crap,' she said, forcefully, squeezing his hand until he made a cry of mock pain. 'It's this business with Mackenzie isn't it?'

'Debbie, I've never seen anything like it. He's like a wild animal. But it only seems to be at night. Jesus, I don't know what the hell is going on.'

'You know that medallion? I was thinking, why don't you take it to an antique dealer? Old Mr Trefoile in the town would be able to date it for you; he might even be able to decipher the inscriptions.'

Lambert nodded. He was silent for a while, rubbing his eyes. He felt a hand trace its way from the top of his knee to his thigh. Debbie pressed herself closer to him, her hand finally brushing through his pubic hair and closing around his flaccid penis. She looked up at him, surprised.

'You really *are* worried,' she said.

He grinned and she tried to pull her hand away but he held it there, feeling the warmth of her fingers as they stroked, coaxing him to hardness. When he was fully erect, she ran her index finger from the tip of his penis to the testicles, now drawn up tightly with excitement. She cupped them briefly before returning to his swollen shaft. He moaned softly as she closed her hand around

134

him and began rubbing gently. As her movements became more insistent he lay back,
thrusting his hips towards the stroking hand. At
the same time, he sought the wetness between
her legs, his fingers teasing her clitoris before
plunging deeper into the oozing cleft of her
vagina. She drove herself hard against him,
finally pulling him onto her, his hard organ
sliding easily into her.

A moment later they climaxed savagely and
clung to one another long after the sensations
had died away. He rolled off and lay on his back,
both of them panting. She leant across and kissed
him, eventually falling asleep with her head on
his chest. He stroked her hair with his hand,
feeling its soft silkiness beneath his fingers.

He returned to staring at the ceiling, wishing
that sleep would come, but the hands of the clock
pointed to four-fifteen before he finally drifted
off into peaceful oblivion.

Kirby stood up as Lambert entered the room.
He had been sitting on a chair next to the cell bed
on which Mackenzie lay. Mackenzie was still, his
eyes closed, arms by his sides. Sunlight streamed
in through the small window in the wall of the
cell. Constable Ferman was also in the room,
standing at the far end of the bed and looking
down at the body of Mackenzie, who was now
securely tied down with thick bands of hemp.

'Morning, Tom,' said Kirby.

The inspector nodded a greeting and looked
down at the immobile figure of Mackenzie.

'What happened?' he asked in awe.

Kirby motioned to Ferman and the constable

135

coughed, clearing his throat as if he were about to make a public address.

'Well sir,' he began, 'I was sitting out there this morning, listening to all the din going on in here and, well, about five o'clock everything went quiet. I looked through the viewing slot and Mackenzie was lying on the floor.'

'Dawn was at five o'clock,' Kirby clarified.

'I waited for about fifteen minutes,' continued Ferman. 'He didn't move, so I came in, put him on the bed and tied him down again.'

'The light,' said Lambert.

Kirby nodded. 'The darkness triggers him off, the light shuts him down. This man is like a light sensitive machine, only, if you'll forgive the flippancy, his mechanism is working in reverse. He comes alive during the darkness and . . .' he shrugged, 'switches off during the daylight.'

Lambert looked down at Mackenzie's body, his mouth almost dropping open in awe.

'His vital signs are practically nil,' said Kirby. 'The heart has slowed to less than forty beats a minute, the pulse and blood pressure are so faint I could hardly get readings. He's in a torpor.'

'What the hell is that?' snapped Lambert.

'Coma if you like.'

'What do we do?'

'I wish I knew.'

'You're a doctor for Christ's sake, John; you must have some ideas.'

'Look. During the night, he's fine.'

Lambert cut him short. 'Fine? He's a psycho during the bloody night.'

Kirby waved away the policeman's protests.

'What I meant was, his life signs are all in order. There's nothing wrong with him bodily.'

'Apart from the fact that he's a maniac with the strength of ten men,' said Lambert, his voice heavy with scorn.

There was an awkward silence then Kirby spoke again.

'I think the problem is in his brain, not his body. It's psychosis of some sort, but we don't know why it's triggered by darkness.'

'This is getting us nowhere,' said Lambert impatiently. 'I want to know what we have to do. This is going to happen again tonight, right? I want an answer quick, John. I'm asking you for a medical answer to this problem. And keep it simple.'

'You've got a number of alternatives, Tom. I either pump him full of Thorazine now and we wait and see if it keeps him out during the night, we keep him locked in here until someone qualified can look at him, or . . .' He hesitated.

'Or what?' Lambert demanded.

'We give him an E.E.G.'

Lambert looked puzzled.

'It's an Electroencephalogram. It tests brain waves.'

'I know what it does,' snapped Lambert, 'I don't see how it would help.'

'It might tell us why the darkness triggers off this savagery at night, why he's terrified of light. That's my last theory.'

The policeman nodded. 'Where would it be done?'

'There's a unit in the hospital in Wellham, about twenty miles from here. I know the

137

specialist in charge of it. If I get in touch with him now, we could have this done before nightfall.'

'Do it,' said Lambert and Kirby scuttled out of the room.

The Inspector looked down at the body of Mackenzie and then at the wrecked cell.

Ferman coughed. 'What if it doesn't work, sir?' he asked tentatively.

Lambert looked at him for a moment, searching for an answer, then turned and walked out.

16

Lambert felt the need to shield his eyes, even though he stood behind a screen of tinted glass. The light inside the examination room was blinding, pouring down from four huge fluorescent banks.

Mackenzie was strapped to a trolley in the centre of the room and, as the policeman watched, two men dressed in white overalls undid the straps and lifted him onto a table. They hurriedly secured him again and one of them, a tall man with blond hair, pulled each of them to ensure they were tight enough. The man turned towards the glass partition behind which stood Lambert, Kirby and Dr Stephen Morgan. The man raised a thumb and Morgan nodded.

He was in his forties. What people like to refer to as 'well-preserved,' for he looked barely older than thirty. He had a carefully groomed moustache which seemed as though it had lost its growing strength when it reached the corners of his mouth and drooped downwards. His blue eyes were obscured somewhat by thin tinted glasses which he removed and began polishing with a handy tissue.

Lambert looked back into the examination

room. Mackenzie was now lying, apparently unconscious, on a hinged couch which could be adjusted by a large screw on the side and, as he watched, the intern with the blond hair twisted it so that Mackenzie was propped up slightly. His mouth opened briefly, as if he were going to protest, then it closed tightly. A tiny dribble of yellowish saliva escaped and ran down his chin.

A nurse dressed in a white smock entered from a door which led off to the right. She paused beside the couch, looking briefly at Mackenzie, then she looked at Morgan. He jabbed a finger towards a trolley which stood beside the couch. The nurse reached for a swab and dipped it into a kidney dish full of clear liquid. She dabbed it carefully onto five places on the top of Mackenzie's head.

'What's that?' asked Lambert, fascinated by the ritual which was taking place before him.

'Conductant,' explained Morgan.

The Inspector nodded abstractedly and continued to watch the preparations. Next, the nurse attached five electrodes to the places where she had applied the swab. She looked at Morgan who swiftly checked his readout. The machine which he stood beside looked, to Lambert, rather like a computer. It had a long length of thin paper running through it and, across this, lay a metal arm which would translate into visual terms, by means of lines, the brain waves received from Mackenzie. Lambert almost laughed. It reminded him of a lie detector he had once seen on an American crime film.

Morgan flicked a switch and a red light came on, signalling that the machine was ready for operation. He raised his hand and the nurse and both interns retreated from the room. A second later they joined Lambert and the others in the observation area.

Morgan flicked another switch.

'We'll test the motor impulses first,' he said.

'I thought the machine usually recorded all the waves at once,' said Kirby.

'Most of them do,' Morgan told him. 'This modification, testing each centre of the brain individually, makes it easier to pin down the trouble and it makes things a damn sight easier for me.'

He pressed the green button and the machine whirred into life.

'Here goes,' muttered Morgan.

Lambert didn't know where to look. His eyes flitted back and forth, from Mackenzie to the machine, from machine to Mackenzie. Morgan stood over the readout, a deep furrow creasing his brow. He readjusted his glasses, as if that act would somehow rectify what he was seeing.

'There's no movement at all,' he said, softly. The arm on the paper was immobile, the tiny piece of graphite it held was stationary. Just one continual black line drawn on the paper, unbroken and unwavering. No loops, no zigzags. Nothing.

'There's no brain impulses at all,' said Morgan, scarcely believing what he saw.

'Perhaps the machine is acting up,' said Lambert hopefully.

Morgan shook his head. He turned to the blond intern, Peter Brooks. 'Turn off the lights.' Brooks slapped a switch and, immediately, the examination room was plunged into darkness. Two huge shutters had been put up at the vast plate glass windows which looked into the room and not a single chink of light infiltrated the blackness.

'Christ,' whispered Morgan, watching as the needle swung back and forth with a ferocity which threatened to tear it loose. It drew parabolas, pyramids, all with vast savage strokes.

'Lights,' snapped Morgan and, once more, the examination room was filled with blinding white light.

The needle on the readout stopped swinging and settled back into its unerring parallel course, never deviating from the straight line it drew.

'That's incredible,' muttered Morgan.

'You see what we mean about the light?' said Kirby. 'In bright light he's dormant, but in darkness he goes crazy.'

Morgan stroked his chin thoughtfully. He looked down at the readout and then across at the still form of Mackenzie. He'd never seen anything like this before and the discovery sent a thrill of excitement through him. He told Brooks to turn off the lights once more.

It happened again. The needle swung crazily back and forth across the readout sheet, never settling into a pattern, just looping and tearing up and down.

Lambert looked worriedly at Kirby. He had noticed that Mackenzie had moved his right hand, was flexing the fingers.

'Put the lights back on,' he snapped.

Brooks hesitated.

'No, wait,' said Morgan, fascinated by the

142

course the needle was taking. So intent on watching it was he, that he didn't notice Mackenzie raise his head and look up.

The nurse stifled a scream as she saw the twin red orbs which had once been eyes, staring at her through the darkness.

Lambert now crossed to the light switch, seeing that Mackenzie was straining against the straps. With a loud crack, one of them securing his arms broke and he began tearing at the broad one which covered his chest and pinned him to the couch.

Morgan looked into the examination room, horrified as he watched Mackenzie breaking free.

Lambert pressed the light switch.

Nothing happened.

Frantic, he pressed it again. Jesus Christ, he thought, what's happened to the fucking lights?

Mackenzie was sitting up now, tearing at the strap which was fastened across his thighs. Another few moments and he would be free.

Lambert slapped the switch frenziedly. For a brief second he thought they were going to work. All four powerful banks flashed with brilliant white light and Mackenzie screamed as the brightness scorched his blazing red eyes. But then, one by one, the tubes blew, exploding in a shower of hot glass, their ends glowing red as they died. Smoke rose from them in silvery wisps.

The darkness was total.

With a last desperate surge of strength, Mackenzie tore free of the final strap and swung himself off the couch. The nurse screamed.

Brooks reached for the door which connected

the examination room with the observation booth.

'Get some light in there,' screamed Lambert, following him.

The Inspector stood no more than three feet from Mackenzie, staring into those bottomless red eyes, riveted by the obscene thing before him. Then Mackenzie leapt.

Lambert, with a speed born of fear, threw himself to one side and avoided the rush. Mackenzie crashed into a surgical trolley but was up in an instant and grabbing for the policeman once more.

'The shutters,' screamed Lambert, 'open the shutters!'

Mackenzie was upon him, powerful hands grasping for his throat, forcing him back over the couch. Lambert smelt the fetid breath in his face, disgusted as the yellow spittle dripped onto him. He struck out, his fist slamming into Mackenzie's forehead. The grip slackened momentarily and Lambert brought his knee up into the man's stomach.

Brooks, meantime, was struggling to tear down the shutters. A chink of light lanced through the blackness and he almost laughed. Another second and the room would be flooded with light. The intern tore at the catches, pulling one of the shutters wide.

Sunlight flooded the room and Lambert suddenly felt the grip on his throat removed as Mackenzie screamed and raised both hands to shield his eyes. The Inspector rolled clear, searching for something to fight back with. It was scarcely necessary. Mackenzie turned towards the window, his red eyes narrowed against the light but fixed on Brooks who was in the process of tearing down the second shutter.

With a roar, Mackenzie ran at Brooks, launching himself at the intern.

He crashed into his prey with the force of a steam train, hurling him backward.

The nurse screamed as both men hit the window.

The glass exploded outward, huge shards flying into the air as Mackenzie and Brooks crashed through the window. They seemed to hang in the air for a second before plummeting the twelve storeys to the ground below.

Lambert scrambled to his feet, hearing the sickening thump as both men hit the ground. Cool air blew in through the broken window and, being careful to avoid the pieces of shattered glass, the Inspector leaned over the sill.

A hundred feet below him, still locked together, lay the bodies of Mackenzie and Brooks. Around them, a spreading pool of blood was mingling with fragments of smashed glass.

'Oh God,' groaned Lambert, bowing his head.

The second intern comforted the nurse who was sobbing uncontrollably.

Kirby and Morgan walked slowly across to the window and also peered down at the smashed bodies.

No one spoke. What was there to say? Lambert ran a hand through his hair and exhaled deeply, suddenly aware of the pain in his neck where Mackenzie had attacked him. He touched a fingertip to it and saw a smear of blood when he withdrew it.

Kirby tilted the policeman's head back and looked at the cut.

'Just a graze, Tom,' he said.

Lambert nodded.

'I don't know what to say,' murmured Morgan. 'I've never seen anything like it. No brainwaves.'

Lambert stood up. 'Is that all that bothers you? Two men have just died, for Christ's sake.' He sighed and sat down on the edge of the couch.

'It would appear our problems are over, Tom,' said Kirby, trying to sound cheerful.

Lambert regarded him balefully for a second and thought about saying something, but held it back. Kirby was right. He had to admit that. Now the only problem he had was finding Gordon Reece. It seemed petty in comparison to the problems he'd had these last few days. The nurse had stopped crying and the second intern was helping her out of the room. Morgan watched them go.

The Inspector got to his feet and headed for the door.

'Where are you going, Tom?' asked Kirby.

'Back to work,' snapped Lambert and walked out.

Lambert drove back to Medworth alone. He felt as if he needed his own company. He didn't want to talk about what he'd just seen and he drove with both windows open as if the fresh air blowing into the car would cleanse his mind. The smell of damp earth and grass was strong, a welcome contrast to the antiseptic smell of the hospital he had just left. He hated hospitals, always had, ever since he was a child, and what he had just seen had done nothing to change his mind.

The countryside rushed past him as he drove, perhaps a little faster than he needed. He inhaled, held the breath and then let it out slowly, trying to calm himself down. His foot eased off the accelerator and he glanced at the falling needle of the speedometer. Finally, he slowed to about twenty, swung the car into a lay-by and shut off the engine.

The road was narrow, flanked on either side by tall hedges. To his right lay hillside, green and shimmering in the early morning sunlight. To his left, down the hill, lay Medworth. He could see smoke belching from the foundry on the far side of the town, but from this distance, it looked like nothing more than a grey wisp. Lambert got out of the car, slammed the door and leant on the bonnet, arms folded. He looked out over Medworth.

'Gordon Reece, where are you?' he said aloud, then smiled to himself. The smile dwindled rapidly as he felt the pain from the scratches on his throat. He rubbed them, remembering the power in Mackenzie's hands. If not for Brooks, he wouldn't have had a chance. Fuck it, he thought, Mackenzie had been a powerful bastard. Lambert thought about the three victims he had claimed. He wondered how they had struggled. He dismissed the thought.

There would be a full autopsy on Mackenzie that afternoon and he had been told, before leaving the hospital, that he would be contacted as soon as the results were ready. Lambert shook his head. Four people had been killed, Mackenzie himself was dead. Their knowledge would do them no good now. He sighed, still unable to believe what he had seen that morning, not wanting to believe what had happened in Medworth during the past week or so.

He suddenly thought of the medallion. Could there be a tie up between *it*, the transformation of Mackenzie, and the disappearance of Gordon Reece? He climbed back into the car and started the engine.

The medallion.

It was time he took a trip to the antique shop.

17

Howard Trefoile prodded the brown mass of liver and onions before him and plucked up the courage to take a bite. He chewed it slowly. Not too bad, after all. He stirred the brown mass around and continued eating. He would have preferred to have gone out to lunch but *that* cost money, and the way things had been for the past couple of months he couldn't afford three course meals every day. The business wasn't exactly floundering in the wake of the recession, more like languishing. Things were stable. That, he decided, was the best way to describe them. He comforted himself with the thought that other businesses in the town had gone broke while his still remained on a paying basis.

The antique shop had been left to him by his father when he died, and Howard had run it successfully for the last eight years since that sad event. He and his father had always been very close and it had been more or less preordained that *he* should take over when his father retired. Unfortunately, cancer had got his father before he could reach retiring age and Howard had been thrown in the deep end, so to speak. But his years of working with his father had stood him in good stead and he found it relatively simple to carry on the business.

His mother had died when he was ten and he could vaguely remember her, but the image wasn't strong enough to cause him pain. He stared across his kitchen table at her photo and sighed quietly. Kitchen. He smiled to himself. It could scarcely be called a kitchen. A small room at the back of the shop which served as dining room, working room, and kitchen. Beyond it lay his tiny sitting room, full of the discarded objects of times gone by. Things which he could never hope to sell in the shop itself, but which he had come to find an affection for. Upstairs was his bedroom and a store room. That was next to the bathroom and toilet.

The building, sandwiched between a shoe shop and grocers, was small, but it was adequate for Howard's needs. He lived and worked alone. There was no one in his life, but he had his work so he needed no one. At fifty-six he sometimes wondered what would become of the shop if anything happened to him, but he knew in his heart what its fate would be. It would be demolished. He felt suddenly sad. Not for himself, but for his departed father. The man had spent his entire life building up the business. The thought that it might someday just cease to exist troubled Howard. Still, he reasoned, what could he do about it now? He couldn't afford to pay staff to carry on running it should he himself pass on, so there seemed no alternative. The shop would become as anachronistic as the things it sold.

He dismissed the thoughts and continued eating. The empty packet which had housed the frozen liver and onions lay on the draining board beside him. Everything for convenience these days, he thought. Speed was of the essence in the modern world. Howard sometimes thought that he had been born twenty years too late.

As he was pushing the last soggy chunk of liver into his mouth, he heard the familiar tinkle of the bell above the door. He tutted. He must have forgotten to put the "Closed" sign up. He often did that. He got to his feet and walked to the door which led out into the shop itself.

The man standing in the shop had his back to Trefoile and, wiping a trickle of gravy from his mouth, the shop owner said;

'Excuse me sir, I'm sorry, but I'm closed for lunch, if . . .'

The man turned and Trefoile let the sentence trail off as he recognized Tom Lambert.

'Inspector Lambert,' said the antique dealer, smiling, 'I didn't realize it was you.'

Trefoile walked past him and turned the sign on the door around so that it showed "Closed" to the street outside.

'I hope I'm not interrupting anything,' said Lambert, apologetically.

'Just my amateurish attempts at lunch,' said Trefoile, smiling. 'What can I do for you?'

'I've got something that I think you might be able to help me with,' said Lambert, reaching into his pocket.

Trefoile perked up. 'Oh yes?'

The inspector laid the medallion on the counter and motioned towards it with his hand. 'What do you make of that?'

Trefoile looked excited as he bent closer,

fumbling in the pocket of his waistcoat for his eyepiece. He stuffed it in and squinted at the medallion.

'Might I ask where you acquired this, Inspector?' he asked.

Lambert sighed. 'Well, let's just say it's part of an investigation I'm working on at the moment.'

Trefoile looked at him for a moment, appearing like some kind of cyclopean monster with the eyepiece still stuffed in position. He bent to examine the medallion once more.

'What exactly did you want to know about it?' he asked. 'The value?'

'Is it valuable?' asked Lambert. 'I mean, it's gold isn't it?'

Trefoile picked up the circlet and hefted it in his hand. He inclined his head and raised his eyebrows. 'This is a *very* interesting piece of work, Inspector. I can only guess at its value of course, but from the age, weight, and purity of the metal, I'd say its value would run into thousands of pounds.' He took the eyepiece out and handed the medallion back to Lambert who looked at it in awe. He shook himself out of the stupor and gave it back to the older man.

'What period would you think it is?' he asked.

'It's very old. I would say, possibly even sixteenth century.'

Lambert scribbled the words down in his note book.

'I'd need to do certain tests of course to ascertain the exact period,' Trefoile added.

'What about the inscriptions?' said Lambert.

Trefoile bent closer. 'Latin. It's medieval script, I couldn't decipher this on the spot. My

Latin isn't up to much anymore.' He laughed and the policeman found himself grinning too, but there was no humour in the smile.

Trefoile frowned. 'You know, Inspector, this might sound ridiculous, but I think I've seen this medallion somewhere before.'

Lambert was instantly alert, his pen poised. 'Where?'

'Not in the flesh, so to speak. But in a book. My father had a large collection of antique books, and this particular object seems to ring a bell.' Trefoile shook his head, as if annoyed at his own loss of recall.

Both men stood in silence, staring down at the circlet of gold on its thick chain.

The antique dealer looked at the inscription around the outside of the medallion and shook his head. 'I don't recognize any of that.'

'Is *that* Latin?' Lambert wanted to know.

Trefoile shrugged. 'I don't know. If only I could think where I'd seen it before.' He squeezed the folds of skin beneath his chin, plucking at them. Lost in thought. Finally he said, 'Look, Inspector, could you leave it with me? I can make some tests on it, check out its authenticity. Perhaps even decipher the inscriptions.'

Lambert nodded. 'That would be marvellous. Thank you.' The two men shook hands. Lambert gave him a number to ring if he should come up with anything, then the policeman left.

Trefoile looked at the medallion, the tinkling of the door bell dying away in the solitude of the shop. Something nagged at the back of his mind. He *had* seen this before. If only he could

153

remember where. And the Latin inscription. He studied it once more, something clicking away in the forgotten recesses of his mind. He looked at the inscription across the centre of the circlet:

MORTIS DIEI

He frowned:

MORTIS

His eyes lit up. He began to remember. Of course, he should have realized. He recognized *that* word at least.

MORTIS

He smiled to himself, its English meaning now clear. The first word in that central inscription stuck out in his mind.

Death.

Lambert sat in his car outside Trefoile's antique shop but he didn't start the engine. He looked up at the sign outside the shop, blowing gently in the light breeze.

The medallion's value must run into thousands. The antique dealer's words rung in his ears. He drove back to the station where Hayes told him that the results of the autopsy on Mackenzie had come through. There were no unusual features about it. Apart from the eyes, everything was normal. Kirby had been wrong though; it hadn't been corneal haemorrhage which caused the redness in the eyes and nothing had been found to indicate why Mackenzie had become psychopathic during the dark hours. In other words, thought Lambert, the entire damned thing had been a waste of time and they were no nearer finding the motive for the killings.

Still, as he drove home he comforted himself

with one thought, Mackenzie was one off the list. Now all that remained was to find Gordon Reece. Men were combing the area under his orders. Maybe he was letting his imagination get the better of him, but Trefoile's words haunted him: the medallion's value must run into thousands.

Lambert frowned as he turned the Capri into his driveway.

Where the hell would Mackenzie get something like that?

PART
TWO

18

Life in Medworth slipped easily back into the deep groove of normality after the tumultuous events of the previous weeks.

The local paper (on Lambert's orders) kept the details of the Mackenzie killings to a minimum and the residents of the town soon forgot the horrors which had gone before. They found new things to talk about. There were things to moan about. More men made redundant at the foundry, and the heavy showers of rain that had been falling intermittently for the last three days. People began to live their lives normally once more, filing away the recollections of the murders in the backs of their minds.

The killings had been a shock for a place as normally peaceful as Medworth. But the human mind is a resilient thing and forgets easily, especially when tragedy touches others rather than the ones close to the heart. There was that curious kind of emotional limbo which comes from discovering that quiet town, a place where many of the occupants had grown up, could house a killer as maniacal as Ray Mackenzie.

There was small mention of his burial, and that of Peter Brooks. Both men were laid to rest in Two Meadows with a minimum of fuss and a noticeable lack of mourners.

Lambert passed both graves, set side by side, as he continued his visits to the resting place of his brother. He found, with a curious mixture of guilt and relief, that he did not feel the need to visit Mike's grave every day. Two or three times a week and always on a Sunday, seemed to satisfy his conscience. The memory faded slowly, like the afterburn of a flash bulb on the retina. He found that he slept better, no longer waking in the small hours with the vision of the accident screaming before his eyes.

Of Gordon Reece there was still no sign and Lambert was beginning to think that the man had just walked out after the death of his wife, unable to face the house which held so many memories. The forensic test on the piece of glass he had found showed that the blood was indeed Reece's. The Inspector was considering closing the case.

The only question which still remained unanswered was the origin of the medallion.

He had heard nothing from Trefoile for three days. Once he had considered calling into the shop to see how things were progressing but, what the hell, it couldn't be that important and, with Mackenzie dead, the thing didn't seem to have such importance about it anymore.

Medworth was well and back to normal.

Lambert had given five of his men leave, secure in the knowledge that his remaining constables could cope with the usual catalogue of shopliftings, bike stealings and complaints about dogs pissing on neighbours' lawns.

As he drove home that Saturday night Lambert felt at ease for the first time in months. He and Debbie were driving into Nottingham that night. Dinner at the Savoy (he'd booked the table a week earlier) and then on to a club or a film. He smiled happily as he swung the car into the drive.

Father Clive Ridley put down his pen and massaged the bridge of his nose between his thumb and forefinger. He shook himself and glanced down at the two pages of notes which lay before him. Tomorrow's sermon. He read quickly through the notes and nodded in satisfaction. It was a job he disliked but, obviously, it had to done. Finding a subject to hold the congregation's interest seemed so much harder now. When he had first become a priest at the age of forty-one, twelve years ago, it had all been so simple. Brimming over with enthusiazm, he had relished his sermons, delivering them with an almost theatrical zest. But lately it was becoming a chore. He seemed to be going over the same ground again and again, and it aggravated him as much as it must have bored the listeners. He looked at his notes again. He had chosen the theme of caring for others, something which he himself knew more than enough about. He had nursed his mother through three years of illness. An illness which had eventually taken her two years ago. She had died peacefully during her sleep and for that, Ridley was thankful. She had suffered a great deal until then, and at one time he had found himself questioning the mercy of a God to whom he devoted his life. For a short

161

time he had begun to question not only his own faith but the wisdom of God. The very memory was painful and he felt almost ashamed to think of it. He looked across his study at the large wooden crucifix hanging on the wall and the silver figure of Christ seemed to stare back reproachfully.

Ridley got to his feet and crossed to the study window, looking out into the gathering dusk. The sky was streaked with brilliant brush strokes of crimson and orange. Colours which signalled the death of daylight and the onset of night. From his window he could see across the road to the cemetery and he decided to take a stroll before he cooked dinner. He often walked through the cemetery during the early evening, in summer particularly he enjoyed his little excursions. The singing of the birds in the many trees which dotted the area, the smell of the flowers in the air. But, as he pulled on his heavy coat and stepped out into the chill evening air, he expected no such sensory feast tonight.

He buttoned the coat, having difficulty with the middle two and promising himself that he would do without potatoes when he cooked his meal later on. He was a big man, tall and thick set. Fat perhaps, at first glance, but on closer inspection it was possible to see that it was only his large stomach which pushed him into the category of obesity. His face, dotted with small warts, was round and red-cheeked, giving him a look of perpetual good health. He blew on his hands, becoming aware of just how cold it was getting, and crossed the road from the vicarage to the cemetery gates.

Despite the chill of the air, the night looked like it would be a still one. The dying sun was sliding from its position in the sky, flooding the heavens with crimson and giving up supremacy to the swiftly gathering blackness. Dusk hung like a blanket over the land, catching it in transition.

A pigeon flew to its nest in the bell tower of the church and Father Ridley watched as it settled on the high sill before disappearing through a gap in the ancient masonry. The weather vane atop the spire twisted gently in the breeze.

He left the gravel drive almost immediately and walked slowly along the muddy footpaths which ran between the rows of graves. Here and there, freshly placed bouquets shone like beacons, their many colours contrasting with the dark earth. Ridley smiled to himself when he saw these, feeling a twinge of sadness when he found plots which bore no flowers or only the dried remains of those left long ago. Perhaps the occupants of the graves had been forgotten. The Reverend sighed. So sad to be forgotten. Death itself was the ultimate horror, but to be forgotten by those who had laid you to rest, that was a tragedy indeed.

He paused at a particularly well kept grave, guarded at all four corners by marble angels whose heads were bent in silent prayer. Engraved on the dark marble slab which covered it were the words:

'I am the Resurrection.'

Ridley smiled weakly and, almost absently, reached for the cross which hung around his neck. He considered it for a second, the tiny figure of Christ seeming to gaze up at him, then he let it slip back into the folds of his clothes.

The breeze had grown stronger now, tugging flowers from their pots and spinning the weather vane atop the spire. The Reverend pulled the collar of his coat up around his neck and decided to return to the vicarage. The sun had almost disappeared now, and besides, he was beginning to feel hungry. He walked quickly, heading for the gravel drive which would take him out through the gates of Two Meadows.

He reached the graves of Ray Mackenzie and Peter Brooks and paused. Such a terrible thing, he thought. He himself had conducted the burial services for all five of the people who had died in Medworth recently, including the entire Mackenzie family, Emma Reece, and Peter Brooks. Ridley shook his head. He noticed that the flowers which covered Ray Mackenzie's grave had been disturbed, scattered across the footpath which ran alongside the plot.

The wind had blown them aside probably, he thought as he stooped to gather the blooms. One by one he retrieved the roses and knelt down to replace them in their position just below the small metal marker which was the only sign that the grave was even there. Its freshly dug earth was already covered here and there with tufts of grass. In a week or so it would be covered completely.

Ridley gently laid the blooms on top of the plot.

A hand shot from beneath the dark earth and fastened iron fingers around his wrist.

The Reverend screamed in disbelieving terror.

His eyes bulged and he felt red hot knives of pain stab at his heart. Shaking his head from side to side, he fastened his horrified stare on the earth-covered hand which protruded from the grave, gripping tightly his wrist.

He could not move.

He tried to rise but his legs wouldn't support him, and all the time the grip on his wrist tightened until he was sure it would snap the bone.

The hand thrust forward, followed by more arm.

The grip loosened and Ridley pulled free, his breath coming in gasps, his head spinning, the pain still stabbing through his heart. He backed off, his eyes threatening to pop from the sockets as he watched the movement from beneath the earth of the grave.

The arm seemed to sway in the air for a second, then, the earth slowly rose and, from below, Ridley saw a face.

The face of Ray Mackenzie.

He was grinning, the blazing red eyes fixing the priest in their unholy stare.

Ridley slipped in a patch of mud and staggered back against a stone cross, hanging onto it for support as he watched Mackenzie drag himself from the grave to his full height. He stood there, the dirt and mud caking his clothing, his eyes (if those two virulent blood blisters could be called that) turned on the cowering cleric.

Ridley was panting, the pain in his chest spreading inexorably to his left arm and up into his jaw. White stars danced before his eyes but he held on to consciousness just a little bit longer.

He might have wished he hadn't, for in his

last agonized minutes, he saw the ground which covered the grave of Peter Brooks erupt and, a moment later, the intern stood next to Mackenzie.

Through eyes blurred with pain, Ridley saw that Brooks too had no eyes, just the hellish red orbs.

A final wrenching spasm of agony racked his body and he crumpled, the sound of his own breathing rattling in his ears.

They were advancing towards him, and, as he lost consciousness, he was grateful for one thing.

He would be dead before they reached him.

19

Lambert stared down at the fried egg on his plate and groaned.

There was a loud crack as the pan spat fat at Debbie who jumped back, brandishing the fish slice at it defiantly. She peered across at her husband who was still considering the egg. He cut into the yolk, watching as it gently spilled its colour onto the plate.

'I don't think I can face this,' he muttered, pushing the plate away from him.

'After three bottles of Beaujolais, three scotches and a brandy, I'm not surprised,' said Debbie, trying to sound stern but fighting to suppress a grin. Her stomach too felt as if it were on a trapeze. As she looked down into the bubbling pan she shook her head and switched off the gas flame beneath it. She had drunk more than usual the night before and she smiled as she remembered how they had tried to undress one another, giggling when they accidentally tore buttons off in their clumsy attempts. They had managed it eventually and slumped into bed, both of them dropping off to sleep before they could even embrace each other.

She crossed the kitchen and sat on Lambert's

knee. He put his arm around her waist, drew her to him and kissed her gently on the cheek.

'Did you have a good time last night?' he asked.

She nodded smiling. 'Fantastic.'

He groaned and put a hand to his forehead. 'I wish my brain would stop trying to climb out of my head; it's using a pickaxe to make its escape.'

Debbie laughed and hugged him and they sat in silence for a moment. Then Lambert looked up at her. 'You know, last night I managed to forget what's happened over the last month or two. It was as if it never . . .' He struggled for the words, '. . . as if it were all unreal.'

She kissed him. 'That's good.'

'Even about Mike,' he elaborated. 'The memory is there, it'll always be there, but not so strong now. I don't want to forget though, Debbie. I won't torture myself with it, but maybe I need that memory.'

She looked at him for a second, puzzled, then said:

'Do you want to drive up there this morning?'

He nodded.

'Mind if I come?'

He pulled her close. 'I think the fresh air will do us more good than this bloody stuff.' He pushed the plate away and imitated the noise of vomiting. They both laughed.

The watery sun had settled in a cloud streaked sky as Lambert guided the Capri along the roads and twisting lanes which led out of Medworth and up towards the cemetery. Sitting alongside him, Debbie clutched a bunch of roses which she sniffed occasionally, enjoying the sweet odour.

'Who'd live in a city?' said Lambert, looking out over the rolling green hills.

'Someone's got to,' Debbie said.

They drove a little way in silence, windows open, enjoying the sight of the countryside around them. The near naked trees added a contrast to the richness of the grass. Here and there a blaze of colour would erupt in the hedgerows where a clutch of wild flowers grew. Above them, where the hillside sloped up gradually into woodland, birds hovered above the trees and Debbie actually caught sight of a kestrel as it glided about looking for prey. The magnificent bird seemed to be suspended on invisible wire as it swung back and forth before finally disappearing from view.

'Are you going into the station today?' she asked, looking at him.

Lambert shook his head. 'Nothing to go in for. The Mackenzie case is closed. Gordon Reece seems to have cleared out. It's back to the normal routine from now on.' He smiled.

'What about the medallion?'

'I haven't heard anything from Trefoile yet, but I doubt if it'll be important. Mackenzie probably just found it somewhere. Maybe he dug it up in his back garden.' Lambert grinned.

'You know better than that,' she rebuked him, letting one hand stray across his thigh.

He swerved slightly and she jumped.

'See what you do to me,' he said, leering exaggeratedly.

They both laughed as he pulled up across the road from the cemetery gates. Debbie squeezed his hand as they sat for a moment, then they both climbed out.

High up on the hill top, where Two Meadows was situated, the wind seemed to blow stronger, and Debbie brushed her hair from her face as the breeze whipped silken strands across it. She shivered slightly but relaxed as Lambert put his arm around her, and locked together they walked in.

'Father Ridley's usually around at this time,' said Lambert, peering over his shoulder towards the vicarage.

'Perhaps he's in the church,' she offered.

'Maybe he's having a lie-in.'

She punched him playfully on the arm. 'Priests don't lie-in on Sundays, you heathen.'

She reached for his hand and found it, their fingers intertwining. As they walked, Debbie found herself prey to that mixed emotion which comes so frequently in a cemetery. The uneasiness mixed with the feeling of almost idyllic peacefulness.

'It makes you aware of your own mortality,' said Lambert, looking at the rows of graves: the ornate, the unkempt, the well-tended.

Mike's grave.

They stood beside it for a second before Debbie knelt and gently laid the roses on top of the marble slab. Lambert smiled as he watched her do it, drawing her close to him as she stepped back. They stood for long moments beside Mike's grave, gazing down at it, aware only of one another and of the wind rustling in the tree which hung above them. Finally, Lambert, squeezed her gently and said, softly:

'Come on.'

They turned and headed back towards the gravel drive.

As they reached the small kerb which edged the drive, Debbie stopped and pointed to something lying no more than ten feet away from them. It was glinting in the sunlight and that was what had attracted her attention.

She pulled away from Lambert and picked the object up.

It was a crucifix.

'Tom,' she called, 'look at this.'

He joined her and peered at the small silver cross which lay on her palm.

'Somebody must have dropped it,' he said, taking the object from her and holding it between his thumb and forefinger.

He dropped the crucifix into his jacket pocket and looked around, searching the ground for something else.

He found it.

A few yards up the path which ran between two rows of graves lay a pile of clods. Lambert hurried to them and kicked at them with his shoe. Then he noticed the flowers scattered around like shredded confetti and trodden into the mud.

'What the hell is this?' he said under his breath.

He took a step closer to one of the graves, noticing that a marble angel had been smashed from its position at a corner of the plot. There was a dark stain splashed across it which Lambert recognized immediately. He knelt and ran his finger through the stain, sniffing the red liquid on his finger tip.

It was blood.

He noticed more of it splashed up the headstone next to the other grave. He read the name on the headstone.

Peter Brooks.

The earth was piled up around the grave and a hollow had been formed in the centre, as if someone had begun digging and then given up half way.

Lambert stood up, his breath coming in gasps.

'Tom, what is it?' called Debbie, advancing towards him along the path.

He ignored the question, looking instead at the small metal marker on the grave next to that of Brooks. Barely readable was the name: Ray Mackenzie. The earth was strewn for many feet around it. Dark, wet earth. Lambert turned and waved Debbie back.

'We've got to find Father Ridley,' he said, tersely.

'What's wrong?' she asked, puzzled.

'I think some sick bastard has been mucking about with Mackenzie's grave.'

He walked past her, then suddenly hesitated.

'You'd better come with me,' he told her, and the two of them hurried across the road to the vicarage.

The curtains were open, and as he headed towards the front door, Lambert hoped that Ridley was in. He rapped hard, three times on the front door, and when he got no answer, went round the back.

'Damn,' he growled. 'He must be in the church.'

Debbie found that she almost had to run to keep up with him.

'Tom, what's going on around here?' she demanded.

'I wish I knew,' he said.

They reached the broken path which led up to the church door and hurried towards it, Debbie's high heels clicking noisily in the silence.

The church towered above them and Lambert pushed the door, noticing, as he did, that there was more blood on the great brass handle of the door. He swallowed hard and popped his head around the door.

'Tom.'

Her single word hung in the air as the policeman stepped cautiously into the great building. His footsteps echoed on the cold stone floor and he shivered at the coldness of the place. Debbie stepped in behind him, pushing the door closed.

The church ran a good fifty yards from door to altar. Pews arranged with soldierly precision on either side formed a narrow aisle down the centre which led straight to the altar. Dust particles danced in the light shining through the stained glass windows on both sides of the building. It smelt musty in there, a smell which reminded Debbie of Madame Tussaud's Chamber of Horrors. She quickly dismissed the thought, making sure she kept close to Lambert as he advanced down the central aisle. To the left stood the pulpit with a huge Bible open on it.

There was no sign of Ridley. Lambert called him, his voice echoing off the walls and ceiling, turning the huge room into a vast stone echo chamber.

'Father Ridley,' he called again.

Silence.

It was then that he noticed the pieces of earth scattered around the base of the altar. The Inspector crossed quickly to them and prodded a large lump with his index finger. He exhaled deeply. Where the hell *was* Ridley? There was one place left in the church he hadn't looked. The bell tower. A flight of stone steps ran up to the belfry from just behind the altar. Lambert looked up. A wooden floor hid the belfry itself from view below. He would have been able to see from where he stood whether or not the priest was up there, but the wooden slats obscured his view. He would have to go up and take a look for himself. He was suddenly filled with a feeling which he took to be fear, but why such a feeling should take hold of him, he didn't know.

'Wait here,' he told Debbie, and set off up the stone steps which would take him into the belfry.

Debbie nodded and watched him go, edging back so that she leant against the altar, looking out into the church. Hundreds of invisible eyes seemed to be fixed on her and she shuddered involuntarily.

Lambert, meantime, found that the staircase spiralled as it rose. The walls on either side hemmed him in so that he could not even extend his arms without touching them.

He slipped and nearly fell, but regained his

footing cursing, and looked to see what had made him stumble.

There was a slippery streak of blood on the step on which he stood. And the one above it. Lambert gritted his teeth. The cold seemed to have intensified and he was also beginning to notice a strange smell which grew stronger as he neared the top of the stairs. Mixed with the cloying odour of damp wood was something more pungent. A coppery, choking smell which stung his nostrils and made him cough.

He reached the top of the stairs and peered round into the belfry.

It was small. No more than ten feet square and Lambert felt as if the walls were closing in around him. The bell, a large brass object, lay discarded in one corner, torn from the thick hemp which secured it.

Lambert gasped and backed against the wall, his heart thumping.

Dangling from the bell rope, the hemp knotted tightly around his neck, was Father Ridley.

His face was bloated, the blackened tongue protruding from his mouth. Blood had splashed down his chest, turning his coat red and the rope which supported him had cut deeply into the thick flesh of his neck, drawing blood in places. He hung like some obscene puppet, his own blood puddled beneath him, soaking into the ancient timbers of the belfry floor.

But, the thing which finally made Lambert turn away in horrified disgust was the face. Splattered with gore, it seemed to glare mockingly at the policeman who noticed with

175

mounting terror that there was something horribly familiar about it.

Both the eyes had been torn out.

Lambert turned and raced down the stairs, almost running past Debbie who caught his arm. Her eyes searched his, looking for an answer which she already suspected.

'He's dead,' said Lambert flatly. 'Come on.'

They ran from the church, chased by a fear beyond their understanding.

They ran to the car and climbed in. Lambert burned rubber as he spun the Capri round. The needle on the speedometer touched sixty as he drove for Medworth, his face set in an expression of fearful resignation. Debbie studied his profile.

'Tom.'

'What?' His voice was tense, sharp.

'What's happening?' There was a note of something near to pleading in her voice.

'The graves,' he snapped, 'the graves of Mackenzie and Brooks were disturbed. It looked as if somone dug them up.' The words trailed off. 'Oh Jesus,' he said, his voice catching.

She reached out and laid a hand on his shoulder.

'What are you going to do, Tom?'

'Open the graves.'

'What?' She swallowed hard, not quite believing what she had heard. 'But you can't. I mean, why?'

'Someone tampered with those graves, Debbie. There must be a reason for that. I want to know what it is.'

'But don't you need an exhumation order?'

'Why?'

'It's the law.'

He looked at her. 'I *am* the law.'

Lambert stood beside Sergeant Hayes, watching as Davies and Briggs threw shovelfuls of earth into the air in an effort to reach the coffin of Ray Mackenzie.

Lambert was smoking. His third that morning. He'd been trying to give up just lately, but the events of the day so far had suddenly persuaded him that he needed something to calm him down. He sucked hard on the cigarette, holding the smoke in his mouth for a second before expelling it in a long grey stream which mingled with his own frosted breath in the crispness of the morning air.

He had driven home after finding Ridley's body, left Debbie there and told her he would be in touch. At first he had been reluctant to leave her alone, a fear which he couldn't understand nagging at the back of his mind. She had assured him that she would be all right and he had driven to the station. Taking a Panda, he, Hayes and the two constables had driven back to the cemetery armed with shovels. As Davies drove, Lambert recounted what he and Debbie had found that morning and when he got to the part about the eyeless corpse of Ridley, Briggs had found himself struggling to keep his poached eggs down. Hayes had said nothing, only looked questioningly at the inspector as if the description of the injuries inflicted had stirred some horrific memory within himself.

The ambulance which removed the vicar's body had been pulling out as the Panda swung into the driveway. Kirby was to do an immediate autopsy on it and ring Lambert with the results as quickly as possible.

Now the Inspector leant on a stone cross and dropped his third butt to the ground, crushing it into the earth with the toe of his shoe.

There was a scraping sound as the shovel Davies was using ran along a wooden surface.

They had reached the coffin.

Lambert stepped forward and watched as the two men scraped away the remaining earth with their fingers. As the last sticky clods were removed, all four policeman noticed the large hole about two feet from the head of the coffin. Splinters of wood were bent outward from it, some mingled with the dark earth.

The Inspector sighed and rubbed his chin.

It was scarcely necessary, because all of them could see through the holes that the coffin was empty, but Lambert gave the order nonetheless.

'Open it up,' he said, jabbing a finger towards the splintered box.

Davies wedged the corner of the shovel underneath one edge of the lid and pushed down. It came free with a shriek of cracking wood.

White satin greeted the men. A few specks of earth had fallen onto it but, apart from that, it was untouched.

No corpse. Nothing.

'Jesus,' said Briggs under his breath.

Lambert noticed some tiny dark specks of colour on the satin of the lid and jumped down into the hole alongside the two astounded constables. Leaning close he saw that the stains were dried blood. There was more smeared on the inside of the coffin. He straightened up and looked up at Hayes. The sergeant was expressionless, his lips and face white, bloodless.

'And the other one,' said Lambert, pointing to the grave of Peter Brooks. 'We've got to be sure.'

Davies groaned and wiped the perspiration from his brow. He gave Briggs a helping hand up from the hole and the two of them set to work on the second grave.

That too was empty.

Lambert bowed his head and, for long moments, no one spoke. Then Briggs said, nervously, 'What's going on, sir?'

'You tell me,' said Lambert, reaching for another cigarette.

Lambert drove home with his mind in turmoil. He told the men to keep quiet about the empty graves until they all had a better idea of what was happening. Probably someone having a sick joke, thought the Inspector. He hoped to Christ he was right. The men were edgy, Hayes too. Lambert had never seen the old sergeant like that. Usually nothing could get him rattled, but this time he strutted around the station trying to find jobs that didn't exist and snapping at the younger constables and making everyone feel all the more uneasy.

Lambert had left them sitting around in the duty room drinking cups of coffee. He had given them no orders. After all, he would have felt slightly foolish asking his men to keep their eyes open for two missing corpses. If the situation had been different he might have laughed about it. 'Just keep on the look out for the missing bodies. They'll turn up somewhere. Probably just been misplaced.' He could hear himself saying it.

He had no answers as yet. No theories floating about in that supposedly logical mind of his. On the other hand, what he had seen that morning defied logic. A priest murdered and hung from the bell rope of his own church. Two empty graves, one of them formerly belonging to a mass murderer, and the last and most disturbing thing, holes in the tops of both coffin lids.

Lambert had no theories but what did make him shudder was the fact that the wood was bent outward in both cases. As if some powerful force had stove it out . . . FROM THE INSIDE.

He was shivering as he swung the Capri into the driveway of the house. He left it in front of the garage and went in the front door.

He found Debbie sitting in the lounge, a steaming mug of tea cradled in her hands. She got up and crossed to him, setting the mug down on the small table beside her chair.

'I could do with one of those,' he said, embracing her and nodding towards the mug of tea.

She hurried into the kitchen to fetch him one and returned to find him slumped on the sofa, head bowed in thought. He smiled up at her as she handed him his tea.

'You all right?' he asked.

She nodded. 'What happened?'

He sighed, staring down into the steaming brown liquid as if an answer lay there. 'Both the graves were empty.'

'Both?' She seemed puzzled.

'Mackenzie and Brooks.' He took a sip of his tea. 'I'm waiting for the autopsy results on Ridley.'

She sat beside him and reached for his hand, squeezing it. 'How about dinner?' she said.

'Not for me, love,' he said, smiling. 'I seem to have lost my appetite.' He took another sip of his tea, watching a tiny brown tea leaf floating on the surface.

Debbie went to the record player and turned it down. Elton John faded into the background.

Lambert hardly noticed and, when the record finally came to an end, neither of them got up to take it off the turntable. It stuck in the run-off grooves, the steady click-click the only sound in the room.

When the phone rang it seemed to galvanize them both into action. Debbie snatched the record up while Lambert grabbed the receiver.

'Hello,' he said.

'Tom.'

He recognized the voice as Kirby.

'John, what have you got?'

'Well,' Kirby sounded tired. 'Not much really. Ridley died of a heart attack.'

'What caused it?'

There was silence on the other end and Lambert repeated his question before Kirby finally, and falteringly, said:

'It's hard to say. He was overweight, anything might have triggered it. I can't be sure, Tom.' A long pause. 'But, from the condition of the arteries around the heart and the condition of the heart itself there would appear to have been

181

massive cardiac failure. His heart burst, to put it simply.'

'You're hedging, John.'

'He died of fright.'

The words came out flatly. No inflection to soften the statement. Cold hard fact. Simplicity itself.

Lambert swallowed hard. 'The other injuries?'

'I compared the scratch marks on the cheeks with those on the faces of Emma Reece and the Mackenzies.'

'And?'

'They match up.'

Lambert inhaled quickly. 'So what does that mean?' His own mind was telling him an answer which he could not, dare not, accept.

'Ridley was killed by the same man who killed the other three. Or so it would appear. That, of course, is impossible.'

There was a long silence. Lambert held the phone down, Kirby's voice seeming far away, as if it were in a vacuum.

'Tom? Tom!'

Finally, the Inspector raised the receiver to his ear.

'Sorry, John.' His tone changed. 'Look, can you come over here tonight?'

'To your house?'

'Yes. About seven?'

'Yes. Tom, what is it?'

'Bring all the papers relating to the previous victims, and those on Ridley. *And* the autopsy reports on Mackenzie and Brooks.'

'Sure, but . . .'

Lambert cut him short, his voice edged

slightly with worried impatience. 'Just do it, John.'

They said their goodbyes and Lambert dropped the phone back onto its cradle. Debbie looked at him and he returned her gaze, their eyes locked together. He sat down beside her and reached for his tea. He took a mouthful and winced. It was stone cold. He put the cup down and crossed to the drink cabinet.

Right now he needed something stronger.

20

It was a minute before seven that evening when there was a sharp rapping on the front door of the Lambert household. The Inspector checked his watch as he crossed to the door. Punctual as usual, he thought smiling. He opened the door to find Kirby standing there, a briefcase in his hand. The policeman ushered him in, his eyes gazing out into the night. The darkness was broken only here and there by the glow of street lamps. He closed the door and led Kirby through into the living room.

There was a pleasing warmth within the room which Kirby enjoyed, and he loosened his tie.

'Sit down,' said Lambert, and the doctor gratefully accepted, placing himself at one end of the sofa.

Debbie emerged from the kitchen. She was wearing a faded old blue blouse and jeans and Kirby ran an appreciative eye over her figure.

'Hello,' she said, gaily.

The doctor tried to rise but she waved him back. 'Would you like a drink? Tea, coffee or something stronger?'

'Tea is fine,' said Kirby, smiling.

She retreated into the kitchen and Lambert

pointed to the briefcase lying beside Kirby. He flipped it open and took out a number of manilla files, each stamped with a number and name. He laid them on the coffee table before him and opened the first one.

'Ridley,' he announced. 'Like I told you over the phone, Tom, it was heart failure. The rest . . .' he hesitated, '. . . was done afterwards.'

There was a long silence as the policeman flicked through the slender report. He closed the file and looked at Kirby. 'You said over the phone that the scratch marks on Ridley's face matched those on the other three victims.'

Kirby nodded.

'What conclusions would you draw from that?'

The doctor shrugged. 'I'm not a policeman, Tom.'

'Imagine you were. What would you think?'

'I would say, against my better judgement, that Ridley was killed by the same man who killed the other three.'

'Which of course is impossible,' said Lambert, something mysterious dancing behind his blue eyes.

'Well of course it's impossible. Mackenzie's dead,' said Kirby, almost smiling.

Lambert got to his feet and crossed to the drinks cabinet. He poured himself a large scotch and downed a sizeable gulp before continuing.

'John, there was another reason I wanted you here tonight. I think it might be linked with Ridley's murder.'

Kirby interrrupted him. 'He wasn't murdered. He died of a heart attack.'

'He died of fright,' said Lambert, his voice rising in volume slightly. 'Besides, some mad bastard did *that* to him. Some fucking headcase tore out his eyes and hung him up.' There was anger in his voice, tinged with something else which seemed, to Kirby, like fear. The policeman drained his glass. 'Look, as I was saying, something else happened up at the cemetery. The graves of Mackenzie and Brooks were tampered with.'

Kirby looked vague.

'Dug up. Desecrated. Call it what you like. The bodies were taken.'

'How do you know?' Kirby swallowed hard.

'I ordered the graves to be opened. Both bodies were gone.'

'So how does this tie up with Ridley?'

Lambert poured himself another drink and inhaled slowly.

'What would you say if I told you I think Ridley was killed by Ray Mackenzie?'

Kirby almost smiled. 'I'd say you should consider visiting a psychiatrist.'

'You said the marks on the faces of all four victims matched.'

'Tom, he's dead. I did the autopsy myself,' said Kirby incredulously.

Debbie emerged from the kitchen carrying a cup of tea which she handed to Kirby. He thanked her and sipped tentatively at it. She got one for herself and joined them, curling up in one of the armchairs beside the fire. Lambert too, sat down, his third glass of scotch cradled in his hand.

Kirby smiled. 'You do realize, Mrs. Lambert, that your husband is a total lunatic?'

'This is no joke,' snarled Lambert. 'What's your explanation?'

Kirby eyed the Inspector warily and stirred his tea needlessly. 'Tom, there must be a logical explanation for what happened. It's some sort of sick imitator. They must have read about the other murders in the paper and well . . .' He let the sentence trail off.

'No details of the murders were published in the paper,' Lambert corrected him, 'especially the taking of the eyes.'

'Coincidence,' said Kirby.

'Bullshit,' snapped Lambert. He took a sip of his drink. 'Look at what we've got here. A man is murdered, or mutilated anyway, in exactly the same way as three previous people. We've got two empty coffins, one of which belongs to a killer. Now, you tell me why anyone would want to steal those bodies *and* kill Ridley.'

There was silence in the room. The glow of the fire and single table lamp which had at first seemed so comforting now became almost oppressive. Shadows in the corner of the room were thick, black, almost palpable, and Debbie drew her chair closer to the fire.

'Tom, you're a logical man, for Christ's sake,' said Kirby.

Lambert held up a hand. 'O.K., let's look at it logically. God knows I *want* to find a logical explanation for all of this. Both coffins were empty, right? Both had large holes in the lids. The wood was bent outward.' He paused. 'Any theories?'

Kirby shrugged. 'Body snatching.'

'But why? Who'd want to steal two corpses? What are you going to do with them? Hang them over your fireplace?'

Debbie suppressed a grin, especially when she saw the pained expression on her husband's face.

'There is another explanation,' said Kirby.

'I'm waiting,' Lambert said, impatiently.

'Have you ever heard of catatonia?'

'I've heard of it, but I don't know exactly what it is.'

Kirby put down his tea. 'It's very rare now; it was quite common at one time but, what with advanced examination procedures it's become more or less obsolete.'

'Get to the point, John,' demanded Lambert, quietly.

'In a catatonic state, sometimes called a catatonic trance, the patient displays all the appearances of death. The bodily functions slow down, sometimes even stop altogether. It can last for seconds or hours.'

'So what are you saying?'

'That Mackenzie could have been in a state of advanced catatonia when he was buried.' A pause. 'He could have been buried alive.'

Lambert shook his head. 'John, he fell over a hundred feet from that hospital room. That's what killed him. He was dead. Dead as a bloody doornail and to hell with your scientific explanations. Besides, the grave of Brooks was empty too. Even if this crap about catatonia was right, the chances of it happening to two men at exactly the same time are millions to one.'

'What else do you have?' said Kirby, wearily.

Lambert shook his head. 'Nothing. Not a goddam thing.'

The three of them sat in silence. Outside, a motorcycle roared past, breaking the solitude for a second before the harsh sound gradually died away. Kirby sipped his tea but found that it was cold. He winced and put the cup down again, declining when Debbie offered him another.

'All right,' began Lambert, 'sticking with this idea of catatonia, how do you explain the holes in the lids of both coffins?'

Kirby shrugged. 'They were trying to get out.'

Lambert shook his head. 'Have you ever felt a coffin lid? It's about two inches thick. Solid oak. You'd need to be bloody strong to punch a hole in that. And then, assuming they managed that, they clawed their way up through six feet of earth?'

'Tom, you've just defeated your own argument. It's impossible. It had to be body snatchers, there's no other logical explanation for it.'

Lambert shook his head. 'Why does the answer have to be a logical one? There's been nothing logical about this whole bloody case ever since it started; why the hell should we start worrying about it now?' He took another hefty swallow from his glass before continuing. 'Look at the facts, John. An ordinary man in an ordinary job with an ordinary family suddenly goes crazy. Butchers his family, tears out their eyes then kills another woman, tears out *her* eyes. During the day he's in a torpor. At night he's like a wild animal. A brain test shows that, to all intents and purposes he's dead, but what happens when the lights go out—he gets up and

189

kills himself and another man. Now, two weeks after he's buried, our vicar is found hanging from his own bell rope, both eyes torn out after having died of fright and the grave of the murderer is empty.' Lambert's voice had been rising steadily as he spoke but now he was almost shouting, his breath coming in quick gasps. Now, the veins on his forehead standing out angrily, he slammed his fist down on the coffee table and shouted:

'Now you tell *me* that's logical.'

He slumped back into his chair, hands covering his eyes, totally drained. No one spoke, then, after what seemed like an eternity of silence Lambert said, 'And there's another thing.' His voice had regained its composure; it was low, resigned almost to the horrors he had just described.

'Mackenzie had a medallion with him. It was old, very old. There was inscriptions on it, in Latin. I think that is the key to all of this.'

'Where is it now?' asked Kirby.

'Trefoile, the antique dealer in town, has got it. He said he recognized it from somewhere.'

'What makes it so important, Tom?' Kirby wanted to know.

Lambert smiled humourlessly. 'Maybe I'm wrong. Perhaps this is what's known as clutching at straws but, right now, it's all I've got.'

'What are you doing about Mackenzie and Brooks?'

'What can I do? Tell my men to be on the look out for two of the living dead? Report in lads, if you happen to bump into anyone who was buried recently, that sort of thing? Frankly, John, I don't know what the fuck to do.' He looked long and hard at the doctor. 'All I know is, it must be kept out of the papers. If the press get hold of this, we'll have half the country crawling over Medworth trying to find out what's going on.'

'Call in help.'

'Where from?'

'Tell your superiors what's going on.'

Lambert laughed bitterly. 'Can you imagine what Detective Inspector John Barton would make of this? He'd have me locked up. No, I can handle it for now.' He exhaled deeply. 'Christ, if only we had a motive. I mean, what kind of person steals corpses?'

The Inspector's eyes suddenly flared. He pointed an inquisitive finger at Kirby.

'Assuming, just assuming, that someone is trying to imitate Mackenzie's crimes and also working on the assumption that that same person stole the bodies, then surely they would have taken the corpse of Emma Reece as well.'

'Why?' Kirby wanted to know.

'Because *she* was one of his victims.'

'Was *her* grave tampered with too?'

'I don't know, I never thought about her at the time.' The Inspector got to his feet. 'We've got to find out now.'

Debbie looked worried. 'Tom, what are you going to do?'

'We have to see if her body has been taken as well,' he said flatly.

'You mean dig her up?' gasped Kirby.

'We've done it twice today already,' said Lambert.

Kirby lowered his head. 'But . . .'

Lambert's tone was soft, but stern. 'We have to know.'

The doctor swallowed hard and looked up at Lambert. He nodded almost imperceptibly. A thin smile creased the policeman's face, and he hurried out of the house to fetch the tools. Debbie and Kirby stared at one another, neither of them able to speak. The cold draft from the open back door blew into the room, temporarily driving away the warmth and making them both shiver.

Lambert returned a second later with a spade and a garden fork. He held them out in front of him.

'Ready?' he said.

Kirby nodded. 'We'll take my car.' He took the tools from Lambert and walked out to his car. Inside, Debbie and the Inspector heard the sound of the engine being started. She pulled Lambert close and he held her head on his chest.

'Lock all the doors,' he said quietly and kissed her on the forehead. He turned quickly and ran out to the waiting Datsun. Debbie, watching from the front window, saw him slide in beside Kirby, and a few seconds later the car disappeared into the darkness.

She hurried to the back door and drew the bolts across then repeated the procedure at the front. Then she walked back into the living room and crouched in front of the fire, suddenly gripped by an icy chill which seemed to cling to her like frost to a window pane.

It was a long time before she was warm again.

21

The drive to the cemetery took less than twenty minutes. Kirby brought the Datsun to a halt and switched off the engine. Both men got out, their breath forming clouds in the cold night air. The doctor unlocked the boot of his car and took out the spade and fork. The latter he kept for himself, the other implement he handed to Lambert. The Inspector reached into his pocket and pulled out a torch and flicked it on, checking the power of the beam. Satisfied, he nodded and the two men set off up the gravel drive which led them into the cemetery. The noise of their shoes on the rough surface sounded all the more conspicuous in the silence.

To their right, the church. A dark mass, the huge black edifice stood surrounded by a sea of shadows. Lambert shuddered as he looked at it, remembering what he had found in there the day before.

'Where is the grave?' asked Kirby, whispering.

'Over near those trees,' said Lambert, motioning with the torch.

They continued up the gravel drive, turning with it as it curved around to the left. Finally, they left the gravel drive and took one of the muddy paths which ran between the rows of plots. It was at this point that Lambert flicked on his torch, sweeping its broad beam back and forth over the marble headstones and crosses. The mud squelched beneath their feet, and once Kirby almost slipped over. Lambert held out a hand to steady him and the two men continued on their way. A row of poplars grew with military precision along the edge of one of the paths, and it was beneath the shade of one of the trees that Lambert's torch beam picked out the chosen spot. In the cold white light, both men read the name on the headstone.

Emma Reece.

There was an urn on top of the grave, withered carnations drooping impotently over the edges. The Inspector removed it, laying it gently to one side. He rested the torch on the headstone itself, the beam giving them a little light to work by.

Standing one on either side of the grave, the men looked at each other and Lambert noted how pale Kirby looked. His face was dark with shadow and, despite the cold, the Inspector could see that there were tiny beads of perspiration on his forehead. They held each other's gaze for a second, then, with a grunt, Lambert drove his spade into the dark earth. The doctor watched him for a second then followed his example, using the fork to tear up large clods which he flung to one side.

In the beam of the torchlight they worked, tearing away more and more earth until mounds of it began to accumulate on either side of the grave.

Lambert felt the perspiration seeping through

his shirt and, twice, he had to stop to wipe it from his forehead. He leaned back, using the handle of shovel as a kind of stool. Kirby too, stopped for a moment and wiped his brow.

'Four hundred years ago we'd have been burned at the stake for this,' he said with a grim humour in his voice.

Lambert nodded and smiled weakly.

They continued with their digging, aware of nothing but the sounds they made as they turned the dark earth and the gentle rustling of the wind in the trees above them. Both men were stooping now to get at the fresh earth.

'Nearly there,' said Lambert, quietly. Almost triumphantly. He felt his heart quicken a little bit.

The earth was piled high on either side of the hole and both men found that it was sticking to their clothes. Kirby tried to pull the clods from his shoes but it was useless. They stuck like lumps of thick brown glue. The prongs of the fork, too, had become encrusted with the wet ground.

There was a dull scraping sound as Lambert's spade struck wood.

He pulled away the remaining clods with his hands, baring the brass plate on the coffin lid. He reached up for the torch and shone it on the plate.

'This is it,' he said.

'How do we get the lid off?' said Kirby, noticing the thick screws which held it firmly in position.

Lambert produced a penknife from his trouser

pocket and, tossing the spade aside, pulled the blade up into position.

'Shine the light here,' he snapped, handing the torch to Kirby who put down his fork and held the beam over the place where the Inspector was indicating. Inserting the wide edge of the blade into the groove in the screw head, Lambert began to loosen it. It turned easily and he grinned triumphantly up at Kirby.

One by one, the screws were removed and Lambert slid his fingers beneath the lid to ease it free. He swallowed hard, not knowing what he was going to find beneath the heavy lid.

'Keep that bloody light steady,' he whispered.

Heart thudding against his ribs, he pushed the lid to one side.

Lying in the coffin, arms folded sedately across her chest, was Emma Reece.

Lambert looked at Kirby who shrugged with the sort of gesture that says 'I told you so.' The Inspector stood up, wiping a hand across his forehead, his eyes riveted to the two empty sockets in Emma Reece's face which had once housed eyes. Gaping black maws now filled with the dirt of the grave. And yet, there was something else . . .

Kirby stepped forward, handing the flashlight to Lambert. He knelt beside the corpse and touched a hand to the face. It was ice cold.

'Curious,' he said, abstractedly.

'What is?' Lambert wanted to know.

'She was buried three weeks ago. The skin usually begins to undergo some minor deterioration within a matter of days. Her skin is still supple.' He prodded it again. 'No deterioration at all.' He reached for the right arm and lifted it a few inches. 'Not even evidence of rigor mortis.' Kirby straightened up, rubbing his chin thoughtfully. 'It must be something in the soil.' He felt a lump between his fingers. 'It is very moist, that *could* account for the preservation.'

Kirby knelt once more, shining the torch into the face of the corpse, bending close until the putrid smell finally drove him back. He shook his head and straightened up again, turning towards Lambert.

'Well, Tom,' he said, brushing the dirt from his hands, 'that seems to put pay to your theory.'

The thing which had once been Emma Reece leapt from the coffin with the speed of an arrow.

Kirby had no time to move and Lambert was momentarily frozen by the sight before him.

The living dead thing fastened both hands around Kirby's neck and pushed him forward, grinding his face into the mud wall of the grave. He struck blindly at it, trying to shake himself free of the vicelike hold. Lambert struck out madly with the torch, shattering the bulb as it crashed against the top of Emma Reece's head. The place was suddenly plunged into darkness, only the vague light from the street lamps outside the cemetery illuminating the unholy scenario.

Kirby was clawing at the bony fingers which encircled his throat, the dirt now beginning to clog his nostrils. He was fighting for breath, his throat being blocked by the crushing fingers while the stinking dirt of the grave filled his nostrils. He felt unconsciousness wrapping its dark blanket around him and his efforts to break free grew more feeble.

Frantic, Lambert drove a fist into the side of Emma Reece's face, hearing bone splinter beneath the impact. It was enough to make her loosen her grip on Kirby, who slumped to the ground sprawled half in and half out of the open coffin.

The living dead thing turned towards Lambert, and he saw with horror the blazing red pinpricks deep within the gaping empty eye sockets. Saliva dripped from her open mouth and he noted, with disgust, that her false teeth were dangling pathetically from her top jaw. Emma Reece leapt at the Inspector across the narrow hole but he caught her by the wrists and held her, surprised at the strength of those apparently frail arms. Her face pressed close to his and he was splattered with the yellowish mucous. A hideous grin began to spread across the creature's face as she forced Lambert back, her talonlike hands reaching for his throat. He stared into those bottomless pits of blackness that had once been eyes and, with a surge of strength aided by fear, forced her back. They both fell, still locked together, Lambert not daring to relinquish his grip on those arms. But now he was on top of her. Still that feral grin sneered up at him.

Kirby, meantime was dragging himself to his feet, his head spinning.

'Kill it,' screamed Lambert, realizing that the Reece thing was squirming free. But Kirby could only stagger against the wall of the open grave, watching the life and death struggle before him. Paralysed with fear he saw Lambert jump back, his hand groping behind him to the lip of the hole.

His hand closed around the spade.

The living dead thing raised both arms and launched itself once more, but this time at Kirby, who, in his dazed condition, went down under the rush.

Eyes wide with horrified revulsion, Lambert saw the thing throttling the doctor, pressing its vile body against him in a manner which made Lambert want to vomit.

With a shriek of rage he swung the spade and slammed its edge into the spinal area just above the pelvis. There was a loud snapping sound, like a branch being broken, and the thing stepped back. Moaning in agony, it stepped away from Kirby, both hands clapsed to the rent in its back. Lambert lashed out again, the powerful stroke catching Emma Reece just below the chin.

The head, severed by the blow, rose on a fountain of dark blood and thudded to the ground several feet away. The living dead thing remained upright for a second, blood spurting madly from the severed arteries, then pitched foward into the coffin. The white satin rapidly turned vivid crimson.

Lambert dropped the spade and crossed to Kirby who was slumped against one of the grave sides coughing. Even in the darkness, Lambert could see the savage cuts around the doctor's throat, bruises and lacerations that would have been normally credited to a garotte. He tried to speak but could only cough, a string-thin trickle of blood running down his chin. Lambert helped him to his feet and then vaulted up out of the dark hole, taking Kirby's hands and pulling him up, supporting him when he was clear.

The Inspector looked down and saw the head of Emma Reece lying nearby. He rolled it gently with his foot, tipping it into the grave where it landed with a thud, the black, empty, eye sockets gazing up at the night sky. He shuddered and turned away, supporting Kirby until they reached the gravel drive. The doctor stood alone for a second then nodded that he was all right. His voice, when he spoke, was dry, like old parchment and every syllable brought a new wave of pain.

'It looks like you were right,' he croaked, touching his throat. 'Drive me to my surgery.'

Lambert nodded and the two of them made their way back to the waiting Datsun.

Kirby collapsed into the passenger seat and gently touched his injured neck. He wound down the window and spat blood onto the road.

'You need a hospital,' said Lambert.

Kirby shook his head and extended his tongue to reveal a deep gash where he had bitten into it. That was the source of the blood, not his throat. Lambert had thought that he might be bleeding inside the throat itself but now he was reassured.

As they drove, Lambert's face was set in an expression of grim resignation.

'Like I said,' gasped Kirby, 'it looks as though you were right about where the bodies of Mackenzie and Brooks went.'

Lambert nodded. 'This is one time I wish I'd been wrong. How the hell are we going to get anyone to believe this?'

They drove the rest of the way in silence. Kirby concerned with his own pain, Lambert tormented by the obscene spectre of Emma Reece. His mind was not quite able to come to terms with the fact that he had just fought a woman who had already been dead for three weeks. He shuddered.

The street lamps had gone out in a number of streets in Medworth that night. The local power station had been inundated with complaints and every caller had been assured that everything was being done to rectify the fault.

Not everyone complained though.

The darkness was a welcome companion to some who walked that night.

To two men in particular.

Emma Reece had been destroyed, true enough. But there were others abroad that night more powerful.

It was eight-twenty. A long time before dawn. There was nothing but darkness.

Darkness.

22

Bob Shaw peered out into the blackness of the night and tried to make out the shape of his Suzuki 750 parked in the road outside.

'All the bloody street lights are out,' he muttered.

He tried one last time to catch a glimpse of his motorbike but gave it up to the all enveloping darkness. Christ, he hoped no bastard pinched it. It had taken him nearly two years to pay for it, fifteen quid a month until he'd paid the five hundred. Still, it was worth it. He was the envy of all the blokes he hung around with. He laughed as he thought of them puttering around on their poxy little 250's. At nineteen, with a stable job as a garage attendant and, most importantly, the bike of his dreams, he was reasonably content.

There was one thing which bugged him.

She was lying on the sofa *now*. One leg drawn up provocatively, revealed by the split in her skirt.

Kelly Vincent was a month or two younger than Bob. She'd made quite a name for herself within the confines of Bob's little circle. Most of his mates had shafted her at one time or another.

Bob seemed to be the only one who hadn't. She hung around with them, she said, because she liked the motorbikes. Bob and his mates liked to think it was for other reasons. After all, as the others had told him, she was a right little nympho. She'd do anything. Even take it in the mouth.

Just the thought made Bob break into a sweat. He stood behind the sofa for a moment, watching her, running his eyes up and down her body: the long, curly hair and full lips, eye make-up which looked as though it had been applied with a trowel. She wore a tight fitting red blouse, undone to the third button. Just far enough to stretch the imagination and whet the appetite. She wore no stockings but her legs were smooth and shapely. As he watched, she scratched the inside of her thigh, revealing just a hint of white knicker.

She looked up and saw him standing there.

'Are you going to stand there all bloody night?' she said.

Bob shook his head and hurried round to join her. She raised her head so that he could sit, then she rested it in his lap. He felt a warm thrill run through him and tried to control the erection which threatened to run riot at any minute. Bob glanced up at the TV screen. There was some crap on about the war. Kelly's old man was always on about the war. Boring old bastard. That was all he ever talked about. Bob hated coming round when he knew Kelly's parents were going to be there. But tonight was different. They were out, possibly for the night. They never moved out of the house usually, that was why it had taken Bob so long to get round to this. His own parents went down the local boozer but he couldn't take Kelly back to his place because his little brothers were always in. Little bastards. He could imagine the cries of derision from them if he arrived home with a girl. They took the piss out of him *now* which was as much as he could stand. He didn't fancy having one of them walking in while he was shagging Kelly.

But tonight it was going to be different. Her parents had gone to a party. Something like that, he couldn't remember exactly what it was. All that concerned him was, they would be out of the way for a few hours.

He looked around the room. A posh place really, he thought. Fitted carpets, brand new wallpaper, colour television. They even had a stereo. Bob compared it to his own house. The threadbare rugs which barely covered the floor in the living room, peeling wallpaper. The stink of damp which seemed to hang in every room. God he hated his home, but as yet he could see no way out. No respite from the rows between his mother and father, the squabbles with the kids. He didn't earn enough to buy a flat of his own, not even to rent one. Property was scarce in Medworth and he didn't fancy moving out of the town and leaving his mates. Bob realized that he was just going to have to learn to accept things as they were. After all, that was life for people like him. He knew it and he also knew that there was nothing he could do about it. It was like having your life mapped out for you, following the same routes as your parents. Only his route led to a dead end.

He tried to push those thoughts to one side and concentrate on the matters at hand. He let his fingers stray to Kelly's breast and he managed a quick squeeze before she knocked it away.

'Get off,' she bleated.

He sighed. He hoped tonight wouldn't be a waste of time. If he didn't get to screw someone pretty soon, his mates would know. They were starting to get suspicious already. Bob shuddered as he thought of their derision if they *did* ever discover he was still a virgin. Of course he had boasted conquests, as do all young men, but he was getting worried. What would they think of him? Some blokes in his gang had fucked more than ten girls. *He* hadn't even got as far as kissing one yet. Bob was a master of bravado but his facade was beginning to crack. If he didn't score tonight he'd be a laughing stock.

He slid his hand once more to her breast and, once again, she knocked it away.

He gritted his teeth and a secondary thought passed through his mind. What if he fucked it up? Kelly would be sure to tell his mates. Bob began to become more nervous.

'Get us another drink,' said Kelly, reaching for the cigarette packet on the coffee table beside her.

Bob got to his feet and scurried across to the drink cabinet. He poured a large measure of vodka into Kelly's glass, hesitated a moment, then filled it right up, adding just a touch of lemonade. Perhaps if he could get her pissed it would improve his chances. He poured himself another beer and returned to the sofa.

She blew a stream of smoke into his face and giggled.

He waved it away with his hand and tugged on her hair. She squirmed.

'You bastard,' she said, smiling, 'don't be so rough.'

'I thought you like it rough,' said Bob, trying to sound experienced.

'Who told *you?*'

'A few people.'

She giggled and took a large gulp of her drink.

'Are you sure your parents aren't going to get back early?' he asked agitatedly.

She put down her drink and slid her arms around his neck, pulling him towards her. He felt her mouth against his, her tongue pressing against his lips. He opened his mouth a little but she pulled away, a grin hovering on her lips.

'You do know *how* to kiss, I suppose?' The question was heavy with scorn.

He grabbed her, more assured now, pulled her towards him and pressed his mouth to hers, his tongue probing. After a moment he pushed her away.

'That better?' he said, smugly.

She giggled. 'What have your mates told you about me?' she wanted to know.

'This and that,' he said.

'What does that mean?'

He felt her hand on his thigh and he swallowed hard, his penis growing swiftly within the tight confines of his jeans. She noticed the bulge and allowed her hand to stray to it, stroking it through the thick material.

'You like sex,' he told her.

'Who told you?' She giggled again, her movements becoming more urgent.

Bob shuffled uncomfortably, aware of his swiftly growing excitement.

'Your mate Dave,' she began, 'he's got a big cock. One of the biggest I've seen.'

'What are you? Some kind of expert?' he said.

She giggled again. 'I've seen enough to know.'

He felt her hand fiddling with his zip, easing it slowly down and he had to grit his teeth to control himself. She gazed at the bulge in his underpants and smiled, holding it firmly in her expert hand. Then, smiling, she backed off and unbuttoned her blouse. Bob never took his eyes from her large breasts, especially when they spilled forth as she unhooked her bra. The nipples were already erect. Bob didn't think he could control himself much longer, but the thought of what his mates would say gave him that extra bit of control that he needed.

Kelly eased herself out of her skirt and stood before him, just the white of her knickers covering that part which Bob sought so desperately. Through the thin material he could see the dark curls of her pubic hair. Swiftly he whipped off his tee-shirt and flung it to one side, kicking his jeans off simultaneously. For one ridiculous second, he realized that he still had his socks on. Hurriedly he pulled them off and knelt on the floor beside her. She pushed him back and tugged his underpants down, revealing his rampant organ.

At first he thought she was going to laugh, but she nodded admiringly and ran her fingers along the hard shaft, pausing for a moment at the swollen, bulbous tip. Bob closed his eyes. He didn't think he could hold back any longer. He thought about anything to distract him from the sensations. West Ham losing the cup final, death, unemployment.

She stopped stroking him and he relaxed, watching as she removed her own knickers. She lay back, waiting for him. Bob hesitated, the uncertainty returning. What if she *did* tell the others?

'Well, come on,' she said. 'I mean, you *do* know what to do?'

He clambered on top of her, trying to force his erection between her thighs.

'Careful,' she said, becoming agitated by his clumsy efforts.

He repositioned himself and tried again. This time she grunted angrily and rolled to one side.

'I don't think you know how to do this,' she chided. 'I think you're a bloody virgin.'

The word stuck in his mind and he could feel himself turning scarlet.

'I know what I'm doing,' he lied, trying to sound forceful.

'Dave knew what to do. He gave me a good fuck. So did Paul.'

'Fuck Dave,' he growled, 'and bloody Paul. I know what I'm doing.'

She rolled onto her stomach and looked away from him. Bob felt the tension growing. He swallowed hard. What were the others going to say? The mouthy little whore was bound to tell them. In a last desperate attempt to save face, Bob grabbed her hips, raising her bottom into the air. Then, with a finesse which he didn't realize he possessed, he slid into her from behind. She moaned pleasingly and pressed back to meet his urgent thrusts. Bob was ecstatic. He knew it wouldn't be long before he reached his climax but he didn't care. He felt like shouting it out:

"Goodbye, virginity!"

There was a scratching at the front door.

Both of them froze, locked together like some kind of surreal statue.

The scratching came again, louder this time. There were footsteps on the front path.

'Oh God,' gasped Kelly, 'it's my Mum and Dad.'

'I thought you said they were going to be late,' Bob blurted, hastily withdrawing and snatching up his jeans. Both of them pulled on their clothes as best they could, expecting the door to open at any moment and to see Mr and Mrs Vincent standing there. Kelly couldn't begin to imagine their reaction. Bob, gasping for breath, tried to force his erection back inside his jeans while pulling on his t-shirt. In his haste he forgot one sock. Kelly stuffed her knickers and bra beneath a cushion, taking care to remind herself to remove them later.

Finally, the two of them threw themselves back onto the sofa, red in the face, waiting for the door to open.

There was no sound.

'I thought that was them,' whispered Kelly.

Bob exhaled deeply. If he'd lost his chance because of a false alarm he'd leave right now. He began to wonder if it was all a set-up. Were Kelly, Dave and the rest of those bastards he called mates playing a bloody joke on him? The thought stuck out strongly in his mind and, when he saw Kelly begin to giggle, his suspicions were confirmed. He got to his feet, pushing her to one side and made for the door.

'You set this up,' he shouted, 'you fucking scab.'

Kelly shrugged, her grin fading.

'I'm going to kill those wankers when I get hold of them,' he snarled. This was it, this was the bloody limit. He wrenched open the hall door, flicked on the light and tore open the front door.

'Right, you cunts . . .'

The words were cut off as powerful hands fastened themselves around his throat.

Bob was driven back into the hall, propelled by the force of his assailant. He slammed into the wall, cracking his head and, for a second, everything went black. But he recovered and grabbed for the hands which were throttling him. He caught sight of the face of his attacker and his stomach contracted. The mouth drawn back in a deathly grin to reveal yellowing teeth, the scratch marks and cuts on the cheeks and forehead and, worst of all, the blazing red eyes of Ray Mackenzie.

The pressure on his throat increased and he felt spittle froth on his lips as he fought for breath. Mackenzie had him against the white wall, slamming his head repeatedly against it until the white paper began to sport crimson smudges. Bob knew that he was blacking out. In his last moments of consciousness he saw another man dart towards the living room. He too had those same burning red eyes.

Kelly heard the struggles from the hall and got to her feet, suddenly frightened. She screamed as the thing which had once been Peter Brooks entered the room. The living dead creature fixed her in that red stare and advanced towards her. Kelly screamed Bob's name. He could not help her. Already lying dead in the hallway, his lifeless form was jerked savagely about as Mackenzie tore his eyes from their sockets, ignoring the blood and vitreous liquid which splashed onto him.

Kelly was weeping with terror, big salt tears pouring down her cheeks. But, with a final surge of strength, she leapt for the kitchen door, vaulting the coffee table in the process. The Brooks thing lunged after her and caught her arm, raking it with broken nails. The girl screamed again but shook free and flung herself through the open door, forcing it shut behind her. Even with her back pressed against it, she knew she would never keep Brooks out. He punched at the door, denting it.

Tears clouding her eyes, she scanned the kitchen for a means to defend herself. She had a choice to make and she had to make it fast.

To try and make it to the back door or to grab the carving knife from the drawer beside her. Her mind spun. It would not give her an answer and the indecision brought fresh tears.

She heard the angry roar from the other side of the door and, a second later, Brooks charged, crashing into it shoulder first. The impact knocked Kelly across the room where she smashed into a chest of drawers. Dazed, she clambered to her feet, sidestepping the living dead thing's lunge and grabbing for the carving knife.

Screaming, she brought it down in a swatting action. The heavy blade caught Brooks on the point of the shoulder and sliced away a large chunk of his coat. He grinned and Kelly swung the knife again, this time scoring a line across his cheek. The Brooks thing roared and put a hand to the wound, blood pouring through his fingers and he backed off. Sobbing uncontrollably, Kelly edged her way towards the beckoning back door. Brooks stood still, watching her.

Praying, she dived for the door, finding to her horror that it was locked. In the split second it took her to turn the key, Brooks leapt at her. The two of them crashed to the ground, his weight pinning her. The knife skidded away.

Kelly screamed, again and again until the sound seemed to merge into one unending caterwaul of terror.

She knew she was going to faint.

Mackenzie appeared in the doorway, that familiar feral grin smeared across his face, his hands dripping blood. And beside him stood another man . . .

Not man so much as youth.

Both of them were grinning.

Kelly stopped screaming for a second, the sobs choking away as she turned her head to look at the two onlookers. The first of them tall, his blazing red eyes like those of the thing which held her down. But beside him, and this was what started her screaming again, stood Bob Shaw.

Where there should have been eyes there were just bloody holes, still weeping crimson. Open sores with pits of congealing gore and yet, somehow, he could see her. Somehow he knew. And he was grinning.

Kelly managed one last scream before all three of them fell on her.

Eight more people were killed that night.

23

There was an expectant hush inside the duty room of the Medworth police station.

Outside a light drizzle was falling, casting a haze over everything and spotting the windows of the room. The windows on the inside were steamy and the place smelled of stale cigarettes and coffee.

A blackboard had been set up at the far end of the room and there was a chair in front of it. The leather chairs which normally were dotted around the edges of the room had been drawn up into two rows, and on these chairs sat the ten men who made up the Medworth force. Facing them was Lambert. To his left, on the other side of the blackboard, sat Kirby, his neck still heavily bandaged from his encounter with Emma Reece a week earlier. He pulled irritably at the bandages every so often and sipped at the luke-warm coffee which Sergeant Hayes had given him earlier.

Lambert lit a cigarette and took a drag, finally expelling the smoke in a long stream. He sighed and turned to the blackboard. There were several names written on it in yellow chalk. He turned his back on the waiting men for a second, reading the names and breathing quietly. The knot of muscles at the side of his jaw pulsed. He felt like a schoolmaster. Finally, he turned.

'Twelve people,' he said quietly, 'have disappeared in the last three days. We can't find a trace of one of them.' He hooked a thumb over his shoulder at the blackboard. 'The pattern is the same in every case. All we ever find at the scene is a lot of blood, scraps of clothing if we're lucky, and other little clues. *Never* any sign of a body, even though all the indications are that there has been a violent struggle.'

The Inspector took another drag on his cigarette, held the smoke in his mouth for a second then blew it out in a long stream. He pointed to the names at the top of the list.

'Bob Shaw and Kelly Vincent. Reported missing by the girl's parents. We found blood in the hall, in the kitchen, on a knife. The blood matched the known groups of the two missing people. Except the blood on the knife. That belonged to a third party, I'll explain more about that at the end.' He pointed to the second name.

'Ralph Stennet. Attacked on his way across a field after leaving a pub. Reported missing by his wife.' Lambert scanned the faces of the watching men. 'Who found the evidence on this one?'

Constable Ferman raised a tentative hand. Lambert nodded.

Ferman coughed, coloured slightly and began. 'I visited the pub where Stennet was last seen and then followed a set of footprints which I thought to be his, across a field. I found blood.' He swallowed hard. 'Lots of it.'

Lambert nodded, and pointed out the next on the list.

'Janice Fielding. Attacked in her own back garden.' He exhaled deeply, finally turning his back on the blackboard. 'There's no point in going on. As I said before, it's the same in every case. The victims are attacked, from the evidence we found, badly assaulted, and then they disappear.' He looked from face to face. 'Any theories?'

A muted silence greeted his enquiry.

'Guv.' It was Hayes. 'You said something about the blood on the knife in the first case belonging to a third party. What do you mean?'

Lambert almost smiled. 'What I'm going to tell you now will probably confirm some suspicions which a few of you have had ever since you've known me. Namely, that I'm a lunatic.'

A ripple of laughter ran around the room.

The Inspector paused, searching for the words. 'Well, maybe that's right. In this case I wish it was.' All the humour had left his voice, his tone now flat, clinical and the men in the room sensed it too.

'The blood on that knife belonged to Peter Brooks.'

There was a moment's stunned silence. Someone laughed, the sound choked off abruptly. No one knew what to say. Hayes found the words.

'But, guv, Brooks is dead.'

Lambert nodded almost imperceptibly and motioned towards Kirby.

'Doctor Kirby,' he continued, 'who, you can see, suffered some injuries the other night, will

216

verify the fact that it *was* Brooks' blood on the knife.'

Kirby nodded and, as the men watched, he slowly began to unravel the bandage around his neck, finally revealing the scars and bruises beneath. The area around his adam's apple and below the ears was a patchwork of black and purple welts and angry scabs.

'Jesus Christ,' murmured P.C. Briggs.

'The doctor's attacker was Emma Reece, Mackenzie's third victim. Father Ridley, who was found hanging from the bell rope of his own church with both eyes torn out, was murdered by Ray Mackenzie.'

The watching men were silent. They heard but could not, dare not, believe.

'All the attacks which have taken place over the last three days,' said Lambert flatly, 'have been carried out by people who were thought to be dead.'

That was it. As simple as that. Lecture finished. Lambert dropped his cigarette butt and ground it into the carpet. He exhaled slowly, as if the movement was painful.

'I don't believe it,' said Constable Davies, flatly. 'It's impossible.'

'It happened, man,' shouted Lambert. 'Look at the marks on his neck.' He pointed to Kirby, his temper now gone. 'They were put there by a woman who'd been buried three weeks before.' He gritted his teeth, his breath coming in short, rasping hisses.

Davies lowered his voice a little, some of the cynicism draining from it. 'Where is she now?'

'She's dead. I cut her head off with a spade.'

217

Lambert raised a hand to his head and ran it through his hair. He exhaled deeply. 'These . . . things, whatever they are, they're strong.' He could say no more. Kirby stood up, seeing that the stress of the situation was beginning to affect Lambert.

'The Inspector and I exhumed the body of Emma Reece; that was when the attack took place,' he said. The doctor smiled weakly at Lambert who nodded and began again.

'At the moment we don't know how many of them there are. The fact that the corpses of each victim disappear would seem to indicate . . .'

Hayes cut him short. 'But how can you be sure that these people *have* been killed if we've found no bodies?'

'I'm assuming, Vic,' said Lambert, calmly. 'Assumptions are the only thing I've got at the moment. Assumptions and twelve missing people.' There was a long silence, then the Inspector continued, 'As I said, there's every reason to believe that the missing victims are now in the same condition as Mackenzie and Brooks.'

'Does that mean they're alive, sir?' said P.C. Briggs.

'I don't know what it means,' said Lambert. 'Alive, undead, living corpses.' He slammed his fist against the blackboard and growled, 'This case gets more insane the closer you look at it.'

'Are you discounting the theory of body-snatching?' wondered Hayes.

Lambert's reply was emphatic. 'Yes. After what happened with Emma Reece, there's no question of it having been that.'

The men shuffled uncomfortably in their seats

and an almost palpable silence began to fall over the room.

'Any questions?' said Lambert.

'Do we get any help on this, guv?' asked Hayes.

Lambert shook his head.

Hayes looked put out. 'But surely H.Q. . . .'

Lambert interrupted, 'And what the hell am I supposed to tell them? Please could I have some reinforcements here as we've got several living corpses walking around? They'd find me a nice cell with padded wallpaper.'

A ripple of nervous laughter broke up the tension. It quickly vanished as Lambert continued. 'No. For the time being, it's up to us. Now, these things only seem to come out at night which gives us a bit of breathing space at least. I want full patrols tonight, no man walking a beat is to be alone. Radio in if you see anything suspicious. Don't go near one of them alone. Understand?'

The men nodded. Lambert stood for a moment, trying to think if there was anything he'd left out. Finally deciding that there wasn't, he dismissed the men. As they filed out he heard young Briggs mutter to Walford, 'It's like something out of a horror film,' and he guffawed as he said it.

'I wish it was,' Lambert called after him, then, softly, 'I wish to God it *was* a bloody film.' He turned to Kirby, 'There's always an expert in a horror film, isn't there? You know, some smart-assed bastard who knows how to deal with things like this.' He almost laughed.

Kirby shook his head. 'Let's not get too paranoid about it, Tom.'

Lambert looked at him for a second, then he headed for the door. When he reached it he turned. 'I'll stop being paranoid when all this is over.' He walked out, leaving Kirby sitting alone in the room gently rubbing the scars on his neck.

Lambert drove home slowly that night, taking a route directly through the centre of Medworth, something which he usually avoided doing. He didn't know why, but the sight of people milling about the town centre reassured him. He drove in silence, not bothering to switch on the radio. He had enough on his mind as it was. The clock on the Capri dashboard showed five o'clock and the shops were beginning to close. Dusk hovered on the horizon, a portent of the darkness which would envelope the land in the coming hours. Lambert wondered what this particular night would bring with it. More deaths perhaps? He pushed the thought to one side and brought the car to a halt at a crossing. He tapped agitatedly on the wheel as the two women crossed, nodding affably to him. He lifted a weary hand in acknowledgement and drove on.

A motorcycle passed him, the driver wearing no crash helmet. Ordinarily, the Inspector would have driven after the youth and maybe even cautioned him, but this particular evening he let the incident pass. He watched as the bike roared away out of sight.

The drizzle which had blanketed the town for most of the day had finally given way to heavier rain and, as large spots of moisture began to splatter the windscreen, Lambert flicked on his wipers. The rubber arms swept away the rain, momentarily blurring his field of vision. By the time he reached home, it was pouring down. He locked the car door and bolted for the house, careful to remove his shoes when he got into the hall. He stood there for a moment then swiftly slid both bolts across, securing the door. Satisfied, he walked into the living room. The smell of cooking beef wafted out of the kitchen to greet him.

'Jack the Ripper's home,' he called, reaching for the local paper.

'Oh good, I thought it might be someone dangerous,' Debbie called from the kitchen.

Lambert took off his jacket and draped it over the back of his chair, his eyes fixed to the column of newsprint beside the headline. The policeman sat down and scanned the small article headline *Police Baffled Over Disappearances.*

'That bastard,' he snarled and threw the paper down.

Debbie appeared in the doorway. 'What's wrong?' she asked.

'Have you seen the local?' said Lambert, motioning to the discarded paper on the coffee table. 'That bastard Burton, I told him not to mention this in the paper. He's called me three times in the past week to ask what's going on. I said I'd issue a statement when the time was right.'

Debbie picked up the paper and read the short column which told of the disappearances of a number of people in Medworth. No names mentioned, though.

'It doesn't seem to give too much away, Tom,' she said, placatingly.

'That's not the point,' snapped Lambert. 'I told him. Nothing to be printed until I found out what was going on. It's bloody scare mongering, that's all it is. If people read this it won't make the investigation any easier.'

'It'll get round by word of mouth,' said Debbie, returning to the kitchen. 'People are talking about it now.'

'What people?' Lambert wanted to know.

'Come on, Tom, it's a big talking point in the town. After all, it's the most exciting thing that's happened here for years.'

'I'd hardly call five murders and twelve disappearances excitement, would you?' He sighed. 'Christ, if they knew the truth they'd shut up.' He flicked on the television and watched the news. The same old stuff. Strikes, Government upsets, the usual batch of robberies and murders. He picked up the local newspaper and read the column again, wondering if Detective Chief Inspector James Baron had seen it. If he had, it would be odds on he'd be on Lambert's back the following day wanting to know what was happening. The Inspector dropped the paper again. How the hell was he supposed to explain if Baron *did* call? Debbie's shout to tell him that dinner was on the table interrupted his chain of thought and he trudged out into the kitchen and sat down. He ate in silence for a time with Debbie watching him. 'I had a lovely day, thank you dear,' she said, sarcastically. 'Oh did you, dear, fine.'

Lambert looked up and smiled. 'Sorry.'

'Welcome back to planet Earth,' said Debbie, softly.

'I was thinking,' he said.

'You always are.'

'I mean, what do you call this? This state that Mackenzie and Brooks are in? How do you rationalize what Kirby and I saw the other night?'

'You can't rationalize it, Tom. It happened, that's all there is to it.'

'But, Mackenzie. I mean to say, it's not life after death in the sense we know it. It's living death. He's dead but he's walking around.' Lambert began to laugh, quietly at first and then more heartily. Debbie swallowed hard as she watched him. He smiled and shook his head, the spasm subsiding.

'I think I'm going insane,' he said, looking at her. 'None of this can be happening. Things like this only happen in bad horror films.' His tone darkened once more. 'And yet I saw Emma Reece get up out of that coffin. I saw her attack Kirby, I felt her strength. I saw that, Debbie. My eyes saw something which my mind can't accept. I saw a dead man walk.' He pushed his plate away from him and rested his head on his hands which he had clasped before him.

'Do you think I'm insane?' he asked.

She shook her head.

'What's happening now, it goes against everything I've ever believed in. Right from the start of your training, they teach you to keep an open mind about things. Never make hasty decisions. Always weigh up all the evidence before making your judgement.' He smiled humourlessly. 'The trouble is, I've made up my mind. All the evidence points to something which, by all the laws of nature, is impossible. The dead are coming back to life.' He paused. 'All those who are victims, in turn, become living dead themselves. Even Brooks, Mackenzie killed *him* in the fall.'

'But what about the first two victims,' asked Debbie, 'and Father Ridley?'

'June and Michelle Mackenzie were cremated. Ridley died of a heart attack. He wasn't actually killed by the living dead. It's only those who are murdered by them that return.'

'Like vampires,' said Debbie, flatly. 'Their victims always become like them.'

Lambert shook his head. 'This is different. There's a pattern, a reason for it. It's almost as if there's a force behind it. Something more powerful than the creatures themselves. Something . . . something that's guiding them.' He rubbed his chin. 'There's a key somewhere, Debbie, a key that will give us the answer. It's just a matter of finding it. I hope to God I can find it in time.'

The phone rang. Debbie got up but Lambert waved her back.

'I'll get it,' he said.

He walked wearily into the living room and picked up the receiver.

'Hello.'

The line was crackly, thick with static and he repeated himself.

'Inspector?' he heard through the hissing. 'It's Trefoile.'

Lambert perked up. 'What have you got?'

224

'It might be easier if you come to the shop,' said the antique dealer, shouting to make himself heard above the roar of static. 'I was right about . . .'

The phone went dead.

'Trefoile!' Lambert flicked at the cradle. There was no sound. Nothing. The Inspector repeated the antique dealer's name.

He held the silent receiver in his hand for a second then gently replaced it on the cradle. His forehead was heavily creased.

'Who was it?' asked Debbie.

'Trefoile,' he told her, then he added, more urgently, 'Come on, let's go.'

She looked bewildered. He explained that they were to visit the antique shop immediately and, from the force with which he gripped her hand, she knew it must be important. Grabbing their coats, they hurried out to the car, and in minutes were speeding towards the shop. Lambert could feel his heart thumping faster as he drove and he pressed down just that little bit harder on the accelerator.

'A key.' His own words echoed in his mind.

Was the medallion the key?

He thought of the phone going dead and shuddered. Perhaps his imagination was running away with him, but, as he swung the car into the main street of Medworth, he prayed that Trefoile would be the only one waiting for them in the antique shop.

Lambert stopped the car and the two of them sat for a moment, watching the sign above the door which was swinging back and forth in the wind. The shop was in darkness, not a light to be seen anywhere. Lambert scanned the other shops along the street. Many had residential flats above and, in most of these, lights were burning. Trefoile's shop, though, was a stark contrast and the Inspector felt an involuntary shudder run through him as he opened the car door. Debbie moved too, but he put a hand on her arm and shook his head.

'Stay here,' he said, softly, reaching for the flashlight on the parcel shelf. He flicked it on, testing the beam, and then stepped out onto the pavement. Debbie leant across and locked the door behind him, watching as he walked briskly to the front door of the shop. Lambert's anxiety was beginning to reach her and she anxiously scanned the street from end to end. Not a living soul to be seen. The light from the dull yellow of the streetlamps reflected back from the wet pavement like pools of liquid gold. The rain bounced hard against the car roof, beating out a tattoo.

Lambert knocked twice on the front door and, when he received no answer, tried the handle.

It opened.

He held up a hand to Debbie to signal that he was going in. She watched as he closed the door behind him.

He flicked on the flashlight and swung it back and forth across the room, aware of the musty smell of the place.

Two gleaming eyes shone at him from a corner and he gasped, suddenly angry with himself as he saw that they belonged to the head of a stuffed fox. He walked behind the counter towards the back room which served as a dining room, workshop, and kitchen.

'Trefoile,' he called.

No answer. Lambert reached for the light switch to his right and flicked it down. Nothing happened. He tried again. The darkness remained. His beam picked out a plate of unfinished mince lying on the table. Beside it was a large book which, upon closer inspection, was revealed as a ledger of some sort. He walked to the back door and tugged at the handle. It was firm, the door securely locked and bolted. The Inspector swung the light around once more and found that there was a door which led out of the room. It was ajar. He crossed to it and cautiously peered round, shining the beam inside. It illuminated a narrow flight of steps which led up into even more impenetrable darkness.

'Trefoile,' Lambert called again, suddenly, and for no discernable reason, wishing he was armed.

Again he received no answer and, slowly, he began to ascend the staircase, finally reaching a small landing which had two doors leading off from it. He shone the flashlight onto each one in turn then made for the nearest one. He opened it quickly and found himself looking into a cramped toilet and bathroom. He closed the door and walked towards the second room.

Something moved above him.

Lambert froze, the breath trapped in his lungs. He shone the beam upwards and saw a trapdoor which he assumed led up into the attic.

Another movement. Heavy footsteps from

above. He edged back towards the head of the stairs, beam pointed at the trapdoor as if it were a weapon. He wished it were a gun he was holding.

The trapdoor opened and Lambert stepped down one stair. Copper he might be, hero he wasn't. If there was something in that bloody attic he didn't intend tackling it alone.

A face appeared in the opening.

It was Trefoile. He smiled affably. Lambert exhaled deeply and almost laughed.

'Bloody fuse blew,' the antique dealer explained. 'I don't know why the hell they had to put the box up here. Won't be a moment.' With that, he disappeared back into the attack and, a second later, the place was bathed in welcoming light.

The antique dealer jumped expertly from the attic and brushed himself down. He smiled at Lambert and said, 'The phone call, it was about the medallion.'

'I thought it might be,' said the Inspector. He explained that Debbie was waiting in the car.

'Bring her in,' said Trefoile. 'We'll have a cup of tea. I think she'll be interested in what I've found too.'

The three of them sat in Trefoile's back room with cups of tea before them. Lying on the table were two huge, leather-bound books. Their pages were yellowed and crusty with age, and one had gold leaf words upon its cover, written in Latin.

Between them lay the medallion.

'As I said to you before, Inspector, this is a most remarkable piece of work,' said Trefoile, prodding the circlet with the end of his pen. 'I sent it to a friend of mine who works in a museum and he verified the fact that it was sixteenth century. He couldn't pinpoint the exact time though.'

'That doesn't matter,' said Lambert, reaching to his coat pocket for his cigarettes.

'You may remember me telling you,' began Trefoile but he broke off as he saw Lambert lighting up the cigarette. 'Would you mind not smoking, please, Inspector? My father never did like it in the house. You understand.'

Lambert shrugged and looked for somewhere to stub out the freshly lit cigarette. Trefoile took it from him and dropped it into the sink where it hissed.

'Sorry,' said the antique dealer, returning to the table.

Debbie suppressed a grin.

Trefoile continued. 'As I was saying, I did mention to you when you first showed me the medallion that I recalled seeing it somewhere before.'

Lambert nodded, watching as Trefoile flipped open the first of the mammoth volumes. He found what he wanted and turned the book so that Lambert and Debbie could see the picture he was indicating. It was an early woodcut of the medallion. Beneath it was a caption in Latin which Lambert pointed to.

'What does it mean?' he asked.

'It doesn't mean anything,' Trefoile said, enigmatically. 'It's a name.'

Lambert read it again, the letters standing out darkly against the yellowing paper.

Mathias.

'I still don't get it,' said the policeman, a slight edge to his voice.

'Mathias was the owner of the medallion. That very medallion which came into your possession.' He paused, watching their reaction carefully to his next words.

'Mathias was a Black Magician. Said, at the time, to be the most powerful ever known.'

Lambert snorted. 'So you're telling me that this,' he poked the medallion, 'belonged to a witch?'

'A Black Magician,' repeated Trefoile, 'a High Priest if you like, a Druid. Does it matter what the name is? It all amounts to the same thing.'

There was a moment's silence then the Inspector said, 'What about the inscriptions? Could you decipher them?'

Trefoile sighed. 'The one across the centre of the medallion was pretty simple. It means Deathday.'

Lambert shrugged. 'The other one?'

'That was trickier, much trickier. You see, it's not like the central one. The inscription around the outside of the medallion is written in reverse.'

'A sort of code?' asked Lambert.

The antique dealer nodded. 'When the letters are transposed, that's when it begins to make a bit of sense.' He pushed the gold circlet towards Lambert, pointing out the letters with the tip of his pen. 'These two words,' he wrote them down on a pad, 'as they are, make no sense. Transposed, they read REX NOCTU.' He paused. 'It means, King of the Night.'

230

'What about the other words?' Lambert demanded.

Trefoile swallowed hard. 'Inspector, don't think me a fool, a coward even, but, if I were you, I'd get rid of this thing now.'

'Why, for Christ's sake?'

'Because it's evil.'

Lambert half smiled. 'Evil.'

'Take these books,' said Trefoile, 'you'll find your answers in there. I want no part of this.'

The Inspector's expression changed when he saw how pale the antique dealer had become. The older man's hands were shaking visibly as he wiped a bead of perspiration from his forehead.

'Trefoile,' he said, 'what the hell is it with this bloody medallion? It's important. People could have died because of this.'

'Does it have anything to do with what's happening here at the moment?' The question hung in the air.

'What makes you think that?' demanded Lambert.

'As I said, it's evil. I can't help you anymore, Inspector.' Trefoile's voice had dropped to a low whisper. 'Just take the books and go. Please.' There was a hint of pleading in that last word.

Lambert looked stunned. He looked at Debbie and shook his head before gathering up the two books and the medallion. He thanked the antique dealer for his help and told him that they would find their own way out. He nodded abstractedly, gazing into the murky depths of his cup, aware only of their departure by the soft tinkling of the bell over the door, lingering like some unwanted nightmare.

231

Lambert and Debbie hurried to the car and climbed in, placing the two huge volumes and the medallion on the back seat. The Inspector started the engine immediately and drove off.

'Tom, he was really frightened,' said Debbie, softly.

'Drive me to the library,' she told him.

'Now?'

'We'll need a dictionary to translate the Latin; there's two or three in our reference section.'

Lambert nodded and swung a right at the next junction. As he drove he noted how few people were on the streets. A couple of lads in leather jackets smoking, standing in a shop doorway. One or two in the fish and chip shop but, apart from that, they hadn't seen above five people since leaving the house two hours earlier.

He brought the car to a halt outside the library and both of them got out. Debbie was first up the stairs, fumbling in her jacket pocket for the master key. Cursing the cold weather, she finally found it and there was a loud click as the heavy lock opened. They stepped in, Debbie slapping the panel of switches near the door. The powerful banks of fluorescents blazed and the library was filled with cold white light. Lambert shivered as he followed her through the maze of shelves towards the reference section.

'Don't you have any bloody heating in here?' he said. He passed a radiator and pressed his hand to it, withdrawing it quickly as it singed him.

'Shit,' he grunted. The radiator was red hot. Yet still he could feel that penetrating cold, an almost palpable chill which encircled him with icy fingers.

Debbie found the dictionaries and hurried out again, turning off lights as she went. Once outside, she locked the door and the two of them hurried back to the car.

Lambert put his foot down and they were home in under twenty minutes. He put the car in the garage while Debbie carried the heavy volumes indoors where she laid them on the coffee table. Once inside, Lambert locked and bolted every door and window in the house then retreated to the comforting warmth of the living room. Debbie already had the books spread open, a notepad by her side.

It was going to be a long job and, as he looked at the first page, Lambert wondered what they were going to find.

The entire book would have to be translated, word for word. They would find one word and, immediately, be forced to look it up in the dictionary. The meaning clear, it would then be transcribed onto a fresh piece of paper.

Lambert looked at his watch as they began. It was eight fourteen p.m.

It took them three hours to do the first page.

Outside, the rain lashed down, the darkness covering the town and countryside like an impenetrable blanket.

24

Charles Burton stubbed out his third cigarette and checked his watch against the wall clock above Lambert's desk. He exhaled through clenched teeth and pulled open the office door.

'When the hell is he getting here?' said Burton.

Sergeant Hayes, who was making out a duty roster, looked up and smiled.

'He shouldn't be long, Mr. Burton,' he said.

Burton slammed the door and Hayes raised two fingers at it. Miserable bastard, he thought, and carried on with the roster.

Burton had never been a patient man, but, at this precise moment in time, seated in Lambert's office, he was on the point of blowing his top. He'd been waiting for the young policeman for more than thirty minutes and he wasn't going to wait much longer. As editor of Medworth's newspaper, he deserved prompt attention. He never had liked Lambert. Cocky young sod, he thought. Burton, approaching his fortieth year, wondered how someone as young as Lambert had ever been put in charge of the Medworth force in the first place. He was never very cooperative, but, regarding recent events, he'd been downright secretive. Burton was determined to get to the bottom of things. It was his right as a newsman, and the people of Medworth had a right to know too. He resolved not to leave until Lambert had told him what was really happening in the town. Burton checked his watch again. *That* was if the young bastard ever arrived.

Burton felt quite exhilarated. He'd never had anything quite *this* big to write about since becoming editor of *The Medworth Herald*, but what with a number of deaths and disappearances over a matter of weeks, this was something new. Usually it was all jumble sales and tedious local events and he allowed his own meagre staff to deal with those trivialities. But this one he wanted for himself. He didn't trust one of his three reporters to cover it adequately. They'd probably miss some important detail here or there. Besides, Lambert would be able to brush them aside easily. Burton was determined not to be pushed away with excuses and half-baked explanations.

He checked his watch again and lit another cigarette. The room was already heavy with the smell of stale smoke and Burton added to it, blowing out a long stream as he dropped the lighter back into his pocket.

His wife had bought it for him for their tenth wedding anniversary. He half smiled, thinking about her. She'd be at home now, up to her elbows in washing up or vacuuming. She was always doing something. Cleaning up, rearranging the furniture. He wondered if there was a medical term for it. Compulsive house cleaning or something like that. She went mad if he even so much as dropped a speck of ash on the carpet. Out came the Hoover straight away. Burton had put up with it for the first couple of years, but, gradually, her mania for neatness had begun to annoy him. He stayed at the office later each night. She never complained about that, though. As long as their house was neat and tidy, she was happy. He often thought that she wouldn't mind if World War Three broke out tomorrow, as long as the house was in good shape. He stayed out until all hours, boozing, sometimes just driving around, even screwing other women, but when he finally got home, she would never question him. Just peck him lightly on the cheek and ask him if he had a good day.

There was a girl at the moment. She worked as a barmaid in 'The Bell,' a pub on the outskirts of the town. Her name was Stephanie (he called her Stevie) Lawson and, although she had never told him, he guessed her age to be around twenty. Only once did it occur to Burton that he was old enough to be her father and that once was after their first bout of lovemaking. Even the recollection exhausted him. Christ, she was a bloody animal he thought, smiling. She was cooking him dinner tonight at her place. It was her night off and Burton was looking forward to it.

His train of thought was broken as he heard footsteps outside the door.

Lambert walked into the station and smiled at Hayes. He held up two, grimy, oil-covered hands.

'Would you believe it,' he said, 'I had a bloody puncture about ten minutes from home.

236

Changed that, and then found out my oil was low so I had to top up with that too.'

Hayes pointed to the closed door of the office. Lambert looked around.

'You've got a visitor, guv,' said the sergeant.

'Who is it?' asked Lambert, lowering his voice.

'Charlie Burton.'

Lambert sighed. 'Christ, I'd forgotten. How long's he been here?'

'Half an hour.'

Lambert nodded and pushed open his office door. Hayes heard the initial greeting then the conversation was cut off as the door closed once more.

'I've been waiting nearly forty minutes for you,' said Burton, irritably.

'Sorry,' said Lambert, smiling, 'I had a blow out.'

He crossed to the sink in one corner of the room and began scrubbing his hands.

'You said nine o'clock,' persisted the newsman.

Lambert gritted his teeth. 'I can't help it if my bloody car gets a flat, can I?' he said, drying his hands. He turned to face Burton, wondering why he ever agreed to meet the man in the first place. If Burton disliked the Inspector then the feeling was more than mutual. Lambert tried to be pleasant. Smiling, he sat down.

'What can I do for you?' he asked.

'You know what I want,' said Burton, impatiently. 'Some information about what's been going on around here during the last few weeks.'

'I told you over the phone that no information would be given until the investigation was over.'

'That's bullshit,' snapped Burton. 'You said there would be press releases.' He emphasized the last two words with scorn. 'Some sort of statement and yet every time me or one of my reporters rings up, you're either not here or you won't tell us anything.'

Lambert picked up a pen which was lying on his desk and began toying with it.

'Like I said,' Lambert said softly, 'I don't want any of this in the papers until the investigation is over.'

'Any of what, for Christ's sake?' said Burton, angrily. 'Just what *is* going on, Lambert? People have a right to know.'

'It's classified.'

'Don't give me that shit. Come on, divulge.'

Lambert sat forward in his chair, the pen pointing at Burton.

'Look, Burton, none of this has anything to do with you or your blasted paper. If I say there'll be no information given about this case, then that's how it'll be.'

Burton smiled cryptically. 'You're a jumped-up little bastard, Lambert, you know that? Just who the hell do you think you are?'

'I'm the law. Who are you? Some glorified bloody paper boy who wants to find out some details so he can stick them in the local rag. I told you, there'll be no info given on this case until it's all wrapped up.'

'So what's all this crap about "Police statements"?' the newsman demanded.

'You'll get them in time,' Lambert told him.

238

Burton laughed. 'I know why you won't tell me anything. It's because you can't. *You* don't know what the hell is going on either. Lambert, you couldn't figure out a fucking crossword puzzle, let alone what's happening here.'

'It's police business. It's none of your concern.'

'People are dying, disappearing in this bloody town. We all have a right to know what's being done about it.'

Lambert reached into the drawer of his desk and pulled out a copy of the previous night's paper. He hurled it down.

'You *don't* have a right to print that,' he snarled, pointing to the column headed, 'Police baffled over disappearances.' 'And, another thing, if you print anything else about this case without my say so, I'll close your fucking paper down.'

'You bastard.'

'Welcome to the club,' said Lambert, angrily.

The two men regarded each other for a moment, the tension between them almost visible. Then Lambert said:

'I mean it, Burton. I want all details, all speculation, kept out of the paper.'

The newsman was unimpressed but, his tone softened slightly.

'Off the record, what *is* going on?'

Lambert smiled at him. 'Off the record?'

Burton sat forward eagerly.

The Inspector pressed his fingertips together and sat back in his chair. 'I don't know.'

'Come on, Lambert, I said off the record.'

'I'm telling you,' the policeman continued, 'I don't know.'

'But it is true that twelve people have disappeared during the last couple of weeks?' asked Burton eagerly.

'Where did you get that information?' the Inspector wanted to know.

Burton was losing his temper. 'People talk. That's the only thing they *are* talking about at the moment. Nothing's happened in this place for fifty years. The biggest event of the year is the bloody Church social. What the hell do you expect them to talk about? It's common knowledge.' He paused, waiting for the Inspector to speak but he remained impassive.

'So, is it true?' he asked again.

'Off the record?'

Burton nodded.

'It's true,' Lambert said, 'but if you print that, I'll have you for disclosure of evidence.'

'What's happened to them?' asked Burton.

'Maybe they just left town.'

'Come on, Lambert, I said this was off the record,' said the newsman, becoming irritable again.

'You want a comment, right?' Lambert said. 'Something to print. An official police statement?'

Burton looked eager, nodding frenziedly.

'All right,' said Lambert, 'got a pen?'

Burton pulled out a notebook, flipped it open and waited expectantly.

'My official statement regarding this case,' began Lambert, 'is simple enough.' He paused. 'No comment.'

240

'You bastard,' snarled Burton.

Lambert had to fight to suppress a grin as he watched the editor turn scarlet with rage. He stood up, slipping the notebook back into his pocket. The newsman headed for the door, turning as he reached it.

'This case will beat you, Lambert, and I'll be the first one to wave goodbye when they wheel you out.'

Burton had the door half open.

'Hey, Charlie,' called Lambert, half smiling, 'for the record.'

'What?' snapped Burton.

'Fuck you.'

The editor slammed the door as he left. A moment later Sergeant Hayes popped his head round the door.

'Everything all right, guv?' he asked.

Lambert smiled, 'Yes thanks, Vic. Just Mr Burton blowing his top. Nothing to worry about.'

Hayes nodded. 'Anything else, guv?'

Lambert smiled, 'Yes. I could murder a cup of tea.'

Hayes scuttled off to make it, closing the door behind him. Lambert exhaled deeply, his forehead creased heavily. He thought of Debbie, at home at this very moment, trying to decipher the two huge volumes which Trefoile had given them. She had taken a few days off so that she could work on them and perhaps find an answer quickly. Time suddenly seemed very important. Lambert just hoped that it wouldn't run out for him. Or for the whole town, come to that. He looked out of the window, pleased to see the sunlight.

He was beginning to dread the night.

25

The wind had grown steadily as the evening wore on. As the sun sank, it had been little more than a gentle breeze, but now, just after midnight, it had grown in ferocity to almost gale proportions.

Charles Burton lay in bed listening to the gate slamming repeatedly in the passageway below. The narrow entrance and stone corridor separated the house from the one next door and it was the wooden door at the head of the passage that was being buffetted by the wind. It smashed sporadically into the lintel, each fresh impact jarring Burton and making him more irritable. If it went on much longer he would have to get up and close the bloody thing. It had a latch but the people next door usually forgot to put it on. That was why the door was slamming now.

Burton exhaled deeply, closed his eyes and tried to sleep, but the insistent banging of the gate disturbed him. Finally he swung himself out, pulled on his trousers and slid his sockless feet into his shoes.

'What's up?' croaked Stevie Lawson, sleepily. She looked up and saw, through blurred eyes, Burton trying to zip up his trousers. He caught a pubic hair in the zipper and yelped in pain.

'Shit,' he snarled.

Stevie smiled. 'What are you doing?'

'It's that bloody gate,' said Burton, inclining his head. As if to add weight to his statement, there was an almighty crash as it cracked into the jamb once more.

'They must have forgotten to lock it, next door,' said Stevie, yawning. 'Can't you leave it?'

'It's getting on my nerves,' he snapped, heading for the bedroom door. He pulled it open and fumbled for the landing light which he slapped on.

'Come back to bed,' purred Stevie, allowing the sheet to drop, revealing her breasts. 'Forget about the gate.'

Burton felt a stirring in his groin at the sight of those firm mounds and he almost hesitated, but the gate slammed again and he was off down the stairs.

Stevie heard him open the hall door and blunder through the living room. She rolled onto her back and stretched beneath the sheets. Burton might be getting on a bit, she thought to herself, but he certainly knew how to treat a woman. Their lovemaking had been even more abandoned that night, animalistic almost, and the thought of it made her tingle. She'd hang onto him for a couple more weeks. He bought her flowers and perfume, anything she wanted really. She only had to ask and he'd get it for her. Silly old bastard, she thought. Couldn't he see she was using him? She'd cooked him dinner that night, listened disinterestedly as he'd prattled on about his day's work. She fussed him, teased him, and finally they had climbed into bed. To her it seemed like a fair deal, he got what he wanted from her, she got what she wanted from him. Sometimes it was difficult to tell who was using who. Still, she thought, next time she'd pick up a younger bloke. Burton had the money and he was good in bed, but she wanted someone nearer her own age. He could only manage it twice in a night and sometimes that wasn't enough for her. Her husband had been the same. She almost laughed aloud as she thought of him. Poor old Ron. He'd joined the army a year before they got married. He was a sergeant in the Signals. Out in Ulster at the moment. She'd had no letter from him for over a week. For all she knew, or cared, he could be lying in some Belfast gutter with an I.R.A. bullet in him. He usually wrote to her once a week to ask how she was, how the family was, and his little joke at the end, to make sure that she was behaving herself. Ha bloody ha, she thought. Dutifully she wrote back, always telling him that she missed him and couldn't wait for him to get home. She smiled to herself. Fucking idiot he was, probably believed her too. She was toying with the idea of moving away from Medworth. It was boring. She wanted to see some life. Ron was happy there, but, of course, he never did have any ambition. London was the place for her. The nightlife. The men. Beneath the sheets she ran both hands over her body, satisfied that she would have no trouble finding someone dumb enough to keep her if she ever should make the trek down there. Any bloke, anywhere, would give his right arm to have her. She was one of that rare breed of women who were not only aware of their good looks but also knew how to use them to get what they wanted. She heard Burton open the back door and wished he would stop farting about and hurry back to bed. She was beginning to feel horny again.

The wind hit him like a cold hammer when he opened the door and the newsman shivered, wishing he'd put on a coat. He stepped out into the darkness and hurried around the corner to the passage. Peering up it, he could see the gate slightly ajar. As he started towards it, a gust of wind blew it shut, plunging the passage and back yard into total darkness. Burton placed his hands on one wall and groped his way towards the door.

He cracked his leg on something which was standing in the darkened passage.

'Jesus,' he groaned, rubbing his injured shin.

The object which he'd collided with was a motorcycle. The lad who owned it lived in the next house and he always put it in the passage on bad nights. Burton cursed under his breath and edged past the bike. He reached the gate just as a gust of wind sent it hurtling back. It slammed into the rear wall with a loud thud and momentarily gave the newsman a view of the street outside. All the lamps were out. It was like a bloody coal mine out there. Burton thought he saw something move at the end of the pathway which led out from the gate, but he dismissed it and fumbled with the latch on the gate, finally dropping it into place and tugging on the metal handle to ensure that the wind wouldn't blow it loose again. Satisfied, he turned and groped his way back down the passage, careful to avoid the motorcycle this time. He edged around the corner into the back yard of Stevie's house and smiled at the sight of light flooding from the open back door. He paused for a moment. He didn't remember leaving the door open when he came out. Burton shrugged. The bloody wind had probably blown that open too.

He heard a scratching sound close by and spun round, trying to make out what it was in the light from the open back door.

A dark shape was moving at the bottom of the garden. Hidden by the large hedge, it was difficult to make it out. The newsman hesitated, squinting into the gloom, trying to distinguish shape from shadow. A particularly strong gust of wind rocked him where he stood and he shivered, bringing both arms up and trying to cover himself while still attempting to make out what exactly was moving about at the bottom of the garden. There was another sound, like that of sticks being broken. Finally, his curiosity getting the better of him, Burton strode off down the garden to find the source of the noise.

Stevie sighed. What the hell was Burton playing at? Surely it didn't take that long to lock a gate? She hadn't heard it banging for the last couple of minutes so she assumed that he had closed it. What the bloody hell was he pissing about at?

She heard footsteps on the stairs and smiled, deciding to play a joke on him. She rolled onto her side, pretending to be asleep. The landing light went off and she heard movement outside the door. She'd frighten the bastard when he came back in. She'd wait until he was leaning right over her then jump up. Stevie suppressed a grin.

Her back was to the bedroom door when it opened.

Burton reached the bottom of the garden, the wind now drowning out all other noises. It gusted around him, roaring in his ears and he began to wish he'd gone straight back into the house. He could hardly see in the darkness and he was freezing but he was determined to find out what it was that was making the scratching noise.

He peered over the top of the hedge, scanning the ground for some sign of movement.

Nothing in sight. He sighed.

Something touched his foot and he jumped back, almost shouting in terror. Controlling the urge to run, he looked down to see a hedgehog scuttling past. It hurried past him and disappeared beneath the wire fence which separated Stevie's garden from the one next door. Burton smiled, amused and angry with himself for his exaggerated reaction. He turned and trudged back towards the house.

He was pleased to regain its warmth and light and he hastily locked and bolted the back door, shivering. Then he made his way back through the darkened house until he reached the hall. Here he paused. The landing light was out, the staircase in darkness. Burton flicked the switch in the hall which also controlled the landing light and the place was illuminated once more. He started up the stairs, slowing his pace as he noticed a strange odour. It reminded him of bad fish and he wrinkled his nose as it became stronger. By the time he reached the landing itself, the stench was almost overpowering. The door to Stevie's bedroom was closed tightly and Burton found that he had to use unexpected force to open it. He stepped inside, reaching for the light switch, the smell now so strong he wanted to vomit. He called her name once and turned on the light.

There were three of them in the room.

Burton froze in the doorway, not quite able to accept what he saw.

The living dead creatures were huddled around the bed like worshippers at an altar. As the light went on, two of them cowered down, trying to hide their blank eyes from the brightness.

Eyes?

It was with mounting revulsion that Burton realized they didn't have any eyes. Just black, empty holes, dark with dried and caked blood. The third of the trio, a man in his thirties, had one hand on Stevie's face, and the newsman saw that one of his bony fingers was still embedded in her, now empty, eye socket. Blood from the torn cavity had run down like crimson tears, staining the sheets. In other places it had splashed over her chest. He noted the wounds around her throat, the bruising and red welts where she had been throttled to death, the numerous other abrasions on her body where the trio of living corpses had attacked her.

Burton couldn't move. All he could do was shake his head slowly back and forth, his eyes gaping wide at the scene before him. Had his mind been functioning properly he would have realized that it was the light that was keeping the things still, but, in his present state, nothing registered. Just the obscene image of those creatures, crouched around Stevie's body like eyeless vultures.

Then, when he seemed beyond horror, something happened which finally galvanized him into action.

Stevie sat up.

Very slowly she turned her head, the bleeding holes which should have been eyes fixing him in a blazing stare.

She was grinning.

Burton screamed and reached down, his fist closing around a hand mirror which lay on the dressing table beside him. He took a step forward and, with all his strength, smashed it into the face of the first living corpse. The impact shattered the mirror and long shards of razor-sharp glass shredded the man's face. So powerful was the swing, it knocked the thing off its feet and it toppled onto the second of the living dead creatures, a woman no more than twenty-five. The third, another man, leapt across the bed at Burton and grabbed him by the throat. Roaring with rage, the newsman pushed the creature away, bringing his foot up. It connected savagely, just below the ribcage and the thing crumpled up. Burton aimed another kick at its head, gratified by the sound of snapping bone as he shattered a cheekbone with the force of his blow.

He staggered for a second, his mind frozen, filled only with one thought. Hatred for the things that had killed Stevie. But now *she* was upon him, her sharp nails tearing at his face, raking his cheeks. Aiming for his eyes. He punched her hard, the blow splitting her bottom lip, but she staggered a moment then was at him again. They fell back against the wall, her hands reaching for his throat.

The second creature, the woman, clambered over the bed and joined in the attack and Burton felt more sharp nails tearing at his face. Blood spurted from three deep gashes and he lashed out, catching the creature in the throat. It made a gurgling sound, yellow mucous spilling over its lips but it continued with its attack and Burton now noticed that the second woman too, was grinning.

They were all grinning.

Even the first of them, staggering towards him with splinters of glass protruding from his torn face where the mirror had cut him.

Burton screamed once more and, with a last desperate surge of strength, hurled Stevie away. She toppled over the fallen creature and the newsman bolted for the door, slamming it behind him and racing for the stairs. The second woman was after him, catching his arm as he reached the top step. He spun around, the momentum of his swing aided by the turn, and slammed both fists into her face. The nose crumbled beneath the impact and bright blood spurted into the air, some of it onto Burton. He grabbed the woman by the hair and hurled her down, watching with something approaching insane joy as she tumbled down the stairs, finally crashing into the table at the bottom. He almost shouted in anguish as he saw her get up, starting towards him once more.

And now the others were spilling onto the landing, all of them sporting that hideous feral grin. Headed by Stevie they lunged at him but he ducked back into the bathroom, slamming the door and sliding the tiny bolt.

One of the living dead men crashed into the door and Burton knew that it wouldn't hold them back for long. His breath coming in gasps, he looked frantically around the tiny room which had become a prison. There was nothing to defend himself with. He couldn't hope to fight off four of them.

There was one chance. . . .

If he could climb out of the window onto the window sill, he might be able to hoist himself up onto the roof of the house. They'd never be able to reach him up there and, even if they did succeed in climbing up, it could only be one at a time. He'd kick the fuckers off as they reached the top.

The bathroom door rocked once more and the bolt began to bend. Burton crossed the room, opened the window and clambered up onto the sill, using the sink as a foothold.

He could hear them moving about outside the room.

Twenty feet below him was a mass of solid concrete and he was thankful he couldn't see it as he scrambled out onto the sill. The powerful wind tugged at him and, for a second, he tottered but he grabbed at the guttering a foot or so above his head and steadied himself. He prayed that it would take his weight.

There was an almighty crash as the bathroom door was smashed in. The living corpses crowded into the room, the first of them rushing to the open window, grabbing for Burton's exposed legs. He shrieked and kicked out at the grasping hand, trying, simultaneously, to hoist himself up. The wind roared in his ears, the hands of the creatures tore at his legs. With almost tired resignation, he realized he wasn't going to make it.

He groaned and tried to pull himself up but the guttering buckled under his weight. For precious seconds it held and he actually managed to hook one leg up onto the slates of the roof, but, with a sickening creak, it gave way.

Burton uttered one mournful cry and plummeted to the concrete below.

The impact broke his back and most of his ribs on the left side, one of which tore through his lung. His head slammed down. Blood burst into his mouth and he sensed a feeling of total awareness before he blacked out. The last thing he saw was the living dead things peering out of the bathroom window, as if, somehow, they could see his shattered body. Even though he couldn't see them clearly, he could sense that they would be grinning.

Twelve more people were to die that night.

26

The night was alive with a kaleidoscope of flashing blue lights as Lambert swung the Capri into Victoria Lane. There were two squad cars and an ambulance, all with their lights spinning, parked in the road outside a house about half way down the street. One of the Pandas was parked on the pavement.

The Inspector rubbed his eyes as he switched off the engine. The clock on the dashboard glowed one-thirty a.m. and Lambert yawned as he stepped out of the Capri and walked hurriedly towards the group of vehicles. There were lights in the windows of houses next door and across the road and he could see people peering out to see just what the hell was going on at this ungodly hour of the morning.

The wind had dropped but there was a biting chill in the air and the Inspector pulled up the collar of his coat, digging his hands deep into the pockets. He recognized Constable Bell, and the policeman smiled grimly as he saw Lambert approach.

'What happened?' asked the Inspector, yawning.

Bell reached for his notebook but Lambert

waved it away. 'Just the shortened version,' he said.

'Well, the house belongs to a Mrs Stephanie Lawson, her husband is in the army, he's away at the moment . . .'

Lambert cut him short. 'I said the short version.'

'Sorry, sir,' said Bell and continued, 'a neighbour rang up about an hour ago to complain about some noises she heard coming from the house. The sarge radioed me and P.C. Jenkins and we came straight over. I knocked on the door but I couldn't get any answer. When I went around the back I found . . .' he hesitated.

'What?' demanded Lambert.

'A body.'

He was about to walk away when Bell called him back. 'He was still alive when I reached him.'

Lambert nodded.

'Dr Kirby is in the ambulance with him now.'

Lambert turned and hurried across to the parked emergency vehicle, its two back doors still open. The Inspector assumed that Kirby must have been summoned at roughly the same time as himself. Hayes had called him ten minutes earlier and told him that there was trouble in Victoria Lane. Now he peered into the ambulance and saw a worried looking Kirby bending over the covered form of a man. There was a red blanket pulled up to his neck but its colour did little to mask the dark stains which had seeped through the thick material in several places.

'John,' said Lambert, climbing up into the ambulance.

'He's dying,' said Kirby flatly.

It was then that Lambert looked down at the prostrate form and saw that it was Charles Burton.

'Jesus Christ,' gasped the Inspector.

At the sound, Burton opened his eyes slightly. When he saw Lambert, they widened to huge orbs, filled with pain and something more. Fear perhaps. The newsman lifted one bloodstained hand towards Lambert and croaked, 'Lambert.' Blood dribbled over his lips and he winced, as if the effort of talking were too much, but he drew in a painful breath and continued. The policeman leant closer.

'What are they?' gasped Burton, his wide eyes fixing the Inspector momentarily in a piercing stare. Then, slowly, he closed his eyes. Lambert looked down at the torn face, the blood-matted hair, a portion of skull shining white amidst the clumps of congealing gore. Kirby pushed him aside and laid his stethoscope on Burton's chest. He felt for a pulse, digging his fingers almost savagely into the wrist. He shook his head angrily.

An ambulanceman appeared in the doorway and looked at Kirby.

'Will you be travelling to the hospital, doctor?' he asked.

'No need,' said Kirby and stepped down, followed by Lambert.

They heard the doors being slammed and, a second later the ambulance pulled away. Its blue light was extinguished. There was no longer an

256

emergency. No hurry to reach the hospital. Not any longer.

Constable Bell appeared again.

'There's blood all over the house, sir,' he said, swallowing.

Lambert nodded. 'What about Mrs Lawson?'

'No sign of her anywhere.'

Bell wandered off again, leaving the two men alone outside the house. Lambert looked up into the dark sky, flecked with hundreds of silver pinpricks of stars. He sighed then looked at Kirby.

'This has gone far enough, John,' he said, flatly. 'We need help.'

27

Lambert and Kirby spoke little on the journey to
Divisional Headquarters in Nottingham. Almost
against his better judgment, the Inspector had
finally decided that he needed reinforcements to
deal with the growing threat which hung over
Medworth like some supernatural cloud. He was
perspiring slightly although the early morning
sun had not yet reached its full power and the
last vestiges of dawn mist still hung, wraithlike,
in the hollows and woods which dotted the route.
There wasn't much traffic on the road and for
that Lambert was thankful. He cruised, doing
an even fifty for most of the journey, causing
Kirby to glance down at the speedometer every
now and then. But he said nothing. He too realized the importance of their journey, and as far
as both of them were concerned, the sooner it
was over, the better.

On the back seat of the Capri was a leather
attache case, filled to bursting point with every
detail they could lay their hands on concerning
the horrors which had taken place in Medworth
over the past month or so. Coroner's reports,
backgrounds of victims, what scant details they
had of the disappearances (there had been

twenty-four up to date) and full reports by Lambert on what was happening.

As they sat in silence, watching the countryside speeding by, both men had the same thought. How the hell were they going to convince Lambert's superiors of the truth of what was going on in the little town?

The journey took less than forty minutes and, at around nine-thirty, Lambert was guiding the Capri through the busy streets of Nottingham, blasting his horn angrily at a cyclist who hesitated too long at traffic lights. The poor woman was so unnerved by the sudden sound that she nearly toppled off into the path of a passing jeep. Lambert swung the car past her and asked Kirby to check just exactly where they were.

'Take a left at the next crossroads,' said the doctor, running his index finger over the inner city map.

The Inspector obeyed, and within minutes they found themselves in a huge car park which fronted the main building, a massive edifice of glass and concrete which seemed to tower up into the very clouds themselves. Sunlight glinted off the many windows which winked like myriad glass eyes, peering down on the tiny car as the Inspector parked it and they both got out. They walked swiftly across the paved area, Lambert looking in awe at the seemingly endless lines of parked Pandas.

They reached the main entrance and climbed the flight of broad stone steps until a row of wire meshed glass doors confronted him. Lambert pushed the first of these, holding it open for

Kirby to pass through. They found themselves in a huge reception area with what looked like a gigantic duty desk at one end. Lambert crossed to it and asked the sergeant on duty where he could find Detective Chief Inspector Baron. The sergeant asked who the Inspector was and Lambert produced his own I.D. card to prove his validity. The sergeant nodded and directed the two men to a lift across the entrance way and told them to take it to the fifth floor.

There was a loud ring as the lift arrived and three uniformed men stepped out, pushing past Lambert and Kirby as if they were in a hurry. The two men stepped into the lift and Lambert jabbed the button marked '5.' There was a humming sound as the lift ascended. It reached five and, with a loud ring, the doors opened. The two men stepped out, feeling the thickness of lush carpet beneath their feet. The corridor was silent, all sounds muffled by the thick cloth on which they walked. At the far end was a desk behind which sat a woman in her thirties. She was reading and, as Lambert drew closer, he could see that the book was called 'Hot Lips.' He suppressed a grin as the woman put the book down and smiled politely up at him.

'Good morning, sir,' she said.

'Good morning,' replied Lambert, 'I'd like to see DCI Baron please. My name is Lambert.' He reached for the plastic card again and showed it to her, 'Inspector Lambert.'

'Just a moment, sir,' she said and flicked a switch on the panel before her. There was a loud buzzing noise and then a metallic voice came through the speaker;

'Yes.'

'Carol. There's a . . .' she hesitated, looking at the name on the card, '. . . Inspector Tom Lambert out here. He wants to see Mr Baron.'

'Send him in,' instructed the voice. 'But Mr Baron is busy at the moment, he might have to wait.'

'That's O.K.,' said the Inspector.

The receptionist showed them a door off to the right and the two men nodded as they walked in.

'It's more like a bloody hotel,' said Lambert under his breath, walking into another office. It was decorated in a lemon yellow, the walls hung with a number of paintings. The area to their left was one huge plate glass window through which the early morning sun was streaming, dust particles swirling in its powerful rays. There were five leather chairs along the opposite wall and an ashtray beside each one. At the far end of the room was a desk and, on either side of the desk, a door. As Lambert approached the desk he could see the two names, which were fastened to the dark wood of the doors, in gold letters. The name on the right hand door was Chief Inspector Mark Dayton. The one on the left read Detective Chief Inspector James Baron.

'Inspector Lambert?' said the receptionist, a woman with a round face and large glasses.

Lambert nodded.

'You'll have to wait, I'm afraid. Mr Baron is busy at the moment.'

'How long will he be?'

The woman smiled, an efficient smile practised over the years. 'I can't say for sure, but if you'd like to take a seat I'll send you in as soon as I can.' She motioned to the leather chairs and the two men sat down. The wall clock said nine forty-five. Lambert lit up his first cigarette of the day.

The hands of the clock had crawled on to ten thirty and there were seven butts in the ashtray before Lambert when the buzzer finally sounded and a little red light flared on the panel before the receptionist. She leant forward and spoke into the intercom.

'Yes, sir,' she said.

Lambert heard something babbled but couldn't understand what it was. He gritted his teeth and exhaled deeply. If there was one thing he hated, it was being kept waiting. He ground out his cigarette angrily and looked across at the receptionist who still wore that perpetual grin.

'There are two gentlemen to see you, sir. An Inspector Lambert and . . .' she looked up, realizing that she didn't know the other man's name.

'Dr Kirby,' he said.

'Dr Kirby,' she repeated.

There were more metallic babblings from the other end and then she nodded and flicked the switch back to 'Off.'

'You can go in,' she said.

'Three bloody cheers,' muttered Lambert. He knocked once and a voice from inside told him to come in. The two men entered the office. It was small, not the grandiose abode which the Inspector had imagined. There were several banks of filing cabinets, a rubber plant on one window sill, and of all things, a tropical fish tank set on a table beside one wall. Baron himself was bending over the tank when the two men entered. He looked up and smiled, extending a friendly hand which they both shook.

'Fascinating things, fish,' said Baron, cheerfully and sat down behind his desk. He pointed to two plastic chairs upon which his visitors seated themselves. So, thought Lambert, this is the great James Baron? The man who had solved more murder cases in this area than *he'd* had hot dinners? Baron's reputation was a formidable one and well known to all those under him. He'd been a colonel in the Chindits during the war and still bore a scar, running from the corner of his left eye to his left ear, as a legacy of those days. Two broken marriages and countless affairs had charted his rise to the very top of his profession, a position which he intended holding until he retired. Another eight years. There was, Lambert had been told by men who had worked directly under Baron, a feeling of ambivalence towards the man. On the one hand he was respected for his abilities as a policeman, but on the other hand he was hated for his hardhearted cynicism, the latter being something that Lambert was all too aware of as he tried to figure out what he was going to say to his superior. Baron was not a favourite with the media either. His policy of releasing only tiny pieces of information had led to him being regarded as uncooperative and rude. *That* at least, was something Lambert could respect about him. Baron had been in the force for nearly thirty years and had held the rank of D.C.I. for fifteen of those. During his term in command, the force in that area had undergone a radical change, dealing with troublemakers in a tougher way which had many crying police brutality. But Baron cared nothing for the reactions of the press and television. As far as he was concerned he was there to do a job and he would do it as he thought best and the way he could best achieve results.

Now, as he sat back in his seat, Lambert studied this powerful man. Well preserved for his age and, considering the responsibilities which he carried, remarkably untouched by the rigours of worry. No wrinkles or grey hairs here. Just the slightest hint of a paunch, visible as it strained against the tightly buttoned waistcoat which he wore. His jacket was hung up behind the door along with his overcoat. Neat.

Baron looked at Lambert and smiled.

'Inspector Lambert, eh?' he said, his voice gravelly.

'Yes sir.'

'You're a young man to hold such a responsible position. You must be good at your job.' He smiled warmly. 'Would you like a cup of coffee?'

'Yes, please,' said Kirby and Lambert too, agreed.

Baron flicked a switch on his intercom and spoke rapidly into it, telling his secretary to fetch three coffees. He sat back in his chair once more, hands clasped across his broad chest.

'Which area are you from?' Baron asked.

'Well, we're based in Medworth, but we cover most of the area round about,' Lambert explained.

'How many men are under you?'

'Ten.'

Baron nodded.

'Married?' he asked.

Christ, thought Lambert, it's like a bloody interview.

'Yes, sir.'

'And you doctor?' Baron wanted to know.

Kirby shook his head. 'No, I'm still a free agent.'

'And quite right too,' said Baron laughing. 'They're more trouble than they're worth, women.'

The other two men laughed nervously. There was a knock on the door and the coffee arrived. Carol set it down on the edge of the desk and left. The three men helped themselves to milk and sugar and Baron sat back in his chair, stirring slowly.

'Well, Inspector, what exactly can I do for you?' said the older man. 'It must be important for you to come all this way.'

Lambert and Kirby exchanged brief glances and the Inspector coughed nervously. He put his coffee cup on the corner of the desk.

'I need your help, sir,' he said. 'I need some of your men.'

Baron took a sip of his coffee and regarded Lambert over the rim of the cup.

'Why?' he wanted to know.

Lambert opened the attache case and fumbled inside until he found what he was looking for. It was a photograph of the body of Father Ridley, hanging from the bell rope. Baron took it and studied the monochrome print, his eyes coming to rest on the damage done to Ridley's face. He nodded gently, looking at the second photo which Lambert handed him. It was of Emma Reece.

'Both the work of the same person?' mused Baron, his gaze settling on the torn eye sockets of both victims.

Kirby reached for two of the manila files in the case with Lambert watching him anxiously. 'The marks on the bodies of the first victims match those on the bodies of the latest ones,' said the doctor, pushing the files towards Baron.

The D.C.I. peered briefly at the files, shaking his head.

'Twenty-four people have disappeared inside a month,' Lambert told him. 'We can't find a trace of them. All we ever find at the scene of the assault is lots of blood.'

'That proves nothing,' said Baron flinging the files back onto the desk.

'People don't just disappear,' said Lambert, his voice rising in volume, 'there's a pattern to it.'

Kirby pointed to the marks on his neck. 'These wounds were inflicted by a woman who had been buried for over a week.' There was a long silence as Baron regarded the two men suspiciously.

'You're both bloody crazy,' said Baron, smiling.

'Sir, for God's sake, can't you at least offer an explanation? We've tried every possible avenue to find a plausible answer. There *is* not a plausible answer,' said Lambert, barely able to control himself.

Kirby returned to the wounds on his neck. 'This woman attacked me. She rose from the grave and attacked me. I was as skeptical as you until that happened but I'm telling you, I was attacked by a living corpse.'

There was a moment's silence, during which time Baron's smile faded. He leant forward, his voice now hard-edged and emotionless.

'Now you listen to me, both of you. I'm a busy man, I've got lots of responsibilities and I haven't got the time to sit around listening to two raving lunatics trying to tell me that they've got a town full of living corpses.' He pointed a stern finger at Lambert. 'If you were a man off the street I might find this whole thing amusing. But you're not, you're an Inspector in Her Majesty's Police force and, listening to what you've just told me, you make me wonder how you ever got past the cadet stage, let alone become an Inspector.' The older man's face was going scarlet with rage. 'How old are you, Lambert?'

'Twenty-two,' he replied, the fury likewise building within himself. He felt like dragging Baron across the desk, strapping him in the car and driving him back to Medworth to leave him at the mercy of the things which roamed the town at night. Perhaps *then* the old sod would begin to understand.

'Well, when you've been in this bloody game as long as I have perhaps you'll have the sense to keep your idiot fantasies to yourself instead of wasting *my* time with them.'

Lambert clenched his teeth, the knot of muscles at the side of his jaw pulsing angrily. He gripped the sides of his chair until he threatened to tear them loose.

'All I want is half a dozen men to back up my

boys,' he said quietly, the anger seething behind his words.

'Forget it,' snapped Baron, returning to his coffee and looking out of the window as if the two men didn't even exist.

'We can't manage on our own,' snarled Lambert, his voice rising in volume.

Baron swung round. 'Get out of here before I have you both thrown out,' he shouted.

Kirby gathered the photos and files and dropped them into the case.

The D.C.I. hadn't finished: 'Another thing, Lambert. If I hear anything more about this . . . ridiculous affair, if I see anything in the paper about it, I'll tell you this now, sunshine, within a week, you'll be back walking a damned beat.' He paused a second: 'Now get out before I have you both locked up.'

Lambert hestitated. 'All right, if you won't give us men at least give us guns.' That was it. The words hung in the air. Make or break.

Silence reigned supreme in the sunlit office. There was a high pitched squeaking sound as Baron leant forward in his chair. The Inspector wasn't sure whether or not a smile was hovering on his lips, and when he finally spoke, his tone was soft, gentle even.

'You know something, Lambert, you really have got nerve, haven't you?'

Lambert swallowed hard. 'The guns sir. Please.'

Another long silence followed then Baron reached forward and flicked a switch on his intercom.

'Carol,' he said, 'have Dayton come in, will you?'

He sat back again, gazing at the two men who stood before him like naughty children in front of an angry headmaster. A second later the door to Barton's office opened and Chief Inspector Mark Dayton walked in.

'You wanted something, guv?' he said, without looking at either Lambert or Kirby.

'Take Inspector Lambert here down to the basement. Issue him with all he wants.'

Dayton looked puzzled, he raised one eyebrow and looked quizzically at the two men then he said, 'Come on, follow me.' The trio turned but, as they reached the door Baron called:

'Lambert.'

The young Inspector turned. 'Sir?'

Baron's voice was low, soft with menace. 'If this turns out to be bullshit, I'll have your fucking head.'

Lambert closed the door gently behind him. 'Cunt,' he muttered under his breath and hurried off to catch up with Kirby and Dayton who were already half way down the corridor.

Dayton leant up against one corner of the lift as it dropped the six floors to the basement. He regarded the men opposite him with indifference. Lambert guessed that the policeman must be ten, perhaps fifteen years older than himself. Dayton was tall but in an ungainly way and his feet seemed to have been designed for someone much smaller than him. That would probably account for his shuffling walk. He had thick eyebrows which snaked upwards giving him a look of perpetual surprise.

The lift came to a halt and the doors slid open. Both Lambert and Kirby were immediately taken aback by the overpowering smell of oil and cordite, an odour which the Inspector rapidly recognized as gun oil.

They walked across the stone floor of the basement, their footsteps echoing on the hard surface and the sounds reminded Lambert of an underground car park. They came to a heavy iron gate which Dayton unlocked. He ushered them in.

The room was small but all four walls held racks which sported row upon row of rifles, shotguns and pistols. There was what looked like a counter over by the far wall and a man in a white smock was cleaning a revolver behind it. He looked up when he saw the trio enter, then looked down again, returning to his task.

'Pete,' called Dayton, 'we want some stuff.'

Peter Baker put down the pistol and nodded. He wiped a hand across his forehead, forgetting it was still smeared with grease, and left a black mark from temple to temple. Lambert looked up at the rows of guns.

'How many in your force?' asked Dayton.

'Ten,' Lambert told him.

'What are they like with weapons?'

Lambert shrugged, 'God knows. I doubt if any of them have even touched a gun let alone fired one. I haven't myself.'

Baker grinned and reached to the rack behind him. He pulled the gun down and handed it to Lambert who was surprised by its weight.

'What is it?' he asked, hefting it back and forth.

'An automatic shotgun,' Baker told him. 'The Yanks call them pump guns.' He looked at Dayton and both men laughed. Lambert couldn't see the joke. He held the gun up to his shoulder and squinted down the sight.

'No need for that,' said Baker, smiling, 'it isn't a hunting rifle. Just make sure you're on target when you pull the trigger and hang onto it tight. Whatever you hit with *that* won't get up again.'

'Let's hope not,' said Kirby, cryptically.

'With just a bit of practice you'll be able to handle it,' Baker assured him. 'But like I said, hang on tight when you pull the trigger, it's got quite a recoil. You could blow a hole in a house with one of those.'

'Give him ten,' said Dayton.

'What about pistols?' Lambert asked.

Dayton looked aghast. 'Are you planning a commando raid or something? This is England. Not bloody New York.' He shook his head. 'Pete, give him a couple of Brownings too.'

Baker nodded and laid down two automatic pistols beside the stack of shotguns and ammunition.

'Bring your car round to the back of the building,' said Dayton. 'We'll have this lot sent up and you can load it straight in.'

By one that afternoon, Lambert and Kirby were on their way back to Medworth, the guns safely stored in the boot of the Capri. Neither of them spoke.

The Inspector put his foot down, anxious to

271

get back. He had to tell his men what had happened, tell them that from now on they were on their own. He realized too that he and the rest of the small force would have to practise with the weapons if they were to be any use.

He sighed. They didn't even know if guns would stop the creatures. Baker's words passed fleetingly through his mind:

'Whatever you hit with that won't get up again.'

Lambert prayed to God he was right.

PART
THREE

PART
THREE

> *'Hast thou found me,*
> *O mine enemy?'*
>
> —1 Kings; 21:20.

28

Dawn rose grey and dirty over Medworth and Tom Lambert shivered as he tugged back the bedroom curtains. He stood in the window for a moment, gazing out into the street below. There were one or two people on the street, on their way to work probably. He wondered if they realized what was going on nightly around them. Shaking the thought from his mind he washed and dressed quickly and hurried downstairs, the smell of cooking bacon meeting him as he reached the living room.

Debbie stood over the pan, stirring with a wooden spatula. He kissed her gently on the lips and ran a hand through her uncombed hair before sitting down. There was a mail, a couple of letters, but he didn't bother to read them. He glanced briefly at the paper, setting it aside as Debbie laid his breakfast before him.

'How long have you been up?' he asked, taking a mouthful.

'Since about five.'

He looked surprised.

'I couldn't sleep, and besides, I thought I'd try and get a bit further through those bloody books that Trefoile gave us.'

275

Lambert nodded. He had read through her transcriptions the night before and, although she was almost half way through the huge volumes, nothing of any importance had turned up yet. Anything of note she had ringed in red marker but, as yet, there were precious little pieces of information to be had. However, on one sheet, one of the most recent ones, the name had appeared for the first time. That name which had caused Trefoile so much distress.

Mathias.

Lambert had studied the name over and over again, finally discarding the piece of paper.

Debbie sat opposite him and sipped her coffee. He looked up at her, concern in his eyes.

'Do you think Trefoile was throwing us a line about the medallion?' he said.

'What do you mean?'

'The secret,' he emphasized the words with scorn. 'I wonder if the answer really is in those bloody books.'

'What reason would he have to lie?' asked Debbie, stifling a yawn.

Lambert shrugged. Now it was Debbie's turn to look at him. She warmed her hands around her mug and watched him as he ate. He had come home late the previous night, looking pale and drawn, as if he were in need of a good night's sleep. They had lain together on the sofa while he told her of what Baron had said. How there was to be no help for them, and she had shuddered involuntarily when he had said that. Lambert had received much the same reaction when he told the men at the police station of Baron's words. A feeling of isolation, but something more, foreboding, had greeted the declaration that they were to fight the menace alone. The guns had given little reassurance to most of them; but the older members of the force, Hayes and Davies in particular, had listened to Lambert's words with grim resolution etched on their faces. Both, fortunately for the Inspector, knew how to use guns. Davies had done National Service and Hayes informed them all, to a great peal of laughter, that his father had been a poacher, and consequently he himself had grown up with guns. Upon hearing this, the tension amongst the men slackened off a little. Briggs and Walford, youngsters that they were, seemed anxious to use the weapons and were positively delighted when Lambert announced that they would all have to practise. They must all become proficient with the weapons. It could, he had told them, save their lives. They were probably all out now in the field at the back of the station blasting away at the targets, under the watchful eyes of Hayes and Davies. Lambert had given the other Browning to Hayes, keeping the first for himself.

The sight of the guns frightened Debbie and she shuddered when she thought to what use they were to be put. Even now, the shotgun stood propped up against the far wall of the kitchen, the Browning hanging in its shoulder holster from the back of the chair on which Lambert sat.

He finished eating, leaving a sizeable portion on his plate, and pushed the remains away from him. They regarded one another across the table, their eyes locked together like magnets. She finally got to her feet and walked around the table to him, reaching for him. He drew her close, squeezing her hard and he could hear her weeping softly. Lambert swallowed, his fingers tracing patterns in her hair. When she sat back, propped on his knee like some little child, tears stained her cheeks and he wiped them away with his finger.

'I love you,' he said, quietly and she smiled a little, fighting back the tears which threatened to spill forth once more.

'Tom,' she said, her voice catching, 'I don't understand any of this.'

He smiled humourlessly. 'Join the club.'

'I don't know why it's happening here. Not here in Medworth. I don't understand why it's happening at all.' Now the strength was returning to her voice and he felt a new power in the soft hands which gripped his.

'Perhaps the answer *is* in the books. Maybe that's the only explanation.' He peered past her into the living room to where the books lay open on the coffee table. Beside them was the medallion. Was it indeed as important as he suspected in getting to the bottom of this horror? Would the inscription finally reveal something of value? Something which they could use to aid them in the coming fight?

He exhaled deeply and kissed Debbie on the forehead.

'I'd better get moving,' he said and she slid from his knee, watching as he strapped on the shoulder holster, finally pulling on his jacket to cover the weapon. He held her close once more, not wanting to let her go. He closed his eyes and felt her arms grip him tight around the waist. Finally he stepped back, still resting his hands on her shoulders.

'As soon as it starts to get dark,' he began, 'lock and bolt all the doors and windows. Don't open them to anyone but me.' He swallowed hard, the next set of words coming out in fits and starts. 'If anything happens, get in touch with the station. Someone will be able to reach me wherever I am.'

'What do you hope to do, Tom? How can you fight them?' she asked, a note of tired desolation in her voice.

He picked up the shotgun, taking a box of shells from the drawer nearby. 'We'll cruise the streets, pick them off as they come out.' She noticed that he was shaking. He saw too, that his hands were quivering and he tried to laugh.

'I don't think there's anything in the rule book about this.' He was scared and he didn't mind admitting it. They kissed a last time and then she closed the door behind him, listening as the Capri started up, its wheels crunching gravel as Lambert reversed out into the street, did a quick three point turn and drove off.

Debbie felt more alone than she ever felt in her life.

She drank another mug of coffee and retreated into the living room. Back to the books. She continued deciphering.

Lambert drove slowly, the shotgun propped up on the passenger seat beside him. He looked at the weapon, its shiny blue-black colour contrasting with the light wood of its stock, the ribbed slide set firmly beneath the huge barrel.

The box of cartridges bounced about beside it as he swung the car into a street, gazing out at the houses on either side of him, many of them now empty. Whether their occupants had been killed to join the ranks of the living dead, or simply just left town, the windows of the houses were as blank and vacant as blind eyes. The toll, both of murders and departures, had been mounting daily and the Inspector wondered how long it would be before there was no one left.

He drove through the centre of town, reassured by the sight of a few more people. By day things were not so bad, but once darkness descended the town became deserted. A ghost town. It was possible, if anyone were foolish enough to do so, to walk the centre of Medworth, in fact the entire town, without bumping into a single living soul. Everyone was secure inside their houses. At least that was what they thought. The only person who didn't mind the current wave of devastation was Ralph Sanders, the local locksmith. He had a little shop in the main street of Medworth and he had virtually sold out of door and window locks and bolts. Those people who had decided to stay seemed intent on keeping out anything that tried to enter their homes. Lambert wondered how many of them had been successful. Hayes would probably have new figures waiting for him when he reached the station but, at the present time, they knew for certain that there were ninety-three people missing. Probably more and, when totalled with the number that had just upped and left, he was staring at a figure closer to three hundred. But, as yet, ninety-three was the figure they had. A question stood out vividly in the Inspector's mind and it was one which was to plague him for a long time to come.

Where the hell did that many people disappear to during the day?

He tapped absently on the wheel as he drove, his mind elsewhere. He was so absorbed in his own thoughts that he almost ran into a woman as she was crossing the road. He braked sharply, making the woman jump back in shock. Lambert raised a hand in a gesture of apology and drove on.

'No, no,' shouted Hayes, 'squeeze the bloody thing.'

P.C. Ferman jerked his finger around the trigger of the shotgun, groaning as the recoil slammed it back into his shoulder, the roar of the discharge deafening him. He worked the pump action, ejecting the spent shell and lowered the weapon, rubbing at his bruised shoulder.

Beside him, Bell was squinting down the narrow sight, trying to line up the bottle before him. He fired, the savage blast nearly knocking him over. The shot missed wildly, leaving the bottle unscathed but peppering the wall above with pellets. Davies groaned and took the weapon from him, demonstrating how it should be used. He swung the shotgun quickly onto its target and fired, smiling as the bottle exploded. showering glass everywhere.

Briggs was having a little more luck. He'd managed to hit two of the bottles lined up before him and was beginning to feel proud of himself. He worked the pump action vigorously and sent three expert blasts tearing into the wall behind, each punching football size holes in the concrete.

'Very flashy,' said Hayes, appearing at his side, 'but let's see you hit the bloody bottles.'

Briggs coloured slightly and returned to the smaller targets, missing twice. He pushed in five fresh cartridges and worked the pump action, chambering one.

'But Sarge,' he protested, 'why do we have to shoot at bottles?'

Hayes shook his head. 'Because, mastermind, if you can hit something that small then you shouldn't have too much trouble hitting a body.'

Both men looked at each other for long seconds, the words hanging on the air. Hayes shuddered. By God, that didn't sound right. Hitting bodies. He coughed awkwardly and rested a hand on Briggs' shoulder. When he spoke again, his tone was softer.

'Come on, lad, keep at it.'

Hayes walked up and down the short line. There were only six of them out there but, even so, in the still morning air, the sporadic explosions of fire from the shotgun muzzles were thunderous. The sergeant remembered the first time his Dad had taught him how to shoot. An old .410 it had been. Hayes had been twelve at the time and he could still remember the clouds of black smoke which belched from the twin barrels as he fired. His Dad had loved that gun, just like he had loved all his other weapons. Particularly the special weapon he had made. A single barrel rifle which, when unscrewed and disassembled, could fit into its own stock. Hayes had that gun at home now, along with the old

.410 and his own under-over shotgun. He had been brought up with guns but never did he imagine that he would need to call upon that experience in a situation like this. He stood still and watched as the men fired, and as he stood he shivered, trying to convince himself that it was the coldness of the wind which caused it.

Davies joined him, his own shotgun still smoking from recent fire.

'Have you tried out the pistol yet, sarge?' asked the constable.

Hayes shook his head and fumbled in his jacket for the Browning. It felt heavy, its thirteen shot clip snug in the butt. He'd only fired pistols a few times and never anything as powerful as this. He drew the weapon and, steadying it with both hands, fired.

There was a loud retort and the pistol bucked in his grasp, the golden cartridge case spinning from the weapon, the bullet tearing a hole in the wall beyond.

'Christ,' muttered Hayes and, excited by the power of the thing, squeezed off two more rounds. Both missed the bottles but he was beginning to get a feel of the thing.

'I hope it's enough,' he said under his breath. And both men looked at each other.

Neither saw Lambert approaching. The Inspector had heard the sporadic gunfire as he had parked his car outside the station. He'd popped inside and found Walford behind the desk. There'd been a couple of calls from people outside the town asking about relatives who they couldn't contact. Walford told the Inspector that he'd informed the callers that inquiries were being made.

'Good lad,' said Lambert and hurried off towards the field behind the station, the shotgun gripped firmly in his grasp, a box of shells in his pocket. That was one thing he was thankful for, at least they had plenty of ammunition. The sound of the savage discharges grew in volume as he neared the line of men.

Davies was the first to see him. The constable nodded and Lambert smiled in return.

'Morning guv,' said Hayes.

'How's it going?' asked Lambert, watching more holes being blown in the wall.

'Not too bad,' said Hayes, trying to smile. 'With a little time . . .'

Lambert cut him short. 'That's one thing we haven't got.'

He strode past the sergeant and Davies and pushed cartridges into his own shotgun before raising it to his shoulder and firing. The recoil cracked savagely against his shoulder.

'Shit,' muttered the Inspector under his breath.

'They're powerful.' Hayes said it as if he were telling Lambert something he didn't know.

The Inspector worked the slide, fired, pumped, fired. The third shot hit a bottle and shattered it. He lowered the weapon and rubbed his bruised shoulder. Hayes was grinning. Lambert felt somewhat reassured, having seen the power of the weapon. He handed the shotgun to Davies and drew the Browning, trying, at first, to sight it with one hand. When he fired, straight armed, the recoil nearly threw the gun from his grip.

'Jesus Christ,' said Lambert aloud and now the other men laughed too. The bullet sped past the wall and disappeared into the distance.

'Two hands, guv,' said Hayes, grinning.

Lambert steadied himself and fired, still surprised by the force of the recoil. He sighted carefully and squeezed off five rounds in quick succession. When he finally lowered the pistol, his ears were ringing and the palm of his right hand felt numb. He exhaled deeply and holstered the pistol. The other men began firing once more and again the morning air was filled with the roar of shotguns, occasionally accompanied by the strident explosion of a shattering bottle.

Hayes and Lambert stood together, watching. The Inspector was pushing more shells into the weapon, hefting it back and forth before him.

'Keep them at it for a couple of hours,' he said. 'No one's asking them to be bloody marksmen, I just want to be sure they hit what they aim at.'

Hayes nodded, watching as Lambert turned to the wall once more and fired the five shells in rapid succession, each one smashing holes in the concrete, two of them even hitting bottles. The Inspector watched as the last empty case fell to the ground, aware finally of the stink of cordite in the air. Then he strode past the sergeant, slapping him on the shoulder as he did so.

Hayes watched the young Inspector leave the field then turned back to the bruised constables before him.

'Well, come on then,' he shouted, 'let's see those bloody bottles get hit for a change. Many more shots off target and you'll have that fucking wall down.'

The intermittent roar of fire continued.

Debbie Lambert reached for the coffee mug and took a sip. Wincing, she noted that it was stone cold. She put the mug down and returned to the two books spread out in front of her. She swallowed hard and scanned the notes she had made. The name Mathias was beginning to crop up with surprising regularity. Debbie felt a twinge of something which she likened to excitement run through her and she almost forgot the steadily growing ache at the back of her neck. She massaged the stiff muscles with one hand, scribbling away frantically with the other. She reached the bottom of another page and turned it, the musty smell of the old book making her cough. She closed her eyes and massaged the bridge of her nose between thumb and forefinger.

'Enough for a minute,' she said aloud and got to her feet, padding into the kitchen where she switched on the kettle. More coffee. She ached all over her body but, somehow, she sensed that she was near her goal. A quick glance up at the wall clock told her it was approaching three thirty in the afternoon.

Lambert stood alone in the field, ignoring the spots of rain which bounced off him. He looked up at the sky, already dark with storm clouds. It would soon be dusk and he felt a shudder run through him. He looked into the box of shells at his feet. Nine left. He'd use them up then go back in. The men were waiting. He raised the shotgun and fired, watching with satisfaction as a bottle exploded under the impact. Again he fired, blasting a huge hole in the wall. His hands and shoulders ached but he kept up the steady fire until the shotgun was empty, the final spent cartridge spinning away as he worked the slide. He laid the weapon gently on the grass and reached inside his jacket for the Browning. He studied the pistol for a second before raising it with both hands and fixing one of the remaining bottles in his sights. Closing one eye he fired. He smiled weakly as he saw it shatter. The grass round about was littered with empty shell cases. It looked like a bloody battlefield. Lambert holstered the pistol and picked up the shotgun before trudging wearily down the hill to the station. He glanced at his watch. Four-fifty. It would be dark in an hour.

Debbie looked down at the medallion. The inscription stood out defiantly, as if challenging her to decipher it. She studied it against the woodcut on the page of the book before her. Beneath it, as Trefoile had shown them, the single word;

MATHIAS.

Owner of the medallion.

She looked at her notes, at the words which she already understood.

MORTIS DIEI—DEATHDAY

REX NOCTU—KING OF THE NIGHT

The inscription around the outside of the medallion still eluded her then, suddenly, she remembered what Trefoile had said, that the words were transposed. The inscription could only be understood when read from back to front. She took the words one at a time:

A

She looked it up in the dictionary. It meant 'to.' Simple as that. She smiled to herself. Now she took the next word. On the medallion, engraved in reverse, it appeared as SIUTROM. She quickly transposed the letters to form the word as recognizable Latin. It came out as:

MORTUIS.

She hunted through the dictionary for that one. Something jumbled here. Not quite right. There were several meanings. Death. Dead. Die. She put a question mark next to the word and looked at the last of the three reversed inscriptions. In its present form it appeared as ERAT-ICXE. She transposed and found that it came out as something more accessible:

EXCITARE.

Another run through the ever present dictionary. Her finger sped over the entries, searching, probing like a doctor in search of some malignant growth. She found it. 'Awake.' She wrote it down then went back to check the second word once more. Perhaps if she could put it into context she could understand. She read her notes, the transcriptions.

A MORTUIS EXCITARE—TO (something) AWAKE.

She frowned. No. That wasn't it. The structure was wrong. The words were in the wrong order. Heart pounding she wrote it out again.

A MORTUIS EXCITARE—TO AWAKE (something).

She re-checked her definitions.

MORTUIS—DEATH. DIE. THE DEAD.

It struck her like a physical blow and she exhaled deeply, quivering slightly as she finally understood. With shaking hand she wrote down the finished translation then transcribed the entire thing onto a fresh piece of paper. When she had done that she read it back, not daring to speak the words aloud. But they were there before her and she was gripped by a strange contradiction of feelings. A feeling of triumph for having deciphered the inscription but overwhelmed by an icy fear which gripped her heart in a vice-like hand and would not let go. She studied the words on the paper. The answer:

A MORTUIS EXCITARE—TO AWAKE THE DEAD.

And beneath that:

REX NOCTU—KING OF THE NIGHT.

Finally:

MORTIS DIEI—DEATHDAY.

Deathday.

And the single word that summed up all that evil.

MATHIAS.

She turned to the second book, searching its age-crusted pages for the information she sought. She looked at the medallion, suddenly distracted from her task. It seemed to glow dully in the dimly lit room and it was a moment or two before Debbie realized that it was nearly dark outside. She crossed to the big bay window at the front of the house and peered out. The street lamps were, as yet, unlit. They didn't come on until six. Another ten minutes. She hurriedly switched on the lamp which perched atop the TV, repeated the procedure with the one on the coffee table and also the taller standard lamp which was propped behind Lambert's chair. The light gave her a measure of reassurance but she found herself still shivering. She hurried upstairs and checked that all the windows were securely closed, particularly the one which looked out over the flat garage roof. She doublechecked that one. Satisfied, she sped downstairs and slid the bolts on both front and back doors before retreating into the living room. She sat in silence, curtains drawn against the darkness outside, surrounded by the paraphernalia of ages gone by. Her nostrils were assailed by an odour of dampness, mustiness.

The medallion glinted wickedly and Debbie found herself staring at it with the same horrified fascination with which a mouse watches a snake. She finally managed, as if it were an effort of will, to tear her gaze from it. She scanned the large yellowed page before her, dictionary at the ready. The page had the name of Mathias at its head and she began to read, intrigued and alarmed in equal proportions. Maybe by the time she finished she would know who this man really was.

She set to work.

The three Pandas were parked outside the station, all facing in the direction of Medworth town centre. From his position in the duty room Lambert could see them, just about. The darkness which had descended was total, almost palpable. He tore his eyes away and looked at the rows of sanguine faces arrayed before him.

Each of the men sat with shotguns across their laps. If not for the circumstances, Lambert could have laughed. It looked like a scene from some bloody western. He cleared his throat and stepped forward. All eyes focused on him.

'Right,' he began, 'I'll keep it simple. Two men to a car, three where possible. Grogan will stay here to take any calls. Bell, Ferman and Davies in Puma One. Vic,' he nodded towards Sergeant Hayes, 'you take Greene and Walford with you in number two. I'll take Puma Three. Briggs and Jenkins, you're with me.' The men didn't speak. Lambert waited, almost hoping for a question but none was forthcoming. He continued, 'Cruise around, that's all you've got to do. If you see anything moving about, anyone . . .' he searched for the word, 'suspicious, don't waste time finding out details, just shoot.'

A hand went up. It was Greene. He was in his early thirties, a capable lad who just happened to be as pale as death at the moment.

'How do we know the guns will work, sir?' he asked.

'We don't,' said Lambert, flatly. 'Try praying when you pull the trigger.' He tried to smile but it faded, washed away like chalk in the rain.

Another hand. This time it was Walford.

'Sir,' he said, 'how do we know that these . . . things will be all that's on the streets tonight? I mean, we might kill innocent people.' He swallowed hard.

Lambert nodded. 'Look, at the risk of sounding melodramatic, anything that's walking those streets tonight *won't* be human.' He became aware that his own hands were shaking and clenched them into fists. 'Whatever you see, blow the fucking thing to pieces.' There was a note of anger in his voice. He scanned the faces once more. Silence hung over the room like some huge invisible blanket. Lambert continued. 'All right, the cars are full of ammunition, you'll have no problems there. It's in the glove compartments, on the parcel shelves, everywhere we could find to put it, it's there.' He tried to smile again. 'One more thing, I want all the cars to keep in touch. Retain contact at all times and radio in to base every thirty minutes. No more than two men are to leave a car at one time. Understood?'

Nodding. Murmurs of approval.

'Right,' he checked his watch, 'it's seven fifteen now, I want this town patrolled until morning.' He finally found the note of humour he'd been looking for: 'Don't worry, you'll all get paid overtime for this.'

A ripple of laughter.

The men rose to their feet and were filing out of the room when Davies turned and raised his hand.

'What is it, Chris?' asked Lambert.

'These . . . things,' said Davies, 'they're living corpses, right?'

Lambert nodded.

'Well, then how the hell do you kill something that's already dead?'

The Inspector had no answer and the words hung in the air.

29

It seemed like they were driving into a huge black pit. That, at any rate, was how young Gary Briggs viewed the slow descent into Medworth. The town was in almost total darkness apart from the time switch lights which illuminated shop windows and a sparkling of house lights, most of which were subdued behind drawn curtains. Beside him sat Lambert, the shotgun cradled across his lap. He was stuffing handfuls of cartridges into his pocket. There was a sudden metallic click from the back seat where Dave Jenkins sat and Briggs felt his heart leap. He realized that it was only the older constable cocking his weapon. The youngster tried to relax, attempting to find some comfort in the fact that, if they did sight any of the things, he would be the one to remain in the car. His own shotgun was propped against the dashboard beside him. Even in the chill of the night air which was flooding in through a partially open window, he could feel the perspiration forming on his back.

Dave Jenkins, the oldest of the trio in the Panda, swallowed hard and ran his hand absent mindedly up and down the sleek barrel of his own shotgun. He peered out into the night, squinting into hedgerows, trying to see through the all enveloping gloom. His mind was elsewhere though. It was with his wife, Amy. He'd packed her off to her mother's when this trouble first began, fearing that it could escalate and he had been disturbed to find that it had. But, besides that, she was pregnant. Near her time by now. Jenkins was overcome by a great feeling of helplessness. Even now it could be happening, she could be having the child. He just prayed that he lived to see it.

Inspector Tom Lambert sat back in his seat and scanned the road ahead, lit only by the twin powerful headlamps of the car. The road which led down from the police station into town was a series of sharp curves and bends and Briggs was constantly braking in order to steer the vehicle safely onward. The car they occupied, Puma Three, had been the last of the three to leave. Lambert had watched the other two drive off, then, after all the men had checked their ammunition, he had climbed into the Panda beside Briggs. They were to patrol the Eastern part of the town, the area which took in the small industrial estate, one or two of the housing areas and Lambert's own home. The other two cars had their designated sectors as well. As he watched the darkened countryside drifting by, Lambert's face was etched in an attitude of grim determination. An act he hoped was working. He'd never been so bloody scared in his life. Frightened not just for himself but also for Debbie, but he drove her fleeting image from his mind and concentrated on the road ahead. It was beginning to straighten out.

Paul Greene sat in the back seat of Puma Two and shivered. He felt sick and could scarcely control his rapid breathing. Once already, Sergeant Hayes, seated in the front beside Walford, who was driving, had looked round at him and asked him if he was O.K. Greene had nodded and clutched his gun tighter as if trying to find some comfort in it. He wondered what his mother was doing. He had personally fitted the locks and bolts to her doors when she had decided to stay in Medworth. He had pleaded with her to go but she had refused. The least he could do now was to make sure she was adequately protected. If indeed, that was possible. They had lived together in that little house just outside the town centre for the last twelve years. Ever since Greene's father had left. In his late twenties now, the young P.C. could still recall the vision of his father standing in the doorway of the house, the night he had left, the car of his 'fancy woman' outside, waiting. Greene remembered how his mother had cried for three days afterwards. He was an only child and the departure of his father brought him and his mother even closer together. He had joined the force partly as an attempt at independence but had finally discovered that he preferred the doting of his mother. Now he wondered what she was doing, fearing for *her* life even more than his own.

Sergeant Vic Hayes closed his eyes and massaged the bridge of his nose between his thumb and forefinger. He felt tired, depressed rather than frightened at the thought of what might confront them that night. He had been sergeant in this peaceful little town for more than fifteen years and now, in the space of a couple of months, all those happy memories had been superceded by the horrors which were occuring daily. He still found it hard to believe.

Tony Walford guided the car slowly through the streets of Medworth's largest housing estate, his eyes alert for the slightest sign of movement. He prayed that they wouldn't come across any of the things that night. Not because of the danger involved but because he didn't think that he could force himself to use his gun on any of them. The very idea of shooting another human being made him shudder. Human being. The words stuck in his mind. Lambert had said that they weren't human. Another thought struck him, one which made the forthcoming task even more difficult. He realized with horror, that he might even recognize some of them. Walford drove on, all the time mouthing silent prayers that they would not see any of the creatures.

'Puma One checking in,' said Chris Davies, holding the transmitter at arms' length to lessen the high-pitched whine of static which had invaded the wavelength. He waited for Grogan's reply, then flicked the switch to 'Off.' He replaced the hand set and returned to gazing out of the window. He and the other two men in the Panda had been given the task of patrolling the centre of Medworth itself. The shopping areas and parks which dotted the town like pieces in a grass and concrete jigsaw. Davies was pleased that they had been assigned this particular sector as there was more likelihood of spotting something. He worked the pump action of the shotgun, chambering a shell; and smiled. God help you bastards, he thought.

In the back, Stuart Ferman was beginning to wish he had never joined the bloody police force. He felt giddy, the smell of plastic, sweat, and gun oil thick in his nostrils. He wished he were at home. He lived alone on the ground floor of a block of flats. Although, strictly speaking, he didn't occupy the dwelling totally without company. He shared it with two enormous Alsatians which he'd had since they were puppies. They'd been handed in to the station by some kid who didn't want them and Ferman had taken them home with him. He had cared for them with a love he didn't think he possessed, watching them grow into the magnificent creatures they were now. He wished he had them both in the car with him at this moment.

Ron Bell, driving, slowed the car as he saw something move ahead of him. He nudged Davies, who had been peering out of the side window and pointed to the area where he had seen the movement. All three men felt the tension rising as Bell edged the Panda closer. Its bright headlamps suddenly swung on the source of the disturbance.

It was a cat.

Caught in the sudden glare it hissed and fled from the blinding light. The trio of men in Puma One felt the tension drain from them and Bell breathed a sigh of audible relief.

They drove on.

Debbie Lambert had found what she searched for.

She had discovered the information about fifteen minutes ago and now she reread it, translating quickly, scribbling the words down like a journalist with a scoop. There were two entire pages about Mathias. She looked back through her notes, found that she was running short of paper and realized that she had more upstairs.

It was as she dashed into the hall that she heard the scratching at the front door.

'Puma Three to all cars. Anything to report?'

Lambert's voice rasped in the closed confines of the other two Pandas. Hayes and Davies responded that, as yet, they had seen nothing.

'Keep in touch,' ordered Lambert, 'over and out.' He replaced the hand set and wound the window down a little further, gulping in the crisp night air. They had now reached the edge of the industrial area and its countless tall chimneys towered above them as Briggs guided the car slowly along the wide roads, keeping it dead centre.

'If you see anything,' said Lambert, 'let me know.'

It was darker than he had imagined, especially in this part of the town, for there were no street lights, just the occasional naked bulb which shone outside a factory entrance. The Inspector made a mental note to have this area checked out in the morning. The things had to be hiding somewhere and out here offered countless possibilities. A thought crossed his mind. There was no evidence to support his own theory that they were, indeed, all holed up in the same place during the day and the thought that they could well be spread out all over town made his heart sink. It would mean searching every empty house, every cellar, every disused shop. He shook his head and sighed deeply.

When Debbie first heard the scratching she paused, heart pounding against her ribs, listening. It stopped abruptly but still she stood in the darkness of the hall until, at last, she sprinted upstairs to their bedroom and found some paper. When she reached the hall again, she switched on the light and stood there for a second. The lock and bolt were secure but she tested them just to set her mind at ease. Satisfied, but nonetheless uneasy, she returned to the living room which was comfortingly aglow with the light of three lamps. She sat down at her desk and reread the passage on Mathias, this time transcribing onto a fresh piece of paper. Her eyes stung from the hours of continual reading but she persevered, realizing that she had reached her goal.

The medallion glinted dully beside her and she looked at it for a second.

There was a rattling from the back of the house. Debbie heard it but ignored it, or tried to. She continued writing.

It grew louder.

A noise now at the front again. That scratching, only more insistent this time.

It stopped.

She looked up, glanced across at the telephone and wondered whether or not to call the station. But, when the sounds didn't persist, she shook her head, told herself that it was her imagination and returned to her work. The transcription was beginning to take shape, almost finished in fact. She read it through twice, struggling with its ancient construction. The meaning was in there somewhere, it was just a matter of finding it. The words on the paper stood out starkly, written in her own neat script. She read them to herself:

This year of the Almighty, 1596, in ground not Blessed of the Church is buried the one known as Mathias. This man did dare to oppose God: buried without tongue or eyes, removed in the sight of those present by hot pincers: Blasphemer, Servant of the Fallen Angel. Buried with him be the symbol of his evil. The instrument with which he hoped to reverse the very rightful process of death; to defy the Almighty; to bring life to the Dead.

Debbie shuddered. My God, that was the tie up. She looked at the medallion.

A MORTUIS EXCITARE—TO AWAKE THE DEAD.

She had more below that first transcription:

May he lie, buried yet whilst alive, forever in the place chosen. Without the Kingdom of the Almighty for the rest of Eternity.

So engrossed was she in her find, she didn't even hear the rattling begin once more at the back of the house. Debbie read on;

And now, though he wear that symbol of his Blasphemy let it not be removed; but, if so done, be it not returned to its owner for there is a power beyond that of man in its presence. Reunited with the symbol of his evil the one known as Mathias may yet attain The Power.

Debbie put down the transcript and looked at the medallion. She felt compelled to reach out and touch it but something told her not to. The gleaming metal winked up at her and she shuddered. 'The Power.' She glanced at her notes once more. At last, they knew the secret of the medallion.

It was then that she heard the rattling.

Breathing heavily, she got to her feet and crossed to the door which led out into the kitchen, suddenly aware of how cold it had become. She pushed the door and peered into the room, taking a step in, the linoleum cold against her bare feet. The rattling grew louder and she looked towards the locked back door.

The handle was being turned frenziedly back and forth.

'Oh God,' murmured Debbie under her breath. She flicked on the kitchen lights, watching as the bank of fluorescents burst into life. The door handle was slammed back and forth with renewed strength and now, a series of dull thuds began to break against it, gradually building to a crescendo which she realized were powerful blows.

She turned, slammed the door behind her and dashed for the phone in the living room. Her shaking fingers found the required digits and she dialled, the pounding growing in intensity. Her breath came in gasps as she waited for the receiver to be picked up at the other end. She heard three words;

'Medworth Police Station . . .'

The line went dead.

'Hello,' gasped Debbie, flicking desperately at the cradle. Her voice grew in volume. 'Hello!' Almost in tears, she flung the useless receiver down. She murmured Lambert's name, ran to the window and dragged back the curtains.

With a mournful puff, the street lamps blew out.

Debbie bit her fist and spun around, the smashing of glass telling her that the window had been shattered. Then, as she spun round to draw the curtains once more, she found herself staring into the grinning face of Ray Mackenzie, those twin blood red blazing orbs fixing her in an unholy stare and she finally summoned her voice for a scream.

Puma Three cruised around the industrial estate five or six times. Every so often Lambert and Jenkins would get out to check an open gate or some movement in the shadows, but each time, to their relief, they found nothing. On such occasions, one man would investigate while the other stood nearby, gun at the ready; never were they far from the car. Lambert told Briggs to keep his engine running whenever they stopped and its idling hum was something of a comfort in the stifling silence of the night.

Finally, satisfied that the area was clear, Lambert told Briggs to head for the outskirts of town with the intention of sweeping the country roads and outlying houses for any sign of activity. After that, they would head back into the built up areas.

As they drove, Lambert fumbled inside his jacket and pulled the Browning from its holster. He pressed the magazine release button and the slim metal box slid from the butt.

'Shit,' muttered the Inspector, noting that it

was empty. He fumbled in his pockets, already remembering that he'd left the extra clips at home.

'Turn the bloody thing round,' he said to Briggs, 'we've got to go back to my house. I left the ammo for the pistol there.' He slid the empty weapon back into its holster, cursing himself. Briggs spun the wheel and the Panda completed a perfect 'U' turn. Within seconds they were heading back into town.

Debbie managed to step back from the window just as Mackenzie thrust a hand at her. It crashed through the glass, showering her with shards of crystal, one of which slashed her cheek drawing a tiny tear of blood. She saw others out there with him. A woman no older than herself, another man. She saw that Mackenzie wasn't looking at her but at the medallion. It glinted invitingly on the desk and the living dead thing grunted, stepping back. Debbie saw him launch himself at the bay window, almost rooted to the spot in awe and terror as his large frame smashed through wood and glass and landed on the carpet a foot or so from her. She screamed once more and grabbed the medallion, vaulting over the stunned man and grabbing at the handle of the hall door. Still lying on the floor, Mackenzie grabbed at her ankle and she felt his clammy hand touch her bare foot as she slipped by.

She didn't even see the kitchen door burst open and two more of the things rush into the living room.

Mackenzie, on his feet now, was racing up the stairs behind her, and Debbie was whimpering

303

as she reached the landing. She could sense his closeness, and smell the fetid stench which came from his body.

A hand closed on her shoulder. Screaming, she fell against Mackenzie, the medallion falling from her grasp. She grabbed the wooden bannister rail to prevent herself from sliding down the stairs.

Mackenzie was not so lucky. The force of Debbie striking him was enough to make him lose balance and with a startled grunt, he fell back, rolling head over heels down the stairs.

Debbie scrambled to her feet, peering over her shoulder.

Mackenzie was on his feet again, coming up at her once more but now there were others behind him. She didn't stop to count, guessing that there were perhaps six. All ages, all sizes. All with one intent.

She grabbed the medallion, bolted for the bathroom and hurled herself inside, slamming the door shut. She slid the flimsy bolt. There were footsteps on the landing and she heard the sound of doors being flung open, then an almighty crash as one of them threw his weight against the bathroom door. She looked around frantically for a weapon. Anything to fight back with but, all she could see was Lambert's safety razor. She grabbed it, screaming as a fist punched through the thin wooden door. Debbie lashed out, slicing open the back of the hand, ripping away a large chunk of skin which stuck to the hooded razor blade. Blood jetted onto her and the hand was hastily withdrawn but the blows kept raining on the door and she knew that they would be in at any second. Big salt tears welled in her eyes and she said Lambert's name over and over again, watching as more of the door was torn away. She could see them all on the landing peering in at her. One of them, a man in his fifties, stuck his face into the gap and, screaming madly, she raked the razor across his lips. Blood burst forth but there was no expression of pain registered in his eyes because he had no eyes. Just those empty, red-rimmed holes. And yet they saw her. Saw the medallion. And they were grinning.

Lambert saw two of the things on his front lawn as Briggs swung the car into the street.

'Oh God,' he shrieked, with pained horror.

Already he was grabbing for the shotgun. Briggs stepped on the accelerator and the car sped forward. It mounted the pavement about thirty yards from the house, smashed through the hedge of the house next door and skidded to a halt on the grass in front of Lambert's house. Oblivious to the danger, with only thoughts of Debbie in his mind, Lambert leapt from the car, swinging the shotgun up as the two things cowered away from the blazing light of the car headlamps. The Inspector fired three times. The first blast hit the leading creature squarely in the chest, blew half its torso away and flung it a good twelve feet across the lawn.

'You fuckers,' screamed Lambert, now joined by Jenkins who also fired.

The second thing was caught in the crossfire and both men were almost joyful as they watched its head disintegrate, a dark shower of blood, brain and shattered bone spraying out into the night.

Lambert saw the broken front window, the front door hanging uselessly from one torn hinge. He dashed into the hall followed by Jenkins. Briggs, shaking with sheer terror, reversed and brought the headlamps of the car to bear on the front of the house, their powerful beams piercing the blackness and pinpointing two more of the creatures in the living room. He reached for his own gun and scrambled out of the car, aiming at the first of them, a man in his twenties.

There was a roar as he fired, the shot missing and blasting a hole in the wall beneath the window. Gasping, Briggs worked the pump action and fired again, screaming in terror as he saw the things scrambling over the window sill. Coming for him. He fired again and the discharge was on target. It hit the man in the lower abdomen, blasting away his genitals, almost severing his right leg. The second creature, a woman not yet in her forties, flung herself at him and the young constable went down under her weight. He felt sharp nails tearing at his face and his screams filled the night.

From his position on the stairs, Lambert could see from the concentration of the creatures clustered around the shattered bathroom door that Debbie was trapped inside.

One of them came at him and he fired from point blank range, ignoring the blood which splashed onto him. He dashed up the stairs, stepping on the body as he did so. Jenkins followed and the two men reached the landing together.

For a second, everything froze. A still frame

in a broken down film. Suddenly, the film was running again. Jenkins raised his shotgun and fired twice, bringing down one of the living dead.

Lambert heard Debbie scream. A scream which was immediately replaced by the sound of snapping wood.

Mackenzie was no more than a foot from Debbie, his fetid breath filling her nostrils. Yellow, bubbling mucous trickling down his chin. He grabbed for the medallion and tore it from her grasp; she expected the grip of his bloodied hands on her throat at any second. But he turned and blundered out, clutching the gold circlet to his chest.

Lambert saw him and lifted the shotgun, jerking wildly on the trigger. The recoil slammed the stock back against his shoulder and the blast blew a huge hole in the wall beside the grinning Mackenzie who bolted for the tiny window at the far end of the landing. Lambert worked the pump action and fired again but he was too late.

Mackenzie launched himself at the window and hurtled through it. The Inspector's shot exploded beside him as he met the cool night air. The living corpse of Mackenzie hit the roof of the garage and rolled once. Lambert dashed to the window and looked out just in time to see him leap from the flat roof and lope off into the darkness.

He turned, cursing, and dashed into the bathroom, throwing the shotgun to one side and grabbing Debbie in both arms. She was sobbing uncontrollably. He closed his eyes and pressed her close to him, his own body shaking. She breathed his name over and over again, sobbing.

He eased the blood-spattered razor from her hand and dropped it into the bath.

Jenkins appeared in the doorway.

'Check outside,' said Lambert softly and the constable nodded, stepping over two bodies as he made his way down the stairs. The house stank of blood and cordite and, Jenkins noted, something else. A carrion odour of corruption. He worked the pump action of his shotgun, ejecting the spent cartridge and walked out into the night. It was then that he saw the woman coming towards him.

She had him fixed in those gaping, empty sockets, and, in the glaring brilliance of the Panda's headlamps, Jenkins could see that her hands were soaked in blood. She raised them towards him and ran, arms outstretched like some kind of obscene sleepwalker.

He took a step back, swinging the shotgun up just in time to get off one shot.

The blast tore through her shoulder, ripping away most of the left breast and splintering both scapula and clavical. She staggered, the wound gaping wide, one arm dangling by thin tendrils of flesh and sinew. Then, to his horror, she started forward once more. He already knew that his gun was empty, realized that he would have no time to reload.

With all the power he could muster, he swung the shotgun like a cricket bat. The butt smacked savagely into her face.

Her jaw bones crumbled beneath the impact. She fell to one side, empty sockets stared up at him. Revolted, Jenkins brought the wooden stock down repeatedly upon her head until it split open like a bag full of cherry syrup. Then he dropped the gun and retched until there was nothing left in his stomach.

He staggered away from the body, avoided the two other bodies laying on the lawn, and gulped down huge lungfuls of air. He leant against the side of the Panda for a moment, his breath coming in gasps, and the bitter taste of his own vomit strong in his mouth. His head was spinning.

'Oh God,' he groaned, rubbing his stomach with a bruised hand. For a second he thought he was going to throw up again, but the feeling passed and he shook himself. He pulled open the passenger side door and climbed in.

The car was empty. No sign of Briggs.

Jenkins sat still for a second and peered out into the gloom, trying to catch a glimpse of his younger companion. Briggs' shotgun was missing from its position beside his seat and Jenkins assumed that the youngster must have got out of the car to help when they had arrived. He pushed open the door and stepped out, walking around to the other side of the car.

'Gary,' he called.

There was no answer. Jenkins stood in the reflected light of the car's headlamps, his face darkened into grotesque shadow. He looked down.

Lying just beside the driver's side door was Briggs' peaked cap. The other constable knelt and picked it up, noting with concern that it was splattered with blood. In fact, there was blood all over the ground near the door, great blotches of it staining the white paintwork of the car.

Jenkins picked up the discarded shotgun, suddenly afraid, and backed off towards the house, the barrel levelled. He stumbled over the body of the woman and nearly fell but he retained his balance and retreated into the welcoming light of the hall.

Footsteps behind him. He turned.

Lambert and Debbie were descending the stairs, the Inspector with his arm wrapped tightly around his wife's shoulders. Her head was bowed and Jenkins could see that she was sobbing quietly—tiny, almost imperceptible movements of her shoulders signalling the tortured spasms. The constable suddenly thought of his own wife, of his child. Had she given birth yet? He drove the thought away.

'You all right?' asked Lambert, the shotgun propped up over his shoulder as if he were off on a hunting trip.

Jenkins, his face the colour of cream cheese, nodded.

'I can't find Briggs,' he said.

Lambert looked puzzled but his expression changed to one of worry when the constable held up the bloodstained cap. The three of them stood in the burning light from the car headlamps, the two policemen looking at one another, Debbie weeping softly. There was a harsh crackling, then a voice from outside.

'The radio,' said Lambert, helping Debbie out, guiding her past the gun-blasted bodies of the living dead.

Jenkins nodded and crossed to the car. He picked up the handset and heard Grogan's agitated voice at the other end:

'Puma Three, come in.'

'Puma Three,' said Jenkins wearily.

'Thank Christ for that,' said Grogan, 'you hadn't called in, I thought something had happened.'

Lambert helped Debbie into the back seat of the car where she lay down, curling up in a fetal position, then he took the handset from Jenkins.

'Puma Three here, this is Lambert. Contact the other two cars, tell them we have encountered a number of the bloody things. Tell them the guns *do* work.'

Grogan muttered an affirmation.

Lambert continued, 'Anything to report, Grogan?'

'No sir, we've had a number of calls from people, sightings and what have you, but nothing from the other two cars. They both reported in a while back to say that they'd seen nothing.'

Lambert nodded as he listened, glancing over to where Debbie lay. Her eyes were closed, her cheeks tear-stained.

'Puma Three, out,' he said and switched off the set.

'What now, sir?' said Jenkins, sliding behind the wheel and locking the door.

'I want to get my wife to Doctor Kirby. Let's go.'

Jenkins nodded and started the car. The wheels spun on the grass but, as they reached the concrete of the road, they caught and the Panda sped off.

Lambert sat back in the seat and closed his eyes. Christ, the vile things had nearly killed Debbie.

311

He prayed that she would be all right. Mackenzie had got the medallion, it seemed to have been the object of the attack. He gritted his teeth. It *had* to be the answer. No wonder Trefoile was frightened of the bloody thing. The Inspector realized that he would have to find out if Debbie had managed to discover the truth about it. He looked around at her. She was still curled up. Asleep.

At least the encounter had proved that the guns were of use. That much he was thankful for. He didn't dare think what would have happened if they had not been . . .

One thing did trouble him though.

Where had Briggs got to?

Run off in fright perhaps? Lambert wouldn't have blamed him if he had. He'd probably stagger in the next morning, ashamed of his own cowardice. Lambert half-smiled; he could quite easily have run off with him.

Even if anyone had noticed, no one would have wondered why there were blood spots on the trunk of the Panda. The whole car was splashed with the crimson fluid after all. What might have interested them was the contents of the trunk.

Gary Briggs had died painfully, his eyes torn from living sockets but now he lay in the boot of the car, fresh blood from the riven sockets still spilling down his cheeks.

He had had no chance against the woman who had attacked him. She had been too strong.

He had crawled into the trunk to escape the blinding lights of the Panda's headlamps. It was dark in there. It stank of petrol and rubber. But he didn't care.

He lay silently.

Waiting.

30

Lambert breathed a sigh of relief as dawn clawed its way across the sky.

Now, as he stood by the window of John Kirby's spare bedroom, he had never been so pleased to see the light of day. He looked down at the cup of coffee in his hand and drained it, replacing the empty vessel on a small sideboard. He watched the sun appear, preceded by golden shafts of light and finally, a tiny portion of it peering over the horizon and filling the heavens with the first glow of morning.

He turned and looked at Debbie who was lying on a bed in one corner of the room. She was sleeping and the slow rhythmic heaving of her chest reassured him. He crossed to the bedside and knelt beside her, reaching beneath the sheets to grasp one of her hands. He stayed there for several moments, gripping her soft hand and gazing at her face. Eventually he got to his feet, kissed her lightly on the forehead and whispered, 'I love you.' Then he carefully replaced her hand under the sheets and left the room. He closed the door behind him and leant against it for a moment, exhaling deeply. The memory of the previous night was still vivid in his mind, burned deep into his consciousness like a red hot brand.

They had arrived at Kirby's at around three that morning. Bleary-eyed, the doctor had let them in and led Lambert, with Debbie's inert form in his arms, upstairs to this bedroom. He had sedated her with Thorazine. Then he and Kirby had gone downstairs to where Jenkins waited. Lambert had told the doctor what had happened and Kirby had listened, his apprehension growing by the second. Finally the doctor had treated their minor cuts and bruises and the three of them had then sat down over a cup of coffee to wait for morning. Jenkins had managed to catch a few hours sleep on the couch in Kirby's surgery. When Lambert walked into the kitchen he found the doctor sitting alone at the table.

'Is she all right?' asked Kirby.

Lambert nodded. 'Still sleeping.'

'She will be for quite a while; it's the best thing for her after what she's been through.'

The Inspector poured himself another cup of coffee and sat down opposite Kirby.

'Where's Jenkins?' he asked.

Kirby hooked a thumb in the direction of the surgery, 'He's still asleep too.' The doctor studied the young policeman's face, the beginnings of stubble on his chin, the dark rings beneath his eyes. 'You look like you could do with some rest yourself.'

Lambert smiled humourlessly and ran his index finger around the lip of his cup. Finally he looked up.

'They could have killed her, John,' he said, his voice softening.

'But they didn't,' said Kirby, trying to inject a note of reassurance into his voice.

'They were like animals. They would have killed her.' His voice broke and he lowered his head, his tone flat, dropping almost to a whisper, 'If I hadn't have gone back to the house, if . . .'

Kirby saw a single tear plop onto the table and, when Lambert looked up, his eyes were red-rimmed, big salt tears pouring down his cheeks. The Inspector clasped his fingers, propped his elbows on the table and rested his chin on his hands.

'I'm sorry,' he said, softly, wiping his face.

'Drink your coffee,' said Kirby, smiling.

Lambert managed to smile back. He coughed, shook himself, blew out a harsh lungful of air. He raised a hand to signal that he was O.K., nodding to himself as if to reinforce the idea.

'What's your next move?' asked Kirby.

'Find them. Find out where they hole up during the day. Find them and kill them.' He finished his coffee. He got to his feet, a new purpose about him, the old strength returning.

'If my theory is right,' he said, 'then they're all in the same place. They seem to function in groups, so it's only logical to assume they sleep in groups too. It's just a matter of finding the right place.'

He went through into the surgery and woke Jenkins. In minutes he was on his feet and the two of them were ready to leave. They paused in the doorway.

'How long before she wakes up?' asked Lambert.

Kirby shrugged, 'It's hard to say, four, five hours perhaps longer.'

'Let me know as soon as she does; it's important.'

Jenkins walked out to the waiting Panda, the blood on it now dried to a dull rust colour, and slid behind the wheel. Lambert paused and extended a hand which Kirby shook warmly.

'Thanks, John,' said the Inspector and he was gone, walking across to the car. Jenkins started the engine and Kirby watched as they disappeared from view down a sharp dip in the road. He went back indoors and poured himself another cup of coffee.

P.C. Bell was distributing cups of tea when Lambert and Jenkins entered the duty room. Mumbled greetings were exchanged and Lambert slumped down into a chair, dropping the shotgun down beside him. The other men looked pale but none looked as downright shagged out as he did. He later learned that they had taken it in turns to sleep as they cruised around. Two men in the front keeping watch while the third snatched a few hours in the back seat.

'We lost Briggs,' said Lambert flatly, taking the cup of steaming tea which Bell offered him.

'How?' Hayes wanted to know.

Lambert shrugged, 'I don't know.' He paused.

'My house was attacked last night; they nearly killed my wife.'

'Jesus,' murmured Walford.

'There were about a half a dozen of them. Ray Mackenzie was one.'

A chorus of sighs ran around the room.

Lambert continued. 'That medallion that we found at his place in the very beginning, my wife was trying to make out the inscription on it. I think she succeeded. Mackenzie stole it, he got away before we realized what was happening.' He finished his tea and stood up, crossing to the end of the room. The men's eyes followed his progress. When he finally spoke, his tone was flat, no inflection at all.

'We've got to find them,' he began, 'and we've got to do it before nightfall. Now that means searching every empty house, every cellar, every shop, every attic; anywhere where they could hide. Now, if you do find one of them I don't want any heroics. Get help, as much as you need and let's wipe the bastards out.' His face was set in deep lines as he spoke. 'Let's just pray that I'm right and that they're all in one place because that'll make our job much easier. Now, to date, there's upwards of ninety people missing. I want them all.' There were a vehemence in his last words which made one or two of the men sit up. 'Every last one of the fucking things has got to be found and destroyed. Understand?'

Nods and murmurs.

'Any questions?'

There were none.

'Right. Work in twos. I'll take my own car, and like before, keep in contact at all times.' Lambert made a mental note to pick up a walkie-talkie on the way out. He looked at his watch.

'It's five-twenty now. That gives us eleven hours of daylight.'

He mentioned something briefly about

checking their weapons to make sure they had enough ammo. Hayes told him that it had already been taken care of. Lambert nodded. He picked up the shotgun and worked the pump action then, checking that this time the magazine was full, he slid the Browning from its holster and pulled the slide back and cocked it. The metallic click was amplified by the silence in the room. He stood before the men, grim determination etched on his face.

'Let's go.'

In the boot of Puma Three the thing that had once been Gary Briggs lay in torpor, hidden from the painful rays of the sun. It lay still.

Waiting for the night.

31

Jenkins brought the Panda to a halt on the dirt track which ran alongside the hedge flanking the garden. The house, invisible behind the tall hedge, belonged to Nigel Moore, Medworth's most prosperous farmer. As Hayes stepped from the car he could see the gleaming metal towers of the pasteurization plant further back.

The farm was large. The house itself formed the apex of a triangle which was made up by a configuration of sheds and outbuildings at one corner and the actual pasteurization plant at the other. The area between the three buildings was part concrete (near to the house) and mud which was thick and clung defiantly to the sergeant's boots as he walked.

He could see cattle and the occasional horse moving lethargically about in the fields beyond. Hayes took a deep breath, enjoying the purity of the early morning air even though it was tinged with the pungent smell of manure. He didn't seem to care.

Jenkins flicked off the engine of Puma One and climbed out, carrying his shotgun at his side.

'You wait here,' said Hayes when they reached the rusty iron gate which opened into the farm yard. 'That way, you'll be able to cover me *and* hear the radio if anyone calls.'

Jenkins nodded, watching as the sergeant strode towards the house, avoiding the worst patches of mud. The constable glanced around him. There were plenty of places out here for the things to hide. He shuddered and looked up at the sun, finding reassurance in its growing heat. The sky was cloudless, a deep blue which promised a beautiful day.

Hayes reached the concrete path which ran up to the front door of the farmhouse and he scraped his boots clean of mud before proceeding. The house itself was traditional in appearance, white-washed, low roofed and covered with climbing ivy. There was a low wooden porch over the doorstep and the sergeant had to duck to avoid banging his head on it. He rapped three times and waited.

There was no answer.

He turned and shrugged at Jenkins who felt his own heart quicken. He gripped his shotgun tighter, his eyes scanning the empty yard furtively.

Hayes sighed wearily and knocked again. Receiving no answer this time, he took the narrow path to the back of the house. The sergeant took time to admire Moore's sizeable vegetable patch before knocking on the back door. After a few seconds he heard bolts being slid back and then the door swung open.

He found himself looking down the twin barrels of a shotgun.

'Morning, Nigel,' said Hayes, grinning and pushing the gun to one side.

Moore shrugged. 'Hello Vic.' He looked down at the shotgun. 'Well, you can't be too careful these days, can you?'

Hayes didn't answer, just looked around the kitchen and asked, 'Have you seen anything suspicious around here lately?'

'Any of those things you mean?' said Moore, his round red face lighting up excitedly.

'Anything?' Hayes repeated, refusing to be drawn.

'I checked all the barns and sheds myself,' he nodded vigorously, 'and the cellar and attic.' He smiled broadly. 'If any of the bloody things come round here they'll get a dose of this.' He lifted the shotgun proudly.

Hayes smiled, aware that the farmer was looking down at his own weapon.

'That bad, is it?' asked the man.

Hayes nodded, 'It's bad.'

Moore shook his head and sighed. 'You wouldn't believe it could happen in a place like this, would you?' There was a tinge of sadness in his voice.

Hayes turned to leave. 'You wouldn't think it could happen anywhere.'

Moore waved him away and closed the door behind him. Hayes took one last look at the expansive vegetable patch and made his way back to the waiting Jenkins.

'Nothing,' he said, 'old Nigel's fine; he says he's checked the place out himself.'

Jenkins nodded, relieved, and they trudged back to the car.

'If one of those things came up against old

Nigel, I'd lay my money on him winning,' said Hayes, sliding into the car. They both laughed.

Davies checked his shotgun, running a hand down the sleek barrel, then he sat back in his seat and gazed out of the windscreen. The houses on either side were empty. The entire street was devoid of people. Those who had not been killed had simply packed up and gone. Redhoods Avenue was as dead as a doornail and there were many more streets in Medworth like it.

'Stop the car here,' said Davies as Greene turned into the road.

Davies sighed. There was no other alternative. Each and every house would have to be checked individually.

'How do you want to do this?' asked Greene, a bead of perspiration popping onto his forehead.

'You take that side, I'll take this one,' said the older PC.

Green swallowed hard, 'That's what I was afraid you were going to say.'

Both men swung themselves out of the car, checking their weapons once more, stuffing handfuls of extra shells in their pockets. Greene prayed that they wouldn't have the need for them. He watched as Davies reached for the radio.

'Puma Two to base.'

Grogan acknowledged.

'This is Davies. We're leaving the car to check every house in Redhoods Avenue, right? Over.'

Grogan said something about reporting in if they found anything.

'Will do. Puma Two out.'

323

The two policemen looked at each other for a moment, both sensing the other's fear.

'How do we get into the houses?' Greene wanted to know.

'Break in,' offered Davies and he walked away, the shotgun slung over his shoulder. Greene watched him walk up the path of the first house in the road, check the front door and then disappear around the back. The younger constable heard the crashing of glass as Davies broke a window and he realized that his companion must be inside by now. He stood still beside the stationary car for long seconds, just looking down the street. A street just like any other on any normal housing estate in any town in the country. A narrow road flanked on both sides by grass verge and carefully planted trees, their branches still, bare. Just an ordinary street.

He was sweating profusely as he set off for the first house. It lay directly opposite the one which Davies had entered, and, like his companion, Greene found that he had to break a window to get in. Using his elbow, he smashed a hole in the frosted pane set in the back door and reached through, fumbling for the key, wondering whether anything were going to grab his exposed hand. He breathed an audible sigh of relief as the lock gave and the door swung open. Clutching the shotgun, he stepped inside.

The kitchen was small, identical to all the others in the street. There was a yellowing calendar on the far wall and Greene noticed that it had not been turned to the appropriate month. It was two behind. He wished that time could, indeed, be reversed, so that all this had never happened. He drove the thought from his mind and continued through into the living room, pleased to find that the curtains were drawn and sunlight was flooding the small room. Tiny particles of dust fluttered in the golden rays. Nothing here. Shaking a little more, Greene made his way upstairs towards the narrow landing.

Three doors faced him. Two open, one closed.

All the houses on the road had either two or three bedrooms as well as an inside toilet. Greene could see through the two open doors that the rooms were both bedrooms. Not much chance of anyone hiding out in a bathroom, he told himself, trying to find reassurance in the assumption. He placed a hand on the knob of the closed door and, praying, shoved it open.

Nothing.

The house was empty. Thankfully, he hurried back downstairs out of the back door and made his way to the next house.

Meantime, across on the other side of Redhoods Avenue, Davies too had found the house he was searching to be empty. Almost disappointed, he left the building vaulting the low fence which divided the adjacent garden.

There was a loud crash, a shattering of glass and Davies looked down to see that he'd landed in a cold frame. He groaned and stepped clear of the wreckage, cursing himself for not being more careful. The grass of the lawn hadn't been cut for a while and it grew knee high, competing for supremacy with large growths of chickweed and dandelions. There was a rusted lawn roller propped up against the fence beside the remains of the cold frame. The constable walked up the path towards the back door which he found was already open. The lime green paint had peeled away in places, leprous slices of the stuff chipped away to reveal the thin wood beneath.

Davies lowered the shotgun, the barrel pointing ahead, and took a step inside. The kitchen smelt damp, the cloying stench mingling with something else. A more pungent odour which caused the constable to cough. He looked around, searching for the source of the odour. There was a white door to his right which he took to be a larder and, as he took a step towards it, he realized that his suspicions were right. The stench grew stronger.

Davies lowered the shotgun and pulled open the door.

'Christ,' he grunted, discovering the source of the smell. On the lowest stone shelf of the larder was a rotting joint of beef. It lay on the place in a solidified pool of blood which spread into a rusty circle around it. Davies heard the somonolent buzzing of flies; some were crawling on the meat. He also noted with disgust the loathsome writhings of maggots on the joint.

He pushed the larder door shut and walked into the living room. The curtains were drawn here, the room in semi-darkness but for the thin beams of sunlight lancing through gaps in the dusty drape. Wary of the darkness, Davies advanced further into the room and tore the curtains down, flooding the room with bright sunlight and throwing up a choking cloud of thick dust. The policeman stepped back, eyes darting round the room. Come on you bastards, he thought, where are you? Satisfied that down-stairs was clear, he pushed open the hall door and made his way up the narrow staircase finally emerging on the landing. Four doors. Two bedrooms, an airing cupboard and a toilet. All empty.

Shaking his head he descended the stairs and made his way across the front lawn to the next house, wondering how Greene was doing across the road.

As it turned out, his younger companion was having as little luck as he in finding anything. There were not even any signs of the creatures and Greene was beginning to think that the search of the street would end up being fruitless. At least that was what he hoped. The perspiration which soaked his back was beginning to stain his uniform as he began searching the fifth house. He didn't even attempt to tell himself that the sweat was heat induced. It was the product of fear. Pure, naked fear. He wiped his brow and pushed the door which he knew led into the living room of the house. The curtains once more were open and he passed through without checking, anxious to scan upstairs and get out of the bloody place. There was a sofa and two chairs in the room, and no carpet on the floor. The sofa was stretched across one corner of the room, a sizeable gap behind it.

It was as the young constable made his way up the fifth staircase that morning, that the sofa was pushed forward and the creature sheltering behind it crept slowly forward.

From his position in one of the bedrooms, Greene didn't hear the slight squeaking of castors as the sofa moved. Having thoroughly searched the upper story, he hurried downstairs once more, his heart slowing a little.

He walked into the living room.

All he heard was a high-pitched rasping sound as the thing launched itself at him.

Greene screamed and swung the shotgun round, his actions accelerated by sheer terror. Luckily, the monstrous discharge hit its target and the young constable slumped back against the wall gasping.

At his feet lay what remained of a cat. It was now little more than a twisted heap of fur and blood, large lumps of it splattered around the room by the horrendous force of the blast. Had it not been for the fact that the partly obliterated head stared up at him, Greene wouldn't have known what he'd killed, so great was the destruction wrought by the gun.

He bolted from the house. Fortunately, he managed to reach the back door before vomiting. Sweating profusely, he leant against the wall, gulping in the grass-scented air and shaking madly. It was some time before he found the courage to move on to the next house.

Across the road, Davies has heard the shot and he smiled. That's one of the bastards gone, he thought. He was surprised that Greene had had the guts to use the shotgun, he seemed such a spineless little sod. Davies himself was more than half way down the street by now, having discovered nothing so far and he, like Greene, was beginning to suspect that all the houses were, indeed, empty. The house he was in this time was built somewhat differently from those further up. He stood in the kitchen, his eyes alert. No pantry here, just a door in front of him, which, he found, led out into a hall. Peeling wallpaper once more, flaking away like dried skin. There was a door to his immediate right and another to the left. Between them lay the staircase. He chose the right hand door first and found that it was a bathroom with toilet. Piss stains up the wall, more flaking paper and a yellowed plastic shower curtain. The place smelt like a urinal.

Davies closed the door behind him and nudged open the other across the tiny hall with the barrel of his shotgun. The living room. He checked it quickly, anxious to inspect the upper floor but even more anxious to get out into the sunlight again. He left the living room and started slowly up the uncarpeted stairs. His heavy boots sounded conspicuously loud in the deathly silence and the policeman swallowed hard, aware that anything up there would most certainly have been alerted to his presence by now. There was a small guard rail running along the side of the landing and, through its wooden slats, he could see the half-open door of a bedroom. It was in darkness, the dirty blue curtains drawn tight against the invading sunlight. He gripped the shotgun tighter and finally stood still on the cramped landing.

Two more doors in addition to the one he had already glimpsed. He kicked open the nearest and walked in. Nothing in there, just bunk beds and an old dressing table. At the far end of the room, a cupboard door had fallen open, spilling toys across the wooden floor. Davies closed the door behind him and crossed to the second bedroom, pulling at the curtains as he did so.

It too was empty.

The last of the three doors was locked tight and the handle twisted impotently in his grasp. He took a step back then threw his weight against it. There was a shriek of buckling metal as the lock broke and Davies tumbled into the room. He sprawled heavily. The shotgun fell from his grasp and skidded across the floor. Suddenly seized by a spasm of terror, he grabbed for the weapon and looked up.

The room was empty. He cursed himself, realizing that the atmosphere was getting to him. Another empty room he thought and shook his head. Where the hell were the bloody things hiding?

It was as he emerged onto the landing that he heard the scraping from above.

His heart leapt, thudding against his chest, the breath catching in his throat. He looked up.

'Oh God,' he gasped.

The trapdoor of the attic was out of place, half of it drawn back, revealing the impenetrable blackness within. The sound came again, louder this time. Davies leant back against the wall, his eyes fixed on the half open hole. My God, he thought, it was so obvious. The attic. What better place for them to hide? It was dark, out of sight, not easily accessible. His heart began racing and he took three deep breaths, forcing himself to calm down. Perhaps his imagination was getting the better of him, maybe it was just birds up there. They very often nested in lofts. Nevertheless, he would have to know for sure.

But how to get up there? He looked around for something to stand on and remembered a chair in the second bedroom. Hastily retrieving it, he positioned it carefully beneath the black hole, his eyes constantly alert for any sign of movement. Cautiously he climbed onto the chair and found that he could reach the wooden surround of the attic entrance. He shook his head. That would mean him hauling himself up gradually, getting a firm handhold and dragging his bulky frame into the enveloping darkness. It was too risky, besides the fact that he would be momentarily unable to use his gun if there were any of the things up there. He shuddered at the thought, leaning against the guard rail which ran along one side of the landing.

That was the answer.

If he could use the guardrail as a further step up from the chair then he could ease himself up into the attic and still retain a firm grip on his gun. Davies set the plan in motion, finding that it was not as easy as he had anticipated. The guard rail creaked protestingly under his weight but he grabbed the wooden lip of the attic entrance, laid the shotgun inside and hauled himself up.

Christ, it was dark in there. He reached for his flashlight, fumbling around inside his jacket. He grabbed it and swung its powerful beam around the inside of the attic.

There were four of them in there and, even though he had half expected it, Davies was still shocked by their appearance. In fact, one, a man in his fifties, was already on his feet and advancing towards the policeman. Davies shone the light in his direction and the man covered his face against the bright light. The eyeless sockets remained open, glaring at Davies through meshed fingers. With a grunt of disgust, the policeman fired.

The blast hit the man in the chest and blew him across the small attic, but now the others were stirring and Davies realized that he couldn't hold the light up and fire at the same time. Praying, he fired off the remaining four cartridges, using each subsequent muzzle flash as a guide. When he'd finished, the room stunk of cordite and his ears were ringing from the swift deafening explosions. Hurriedly, he reached for the light and shone it in the direction of the living dead things. Joyful at first, he counted three bodies but then suddenly the awful realization hit him. He had seen four when he first entered the attic. Where was the fourth creature?

He swung around in time to catch it in the beam. What had once been a girl in her twenties, her eyeless sockets still caked with dark dry blood, ran at him, dark liquid gushing from a savage wound in her side which had exposed the intestines. Her mouth was open in a soundless scream of rage and, arms outstretched, she lunged at Davies. He rolled to one side and the girl tripped, falling head first through the open trapdoor. There was a sickening thud as she hit the landing below. Davies leapt down after her, his full weight landing on her torn body. His gun now empty, he snatched up the chair and brought it crashing down on her head. The one blow was all that was needed. Her skull collapsed like an egg shell, greyish slops of brain plopping onto the carpet. Seized with an almost insane hatred, the policeman reloaded his shotgun and fired two more shots into the inert form as if not quite satisfied that the creature was finally dead. The second blast tore off her head. What remained of it.

He stared down at the body, shaking with rage and fear.

'Bastard,' he said. 'Bastard. Fucking bastard.' It was a moment or two before he recovered his composure and left the house, wondering what he would find in the next.

Walford brought Puma Three to a halt in the car park at the back of the block of flats where constable Ferman lived. The two of them had been ordered to check out the block with its twelve storeys and ninety flats. The two men sat in the car for a moment, gazing upwards to the top storey.

'Shit,' muttered Walford, 'we'll be here all day checking this lot.'

Ferman grinned and climbed out of the car. Walford followed a second later, wondering what his companion found so amusing.

'Don't worry about it,' said Ferman, 'we'll have this done in less than half an hour.'

They were already inside the main entrance hall, the lifts in front of them, two corridors on either side stretching away for hundreds of yards.

'Half an hour my backside,' said Walford, indignantly.

'Just shut up and come with me,' Ferman told him, heading for the flat nearest them. He fumbled in the pocket of his trousers and produced a key. 'My flat,' he announced. He opened the door and Walford shrank back. Curled up in front of the dormant gas fire were two of the biggest Alsatians he'd ever seen. The first animal looked up, saw Ferman and bounded across to him. He smiled and grabbed the dog, patting it and running his hand along its sleek body. 'This is King,' he announced, stroking the animal which looked at Walford lazily, regarding him as if it were looking at its next meal.

'They're big bastards, Stuart,' said Walford, trying to hide his apprehension. He wasn't too keen on dogs at the best of times and these bloody things looked like ponies, he'd never seen any as big.

'I look after them,' said Ferman proudly, stroking the second dog which licked at his hand. 'This one is Baron. If they can't sniff out those bloody things then no one can.'

'You know, you're not as daft as you look,' said Walford, smiling.

Both men checked their weapons. Ferman led the dogs out into the corridor and hastily locked his flat door behind them.

'What makes you so sure they'll be able to find anything?' Walford asked as they set off up the first corridor, the dogs leading.

'Dogs can usually sense when something's wrong,' Ferman said. 'It'll save us a lot of time if they can.'

They checked the place, floor by floor, all the time their ears and eyes alert. Ferman watching the two dogs, observing their reactions as they paused now and again at a door, one of them sniffing around, the other pacing back and forth.

On the fifth floor a door opened and a woman stuck her head out, suddenly alarmed by the sight of gun-carrying policemen and dogs.

'What's going on?' she asked, worriedly.

'Nothing to worry about,' lied Walford, 'just a check. We got a call from someone in the flats who'd reported someone suspicious hanging round.'

The woman looked at the two men and then at the dogs. She hesitated a moment then closed her door and both policemen heard a bolt being slid into place on the other side. They walked on.

'Mrs Cole,' Ferman announced, 'we probably interrupted her and one of her customers.' He laughed to himself. Walford looked puzzled. 'She's a bit of a goer if you get my drift.'

Walford did.

'Her husband's in the nick, some big black bloke. Right fucking headcase, alcoholic too. He used to knock the shit out of her. I dragged him in twice for assaulting her but she stayed with him. I suppose she's making up for lost time now. There's a different bloke in there every night.'

Walford started to sound interested. 'How old is she?'

'Thirty, maybe younger. Who knows?'

They reached the flight of steps which led up to the sixth floor and the dogs raced ahead. Ferman watched them go, wondering if they'd found something at last. When he and Walford finally caught up with the animals he saw that it was a false alarm. They continued their endless trekking along the maze of corridors. Doors were tried; those that were open they investigated, the ones that were locked they bypassed.

'I hope you're right about these bloody dogs,' said Walford. 'I mean, what if they've missed something?'

Ferman shook his head. 'No chance. If there's anything here, they'll find it.'

Someone else popped their head out of the doorway on the tenth floor. Mr Wilkins. A retired solicitor, Walford was told afterwards.

'Pompous old sod,' said Ferman as they walked on. 'He's a nosey old cunt, too. There's not a thing goes on in this bloody block that he doesn't know about.'

'Do you know everyone who lives here?' asked Walford, irritably.

Ferman smiled.

Eleventh floor and still nothing. The sun was beaming in through the huge picture windows at either end of the corridor and Walford leant back against the wall to rub his aching thighs.

'Only one more floor,' Ferman told him.

'Thank Christ for that. My bloody legs are killing me, all these stairs.'

It was King who started barking first. Walford looked around to see the animal standing at the far end of the corridor, hackles raised, barking madly at something which he couldn't see. A second later, Baron joined in and the entire corridor was filled with a cacophony of harsh yapping and growling. King began scratching at the door, growling, backing off then barking once more. The two policemen ran to where the dogs stood and Ferman grabbed their collars, pulling them back, finding that he needed all his strength to do so.

'Try the door,' he said, watching as Walford gently turned the handle. The dogs' frenzied barking had now subsided to a low guttural growling; both had their sharp eyes fixed on the door as the policeman turned the handle and pushed it open a few inches.

'What do we do?' asked Walford. 'Let them go in?' He nodded towards the waiting animals.

Ferman bit his lip contemplatively. 'There is the chance they could be wrong.'

'You said . . .'

'All right. But I'll go in with them.' Ferman swallowed hard. He told his companion to hold the two Alsatians while he himself worked the pump action of his shotgun, chambering a shell. Walford held the dogs as best he could, stunned by their power.

'Let them go,' snapped Ferman, simultaneously kicking open the door.

The two animals hurtled in, Ferman following. There was a flurry of barking and howling from the room beyond him as he ran to catch up with the dogs. They had barged through a half open door inside which the policeman knew led into one of the bedrooms. All the flats were built the same; this one was no different to his own. He kicked open the second door and froze.

What had once been a man in his forties was struggling with the two animals, yellow spittle dribbling over his chin. He snarled and bit like they did, uttering the same harsh animal sounds so that it was difficult to determine who was making the noises. He had one hand clamped

337

round Baron's throat, while the bulk of King clung to his other arm, teeth firmly embedded in the flesh. The living dead thing grunted and hurled Baron away, the animal smashing into the far wall, staggering for a second then racing back at the creature. He tried to bludgeon King away and, by turning, left his face exposed. Baron launched himself at the man's unprotected side and tore away a large chunk of skin. Blood spurted into the air and the dog fell away. The living dead thing spun round, bringing one hand down hard on King's head. The animal dropped like a stone and Ferman raised his shotgun, anger boiling within him.

'You bastard,' he muttered, and fired twice. Both shots hit their target and the man was slammed back against the wall. He stood there for a second before slumping forward, a huge crimson smear trailing out behind him, his entrails spilling in an untidy pattern on the floor before him.

Ferman dropped his gun and ran to King. He knew before he reached it that the animal was dead, its skull crushed to pulp by the powerful blow it had received. Baron, whimpering softly, licked at the policeman's hand and he had to fight hard to keep back a tear.

Walford appeared in the doorway. He looked in, saw the dead dog and the corpse and left, staggering into the corridor outside. Ferman finally emerged, carrying the body of the dog, Baron close behind him. The policeman's face was set, his jaw firm, the knot of muscles at its side pulsing angrily.

'I loved that dog,' he said, softly. And Walford reached out to touch his shoulder.

'Come on,' he said, still shaking from what he'd just seen, 'we'd better report in.'

Lambert was surprised at how many people there were in the centre of Medworth that morning. Perhaps they just chose not to hide or realized that they were not in so much danger during the daylight hours. The sun shining brightly overhead seemed to add much needed reassurance.

He had just received the reports from the three other cars, well over half the town had been covered now and, as yet, only eight or nine of the things had been found. The evidence seemed to support Lambert's own theory that the bulk of them hid together during the day. But where? . . .

He glanced up at the clock on the council offices as he guided the Capri along the main street. It was 1:30 p.m. They had less than five hours of daylight left. Bell and he had covered an extensive area themselves that morning but had found nothing. A search of two pub cellars had revealed nothing, neither had a house to house probe which had taken in most of Medworth's largest estate.

Lambert swung the Capri round the roundabout at the top of the main street and guided it into the narrow delivery road which led up to the back of the suupermarket which was the next sight of their quest. It had, up until three days ago, been a large branch of Sainsbury's but, as events in the town had become progressively worse, the management had pulled out, closing the store down. The Inspector brought the car to a halt in one of the loading bays and shut off the engine. Better to go in the back way, he thought. The people in the town were jumpy enough without seeing two coppers walking around with shotguns. He radioed in to the station, telling Grogan that they were going in. The Inspector hesitated a second, considering the handset which he held, then, almost as an afterthought, he said, 'Any word from Doctor Kirby yet?'

Grogan said that there wasn't and Lambert switched off the set. He sat for a second then reached for his shotgun and swung himself out of the car. Bell followed. As they reached towards the twin doors which marked the back of the supermarket, the Inspector's thoughts returned to his wife. Kirby had promised to contact the station as soon as Debbie woke up. He must have given her a pretty strong dose of sedative if she was still out. Lambert hoped that she would wake up in time. She was, after all, the only one who knew the horrendous truth behind all that had transpired these last two months. He hoped that her knowledge would be enough.

The two men reached the large doors and Lambert pressed down hard on the locking bar. It wouldn't budge an inch either way.

'Stand back,' he said, working the pump action of the shotgun.

Bell took several steps back and watched as his superior fired a blast, point blank, into the end of the bar. Lumps of metal and pieces of shot ricochetted into the air. Lambert kicked at the bar and it gave. The door swung back.

Both men looked at one another and, with the Inspector leading, walked in.

From the piles of boxes and cans, both men realized that they were in the supermarket's vast storeroom. On all sides, every kind of tinned and packaged food rose in huge towers and Lambert almost smiled to himself. Christ, the owners must have been anxious to get out to leave this amount of stuff behind. There was a fruity smell in the room, a more pleasant odour than the perpetual mustiness they had encountered nearly everywhere earlier in the day. They separated, ensuring that every inch of the storeroom was searched.

Away to his left, Lambert heard a crash and spun round, the shotgun at the ready.

'Bell,' he called.

'I'm all right, sir,' came the reply. 'Just tripped over a box of bloody baked beans.'

Lambert smiled and made his way cautiously towards the next set of doors which confronted them. Bell joined him and the men found themselves faced by row upon row of shopping trolleys, all arranged in front of the doors. They heaved them to one side, making a path. Lambert pushed the doors, relieved to find that they opened easily. The two policemen found themselves in the supermarket proper. He remembered it when it had been full of people, bustling up and down the aisles like ants moving around the nest, snatching things from the shelves to put in their baskets and trolleys. Now the place was deserted, as quiet as a grave, its once powerful banks of fluorescents now dead, leaving the entire huge amphitheatre in a kind

341

of semi-darkness. Lambert thought about turning on his flashlight but realized that he could see perfectly well without it. Away to their right was another doorway, this one open; it led into the meat storage area. There would be time later to check that.

'You take the end aisles,' said the Inspector, softly, almost reluctant to disturb the peace and solitude within the vast empty building. 'Work your way to the middle. I'll do the same from that side.' He hooked a thumb over his shoulder. Bell nodded and walked off, his boots echoing conspicuously on the tiled floor.

As he made his way slowly down the furthermost aisle, Lambert had already made the assumption that *this* was not the resting place of the creatures. It was too open, even the fridges didn't have tops. He reached the bottom of the aisle and peered across through the gloom to see Bell emerge at the far end of the supermarket. The constable raised a hand and Lambert nodded. They both started up the next aisle, giving mutual signals when they reached the end.

This procedure continued until they met in the central aisle.

'What now?' said Bell, relieved that nothing had turned up.

'The freezers,' said Lambert, motioning with the barrel of his gun, 'where they keep the meat.'

The two men headed for the storage room, Lambert noting that a pile of cans was strewn across the floor near the entrance. Probably someone had knocked them over in their hurry to leave. Or perhaps. . . .

The door to the cold storage room was open

and the Inspector walked in. The place was larger than he'd expected. All down the left hand wall was a stainless steel topped work bench, the butchers' implements still spread out upon it. Carving knives, cleavers, saws and the Inspector could see that some of it was still dark with dried blood. Running the full length of the room were six metal rods, each about four inches thick and placed more than six feet from the ground. A number of meat hooks hung from them, suspended from one of which was a whole pig. Lambert wondered why just one carcass should have been left behind. Probably no reason at all; maybe his imagination was getting the better of him again. The far end of the room was made up entirely of fridges, huge coffin-like things which must have been more than four feet deep. The white tiled floor was spotted red in places and, with the coolant turned off, both men began to notice the pungent odour of putrifying meat. It was dark in there, very dark and now both of them switched on their torches. Lambert smelt another odour, the sharp smell of sweat which he realized was his own. He swallowed hard and walked slowly towards the waiting fridges at the far end of the room, gun in one hand, torch in the other. Bell followed his example. They reached the first of the freezers and Lambert laid his flashlight on top of the adjacent fridge.

'Shine the light here,' he told Bell, both men's faces looking white in the powerful beam. The constable obeyed, watching as Lambert hooked one powerful hand under the lid and flipped it back.

Empty.

Both men breathed heavily and Lambert's voice was low when he spoke:

'I'll start at the other end. We'll check each one. Then we'll get the hell out of here.' He was nervous and he didn't mind admitting it. He retrieved his flashlight and hurried to the end of the line of fridges. There were eight in all. He laid his light on top of the metal lid of the next freezer along and, propping the shotgun up against the wall, raised the first lid.

Empty.

Further along, Bell was repeating the procedure. He too, found nothing. Both men moved along, hearts thumping and, twice, Lambert was forced to wipe beads of perspiration from his forehead.

He opened his third fridge and found it empty.

Bell actually had his hand on the lid when it shot up, knocking the shotgun and the torch from his grasp. He shrieked and Lambert spun round, the torch beam highlighting the horror before him.

The creature, a woman (Lambert wasn't sure because of the long hair and bad light), had one powerful hand clamped around Bell's neck and was dragging him into the fridge. He clung to the sides, fighting against the strength which held him, his eyes bulging wide in pain and terror. Lambert reached for the Browning but, as he pulled it free of the holster, he realized that he dare not shoot for fear of hitting his companion. He shone his flashlight full in the face of the thing which he now saw was a youth in his early twenties. The creature opened its mouth in silent protest, trying to shield its eyeless face with one hand while throttling Bell with the other. Lambert ran forward and struck the thing full in the face with the flashlight. The room was plunged into darkness and Bell fell to the ground. Lambert flung himself down, his desperate fingers searching the floor for the dropped light.

Grinning, the thing was dragging itself out of the fridge.

Lambert saw the light, lying not more than ten feet from him. He threw himself towards it, hearing Bell shriek again as the thing grabbed for him. The constable rolled clear and the living dead creature was caught in two minds for a second, not sure which of the two men to pursue. It saw Lambert reach the light and came after him, anxious to extinguish it. The light which brought so much pain.

The Inspector felt the crushing weight of the creature on him and powerful hands snaked around his neck, choking him. He gripped the hands and tried to pull them free. Bell stood motionless, watching the tableau, too frightened to move.

'For fuck's sake get it off,' screamed Lambert, his shout finally galvanizing the stunned constable into action. He looked around for a weapon, squinting through the gloom to the table of butcher's implements. His eyes sought, and found, the cleaver. Whimpering, he grabbed it and brought it crashing down on the living dead corpse, aiming for its head. But the blow missed by inches, sliced off one of its ears and powered into the shoulder at the point of clavicle and jugular vein. There was an enormous fountain of blood which sprayed out like a crimson jet.

Lambert felt the pressure on his throat eased and he struck out, knocking the creature off. It fell back, the blood still spouting from its neck but, in the darkness, both men saw it wrench the cleaver free and, despite the frenzied spurtings of dark fluid from its wound, come at them once more. Scarcely believing what he saw, Lambert backed off. The thing made a last desperate charge and brought the cleaver hurtling down with the force of a steamhammer. Bell, retreating also, slipped in a pool of blood and raised his hand to shield himself from the attack.

The bloodied blade sliced through his arm just above the wrist, the severed limb flying into the air. He began screaming, holding up the shattered stump as if it were a prize, blood pouring from the remains of his arm.

Lambert at last had a clear shot and, with Bell's screams ringing in his ears, he squeezed off two, three, four shots.

Moving at a speed of over 1,100 feet a second, the heavy grain bullets tore into the living corpse, blasting exit holes the size of fists. The impact hurled it across the darkened room where it slammed into the fridges, blood spattering up the smooth white sides. Lambert fired again, again, again. Blasting the body into an unrecognizable bloody rag. Finally he lowered the gun, the muzzle flashes still burned onto his retina, the roar of fire in his ears but, above all that, the delirious screams of Bell as he staggered a couple of feet before dropping to his knees still holding up the stump of his wrist.

Screams. Screams.

Lambert vomited. Only by a supreme effort

of will did he manage to stop himself fainting. Leaving Bell alone in the store room, he staggered out.

He managed to reach the Capri and radio for help, but then, as he dropped the handset, he lost his fight and finally did pass out.

32

Lambert sat up, felt hands on his shoulder. He grunted and reached for his gun, suddenly frightened. But slowly, as his wits returned to him, he saw the face of Hayes looking in at him.

'You all right, guv?' he asked, his big hand still on the young Inspector's shoulder.

Lambert was still dazed. He saw the two dark uniformed men carrying someone to the back of a waiting ambulance. Its blue light was spinning and the engine was humming but there were no other sounds. He caught a brief glimpse of Bell's face, milk-white as they manoeuvred him inside the vehicle. The Inspector exhaled, running a hand through his hair.

'Where the hell did you come from?' he asked, groggily.

'Grogan picked up your message. We were the nearest car, so here we are.' The sergeant smiled.

'I blacked out,' said Lambert, not that the explanation was really necessary.

One of the ambulancemen, a tall man with sad eyes, walked across to the car and looked in at Lambert.

'Will you be O.K.?' he said.

The Inspector nodded. 'Thanks.' He paused. 'What about Bell?'

'He'll live, but he's lost a lot of blood.'

Lambert nodded again and rubbed his face in the imitation of washing. The ambulanceman took one more careful look at him then walked away and got into his vehicle. In seconds, it was pulling out, the scream of its siren now filling the air. Lambert shook himself, then felt something being pressed into his hand. He looked down to see that it was a silver hip flask. Hayes nodded towards it and the Inspector drank, allowing the liquor to burn its way to his stomach.

'Purely medicinal of course,' said Hayes, smiling.

Lambert too found the strength to grin, handing the flask back to the sergeant. A thought suddenly struck him.

'Any news of my wife?' he asked, hopefully.

'Grogan called about ten minutes ago. You must have been in there,' he pointed to the supermarket, 'at the time. Doctor Kirby says that she's conscious.'

Already Lambert was starting the engine but the sergeant reached out a hand and switched it off.

'What the hell are you doing?' snarled Lambert angrily.

'Let me drive, guv,' said the sergeant softly.

The Inspector nodded. 'I'm sorry.' He slid across, allowing Hayes to settle his considerable bulk behind the wheel. He called to Jenkins to follow them and the constable nodded, gunning Puma One into life.

The two cars swung out of the loading bay

and, within minutes, were on the road leading to Kirby's house.

Kirby had hardly got the door open when Lambert barged in.

'Is she all right?' he demanded.

Already he was bounding up the stairs to the bedroom where he knew Debbie to be. He flung open the door and she turned her head and smiled at him. Lambert rushed across to her and took her in both arms. They hugged each other for long minutes. Finally, he let her go and he saw the tears in her eyes. She gripped his hand and he reached out to brush her cheek with his finger tips.

'Are you O.K.?' he asked, his voice little more than a whisper.

She nodded, squeezing his hand harder. 'Tom, those things.' He saw more tears welling up and ran his hand over her forehead.

'Don't worry, we found some of them this morning.'

'And?'

'We killed them.'

She seemed reassured and her tone brightened a little, but her voice was still croaky. He saw a jug and glass on the small bedside table and poured her some water. She drank and handed the glass back to him.

'Tom,' she said, 'I found out about Mathias, about the medallion. What Trefoile told us about him was true. He *was* a Black Magician, and that medallion belonged to him. He'd found the secret of reversing death, bringing the dead back to life. That's what the inscription on the medallion means; "To Awake the Dead." ' She gripped his hand and he edged closer, putting one arm around her shoulder as she continued.

'Mathias was buried alive for his crimes, his blasphemies they called them, but before that, his tongue was torn out and he was blinded. They gouged out his eyes. It was some old superstition, so that he couldn't see or speak of the evil he'd committed. It's all in my notes at home.' As she mentioned the word he felt her body stiffen.

'Oh God, I don't think I can ever go back there, Tom, not after what happened last night.' She hugged him, fighting back the tears. He ran his hand through her hair, kissing the top of her head.

Kirby appeared in the doorway.

'Come on, Tom,' he said, quietly, 'don't tire her too much.'

Reluctantly, Lambert broke away but Debbie held onto his hand. 'What are you going to do?'

'I'll drive back to the house,' he told her. 'See if there's any clue in your notes as to where Mathias's grave might be.'

'It said he was buried in ground not blessed by the church. Unconsecrated ground.'

Lambert nodded.

'Tom.'

He looked at her.

'You know why they took the medallion?'

He looked vague.

'If it is ever returned to Mathias, it'll enable him to rise again. They must know where he's buried.'

Lambert looked across at the clock on the dressing table. It said 4:30 p.m.

They had ninety minutes of daylight left. Lambert's mind was spinning. He had to drive back to the house, pick up Debbie's notes, praying that there might be some clue as to where the grave of Mathias was, but, above all, he had to find the remaining living dead before nightfall. He shuddered. Debbie pulled him close one last time and this time the tears flowed in an unceasing river. They held each other for a long time, Debbie sobbing softly, her head buried within his arms. Finally he pulled away, supporting her head in his hands. He kissed her.

'I love you,' he said, softly.

'Tom, for God's sake be careful,' she sobbed.

He kissed her on the forehead and then he was gone, his heart seized with the icy conviction that he might never see her again. But overriding that feeling was one of grim determination. As he left Kirby's house, the doctor heard him muttering one phrase over and over to himself, like some kind of litany—

'I'll get you, you bastards. All of you.'

He bypassed Hayes and Jenkins and climbed into the Capri, shouting at the two other policemen to keep up their search. Then he drove off, not even thinking to look up at the bedroom window where Debbie stood, watching as the car disappeared out of sight.

Already, the first warning clouds of dusk were beginning to gather on the horizon.

33

Lambert sat in the Capri for precious minutes before he could actually pluck up the courage to walk up to his house. The memory of the previous night was burned indelibly into his mind and he wondered if the image would ever fade. But, at the moment, time was the important factor so he swung himself out of the car and headed up the path towards the front door. There were tyre tracks on the front lawn, patches of dark blood spattered over the front of the house. He walked in, through the still open front door, hanging by its single remaining hinge. He cast a furtive glance up the stairs as if expecting to see the things waiting for him once more. There was more blood on the stair carpet and up the white walls. He entered the living room, a cold breeze blowing through the smashed bay window. It stirred the papers scattered across the floor.

More blood and the pervading stench of death. Lambert hunted quickly through the papers strewn across the carpet and desk. Even some of these bore tiny specks of dried crimson. It took him about ten minutes to find what he sought. He gathered up the necessary information and hurried from the house back to the warmth and safety of the car. There, he read through Debbie's notes, found it all just as she had told him earlier. He reread, his eyes straying back to that one phrase:

. . . in ground not Blessed of the Church is buried the one known as Mathias.

Unconsecrated ground. Christ, that could mean anywhere. He laid the notes on the passenger seat and started the engine, swinging the Capri round and driving back into Medworth.

As he drove, reports came in periodically from the other cars. All of them the same. Nothing to report. Not one of the things had been sighted since the morning. Lambert glanced at his watch. Nearly five o'clock. Less than an hour until nightfall.

He took the route through the already quiet town centre. There were only a few people about, all of them anxious to be home before darkness. The Inspector drove past the huge silent edifice of the deserted cinema, glancing at it as he did so. The letters above the entrance had fallen in places, blown down by the wind. He smiled as he read the sign:

TH EM IR C NEM.

It towered over him as he drove past, a monument to obsolescence.

Lambert slammed on the brakes, the Capri skidding to a halt.

One of the cinema's side doors was slightly ajar.

He sat still, his breath coming in gasps. The place had been closed for over two years now. And yet, the wooden door was propped open,

354

wide enough for a man to squeeze through. Lambert snatched up the shotgun from beside him, made sure the Browning was loaded and got out of the car. There were two sets of doors facing him. He had been in the cinema a number of times before it closed down and he knew that both sets of doors were exits. One from the stalls, one from the balcony. But right now he couldn't remember which was which. He pushed the open door and it moved slightly, the hinges shrieking in protest. Lambert squeezed through, surprised at how light it was inside. He knew immediately, from the wide flight of stone steps which faced him, that this exit led down from the balcony.

Moving slowly, his ears alert for the slightest sound, he began to climb.

Half way up, the staircase turned in a right angle, flattening out into a small landing before rising, in another flight of steps, towards the doors which led into the balcony itself. There was a large frosted glass window set in the wall and that was where the light was coming from. The window itself had been broken in two places and a cold draught blew through, creating an unnerving high pitched moan.

A few feet away from him, its door cracked and peeling, was the toilet. A rusty sign on it proudly proclaimed—Gentlemen. The door was closed. Lambert crossed to the door and, swallowing hard, pulled it open. He stepped in. The place stank of damp and blocked drains. The single window had been bricked up and the Inspector found it hard to see in the gloom. There was a tiled urinal area and a single cubicle. He pushed the door open and found, to his relief, that it was empty. The persistent drip, drip of water from the old cistern added background to the Inspector's laboured breathing. He left the toilet and began climbing the second flight of stone steps which would take him into the balcony itself. The twin doors which led into it were firmly closed. Heart thudding against his ribs, he pulled open one of the doors and stepped inside.

The darkness was total. Almost palpable, like some thick black fog, totally impenetrable and clinging around him like a living thing. Lambert, literally, couldn't see his hand in front of him. He fumbled in his jacket for his flashlight and realized, angrily, that he'd lost it earlier that afternoon in the supermarket. He fumbled for his lighter and found it, the yellow light giving him a few precious feet of visibility.

Using its light as a guide, he climbed the steps which eventually levelled out onto a kind of walk way, separating front from rear balcony. He knew, from memory, that the main entrance was about twenty yards to his right, but in the all enveloping darkness he could see no farther than the glow his lighter allowed him. He walked on, heading for the entrance, becoming more aware of the stench which filled the place with each passing second. Not just the odour of dampness which he expected, but something more powerful. The carrion odour of rotting flesh. Excrement. Death.

There was a movement behind him and Lambert spun round, the dim light from the lighter totally inadequate for the task. He saw nothing but remained in that position, gun at

356

the ready. Waiting and listening. Then finally, slowly, he turned again.

The dull glow of the lighter shone straight into the grinning face of Ray Mackenzie.

Lambert shouted in sudden terror, dropped the lighter and was plunged into total darkness once more. He rolled away, knowing that Mackenzie was coming for him. The Inspector fired one blast into the air.

In the thunderflash explosion of the discharge, the entire vast amphitheatre was momentarily illuminated and Lambert saw an image which he had always suspected. Always feared.

In the swift blinding light he saw them. Fifty. Sixty. Probably more. Living corpses all around him. He cursed himself for not having had the place searched before. It was so simple.

But now, in that brief moment of light, he knew he had found them.

34

For untold seconds nothing happened, then Lambert fired again, using the gun as a source of light. He fired off the five cartridges in rapid succession, moving towards the area where he knew the stairs to be. He didn't even know whether he hit any of the creatures with his blasts, but as his finger jerked a last time on the trigger, something warm and wet splashed across his face. His hand found the banister which led down the short flight of steps to the balcony entrance. He tried to jump the distance, tripped and tumbled to the bottom of the stairs, losing the shotgun in the process. He pushed open the door and a kind of dull half light flooded the bottom of the staircase. Lying at the bottom, Lambert looked up and saw the things crowding above him, Mackenzie at their head. The light stunned them for a second, long enough to enable Lambert to clamber to his feet and burst out of the balcony doors. He heard them thundering after him.

A few feet of carpeted landing and he was at the stairs which led down into the foyer.

Mackenzie burst from the doors in pursuit, others behind him and Lambert could smell their stench as he ran, taking the stairs two and three at a time. He reached the bottom and flung himself the last few feet, skidding across the tiled foyer floor.

The living dead pounded down behind him, one or two of them reaching the ground floor a mere second after him.

Lambert spun round, pulling the Browning from its holster. He fired with one hand, the recoil almost breaking his wrist, but by some miracle the shots hit their target and two of the creatures were felled. But now more were flooding the foyer and Lambert dashed for the twin sets of double doors, smashing the glass in one as he slammed into it, desperate to reach the main doors of the cinema. The things clattered after him, pausing a moment when he shot down two more. But now it was Lambert's turn to pause.

He turned to the great, steel braced glass doors and almost shrieked when he saw the chains and padlocks which held them firmly shut.

The first of the creatures came at him through the double doors and he blew half its head off, then another, recoiling from the light, shielding its eyeless sockets in pain. Lambert realized that the light was his only hope. He tore down the curtains which masked the twin sets of double doors, flooding ten feet from him. The Inspector felt sick, overpowered by the collective stench which emanated from them. He gave himself a moment's respite and fired at one of the padlocks. The heavy grain bullet shattered it and Lambert tore the chain free, kicking at the heavy door, shouting when it stuck. He threw all his weight against it, aware that the bolder of the creatures were drawing closer to him. He fired. The first of them went down, blood jetting from the wound in its throat.

Mackenzie ran at Lambert, his lips drawn back in that familiar hideous feral grin.

It was the force of his charge which finally catapulted Lambert through the half-open door and onto the pavement outside.

The other creatures cowered back from the light which flooded in through the glass and Mackenzie was left outside. Lambert felt his weight on him and struggled to free himself, aware that his attacker was becoming weaker in the light. Lambert remembered that he still held the length of chain and he lashed out savagely with it, catching Mackenzie across the cheek and laying it open to the bone. Those burning red orbs glowed intensely, defiant to the end. Lambert brought the chain whipping down across the man's skull. The heavy links split the flesh of his scalp, tearing away hunks of hair. Mackenzie dropped to his knees, his blazing red eyes still fixed on Lambert who had retrieved the Browning.

From point blank range, the policeman fired, almost shouting his delight as the bullet slammed into Mackenzie's jaw just below the ear, tearing it off before erupting from the back of his neck. Mackenzie sagged forward in a spreading pool of blood and Lambert put three more into him, finding something akin to pleasure in the damage the bullets wrought. He stared down at the body, frightened it would get up. At last he bolted for his car and snatched up the handset.

'Grogan,' he barked, continuing before the man had even had time to acknowledge, 'get all the cars to the Empire in town. The cinema. They're here. All of them. They're here.' He was shouting now. 'And I want petrol, lots of petrol and tell them to hurry, for fuck's sake tell them to hurry.' He threw the handset back inside the Capri and dashed back to the front of the building, peering in at the remaining living corpses. Jesus, there must be upwards of eighty, he thought. He looked at his watch.

5:30.

Night was drawing in fast. Lambert prayed they would make it in time.

The three police cars arrived within minutes of one another. Lambert told all of them to switch on their headlights and keep them trained on the front of the cinema.

'What about the petrol?' asked the Inspector, looking at Hayes.

As if in answer to his question, a Shell delivery tanker rumbled up the street and Lambert caught sight of Grogan behind the wheel. The policeman drove up onto the pavement in front of the cinema and leapt down from the cab. Together, he and Lambert pulled the hose free and Lambert placed the nozzle just inside the main door of the building.

'Turn it on,' he shouted.

Clambering back into the cab, Grogan flicked a switch and gallon after gallon of petrol pumped into the foyer of the cinema. The policemen in the cars could see the living dead cowering back from the blazing headlamps, stepping in the

361

flooding petrol, falling over one another in their attempts to reach the darkness. Many stumbled into the stalls for shelter but Lambert had men posted at each exit with orders to shoot anything that came out. Nothing would come out of that place tonight.

A red light winked on the dashboard of the tanker and Grogan yelled that the tank was empty.

Lambert ran to the safety of the nearest car then, taking a shotgun from Walford, fired four times into the petrol flooded cinema foyer.

There was an ear splitting roar and a blinding flash as the flammable liquid went up with a high-pitched shriek.

The creatures not immediately incinerated in the conflagration were either burned as the fire took hold throughout the entire building or shot down as they bolted from the exits.

Almost in awe, the men of the Medworth force watched as huge tongues of flame licked up the outsides of the building, the entire place transformed into a huge oven. For four hours it burned, the smoke rising thickly into the night sky until at last, gutted and destroyed, the roof collapsed, sending out a blistering shower of sparks.

By first light the next morning all that remained was a gigantic blackened ruin, like some huge pile of charcoal, choking black smoke still drifting from the remains.

The men had stood silently for a while, not daring to believe that it was all over but then Lambert had given the order for them to leave and, led by him, they had driven off.

Lambert felt no elation, merely a crushing weight of weariness, of total emotional and physical exhaustion. His desire to rest overwhelmed all but one feeling.

He thought of Debbie.

No one had seen the thing which had once been Gary Briggs crawl from the boot of Puma Three that night. All had been too intent on watching the incineration of the living dead.

When they left, the Briggs thing crept into the ruins of the cinema, searching. It knew that it would have to be quick for the sun would be at its zenith soon and the pain would be too great. But it found what it sought and it left the blackened hell where the other living dead had sought refuge.

Now it hid in the church up at Two Meadows, sheltering from the light. At home in the bell tower where no sun could reach it.

It knew what it had to do and knew how to do it. It rested, clutching the medallion to its chest.

It waited for the coming of night.

35

'You'll do,' said Kirby, tucking away his stetho-scope. Lambert pulled his shirt back on and began fastening it.

'What about the rest?' asked the Inspector, tucking the shirt into his trousers.

'They were fine too,' Kirby told him. The two men looked at each other for a moment then the doctor said, 'Back to normal eh, Tom?'

Lambert shrugged, 'I don't think anything will ever be bloody normal after what's happened here these past couple of months.' He ran a hand through his hair, 'I'm just pleased it's all over.'

'Amen to that,' said Debbie, who was sitting in a chair across the room from the couch on which Lambert perched. They were in Kirby's surgery.

'I hear Jenkins' wife had a little girl,' said the doctor, smiling.

Lambert nodded, 'I sent him on leave to be with her. Walford and Hayes are off too. They deserve the rest after what they've been through. The others will get their chance in a couple of weeks.'

'And what about you?' asked Kirby.

'What about me?'

'When do you take your leave?'

Lambert slid down from the couch, 'I don't. There's still work to be done, John. I'm in charge of the force here; it's my job to see that it gets done.'

'Tom, be sensible. After what you've been through, you more than anyone need a couple of days off.'

'We all went through the same. What about Bell, what about Briggs? At least *I'm* still alive.'

Kirby turned to Debbie. 'Can't you talk some sense into this hard-headed bastard?'

Debbie smiled humourlessly and shook her head, 'I gave up trying to do that a long time ago.'

Lambert extended a hand which Kirby shook warmly. 'Thanks for everything, John,' said the Inspector.

'You can stop here as long as you like, you know,' Kirby told him.

Lambert shook his head.

'You're not going back home, then?'

'Not after what happened there,' Lambert told him. 'I don't think either of us could face it again. There's a little place in Bramton, about twenty miles from here. I don't mind the journey every day. We couldn't stay here after what's happened.'

Kirby nodded. Debbie got to her feet and joined her husband and they walked out to the car with Kirby at their side. He kissed Debbie lightly on the cheek and watched as both of them climbed into the Capri. Lambert rolled the window down and looked up at the doctor.

'I'll be in touch,' he said, and started the

engine. The Capri moved off and Kirby watched it disappear out of sight over the hill. He stood for long moments alone on the hillside, until at last the cool breeze drove him back inside. Into the warmth.

'Are you really going back straight away?' said Debbie, studying Lambert's profile as he drove.

'What choice do I have?' he asked.

'Can't you put someone else in charge for a couple of days? Christ, Tom, two days won't hurt will it?' There was a note of exasperation in her voice. He reached across and placed his hand on her thigh.

'We'll see,' he said, smiling.

They drove for a long way in silence, the policeman taking back roads, dirt tracks, anything he could to avoid the hustle and bustle of main roads. When they had reached a particularly secluded spot he stopped the car and got out. Debbie followed him. He walked away from the vehicle, catching her hand and pulling her close to him. They stood on the hilltop, the whole of Medworth and its surrounding countryside spread out before them. The air was fresh, filled with the scent of damp grass and wild flowers which added an occasional clutch of colour in the all encompassing greenery of the fields. Lambert bent and picked a single bloom, sniffing it before he handed it to Debbie. She kissed him, pulling him down on top of her in that damp field. Their hands sought each other's bodies, their tongues eager for the taste of the other's mouth.

There, in that open field, high on the hill side,

they made love with a passion they had never before experienced.

High above the sun shone down, its warming rays covering them.

Lambert woke with a start and looked at his watch. He sat up, startled, shivering. Beside him, Debbie stirred and nestled closer to him for warmth. Lambert began to laugh. He laughed until the tears ran down his face. Debbie looked up at him, his own merriment contagious. She too began to laugh.

She realized what he was laughing at. They were naked. Both of them, there on the hillside. They'd fallen asleep after their lovemaking, beneath the comforting warmth of the sun. She checked her own watch.

Four-fifty.

Still giggling, they dressed quickly and retreated to the safety of the car just as spots of rain began to fall from the rapidly darkening sky. They sat there for a moment, both now free of the tension which they had felt for so long.

'Maybe just two days,' said Lambert, smiling.

Debbie leaned across and kissed him.

He started the car and drove off. It wasn't until they reached the centre of Medworth itself that she realized what he was doing. Even after all he had gone through, the memory was still with him. She realized he was heading for the cemetery. To take one last look at his brother's grave. Lambert still bore the sting of guilt, but now, somehow, he had managed to come to terms with it. He had to see Mike's grave once more.

By the time they reached the cemetery, the sun had retreated from the sky, driven away by a combination of gathering storm clouds and the onset of night. Twilight hovered like a hawk in the darkening heavens.

Lambert shut off the engine and looked across at Debbie.

'Stay here.' He smiled, warmly.

But she was already out of the car, reaching for his hand, their feet crunching on the gravel of the driveway. An icy wind had sprung up and the first large spots of rain were beginning to fall as they left the driveway and walked the pathway which led to Mike's grave.

A silent fork of lightning split the clouds and Debbie jumped. Lambert smiled and hugged her tighter as they walked. They finally reached the grave and stood beneath the big oak tree which hung over it, listening to the rain pelting down. Lambert read his brother's name and felt no pain, just a deep sense of loss. The wound was healing and he knew it. He had at last found the strength to come to terms with his brother's death. It was as if the destruction of the past two months had somehow put it into perspective. What was the phrase . . . ?

Just a drop in the ocean . . .

They stood for long moments, close to one another, ignoring the rain which dripped onto them. Then finally, Lambert said,

'Come on.'

It was as they turned that they saw the figure emerge from the church.

At first neither moved and it was obvious that the person hurrying across the cemetery had not seen them. The oak hid them from its view. Lambert squinted through the pouring rain to get a glimpse of the figure, which seemed to be dressed in a uniform of some sort. And it was carrying something. . . .

There was a blinding explosion of lightning and Lambert saw who the person was.

'Oh my God,' he breathed, 'it's Briggs.'

Debbie didn't understand but she felt a sudden, ungovernable terror rise in her.

'He's got the medallion,' gasped Lambert, watching, riveted, as the living dead thing shambled quickly towards the patch of waste ground a hundred yards away. Waste ground. Outside the boundaries of church land.

The realization hit them both like a steam hammer, but it was Debbie who spoke first.

'Tom, the Unconsecrated Ground. Mathias's grave must be there.' She was pointing to the line of trees which marked the outskirts of the scrubland. Lambert was running, screaming at her over his shoulder to get back to the car, bellowing to make himself heard above the driving rain and persistent roaring of thunder. Debbie watched him for a second then she too ran, the breath rasping in her lungs, heading for the cemetery gates and the safety of the car.

Lambert reached the crest of the ridge in time to see Briggs tearing clods of earth up with his hands, furiously digging deeper.

The Inspector paused and pulled the Browning from his holster. He steadied himself, aimed and squeezed off a shot. It threw up a small geyser of earth a foot from the rapidly digging Briggs who paid it no attention. Lambert fired again.

This time the shot sped past its target and disappeared into the distance.

The rain seemed to have intensified and even the loud retort of the Browning was drowned by the persistent rumbling and crashing of thunder.

The Briggs-thing felt its fingers connect with wood and it redoubled its efforts, tearing the coffin lid free and exposing the mouldy skeleton of Mathias. Grinning madly, the living dead corpse picked up the medallion, holding it aloft for a second, then placed it carefully on the chest of the skeleton.

Lambert fired a last time and ran towards the thing crouching in the centre of the waste ground.

His final shot was on target. It powered into Briggs' side just below the right armpit, tearing through the rib cage and exploding from the other side to send a confetti of shattered bone and gobbets of lung tissue flying into the air. The impact toppled the creature but didn't kill it. Blood pumping from its wound, it staggered to its feet to meet Lambert's onslaught. The Inspector used the butt end of the pistol like a club, smashing it down on Briggs' head with a force that buckled the metal. The head split open and the creature keeled over.

Lambert, gasping for breath and almost blinded by the rain turned and looked down into the coffin where Mathias lay. He saw a bony hand grab for his ankle, but as he backed off he realized that he was too late.

Debbie had never worked a handset before and now, in the moment when she most needed it, she couldn't find the knowledge what to do next. She suddenly had an idea. The Capri roared into life as she twisted the ignition key. She stepped hard on the accelerator and it shot forward, spraying gravel out behind it.

Mathias stood erect in the centre of the waste ground, the medallion gleaming around his neck.

Lambert was shaking, his eyes riveted to the spectre of pure evil which confronted him.

It must have towered a good six inches above him, and he guessed its height to be somewhere around six feet six. The tattered shroud which was the only thing that covered its body hung in gossamer wisps, scarcely hiding the yellowed flesh which was stretched over thick bones like parchment. And yet there was a power there which Lambert could almost feel, not least in those gaping black eyeless sockets which fixed him in their stare, tiny pinpricks of red light at their centres gradually expanding until they filled the whole gaping maw. Two blazing red orbs which glowed like the fires of hell and made the Inspector stagger. He was gripped by a cold so intense it penetrated every fibre of his body until even the slightest movement seemed a monumental effort.

He realized he still had the Browning and he fumbled in his pocket for a fresh clip, slammed it in and raised the weapon. The trigger wouldn't move. The impact on Briggs' skull must have damaged the firing pin in some way.

With a shriek of terror, he flung the pistol at Mathias and finally found the strength to run.

He knew without looking round that the thing was after him.

Gasping for breath, Lambert climbed the short incline and went sprawling on the gravel drive, cutting his palms. Then, all at once, he saw the twin beams of the car headlights speeding towards him.

'Oh God,' he gasped.

Debbie saw him and slammed on the brakes. Then she saw Mathias behind him, no more than a yard behind him, and she screamed. The Capri skidded on the gravel, spinning round once. Lambert grabbed for the handle of the passenger door and flung himself in. Debbie immediately drove her foot down on the accelerator and the car burned rubber for precious seconds.

There was a fearful explosion of glass which showered them both as Mathias broke the back window with a single blow of his fist.

The car jerked forward and the Black Magician pulled his hand free just in time to prevent it being torn off at the wrist. Lambert looked over his shoulder and saw the vision of the creature receding, but just as it was leaving his field of view he saw it raise both arms skyward.

He heard Debbie scream and turned round in time to see that the cemetery gates had slammed shut. She twisted the wheel, stabbing at the brake simultaneously. The car slowed down a little but not enough. It left the driveway, the wheels skidding on the wet grass, sped a few yards and slammed into the high wall surrounding the cemetery. Lambert felt his head snap forward, crashing hard against the dashboard and blood ran down his face. Debbie slumped back in her seat and he had to shake her out of unconsciousness, gratefully realizing that she had only fainted. She shook herself and looked at him, the blood pouring down his face.

'We've got to get out,' he panted, throwing open the door and taking her hand.

As she clambered after him she saw the image of Mathias filling the rear view mirror and she could swear that he was grinning.

'The church,' shouted Lambert as another bolt of lightning tore open the clouds.

They ran with a speed born of terror and reached the hallowed building, praying that the door wasn't locked.

Lambert pulled on the metal handle and the door gave. They tumbled in, immediately enveloped by a stench of dampness. The sound of their footsteps reverberated throughout the ancient building as they ran towards the altar. Within seconds, Mathias was driving the first of a series of powerful blows against the massive oak door of the church.

Lambert looked around, searching desperately for something with which to defend them. He glanced at the door.

'That won't hold him for long,' he said.

Debbie was close to tears and Lambert found his own breath coming in gasps. He scanned the building frantically. There was another powerful blow on the church door and the wood bent inward a fraction.

'The medallion is giving him his power,' said the policeman. 'I've got to get it away from him somehow.'

Debbie grabbed his arm, 'Tom, he'll kill you.'

The tears were streaming down her face. 'That's no man out there.'

Another thunderous bang and a large portion of the church door showed a split from top to bottom. A minute more and Mathias would be in. Lambert's head was throbbing, both from the pain of the gash and also from the effort of trying to find some way of saving them from the horror awaiting them. He held Debbie tight and looked into her face.

'You must get out, understand? When I distract him, you run for the door. Get help, just get out of here.'

She shook her head despairingly, the tears coming with renewed ferocity.

'Do it,' he said, his voice low but full of power.

He pushed her behind him as the first panel of the door splintered inwards.

'Behind the altar,' he told her, his gaze now fixed to the sight before him.

With four powerful blows, Mathias demolished the door, huge lumps of metal and oak flying into the church under the impact of his onslaught. He passed through what remained of the door and stood in the entrance, peering into the church. In the cold light cast by the frequent flashes of lightning, the golden medallion winked evilly at Lambert who reached behind him and grasped a metal candelabra for protection. He also found a heavy golden cross which he picked up.

Mathias advanced slowly down the central aisle, heading straight for the waiting Inspector.

Lambert gripped the puny weapons until his knuckles went white, then, with a scream of angry fear, he ran at the Black Magician and swung the candlestick. The creature raised one hand to shield its face and the metal cracked savagely against its forearm. There was a snapping sound as the bone broke and Lambert pressed his advantage, using his own body as a battering ram, actually managing to knock Mathias to the ground. The two of them crashed into a row of pews and Lambert felt a powerful hand hurl him effortlessly to one side. He rolled once then was on his feet, brandishing the cross and candlestick before him. Mathias lunged and managed to grab the candlestick and Lambert felt the power in that ancient hand as it forced him back. And all the time, those blazing red orbs fixed him in an unholy stare. The thin, almost transparent lips drawn back to reveal rotted teeth, the mouth opening occasionally to reveal the gaping maw within. The stench was unbelievable.

The Inspector felt himself being forced to the ground and struck out with the golden cross, driving the end towards the empty socket which had once housed an eye. The top of the cross disappeared into the hole, swallowed up in the red light which filled the eyeless pit. Mathias only grinned and struck the weapon away, seizing Lambert in a vice like grip, and lifting him by his throat in one huge powerful hand.

'Run,' shrieked the Inspector, and he caught sight of Debbie dashing past them towards the remains of the door. Wind and rain blew in and she could feel them on her face.

Mathias turned, still holding Lambert and pointed his other hand towards the escaping

Debbie. The Inspector felt a force like an electric shock run through his entire body as, through pain-clouded eyes, he saw one of the huge wooden pews at the back of the church lift a good six feet into the air and hurtle across the entrance of the church.

Debbie screamed and fell back. Mathias now seemed to have tired of the Inspector and, with a contemptuous heave, flung him to one side. Lambert struck the cold stone floor of the church and looked up, stunned, to see the figure of Mathias raise both arms skyward.

There was an earsplitting roar and a large rent appeared in the church roof. Masonry tumbled down. A particularly large lump hit a pew and splintered it to matchwood. Rain poured in through the hole but the Black Magician was oblivious to it and remained where he stood.

Lambert looked on in horror as a large crack appeared in one of the thick stone columns supporting the roof. Dust and ancient stone fell to the floor, mingling with the rain that was now pouring in through the roof.

And the cold. Lambert felt it once more, seeping into his bones, a cold the like of which he had never known, and with it, came the overpowering stench of rotted flesh.

Mathias was grinning, those blazing pools of blood glowing with even more vehemence.

There was an explosion as the stained glass windows shattered inward as if pushed by some giant hand from the outside. Huge jagged shards of coloured glass rained into the church, some remaining intact, others splintering again as they hit the ground. The wind rushed in through the

holes, drowning out all other sounds. Lambert
tried to stand and found the effort impossible.
Debbie too, found herself pinned to the ground
by the enveloping force which was invading the
church with each second. She could only gasp as
she saw her husband dragging himself across the
church towards one of the broken windows.

Lambert felt as if he had lead weights secured
to every limb and the act of crawling seemed
an impossibility. His teeth were chattering, the
combination of the driving rain and unbearable
cold making his task all the more difficult. Glass
cut his hands and knees as he crawled but he
ignored the pain and reached out to grasp a long
shard of glass which bore the face of Christ.
The policeman gripped it, disregarding the blood
which ran from his cut palms. He wanted to
scream. He felt the cold growing more intense.
The sound of the rain and the intensifying storm
outside deafened him but he crawled on. Finally,
by a monumental effort of will he dragged
himself to his feet.

'Our Father, who art in Heaven,' he began,
under his breath. Each agonized step brought
him closer to Mathias who still stood with his
arms outstretched. His back to the advancing
policeman.

'Hallowed be thy name.'

The cold wrapped itself around Lambert like
a blanket, slowing his already faltering steps.

'Thy Kingdom come, thy will be done.'

He drove himself on, tears of fear and frustration now coursing down his cheeks. The blood
from his head wound still dribbling down his
face. His hands, slashed open to the bone,

gripped the dagger-like shard of glass. The face of Christ suddenly ran red with Lambert's blood as it cascaded over the coloured crystal.

'Give us this day our daily bread and forgive us our trespasses, as we forgive those . . .'

Mathias was no more than a yard away, his back still to the Inspector.

There was another resounding explosion as a further crack appeared in the central roof support pillar. More masonry sped down, shattering on the stone floor and spraying out like shrapnel.

'. . . Who trespass against us. And lead us not into temptation, but deliver us from evil.'

Deliver us from evil.

Mathias turned, bringing the full fury of those burning red pools to bear on Lambert.

The Inspector gave a last despairing scream and lunged forward.

Mathias couldn't avoid the thrust and, as Lambert drove forward, the Black Magician opened his mouth in silent agony as the razor sharp shard of glass pierced his heart. Lambert twisted it, indifferent to his own pain. Blood from Mathias' torn heart sprayed him, a thick, almost black ooze which stank of corruption. Lambert staggered back, watching the pus-like fluid spouting from the creature's chest.

Mathias made a desperate attempt to tear the glass free but his hands could gain no firm grip on the slippery weapon and he staggered drunkenly for a second before toppling back.

The blazing red of his eyes dulled momentarily before glowing even stronger and then, as Lambert watched, twin fountains of blood, brighter than that gushing from the creature's heart, spurted from the empty eye sockets. Mathias opened and closed his mouth, speaking silent curses, then, that too filled with dark blood.

Lambert swayed, thought he was going to faint, but Debbie's screams brought him back to his senses and he looked up in time to see that the central roof column was crumbling.

Finding new strength, he ran, vaulting the transfixed body of Mathias and reaching the door of the church just as the roof folded inward.

Debbie and he ran outside, the rain and wind buffeting them about like leaves in a gale, but they fought against it, not even turning to watch as the last remnants of the church roof crumbled inwards. Tons of old stone and rubble crashed down, shattering pews, altar, everything. Burying the body of Mathias for the last time.

Lambert collapsed on the wet grass, finally aware of pain in his hands and head. Every muscle in his body ached and, even with Debbie supporting him, he could hardly make it to the car. She helped him in and then went and hauled back one of the heavy gates at the cemetery entrance.

The engine spluttered as she started the car, and for a second, she wondered if it would move. Its wheels spun only for a second before catching and she guided it out of the cemetery.

Beside her, Lambert was barely conscious. He was covered in blood, his own and that of Mathias. The stench in the car was unbearable and Debbie wound the window down, ignoring the rain which spattered her. She looked across at him every few seconds, the tears filling her eyes.

He smiled weakly and reached for her knee with a blood-stained hand.

'Now it *is* over,' he croaked, the smile still on his lips.

When she looked back again, he'd passed out.

36

Time passed slowly in Medworth and it was nearly two years before the town finally returned to something like normality. It grew in size, its small industries expanding and attracting new inhabitants, becoming a part of the progress which it had always resisted.

Those who moved there never knew anything about what had happened. Nothing had been printed in any papers about it. The deaths were never explained. Indeed, how could they be?

Lambert was promoted. He and Debbie moved further North where he took over command of a force three times the size of the one in Medworth. Once a month they returned to the town to visit the cemetery, to plant fresh flowers on Mike's grave. Lambert had finally found the peace within himself which he had always sought.

The church was never rebuilt. It remained a roofless shell, home only to those animals who would enter it. Moss and lichens invaded it, and, some said that there were rats as big as cats in there. Visitors to the cemetery gave it cursory glances as they passed by.

As time passed, it was forgotten.

EPILOGUE

The boy was frightened. Not only of the church but of what his mother would say when he got home. He looked at his watch and saw that it was approaching eleven p.m. God, she'd skin him alive when he got in. She'd warned him before about hanging around with those Kelly boys. They were always in trouble with the law, she'd told him. The boy knew she was right but he also knew that if he ducked out of this prank, he'd be a laughing stock at school next day. That fear overshadowed anything his mother would say. So now, he stood in the ruined church staring around him, his body coated in a light film of perspiration. But this was part of the initiation ceremony. The Kelly brothers had told him so. Enter the church and bring something out to prove that you've been in there. All the other gang members had done it at one time or another.

The boy was sixteen, his imagination vivid. He had heard the stories of the giant rats nesting in the ruins and that thought was strong in his mind as he rooted amongst the rubble, shining his torch before him as he tried to find a likely prize.

The beam alighted on something golden lying at his feet. He bent to pick it up.

It looked like a medallion of some sort and there were funny signs on it. This would do perfectly. The boy snatched it up, anxious to be out of the church. It was only as he lifted it that he felt the heat.

It intensified until he dropped the gold circlet. He rubbed his palm against the seat of his dirty jeans and picked it up again, more cautiously this time. No trouble. No heat. He dropped it into his pocket and ran out.

The Kelly brothers accepted him as a member of the gang and that pleased the boy. He kept the medallion in his pocket, careful to hide it from his mother when he finally did get home. She shouted at him just as he'd expected and so did his father. The boy ignored them and went to bed.

He sat up for a long time looking at the medallion, but finally he switched off his bedside lamp, surprised at how much the light hurt his eyes.

Besides, he had a terrible headache.

Renegades

This book is dedicated to Liverpool Football Club. Its players, its staff, its fans and everything it stands for. For bringing me so much pleasure over the last twenty-five years, I thank you.

Acknowledgements

As ever, no book is written without a certain amount of help, inspiration and support for yours truly. So, here are most, if not all, of the people who provided those three commodities (or who paid me money to see their names in print ... just joking).

Extra special thanks to Gary Farrow, my Manager, the man who kicks arse whether it needs kicking or not, the man whose epitaph will read 'How much' or 'Only if we get the cover' ... Thanks, mate. Also thanks to Chris and Damien at 'the office'.

Very special thanks to Mr John O'Connor, Mr Don Hughes, everyone in Sales and, most of all, to my sales teams for their untiring efforts and for putting up with me 'on the road'. To Nick Webb who'd been pursuing me for years and finally nailed me ... (you're stuck with me now, Nick). To Barbara Boote, to Nann du Sautoy, to Jane Warren and Rosalie Macfarlane and everyone in publicity, in fact thanks to everyone at Macdonald/Futura/Sphere for their support. To John Jarrold for the first of many gut-busting lunches ... Thank you all.

Special thanks to Mr Ray Mudie and Mr Peter 'prisoner of Gotham City' Williams. Always respected, always friends. I owe you.

Very special thanks to James Hale who edits with a pencil not a hatchet. Thanks also to Vanessa Holt and Carole Blake and Julian Friedmann.

Thanks to Bill Young (No threats this time, Bill)

and Andy Wint. To Brian 'there's another one in the post' Pithers, to 'Mad' Malcolm Dome at 'RAW' and to everyone at 'Kerrang' too.

Many thanks to Gareth 'still overworked and trying to practice' James, to John 'respectable at last' Gullidge and 'Samhain', to John Martin, to Nick Cairns and Andy Featherstone (beware, these men carry tape-recorders). Thanks for your support and interest.

Thanks to Alison at EMI, to Trish at BMG (thanks and don't forget your thermals ...) to Shonadh at Polygram, to Georgie, to Susie (for keeping me fit ...). To Broomhills Pistol Club, especially Bert and Anita, Mike 'Just call me Travis' Kirby and everyone else. To Ian 'I've brought the tape back' Austin, the man with the biggest phone bill in the world ... cheers, mate. To Dave and Malcolm in Manchester (I'll tell you when it's lunch-time, Malc ...), to Roger who is probably on a boat or plane somewhere and to Dave 'I'm going to use all the tape on your answering machine' Holmes.

Many thanks to all the management and staff at The Holiday Inn, Mayfair for their friendliness. And, for no other reason but I feel like mentioning them, thanks to Fouquet's in Paris, to the Barbados Hilton, Dromoland Castle in Ireland and Bertorelli's in Notting Hill Gate.

As ever, thanks to Steve, Bruce, Dave, Nicko and Adrian for letting me repeat the experience of a lifetime. Thanks also to Rod Smallwood and everyone at Smallwood Taylor. Many thanks to 'Big' Wally Grove (get some etiquette, mate ...).

Indirect thanks to Queensryche, Great White, Thunder, Tangier, Black Sabbath, Clannad and Enya. Also thanks to Michael Mann, Sam Peckinpah and Martin Scorsese.

Thanks to Croxley typing paper for the free sheets.

This novel was, as ever, written on Croxley paper, wearing Wrangler jeans and Puma trainers (well, it worked with Croxley ...).

I don't think I've left anyone out except to say a quick word of thanks to Amin Saleh, Jack Taylor and Lewis Bloch.

The most important people I leave until last and that means my Mum and Dad without whom none of this would be possible (the day I slow down, Mum, will be the day Dad gets a treble up ...). And to my wife, Belinda, who over the past few years has saved my sanity, my soul (maybe), my national insurance stamps and my twenty pence pieces. This one is with love too.

That leaves one group of people to thank and that's *you*. To every person who has ever bought, borrowed or stolen one of my books, thank you. What follows is for you, and always will be.

Shaun Hutson.

'What does not kill me makes me stronger.'
— Nietzsche

Prologue

It was the darkness of the blind.

A blackness so impenetrable, so palpable he felt as if he was floating on it. Surrounded by it. As if the tenebrous gloom were infiltrating every pore of his body, shutting out the light as surely as if his eyes had been removed.

But amidst that darkness there was pleasure.

Pleasure he had felt before and knew he would feel again. Sometimes so exquisite it was almost unbearable.

The inability to see heightened the sensations he felt.

His sense of smell was sharpened.

The odour was strong in his nostrils, pungent, sweet, occasionally somewhat rancid.

A powerful coppery odour which he knew well and which he welcomed.

His ears seemed more sensitive than usual, too, his hearing attuned more intensely to the sounds that filtered through the blackness.

It was like some kind of chorus.

His own sighs and grunts of pleasure mingled with the other noises.

The more strident cries.

Cries of pain.

He smiled in the gloom, running his own fingers over his features, pushing one index finger into his mouth and tracing the outline of his lower lip.

He tasted the blood on it and licked it off.

His body felt as if it were on fire, despite the coldness

inside the building, and he grinned as he thought about the luminosity which his body might be giving off as that warmth seemed to intensify.

But there was no glow.

Only that blackness which he loved so dearly.

Almost as dearly as the objects that surrounded him.

He ran his hands over them with greedy relish.

He was close to ecstacy.

His own breathing was low and guttural, rasping deep in his throat as he continued to run his fingers over the thing beside him.

Then finally he lifted it. Smoothly, effortlessly.

The smell seemed to grow stronger as he brought the object close to his face.

It was invisible in the darkness but he ran his right index finger across it, feeling every fold and crease.

Every unblemished inch.

It felt like velvet.

He smiled broadly, knowing that this pleasure could continue for hours yet.

They would not come for him until morning and by that time he would be satiated. Glutted on pleasure.

Until the next time.

He shuddered with anticipation and brought the object closer to his face, feeling something run slowly down his right arm.

Fluid which dripped from his elbow onto his naked thigh.

He opened his mouth slightly, preparing himself, his tongue flicking across his own lips before snaking out to weave tight patterns over the other object.

He tasted. He smelled. He felt. He heard.

The low cries.

The dripping of fluid.

His tongue touched lips.

viii

And those other lips were warm.

Despite the fact that the head had been severed over an hour ago.

PART ONE

'No life that breathes with human breath,
Has ever truly longed for death.'
                    – Alfred Lord Tennyson.

'For a price I'd do about anything, except
pull the trigger. For that I'd need a pretty
good cause.'
                    – Queensryche.

One

STORMONT, NORTHERN IRELAND:
They would kill him.

Chris Newton had no doubt about it.

He was a dead man.

If he fucked up on this assignment then they would kill him. He shoved a fresh roll of film into the back of the Nikon which hung around his neck, checked and re-checked the other two cameras which he carried then peered through the one with the telephoto lens that was perched on the tripod before him. He adjusted the lens, trying to bring the Parliament building into sharper focus, aware that he'd already performed this task a dozen times in the last fifteen minutes.

His hands were shaking, and not just from the chill wind which swept across the great lawns fronting the building. He was nervous. No, that was an understatement. He was scared shitless.

Had he taken all the lens caps off? Were all his exposures set right? Was the shutter speed correct?

Check.

Check.

He felt like a bloody astronaut running through the final details of take-off prior to being fired into space. And again the thought crossed his mind that, if he didn't get the pictures he'd been sent here to obtain, space probably offered his only safe haven.

The editors of The *Mail* had seen fit to give him this

assignment on the strength of the work he'd been doing on the paper for the last seven months. He'd covered everything for them from football matches to society parties and they had been impressed. Impressed enough to send him here.

The men around him were probably just as nervous as he was, Newton tried to tell himself. Most of them were smoking; one was sipping from a hip flask. Newton could have done with sharing the liquor. Anything to calm his nerves.

The assembled politicians were expected out onto the lawn within the next fifteen minutes.

He checked his watch.

Close by a film crew were setting up, the reporter tapping the end of his microphone, complaining that it didn't work. The cameraman was swinging his hand-held camera back and forth as if it were some kind of weapon, sweeping it across the ranks of newsmen and women, pausing occasionally to wipe the odd spot of rain from the lens.

The sky was overcast, threatening a downpour. It had been raining on and off since Newton arrived in Northern Ireland two days ago. In fact, Belfast reminded him of Manchester with its almost constant rainfall, the main difference being that British soldiers didn't patrol the streets of Manchester.

Not yet, anyway, he mused.

There were soldiers ahead of him, mingling with the scores of Ulster Constabulary men, the mosaic of uniforms incongruous against the regal background of Stormont itself.

'You ready?'

The voice startled him and he glanced round to see Julie Webb looking at him.

4

She had flown out with him, reminding him all the time (as if he needed it) of the importance of getting good pictures.

The Stormont Summit was the most important meeting of its kind in the history of the Six Counties: a final opportunity to end the bloodshed which had torn the country apart for over four hundred years. At this very moment inside the building there were members of the British Cabinet, the Irish Government, Ulster Unionists. Even representatives of Sinn Fein, for Christ's sake.

A meeting of ideologies which, a year before, would have been unthinkable.

But it was happening right now and Chris Newton had been sent here to record it on film.

And if he fucked up his editors would kill him.

It was as simple as that.

Julie stamped her feet trying to restore circulation, her boots crunching gravel.

'They're coming out soon,' she told him, sipping from a plastic mug she'd taken from a thermos flask. The flask itself she held to her chest as if it were a new-born child. She poured herself another cup of the steaming coffee and offered some to Newton.

He declined, shaking his head, blowing on his hands instead, trying to induce some warmth and also to stop himself trembling.

A few feet away he heard the quick-fire rattle of several shots from a Pentax.

To his left a reporter from one of the major news shows on television was recording his location and time indent. That done, he turned towards the Parliament building and muttered something under his breath before looking at his watch again.

The troops and security men watched the swarms of newsmen intently. Security at the gathering was even more stringent than usual, the presence of the security forces more in evidence than Newton could ever remember. As well as troops and R.U.C., it was rumoured there were a number of S.A.S. men present, invisible amongst the crowd. Newton glanced to his right and left, wondering if the very men he stood beside were in fact S.A.S. men in disguise.

His own press card had been double-checked, the guards at the press entrance apparently unconvinced that the likeness on his card matched his actual identity. Newton had thought for one awful moment that he was going to be refused entry but the guards had finally relented and allowed him to pass.

He continued rubbing his hands together, looking around.

The media interest in the summit was, naturally, immense. Newton wondered if there were any reporters left in Fleet Street. Everyone, it seemed, was gathered here; they wanted to be part of the momentous event, irrespective of whether it was part of their job or not. There were foreign film crews from as far afield as Japan, though what they made of it all Newton couldn't imagine. Probably spies from Nikon wanting to see how sales were doing, he mused, checking his own equipment again.

Larger spots of rain began to fall sporadically and a number of the assembled throng glanced upwards towards the swollen clouds and passed less than flattering comments about the weather in the province.

Newton pulled a baseball cap from the pocket of his coat and jammed it on. He bent forward to peer through the mounted camera once more, annoyed when someone bumped into it.

'Careful,' he hissed irritably, glaring at the offender.

The man met his gaze with unblinking eyes, almost challengingly. He was stocky and in need of a shave. He stood looking at Newton for long seconds before passing off into the crowd.

'Prat,' the photographer muttered, making sure the other man was out of earshot. He re-adjusted the camera, peering through the telescopic lens as a sniper might study his prey.

He was one of the first to see the main door of the building open.

'Jesus,' he muttered, noticing the armed security men who emerged ahead of the first of the politicians.

And then the whole cold, wet and irritable throng of media saw what they had come to see. The weather and the conditions were momentarily forgotten.

More politicians emerged, some joking about the weather, others wondering whether or not it might be more prudent to remain inside the building until the rain had stopped.

The air was filled with the quick-fire rattle of a hundred cameras firing off an almost synchronized volley. Reporters tried to move forward but were held back by the line of security men and now the waiting media saw that the politicians were coming towards them anyway, sticking to the pathways wherever possible.

Newton, snapping away as if his life depended upon it, caught sight of the Irish Prime Minister walking alongside two Unionist MPs. Behind them the British Foreign Secretary strode between two security guards, chatting animatedly with a member of Sinn Fein. Newton shook his head in wonderment.

7

The politicians drew closer, grouping together for the benefit of the posse of media. The reporters now began firing questions with a verbal rapidity that almost matched the high-speed salvos coming from the cameras. Television cameras cast cyclopean eyes over the entire gathering as the questions rained down and sound men struggled to push boom mikes close enough to catch the responses.

'How much progress had been made in the talks?'

'Is it possible that a settlement could be reached before the end of the week?'

'What do the talks mean to both Northern Ireland and Southern Ireland?'

'Will the troops be withdrawn soon?'

Newton kept firing away, happy that he was covering every angle, framing every face. His nervousness seemed to have gone. He was doing what he did best now. Moving alternately between the mounted camera and the ones he carried around his neck he expertly and swiftly changed rolls of film, not wishing to leave any possible history-making shot to chance.

The questions continued to pour forth, their answers sometimes vague, sometimes encouraging, sometimes non-committal. Newton himself realized that one summit meeting and four days of discussion were insufficient in themselves to cure a disease that had afflicted the province for so long but, if the troubles in Ulster were an open wound, then this summit was going some way to at least dress that wound. The healing process would take much longer.

He was preparing to take another photo as the politicians gathered together when he was almost knocked to the ground.

He spun round angrily.

'What the fuck …' he snapped, seeing that it was the same unshaven man who had bumped into him a moment or two earlier. 'Watch it, mate,' Newton said angrily. 'We're all in the same boat here, you know.'

The man again said nothing. His eyes were fixed on the assembled politicians who were now all but surrounded by reporters, the heaving throng kept a respectful distance by the security forces. Maybe he was one of the plain-clothes S.A.S. men, thought Newton, his job to mingle with the crowd and check for any trouble. He carried a camera around his neck but it was not the camera he was reaching for.

It was the gun that he pulled from inside his coat.

Two

Scarcely had the barrel left the folds of the jacket when Newton heard a deafening blast of fire.

He hurled himself to the ground, covering his head, but as he looked around, the roar of the retort still ringing in his ears, he saw that the unshaven man was lying close to him on his back, a massive hole in his forehead.

Two or three other men stood around him, each with a pistol in his hand. Newton noticed the thin plume of smoke rising from the barrel of one of the hand-guns.

If the unshaven man had been an assassin, it appeared he'd been shot before he could complete his mission. The plain clothes S.A.S. men were rummaging through his pockets, ignoring the blood which was still spouting from his head.

Amazed and relieved at the speed with which they had acted, Newton scrambled to his feet.

The burst of fire from behind him sent him sprawling once more.

Away to his right another man was advancing on the group of politicians, a Skorpion machine-pistol gripped in his hands. He swept it back and forth across the line of pressmen and security men.

To the left was another man, similarly armed.

And another.

Newton had one ridiculous thought as he hugged the ground, his ears ringing from the constant rattle of automatic fire.

How the hell did they get the weapons past security?

As more and more bullets ploughed into the assembled throng Newton saw men fall, clutching wounds. There were screams of fear. Of surprise.

Of pain.

Newton saw one of the Unionist MPs hit, the bullet catching him in the chest and punching through his ribs before erupting from his back.

One of the Sinn Fein men dived for cover, yelling in pain as another bullet took off two of his fingers, the shattered digits spinning into the air. He rolled over on the wet grass. A third high-velocity shell blasted away part of his face.

Soldiers tried to force the politicians back towards the relative safety of the Parliament building. Not that many needed persuading.

Those bullets which didn't strike flesh whined up off the gravel pathways around Stormont or ricocheted off the statues that adorned the ornate gardens. Lumps of stone were blasted from the carvings, the squeal of spent cartridges mingling with the constant roar of fire and the shouts and screams of those being shot.

Another of the attackers was hit but not before he managed to send a stream of fire into the S.A.S. man who'd shot him. Both crashed to the ground. But the gunman's two companions continued pumping bullets into the fleeing politicians. Indeed, into anything that crossed their path.

Newton, who was trying to crawl to a nearby hedge, glanced behind him to see that there were already more than a dozen bodies scattered on the lawn, motionless. He finally reached the hedge and dragged himself behind it, panting like a carthorse, perspiration mingling with the rain which was falling rapidly now.

The air stank of cordite, great bluish-grey clouds of it swirling around gunmen and security men alike. Heaving banks of malevolent fog which grew thicker as the firing continued.

An R.U.C. man fell to the ground, blood jetting from a wound in his neck.

One of his colleagues was shouting into a two-way radio, shielding a member of the Irish Cabinet with his body. The same burst of fire took them both. The radio fell uselessly to the ground a few feet from its bullet-riddled owner.

Some of the politicians had managed to run back towards the building and were joined in their flight by the media.

Newton caught sight of Julie Webb, tears streaming down her face, arms clasped around her head as if to keep her safe. Curled up in a foetal position, she could only scream in terror as bullets tore up the ground around her, little geysers of earth erupting as the 9mm slugs drilled patterns across the ground.

And then one hit her.

It shattered her right wrist, powering through into the top of her skull.

Newton saw her body jerk uncontrollably for a second; then she was still, like so many others around her.

Still the air was filled with the roar of machine-gun fire, spent cartridge cases spraying into the air and rattling on the gravel as they rained down from breeches now hot from so much fire. Muzzle-flashes blazed as the weapons continued to spew forth their deadly load, cutting bloody swathes across those in their path.

Another S.A.S. man was hit, catapulted backwards by the impact of the bullet which stove in his breastbone and left him writhing on the wet grass that, in places, was now slicked crimson.

Then Newton heard another sound, a loud strident wail he recognized as a siren.

Away to his left, two police cars were roaring towards the scene of carnage. It seemed like an eternity to Newton since the firing had begun. It would have surprised him to know that the slaughter was just forty seconds old.

To his right another car, this one unmarked, also sped towards the fire-fight. Its driver was hunched over the wheel.

One of the gunmen shouted something to his companion and pointed first at the police cars then at the other car. The taller of the two men jammed a fresh magazine into his Skorpion and turned it towards the onrushing R.U.C. vehicles, gritting his teeth as he kept his finger tight on the trigger, grunting in pain as an S.A.S. bullet tore through his shoulder.

Bullets spattered the windscreen of the leading vehicle and glass exploded inwards, showering the driver and his companion. The car skidded off the road and ploughed across one of Stormont's immaculate lawns, leaving great furrows in the sodden grass.

The second vehicle kept coming.

As did the unmarked one.

It was as the two cars bore down on the men that Newton suddenly forgot his fear and remembered the camera around his neck.

He fumbled for the Nikon, peering through the view-finder, pinning the two gunmen in his sights as surely as they had their victims.

He clicked off half a dozen shots.

It was the taller man who saw him.

For an agonizing second it seemed to Newton as if time had stood still. Everything was frozen.

The gunman turned towards him, a slight smile on his face almost as if he were posing for the photograph.

Then he opened fire.

The first two shots missed Newton. The third was more accurate.

The bullet from the MP5 hit the camera dead centre, blasting through the lens, piercing the single eye, blowing the camera apart before it thundered into Newton's temple, shattering the frontal bone. The photographer felt a second of agonizing pain, as if he'd been hit with a burning hammer, then the bullet tore through his skull, erupting from the back, carrying a confetti of brain and pulverized bone with it. The impact lifted him off his feet and he crashed to the ground, his hands still gripping what remained of the camera. Pieces of it had been driven back into his head by the passage of the bullet. Blood spread rapidly from what was left of his shattered cranium, his body quivering madly as the muscles finally gave up their hold on life.

The taller man spun round to see that the unmarked car was almost upon them. It skidded to a halt, great geysers of gravel flying up behind it as the rear wheels spun and the driver roared at the two gunmen to get in.

The taller man hurled himself into the passenger seat. His companion, already hit, was not so lucky. One of the S.A.S. men shot him in the back of the head and his body fell heavily on the gravel as the Granada sped off.

The R.U.C. car bore down, hurtling directly towards them, one of its occupants firing out of the window at the oncoming Granada.

The tall man gripped the Skorpion in one fist and opened up, smiling as he saw bullets ripping into the police car. He saw one pierce the windscreen and catch the driver in the face. The car immediately went out of control, skidding madly before ploughing through a hedge, its tail end spinning round.

The driver of the Granada tried to avoid the other vehicle but couldn't. He slammed into its rear end as he passed, the jolt shaking the men in the car.

The remaining policeman struggled from the car, lifting his gun, trying to get a couple of shots at the escaping assassins.

A burst from the MP5 cut him down, bullets ripping into the side of the police car, one of them hitting the petrol tank.

There was a deafening roar and the police car disappeared in a searing ball of orange and yellow flame. Pieces of chassis were sent spinning into the air like blazing shrapnel. A mushroom cloud of dense

14

black smoke billowed upwards into the sky, darker even than the rain clouds which wept over the scene of destruction below them.

Pieces of broken equipment littered the ground, scattered amongst the bodies of the dead and dying and those who might still be too terrified to move. Moans of pain mingled with the roaring flames belching from the wreck of the police car. Politicians, security men and members of the media crawled amongst the bodies, ignoring the rain which drenched them and the blood which spattered their clothes.

A television camera, its operator dead from a wound in the back, continued to turn, recording the scene of devastation until someone inadvertently bumped into it and sent it crashing to the ground.

The sound of more sirens filled the air, adding to the cacophony. The pain, the roar of flames.

The Granada was long gone.

Three

BRITTANY, FRANCE:
Even in bright sunlight the church looked dark.

Its bell-tower thrust upwards into the air like an accusing finger, pointing at the blue sky where a blazing sun was suspended like some burnished ring. There was very little cloud in the sky and what there was appeared only as thin white wisps against the watery blue of the heavens. A light breeze stirred the long grass that grew all around the church and also on the hills that overlooked it.

Instead of being raised high on the hilltop, the building seemed to have been relegated to the valley floor, as if it were something to be hidden from view; to be shunned instead of exalted.

A house of God where few had been and which, it seemed, God himself had decided to pass by.

The church was old and the passing years had not been kind to it. The stonework was worn, cracked in places so deeply that the entire structure looked to be in danger of collapsing. The remnants of a weather-vane twisted on top of a bell-tower which had housed no bell for hundreds of years. Where it was no one knew and no one cared.

No one ever visited the church.

The nearest village was over five miles away, the church itself set back from the narrow road which wound through the Brittany countryside.

No birds nested in the eaves. No rats frequented the hollow shell of the building.

Neither man, animal or God, it seemed, was interested in the place.

Carl Bressard stood on the hilltop looking down at the church, feeling cold despite the warmth of the sun on his skin. He looked up briefly as if to remind himself that the burning orb was still there and, as he did, a thicker wisp of cloud drifted slowly in front of it, casting a momentary shadow over the valley and the church.

Phillipe Roulon saw the look on his companion's face and smiled.

'You're afraid,' he said scornfully, sticking his face close to his friend's.

Carl would have liked to tell Phillipe he wasn't, but if he had he would have been lying.

But, he thought, what was there to be afraid of? The church was empty and had been for years, far longer than the ten years he had been on the earth. Hundreds of years, his parents had told him, when he asked them about it. They'd told him it had not been used for more than two hundred years.

Then they had told him to keep away from it.

He had asked why, but they had told him not to question their word. He was to keep away from it. It was as simple as that.

Phillipe had been told the same thing by his mother. He had no father. In fact he could scarcely remember the man who had died when he was just five years old. The intervening six years had served to blur the vision of the man in much the same way as an old photo gradually fades.

He had seen the church himself before but, as now, only from a distance. As he looked down at it he felt the goose pimples rise on his flesh. But he couldn't back out. Not now. They would go in together.

Into this place which had been forbidden to them.

Perhaps to discover why it was forbidden.

The two boys looked at one another for a moment then set off down the hill, Carl almost tripping in the long grass as they ran. But, giggling now, they hurtled down the slope, their speed increased by the sharp decline in the land.

As they reached the valley floor they slowed their pace.

The church was less than two hundred yards away now.

It had seemed small from the hilltop but now, as they looked at it, the structure seemed massive. Its walls were dark and it looked as if it had been built not from

17

individual pieces of stone but hewn from one single lump of rock. The monolithic edifice may well have been spewed up from the earth itself, disgorged by the land. Unwanted by nature as well as by God and man.

The two boys took faltering steps towards the church, their eyes fixed on it.

Carl could see that, where there had once been stained-glass windows, there were now only yawning holes in the rock. Wounds in the stone which had been given temporary scabs in the form of boarding, nailed haphazardly across the gaps with little care for appearance. The nails which held the boards in place were rusted and broken. Some of the boards were hanging free. One swung gently back and forth, pushed by the wind which now seemed to be much stronger.

The sun burned with continued radiance but both boys felt the chill grow more intense the closer they drew to the church.

Neither dared stop walking. Neither wanted to show his fear to the other.

Besides, what was there to fear in an empty stone building?

Carl tried to comfort himself with that thought but it did little to lessen the speed at which his heart was beating.

Another cloud passed close to the sun, throwing the valley into shadow once again. This time both boys froze until the warmth returned.

They moved closer.

The grass around the church was even longer and the boys had to lift their feet high to prevent themselves tripping over the green tendrils that seemed to grasp at their shoes.

A strong gust of wind sent the weather-vane

spinning. The dull creak of rusty metal cut through the silence like a blade. There was a narrow gravel path around the church, also overgrown with weeds and grass, but at least it made walking easier. The two boys, now moving side by side, made their way along the building towards the front of the church.

The huge double doors loomed over them. The wood was rotten in places, the metal bracing rusted and flaking like dry, scabrous skin. Two massive circular rings hung down from the doors. It was over one of these that Carl's hand hovered.

All he had to do was pull the door open and the church could be entered.

'Go on,' Phillipe said, his voice soft now, the bravado gone from it.

Carl touched the rusted ring and pulled.

The door wouldn't budge.

'I knew it would be locked,' he said, stepping back with relief.

'Try the other one.'

He shrugged, felt the colour draining from his cheeks.

'Come on,' snapped Phillipe.

'You open it,' Carl hissed, standing back, watching as his companion steadied himself and gripped the iron ring in both hands.

There was a muffled groan of protest from the rusted hinges as the door opened a fraction.

Phillipe let go of the metal ring as if it had suddenly become hot. He wiped his hands on his jeans, noticing how the rust stains looked like dried blood.

The door was open wide enough to allow them to slip inside.

Both boys stood looking up at the open door, waiting

for some kind of signal it seemed, to tell them what to do next.

They could see into the church now, or at least as far as the impenetrable blackness which filled it.

Phillipe was the first to move towards the door, urging Carl to follow him, snapping an insult when he hesitated.

The sun was still obscured by a cloud although Carl suspected the chill he felt was more the result of fear than from the absence of the warming rays. There was no turning back now. He had to enter. Enter this empty church which his parents had warned him not to go near.

Empty.

He tried to cling to the word, seeking comfort in it.

Empty.

He moved closer to the door.

Empty.

Both boys slipped inside.

It stank. Of neglect. Of decay. Of damp. As if the passing years had caused the very air itself to decay and rot so that each inhalation the boys took was rank. Carl felt as if he was swallowing some particularly vile medicine. He wanted to spit it out.

More than anything he wanted to be back out in the light again.

Shafts of sunlight pierced the gloom in places, poking through cracks in the boarding which covered the holes where the stained glass windows had been, casting enough light for the boys to see where they were going but not sufficient to illuminate the interior.

The watery shafts seemed incapable of penetrating such overwhelming blackness.

It was as if even the sunlight sought no access to this place.

The two boys moved slowly down the central aisle of the church, peering around them into the gloom.

Pews, unfrequented for years, were overturned on either side of them. Rotten. Broken. In places they had been piled up against the wall, like bonfires waiting to be lit.

As the boys walked they found that their footsteps were curiously muffled. Suffocated by the thick layer of dust and dirt which carpeted the church floor like a noxious rug. They left footprints in the dust.

They moved towards the chancel. Here, the air itself seemed to be black. It was more difficult to breathe.

Carl coughed, the sound echoing around the confines of the church before being swallowed by the silence and the gloom.

There was a doorway in the wall which separated the chancel from the nave.

The door was slightly ajar.

'Let's go now,' Carl said, his voice low.

Phillipe moved towards the doorway, which was momentarily illuminated by the intrusion of a shaft of sunlight forcing its way between two boards on a nearby window.

'The altar is through here,' Phillipe said. 'That's where it happened.'

'You go,' Carl said, finally unashamed of his fear.

He stood watching. He didn't care if Phillipe and all his friends called him a coward when he got back to the village.

He did not want to go through that door. Even if the church was empty.

Empty.

Perhaps just a quick look.

Empty.

Phillipe was about to push open the door.

Encouraged by his friend's bravery and curiosity, Carl moved alongside him and they prepared to pass through together.

The door suddenly swung open, a particularly bright shaft of sunlight slicing through the darkness.

And in that moment they both saw the figure.

The figure moving towards them.

Four

He had heard the sounds inside the church and wondered who had come to disturb his work.

Now Mark Channing watched as the two small boys ran screaming from the building.

He stood still for a moment, scratching his chin, wondering why his appearance had so terrified the visitors. Hadn't they noticed his car parked on the Western side of the church? Obviously not, he reasoned, watching as the two figures hurtled from the door and out into the sunshine beyond. The church was silent again, the way Channing liked it. He smiled to himself and turned back into the chancel, pushing the door shut behind him.

Two battery-powered lights illuminated the chancel itself, throwing out a cold white glow which cast everything into deep shadow. Channing poured himself a cup of tea from the thermos flask in his bag and stood sipping it, looking around him.

To his left the stairs which led up into the belfry

thrust upwards into even more cloying darkness. To his right, supporting the two lamps, was the altar. Or what had once been an altar.

It was a piece of flat stone, marble-smooth and relatively unmarked. He had spread several of his notepads out on it. A package of sandwiches and the remains of a half-eaten pork pie he'd consumed about half an hour ago also lay there, like offerings to some culinary deity.

The windows on either side of the chancel were, like the windows in the remainder of the church, now missing. Boarded up like those in the nave.

Channing's work on the church had revealed that the stonework around the windows had been chipped away, indicating that the windows had been removed. Actually physically taken from their place in the stone, frames and everything. Their absence was not the result of an act of vandalism but of careful, reasoned thought.

But thought which had its basis in superstition and fear.

Channing knew the church and the surrounding area well. He knew them by association. By what he'd read and what he'd written. This was the first time that he'd ever been inside the place, though.

He'd arrived in France five days earlier and he'd been working at the church for the last three. He didn't have to seek anyone's permission to enter the building. No one in any of the towns or villages close by seemed to care that he was going to be working there and Channing had been unable to discover who owned the land on which the old building stood. The church was one of the few remaining testaments to the fact that, at one time, this part of Brittany had been the domain of that province's richest inhabitant.

But that had been over four hundred years ago.

Channing had sought out the church for a number of reasons. He had been owed some holiday from his post as a senior lecturer at Balliol, so he'd taken the opportunity to come to Brittany for a break as much as anything else. But his main objective had been to see the church he'd previously only read about.

Its owner, however, was more familiar to him, having been the subject of a treatise he'd written two years earlier. It had been featured in a book produced by one of the country's top publishers. The book's title escaped him (although he remembered it as a flippant, under-researched tome; apart from his own piece, of course). The name of his subject didn't.

The former owner of this dank, deserted place had been Gilles de Rais.

During the fourteenth century, de Rais had been responsible for the ritual murders of over two hundred children, many of them in the church where Channing now stood. The church had merely been part of de Rais' vast estate called Machecoul. The man had been a hero in his native country; he was made a Marshal of France for his part in the fighting against the English during the Hundred Years War and, at the height of his power, he had been rumoured to be the richest nobleman in all of Europe. But his love of expensive living and a horde of parasitic advisers, all syphoning money from de Rais' coffers, had eventually turned him from rich man to bankrupt.

It was then that he had turned to alchemy.

Then that the killings had begun.

Channing sipped more tea and again glanced around the chancel, his attention focused on the boarded-up windows.

As he turned he saw something glinting dully; one of the rapier-like spears of sunlight, forcing its way into the gloom, bounced back off something to his left.

The historian put down his cup and crossed the chancel, careful not to obstruct the shaft of light.

Below a gap in the stone left by the removal of a window there was a tiny square of luminosity, as if something within the stone itself were burning.

Channing took a small chisel from the bag which lay beside the altar and began tapping at the area around the glowing square, gradually realizing that the sunlight was striking glass.

Coloured glass.

He frowned.

The stonework was old and brittle but still remarkably strong and resistant to the chisel, so much so that Channing hit it with the heel of his hand.

A crack appeared in the wall, running rapidly from one part of the stonework to another for a distance of about two feet. Several small pieces of rock fell to the floor, their sound amplified by the silence within the chancel.

Channing reached for the small mallet that lay on the altar and, steadying himself, used it to strike the chisel.

Another crack appeared in the stone.

A larger lump fell away.

He was breathing heavily now as he continued to chip away at the crumbling stonework.

More rock came away, falling at his feet.

Then finally he saw what the stone had hidden.

Channing swallowed hard, his eyes widening as he peered through the gloom, the sunlight which had forced its way into the chancel now fading.

Only the light from the battery lamps illuminated what he saw.

He licked his lips, his heart thudding hard against his ribs as he stared.

Only two words escaped him, muffled by the darkness and silence within the church, but low because of his own shock. He stared on, unblinking.

'Jesus Christ,' he murmured.

Five

Channing's hands were shaking as he twisted the key in the ignition.

The car roared into life at the first attempt and the historian jammed it into gear, guiding it over the gently undulating land towards the road that would lead him back to the nearby village of Machecoul. The sun was still high in the sky but more clouds were beginning to fill the heavens, some dark. Every now and then they would obscure the sun and the land would be momentarily cloaked in shadow. The wind which had been blowing all day seemed to have strengthened. As he drove, Channing saw that the trees by the roadside were swaying more violently with each gust.

He gripped the wheel tightly, aware that his palms were moist. Tiny droplets of perspiration had beaded on his forehead.

Not all of them the product of the warmth inside the car.

What he'd found in the church had surprised him.

No, he corrected himself, it had shocked him. Shaken him. Not merely because he had not been expecting it but also by its nature.

The vision of what he had left behind there was still strong in his mind, seared into his consciousness like some kind of brand.

He shuddered as he drove, angry with himself for his initial reaction, but unable to shake the feeling of shock nonetheless.

He administered a swift mental rebuke, angered that his own professionalism had been tested and found wanting. His self-control had cracked just like the stonework in the church.

He turned the car swiftly along the winding road, anxious to reach the village and the small inn where he was staying. Anxious to get to a phone.

There was a call he had to make.

He slowed his speed slightly as he reached the outskirts of Machecoul, guiding the car around the stalls which occupied the market place. The residents of the village were busy going about their business. Farmers had brought produce in from local farms to sell and, as he parked the car outside the inn, Channing could hear voices filtering through the air, arguing good-naturedly, bartering, laughing.

But that scene of rural life was not for him. He had more important things on his mind.

He scuttled into the small, white-painted inn, noticing how cool it felt compared to outside. The plump woman who ran the place gave him the key to his room and was about to ask him if he was all right when he disappeared in the direction of the stairs that led up to his bedroom.

There were only about ten rooms let to guests and

27

most of those, at the moment, were empty.

Channing let himself in, crossed straight to the phone beside his bed and picked up the receiver.

He dialled, cursing under his breath when he realized he'd forgotten the international code for England. He dialled again. The international code, then the code for London, then the number he required.

His hand was shaking slightly.

He held the receiver to his ear, listening to the assortment of pops, crackles and hisses that ran down the line as his number was connected. At the far end the phone was ringing.

And ringing.

'Come on,' he murmured, impatiently.

And ringing.

'Hello,' a feminine voice began.

'Hello Cath,' he said breathlessly.

The other voice continued.

'This is Catherine Roberts. I'm afraid there's no one here at the moment …'

'Shit,' rasped Channing, slamming the phone down. Bloody answering machine. He waited a second then dialled again and waited.

The same metallic voice greeted him and he was about to replace the receiver a second time when he heard a buzz as the machine was switched off. 'Hello,' the voice repeated.

'Cath, is that you?' he said.

'Yes, who's that?' the woman on the other end asked.

'It's Mark Channing. I didn't want to talk to that bloody machine.'

'I just walked through the door,' she explained. 'I thought you were in Brittany.'

'I am. Listen to me, Cath. I've been to the church at

Machecoul,' he told her, his voice low, almost breathless. 'There's something there. You have to see it.'

'What is it?' she wanted to know.

'When can you fly out?'

'Mark, for God's sake,' she began, almost laughing. 'I can't just drop everything.'

'You have to,' he insisted, and she was aware of the anxiety in his voice. 'This is important. It's in your field.'

'My field?' she said vaguely, puzzled by his urgency.

'You're an art historian, for Christ's sake,' he snarled, as if he needed to remind her of her profession. 'A medievalist. I need you to look at what I've found. I need your help.'

Six

COUNTY CORK, THE REPUBLIC OF IRELAND:
The line of cocaine seemed almost phosphorescent in the dimly-lit bedroom.

Laura Callahan, her naked body covered by a thin sheen of perspiration, swept the long brown hair from her face and knelt beside the table where the coke was waiting. Two razor-blades lay close by.

She pressed the first two fingers of her right hand against her right nostril and carefully, lovingly pushed the tip of her nose into the line, smiling broadly as she caught the first few grains of powder. Laura inhaled, sliding over the table as she drew the fine white powder

29

into her nostril. She writhed, her eyes closed in ecstasy, feeling the coldness growing inside her nostril as she took in more and more of the coke. As she slithered over the polished wood she looked down and saw her reflection. The sight pleased her.

Her body was firm, her breasts small but the nipples hard. She paused for a moment to admire her reflection. The flat stomach, the smooth hips and the tiny triangle of dark hair between her legs. She allowed one finger to stir the tightly-curled pubic hair, teasing herself for a second before returning to the line of cocaine.

She snorted the remainder then rolled off the table, her breath coming in gasps.

As she rolled over she pressed her legs tightly together and felt moisture beading on her upper thighs. She sat up, one finger stirring the swollen outer lips of her vagina, tracing a pattern over the warm wet flesh until she reached the hardened nub of her clitoris.

She gasped as she stroked it.

Cocaine flecked her nose and her upper lip and she flicked her tongue out to remove it, feeling the same momentary numbness in her mouth as she did in her nose. She giggled, then crawled across towards the bed, towards the man who lay there waiting for her.

He too was naked, his erection throbbing against his stomach as he lay back, a drink cradled in one of his large hands.

She kissed his right foot as she pulled up onto the bed. Then, moving higher, she kissed his shins, his knees, his thighs. Only here she paused, allowing her tongue to dart out and taste the flesh of his leg. She bit it gently then licked, leaving a trail of saliva as she moved closer to his groin.

David Callahan watched, an amused smile on his face. He reached down and slowly entwined some of her long hair around his hand, gripping it, pulling her up higher until her mouth was in line with his penis.

He grinned as she kissed the bulbous head, allowing her tongue to creep into the narrow eye of the glans, licking away a dribble of clear fluid.

As she sat up she saw the lines of coke on his body.

One ran from each of his shoulders down as far as his groin.

She looked at him and laughed, kissing his chest, careful not to disturb the precious white powder. Then, beginning with the line at his left shoulder, she snorted her way down his body until the musky smell of his pubic hair, already matted with her own secretions from earlier on, mingled with the coke.

She laid her head on his stomach this time, careful not to displace the other line with her hair. Then, slowly, she moved her head forward, her lips enveloping his penis, her tongue slithering around the shaft. With one hand she began to massage his swollen testicles, allowing her free hand to reach back between her own legs, to stir the wetness there.

She felt other fingers alongside her own and then Callahan himself was pushing first his index finger then his middle finger into her dripping cleft, his thumb rubbing her clitoris, making her moan softly as she continued to suck his erection.

She sat up, his fingers still inside her, anxious to reach the second line of cocaine.

Laura took it into her other nostril this time, breathing it in as she slid down once more towards Callahan's groin. This time, she took his penis into her mouth and kept it there. Sucking and kissing as he

31

pushed his fingers into her with increasing speed, smiling as he felt the liquid pleasure covering the probing digits.

She stroked his thighs and rubbed his scrotum, aware that he, like she herself, was reaching a climax. Laura prepared herself for his ejaculation, clamping her mouth more firmly onto his throbbing organ as she felt his penis jerk, heard him grunt with pleasure.

And then her mouth was flooded with the oily, white fluid, gouts of it shooting into her throat. She swallowed as fast as she could until her mouth was full and some of the sticky liquid dribbled from the sides of it.

She felt her own orgasm surge through her and opened her mouth to gasp her pleasure as his fingers rammed deeper into her and she too spilled her ecstacy onto his hand.

Callahan gradually withdrew his fingers from her and held them before her.

She sucked at them, licking the slicks of fluid, sucking his fingertips like a hungry child would suck a nipple.

She tasted herself. She tasted his emission on her tongue.

They laughed loudly as they embraced, both coated in sweat from their pleasure. Then they both looked towards the bottom of the bed and grinned.

The image disappeared instantly as David Callahan pressed the 'Stop' button on the video.

Lying beside him on the huge bed, Laura Callahan took a sip of Jack Daniels and smiled. She moved closer to her husband, one hand reaching for his stiffening penis.

'You were great,' said Callahan, smiling. 'You should get an Oscar.'

32

'I don't want an Oscar,' she purred, nuzzling his neck. 'I want you.' She closed her hand around his erection.

Callahan thrust into her hard and she raised her legs, allowing him deeper penetration, finally locking her ankles behind his back as his movements became more forceful.

The video camera at the bottom of the bed regarded them impassively this time, their lovemaking reflected in its single glass eye.

Seven

In the silence of the bedroom he could hear her breathing.

There was a slightly nasal quality to Laura's exhalations, a product of more than five years on cocaine.

Callahan didn't know exactly what it did to the nasal passages. He didn't really care. She enjoyed it. Who was *he* to deny her pleasure?

He sat up in bed, careful not to disturb his wife. For long moments he watched her sleeping: the steady rise and fall of her chest, the gentle pulse in her throat. Then, carefully, he swung himself out of bed, pulled on his bathrobe and padded across the bedroom towards the bathroom. Once inside he flicked on the light, wincing as the fluorescents buzzed into life. Callahan turned on the tap, scooped some water into his mouth and smoothed his hand through his short dark hair. He stood before the mirror gazing at his reflection, pleased with what he saw.

He was thirty-six, four years older than his wife, and his body was still lean and muscular. He opened the bathrobe to inspect his pectoral muscles. He worked out every morning in the small gym which he'd had built into the house when they'd first bought it two years ago. The house and the fifteen acres of land which went with it had been relatively cheap, certainly to a man of Callahan's means. He wasn't sure exactly how many million he was worth. He didn't think that much about money. He had more than he'd ever need so there wasn't the necessity to think about it. Only those who didn't have enough were obsessed with the stuff, he thought, amused by his own philosophy.

He splashed more water onto his face, wiping the excess moisture away with the sleeve of his bathrobe. Then he tugged on the string and the bathroom was plunged into darkness again.

Callahan moved back into the bedroom, glancing across at Laura.

She had rolled onto her side now, her legs drawn up to her chest.

Callahan stood gazing at her for a moment then crossed to the window.

Their bedroom was at the front of the house and, with the aid of the large spotlights which blazed from the roof, Callahan could see about twenty or thirty yards down the wide driveway which approached the massive house.

Visible through the gloom were the stables which housed half a dozen horses. To the right of them stood a couple of barns. Another gap of ten yards or so and the west wing of the house was visible.

The whole building was white-washed, in places its walls covered by ivy that grew so densely the stonework was almost totally obscured by the parasitic plant. Elsewhere dozens of windows reflected the night like scores of blind eyes.

All except one.

Callahan gazed out over the driveway in front of the house, peering close to the glass of the window to get a better view.

A light came on in one of the downstairs rooms.

He looked at his watch, the hands glowing sickly green in the darkness.

3.32 a.m.

Surely none of the staff would be up at this time of the morning.

The light went off again and Callahan relaxed for a moment.

He rubbed his eyes, as if he'd just woken.

The light came on again.

Went off.

Came on.

Callahan turned and headed for the bed, stopping short, pulling open the drawer of the cabinet beside it.

From the top drawer he pulled out a Smith and Wesson .38.

He flipped out the cylinder, checking that the weapon was full, then, satisfied that it was, he crossed back to the window and looked out.

The light was still on in the downstairs room.

Callahan gripped the revolver in his fist. Glancing back at Laura, he headed for the bedroom door.

Eight

The silence inside the house was almost oppressive, the only sounds coming from Callahan himself as he moved quickly but quietly across the vast landing towards the head of the stairs.

As he reached the balustrade he stopped and peered over, looking down into the hallway. Without lights it was like looking into a well. He thought about flicking on the switch at the top of the stairs, flooding the flight of steps and the hall beneath with bright light, and his finger hovered for a moment before he decided against that course of action. Instead he gripped the .38 more tightly and began to descend.

The fourth step creaked loudly in the silence and Callahan muttered something under his breath, pausing for a moment in the stillness.

The room where he'd seen the light, however, was well away from the stairs. Even if there were anyone in there it was unlikely they'd heard the groaning stair.

He pressed on, taking the steps more quickly now, anxious to reach the bottom.

Could it be an intruder, he wondered?

That possibility seemed unlikely.

The house itself was more than fifteen miles from the nearest village, the grounds protected by a stone wall twelve feet high.

Any intruder met a sophisticated alarm system wired to every door and window inside the house itself and

36

there was also the distinct possibility that they might disturb one of the members of staff.

If there was an intruder in the house then they were both determined *and* expert.

Unless it wasn't a burglar.

Callahan paused a moment longer, feeling the sweat on his palms. He let go of the revolver and wiped both hands on his bathrobe before seizing the gun once more.

Not a burglar.

Maybe the intruder didn't want his money or his valuables.

Maybe they wanted *him*.

Callahan had made enough enemies in his time, on both sides of the law and on both sides of the Irish sea. He knew there were men who, even now, would pay a great deal of money to see him dead.

That was one of the reasons he'd been forced to leave London. The situation there had simply become too dangerous for him. He'd had too much to lose, his life not being the least.

He gripped the pistol tighter and moved out of the hall towards the door on his right.

It led through into a long corridor flanked on either side by more closed doors.

Callahan paused beside the door, then swiftly turned the knob and stepped through.

The room where he'd seen the light was ahead of him, around a bend in the corridor.

On the walls on both sides paintings hung: here a Matisse, there a Dali. Further down there was a Goya. They were all originals. All priceless now.

Callahan moved slowly down the corridor, his footsteps muffled by the thick carpet. He was aware of his own low breathing as he moved further towards the bend.

As he reached it he stopped again, a single bead of perspiration squeezing itself onto his forehead.

There were more light switches at hand but he resisted the temptation to flick them on. He saw the thin band of light beneath the door directly in front of him.

Callahan approached slowly, his eyes on the thin strip of luminosity.

The light went out.

He froze.

Had whoever was inside heard him?

The brightness returned.

Callahan gritted his teeth, pulled the .38 from his pocket and moved towards the door again, his hand hovering over the knob.

There was no sound from inside.

Except ...

What the hell was that noise?

He stood close to the door, listening, a frown creasing his brow.

The light went off once more.

Callahan actually had his hand on the handle now, turning it slowly, praying to a God he didn't believe in that it wouldn't squeak.

'Right, you bastard,' he whispered under his breath.

He threw the door open, the pistol raised before him.

As he did the light came flickering on and, as it did, he heard the noise again.

A buzzing, puttering sound.

It came from above him.

From the fluorescent light which was flickering on and off.

It was faulty. The bloody light was faulty.

Callahan chuckled, shook his head and exhaled deeply, annoyed with himself for having allowed fear to take such a hold on him. Christ, what the imagination could do to you! But there was also relief in his exhalation.

Relief that there had been no one in the room.

He looked at the .38 in his hand and slipped it back into his pocket. No one this time, but next time who could tell? He wondered how much longer he would have to wait.

Callahan flicked off the faulty light, making a mental note to get one of the staff to fix it in the morning. He turned and headed back down the corridor, past the Matisse and the Dali and the Goya and the sculptures. Past all the possessions that testified to the magnitude of his wealth.

As he closed the door he could not help but glance over his shoulder, as if this had been some kind of warning. A portent.

He knew they would come eventually.

But when they did, he'd be ready for them.

Nine

The house in Porten Road, Hammersmith was unremarkable; a simple terraced place badly in need of some exterior decoration.

Sean Doyle sat in the Datsun, one foot up on the dashboard, alternately glancing out of the window and flicking at the laces that hung from his baseball boots.

Doyle noticed how some of the houses, formerly council, had been bought by their occupants. Many sported the mock-stone frontages that seemed the mark of new owner-occupiers. All taking advantage of the Government's wonderful offer to own the houses they'd lived in since rent was ten shillings a week, thought Doyle, gazing at the rows of houses.

Lights burned in many front windows, promising warmth beyond their closed curtains.

It wasn't too warm inside the car and Doyle turned up the heating, massaging his left leg as he felt a twinge of cramp in his calf. He lowered his leg, raising his right instead, propping that against the dashboard.

He flicked on the radio, tired of the silence.

Doyle twisted the frequency dial but found only vacuous pop music, the same sanitized crap on every station, it seemed. There was a play on Radio Four but he skipped by that and finally found the tail end of a Black Sabbath track, but the static was so bad he decided to turn the set off again.

Doyle was bored. He'd been sitting in the car for nearly two hours already. His back ached, his arse ached and his head was beginning to ache. He fumbled in the glove compartment for the remains of a Mars Bar he'd started devouring earlier. He hadn't eaten for over six hours, apart from the few mouthfuls of chocolate. At two-thirty that afternoon he'd bought a hamburger but now his stomach was growling loudly. He patted it in a gesture of placation, then yawned and tried to stretch in the confines of the car, hearing his shoulders and elbows crack.

He coughed and looked around once more, catching sight of his own reflection in the rear-view mirror. He ran both hands through his shoulder-length brown hair. His eyes looked sunken, as if someone had coloured in the area beneath his lower lids with dark ink. His haggard look was negated somewhat, however, by the gleam of his dark grey eyes. They seemed to glow in the dull light of the street lamp, darting back and forth with an alertness and energy that seemed to have deserted the rest of his body.

He rubbed his hands together and stuck them in the pockets of his leather jacket, slumping back in his seat and gazing out into the street. He could feel the ache beginning to creep up from the small of his back. He fidgeted, trying to make himself comfortable. Thirty years old and you're a fucking wreck, he told himself, a slight smile creasing his lips.

Unlike most of the other houses in Porten Road, no light burned in the window of Number 22.

In fact, no light burned anywhere in the place. Not that he could see, anyway. He knew, however, that there were people inside. He'd seen three enter in the last thirty minutes. The first had arrived in a battered old Capri which he'd parked across the street from where Doyle now sat. He'd let himself in by the front door, glancing furtively around before opening it.

The other two had arrived together about ten minutes ago.

Doyle checked his watch.

8.36 p.m.

On this side of the road a man was walking his dog, trying to keep the wretched animal under control as it jerked and pulled on the end of the lead. Doyle smiled to himself as the man swore at the Alsatian which, it seemed, had decided to cross the street, tugging its reluctant owner with it. He watched them in the rear-view mirror and caught sight of another man.

41

The newcomer was short and stocky, hands tucked deep into the pockets of an overcoat. He glanced at the Alsatian, quickening his pace when it seemed to be making for *him*.

Doyle saw the man turn into the short pathway that led to the door of Number 22. He walked up to the door and knocked once. The door was opened a fraction and the man entered.

Quite a gathering, Doyle thought, checking his watch again.

Another five minutes.

He yawned and rubbed his eyes, blinking myopically through the gloom.

'Panther One, come in.'

The voice sounded loud in the confines of the car, despite the fact that there was a newspaper laid over the two-way radio.

'Panther One, do you read me, over?'

Doyle picked up the newspaper, glancing again at the photo of the topless model. Her name was Tina and she was a hairdresser; the caption said, 'Guaranteed to make your hair curl.' Doyle grinned and tossed the paper onto the back seat.

'Panther One, for Christ's sake …'

He picked up the two-way.

'Panther One. Don't have a fit, I can hear you,' Doyle said quietly, eyes still scanning the street ahead of him.

'Then why didn't you answer?' the metallic voice demanded.

'I did answer. I'm speaking to you now. What the fuck do you want?'

'We're in position.'

'Good for you,' said Doyle disinterestedly, eyes still roving.

42

'Porten Road, Ceylon Road and Milson Road are all closed off,' the voice told him.

Doyle didn't answer. He'd spotted another man approaching the front door of Number 22.

'Doyle, I said …'

'I heard what you said. Stand by.' Still gripping the two-way, Doyle watched as the man advanced towards the door and knocked twice. He bounced up and down on the balls of his feet as he waited for it to be opened. When it finally was, he walked in, disappearing from view. Doyle held on to the two-way with his left hand; with his right he reached inside his jacket.

The rubber grips of the CZ-75 automatic brushed against his finger-tips as he felt the shoulder holster.

In another holster, worn around his waist, hidden by his leather jacket, he carried a much more formidable weapon. The .44 Bulldog, despite its small size, could put a hole in a wall at two hundred yards.

'You and your men ready?' Doyle asked, eyes now fixed on the front door of Number 22.

'I told you we're in position,' the voice replied irritably.

'Well, tell them to stay out of my fucking way. Let's go. It's party time.'

Ten

As Doyle swung himself out of the car he saw other men running towards Number 22.

Some were in uniform.

Doyle made it to the door first, vaulting the gate as if there were some kind of prize for reaching the house ahead of his colleagues. He didn't slow his pace, merely ran at the door and launched himself at it, slamming against the wood, which creaked protestingly. He took a step back and drove a powerful kick against the lock, grinning when the door crashed back on its hinges. He dashed into the hallway, followed by two of the uniformed men.

The place smelt of damp, neglect and something more pungent which Doyle recognised as urine. But smells didn't bother him. He heard raised voices from a room to his left and he turned.

'Upstairs,' came a shout from behind him.

Two of the uniformed constables thundered up the stairs. Doyle kicked the door ahead of him open, the CZ now gripped in his fist. He stepped away from the door, heard more shouts from inside.

From the rear of the house there was the sound of breaking glass. Curses.

He ducked into what was supposed to be the sitting room. There was a battered old sofa, the stuffing spilling out of one arm. Two wooden chairs. Nothing else. The floor was bare board.

There were three men inside the room and Doyle levelled his pistol at the closest one.

The man immediately raised his hands in surrender, his face losing its colour as if the blood had been sucked from his cheeks.

Doyle heard more shouts coming from the rear of the house then, suddenly, there was the ear-splitting roar of a gun.

He glanced to his right and, in that split second, one of the men facing him dashed towards the window.

He hit the glass with the force of a steam-hammer, crashing through the dirtied panes, shattering the wooden slats and sending crystal shards flying into the air. He hit the ground, rolled over once and ran for the road.

'Watch them,' shouted Doyle and hurtled after the fleeing man. He vaulted the fence and sped after the escaping figure, who glanced over his shoulder to see his pursuer gaining.

Up and down Porten Road curtains were being drawn to one side as the commotion roused neighbours. Curious faces peered out into the night and saw the chase unfolding before them.

The man Doyle was pursuing was several years younger, but he had not counted on the other man's fitness. He ran round a car and into the street. Doyle merely leapt up onto the bonnet then launched himself at his foe, missing him by inches. He rolled over and got to his feet, seeing the other man, dressed in a blue jacket and jeans, heading across the street towards a passageway between two houses.

Doyle followed as the man battered his way through a wooden gate at the head of the passage.

Blue-jacket ran on, spinning to his right, into the garden at the rear of the house. There was a high fence partitioning the back yards and Blue-jacket began scaling it. Doyle skidded around the corner in time to see the other man scrambling over the fence. Doyle holstered his pistol, allowing himself the use of both hands, threw himself at the partition and clambered up and over it. He dropped down beside a fish pond as he continued his pursuit.

A hedge was the next obstacle and Blue-jacket leapt it easily.

Doyle followed, his eyes never leaving his quarry, homed in on the fleeing man as if they were locked on by radar.

The man looked back, surprised to see Doyle still in pursuit. He was no more than ten yards away now and Blue-jacket could feel his own breath rasping in his throat as he desperately sought some way back into the road, some passageway.

If only he could get to the car.

Ahead of him there was another fence and a greenhouse, and beyond that a much taller wall. He leapt the fence, almost falling as he landed.

Doyle saw the obstacles too but he slowed his pace.

There was no way his quarry was going to get over the wall. This was the end of the road, he thought, grinning.

He pulled the CZ from its holster and stood still.

'Stand still,' he roared, settling himself, drawing a bead on his foe.

Blue-jacket spun round, saw the gun and slowed his pace slightly.

'Fuck you,' he bellowed back, stepping slowly towards the greenhouse, not really knowing where he was going but knowing that the Englishman would not fire.

His eyes widened in a mixture of shock and terror as he realized he was wrong.

Doyle fired twice.

The first bullet hit the man in the chest, the second in the throat.

The impact lifted him off his feet and his body catapulted several feet backwards, as if punched by an invisible fist. He crashed into the greenhouse, which promptly collapsed around him, showering him with huge fragments of glass. The noise was deafening as the crystal shards rained down around him, cutting his flesh. Blood from the lacerations mingled with the crimson fluid already spurting from the two bullet wounds.

Doyle walked across to the body and looked down at it, kicking one of the man's outstretched legs. He noticed that the body was lying on some tomato plants, and blood had spattered the fruit.

Doyle, ignoring the smell which rose from the corpse, pulled a tomato free and began chewing on it, looking down at the dead man.

The back doors of the house opened and a man emerged. He looked at the scene of carnage and shouted something Doyle didn't catch. Then, as the man repeated it, he heard the words more clearly.

'Call the law,' the man shouted to someone inside the house.

Doyle took another bite from the tomato, wiping the juice from his chin.

'No need,' he said, holstering the CZ. 'I *am* the law.'

Eleven

The blue lights of the ambulance turned in silence, bathing the area in a dull glow. Without its siren the vehicle seemed curiously serene. Doyle leant against the bonnet of his car, smoking. The tableau before him looked like a film to which someone had forgotten to add the sound.

There were policemen, uniformed and plain-clothes,

47

milling about in the road, some gathered around in groups, others talking to the occupants of other houses. Many were standing on their front doorsteps peering out at the activity. Two police cars were parked outside Number 22. Ten minutes earlier a van had arrived and the four remaining occupants had been bundled inside and driven off. The battered Capri had also been towed away by a police pick-up truck. Doyle sucked gently on his cigarette and watched the other men scuttle to and fro, his attention finally drawn to some movement off to his left.

Two ambulancemen emerged from the passageway between the two houses carrying the body of the man Doyle had shot.

His body was covered by a blanket.

A tall, slightly overweight policeman walked alongside the stretcher. He glared at Doyle as he passed but the younger man merely took a final drag on his cigarette and ground it out beneath his foot. He wandered across towards the rear of the ambulance, where the body was being lifted in.

As the men were about to lay it down inside the vehicle Doyle reached for the blanket, pulling it back.

He looked down at the waxen features, the eyes still open and staring, fixing Doyle in a blank accusatory stare.

'Any I.D. on him?' Doyle wanted to know, flipping the blanket back over the dead man.

'Why did you kill him?'

The question came from the tall man standing beside him. Chief Inspector Ian Austin drew in an angry breath and puffed out his considerable chest. He was taller than Doyle and looking down on the younger man suited him.

'Is it important?' asked Doyle matter-of-factly.

'Yes, it's important,' hissed Austin through gritted teeth. 'He was unarmed, for God's sake!'

'I didn't know that at the time.'

'Would it have made any difference if you had?'

'No. I'd still have shot him.'

Doyle dug in the pocket of his jacket for his cigarettes, pulled one out and lit it, flicking the match into the road. He stepped back as the ambulance doors were closed.

'So what *was* his name?' he asked.

'Galbraith. Martin Galbraith,' said Austin wearily. He walked with Doyle as the younger man headed for his car.

'Any form?'

'Suspected arms dealing, robbery. He did a couple of years inside, over here *and* in Ireland,' said Austin.

Doyle nodded and drew on his cigarette.

'What about the rest of the boys?' he said, slipping into an Irish accent.

'They've been taken to a police station for questioning,' Austin told him.

'Which one?'

'That's none of your business, Doyle. This is *our* game now,' said the policeman irritably.

'Bollocks,' snapped the younger man. 'Which nick have they been taken to? I want to speak to them.'

'I told you, it's *our* province. This was a joint operation between the anti-terrorist squad and the flying squad. It has nothing to do with you or your department. You were here tonight to observe and advise. Not to shoot the bloody suspects.'

'You're lucky I only killed one,' Doyle told him. 'You don't know how to handle them, Austin.'

'And I suppose shooting them is the answer?'

'It's *my* fucking answer,' snapped Doyle. 'Now, which nick have they been taken to?'

'Why do you need to know? So you can torture information out of them? You'll need official clearance before you interrogate prisoners of this nature.'

'I've got clearance. Call my superiors if you don't believe me. Why do you think I *was* here tonight? I'll tell you. Because no one trusted you and *your* boys to do this job without fucking it up.' Doyle pulled open the door of his car. 'Now, if you won't tell me where they've been taken, I'm sure someone else will.' He slid behind the wheel, winding his window down, looking up at Austin. 'What did they find in the house, anyway?' He hooked a thumb over his shoulder in the direction of Number 22. 'And don't tell me *that's* none of my business.'

Austin regarded the younger man angrily for a moment, the knot of muscles at the side of his jaw throbbing.

'Two AK-47's, three thousand rounds of ammunition and some Semtex,' he said.

'How much?'

'About seventy pounds.'

Doyle nodded.

'Enough to make half a dozen bombs. Enough to kill Christ knows how many people.' He smiled humourlessly. 'And you moan because I shot one of the fuckers.' Doyle started his car, stepping on the accelerator, allowing the engine to roar for a moment. 'I'm going home to change. I'll probably see you later.' He let off the handbrake. 'Just for a little chat with our Irish friends.' Doyle winked at the Chief Inspector and guided his car away from the kerb, banging his hooter as two men blocked his path. They jumped aside hastily as he drove by.

Austin stood and watched the Datsun disappear around a corner. He was clenching and unclenching his large fists, his eyes fixed on the path taken by Doyle.

'Bastard,' he murmured under his breath.

Preparation

The man had been hanged three days earlier.

His body dangled from the rope, twisting gently in the breeze. The wood of the gallows creaked mournfully, offering a final lament.

It was difficult to tell his age; most of his features were gone.

The crows had done their work thoroughly.

The eyes had been taken first, devoured hungrily by the carrion birds.

Flies had feasted on the open wounds, laying eggs in the lacerations so that now portions of the face seemed to move. As if muscles were still twitching in that dead visage.

Maggots writhed beneath the flaps of skin, eating their way free.

One eye-socket was bulging with them; the wriggling forms spilled down a torn cheek like living, parasitic tears.

The body continued to turn slowly as the night breeze stiffened, hauling the clouds around the moon like a cloak, bringing an even greater darkness over the countryside.

The two men who stood looking up at the dangling corpse did so with indifference.

They didn't know the man's name, they didn't know why he'd been hung. They didn't care.

The first was a tall, slender individual with bony fingers which he kept shuffling together as if they were playing cards. His companion was also tall but more stoutly built.

He was the one who carried the knife.

The moon disappeared behind another bank of cloud and the darkness returned.

The second man stepped towards the corpse, noticing, at last, how low to the ground the dead man's legs were. His feet were only a foot or so clear. Indeed, whoever had tied the knot around the man's neck had been no expert. The second man glanced at the dangling body more closely, noticing how the neck was stretched. The flesh was taut over the withering muscles.

The man had been choked to death, denied the mercy of a broken neck.

The second man was aware too of the stench that came from the body. The smell of putrefying flesh.

The hanged man's clothes had been taken so there was nothing to contain the odour. He wrinkled his nose as he moved closer to the corpse, his gaze resting for a second on the ravaged, shrunken genitals.

Probably the crows again, he thought. The dead man's scrotum had been torn open, most likely by a powerful beak. The testicles had been devoured, the penis savaged.

The feet of the corpse bore several bad cuts, too. Probably foxes or badgers, unable to reach the rotting carcass, had taken bites from the most accessible part. Three toes were missing.

The man seemed to tire of his appraisal of the dangling body and, instead, set to work. He seized the left arm in one powerful hand. Then, with the other, he pressed the knife against the wrist.

The dead man's skin felt soft and pliant and he found it relatively easy to cut.

Until he reached the bone.

The knife blade grated against the radius and the ulna but the man persevered, smiling when he heard a dull crack. He continued with the knife, using a sawing action until finally, tugging on the appendage simultaneously, he severed the hand.

He held it up like some kind of trophy and walked back towards the first man, who had watched the whole episode unmoved.

Now he reached inside his jacket and took out a small wooden box about six inches by eight. He flipped it open and watched as his companion laid the hand inside. Then, satisfied, both men walked across to the horses that were tethered nearby, swung themselves into the saddle and rode off.

The hanged man twisted gently in the breeze.

Twelve

The green light was flashing on the answering machine when Doyle walked in.

He flicked on a light as he walked into the flat, crossed to the machine and pressed the button marked 'Incoming Messages'. As he waited for the machine to rewind he pulled off his leather jacket and tossed it onto the sofa, walking across the sitting room of the flat towards the hi-fi.

The first message began to play back.

'Is that Carol …? Is Carol there …? …' Then silence and a click.

Wrong number.

'Prat,' murmured Doyle, annoyed at the anonymous caller. There was a beep then the second message began.

'Sean, this is Angela. Angela O'Neal. I hope you remember me.' A chuckle. 'I hope you enjoyed the other night as much as I did.'

Doyle turned and headed back to the answering machine.

'I'm sure I gave you my number, but in case you've forgotten it I'll give it to you again so you can call me. The number …'

Doyle switched off the machine, turned and headed back to the hi-fi. He switched it on, the tape inside the machine turning immediately.

'… *In a hotel room I remember the way, we'd do what we do* …'

Doyle passed through into the kitchen, pulling off the shoulder holster as he did so.

'*Too long, without your touch, too long without your love* …'

The singer roared on from the sitting room as Doyle pulled a pint of milk from the fridge, removed the top and swallowed great gulps. He wiped his mouth with the back of his hand, took a glass from the draining board, blew in it to remove some dust, and filled it with the white fluid. He carried it back through into the sitting-room, putting the glass down for a moment as he undid the holster around his waist. He dropped the Charter Arms .44 onto the sofa alongside the CZ, glancing down at the two weapons for a moment before walking on through into the narrow corridor which led to the bedroom and bathroom.

54

Inside the bathroom Doyle turned on the shower, testing the water temperature with his hand as it spurted from the head. He sat down on the stool in the bathroom and pulled off his baseball boots and socks. Then he stood up, looking at himself in the mirror opposite. He pulled off his T-shirt.

His torso was a patchwork of scars, some running from his shoulder to his navel, others shorter, sometimes deeper, cutting across his chest and stomach. He turned, glancing at the back where there were more. One in particular ran from his left scapula, across his back, then diagonally down to his lumbar region.

It was that wound which had almost killed him.

Doyle turned round once more, running the tip of his index finger over a particularly deep scar which had bisected his right pectoral muscle. There was no nipple there either, just a ragged hole which looked dark in the brightness of the fluorescent light above.

He pulled off his jeans and tossed them to one side.

There were more scars on his legs and buttocks. Even his left shin was heavily marked, the scars looking white beneath the hair on his legs.

He looked like a road-map.

He accepted the scars now. In the beginning it had been difficult. Many times, especially when he'd first seen the extent of his injuries, he'd felt like weeping, not in self-pity but at the damage which had been wrought on his frame. He was grateful that his face had escaped relatively unscathed, but for a deep scar which ran horizontally from the corner of his left eye to his jaw. He had been lucky. His torso and legs had borne the worst of the damage.

Doyle stood staring at his body for long moments,

memories flooding back into his mind, still uncomfortably fresh even after five years.

The man he'd been after had been responsible for three murders. All politicians. He'd been one of the IRA's top hit men and it had taken Doyle more than three months to pin the bastard down. Weeks of trekking round Londonderry and Belfast looking and listening for any sight or sound of his prey until, finally, he'd found the man. McNamara. He could still remember him. Doyle had been given orders to bring the man in alive and that was precisely what he'd been trying to do when McNamara realized that he'd been cornered. The chase had taken them through the Creggan and Bogside estates but, by the time they reached the Craigavon bridge, McNamara had taken his fill of being chased by this maniac Englishman.

He'd been carrying a couple of pounds of explosive on him, possibly for an impending job. He'd jumped into a car on the bridge and, as Doyle had drawn closer to him, gun already aimed at the fugitive, McNamara had detonated the explosive he'd been carrying.

The car had been blown to pieces and the Irishman with it. Two passers-by had been killed by the flying pieces of pulverized car, many injured.

Doyle amongst them.

He could still remember lying on the bridge, unable to move, his body feeling as if it were on fire, yet being perfectly able to take in every detail of what was going on around him.

A small child had peered down at him, at the blood which he could feel running from his own wounds, which he could see puddling around him. Most ridiculous of all, there had been an empty cigarette packet lying in the gutter beside him, and all Doyle could seem to focus on were the words: SMOKING CAN SERIOUSLY DAMAGE YOUR HEALTH. *But not as much as gelignite*, he said to himself, and that had been his last thought before passing out.

He'd woken three days later in hospital (in an army hospital, he'd later learned) and he'd suffered as much pain then as he'd ever thought imaginable.

One lung had been punctured by a piece of sharp metal; fragments of it, still lodged in his back, were waiting to be removed. His left kidney had been badly damaged, perhaps irreparably, the doctors had thought at the time. Another piece of burning steel had hamstrung him. Another had torn away most of the flesh on his left quadricep and also shattered his femur in two places.

Eight ribs had been broken, two smashed beyond saving. A portion of one had been taken from inside the punctured lung. He remembered someone telling him he'd lost over thirty pints of blood. The right scapula, the left clavicle, the ulna and radius of his left arm had all been broken.

Apart from a hairline fracture of his right sphenoid bone and the gash on the left hand side of his face, his head was unmarked.

A doctor told him he'd been lucky.

With most of the bones in his body broken and more pain than he'd thought it possible to endure, Doyle had been somewhat at odds with that particular diagnosis. Let someone blow the fuck out of you, then see if *you* feel lucky, he'd thought, gazing up at the doctor through eyes clouded with pain and morphine.

Still, he'd been told, he was out of action, out of danger now. All he had to do was get well. It was a miracle he'd survived. Somebody up there liked him.

They'd rolled out the clichés for him.

Somebody liked him, did they? Well, if it was God, he had one hell of a sense of humour.

Doyle took one last look at his ravaged body in the bathroom mirror and stepped into the shower, enjoying the feel of the water on his skin.

From the sitting room the music thundered on, but beneath the stinging jets of water Doyle couldn't hear it.

He didn't hear it when the phone rang either.

Thirteen

When he finally stepped from the shower he stood, head lowered, on the towel he'd spread on the bathroom floor. It was like some kind of meditative act. Eyes closed he stood there, water running in rivulets from him, some of it coursing down the deep scars like a stream through rock. He sucked in several deep breaths and finally reached for the bath towel nearby and began drying himself. From inside the sitting room he could still hear music. Wrapping the towel around himself he headed for the source of the sound, picking up the glass of milk as he did. Water was dripping from his long hair and Doyle wiped it away as it trickled down his back.

He crossed to the stereo and eased the volume down slightly. Then he reached for the phone and jabbed out some digits.

It was picked up almost immediately. Doyle smiled as he recognized the voice.

58

'Yeah, who is it?'

'Ron, it's Sean.'

'Doyle, what the fuck do *you* want?' Ronald Wyatt wanted to know. 'I hear on the grapevine you've been a naughty boy.' He chuckled. 'Old Austin was spitting blood about that mick you blew away.'

'Fuck him,' snapped Doyle. 'It's the others I'm interested in. I want to know where they took them; Austin wouldn't tell me.'

'Why do you want to know?'

'Why the hell do you think I want to know? I want to talk to them.' Doyle wiped some droplets of water from his face.

'About what?'

'Come on, Ron, what is this? Twenty fucking questions? Just tell me where they took them,' snapped Doyle.

'Shepherd's Bush Road police station.'

Doyle smiled.

'Thanks,' he said.

'By the way, if anyone asks how you found out, remember ...'

'I know, a little bird told me,' Doyle chuckled.

'A little blonde bird with big tits.' Wyatt erupted into a spasm of laughter. Doyle held the phone away from his ear for a moment.

'Cheers again, Ron,' he said and was about to replace the receiver when Wyatt spoke again. There was a sudden unexpected sobriety in his tone.

'Sean, what the fuck *is* going on?' he asked. 'I mean with the IRA. You know that they were as keen on a peace plan as anyone. Now, first we've got that bloody massacre at Stormont and then piles of Semtex here in London. It doesn't make any sense.'

'Since when did any of this shit in Ireland make sense, Ron?'

'Right,' Wyatt murmured wistfully.

'I'll talk to you soon,' said Doyle. This time he did put down the receiver.

Shepherd's Bush, eh? It made sense. It was the closest police station to the scene. Doyle should have realized.

He turned and headed back towards the bedroom where he quickly dried himself. He took clean jeans and a clean T-shirt from his wardrobe, pulled them on and dragged on a pair of cowboy boots. He glanced briefly at his reflection in the mirror and wandered back into the sitting room. There he took the .44 from its holster and flipped open the cylinder, emptying the weapon. He gathered up the rounds and crossed to a cabinet next to the stereo which was still roaring out music.

'*... Let me keep on sleeping, forget that I'm alone ...*'

Doyle opened a drawer and pulled out a box which he carried back to the sofa. Then, squatting on the arm of the settee, he slid the box open to reveal the shells inside.

'*... One day of faceless living is twenty four hours too long...*'

The copper casings reflected the light, glinting as Doyle removed six of them. He glanced at the bullets admiringly for a moment and slowly pushed one into each chamber of the .44.

These were his pride and joy.

Number twelve shot suspended in liquid teflon in a copper casing.

Beautiful.

Twice the explosive power of any dum-dum bullet. These didn't need to strike bone first; they exploded

60

immediately they entered their target. One was always enough.

He pushed the final shell into the cylinder and snapped it shut, jamming the weapon into the waistband of his jeans. He pulled on his leather jacket, turned off the stereo and headed for the door, car keys already in his hand.

He was half-way down the stairs when his phone rang but he hesitated only a second, knowing that the answering machine would pick up the call.

After two rings, however, there was silence.

For the second time that night the caller had chosen not to leave a message.

What had to be said should be said to Doyle himself. For now it could wait.

Fourteen

BRITTANY, FRANCE:
It was hideous.

Channing had no idea what it was but the creature was repulsive. Despite its vile appearance he looked at it more closely, marvelling not so much at the grotesqueness of the creation but at the skill which had gone into its construction.

He had guessed that the stained glass window must be at least five hundred years old but the workmanship was remarkable. Now, as he dipped the piece of rag in surgical spirit and began working carefully on one portion of the glass, he began to see the colours more clearly.

Lit only by the glow of the hurricane lamp, the image appeared from beneath the grime with infinite slowness as Channing worked intensely to remove the dirt that obscured it. Outside the sun was sinking low behind the hills, bleeding its colour across the sky. Channing could see none of this. All he was aware of was the window before him.

And of the face which was becoming clearer by the second.

This was not right, Channing thought. He had seen enough stained glass in his time to realize that the artefact before him was not the product of a God-fearing mind. No man of God would create an image so repulsive.

Who, then, had created the window?

Ninety per cent of it was still covered by dust and dirt, much of it so thick that not even the surgical spirit would remove it.

Catherine would know how to reveal the other panels, he thought. She would know. Once the entire window could be viewed he might be able to find some answers.

Encased in stone, as it had been when he'd first found it, the window had looked as if it had been hidden. As if whoever had constructed it had secreted it away within the church at Machecoul. As if only certain eyes were meant to gaze on it.

From what he uncovered so far he couldn't think of many who would want to.

The face was becoming clearer.

The dirt of ages, the filth of neglect was thick on the rag he was using. Channing tore off another piece, discarded the first and continued with the cleaning process.

More of the face now became visible and he moved back slightly, trying to see exactly what he had discovered.

The hurricane lamp flickered and Channing looked at it warily for a moment until the full glow was restored.

The face within the panel glared back at him.

It was shaped like that of a man but the head seemed to broaden, to swell at the temples, and across the forehead there were several protruberances. *Horns, perhaps?*

The hurricane lamp flickered again.

Channing moved closer to the window, staring at the face more intently.

A large mouth yawned open, long teeth prominent in both upper and lower jaws. From inside that mouth a thick barbed tongue flickered, but there was nothing else reptilian about the appearance of the monstrosity. The most striking thing about it were its eyes.

As Channing held the hurricane lamp close to the window the glass eyes seemed to glow. Both had been formed from single chips of red glass and now, with the light on them, they seemed to burn as if lit from within, shining with a lustre that must have been quite awe-inspiring when they were first created.

Channing shuddered, aware that the hairs on the back of his neck were rising.

Even his rudimentary knowledge of stained glass told him that the windows were originally constructed as learning aids as much as offerings to God. Peasants, unable to read, would be taught by monks or priests using the panels of the windows as a kind of storyboard. But the depictions were usually Biblical or philosophical. Channing shook his head slowly as he gazed at the creature depicted in the part of the panel he had uncovered.

What kind of story would feature a beast like this?

And what kind of man had invented such a monstrosity?

Again the hurricane lamp flickered.

Channing reached out and gently touched the glass, running the tip of one index finger around the perimeter of a red eye.

The glass felt ice-cold.

He felt the goose-pimples rise on his flesh immediately.

He traced the outline of the face with his finger, finally touching the gaping mouth, running his hand over the grimy glass.

The mouth opened.

As if the glass itself had suddenly become animated, the mouth seemed to collapse in on itself.

In that second Channing felt his hand slipping through.

Through the glass.

Between those painted lips and teeth.

He jumped back in panic, his heart hammering uncontrollably in his chest, but as he moved his hand remained inside the mouth. His eyes bulged in their sockets as he tried to pull himself free.

Then he felt mounting pressure on his wrist.

As if something was biting him.

The pieces of glass that formed the lips of the mouth seemed to be closing around his arm, chafing skin.

They snapped together with a loud crack.

And finally Channing was free of the grip.

Free because his hand had been severed.

He fell back onto the floor of the church screaming,

the torn arm held before him like a bizarre trophy, blood spouting madly from the stump of the wrist.

The thick crimson fluid was pouring down the front of the window too, smeared copiously around the mouth of the creature depicted there.

The mouth was now closed.

Channing gaped at his shattered wrist and at the pieces of pulverized bone and the tendril-like lengths of vein and artery still spurting scarlet.

And he screamed again.

He was still screaming when he woke up.

Dragged from the dream by his own bellowing, he sat up, his body sheathed in sweat, his hands shaking madly.

He held them both out as if to check that he still possessed two. The residue of the nightmare was still strong in his mind.

He tried to control his breathing, realizing now that it had been a dream. Gradually he felt his heart slowing, the rushing of blood in his ears diminishing. He was aware that he was in his bedroom at the inn and not inside the church of Machecoul. Channing heard movement outside his room, a gentle tapping on the door followed by some urgent enquiries about his well-being from the lady who owned the place. His screams must have awoken her, he reasoned. He called back that he was fine. It was just a nightmare.

Just a nightmare. Jesus Christ!

Channing finally slumped back onto pillows which were drenched with sweat. He ran both hands over his face, closing his eyes momentarily, relieved when he saw no more of the vision he'd witnessed in his dream.

He sucked in a deep breath, held it for a moment and let it out slowly, aware that his heart had ceased its frantic pounding. He began to relax.

Sleep came to him again, but slowly. He accepted its embrace almost unwillingly, wondering what else he might find inside his mind once the peaceful oblivion settled upon him.

He was just drifting off when the phone brought him hurtling back to consciousness.

The ringing continued for a moment or two as Channing tried to re-orientate himself. Then he reached for the receiver.

The hands on his watch showed 2.14 a.m.

Fifteen

LONDON:
The desk sergeant at Shepherd's Bush Road police station didn't look up as he heard the footsteps approaching his counter. He continued sipping at his tea and filling in names on a form he had laid out in front of him.

Only when the newcomer coughed theatrically did Sergeant Raymond Nyles deign to glance up.

His first impression was one of surprise. The man facing him was in his early thirties, he guessed, dressed in a leather jacket, T-shirt and jeans. As he took a step back, Nyles peered over the counter and saw that he wore cowboy boots, too.

What a bloody sight, the Duty Sergeant thought.

'Can I help you?' he said wearily.

'Some men were brought in earlier tonight,' Doyle

told him, as if imparting some information Nyles wasn't aware of. 'Four of them. Irish.'

Nyles was non-committal. He merely frowned slightly, pulled at the end of his nose and continued looking appraisingly at Doyle.

'If they were, what do you want to know for?' he asked.

Doyle dug inside his jacket and pulled out some I.D.

'Don't play games with me,' he snapped, tossing the slim leather wallet in front of Nyles. 'I need to see them.'

Nyles inspected the I.D., checking the photo inside against the face of the man who stood before him as if he doubted the validity of the picture.

'C.T.U.,' he muttered, his frown deepening. 'The Flying Squad are already here, they were the ones who brought them in. No one told me the Counter-Terrorist Unit were involved too.'

'Perhaps they forgot,' said Doyle, gathering up the leather wallet. 'Now can you just tell me where the men are being held?' Irritation was creeping more noticeably into his tone. Nyles regarded him a moment longer, then reached for the phone on his desk and flicked a switch. Doyle leant against the counter and lit up a cigarette, ignoring the NO SMOKING sign emblazoned on the far wall.

Nyles spoke into the phone and, a moment later, a uniformed constable appeared. He looked at the sergeant and then at Doyle.

'Take this ... gentleman through to the cells,' said Nyles, glancing once more at the counter terrorist before returning to his form. 'Stay with him.'

'There's no need for that,' Doyle said, nodding for the constable to lead on.

They walked along a wide corridor with rooms on each side, finally pausing at a heavy iron door set in the far end. The constable unlocked it and led Doyle through.

'Are you Flying Squad?' asked the uniformed man.

Doyle grunted indignantly.

'No. Why?'

'It's just that there are two or three of them here already. I thought you …!'

'No. Not me,' Doyle interrupted.

The constable paused at a door, knocked and opened it when he heard the order from inside to enter. He held the door for Doyle.

The room smelt of cigarettes and strong coffee. There were two men inside, one of whom he recognized immediately.

'What are *you* doing here?' asked Chief Inspector Austin. 'I told you to keep out of this.'

The other man in the room glanced at Doyle, then returned his attention to the two-way mirror which looked into a small room beyond. It was about half the size of the one in which the men stood, about six feet by six, containing only a table and two chairs.

Seated in the room was a man in his early forties, greying at the temples. Red in the face, he was constantly looking round the room as if expecting a hole to open up in the wall and allow him to escape. He chewed on his thumbnail constantly.

'Who is he?' said Doyle, pouring himself a cup of coffee.

'His name is Sheehan,' said Austin. 'Thomas Sheehan. Known member of the IRA. Served three years in Long Kesh in the late seventies for possession of explosives.'

'What about the others that were brought in?'

'Same. All known IRA.'

'Has anyone spoken to any of them yet?' Doyle asked, sipping his coffee, never taking his eyes from the man in the room beyond.

'We've spoken to all of them,' said the other man with Austin. 'They won't speak.' He said it with something approaching smugness.

'I heard your boss was on his way down here,' Austin informed the counter-terrorist.

'Donaldson? What does he want?' Doyle enquired, his gaze still fixed on Sheehan.

'The same thing we all do. Information,' said the policeman. 'It seems unlikely we're going to get it just yet. Perhaps when the bastard's sat there for a few more hours without a cigarette or the chance to have a piss he'll feel like talking.' Austin and his companion smiled at each other.

'Bollocks,' said Doyle. 'It's going to take more than a bursting bladder to make him talk.'

'Why don't *you* have a word with him?' said the other policeman, a note of sarcasm in his voice. 'Perhaps he'll be so scared he'll tell you everything.' The man chuckled.

'Look, mate, I guessed you were a prick,' said Doyle. 'You don't have to advertize the fact.' He took another sip of his coffee, not even giving the other man the benefit of a glance.

The policeman was on his feet in seconds, lunging at Doyle, who merely moved to one side, allowing Austin to grab his furious companion.

'Cut it out,' the Chief Inspector snapped, holding the other man by the shoulders and finally shoving him back towards his seat. The man, Garner, looked angrily at Doyle.

69

'They won't talk, Doyle,' Austin said, with an air of finality. 'None of them.'

'They'll talk to me,' said the counter-terrorist, putting down his cup.

'No way. You set one foot in that room and they'll be crying police brutality.'

'Let them,' said Doyle. 'Who's going to hear?' He turned and headed for the door which led through into the smaller room.

'Doyle, I'm ordering you,' shouted Austin.

'You can't order me. Donaldson *can* but he's not here, is he?' said the younger man, one hand on the door knob. 'I told you, I just want a chat with him.'

'Go on then, big shot,' hissed Garner.

'You shut up, too,' Austin rasped, rounding on his companion.

Doyle turned the knob.

'Who do you think you are, bloody Clint Eastwood?' snapped the C.I.

The door was closed.

Doyle was inside the room.

'Mouthy bastard,' said Garner, watching Doyle as he approached the table where Sheehan sat. 'The mick won't talk to *him*. Who does he think he is, anyway?'

'Shut up, Garner,' Austin said wearily. 'Just shut up.'

Both men watched in silence as Doyle went to work.

Sixteen

Thomas Sheehan looked up as the door opened, his eyes flicking appraisingly over this newcomer. If the

Irishman was surprised by Doyle's appearance it didn't show in his face but for a slight narrowing of his eyes. He chewed part of his thumbnail away and spat it onto the floor in front of Doyle, who merely walked around to the other side of the table and rested one booted foot on the chair.

His eyes never left Sheehan's.

The man was sweating slightly but not, Doyle guessed, from fear. He'd seen men like Sheehan before. Hard bastards. Prepared to take it rough, if they had to. Fear of their own colleagues was sometimes a more potent obstacle to communication than fear of the authorities.

Doyle meant to change that.

'You've probably had the nice copper, bad copper routine already,' said Doyle, lighting up a cigarette and blowing the smoke in the direction of the Irishman. 'Been sitting here a while, busting for a piss, dying for a fag, wondering how much longer they're going to keep you sitting here. Well, Tommy, that's all down to you. You can sit here for another few hours, you can sit here for another few days, for all I care. You might have got time to waste but I haven't. I need to talk to you, or, more to the point, I need *you* to talk to *me*. If you want to make it easy, that's fine; if you want to make it hard on yourself I really couldn't give a fuck either way. I want some answers before I leave this room.'

'Nice speech. Go fuck yourself,' said Sheehan, looking around the room, anywhere but at Doyle.

A slight smile creased Doyle's lips.

Well, well, no wonder Austin could get nothing from him, thought the counter-terrorist.

'I'm not answering your fucking questions. Go to hell,' Sheehan said dismissively, this time looking at the younger man.

71

'If I go, you're coming with me,' Doyle told him, noting the surprise in the Irishman's eyes as he heard the words spoken in his native tongue. 'Now, start talking. Why the meeting?'

'Fuck you.'

Doyle drove his boot against the edge of the table, propelling it with great force and power into the chest of the Irishman who was knocked from his chair by the impact. He crashed heavily against the wall, banging his head. Doyle was on him in a second, dragging him to his feet and slamming him upright against the white tiled wall.

'What's going on?' he snarled, in English this time. 'Talk to me, you bastard.'

Sheehan felt his feet being lifted from the floor as Doyle exerted more pressure on his throat. The Irishman summoned a mouthful of spittle and spat into the Englishman's face.

Doyle's eyes blazed with rage and he drove a fist into Sheehan's stomach. The blow tore the breath from the man and also released the last shreds of control he was keeping on his full bladder. As he sank to the floor a dark stain began to spread across the front of his trousers.

Doyle placed one foot on the man's chest, watching as the urine soaked through his clothes, some of it puddling beneath him.

'Messy boy,' he chided, digging the heel of his boot into Sheehan's chest more firmly. The knot of muscles at the side of the Englishman's jaw pulsed angrily.

'Talk to me, shithead,' Doyle rasped. The acrid stench of urine reached his nostrils. 'You're starting to stink and I don't want to spend any more time in here than I have to. So, tell me what the fuck is going on?'

He slammed Sheehan back against the wall even harder.

The Irishman raised his hands and tried to pull his tormentor's arms down, anything to relieve the pressure on his throat but Doyle merely pressed his thumbs in harder, watching with relish as his opponent's face began to turn scarlet.

It looked as if Sheehan was trying to speak but the only sounds he could make were strangled gasps. Doyle held him a moment longer then hurled him across the room where he rolled once, then crashed into the other wall, right beneath the two-way mirror. Doyle took two paces and was on him again. This time he simply drove the toe of his boot into the Irishman's side, satisfied when he heard a dull crack.

One rib gone, he thought.

Sheehan groaned and reached for his injured side but Doyle dragged him upright again, staring deeply into his eyes.

'You can't do this,' the Irishman groaned. 'I've got rights.'

'You've got nothing,' Doyle hissed, slamming him back against the wall again.

This time the impact was so violent that it opened a cut on the back of Sheehan's head. Blood began to well from the gash and trickle through his hair. Doyle glanced at the crimson smear on the wall without a flicker of emotion. He slammed Sheehan down into the one seat which was still standing and grabbed the back of his head, getting a handful of hair in his fist, ignoring the blood that stained his palm. He jerked Sheehan's head back so sharply it seemed he would break his neck.

'Why don't you talk to the others?' Sheehan rasped.

'Because they're small fry. *You* organized that meeting tonight. You're the one who knows what's going on and why. Now tell me or I swear to Christ I'll break your fucking neck.' As if to reinforce the conviction of his statement, Doyle jerked even harder on the Irishman's hair, almost causing him to overbalance.

'I can't talk,' said Sheehan with difficulty. He felt close to fainting.

'Can't or won't?' snapped Doyle and suddenly hurled Sheehan forward, driving his head against the table top with such force that it broke his nose. Blood exploded from the shattered appendage and ran down the Irishman's face and shirt, mingling with the urine that had already stained his trousers.

Doyle stepped back. Sheehan was burbling incoherently now, his face was a crimson mask. He finally managed to sit up, one hand held to his face. Blood seeped through his fingers. He looked at the counter-terrorist with hatred in his eyes but Doyle saw something else there too.

Fear, perhaps?

The Irishman was breathing heavily, deep gasping breaths through his open mouth as he held his pulverized nose, occasionally taking his hand away to inspect the amount of blood on his fingers.

'You bastard,' he hissed at Doyle. 'And you expect me to talk?' He tried to grin but it appeared as a leer.

'I don't expect you to,' Doyle informed him. 'But I *advise* you to, unless you want your cheek bones and your jaw to end up like your nose.' There was no inflection in the words, no threat. Merely the statement of the inevitable.

'So what do you think I know?' Sheehan asked,

74

wincing as he wiped his shattered nose with one shirt sleeve. Blood still dripped from it, puddling beneath him.

'Just tell me what's going on.'

'What the fuck are you talking about? What *is* going on?' Sheehan said, almost mockingly.

Doyle's expression didn't change.

'Don't be a smart-arse, Tommy,' he said. 'Two days ago in Northern Ireland, as you well know, twenty-three politicians, including some Sinn Fein men, were murdered. Nobody knows *who* shot them, or why, and now, tonight, we find you and your cronies with enough Semtex to start a fucking war.' Doyle rested one boot on the edge of the chair and leaned closer to Sheehan. 'Ten days ago the Provisional IRA said that they were willing, if their leaders found the terms favourable, to stop all hostilities against the British army and to cease any activity on the mainland against military and civilian targets.' He paused a moment, glaring at the Irishman. 'Your fucking lot were ready to call it a day. No more bombings, no more shootings, no more knee-cappings. Nothing. And now what happens? In the space of forty-eight hours twenty-three people are murdered and we find your explosives store. Now tell me you don't know what's going on.'

Sheehan eyed the counter-terrorist warily, still dabbing at his nose with his shirt.

'You can't blame me for what happened at Stormont,' he said.

'I can blame you for any fucking thing I want unless you come up with some info to tell me otherwise,' Doyle snapped irritably. 'Who was behind that shooting? Who told you to call a meeting tonight?'

'What the fuck are you talking about, *meeting?*'

'You and the others have worked together before as a team. Thinking of going back into business?' The two men looked at each other in silence for a moment. 'Who told you to call that meeting? The same bloke who organized the shooting at Stormont?'

'Why don't you talk to the fucking Protestants?' snapped Sheehan. 'How do you know the fucking UVF aren't to blame?'

'A hunch,' said Doyle flatly. 'Now I'll ask you once more,' he stepped back a pace, one hand reaching around to the back of his jacket. 'Who ordered the shooting at Stormont?'

'You want me to turn tout?' Sheehan chuckled, dabbing at his nose. 'You know what they'd do to me if I did? A bag over the head and two bullets in the skull.'

'If you're worried about turning tout then there's somebody to grass *on* isn't there?' Doyle said, flatly.

'You're quick,' snapped Sheehan.

'No, I'm impatient. Give me a name.'

'No way.'

'As you want.'

It was then that he pulled the gun.

Seventeen

The Charter Arms .44 looked huge as Doyle pulled it free, aiming it at Sheehan's head.

Chief Inspector Austin saw the weapon and shouted, realizing that Doyle couldn't hear him through the two-way mirror.

'He's going to kill him,' said Garner incredulously. 'The mad bastard is going to kill him.'

Austin shouted once more then spun round, heading for the door into the small cell beyond.

This time Doyle *had* gone too far.

'Leave him.'

The voice startled Austin, both its intrusion and the feeling of power it seemed to carry. He turned to see who had spoken.

Jeffrey Donaldson stood inside the room, looking past Austin at the counter-terrorist and his adversary. He watched as Doyle pressed the gun against the remains of the Irishman's nose, fresh blood spilling down his face.

'He could kill the man, for Christ's sake,' Austin protested.

'He *could*,' said Donaldson, moving closer to the two-way mirror. Garner looked at the newcomer. He was in his mid-forties, tall and lean. His face had a somewhat pinched appearance due to his hollow cheeks. Even the greying beard he sported did nothing to make his features appear fuller. He was dressed in an open-necked shirt and trousers, with an overcoat around his shoulders. As he watched the tableau behind the glass he plucked absent-mindedly at his beard, as if trying to tease each bristle free.

'How long's he been in there?' Donaldson asked.

'About fifteen minutes,' Austin told him. 'I suppose we should be grateful Sheehan lasted *that* long.' He glanced at the two men in the smaller room once more. 'He wouldn't speak to us but Doyle insisted on trying for himself.'

'He uses different methods,' said Donaldson matter-of-factly.

77

'Brutality being the main one,' Austin snapped. 'You're his superior, *you* stop him.'

Donaldson had been head of the Counter-Terrorist Unit for the last four years. He had been one of the few in that unit who had actually encouraged Doyle to return to the fold after he'd been advised to quit for good. The injuries he'd sustained after the bomb blast had looked like forcing him into early retirement and Donaldson could still remember visiting the younger man in hospital, wondering if he would ever walk again, never mind return to the job. When, against all medical and official advice, Doyle had returned, Donaldson had seen what a changed man he was. Before, he'd been cautious. Since the blast he'd been positively reckless with regard to his own safety. He seemed to care nothing for life any more, his or anyone else's. There was a ferocity about him which was sometimes quite terrifying.

Donaldson was witnessing it now.

'Get him out of there,' Austin said. 'He'll kill Sheehan, then we'll never get anything out of him.'

'I read his file in the car on the way here,' Donaldson said. 'What makes you think you'll get anything out of him anyway?'

'There are certain procedures which must be followed ...!' Austin began but Donaldson cut him short.

'Certain procedures,' he said scornfully. 'You mean, do it by the rules? Well, the rules are different with men like Sheehan. You should know that. Doyle plays by *their* rules.'

'Doyle doesn't play by anybody's rules,' Austin snapped. 'How the hell can you trust him, anyway? His family were Irish, weren't they?'

78

'That's one of the things that makes him perfect for the job. He understands their mentality.'

Doyle had just pushed Sheehan up against the wall. He now shoved the gun under his chin.

'I don't trust him,' said Austin.

'I don't trust anyone,' Donaldson said, looking directly at the policeman.

'He's insane.'

'He gets results.'

'That's as maybe. I still think he's insane.'

Donaldson smiled thinly.

'You could very well be right,' he said quietly.

Austin had no answer. All he could do was watch as Doyle moved the barrel of the .44 up towards Sheehan's mouth.

Eighteen

'You can't kill me.'

There was a note of desperation in Sheehan's voice as Doyle prodded the gun against his cheek.

'Who ordered the shooting?' asked the counter-terrorist flatly.

'Fuck you,' shouted the Irishman.

Doyle grabbed his hand and slammed it down on the table top, gripping the wrist firmly, spreading the fingers.

With a movement combining lightning speed and demonic force he brought the butt of the pistol down onto the tip of Sheehan's index finger.

The fingernail splintered under the impact; bone crumbled easily. Blood burst from the end of the pulped digit.

'I don't know,' Sheehan wailed.

Doyle smashed the tip of his middle finger.

A fresh scream of pain filled the room.

'Talk to me,' Doyle said through clenched teeth.

'I can't tell you,' Sheehan insisted.

Doyle smashed a third finger tip.

And a fourth.

It looked as if someone had slammed the Irishman's hand repeatedly in a car door.

Doyle aimed for the thumb.

The nail actually came free along with a small chip of bone in a spurt of blood as the thumb was pulverized.

'You've only got one hand left,' hissed Doyle. 'You won't even be able to wipe your own arse if you don't give me some answers. Who ordered the shooting at Stormont?'

He hurled Sheehan across the room once more, advancing on the fallen man who was trying to protect his injured hand.

'No more,' he gasped, blood still running from his broken nose.

'Then talk,' said Doyle flatly. He knelt beside the Irishman, the .44 pressed against his chest. 'Who ordered the Stormont shooting? Was it the IRA?'

Sheehan sucked in a deep breath.

'Jesus,' he murmured softly. 'If I tell you …'

'Was it?' rasped Doyle.

'No.'

If Doyle was surprised it didn't register on his face.

'Not officially,' Sheehan told him.

Doyle grabbed him by the front of his blood-stained

shirt, dragged him to his feet and dumped him on one of the chairs again.

'Not officially,' he mimicked. 'What the fuck is that supposed to mean? Was it the IRA or not?'

'They *were* IRA men who did the shooting but they were acting unofficially. *Against* Sinn Fein orders.' He looked down at his hand and what remained of the finger tips.

'Tell me more,' said Doyle.

'You were right in what you said; Sinn Fein were all for this peace settlement in the six counties. They even gave orders that hostilities were to stop until the politicians had had their say. The men who did the shooting at Stormont didn't want that. They wanted the war to go on. No peace settlement. They wanted to carry on fighting. They wanted the money, too.'

'What money?' asked Doyle sharply, his attention now fully focused, his curiosity aroused.

'The group that did the shooting were privately funded. Someone paid them a huge amount of money to carry out that shooting at Stormont.'

Doyle stroked his chin thoughtfully.

'And you; where do you figure in all this?' he asked. 'Was it the same man who ordered the shooting that told you to call the meeting tonight?'

Sheehan nodded slowly.

'We were supposed to start bombing civilian targets, cause as much disruption as possible, create anti-Irish feeling again and stop the peace initiative going through,' he confessed.

'How much were the gunmen paid to do the shooting?' Doyle wanted to know.

'I heard about a million, maybe more.'

'Jesus,' muttered Doyle. 'Who paid them?'

'That I *don't* know.'

'Do you want to lose your other hand?' the counter-terrorist hissed. 'Who paid them?'

'I swear to God I don't know.'

'How many gunmen were involved in the shooting?'

'I don't know that, either. All I know is there are five or six men working in the squad.'

'Who's in charge of them?'

'His name's Maguire. James Maguire. That's all I know. I swear.'

'I need to know who paid him the million quid and why,' said Doyle.

'I told you, I don't know,' Sheehan insisted.

Doyle took a step back.

'Bullshit,' he hissed, aiming the gun at the Irishman. 'Who paid them?'

'I don't know.'

'Then you're no use to me any more,' the counter-terrorist said, drawing a bead on Sheehan. The sight was over his forehead.

'I've told you all I know,' Sheehan shouted frantically, his eyes bulging in the sockets. 'You can't kill me.'

Doyle smiled.

'Wrong,' he said quietly, and thumbed back the hammer.

It was then that Sheehan fainted.

'And you have no doubt that he was telling the truth?'

Jeffrey Donaldson's words seemed to echo around the small room inside the police station. He chewed on the stem of a pipe as he spoke, the fumes from the bowl mingling with air already heavy with cigarette smoke. It looked as though someone had draped the air with a shroud.

Doyle took a sip of his coffee, wincing when he found it was cold.

'He didn't know anything else,' he said. 'He doesn't know who hired Maguire and his men.'

'Who the hell would want to do that?' said Austin.

'Who could *afford* to do it?' Garner asked.

'Another terrorist organisation? Someone with a vested interest in seeing that there *is* no peace settlement in Ireland,' Donaldson suggested. 'Maybe even another country.'

'Like Libya or Iran?' Doyle mused.

'Or someone bigger,' Donaldson said, raising his eyebrows.

'What do you mean?' Austin said.

'Most IRA weapons and funds come from outside sources,' Donaldson told him. 'The Middle East, America, Russia. Some IRA men are even sent to the Middle East to learn their trade. What we have to find out' – he looked at Doyle – 'is who paid the money and why.' He got to his feet. 'I want you at my office tomorrow morning at ten o'clock, Doyle. We'll go over this again there.'

The younger man nodded and ground out his cigarette in a nearby ashtray.

'What about me?' Austin asked. 'I have a right to know what's going on. What you decide to do.'

'This is out of your hands now, Austin,' Donaldson told him. 'It's beyond the Flying Squad. You haven't the resources or the capabilities to deal with this situation. We'll take over from here.' And then he was gone.

Doyle also got to his feet and headed for the door.

'It might interest you to know that Sheehan is in hospital,' said Austin. 'You could have killed him.'

'I wish I had,' the counter-terrorist said flatly as he paused in the doorway. 'Maybe next time I will.' Then he too was gone.

Séance

There were five of them seated around the table, their faces cast in deep shadow.

The only light in the great hall came from the hundreds of candles arranged in various patterns on the floor. The entire room was filled by sickly yellow light and the acrid smell of a thousand burning wicks. Smoke rose in small ethereal plumes every once in a while when a gust of wind extinguished a candle. Each time it was rapidly re-lit by one of the three men who looked on.

The quintet seated at the table remained where they were, heads bowed, fingertips touching gently.

In the centre of the table, framed by yet more candles, lay the body of a child.

The boy was naked. Unconscious.

The drug had taken a very short time to work on him and now, exposed to their prying eyes, he lay spread-eagled in their midst.

One of the men kept looking at the boy but a word from one of his companions forced him from his pleasure and he closed his eyes once more.

Outside the wind was whipping around the building, screaming at the windows and snuffing out more candles. Again they were re-lit.

The man who had been staring at the unconscious child

heard movement to his right but did not look up. He knew what was happening. Knew that one of his companions had risen and was now standing, arms outstretched in a gesture designed to encompass all those who sat at the table.

The man standing began to speak but his words were not always easy to understand. Not because of any speech impediment but because of their nature.

Strange, apparently meaningless phrases spilled from his lips. The others heard the words but did not understand.

It began to get colder in the room.

In the centre of the table the child stirred for a moment, perhaps momentarily roused by the chill, but after a short moan he drifted into oblivion again.

The cold intensified.

It was as if every ounce of warmth was being sucked not only from the room but from the men who sat at the table. They began to shiver, not least the one who sat at the head of the massive oak table. He raised his head to see that his companion was still speaking but his words now seemed to have changed from a series of phrases into a chant.

The chant grew louder.

The cold grew more palpable.

A breeze seemed to sweep through the room and many of the candles were blown out, their yellow lights snuffed as surely as if invisible fingers had nipped the wicks.

As the men who looked on made to re-light them the individual who was chanting held up a hand to stop them. They sank back into the shadows, grateful to hide in the gloom.

The chanting stopped.

There was a low rumbling sound which seemed to come not from one particular source but from all around the table.

All around the hall.

It was as if the entire place and all its occupants were

about to be engulfed by an earthquake.

A candlestick fell to the ground, clattering noisily on the stone floor. It was followed by another.

And another.

As each fell so their candles went out and the darkness in the room deepened.

So did the cold.

The man at the head of the table, squinting through the gloom, saw something.

At the far end of the hall, even through the tenebrous darkness, he could discern a shape. Somehow blacker than the night itself, it was as if a portion of the umbra had taken on tangible form and detached itself from the remainder of the shadows.

That shape was now moving towards the table.

The man narrowed his eyes, both to see through the gloom and also to try and pick out exactly what the shape was.

He swallowed hard as he realized that the one they had sought was among them.

Nineteen

Bright shafts of sunlight thrust their way through the windows of the Mayfair office. Motes of dust caught in the golden shafts as if magnetized.

The sunlight was shining onto Jeffrey Donaldson's polished desk top. He was sitting back in his swivel chair, puffing contentedly on his pipe. Smoke rose in small clouds, dissipating high above him, swirling around the huge crystal chandelier which hung from the centre of the ceiling.

The chair made little noise as he moved back and forth in it. In fact the entire room seemed unnaturally silent; even the footfalls of the other man in the room were muffled by the thick pile of the carpet.

Tom Westley wandered back across the office and set down a crystal tumbler close to Donaldson, who glanced up from the file he was reading and inspected the contents of the glass.

'It's a bit early for this, isn't it, Tom?' he said, smiling.

'If you don't want it I'll drink it,' Westley said, sipping his own Scotch.

He was a year or two older than Donaldson, and much more powerfully built; a broad, muscular man with a tanned face and large hands that not only dwarfed the glass but threatened to crush it if he squeezed too hard. He stood at the window, looking out over the paved area beneath. There was a patio and a small pond which boasted a fountain. Sunlight glinted on the surface of the pool, the warmth of the water coaxing movement from the fish which populated it.

Westley took another sip of his drink, then wandered back across the room and added a squirt of soda.

'What's wrong?' Donaldson asked.

'I don't like this situation, Jeff. This business with the IRA,' he said, turning to face his companion. 'I read Doyle's report too.' He shook his head. 'This … antagonism between himself and the IRA seems to go beyond the job. He treats the fighting as if it's something personal between *him* and the Provisionals.'

Westley drained the contents of his glass and poured himself another.

This time he didn't bother with the soda.

Donaldson eyed his companion guardedly for a moment, watching as he downed half of the fiery liquid in one gulp. He had always disapproved of his companion's sometimes excessive drinking habits but, as they never interfered with his work, he thought it churlish to make an issue of it. When his twenty-year old daughter had been killed in a car accident two years earlier Westley had hit the bottle hard; even now, when he felt too much stress he was a little too easily tempted to reach for the Scotch.

Donaldson smiled thinly.

'Doyle's *passion* for his work might be to our advantage,' he said.

Westley grunted.

'If you ask me, the bastard is insane,' he said. 'Since he was injured he's changed. His attitudes, his methods, everything.'

'He was always a little over-zealous,' Donaldson said, reaching for his own drink and taking a sip. 'Even before the accident.'

'Well, he's much more than that now. I think he's dangerous to others as well as himself. Some of the other agents think he has divided loyalties.'

Donaldson raised one eyebrow quizzically.

'I mean, with his family being Irish,' Westley continued.

'His family are dead. He has no one. That might account for his state of mind.'

'Does it account for his death-wish, too?' asked Westley cryptically.

The two men looked at each other for a moment.

Then Donaldson leant forward and flicked a switch on the console on his desk.

'Send Mr Doyle in, please,' he said and sat back.

Westley held his companion's gaze a moment longer, then poured himself another drink.

There was a knock on the door and Doyle entered. Greetings and handshakes were exchanged and Doyle sat down opposite Donaldson. He also accepted the drink Westley offered him, cradling the fine crystal glass in his hand as he sat there, waiting for the older man to take up his position on the other side of the desk. It was as if Westley felt he needed that distance between himself and Doyle.

'We'll keep this as brief as possible, Doyle,' said Donaldson, flipping open another file. He glanced at it, then turned it towards the younger man. On top of a pile of papers was a photograph. The man in the picture was in his mid-twenties, strong-featured, his face framed by a mop of curly hair. There was a sparkle in his eyes which looked like defiance.

'James Maguire, the man responsible for the shootings at Stormont,' said Donaldson. 'That's the man we want. Him and as many of the men operating with him as possible.'

Doyle glanced at the photo and nodded almost imperceptibly. Then he looked at his superiors.

'He'll never let himself be taken alive,' he said.

'We know that,' snapped Westley. 'But you could at least try.'

Doyle shrugged.

'I'm telling you, he won't let himself be taken, and if that's the way he wants it ...' He allowed the sentence to trail off.

'You'll be working with another agent,' Donaldson

89

told him.

'No way,' Doyle snapped. 'I work alone. I don't need anyone else getting in the way.'

'This isn't a bloody western, Doyle,' Westley reminded him, 'or some bad American cop show. All this maverick crap doesn't wash here. You're working with another agent.'

'Then find some other prat to do the job,' snapped Doyle, getting to his feet.

'Wait,' hissed Westley.

'Who *is* the other agent?' Doyle demanded.

'Willis,' Donaldson told him.

A thin smile flickered on Doyle's lips.

'Why Willis?'

'Because no one else will work with you,' Westley said. 'And quite frankly I don't blame them.'

Again Donaldson flicked the switch on his console.

'Tell Willis to come in,' he said.

Doyle turned as the door opened, the smile hovering once more on his lips.

'You know Doyle, don't you?' Donaldson said as the other agent approached the desk.

Georgina Willis nodded.

Twenty

The four of them sat in the office while Donaldson ran over the briefing. Doyle seemed uninterested, his attention fixed more firmly on his companion.

Georgina Willis was three or four years younger than

Doyle. She had a thin face which tapered off into a neatly pointed chin. Blonde hair flooded onto and beyond her shoulders, and every so often she would run a hand through it, occasionally glancing at Doyle. When she did, he looked deeply into her green eyes, noting how clear and alert they were. She was dressed in a sweatshirt and jeans, and as she sat listening to Donaldson she curled the lace of one trainer around her index finger. She was pretty and Doyle couldn't help but wonder how the hell she had ever come to be in this line of work. Maybe he'd take the time to find out, he promised himself.

Maybe.

Donaldson finally finished speaking and looked at the two agents as if expecting some response from them.

They merely looked at each other. Then Doyle glanced at his watch.

'If the lecture is over, I think I've heard enough,' he said.

'Take the files on Maguire. Study them,' said Westley. 'Find out all there is to know about him.'

'He's the enemy,' Doyle said flatly. 'What more do we *need* to know?' He got to his feet.

Georgina picked up one of the manilla files and followed Doyle towards the door.

'You'll leave for Belfast on separate planes tomorrow morning,' Donaldson told them. 'Once you get there, you're on your own. How you find Maguire, that's your problem. There's nothing more we can do for you.'

'Nice to know we've got your support,' Doyle said acidly and walked out. Georgina followed him, closing the door behind her.

Westley waited a moment then slammed his fist down on the desk top.

'Insubordinate bastard,' he snarled. He wandered across the room to another door in the oak-panelled wall. He opened it and two men stepped into the office. Both were dressed casually, both in their mid-thirties. One was smoking a cigarette he'd rolled himself. Peter Todd took the cigarette from his mouth and removed some tobacco from the tip of his tongue.

George Rivers glanced down at the file on the polished desk top, catching sight of the pictures of Maguire.

'Nasty piece of work, isn't he?' he said, smiling.

'You heard what was said in here?' Westley asked.

Both men nodded.

'You will follow Doyle and Willis until they've tracked down Maguire and his renegades,' Westley said. 'Then you will kill Doyle *and* Willis. Clear?'

The two men nodded.

Twenty-One

There were relatively few people in the pub. It was still too early for the office lunchtime trade, and for that Doyle was thankful. He didn't like crowds, didn't like people crowding him. He picked up the drinks from the bar and made his way across to the table where Georgina Willis sat. She thanked him, then watched as he wandered across to the juke-box, fed in some change and punched in his selections. He returned to the table and sat down just as the first swelling roar of guitars began to blast from the speakers. One or two other drinkers looked up irritably.

Georgina glanced at him as he sipped his drink, studying the hard lines of his face, her eyes finally alighting on the deep scar which marked the left side of his features. Doyle scratched at it unconsciously and took another swallow from his glass. He'd asked her if she wanted a drink when they'd left the office but he didn't seem to be in the mood for conversation, she thought, sipping at her own drink and running one index finger around the rim of the glass.

'If we're going to work together we might as well try and get on,' she said finally, tiring of the silence between them and Doyle's apparent indifference. He seemed distant, his mind focused on something far beyond the pub and the music that filled it.

He nodded slowly.

'Is it me?' she asked.

He looked puzzled.

'You've hardly said a word since we left Westley's office,' she told him.

'I was thinking about something,' he told her.

'Maguire?' she wondered.

'Maguire. His renegades. This whole fucking job.' He took another swallow from his glass. 'Westley and Donaldson are crazy if they think we'll be able to catch him.'

'You think he's going to be that hard to track down?' she said.

'Finding him won't be a problem, but I'm damned if I'm going to waste valuable time trying to make him see the error of his ways.' Doyle emphasised the words with scorn. "Or that it would be in his own interests to give himself up. When the time comes I'm going to kill him, because you can bet your arse he's going to try and kill *us*.'

'Donaldson and Westley won't like it.'

'Then let *them* find him and bring him in.' Doyle finished what was left in his glass, then got himself another. Georgina watched him as he stood at the bar, telling the barman to make it a double Scotch this time. He paid and returned to the table.

'How do you want to play this one?' she enquired. 'Once we're there.'

He shrugged.

'Married couple,' he suggested. 'Boyfriend-girlfriend. Something like that. Mr and Mrs Average.'

She nodded and ran a hand through her hair, her green eyes fixed on him.

'I heard they wanted you to retire after what happened,' she said. 'Why didn't you?'

'Retire to what? Sitting around in some fucking nursing home counting my scars and drawing a disability pension once a month?' He shook his head. 'They wanted me to retire because they didn't like my methods. When I got hurt it just gave them some extra leverage to get me out. So they thought.'

'You were lucky to survive. Why put your life on the line again and again? And don't tell me it's patriotism.'

'I never pretended it was. I enjoy what I do.' He looked directly at her, almost surprised when she held his gaze. 'What about you? Why did you get into this line of work in the first place?'

'I went through the usual channels,' she told him. 'Undercover, plain-clothes. When the chance came to join the Counter-Terrorist Unit I took it.'

'Why?'

'My brother was killed by the IRA two years ago. A bomb had gone off in Belfast city centre; he was helping get people into an ambulance when one of

94

their snipers shot him. He was only twenty.'

'So it's a revenge thing for you?'

'I suppose you could say that. Isn't it with you?'

'It's not revenge, it's hatred,' he told her flatly. 'I should have died that day in Londonderry. The doctors said I didn't have any right to survive, considering the extent of the injuries.' He looked down into his glass, as if seeking his next sentence in the liquor. 'I've been living on borrowed time ever since. It's just a matter of how long before that time runs out. That's why I live life day to day. I could be dead tomorrow, why worry about it? There's no point looking beyond tomorrow.'

'I can see it's going to be a bundle of laughs working with you, Doyle,' she said, smiling thinly.

'Then don't work with me. Why did you volunteer in the first place?'

'Because no one else would work with you.'

'And what makes you so different?'

'I know how you feel.'

'Because of what happened to your brother?' He shook his head. 'No one knows how I feel, Georgie. I don't expect them to. I don't want them to *try*.' He tapped his temple. 'What goes on in here is my business, nobody else's.'

She sipped her drink, studying him over the rim of the glass.

'So we're agreed, then,' she said finally.

'On what?' he asked, looking puzzled.

'When we find Maguire, we kill him.'

Doyle smiled, and for the first time she saw something approaching warmth in the gesture.

It passed as rapidly as it had appeared.

'Cheers,' he said, raising his glass.

They left the pub together, separated on the corner

of the street and went in different directions, Doyle towards Hyde Park corner, Georgie towards Green Park.

It was 12.36 a.m.

And that time was duly noted by the figure who had sat patiently at the wheel of the Granada since they'd entered the pub.

Watching.

Waiting.

PART TWO

'We are born into a world where alienation awaits us.'
– R.D.Laing

'Eternity! thou pleasing, dreadful thought.'
– Joseph Addison

Twenty-Two

BRITTANY, FRANCE:

The cyclist tottered uncertainly, swaying from side to side as he struggled to negotiate the hill.

Catherine Roberts slowed down, watching the man warily in case he fell off into the path of her car, then finally accelerated past him, glancing at his face in the process. He looked ready to drop.

Not surprising in this heat. It poured through the windscreen as if the Peugeot were some kind of mobile greenhouse. She wiped a hand across her forehead, annoyed that the window on her side was stuck fast and could not be wound down. The air being blown into the car was hot and dry. She shifted uncomfortably in her seat as she drove, feeling the perspiration on her back and her legs. She drove barefoot, the pedals of the car warm beneath her skin.

She'd rented the car at the airport when she'd landed about an hour ago; now she was nearing the end of her journey.

Signposts, standing there like count-down markers, told her that the village of Machecoul was close.

On the back seat of the car was a small suitcase containing the bare minimum of clothes and necessities. She didn't know how long she was going to be in France.

She didn't even know why she was here, or what she was going to see.

Channing's brief phone conversation with her hadn't exactly been exhaustive in its detail.

The call had come unexpectedly; she hadn't seen him for months. She wondered what had made her agree to come. Curiosity? Perhaps she wanted to see him again. She shook her head, answering her own unspoken question. No, it wasn't that. What had happened between them was in the past now, dead and buried, and she, for one, had no wish to resurrect it. Her journey, she told herself, was in the pursuance of professional interest. It was an answer pretentiously contrived enough to persuade her.

Despite the heat that filled the car, ahead of her the clouds were dark, looming over the hills that surrounded Machecoul like gloomy portents of rain to come. Perhaps the weather would break up. She hoped it would, right now, so that she could be free of the stifling heat inside the car. Her long dark hair was tied back, pulled back a little too severely from her thin face. Yet to enter her thirty-fourth year, she was a little concerned to see the lines around her eyes. Some were uncomfortably deep to be passed off as laugh-lines. There were others under her chin, too. Irritated by her own vanity she drew her attention away from the rear-view mirror and concentrated on the road once more.

She passed a sign which proclaimed she was just five kilometres from the village she sought.

Again the thought slipped to the forefront of her mind.

What did Channing want her to see?

What had he found here that was so important?

She noticed that the road was beginning to slope downwards now. She could see the tops of houses as she turned a corner. The hills levelled out beneath her, sloping down towards the village itself. Most of the buildings were on the valley floor, others clung to the hillsides as if some frantic architect had flung them there.

Two children playing by the roadside glanced inquisitively at the car as she passed. One waved and Cath smiled and waved back. She wondered if all the natives would be as friendly.

She drove slowly through the centre of the village, glancing around the market square, looking for the inn where she knew Channing was staying and where he had booked her in, too. She finally found it and parked, glad to be out of the baking confines of the Peugeot. She picked up her suitcase and wandered into the small reception area which was delightfully cool and smelt of freshly-picked flowers.

The plump woman who owned the place greeted her warmly and Cath responded, using what little French she could remember to good effect.

She asked if Mr Channing was around.

He wasn't, she was told, as she was led up to her room. Once inside she thanked the plump woman, closed the door and headed straight for the bathroom, where she stripped and stepped beneath the shower, washing away the perspiration and also the grime of the flight and drive. She dried her hair quickly, wrapped a towel around herself and padded back into the bedroom where she began unpacking.

She had just pulled on a clean blouse and skirt when there was a knock on the door. Cath crossed to it and found she had a visitor.

Mark Channing smiled thinly when he saw her, stepping into the room, pulling her to him and kissing her on the cheek.

101

The greeting of a friend, not a former lover.

He asked how her flight and the drive from the airport had been. He told her she looked well. The usual bullshit, she thought, polite conversation.

She thought how terrible he looked.

Channing looked pale and his eyes were sunken, the lower lids puffy. He hadn't shaved for a couple of days.

'Are you feeling ok?' she asked him, genuinely concerned at his haggard appearance.

He smiled but it looked more like a sneer.

'I haven't been sleeping very well,' he told her, the smile fading as if even the recollection of the nightmares was painful.

'Well,' she said, 'are you going to put me out of my misery? Tell me what you dragged me over here for?' She smiled.

The gesture wasn't reciprocated. Channing got to his feet. Already he was heading for the door.

'Mark,' she said, surprised. 'What have you found?'

He swallowed hard.

'It's simpler if I show you. Come on.'

Twenty-Three

COUNTY CORK, THE REPUBLIC OF IRELAND:
The accident had happened less than ten minutes ago.

Looking at the wreckage, Callahan could only guess at what had happened.

The road which led past his estate and into the nearby village of Glengaire was narrow, flanked on both sides by tall hedges and trees. Scarcely wide enough to accommodate two cars side by side, let alone a car and an articulated lorry.

The huge Scania had skidded across the road, flattening about twenty yards of hedge in its wake.

It looked as though it had hit the car head-on.

He thought it was a Sierra but, from the damage the vehicle had sustained, it was virtually impossible to tell. The car looked as if it had been put into a huge vice and crushed.

As yet, there was no sign of the passengers.

The only signal that there had even been anyone in the pulverized car was the amount of blood on the road.

Callahan sat intently behind the wheel of the Mercedes, window wound down, eyes fixed on the scene of carnage before him.

In the passenger seat Laura wriggled slightly, her short skirt pulled up almost to her thighs. Beneath it she wore no underwear and, as she too looked at the scene of devastation, she felt a warm glow spreading between her legs. She leaned forward to get a better look, her breath coming in low gasps as she watched the blood running across the road.

A member of the Garda walked across to the cab of the lorry and looked up into it.

The windscreen was shattered, spider-webbed where the driver's head had connected so forcefully with it. There was blood inside the cab, smeared on the shattered glass.

The Garda man opened the driver's side door and peered in.

The driver was slumped across the seats, blood pouring from his face and head. Both his eyes were closed, sealed shut by the congealing gore, it seemed.

Laura shifted in her seat once more, aware of the growing wetness between her legs. She glanced quickly across at her husband and smiled, one hand slipping onto her own thigh, stroking the smooth flesh, increasing her excitement.

From where they were parked, the Mercedes was hidden from the view of those on the road by a low hedge, but the Callahans had an excellent sight of all that was unfolding before them. One of their gardeners had heard the crash while working out by the perimeter wall which ringed their estate. He had mentioned it in passing to Callahan and the Englishman and his wife had driven to the scene immediately.

It had been worth it.

They had even beaten the ambulance and fire brigade to the crash.

'I wonder how many are in the car?' said Laura quietly, one hand now gliding up between her thighs, the fingers brushing her tightly-curled pubic hairs.

How ever many there were, Callahan thought, there wasn't going to be much of them left.

'I wonder if the driver's dead in the lorry,' Laura breathed, taking her index finger and slowly licking the moisture from its tip. She could see the Garda man walking back to his car, speaking into his radio. His feet left bloodied imprints on the tarmac where he'd walked through the blood that had spilled over the road.

In the distance they heard a siren.

The ambulance had come from the village, Callahan reasoned. It pulled up beside the lorry and two uniformed men jumped out, hurrying across to the cab. One climbed up into it, the other crossed to the car and inspected the wreck. He turned away swiftly, his face pale.

Laura felt the wetness between her legs increase.

More sirens.

Another ambulance. A fire engine.

They too pulled up next to the stricken vehicles, their crews spilling out, swarming around the wreck like ants round a piece of raw meat.

Callahan looked on intently as two of the firemen began cutting into the wreck with oxy-acetylene cutters, working their way around a shape in the front of the car.

The Garda man had taken off his hat and was leaning back against the bonnet of his car, breathing heavily into one hand as he watched the rescue operation.

The fireman removed a panel in the side of the car about four feet square.

The body didn't so much fall as ooze out.

From the shape of the corpse, Callahan guessed that nearly every bone in the man's body must have been crushed in the horrendous impact with the lorry. The steering column had been driven back into his chest, shattering his ribs. The top half of his body looked as if it had been wrapped in a crimson blanket. And yet his eyes were open as they pulled him out. Stretched wide in terror, perhaps, as he'd realized the inevitable end seconds before it had happened?

One arm had been almost severed at the shoulder.

Laura rubbed her thighs more tightly together, her breathing growing deeper, the wetness from her vagina now beginning to seep onto the material of the seat beneath her.

When the driver was lifted onto the roadside she could see that his stomach had been split open as surely as if it had exploded from inside. Thick lengths of intestine throbbed in the hole, spilling free as he was laid on the grass beside the road.

The Garda man finally lost his battle of will and vomited down the side of the car.

The firemen began to remove the second body.

It was a woman.

At least Callahan thought it was.

Glass from the smashed windscreen had flown back into the car and effectively shredded her face, ripping the skin beyond recognition. Portions of her features merely slid from her skull as she was lifted free.

The force with which she had been thrown forward had ensured that her body had been crushed up against the dashboard, her hips and legs pulped, one of them little more than tendrils of dripping muscle and flesh. But her head was where the worst damage had occurred.

As she was laid on the blood-spattered road, part of the top of her skull seemed to fall away and a thick slop of brain spilled from the mashed cranium. The fireman holding her head wiped his hands on his tunic and turned away. It must have been like touching an overripe rotten peach, Laura thought, watching as more sticky brain matter dribbled onto the road.

Laura was breathing loudly now, rubbing her thighs together with almost rhythmic precision as the feeling grew more powerful. She could feel the sensations building, the moisture between her legs flowing freely. Her nipples were achingly erect and she leant forward an inch or two more, her eyes fixed on the wrecked car, her body now quivering all over.

She sucked in a breath which rasped in her throat; she wanted to close her eyes, to enjoy the feeling more fully but she did not want to deprive herself of the

106

sights before her widening eyes. She ground herself more strongly into the seat, her thighs clenched tightly together as she rocked back and forth, flicking her lips with her tongue, knowing that the moment of supreme pleasure was almost upon her.

Callahan glanced across at her and smiled.

As they lifted the remains of the baby from the wreckage, she climaxed.

Twenty-Four

BRITTANY, FRANCE:
'How did you find it?'

Catherine Roberts' voice echoed inside the still confines of the church. Her eyes never left the object before her.

'Virtually by accident,' Channing explained. He described how he had inadvertently uncovered the window.

She took a step closer, touching the small section of exposed glass with her index finger.

'What is that thing?' Channing wanted to know, indicating the features of the creature on the window.

Cath could only shake her head. She peered closer, gazing at the glass itself rather than the shape that had been exposed.

'I won't be able to tell which method was used to make the window until we've uncovered it fully,' she said, still gazing at it.

'What do you mean?' Channing was rubbing his hands together, feeling cold.

'Once I've determined the method, I'll be able to give you a more accurate dating. Some of this seems to have been constructed using the *cloisonné* technique.' She tapped the glass. 'Coloured glass would actually be poured into compartments that were shaped to form images. But the rest of it ...' She allowed the sentence to trail off.

'I'm still not with you,' Channing said somewhat irritably, annoyed that Cath had not taken her eyes off the window since first meeting it.

'If some of the glass was prepared using the *cloisonné* method and some was done by painting onto glass then it means the window was put together by more than one man. And possibly over a period of years.'

'Is that so unusual?' he wanted to know.

She frowned and nodded.

'A window was as individual to its maker as, say, a novel is to its writer. It was unusual to find glass-makers working together on one window,' she told him, her eyes still fixed on the glass.

'What about that image?' he persisted, pointing at the grotesque creature depicted on the piece of window visible. 'I don't recognize it. I realized that the windows were used as teaching aids but that figure isn't biblical or mythological.' Channing found himself looking at the dull red, glass eyes. His mind flickered briefly back to his nightmare of the night before.

The mouth opening.

His hand disappearing into that yawning, fanged chasm.

He shuddered.

The dream had come to him almost every time he closed his eyes for any length of time. He knew it was a dream but the ferocity of the nightmare had not

108

abated. If anything, each successive experience burned it more vividly into his mind. He turned away for a moment.

Catherine, on the other hand, remained crouched before the glass.

'We have to uncover the rest of it,' she said.

'I agree with you. If we come back in the morning ...'

'No, Mark, I want to start now,' she said sharply, still not looking at him.

'You mean drive back into the village for your tools?'

She cut him short once again.

'You called me out here to work on the bloody thing,' she rasped, finally turning on him angrily. 'So let me work on it.'

They faced each other in silence for a moment, the cloying solitude of the church wrapping itself around them like a blanket. 'You go back, fetch my tools. Now,' she said. Then her tone softened a little. 'Please, Mark. It is important. You were right when you called me. I have to see it all. The sooner I can start, the sooner I can uncover it, decipher it.' She even managed to smile. 'Maybe even tell you what the significance of this little darling is.' She pointed to the image of the creature etched in glass.

Channing stood looking at her, then nodded and left the chancel.

Cath heard his footsteps echoing away. She turned back to look at the piece of glass he had uncovered.

At the monstrous face.

The red eyes seemed to fix her in a blank stare.

She reached out to touch one with her finger.

As she did, she smiled.

Twenty-Five

Channing yawned and looked at his watch.

10.34 p.m.

They'd been at the church for more than four hours now. Outside, the pleasant sunshine had long since been forced away by the onset of evening then the thick blackness of night, and with that blackness had come a cold wind that seemed to permeate even the stone of the church. He could hear it whistling around the old building as he stood in the chancel. It rattled the boarded-up windows too, poking cold fingers through into the church interior. Yet despite the cold Channing's shirt was damp with perspiration.

The effort of moving so much stone, so carefully, had drained him.

Upon returning from the village with some of Cath's tools they had set to work on the window, on the most important task first.

It had to be freed from the stonework which held it in place. They had no way of knowing if the window wasn't, like the others in the church, already smashed. Or perhaps they were only dealing with a fragment of a much larger window, the rest perhaps destroyed. Only by removing the encasing stone would they know the first of many answers posed by the discovery.

The work had not been strenuous so much as nerve-wracking. Encased in stone as it was, the window was still highly vulnerable to any over-zealous attempt to free it. It was like, Channing thought, trying to free a human body from ice with a pneumatic drill.

This task was ten times more delicate.

The glass was old, fourteenth or fifteenth century, Catherine was sure of that now. One slipped chisel or misplaced mallet blow and the entire thing could be smashed into a million pieces.

They had worked diligently, almost nervously, to chip away the stone from around the prized discovery, laying pieces of masonry on the floor of the church, occasionally stepping back to see how far their work had progressed.

After an hour they had uncovered the top three panels of the window.

The section now exposed to the dull light of the hurricane lamps was virtually impossible to see, however. The covering of masonry, the ravages of time and some defects in the glass itself served to ensure that they could not see through the patina of muck which coated the glass. The iron and lead strips used to separate the coloured panels were rusted and discoloured, too.

But they worked on, satisfied that the window was standing up to their attentions adequately, although Channing couldn't banish from his mind the thought that when they removed the final piece of stone the entire structure would topple forward and shatter on the church floor. He pushed the thought to the back of his mind.

As they worked, certain puzzling anomalies began to emerge.

Not only was the glass apparently the work of more than one glazier, but the stone which held it so firmly was of a different period to that from which the building itself had been constructed.

'It was added at a later date,' Channing had said.

'But why hide it?' Catherine had wanted to know, her attention riveted to the window and growing as more of it was revealed.

Channing had no answer to that particular question. Perhaps once it was uncovered and deciphered that riddle would be solved.

As more panels were revealed it became obvious that the glass so far discovered was not merely part of a larger window.

What Channing had found was complete.

The window was about forty-eight inches wide, perhaps anything up to six feet in height. Catherine had paused for a moment, wiping perspiration from her face with the back of her hand, then, with infinite care, she had scraped away some dirt from one of the panels, examining the glass beneath with the aid of a jeweller's eye-piece and a spot-light.

'It's crown glass,' she had told him. 'At least, this part is.' Without waiting for his question she had continued. 'A bubble of glass was blown onto an iron tube and then spun until it formed a disc. Then they'd use a grosing iron to chip away the edges until they'd formed the glass into the right shape.' She prodded the glass with a tracer, indicating the tiny bubbles still visible in the glass. 'The bubbles in crown glass always run in concentric circles.'

'Does that tell you anything about the man who made it?' Channing had wanted to know.

'That's one of the oldest methods of making stained glass. Other parts of it seem to have been made by other means. That's what makes me think it was constructed by more than one glazier.' She had uncovered another part of the design beneath the film of dirt.

112

A clawed hand had been revealed.

The huge claw was holding a child.

Channing had frowned, but somehow it made sense.

If this window had indeed been commissioned for Gilles de Rais then the inclusion of a child in its design was almost predictable.

What else could be expected of a man responsible for the deaths of over 200 children?

'The colouring methods are different, too,' Catherine had said, looking first at the clawed hand then up at the red eyes which still seemed to glow so luminously from the face of the first creature. 'That,' she pointed at the creature's face, 'looks as if it was fixed. The glass was coloured before it was put into the panel. This,' she tapped the claw very gently, 'looks as if it was painted onto the glass once it had cooled.'

'How did they colour the glass?' Channing had enquired.

'They added different metal oxides to the pot metal, that's what they called the molten glass.' She wiped her face once more. 'If they wanted red glass they added copper oxide. For green they'd add iron oxide. Cobalt oxide, blue. Manganese oxide, purple. If they wanted yellow they added sulphur.'

He had listened intently, his eyes flicking alternately between the window and Catherine.

Now, as the hands of his watch crawled round to 11.00, he leant back against the altar and looked at the window.

The glass might as well have been opaque for all they could see.

Just the claw and the face of the other creature; the rest was still encrusted by a thick layer of dirt.

Channing was tired, more tired than he could

113

remember. He felt as if the strength had been sucked from him, as if, instead of blowing wind into the church, the elements outside were drawing it away, creating a vacuum inside the chancel which made it difficult to breathe. He attributed it to the clouds of dust which hung in the air.

It was getting colder.

He rubbed his arms and shivered, looking again at his watch.

'We ought to get back to the inn,' he suggested.

Cath continued staring at the outline of the window, amazed that it was intact.

'Cath,' he said quietly, 'I said ...'

'I heard you,' she snapped, not looking at him, not taking her eyes from the casement.

'We can carry on working tomorrow morning,' Channing persisted.

Still she didn't answer him, her eyes fixed on the face of the creature in the top left-hand panel. Every now and then she would glance at the clawed hand which clutched the child but it was the red eyes that held her gaze. Finally she managed to tear her attention from it. She massaged the bridge of her nose between her thumb and forefinger and nodded.

'Maybe you're right. A good night's sleep wouldn't hurt,' she said, even managing a thin smile.

A good night's sleep. Channing couldn't remember when he'd last enjoyed that luxury.

They began to gather up their tools.

'Something's been puzzling me, Mark,' she said. 'About the church itself. How did you manage to get permission from the local authorities to work here?'

He shrugged.

'They class it as a derelict building,' he told her.

114

'They don't care who comes here or what they do when they get here. If it fell down tomorrow I don't think it would bother them.'

The wind seemed to increase in intensity. Channing shivered.

It was definitely getting colder.

Through a gap in one of the boarded-up windows he saw the moon appear momentarily in the sky before a bank of black cloud swallowed it up.

One of the hurricane lamps flickered and died, then glowed again.

Channing looked across at the window.

A dull thud reverberated throughout the church, the sound carried on the stillness.

He must have forgotten to secure the church door when they'd first entered, he told himself.

'Leave it for tonight, Cath,' he said.

The thud came again.

Twice in quick succession.

What the hell was going on here?

Twenty-Six

Channing looked around towards the door which led into the chancel. Perhaps the main door of the church had been slammed shut by the powerful wind. He crossed to the chancel door, opened it and peered out, his torch beam cutting a swathe through the gloom, picking out the main door.

It was shut tight.

Another thud, this time from above them.

In the belfry.

'Let's get out of here,' Channing said, his voice catching. 'Come on. I think we've done enough for tonight.' *Had she detected the note of fear in his voice?* He didn't really care if she had. He was tired, cold and something else he didn't care to admit. *No, what the hell?* He was frightened. The place made him uneasy at the best of times and now these bloody noises ...

'Let's go, Cath,' he said again, more forcefully this time.

She was still gazing at the window, moving towards it as if she had spotted something in the glass which Channing couldn't see.

'For Christ's sake,' he snapped. 'We'll come back in the morning.'

That thud again, and now he knew it was coming from above them.

A rational part of his mind told him it was the door which led into the belfry. The wind must have blown it open and now, with each fresh gust, it was slamming it back on its hinges. That was the answer. He suddenly felt angry with himself for even entertaining any solution but the most logical one. Lack of sleep fuelled the imagination, he told himself, thinking how late at night it was for home-spun philosophy.

Cath was kneeling beside the window now, looking more intently at the face of the child held in the clawed hand. She wiped more dust away from it.

'I'll wait for you in the car,' said Channing irritably, and she heard him clatter through into the main nave.

Cath looked at the face on the window, running the tip of her index finger around it, trying to make out the features.

116

Something …

Channing muttered to himself as he tripped and almost fell over a pew in the nave.

… *familiar* …

He heard a strident screech ahead of him as the church door opened.

For fleeting seconds he blinked in the gloom, the wind roared outside and the moon broke free of the clouds.

… *about the face* …

A dark shape filled the doorway of the church.

Dark and massive.

'Oh, Jesus Christ,' murmured Channing, fumbling for his torch.

'Cath,' he called, flicking on the torch, swinging it back and forth.

The church was filled with a smell unlike anything he'd ever encountered before.

A stench of decay.

And it was drawing closer to him, filling his nostrils.

He heard footfalls, sensed movement.

'Cath.'

He backed off.

In the chancel, Cath squinted as she continued to trace the features of the child in the window.

She knew that face.

She heard her voice being called. She smelled the vile stench.

As she heard the scream from inside the nave she looked around.

'Mark,' she called, getting to her feet, taking one last look back at the window. At the face of the child.

As she did the breath caught in her throat.

The face of the child was contorted into an attitude of terror. The child was screaming.

But it was no longer a child.
It bore the face of Mark Channing.

Twenty-Seven

She called out his name as she sat up, her body sheathed in sweat.

As she was flung from the nightmare she let out a low gasp, a combination of fear at the images which had invaded her mind and also of relief that the experience had been within the confines of her subconscious.

Now she sat forward, one hand to her throat, feeling the sweat on her fingers.

She almost screamed again when she saw the figure standing beside her bed.

In the semi-darkness, her mind still reeling from what she'd dreamt, she was unable to focus on the figure and the newest intrusion sent her heart pounding even more furiously.

It took her a second to realize that it was Channing.

'Jesus,' she murmured, her hand falling from her throat to her chest. She could feel her heart thudding against her ribs.

'Are you ok?' he asked, looking down at her. 'I heard you shout.'

She swallowed hard and nodded, looking at her watch.

2.14 a.m.

'I'm ok,' she said. 'Just a bad dream. I haven't had a nightmare since I was a kid.' She sucked in a couple of deep breaths, aware that only the sheet around her protected her nakedness from Channing's gaze. She pulled it higher, up to her throat in a gesture of exaggerated modesty. The gesture seemed somewhat inappropriate, considering they had once been lovers. The thought was pushed from her mind rapidly. The images of the dream returned and she switched on the bedside lamp, as if the coming of light would hasten the banishment of those images.

As it illuminated Channing's face she saw how pale and drawn he looked; the rings beneath his eyes were so dark and deeply etched as if a manic tattoo artist had been let loose with dark ink around the blood-shot orbs.

'You look pretty bad, Mark, if you don't mind me saying,' she said, aware of how clumsy the words sounded. 'Sorry if I woke you.'

'I was already awake,' he explained. 'Bad dreams too.'

She shrugged.

'I dreamt I was in the church,' she told him. 'I could see it as clearly as I can see you now.' She looked up at him and he squatted on the edge of the bed.

'What did you see?' he wanted to know.

'The window. Uncovered. At least another part of it.'

'A clawed hand,' he said flatly.

She nodded.

'A clawed hand holding a child,' he continued.

She looked at him, a frown creasing her brow.

All she could do was nod gently. She felt cold.

'What time did we get back from the church tonight?' she asked him, as if her own memory were suddenly untrustworthy.

'About eleven-thirty,' he told her.

Outside the wind whipped through the village square, catching one corner of an unsecured market stall awning. It began flapping in the breeze like the wings of a massive bat.

'What else did you dream?' Channing wanted to know.

'We were in the church, it was after we uncovered the window. It started to get colder in there. It was as if I could feel it.' She rubbed one arm where the flesh had risen in goose-pimples. 'There were noises. I saw something on the window. The hand you mentioned, holding a child.' The realization seemed to strike her like a slap across the cheek. 'You saw the hand, too?'

He nodded.

'On the window?' she asked.

'I think so.' He massaged the back of his neck with one hand.

'The noises carried on so you went out into the nave, left me with the window. I saw the child's face in the glass, it seemed to get clearer. I heard you calling me but I couldn't look away from the glass.'

'You felt the cold, heard the church door open.'

These weren't questions, they were statements.

'You heard me scream, you called to me, you were about to come through into the nave when you looked back at the painting and saw that the face of the child was really *my* face.'

She could only look at him blankly.

'We shared the same nightmare, Cath,' he told her. '*I saw what you saw.*'

'That's not possible,' she said, but there was no conviction in her voice.

'Then you give me another explanation.'

120

She couldn't.

Outside the wind continued to whip the awning loudly. It sounded like some huge carrion bird coming closer.

Twenty-Eight

ENNISKILLEN, COUNTY FERMANAGH, NORTHERN IRELAND:

He moved the rifle slightly to the right until the cross-threads of the telescopic sight rested squarely on the woman's head.

She bent down and he followed her with the rifle, never losing his aim, his finger resting gently on the trigger of the HK91 rifle.

Maureen Pithers knelt down beside the flower-bed and pulled some weeds from the dark earth, dropping them into the bucket beside her. She carefully worked her way round, removing any offending piece of foliage which spoiled the look of her garden. She enjoyed the task. Her weekly war on weeds, she called it. Now she continued with her own war, unaware of the rifle pointed at her head.

Billy Dolan lowered the rifle for a moment and lit up a cigarette. From where he lay he was well hidden from the house and garden by almost one hundred and fifty yards of gently sloping hillside, tall grass and trees. He'd found the best spot about an hour ago, ensuring that he had the front door of the house in clear view. The house was at the bottom of the slope, a white-painted, red-tiled building that seemed to shine in the sunlight. Nice place, Billy thought as he lit his cigarette, puffing contentedly on it for a moment before rolling over back onto his stomach, resting the stock of the rifle against his shoulder and drawing a bead on the woman once again.

She was in her mid-forties, a little plump, dressed in a green plastic apron to stop the earth from the garden getting on her clothes. He watched her pull vigorously at the weeds, tossing each one into the bucket.

Yes, it was certainly a nice place. Beat the fuck out of his home in the Turf Lodge area of Belfast. Fast approaching his twenty-second birthday, Billy had foreseen for himself the same life as his father. Jobs here and there if he was lucky, sucking up to some fucking Proddy foreman, then on the dole, drawing thirty quid a week if he was lucky.

Billy didn't want that. He didn't want to spend the rest of his days signing on and then drinking the money away in the pub on a Saturday night with the rest of his mates, who were also out of work. Fuck that.

He shifted position on the hillside and drew deeper on his cigarette.

Most members of the IRA had brothers, fathers, grandfathers or kin of some description in the ranks. Or they had followed family members into the arms of the cause. Not Billy. He had made the decision on his own because that was the way he chose to spend his life. Not bowing and scraping to anyone. Fuck the lot of them. He only took orders from one man now.

That man was lying next to him on the hill, gazing at the white house through a pair of binoculars.

James Maguire was about eight years older than Billy, a dark-haired, hard-faced man who was short yet so powerfully built his appearance could almost be described as brutish. He scanned the house and garden with the binoculars, aware that Billy had the woman pinned in the sight of the HK91.

When the time came, he would not miss.

'The car's waiting,' said Maguire. 'There's no hurry. Bring the gun with you when you've finished.'

Billy nodded.

'Company,' said the younger man, spotting a new arrival through the telescopic sight.

Maureen Pithers had stopped her war on the weeds to speak to another woman who had approached the hedge which separated the immaculately kept garden from the narrow country lane in which it stood. The house was about two hundred yards from its nearest neighbour.

Billy began moving the rifle back and forth, fixing first one woman then the other in the sights of the weapon.

'Billy.'

The sound of his own name broke his concentration.

'Front door,' said Maguire, still peering through the binoculars.

Billy looked across and saw a man emerging from the house. He was in his late forties, tall, balding. What hair he had was grey. His face was full, jovial.

Reverend Brian Pithers stood on the front doorstep for a moment, briefcase in hand, smiling across at his wife and her friend, then he crossed the lawn to the women and began speaking animatedly to them.

'I can imagine what he's saying,' said Maguire, a slight smile on his lips. 'We should never have trusted the IRA. I warned everyone about them. Now there'll be a price to pay.'

Billy chuckled.

'Have you been reading his speeches, Jim?' he said, squinting down the sight.

'It's all he's been saying since the business at Stormont,' Maguire said quietly.

'It's all he was saying *before* it,' Billy added. This time both men laughed.

Billy was still chuckling when he drew a bead on Reverend Pithers and fired.

The bullet, moving at a speed in excess of two thousand feet per second, struck Pithers just above the left eye, blasting a path effortlessly through his frontal bone before ploughing on through his brain, finally exploding from the rear of his skull, carrying a massive portion of the parietal and occipital bones with it. A thick flux of brain spewed from the wound, propelled by the force of the bullet which lifted the clergyman off his feet and catapulted him several yards backwards. He hit the ground, spraying blood all over his wife's carefully tended lawn.

Both women screamed, Mrs Pithers running to her husband's side, the other woman bursting through the gate and hurtling towards the house. Presumably to call an ambulance.

Save your strength, thought Billy, studying his handiwork through the sight.

Pither's eyes were still open, although blood from the entry wound had run into the left one. It was spreading rapidly around what remained of his head while his wife could only kneel beside him shouting something neither Billy nor Maguire could hear. There were slicks of crimson on her apron, no doubt splashed there when the bullet had first blasted away part of her husband's cranium.

The two IRA men got to their feet and sauntered away, spotting the car which waited for them at the other side of the hill, its engine idling. They'd gone less than ten feet when Maguire took the rifle from Billy and wandered back to the crest.

'Jim, what's wrong?' Billy asked, looking at his companion.

Maguire raised the rifle to his shoulder.

'He's dead,' the younger man protested.

'I know he's dead.' Maguire took aim. 'But I'll tell you something, Billy,' he said quietly. 'My mother always used to say it to me. There's nothing in this world so sad as a widow.'

And he shot Mrs Pithers once in the head.

Twenty-Nine

COUNTY-CORK, THE REPUBLIC OF IRELAND:
Night had brought with it the first spots of rain.

David Callahan stood before the huge picture window that ran virtually the length of the sitting-room and glanced out, watching the droplets spattering the glass.

After a moment or two he pulled the cord and drew the thick velvet curtains across, shutting out the darkness and elements. He crossed to the drinks cabinet and poured himself a large brandy, warming it in the large crystal tumbler.

'Do you want anything?' he asked, glancing across at Laura, who was stretched out on one of the sofas in the lounge reading. She shook her head but he poured her a vodka anyway and placed it on the table beside her.

Callahan crossed to the leather chair facing the TV and sat down, glass in hand. He reached for the remote control, pondering whether or not to switch on the set. He decided to finish his drink first.

Laura looked up from her book and caught his pensive expression.

'What are you thinking about?' she asked, reaching for the vodka and taking a sip.

'This and that,' he said enigmatically.

She folded over one corner of the page and tossed the book onto the coffee table.

'You miss London, don't you?' she said.

Callahan smiled.

'Is it *that* obvious?'

'What's there to miss, David? We've got everything here. Money, freedom to do just what we want. To experiment.' She smiled at him over the rim of the glass. 'Besides, it was too dangerous there, you know that.'

He nodded, staring down into the brandy glass. He knew she was right. They'd had no choice but to get out of London. The police had been after him; two other gangs had threatened to kill him. One had even tried. His customers had complained about the quality of the merchandise he'd been supplying. With good reason, he thought, smiling thinly. The last batch of heroin he'd sold had been only thirty per cent pure.

The rest had been made up of vim and talcum powder.

Callahan had no way of knowing how many had died as a result of taking the inferior stuff. He didn't really care, either. He'd made in excess of three million on

126

the load. However, even that was chicken-feed compared to the other rackets.

The gun-running had been so far the most lucrative, with over sixteen million netted in just over a year. When he offset the police pay-offs it still left him with close to fourteen million. The odd two or three million here and there was a small price to pay for being able to run such a lucrative business.

However, with the money came danger. Selling guns to terrorists brought its own risks. A group of French radicals had threatened to kill him over a shipment of inferior Sterling rifles he'd sold them. He'd had trouble collecting money from an over-ambitious group of Chinese youths who'd fancied their chances against one of the Triads in London.

Three of them had finished up decapitated, their bodies found in Soho Square, their heads jammed onto the railings in Leicester Square.

No one ever discovered what became of their genitals.

Callahan smiled at the recollection.

He had seen the signs early enough. He and Laura had slipped out of the country and travelled the world for eight months: the States, the Far East and the Caribbean. Finally they bought the estate in Ireland, where they now lived like throw-backs to a feudal age.

Callahan employed six house staff and four others to work the estate. At first he and Laura had both thought that Ireland, with its relaxed way of life, might be too slow for them. But they had found diversions.

And there were always the drugs.

One thing remained elusive, though. Not so much because of its unavailabilty but because it was intangible.

The ultimate thrill.

The supreme experience.

Callahan had searched for it all his life, experimenting with every substance and experience he could imagine. There were things he hadn't tried, of course, but that time would come.

He and Laura had made it their quest.

It was their Holy Grail.

He chuckled at the analogy. There had been nothing holy about most of their indulgences.

In Laura he had the perfect companion, as devoted, as obsessive in her search for that ultimate thrill as he was. Together they had run the gamut of perversion, exhausting their minds as well as their bodies in their singular quest, never really knowing how close they were to achieving the elusive dream. Neither of them knew which form it would take. They lived in a state of almost constant expectation, existing in a world of heightened arousal.

Callahan knew that the ultimate thrill was not in taking a life.

He'd done that twice before, one by shooting, the other by strangulation. Watching, feeling a man's life ebb away was a powerful sensation indeed but he knew that there must be something beyond it.

Beyond death itself, perhaps.

Callahan smiled to himself and flicked on the TV.

There was a photo of a clergyman behind the newsreader. Something looked vaguely familiar about the man's face. Callahan got to his feet to re-fill his glass, turning the volume up as he did.

'... *earlier today. The shooting happened outside Mr Pither's home in County Fermanagh and was seen by a neighbour ...*'

'David, do we have to watch this?' Laura said wearily.

128

Callahan raised a hand to silence her, his attention focused on the screen. He made his way back to the chair and gazed rapt at the television.

'... *Reverend Pithers was dead upon reaching hospital. His wife was also killed in the attack* ...'

Callahan sipped his drink slowly.

... '*The attack has been condemned by all sides including the Provisional IRA, who were anxious to stress that none of their men were involved in the killing* ...'

Laura rolled onto her stomach, her chin resting on her arms as she looked disinterestedly at the television.

'... *Coming so close to the massacre at Stormont it would appear that any permanent solution to the military and political problems in Northern Ireland is now fading fast. Police suspect that the same men responsible for the shootings at Stormont were responsible for the killing of Reverend Pithers and his wife* ...'

Callahan took a long swallow from the brandy glass, feeling the amber fluid burn its way to his stomach.

'... *the hunt for the killers continues* ...'

Callahan was on his feet, making for the drinks cabinet again when the maid appeared in the doorway of the sitting-room to announce that dinner was ready. Laura thanked her and got to her feet, preparing to switch off the TV as she passed.

'Leave it,' said Callahan, his eyes still fixed on the screen.

Laura shrugged and wandered out of the room.

The phone rang and Callahan picked it up.

'Hello,' he said, eyes still on the television, flicking it off when he realized the item had finished. 'Hello.'

No answer.

'Who's there?' he said irritably.

There was a click as the phone was put down.

He held the receiver for a second then dropped it back on the cradle and followed Laura through to the dining-room, where they both sat down.

The first course had barely been laid in front of them when the phone rang again.

'Let Julie get it,' said Laura but Callahan was already on his feet and heading for the phone in the hall.

He returned a few moments later, his face a little pale. Laura frowned as she saw his expression.

'Are you ok, David?' she asked.

He nodded briskly but didn't look at her.

'Who was that on the phone?' she wanted to know.

'Wrong number,' he said dismissively.

Laura shrugged and continued eating. As Callahan raised his fork to his mouth he noticed that his hand was shaking slightly.

Wrong number.

He wished it had been.

Thirty

He paused by the entrance to the cellar.

Callahan knew that no one else would be awake in the house at such an hour; he also knew that no one else was allowed access to the cellar. Even so, he stood for what seemed an eternity with his hand on the door knob, looking around him.

The door of the cellar was in the kitchen, and it was through this first barrier that he now passed, locking it carefully behind him. He flicked on the light switch and a narrow stairway was illuminated below him. It smelled of damp down there despite the fact that the walls were relatively free of mould, the paint still uncracked.

He descended the first flight of steps and came to another door.

Selecting a second key, Callahan let himself through and emerged into the room beyond.

More stairs stretched away before him and he snapped on more lights. A bank of fluorescents burst into life illuminating the sub-cellar. It was large, over twenty feet square. On all four sides wooden boxes were piled as high as the ceiling. As he descended he saw the words on the sides of the boxes, sprayed there with the help of a stencil.

Some of the words were foreign.

The writing was Russian. French. German.

As Callahan reached the centre of the sub-cellar he could smell the familiar odour of oil. As he crossed to the box nearest him the smell became stronger. The lid had been partially removed using a crow-bar, which lay nearby. Callahan completed the task, pulling the lid free, removing the straw which covered the contents of the box.

Four Heckler and Koch Model 33 assault rifles lay on top of the straw. Beneath them, four more.

Piled beside the crates were smaller wooden boxes full of ammunition.

Bullets of every calibre imaginable.

.45. 9mm. 5.45mm. 7.62mm. .357. .38. .44 Magnum rounds (half and full metal jacket). Hollow tips. Wad-cutters. Even a case of .223 'Duplex' cartridges.

Every type of bullet to fit every type of pistol and rifle and machine gun.

The crates were storehouses of death.

Combat Magnums, Smith and Wessons, Rugers, Walthers, Berettas, Brownings, Heckler and Koch, Remington.

And the sub-machine guns.

Ingrams, Berettas, Uzis, Skorpions, Steyrs.

The shotguns were there, too. The Ithacas, Brownings and Spas.

For the right price Callahan had always said he could get a tank. Now he smiled and picked up one of the HK33's, working the bolt action as if he were chambering a round. He pressed it to his shoulder and squinted down the sight, peering around the subterranean room.

He squeezed the trigger and the hammer slammed down on an empty chamber. The metallic click sounded thunderous inside the sub-cellar.

He had seen a young lad dressed in a T-shirt once which had borne the slogan, 'Killing is my business ... and business is good.'

It might have been invented for Callahan.

He couldn't begin to imagine how many hundreds of thousands of pounds worth of weapons were stored here below the house; it might even run into millions. Brought to him by private plane or boat from his many contacts around the world. Sent out the same way when they were needed. And there were many who paid for what he had to sell.

He re-cocked the HK33 and held it before him, finally pressing it to his shoulder and bringing the sight to bear on the sub-cellar door.

He knew he would have need of these weapons himself soon.

The time was drawing closer.

Thirty-One

BRITTANY, FRANCE:

As she drove, Catherine Roberts caught a glimpse of herself in the rear-view mirror, and what she saw wasn't very pleasing.

She was pale through lack of sleep, her eyes swollen and puffy as if she'd been crying. There were bags beginning to form, she thought, annoyed at this sudden attack of vanity. She ran a hand through her hair and concentrated on the road instead.

Beside her Mark Channing lay back in the passenger seat, his eyes closed as if hoping that the sleep which eluded him at night would come now. And yet he knew that with sleep would come dreams.

Those dreams.

He opened his eyes and rubbed them with his fists, blinking myopically at the passing countryside. Then he glanced across at Cath, who seemed unaware of his gaze. He noted every detail of her appearance and attire. Her thin face with its high cheek bones, her long hair which was whipped by the wind flowing through her open window. She wore a simple plain blouse which successfully concealed her breasts. Her jeans were tight, marked in places with the dust of the church.

The church.

It seemed that he could not escape the building whatever his train of thought and, at the moment, those thoughts were *not* on some relic of the past. They were firmly on the present.

'I don't think I've had time to thank you for coming out here, Cath,' he said, finally. 'I appreciate it.'

She smiled.

'I didn't think you'd come,' he continued, 'after what happened between us. I thought you might find it difficult.' He shrugged.

'What happened is in the past, Mark,' she said.

'Meaning you've forgotten about it?'

'I didn't say that. I haven't forgotten about it. You can't wipe out memories that easily.'

'Do you *want* to wipe them out?'

'Our affair is in the past. We were different people then.'

He looked a little disappointed.

'It was good at the time but that time has gone,' she told him.

'And you don't want it to happen again?' Channing asked, his tone lower.

'No.'

Cath was amazed she'd managed to say it quite so directly. She hoped she hadn't hurt him, but if she had then he would have to learn to live with it.

'Is there anyone at the moment?' he wanted to know.

'Is it important?'

'I'm just curious.'

'You're more than curious, Mark,' she said wearily. 'But in answer to that question, no, there isn't anyone at the moment.'

'Are you going to tell me your work comes first?' he said. She wasn't slow to pick up the hint of sarcasm in his voice.

'What's so bad about that?' she snapped.

'Nothing. I just didn't picture you as a career woman,' he told her, and again there was that edge to his tone she didn't care for. She thought about saying something but resisted the temptation.

'Don't you think we'd be better off discussing the real reason I came here, instead of raking over the past?' she said finally.

Channing was silent for a moment, looking out of the window distractedly. Finally he nodded briskly.

'So give me your *expert* opinion,' he said.

Again that edge to his voice.

'The date of the window and as much as you can tell about its manufacture.' He reached into his pocket and pulled out a packet of Rothmans, offering her one before lighting up himself.

'It's too early to tell without a thorough examination of the glass,' she began. 'But from what little I've seen I'd say that it was early fifteenth century.'

'Which would place it around the time of Gilles de Rais,' he said quietly, a softly-spoken affirmation of his own original theory. 'What I can't understand is, if de Rais was a necromancer, black magician, whatever, why would he have a stained-glass window put into a church he'd already desecrated?'

'From what we've seen of the images in the glass so far the window isn't exactly an offering to God,' said Cath. 'Stained-glass windows were usually offered as dedications to God by the men who commissioned them.'

'Jesus Christ,' murmured Channing. 'Maybe that's what the window is. An offering. An offering to the deity de Rais worshipped.' He sucked on his cigarette. 'Stained-glass windows usually told a story of some kind, right? Perhaps this one does too.'

'I won't know that until we've uncovered it all,' she

told him. 'There has to be somewhere else to work, Mark. I need to do more detailed tests on the glass.'

'Where would you suggest? Back at the inn?' he said, acidly. 'The work has to be done inside the church. Also, the fewer people who know about it the better.'

'Jealous of your little discovery, Mark?' she said, and now it was *her* turn to inject scorn into her words.

He didn't answer.

She swung the car around a curve in the road.

The church came into view, momentarily enveloped by deep shadow as a cloud passed in front of the watery sun.

Neither of them spoke as they drew nearer the building; both had their eyes fixed on it, a mixture of anticipation and unease flowing through them.

It was Cath who spotted it first.

'Mark, look,' she said, pointing ahead.

Outside the church, close to the main door, another car was parked.

Thirty-Two

Cath slowed down as they approached the car, able to see that its owner was not in evidence.

'Drive past it and stop,' said Channing, scanning the area around the church.

She did as she was instructed then they both clambered out of the Renault, eyes and ears alert to the slightest sight or sound of movement from the church. Clearly the owner of the vehicle was inside the building.

Channing headed for the door.

He was less than two feet from it when the figure emerged.

Channing took a step back, startled by the sudden appearance of the man. He was in his late twenties, tall and slightly built, with short dark hair. He smiled politely and moved out into the open, nodding a polite greeting to Cath.

'Who are you?' asked Channing.

The man looked stumped for a moment and Cath wondered if he was unable to understand English. Her French wasn't up to much but it might do in a crisis. She took a step forward.

'*Qui êtes vous?*' she asked.

'*Pardon,*' said the man, smiling. 'You may speak English if you wish. I have enough of your language to prevent difficulties.' He smiled again and Cath found herself smiling back, amused at his accent.

'What are you doing here?' Channing said, less charitable in his approach.

'My name is Claude Lausard,' he said, extending a hand which Channing declined to shake. 'I was visiting the church.'

Channing eyed the man suspiciously.

'Have you been inside?' he wanted to know.

'Only briefly ...'

'What did you see?' Channing interrupted.

'What should I have seen? Tell me, Mr Channing, you have spent more time here than most in the past few days. Miss Roberts, too.'

'How do you know our names?' Cath asked him.

'Madame Chabrol, the lady who runs the inn, *she* told me,' Lausard admitted, the smile never leaving his lips.

'We still don't know who you are,' Channing said irritably. 'Why have you been prying, finding out our names? What the hell do you want?'

Lausard held up his hands to calm Channing.

'I want a story, Monsieur Channing,' he said, still smiling.

'You're a reporter,' Cath said flatly.

The Frenchman nodded.

'Only from a humble regional newspaper, I admit, but we all have to work. What is the attraction of Machecoul?' he said, motioning to the church, his smile finally fading. 'No one ever comes near this place; you should have known that your work here, I presume it is work, would not go unnoticed by the locals. What happened here may have happened over four hundred years ago but the stigma remains. The name of Gilles de Rais belongs to history, Monsieur Channing. Perhaps for the wrong reasons, but it does nonetheless.' Lausard lit up a cigarette and walked across to his car, leaning on the bonnet. 'What were you hoping to find here?'

'Information,' Channing told him tersely.

'About de Rais? Why?'

'For a book I'm writing. I'm a historian.'

'And you, Miss Roberts? What is your interest here?'

'It isn't really any of your business, Mr Lausard,' she told him flatly.

The smile returned to the reporter's lips.

'You are certainly very protective of your discovery, whatever it may be,' he said, reaching for his lighter. As he held it up to relight his cigarette Cath noticed it was in the shape of a silver horse's head. 'Have you found de Rais' treasure?'

A heavy silence descended, broken finally by the Frenchman.

'I am not here to interfere,' he said, 'but to discover, like you.' He eyed them both. 'Is it the treasure you've found? Don't pretend you don't know what I'm talking about. If you know about Gilles de Rais then you know about the treasure he supposedly had.'

'No one knew what form that treasure took,' Channing said.

'That is what you are here to find out, I presume?'

'Look, why don't you just leave us alone to get on with our work?' snapped Channing.

Lausard continued to smile.

'Don't let me stand in your way. I'll come back when you're not so busy.' He tossed away his cigarette and slid behind the wheel of his car, starting the engine. He wound down the window and looked at the others. 'I will see you again,' he said and drove off, gravel spinning up behind the car as he sped away. Cath and Channing watched the car disappear up the dirt track then around a bend.

'That's all we need,' said Channing wearily.

The sun was sinking slowly when Lausard returned to Machecoul.

He parked his car on the crest of one of the hills which sloped down to the valley floor, got out and sat on the bonnet, looking down at the church. He reached into his pocket, pulled out first a packet of cigarettes then the silver lighter. Lausard sucked hard on the Gaulois, inhaling the smoke, allowing it to burn its way into his lungs.

From his vantage point he could see the Renault parked outside the church. He knew that Cath and Channing were still inside. What they were doing he could only guess at.

A chill breeze had sprung up; it whistled around the car, making Lausard shiver. He decided that it would be warmer waiting inside. He glanced at his watch.

7.26 p.m.

It might be a long wait.

Thirty-Three

It was almost eleven-thirty when Lausard saw the headlights of the Renault cutting through the blackness of the valley floor away from the church of Machecoul. He sat behind the wheel of his car and finished his cigarette, finally tossing the butt out of the window. Then he started the engine and guided the Citroen down the narrow road towards the building.

He didn't put on his own headlamps, relying instead on the side lights despite the unevenness of the road. No point in announcing his arrival, he thought, smiling.

The moon was hidden behind vast rolling banks of dark bilious cloud but Lausard welcomed the darkness. It aided his secretive approach.

He pulled up close to the main door of the church and switched off the engine, sitting there a moment, looking up at the church. It towered above him like some predatory animal. He finally swung himself out of the car, reaching over to the back seat in the process to pick up the camera that lay there. Checking that it was loaded with film he proceeded towards the main door, pausing before it, listening for any sound from inside.

Maybe only one of the English couple had left; perhaps the other one was still inside?

He moved closer, pressing gently against the door which opened a couple of inches.

The smell of damp enveloped him as he stood on the threshold and he stifled a cough, so strong was the odour of neglect.

It was as quiet as the grave.

He was sure he was alone.

Lausard moved into the nave, pulling a torch from his jacket pocket, flicking it on as, for the second time that day, he wandered through the derelict building. The torch beam picked out overturned pews. Dust swirled as he walked, the motes pinned in the roving light like flies on paper. He moved down the central aisle of the church towards the door that led into the chancel.

Christ, it was cold.

His breath clouded in the air as he exhaled. He stopped for a moment to breathe on his hands. It hadn't felt this cold outside, he thought, as he moved closer to the far door.

His inspection of the building earlier in the day had not taken him beyond the nave. In fact he'd been on the point of investigating the chancel when he'd heard the car with Cath and Channing in pull up. Now, however, there was no one to interrupt him.

Keeping the torch at chest height he moved on.

He knew they'd found something inside the church. Otherwise what reasons would they have for being so secretive?

Had they really found de Rais' treasure?

Lausard reached the chancel door and pulled at it, relieved when he found it wasn't locked.

141

As he opened it a blast of cold air hit him like a freezing hammer. It was as if all the warmth had been sucked from his body. He paused for a moment, trying to re-acclimatize himself to the sudden, savage drop in temperature.

The darkness inside the chancel was almost palpable. Lausard felt as if he were drowning in it, as if the gloom was filling him as he breathed. He slowed his breathing and shone the torch around the inner sanctum of the church, picking out the altar, the boarded-up windows, the door which led to the stairs and belfry beyond, the shape ...

To his left was an object draped in a piece of cloth.

An object about six feet high.

He shone the torch over it, unable to make out any contours.

Aware of his own heartbeat thudding more insistently, Lausard moved towards it, reaching out to grip the cloth.

He pulled and it came free.

Lausard frowned.

Was this what they were being so secretive about?

A *stained-glass window*.

The top third of it had been uncovered by painstaking work and the images seemed to glow in the light of his torch with surprising brilliance. Exactly what they were he didn't know.

Some of them disgusted him.

He moved closer, shining the torch over the glass, gazing long and hard at the features of the creature in the top right-hand panel, then turned away and headed towards the door that led to the belfry stairs. If they'd found something, he reasoned, it had to be more than the window.

Surely.

The door opened with difficulty, its ancient hinges creaking protestingly as Lausard pulled.

A gust of cold wind blew down the spiral stairs and ruffled his hair. He shone the torch up and saw that the stairs curved around to the right, the spiral apparently growing tighter the higher the staircase rose.

He pressed on the first step, putting all his weight on it, satisfied when the old timbers merely groaned under his pressure.

The stairs were safe to climb.

He began to ascend.

Lausard was halfway up when he detected the stench.

It was noxious beyond belief, a nauseating smell which made him feel faint, such was its intensity. He stopped on the stairs, putting one hand across his mouth in an effort to minimize the effect of the choking fetor.

It was then that he realized it was coming from below him.

From the chancel.

He turned on the stairs and headed back down, the torch beam swaying back and forth as he hurried down the creaking steps, almost retching now, such was the vehemence of the stench.

As he stumbled into the chancel itself he felt his legs give way and he fell to the ground, his lighter skidding across the floor.

He didn't attempt to retrieve it.

All he wanted to do was get out of the church, get away from this rancid atmosphere.

He dragged himself to his feet, his torch beam settling briefly on the window again.

The smell was momentarily forgotten as he stood gaping at it.

At …

Lausard wanted to shake his head, wanted to register some gesture but it seemed as if every muscle in his body was frozen.

Thirty-Four

Callahan was half way up the stairs when he heard the phone ring again.

Callahan called that he would answer it, anxious that Laura should not retrieve the receiver. He snatched up one of the extensions in a spare room, pressing the phone to his ear, his hand shaking slightly.

'Hello,' he said.

The line was crackly, alive with static.

'Who is it?' Callahan repeated, trying to steady the quivering in his voice.

'Callahan,' the voice on the other end said. 'It's me. It's Lausard.'

Callahan swallowed hard and his grip on the phone relaxed.

'What do you want?' he asked.

'I might have something for you,' the Frenchman said.

'What is it?'

'It should fit nicely into your collection,' the Frenchman said.

'Just stop pissing about and tell me what it is,'

Callahan snapped. 'I don't pay you to play games.'

'It's a stained-glass window.'

Callahan didn't speak.

'Did you hear what I said?' Lausard repeated. 'Probably commissioned by Gilles de Rais himself.'

'Who else knows about it?' Callahan wanted to know.

Lausard explained about Channing and Catherine Roberts.

'I want it Lausard. Do you understand? No matter what, I want it.'

'It's going to cost you a lot of money.'

'I don't care how much it costs, I want it.' There was a steely determination in his voice. 'We'll come over as soon as we can.' He hung up.

Callahan smiled to himself.

Gilles de Rais.

The man had murdered over two hundred children, many of them in the church at Machecoul. Ritual killings, the children had been between the ages of four and ten, rarely older. De Rais himself had been burned at the stake as a witch. Again Callahan smiled. He climbed the rest of the stairs to the bedroom, where Laura lay naked on the bed glancing at a magazine.

'Lausard's found something in the church at Machecoul,' he said quietly.

She turned to look at him.

'To do with de Rais?' she said.

He nodded.

'Machecoul.' She said the name softly, with something bordering on reverence.

They had visited it many years ago. Just as they had visited countless other places around the world where murders, and sometimes much worse, had taken place. They visited and they photographed and they studied.

145

Their interest had often taken them far afield but they had visited sites and soaked up atmospheres others would have shunned.

Auschwitz.

Belsen.

10050 Cielo Drive in Los Angeles, scene of the ritual murders of Sharon Tate and four others by Charles Manson's family.

Dealey Plaza in Dallas. (They had stood on the spot in the road where the car had been when President Kennedy had been shot.)

Saddleworth Moor in Yorkshire. (Laura had been excited by the fact that she might actually be *standing* on the grave of one of the victims of Ian Brady and Myra Hindley.)

The German Embassy in Stockholm, fire-bombed by the Baader-Meinhof gang.

Cranley Gardens, Muswell Hill, London. (They had wanted to look inside the flat where Denis Nilsen had killed and mutilated his victims but had been turned away. Still, Laura had taken plenty of pictures of the outside of the building.)

Jeffrey Manor, Chicago. (Richard Speck had killed eight nurses there in one night of madness.)

Buhre Avenue, New York City. (David Berkowitz, known as 'Son of Sam', had shot his first victims there.)

The list was endless. They had travelled the world to sample these delights, bringing back with them souvenirs wherever possible. Pieces of wire from Auschwitz. Turf from Saddleworth Moor. Stones from Buhre Avenue. Usually, however, they were content with photos; they had hundreds in one of the rooms close to their bedroom. It was like a shrine.

Laura often sat in there alone, staring around at the walls, surrounded by images of death and pain, excited sometimes beyond endurance.

Sex in that room was beyond belief.

It was pleasure without measure, or equal.

'How many did de Rais kill?' she asked, letting one hand slide across the bed towards Callahan's groin.

'Over two hundred,' he said, feeling his own excitement growing as she rubbed his penis, feeling it stiffen.

'All children,' he continued.

He was fully erect now.

She leant over and took him in her mouth, allowing her saliva to coat his purple glans, licking down the length of the hard shaft to his testicles.

'He killed them slowly,' Callahan said, feeling urgently between her legs, smiling as he felt the hot wetness there.

'How did he kill them?' she asked, swinging herself around, lowering her dripping sex onto his organ with infinite slowness, allowing just the tip to penetrate her, teasing both herself and her husband.

'He cut them at the base of the skull, then he'd masturbate over their bodies,' Callahan said.

She lowered herself sharply, allowing him to slide up inside her. The glorious insertion ripped the breath from her and she moaned loudly, pausing only a second before beginning to move up and down on his rigid erection.

'He timed it so that his own climax would arrive as they died,' she gasped, perspiration beginning to form on her forehead. Machecoul.

The window.

He had to have it.

147

Had to possess it. To put it alongside the pieces of masonry he and Laura had taken from the building on their last visit.

Laura began to come.

Callahan was close behind her.

The window.

He *would* have it.

Thirty-Five

STRABANE, COUNTY TYRONE, NORTHERN IRELAND:

'It's a fucking disgrace.'

Joseph Hagen spat the words out as if they were poison, aware that all other eyes in the room were upon him but revelling in that knowledge.

'These bastards have put back the name of the IRA twenty years,' he continued. 'And after all we've done. All the sacrifices. All the compromises. Something has to be done and done fast.'

There was a babble of agreement from the other men in the room.

It was a small room over the top of a bar called 'The Mean Fiddler'. The pub stood about twenty miles from the border with Donegal. It had been used countless times by the men who sat in it now and by their fathers and grandfathers before them. It was perfect, the location, the surroundings. Jobs had been planned here for as long as anyone could remember. Any hint of police or army interference and they could be back across the border into the Republic within twenty minutes.

But now the members of the IRA high command were meeting for a very different reason. The target was not to be an RUC outpost or an army border patrol.

It was much closer to home in all respects.

Joe Hagen took a hefty swig from the glass of Jameson's and shook his head. He looked down at his large hands.

'I agree with Joe,' said another man, a smaller man with thin, pinched features and the beginnings of a beard. 'We all know who's to blame for what's been going on. The longer we leave the problem, the worse it's going to get.'

Another babble of agreement.

'Jerry, make a decision now. It can't be that hard, especially for you,' Eamonn Rice said. 'Christ, you were at Stormont, you could have been killed along with the others. We all know what has to be done.'

The words were directed at the man who sat in one corner of the room, head down, the collar of his flying jacket pulled up high so that he looked like an owl. When he glanced around the room he saw expectation in the faces of his colleagues.

Gerard Coogan clasped his hands together on the table in front of him and tapped his thumbs together. Mention of Stormont brought pictures flooding back into his mind like forgotten photos dredged up from an unwanted album. The gunmen. The bodies. The blood. Coogan had seen it all before but he'd never been on the *receiving* end before. He was thirty-five, dark-haired, sallow-faced. The most striking thing about him were his eyes, a blue so vivid they glowed as if lit from within his skull. He moved his gaze over the men in the room, those eyes roving like sapphiric searchlights.

'You're right,' he said finally, his voice deep and rumbling. 'I do know what has to be done but that doesn't make it any easier. For as long as I can remember the British Government have been our enemy. It's their soldiers who patrol our streets, it's their policies that govern the six counties. But now, all that's different. The enemy doesn't wear a khaki uniform anymore. We've got no fuss with the British now, or the fucking Protestants. For all I know there are British agents in Ireland already. If there are I don't really care. This is *our* problem and we'll solve it *our* way.' He cleared his throat, using the back of one hand to mask the cough. 'We know Maguire and his men did the shootings at Stormont. We know they killed Pithers and his wife. What we don't know is *why*.' He glanced around the room. 'We need to know who paid them. Joe's right; what they've done, what they might do has damaged the image of the IRA badly. That's why *we* need to catch them. Catch them and destroy them.' He smiled thinly. 'We're not fighting the British anymore. We're fighting ourselves.'

'Who do *you* think was behind it, Jerry?' Rice asked.

'Probably the fucking Protestants,' Hagen snapped.

'Why should they be?' Coogan said challengingly. 'They wanted peace here more than most.' He shook his head. 'I haven't got a clue. I really haven't. Whoever set it up knew what they were doing, though. We're all at the stage of not trusting one another again. If something isn't done quickly then relations will break down and we'll be back to square one.'

'Maybe that wouldn't be such a bad thing,' Hagen rumbled.

'Don't talk shite, Joe,' Coogan snapped. 'We couldn't fight this war against the British indefinitely and, besides, our demands had been met. We've all fought too long to get where we are now. Not just us but our fathers and grandfathers too. We'd *won*.' He looked icily at Hagen, fixing the man with the full ferocity of his stare. 'If we get Maguire then all the suffering over the years will have been worthwhile. But we have to get him fast.'

'How many men has he got with him?' Rice asked.

'Four or five,' said Hagen. 'We have their names.'

Coogan nodded and Hagen reeled them off like a roll-call.

'Billy Dolan. Damien Flynn. Paul MacConnell and Michael Black. And Maguire himself of course. There could be a couple more but I doubt it.' Hagen drained what was left in his glass.

'Like I said, the British have probably got someone on their trail too,' Coogan said. 'But it's important that we find them first.' His gaze travelled in the direction of the man in the far corner of the room. So far he hadn't spoken, merely sat listening, his face impassive. His features looked as if they'd been carved from granite. He regarded Coogan from beneath heavy-lidded eyes. The lines across his forehead looked as if someone had drawn a fork through the flesh. There were deep creases around his eye corners, too. He looked older than his twenty-seven years.

'We'll get them,' Simon Peters said quietly. 'I've got men checking them out now; their homes, where they were last seen. We'll get them.'

'And whoever paid them,' Coogan reminded him.

Peters nodded.

'What about the British?' he said. 'You think they've

already got men chasing Maguire. What if they get in the way?'

Coogan stroked his chin thoughtfully for a moment.

'Kill them too,' he said, flatly.

Thirty-Six

The crack of pool balls was scarcely audible above the noise coming from the juke-box.

Sean Doyle sat at the bar of 'The Standing Stones', alternately gazing around at the other drinkers and staring into the bottom of his glass.

To his right two men were playing darts. Behind them one of the two pool tables was in use. The men playing looked like father and son. Both had bright red hair. The pub was relatively busy, most of the booths taken and many of the bar stools occupied. A concentrated buzz of chatter filled the air, competing with the juke-box. There was a television set at one end of the bar, set high up on a shelf, and that too was on but the sound was turned down and images appeared in silence.

The air smelt of smoke and alcohol.

It was a smell Doyle had grown accustomed to during the past two days. Ever since arriving in Belfast it seemed that he'd spent all his time drifting from pub to pub. From the Ardoyne to New Lodge. From the Lower Falls across to Short Strand. Now he found himself in Ballymurphy.

His procedure, such as it was, had been simple and

unwavering in every place. Order a couple of drinks, sit at the bar or close to any large group of drinkers. Just observe and listen.

He was like a gull following a trawler, waiting for any tit-bit to fall in front of him. The talk was the usual pub talk, had been in every one of the places he'd visited so far. Sport. Politics. Women.

Never religion.

Each pub, each face had seemed to blur into one as he'd ceaselessly trekked around the city in search of that elusive piece of information he sought. If any of the locals knew anything about Maguire and his renegades they weren't saying. In fact, they weren't even voicing opinions about it. Not as far as he knew, anyway.

He ordered himself another drink and swivelled around on his stool to watch the two men who were playing darts, but his gaze darted around the bar constantly, alighting on each new face as it entered the bar.

How beautifully simple it would be, he thought, if Maguire were to walk in now.

Doyle smiled to himself.

So simple.

The counter terrorist had a .38 special strapped to his leg in an ankle holster, hidden by his jeans and boots. Yet, if Maguire walked in, how easy it would be to retrieve the pistol. The weapon was loaded with Blazer .357 rounds. Hollow tips to ensure that one or two shots at the most would be enough to stop his quarry. The .44 which he usually carried was too bulky for the ankle holster. It lay back at the hotel along with the CZ automatic and the extra special little item he'd brought along.

Back at the hotel.

Donaldson had fixed both him and Georgie up with

jobs at the Excelsior hotel in Belfast city centre, Doyle as a night-porter, Georgie as a bar-maid. They were posing as an engaged couple.

Since the relaxation of hostilities between the IRA and the British in the last few months, the curiosity and mistrust which newcomers usually faced was not so apparent. Doyle had been able to move unhindered through areas where, twelve months before, he would have been risking his life travelling.

Ballymurphy was one such place. The Catholic stronghold had been infiltrated a number of times in the past by Secret Service men but, more often than not, they were discovered. Their fate was invariably a savage beating and torture; then they were bagged and dumped on waste ground.

Doyle had been working undercover in the same way when he'd been so badly injured in Londonderry two years earlier.

Now he sipped at his drink and continued looking around the bar. Darts continued to thud into the board. Pool balls cracked loudly against each other. The cacophony of conversation grew in volume.

The man next to him had a newspaper laid out on the bar and he was running his index finger down a list of horses, looking vainly for a winner. He picked out a couple of possibles, then folded the paper up and dropped it down, front page up.

MORE MURDERS AS PEACE PLAN FACES CRISIS

proclaimed the headline of the *Evening Herald*. There was a photo of Reverend Brian Pithers' house with an ambulance outside and several police cars. Doyle pulled the paper towards him.

'Do you mind?' he asked the owner of the paper, his

Irish accent unfaltering.

'Help yourself,' the man replied, smiling amiably.

Doyle scanned the headline again then quickly read the report on the clergyman's death and that of his wife.

'Terrible business,' said the man next to him, nodding in the direction of the paper.

'He had it coming,' said Doyle flatly, smiling at the man. 'He's been doing nothing but putting down the Cause for the last five or six years.'

'You'll be telling me his wife had it coming too,' said the man irritably.

Doyle shrugged and pretended to look at the paper.

Pick your words. Play it carefully.

'Maybe she did,' he said indifferently. 'Her *and* those fellas at Stormont. Why did they have to interfere, anyway? What makes *them* think they can put the bloody world to rights?'

'Ah, you're bloody crazy,' said the man dismissively.

'What's wrong, George?'

Another voice joined the conversation. It belonged to a tall, brown-haired man who was leaning against the bar as if for support. Doyle could tell from the slight slur on his words that the man had had too much to drink.

Perfect, he thought.

'Your man here,' said the first drinker, hooking a thumb in Doyle's direction. 'He reckons that old Pithers had it coming.'

'Him and the others,' Doyle said loudly. 'Who the fuck do they think they are, anyway? A peace plan. To hell with it. It's a pity the IRA ever sat down at the same table with the bloody Brits and the Proddies. They should have carried on as they were.'

'How long have you lived in this city, man?' said the drunken individual, pushing past his companion. 'Long enough to see the fucking bombs going off and people being shot down? There was a chance of peace and these fucking rebels or whatever they call themselves might have ruined that chance.'

Come on, sunshine. The bait's laid, you've picked it up, now I've just got to reel you in.

'So what?' Doyle said, scornfully. 'I hope they kill a few more.' He raised his glass in a toast. 'Here's to the rebels,' he said, smiling.

'You bastard,' snarled the drunken man, lunging at him.

Bingo.

Doyle moved away from the bar, side-stepping the clumsy dive with ease, but the man rounded on him, preparing to throw a punch.

'Cut it out,' shouted the barman, seeing the impending trouble.

'You've got a fucking big mouth,' snarled the drunk, glaring at Doyle.

'Then make me shut it, shithead,' he rasped, waiting for the inevitable onslaught. Doyle took a step backwards towards the unused pool table. Two cues were lying on it.

'Leave him, Tommy,' said someone further down the bar but the drunk was incensed, his reason clouded by the amount of booze he'd consumed.

'I'm going to knock your fucking head off,' he hissed at Doyle.

'Then do it,' he snapped back.

The man ran at him.

From a booth in the corner, Billy Dolan looked on with interest.

Thirty-Seven

The attack was clumsy.

Doyle side-stepped the drunken man's charge with little difficulty, his hand closing around a cue on the pool table.

As the man rose Doyle gripped the long piece of wood tightly and swung it with savage force.

The blow caught the man full in the face as he was rising. The thick end of the cue shattered two of his front teeth as it hit him squarely in the mouth. The enamel disintegrated under the impact, one tooth torn from the gum and forced through his upper lip. Blood poured from the hideous injury and the man dropped to his knees, both hands held to the bleeding cavity, moaning in pain as others came to his aid.

Doyle thought about bringing the cue down on the top of the man's head but finally he threw it to one side, his eyes on the two other men by the bar who'd been with his opponent before the fracas began. One of them took a step towards him but Doyle shook his head, his hand going to his jacket pocket.

The man didn't know there was nothing in there but he backed off nonetheless.

Shouts now filled the pub. Of rage. Outrage.

'Get out of here,' shouted the barman, flipping open the bar and ambling towards Doyle. 'Go on, get out of my fucking pub.'

The counter-terrorist had every intention of doing

so; he even tolerated a half-hearted push from one of the injured man's colleagues. Then, suddenly, he was in the street, the sounds of bedlam closed off as the main doors of the pub shut behind him. He began walking immediately, hands dug deep in his jacket pockets, his pace even and unhurried.

He smiled as he remembered the sight of the drunken man's face after he'd hit him with the cue. It had felt good, all the more amusing to Doyle because he'd inflicted the damage defending the name of an organization he'd spent a good portion of his life fighting. The irony kept the grin on his face as he walked.

He wandered down streets of terraced houses, each one looking as if it had been deposited from the end of a huge conveyor belt. They had a depressing uniformity; the only concessions to individualism were different coloured curtains or front doors.

On the other side of the road there was a shop, a small general-purpose store. Its windows were heavily boarded up. Slogans had been sprayed over the metal guards.

FREEDOM FOR IRELAND
BRITS OUT
GOD BLESS THE CAUSE

A group of children were kicking a ball about, bouncing it off a parked car nearby. The ball spun loose and skidded in Doyle's direction. He trapped it expertly with one foot, flipped it up into the air and began knocking it from one foot to the other then from one knee to the other, finally balancing it on his head as the youngsters watched. He finally flipped it up, caught it on the volley and sent it crashing against a lamp post.

'Flash bastard,' said one of the children as he passed.

Doyle grinned broadly and walked on.

Two women standing in the doorway of a house

looked across at him, perhaps not recognizing his face, wondering who this newcomer to their community was. Life on the estates of Belfast was very insular; everyone knew everyone else's business. There were no secrets. It was as if the whole country were part of one gigantic conspiracy.

He stopped to light a cigarette, tossing the spent match into the gutter.

It was as he turned into Whiterock Road that he realized he was being followed.

He had suspected as much when he stopped to kick the kids' football but he had only glimpsed the man briefly out of the corner of his eye. To a less trained man the tail probably would have been anonymous, as it was intended, but to someone in Doyle's profession the pursuer might as well have been wearing a sandwich board proclaiming the fact.

A friend of the injured man's, perhaps?

A plain-clothes policeman even, suspicious of such open support for the IRA renegades?

A number of alternatives passed through Doyle's mind as he walked on.

He crossed the road, glancing back supposedly to check for traffic.

His pursuer was still there.

Gaining, if anything.

Doyle reached the other side of the road and slowed his pace. Fuck this; he wasn't going to wear himself out for nothing. He dropped to one knee and pretended to adjust his boot, aware how easy it would be to slip the .38 from its holster should he need to.

He heard footsteps quickening behind him.

There were about a dozen people on the street but Doyle didn't care. If he had to he would use the gun.

159

The footsteps drew closer.

'Hey,' a voice called.

Doyle got to his feet, his pursuer now less than ten feet behind him.

'Hey, you,' the voice called again, much closer this time.

Doyle turned, not wanting to be caught off guard.

The man who approached him was in his early twenties, a little shorter than Doyle.

He was smiling.

'I saw what happened in the pub, back there,' said Billy Dolan.

'What if you did?' said Doyle challengingly.

'I just wanted to tell you that if you're in there again I'll buy you a drink.'

Doyle's facial expression didn't change.

'Why?' he asked.

'I heard what that mouthy bastard was saying about the IRA before you put one on him. I wanted to thank you. The Cause doesn't have too many friends right now. One more never hurts.' He smiled that broad, infectious smile again.

'Thanks,' said Doyle. 'I'll take you up on that drink.' He faltered, realizing he didn't know the man's name.

'Billy.'

Doyle extended a hand which Dolan shook warmly.

'Good to meet you, Billy,' he said, looking closely at the man's face, taking in every detail, every furrow and line, every nuance of expression. 'My name's Sean.'

'I'd buy you one now but I've got to be off,' said Dolan. 'But, like I said, if you're in there again the offer stands.' He turned and headed back across the road, raising a hand as a gesture of farewell.

Doyle watched him go, looking down briefly at his

own right hand as if he could still feel the strength of the man's grip.

'Well, Billy,' he said, softly, his Irish accent now gone. 'Maybe I will let you buy me that drink after all.' Then, smiling, he turned and headed towards the bus stop at the bottom of the road.

Thirty-Eight

She wanted to see where he'd died.

That had been her first, irrational, ridiculous thought, looking out of the plane onto Belfast.

She had wanted to see the place where her brother had been murdered.

Now Georgina Willis stood against the window of her room on the tenth floor of the Excelsior Hotel and looked out across the city where her brother had been killed.

It was late afternoon; the sky already dark with approaching rain clouds. The weather forecast even spoke of some localized fog. She pressed her face to the cold glass and sighed, glancing down at the people milling about in the streets below, at the cars and buses which clogged the roads. From here, Belfast seemed like any ordinary city, full of shoppers and business people, tourists and visitors. But since 1969 it had been a battleground. And, just when that conflict had looked like reaching a final conclusion, the threat had risen once more to cloud the minds of those who lived in the province. It seemed as if so much hope was to be dashed, already had been dashed, in the blaze of automatic weapons at Stormont less than a week earlier.

But those that had died at Stormont had been faceless to her in the widest sense. Yes, she knew their names, but their deaths had been unfortunate. Their passing had not touched her life. They had been strangers.

She thought that most of the pain of losing her brother had passed by now, but as she stood gazing out over the city she found the hurt rising again inside her, swelling like a blister on her consciousness. She finally moved away from the window, walking across to the bed. There she sat on the edge and took off her shoes, massaging her aching feet. The shift had seemed unusually long behind the main bar of the hotel. She'd been working for over four hours, pulling pints and measuring shorts, cleaning glasses, chatting with the other bar-staff and customers alike.

There had been little information worth storing, little worth telling Doyle when he returned. If he ever did.

She had seen little of him in the past two days. He had a room next to hers, but when he wasn't posing as a night porter he was out and about in the city. She'd seen him for less than an hour since they'd arrived in Belfast two days before. He was becoming restless, angry that no leads were turning up. It seemed that Maguire and his men had disappeared into thin air after the killing of Reverend Pithers. There had been talk of the latest murder in the hotel and Georgie had probed and cajoled her colleagues to speak their views on what had happened in the vain hope that one of them might have some shred of information worth following up, but so far she had heard nothing.

She unbuttoned her blouse and tossed it onto the bed, slipped off her skirt and threw that to one side as well.

She wandered through into the bathroom and turned on the shower, testing the water with her hand. Then she pulled off her bra and knickers, wrapped a white housecoat around her and padded back into the bedroom. She put her skirt and blouse on a hanger and crossed to the wardrobe.

As she opened the door she looked down at her handbag.

The gun was inside.

While she waited for the shower to heat up she took the pistol from her bag and walked across to the bed with it, where she sat, one leg drawn up beneath her, the gun cradled in her hand.

The Sterling .357 Magnum was surprisingly light; it was one of the reasons she had chosen it. It was chambered for either .38 or .357 rounds. Georgie flipped out the cylinder and spun it, checking each chamber. In her bag she had the ammunition. She was using Blazer rounds, light and hollow-tipped.

She raised the pistol and squeezed the trigger, smiling at the smoothness of the action. The hammer slammed down on an empty chamber, the metallic crack echoing around the room. She replaced the weapon, wandered through into the bathroom, took off her robe and stepped beneath the shower, enjoying the feel of the water on her skin. She adjusted the spray so that the jets stung her skin and stood beneath the spray, eyes closed, allowing the water to bounce off her. It ran over her breasts and down her stomach, through her light pubic hair. The hiss of the shower was loud.

Loud enough to mask the sounds outside her door.

Georgie did not hear the rattle as someone tried to turn the handle.

She stood beneath the shower, allowing the water to wash the smell of smoke and drink from her hair, to scour the tiredness from her muscles.

The door-handle twisted.

She heard nothing beneath the pounding spray.

She reached for the soap.

'Shit,' she murmured, noticing that she had left it by the sink.

She stepped from beneath the shower, almost slipping on the tiled floor as water ran down her legs, one hand wiping moisture from her eyes.

She was about to step back into the shower when she heard the rattle of the lock.

Through the open bathroom door she could see the handle moving very slightly.

Without a second thought she sprinted through into the bedroom, naked, leaving soggy footprints on the carpet as she scuttled towards the wardrobe.

Towards the revolver.

The sounds outside the door had ceased for a moment and Georgie opened the wardrobe quietly, wincing when the hinges creaked. She kept one eye on the door, pulling the gun and ammunition from her bag.

The handle moved once more.

She slid six bullets quickly and carefully into their chambers and snapped the cylinder shut. Then, raising the gun before her, she pressed herself against the wall and moved towards the door, leaving wet slicks against the wallpaper.

She heard a click as the lock was slipped, she guessed with a credit card.

The door began to open.

Georgie steadied the gun in both hands, making sure

that, if the door was pushed, she would still have clear access to the intruder.

The door opened a little more; she saw the outline of a shadow fall across her threshold.

A figure took a step inside.

She lowered the .357, her heart pounding that little bit faster.

The intruder was in now.

Georgie smiled and thumbed back the hammer, pushing the barrel of the weapon against the intruder's head.

'You move and I'll blow your fucking head off,' she whispered.

Thirty-Nine

It took Georgie a couple of seconds to realize what was happening.

To recognize the long hair, the leather jacket.

'For Christ's sake, Doyle,' she hissed, lowering the pistol. 'Couldn't you just knock?'

The counter-terrorist turned to face her, a smile spreading across his lips as he saw that she was naked, her body still dripping water. Georgie suddenly seemed to realize as well and tugged the blanket from the bed, wrapping it around herself. Her cheeks flushed.

'What the hell are you doing creeping around breaking into my bloody room, anyway?' she said, irritably, returning the .357 to the wardrobe. As she turned her back on him he saw that the blanket didn't serve as a very good wrap around. Her buttocks were bare. Doyle raised his eyebrows approvingly. He walked across to the bed and sat down.

'We are supposed to be a couple,' he said, still smiling, stroking the scar on the left side of his face.

It was as he raised his hand she noticed there was blood on it.

'What happened to you?' she asked, nodding towards his hand.

Doyle noticed it now too and shrugged.

'It's not my blood,' he told her. 'It's from some mouthy mick I met in a pub.'

She walked back into the bathroom, pushing the door shut behind her, finishing her shower quickly. She emerged a moment later, dressed in the bath robe, her hair dripping. She wiped it with a towel.

'Have you heard anything?' he asked.

'Just the usual chit-chat,' she said. 'Everyone's outraged by what's happened, can't understand why the killing took place. The usual sort of thing. Nothing to go on. What about you?'

'If anyone knows anything about Maguire they're keeping it bloody quiet,' he said, lying back on the bed, arms folded behind his head. 'No one even wants to admit allegiance to the IRA since what happened.' He paused for a moment. 'Apart from one guy I met today in a pub in Ballymurphy.' He told her briefly what had happened in the pub.

'Who was this guy who followed you?' she wanted to know, running fingers through her hair to dry it.

'His name was Billy. I didn't get his last name, unfortunately. Young. Early twenties, about five-eight, dark-haired, grey eyes. I'm going back tomorrow, see if I can find him. It's not much of a lead but it's all we've got at the moment.'

She finished drying her hair, perched on the end of the bed looking down at Doyle.

'Where the hell have you been for the last two days? I've hardly seen you?'

'Doing my job,' he said. 'We came here to find Maguire, not go on a sightseeing trip.' He regarded her coldly for a moment.

'You don't have to be so hostile, Doyle. I'm on *your* side, remember?' she said quietly.

He swung himself up and prepared to get to his feet.

'If it hadn't been me coming through that door just then,' he said. 'What would you have done?'

'Fired, if necessary. Does that surprise you?' she asked.

'No.' He smiled at her.

'You're off tonight, aren't you?' she said. 'I know because I checked the rotas. I'm off too.'

'Want to go out somewhere?' he asked, almost as if it were a natural thing to do. 'A meal, perhaps? You never know, we might even overhear something.'

She smiled.

'That would be nice,' she said.

He was already heading for the door.

'I'll be back in half an hour, I want to get cleaned up,' he told her. He paused as he reached the door. 'Have you got anything else with you except that Sterling?'

She nodded.

'I've got a PD Star. Why?'

'Bring it,' he said flatly. 'Slip it in your stocking top.' He winked at her. 'Just in case.'

Then he was gone.

Georgie went back to the wardrobe and found the Star in a side compartment of her handbag. At less

167

than four inches in length it fitted into the palm of her hand, but its 9mm calibre meant that, should it be needed, it was more than adequate for bringing down a man. She laid it beside her on the dressing table as she began to apply her make-up.

Doyle was bang on time.

At 8.36 p.m. they rode the lift to the ground floor where he invited her to take his arm.

'We *are* supposed to be a couple,' he reminded her.

Arm-in-arm they walked through the foyer and out into the bustling streets of the city, which was now under a blanket of darkness.

Doyle hailed a taxi and they climbed in.

Neither of them spotted the car which pulled out behind them and settled in traffic two car-lengths behind.

The driver never let the cab out of his sight as he followed.

Forty

The restaurant wasn't very crowded, and for that Doyle was grateful.

It was small, what the tour guides like to call 'intimate'. Subdued lighting, plush seats and mirrors on the wall reflecting the glow from the lamps on each table. Every now and then Doyle would catch a glimpse of himself in the mirrors and avert his eyes, as if the sight of his own reflection was somehow unpleasant.

He sat alone, waiting for the first course to arrive and

for Georgie to return from the ladies room. There were two other couples in the restaurant and one portly man on his own in a corner. He constantly looked round as he ate, although invariably his gaze met Doyle's and he would hastily return his full attention to his meal.

What do you know?

Why are you on your own?

Businessman? Out for a quiet dinner because there's no one at home to cook you one? Had a row with your partner? Wife out with the girls?

Doyle smiled at his own curiosity. Perhaps it was a hazard of the job, he told himself.

A bit like being blown up by suicidal IRA men?

Another occupational hazard?

His musings were interrupted by Georgie's return. Doyle ran appraising eyes over her, liking what he saw.

She wore a tight-fitting black dress open in a 'V' down the back just above the small of her back. It was too tight to allow underwear beneath, something he was convinced of by the way her nipples pushed against the material. She walked with grace on a pair of precipitous high heels.

As Georgie arrived so did the starter and they both began eating. Her clutch bag lay on the seat beside her, the Star automatic nestled inside.

Doyle wore the Charter Arms .44 in a holster around his waist, hidden by his jacket.

'How did you find this place?' Georgie asked. 'It doesn't look like *your* style.'

'And what does my *style* mean?' he said somewhat scornfully. 'You mean you think I'd be better suited to a MacDonalds?'

'I didn't say that,' she murmured, looking a little embarrassed.

'Appearances can be deceptive, Georgie,' he said. 'I mean, look at *you*. You don't exactly look like a counter-terrorist.' He lowered his voice as he spoke the last two words.

'What do I look like?' she wanted to know.

'Tonight?' He smiled. 'You look like a model.'

She was taken aback by his remark. Surprised and flattered by it.

'You're full of shit, aren't you?' she chuckled.

'The best quality bullshit,' he reminded her.

'And do all the girls fall for it?'

He shrugged.

'Some.' He looked at her unflinchingly. 'What about you?'

'If you mean do I fall for bullshit, the answer is sometimes. I'm going to take what you said as a compliment, though. It's probably the closest I'll get from *you*.'

They continued eating.

'So are there any women in your life, Doyle?' she wanted to know. 'Is it true what I've heard about you?'

'Tell me what you've heard and I'll tell you if it's true.'

'You're a womaniser. An irresponsible, violent, disrespectful and possibly disturbed man. You've got a death wish. You treat everyone with equal contempt, men and women. A loner. You drink too much, you're unpredictable, single and, as I said, a womanizer.'

'You've been reading my file,' he said. 'Or is that what Donaldson told you?'

'I read your file *and* your psychological evaluation. When I found out I was working with you I wanted to know more about you.'

'So you found that out and you *still* wanted to work with me. Why?' he wanted to know.

She shrugged.

'Perhaps it was a challenge for me,' she said, smiling.

'Now who's full of shit?' he muttered, sipping from the glass of Scotch beside him.

'So *is* it true? What it says in the file?'

'Believe what you want,' he said, flatly.

'What about me? Did *you* check up on *me*?'

He shook his head.

'I didn't feel the need,' he said. 'I couldn't see the point in getting to know about your past and you might not have a future. All that matters is *now*. What's the point in me getting to know you when you could be killed tomorrow?'

'What a cheerful thought. Thanks, Doyle.'

'I'm being realistic, Georgie. You could be killed, we could both be killed. That's why I never look ahead. What's the point in making plans when you could get shot tomorrow? I take each day as it comes. If I'm still alive when I get into bed at night then I've had a good day.' He took another sip of his drink and ordered a fresh one. 'It's just my way of coping with life.'

'Have you only been like this since the accident?' she wanted to know.

'What is this? Twenty questions? What does it matter? And anyway, it wasn't an accident. I was bloody careless. I shouldn't have got that close to McNamara. I should have killed him before he had the chance to spread himself all over the Craigavon bridge.'

She finished eating and pushed her plate away. The waiter came scuttling over and removed their plates, bringing a bottle of wine when Doyle asked. He prepared to pour but Doyle waved him away and did the honours himself, filling Georgie's glass. A moment later the main course arrived and they were left alone again.

171

'What do your family think about what you do?' Doyle asked.

'I thought you didn't want to know anything about me,' she said somewhat sarcastically.

'I'm just making conversation,' he said flatly.

She nodded.

'I don't have a family,' she told him. 'My mother and father were killed in a plane crash when I was ten. An aunt brought me up. She died the day before my twentieth birthday. My brother, I told you, was killed by the IRA.' She laughed bitterly. 'No one would miss me either if I *was* killed.' She took a sip of her wine.

'What about boyfriends?'

'There've been a few. Nothing serious, though. Perhaps I'm like you in that way, Doyle.'

He grinned.

'Maybe.' He exhaled deeply. 'So we're just two lonely little souls pursuing our own goals. You want revenge for your brother ...' He allowed the sentence to trail off.

'And you? What *do* you want? What do you get out of this? Out of knowing that you could be killed any day? Why do you do it?'

'Because it's all there is for me,' he told her, his face impassive. 'Some days I used to *wish* that I'd get caught in a fight, a gun battle or something.' He smiled. 'So I could go out blazing like some fucking cowboy. Maybe it's because I haven't got the guts to get into a car and drive it into a wall. At least if I get shot or blown up then my death is someone else's responsibility.'

'Why do you want to die?' she asked him.

'Because there isn't a better alternative,' he told her. 'Like it says in the song, "*No happy endings like they always promised*".' He chewed his steak for a moment.

172

'That's right, you know. Perhaps we do share one thing in common. We're alone in the world. My parents are both dead, too. My mother had a stroke, my father had a heart attack. They both hung on longer than they should have and I watched them die, lying there in fucking hospital beds. There's no way I'm going out like that, Georgie. Better to burn out than fade away, they say. Fucking right.'

She sipped her drink, looking across the table at him, realizing that there was something not only dangerous about him but also something very sad. It touched her deeply. More deeply than it should have done. His arrogance, his anger and his attitude were the qualities which made him attractive to her. She looked across the table at him and she wanted him, wanted to share that rage, that ferocity. But she feared that she couldn't. She wondered if Doyle was already dead as far as his emotions went. Was he capable of feeling anything other than hatred and anger? She wanted to know.

But she knew that now was not the time.

'How are you getting on working as a barmaid?' he asked after a long silence, a slight smile on his face.

'I'm managing,' she replied, also smiling.

The rest of the evening was spent passing good-natured conversation and Georgie was surprised at the occasional warmth that crept into Doyle's tone. For all that, he was guarded about himself. He told her jokes, anecdotes. They swapped stories about their experiences in the C.T.U. They talked business.

They talked about killing men.

It was almost 11.30 p.m. when they finally left the restaurant.

Doyle suggested they walk and she was pleasantly

surprised when he draped one arm around her shoulder. She responded by slipping her own around his waist. *Well, it had to look convincing.*

They spoke quietly as they walked, as if not to disturb anyone.

It was as they passed the City Hall for the second time that Georgie realized they were walking in circles.

She slowed her pace and turned to him, smiling, but Doyle's features were set firm and he was gazing ahead as if at something she couldn't see.

'Sean, we're walking in circles.' she said. 'The hotel ...'

'Just keep walking,' he hissed.

She felt the .44 inside his jacket as she snaked her arm around his waist again.

'Are you carrying your automatic?' he wanted to know.

'Yes,' she told him.

'Good. You might need it. We're being followed.'

Forty-One

'How many are there?' Georgie asked almost nonchalantly, keeping up the same steady pace, not looking back.

'I don't know,' Doyle told her. 'I spotted a car and one guy on foot as we passed City Hall first time. The car went through a red light to keep close.'

'How do you want to play it?'

'Let's keep walking for now, see if they move on us.'

'And if they do?'

'We kill them. It could be anyone. IRA. UVF. It could even be one of Maguire's mob.'

'Sean, there's no reason for it to be the IRA or the UVF. Since the peace talks started, guerilla activity has ceased. You know we couldn't have infiltrated as easily as we have otherwise.'

He nodded.

'Then it has to be Maguire,' he said.

They came to a turning in the road.

'Right,' he said, pausing to light a cigarette. 'We'll split up, try to lose them. I'll meet you back at the hotel. Don't forget, Georgie; if you have to, shoot.'

She nodded then snaked her arms up around his neck, drawing him to her, pressing her lips against him. He felt her tongue probing and opened his mouth, allowing it to stir the warm wetness within. They remained like that for long moments, then she pulled away, smiling.

'If you're saying goodnight we might as well make it look convincing,' she told him and turned away.

Doyle smiled and walked off in the opposite direction.

The car followed him.

The man on foot pursued Georgie.

Doyle knew that the driver of the car dared not drive too fast. As far as *he* knew, Doyle was still unaware he was being followed. He didn't know the counter-terrorist was aware of the tail.

He walked briskly but unconcernedly. If his tracker was going to try and kill him then he'd have to pull level with him or, better still, in front of him.

Then Doyle would be able to use the .44.

He smiled at the prospect, but for the moment he

merely kept walking, keeping his pace slow enough to allow the driver to track him.

The time for speed would come soon enough.

Georgie meanwhile was also walking slowly, her high heels beating out a tattoo on the wet pavement. She pulled her jacket around her to ward off the cold, her clutch bag held before her, the comforting shape of the automatic nestled within.

There was an alley up ahead to her right.

She ducked into it.

It ran for about three hundred yards along the back of shops and houses.

It was as black as pitch down there, the only vague light coming from some of the rear windows of the houses or their yards. Dustbins were lined up on both sides of the narrow alley like sentinels.

Georgie scuttled along it, heading for a pile of old boxes stacked high against one of the shops. The place stunk of rotting vegetables and cats' piss but she pressed herself against the wall, eyes fixed on the opening of the alley, watching to see if her pursuer followed her.

She saw his shape loom in the alley entrance.

He paused for a moment, then began walking tentatively down the narrow thoroughfare, cursing when he tripped over the rusted frame of a child's bike.

He drew closer, slowing his pace now, eyes and ears alert for the slightest sound or movement.

Doyle crossed the street, quickening his pace slightly, not even glancing back over his shoulder as he walked. He knew the car was still there, its driver watching him through the windscreen.

There were a set of traffic lights up ahead, showing green.

Doyle paused and lit another cigarette, one eye on the lights.

They changed to amber.

He sucked hard on the cigarette and walked on.

Red.

Doyle broke into a run, hurtling across the junction, narrowly avoiding a car which came from his right. The driver banged on his hooter angrily as the counter-terrorist dived across in front of him.

The man in the pursuing vehicle swore under his breath as he glanced up at the red light then at the figure of Doyle disappearing around a corner on the far side of the road.

He stepped on the accelerator and shot across the junction, ignoring the traffic signal, swerving to avoid a van which was forced to brake hard to prevent a collision.

'You fucking idiot,' the driver of the van bellowed as the other car sped after Doyle.

Doyle himself had ducked into a side-street. He watched as the pursuing car shot past, skidding to a halt at the end of the street, its engine idling as the driver looked around for his quarry.

Whoever was driving was no expert, Doyle thought. A blind man would have known by now that he was being followed. In the glare of street lamps, Doyle could see that there was just one man in the car.

Just the one in the car and the one following Georgie.

He frowned.

Who the fuck *were* these guys?

He watched the car finally turn left and drive off in the direction of Sandy Row.

Doyle waited a moment longer then turned and headed back the way he'd come.

Georgie lost sight of the man momentarily as he entered the alley-way, so impenetrable was the darkness. She could hear his footfalls on the cracked concrete but she couldn't see him.

She thought about easing the .45 from her bag but resisted the temptation.

The man was closer now.

Georgie carefully stepped out of her shoes, anxious that the click of her heels should not give away her hiding place.

As she did so she put her left foot into something soft. It felt cold and she winced as she felt it ooze up between her toes. What it was she didn't even *want* to think about.

The man was on the far side of the alley, drawing closer all the time. He pressed against the door of a yard and the hinges creaked loudly.

From inside the yard a dog flew at the door, barking madly.

The sound startled the man and gave Georgie the opportunity she was looking for.

She hooked one hand through a dustbin lid handle and ran at the man who turned, stunned, to meet her charge.

His reactions were too slow.

Georgie smashed the dustbin lid into his face, a loud clang echoing around the alley, joining with the frenzied barking of the dog to create a deafening cacophony.

The man fell back against the gate, his nose broken by the impact, his head spinning.

She dropped the dustbin lid and brought her bare foot up into his crutch with stunning force.

He let out a strangled cry and dropped to his knees.

Georgie retrieved the dustbin lid and hit him again, across the back of the head this time. The blow opened a hairline cut across his scalp. Blood ran through his hair as he pitched forward, his face connecting with the ground, the impact lessened as he fell into the contents of a spilled dustbin.

Georgie prodded him with her foot, dropped to one knee and hauled him over on to his back.

The dog was still barking madly, throwing itself at the gate as if anxious to get through to the people in the alley.

She knew she had to move fast; so much noise would attract attention.

She rummaged through his pockets, finding it difficult to see anything in the pitch blackness. Even his features were hidden from her in the gloom.

She found a wallet in his trouser pocket but nothing other than money inside.

Not even in his jacket or inside pockets.

No I.D. Nothing.

She paused for a moment then wiped her bare foot on his jacket, retrieved her shoes and bolted down the alley-way, the sound of the dog echoing in her ears.

As she reached the other end of the alley she slowed down, breathing deeply to restore her composure, wiping her foot with a tissue before slipping her shoes back on.

She set off at a steady pace, and in fifteen minutes she was back at the hotel.

She wondered what had happened to Doyle.

Forty-Two

The night porter in the Excelsior Hotel nodded politely at Georgie as she passed him heading for the lifts. She returned the gesture, aware that his eyes were following her every movement, his gaze centred on her legs and backside as she entered the lift.

She rode it to the tenth floor and got out, passing two middle-aged men about to descend. One of them said something to his companion and she heard their raucous laughter inside the lift.

She reached her own room, fumbled in her bag for her key and was about to let herself in when the door next to her opened.

Doyle stuck his head out and smiled, motioning her inside. She closed the door behind her as she entered, then walked to the bed and sat down, kicking off her shoes. She sat cross-legged, watching him as he went to the dressing table, poured two glasses of Scotch from the bottle of Haig which stood there and handed her one.

'What happened?' he asked, listening intently as she relayed the story, waiting until she'd finished then stroking his chin thoughtfully.

'And he was carrying no I.D. at all?' Doyle said, perplexed.

'No driver's licence, no credit cards, nothing,' she said, taking a sip of the Scotch. 'What about your bloke?'

'I lost him easily. Maybe *too* easily.' He pulled at the top button of his shirt, loosening it, then pulled off his tie and tossed it to one side. 'You know, the more I think about it the more I reckon they *wanted* us to know we were being followed.'

'You mean, whoever put them on to us was warning us? Letting us know we're under surveillance? It doesn't make any sense, Sean. If it was the RUC they'd have come straight out and confronted us. The IRA or the UVF or any other of the para-military organizations aren't actively functioning at the moment, and if it'd been Maguire and his men they'd have killed us.'

'That doesn't leave many alternatives, does it?'

'It doesn't leave *any*.'

Doyle took a swig of his drink and looked at Georgie still sitting cross-legged on the bed.

'Are you OK?' he asked her.

'I'm fine. Just curious, like you.' She smiled at him, noticing that he was moving closer to her.

'You've cut yourself,' he said, pointing to a graze on her shoulder. He wet the tip of his finger and wiped the dried blood away gently.

'It must have been in that alley-way,' she said as he bent closer, inspecting the small cut.

Their faces were inches apart. She could smell the faint scent of after-shave on him, could feel the heat from his skin close to her.

'Sean ...'

She spoke his name, then whatever words she intended to speak were lost as he turned his face and kissed her. Their lips crushed together, his tongue probing, met by hers with equal if not increased vigour. She uncrossed her legs, allowing one to slip down and her foot to touch the floor. He pushed her back onto

181

the bed as she fumbled with the buttons of his shirt, their mouths still locked together in the kiss.

She felt his left hand sliding slowly, gently, up inside her dress, stroking the smooth flesh of her inner thigh, his fingers brushing briefly against the tightly curled down of her pubic mound. Then the fingers were gone again, tracing paths over her thighs.

He was aware of the warmth radiating from her sex and it seemed to spur him on but there was no impatience in his touch. Only tenderness. A gentleness which seemed almost alien but was all the more arousing because of that.

He took his hand from beneath her dress and stroked her cheek as he lay down beside her.

She fumbled with his shirt, pulling it open.

As he rolled onto his back she saw the scars that criss-crossed his torso.

If they shocked her she showed no signs. Instead she bent forward and kissed his chest, allowing her tongue to flick gently against a scar which ran across his chest, licking it, following it down to his belly where she found another. She kissed it.

And another.

She kissed that too, sucked the white flesh into her mouth, her saliva running into the deep scar, trickling down to the waistband of his trousers which she began to undo.

He pulled her up and kissed her again, more forcefully this time, gripping her head between his hands as if he were going to crush it.

She reached out with her right hand and unzipped his trousers, feeling for his stiffness, aware of the moisture between her own legs, of the aching in her nipples which pressed against the material of her dress almost painfully.

She sat up and pulled the dress over her head, throwing it to one side then, naked, she slid onto him, allowing him to raise one thigh so that it was rubbing against her moist cleft. She left a stain on his trousers as she manoeuvred herself down his body, licking the line of the scars as if they were guides for her. She slipped his trousers and pants off in one movement so that they were both naked.

She saw other scars on his thighs and those too she kissed before trailing her tongue up to his swollen testicles, one of which she took into her mouth, sucking so gently on it. Then she swivelled around, lowering her slippery sex towards his face, offering it to him as she took the head of his penis into her mouth, licking the clear liquid from the swollen glans.

Doyle parted her pink, puffy lips with his index finger and ran his tongue over their outer edges, feeling her shudder as he flicked his tongue deep into her. He stirred her wetness for a moment before transferring his attentions to the hard bud of her clitoris, drawing back the fleshy hood to reach it, raking it gently with the edges of his teeth.

He felt her release his penis and gasp her pleasure as he licked faster, sensing her urgency, sensing her desire for release.

He kissed her inner thighs, brushed his nose through her dewy pubic hair and smelt the musky odour of her sex and she began to suck him once more, her hands rubbing his thighs and testicles, knowing that he too was close.

Doyle grabbed her slim hips in his powerful hands and lifted her off him, slithering around so that he was beside her, looking down onto her.

He raised himself up and she parted her legs to

183

welcome him, moaning softly as she felt the head of his penis probing against her vagina. He inched forward, penetrating a fraction then withdrawing. He repeated the action half a dozen times, each tiny stroke greeted by a gasp of pleasure from Georgie as she raised her hips in an attempt to coax him into penetrating her fully. Instead, he merely moved his swollen organ over and around her slippery sex, placing his glans against her clitoris for glorious seconds before pushing a little more deeply into her.

'Please ...!' she whispered, stroking his face, her breath coming in great racking gasps.

And he slid into her fully.

The feeling was exquisite and she arched her back, both because of the sheer pleasure but also so that he could penetrate her further.

He began to move rhythmically, each thrust of his met by her raising her hips. She gyrated them gently, her eyes now closed. Lost in the pleasure of the moment she was aware only of his penis deep inside her and of the growing pleasure, the feeling which was building inexorably.

He held her breasts gently, running his thumb over the stiff nipples then bending his head to take first one then the other between his lips.

She whispered his name again as she felt the warmth begin to spread across her thighs and belly, at its hottest between her legs.

She raised her legs, locking them around the small of his back, drawing him deeper as the feeling finally reached its peak.

She clawed his back, her nails scratching him, skimming over deep scars which had long since healed. He licked the perspiration from her cheek as he thrust harder, his own release now seconds away.

Georgie called out his name loudly as she climaxed and the sound, coupled with the vibrations he felt beneath him, pushed him over the edge into ecstacy. She moaned more loudly as she felt his thick fluid filling her, his thrusts still perfectly rhythmic as he poured his liquid lust into her, his body trembling.

She kissed him, the feeling only barely subsiding. She was quivering all over.

'Oh God,' she murmured, her legs finally slipping from around him, her eyes still closed.

He licked more perspiration from her cheek, tasting its saltiness, his own pleasure now spent for the time being. He eased himself free of her, their fluids mingling, dampening the sheet beneath them.

He lay beside her, listening to her breathing, his own deep and guttural. Gradually it subsided as the burning became a pleasant glow.

She rolled across to him, looking down at his back, at the scars there too. She kissed one on his shoulder, licking it with her tongue, brushing his long hair away with one hand.

She wondered what he'd looked like an hour after the explosion.

He glanced across and saw her smiling at him.

'What are you smiling at?' he asked, touching her lips with his index finger.

'You. You're full of surprises.'

He looked vague.

'You're very gentle, considerate.'

'What did you expect me to do? Tie you to the headboard?'

She laughed and kissed his back, just above a particularly deep scar over his kidney.

'Do they ever give you pain?' she wanted to know.

'Life's full of pain, Georgie. You just learn to live with it.'

He reached out and stroked her blonde hair, feeling how soft it was as his fingers slid through it. She stroked the backs of his thighs, tracing one or two more scars.

He must have bled badly.

She finally shifted around so that she was lying beside him, also on her stomach. He began to run one hand up and down her back, pausing every so often to enjoy the gentle curve of her buttocks. She kissed him softly on the forehead, then the nose, then the lips.

When she felt cold he pulled the blanket over them.

After a while they made love again.

Eventually Georgie drifted off to sleep.

Doyle lay awake gazing at the ceiling, his mind thankfully clear of thoughts. Finally he eased himself out of bed, careful not to disturb her, and walked across to the window. He peered out over the city below, looking down on cars which showed little more than pinpricks of light from their headlamps, moving along roads that looked like the illuminated lines on a map.

Somewhere in that city were the men who had followed them and they had answers which he needed.

Doyle stood by the window and glanced back at Georgie as she lay sleeping. Then he faced the glass once more, seeing his own reflection. He raised his arms, putting one on either side of the frame, resting his head against the cold glass.

Don't let her get close.

He gritted his teeth until his jaws ached and he lowered his head a fraction, as if he didn't want to see his reflection.

Keep her distant.

He drew his head back a few inches and slammed it forward against the toughened glass, so hard it made his forehead throb.

'Bastard,' he hissed and headbutted the window again.

And again.

Forty-Three

BRITTANY, FRANCE:
The window was fully exposed.

As if every single piece of stone had been meticulously chipped from around it, as if every panel had been painstakingly cleaned.

The window in the church at Machecoul was as vivid and visible as the day it had been created.

It stood amongst the dust and dirt of the old building like a beacon, the colours in its glass apparently glowing, such was their intensity. Reds looked like liquid fire, blues like sapphires, yellow like freshly polished gold.

The window seemed to be glowing.

Mark Channing stood staring at it, his jaw slightly open.

Catherine Roberts was beside him, her own gaze rivetted on the window, her emotions in turmoil. She felt a curious mixture of elation, bewilderment and two other feelings which she didn't care for so much. One was awe at the sheer magnitude of the craftsmanship in the window.

The other was fear.

When they had left the window the previous night it had been partially encased in stone, its panels still covered by the dirt of ages, yet now it stood in all its original glory.

The question they both wanted to ask was, How?

Yet each knew that to voice that question would merely confuse matters even more. They had the clichés in their minds and on their lips, ready to roll them out like bit-players in a bad B-Movie.

'Who could have done this?'

'What has happened to the window?'

'What we are seeing is impossible.'

They were like atheists trying to explain a miracle.

It couldn't have happened. It wasn't possible.

And yet they saw it.

For a moment Cath wondered if it was a dream, an extension of the nightmares they had shared for what seemed like an eternity. She almost pinched herself.

Instead she took a step towards the window, narrowing her eyes against the brilliance of the colours contained in the glass.

Come on, there had to be more clichés to describe the way she was feeling.

Amazed. Incredulous. Dumbstruck.

The list was endless.

Channing also moved closer, his jaw still slightly open.

Should he look for scientific explanations? Perhaps it *was* a fucking miracle, he thought. Perhaps God had seen fit to restore a window dedicated to him to its full splendour.

One look at the design on the glass told Channing that God did not figure anywhere in this tableau.

If he had seen what the window bore he would have destroyed it, not renewed it.

He wanted to speak but the words would not come. They eluded him with the same stealth as rational thought. He didn't know what to say, he didn't know what to think.

He could only look at the window, take in its details, marvel at its appearance.

If only he could stop shaking.

Cath moved to within a foot of the window, then stepped back lightly, as if to take in every panel, every mullion, every trefoil and quatrefoil. Every line, every colour, every shape. They seemed to converge on her like a manic kaleidoscope, searing her retina, implanting their forms on her mind as well as her eyes.

She felt faint and backed off a little, as if direct confrontation with the window was somehow too overpowering, too difficult to contend with.

The feeling passed gradually and she was able to look once more, mesmerized by the radiance of it.

The sun had pierced the gloom of the church, cutting through the darkness as it fought its way past a broken slat in one of the boarded up windows.

The shaft struck something lying close by the window.

Something silver.

She took another step backwards but kept her eye on the glinting object, not sure if Channing had seen it or not. He mumbled something under his breath about the camera and left the chancel, his unsteady footsteps echoing away within the main body of the church.

And now Cath saw that silver object glinting again and, this time she moved towards it.

It lay close to the base of the window at its left hand

side, almost hidden in dust and crumbled stone. She knelt and picked it up, brushing the grime from it, cradling it in her hand.

It was a cigarette lighter in solid silver, shaped like a horse's head.

Lausard's lighter.

She regarded it impassively for a moment until she heard Channing re-enter the church then, quickly and surreptitiously, pushed it into the back pocket of her jeans.

Out of sight.

Lausard had been here after them, that much was obvious. But why? How had he come to drop the lighter; or, more to the point, to leave it?

Another mystery?

She looked at the window again, feeling the lighter in her back pocket.

Channing didn't notice the slight smile on her lips.

Forty-Four

The creature was almost six feet tall.

It rose in the centre of the window, arms outstretched and upraised. In its left hand sat a child, in its right another, smaller apparition.

It stood on the heads of two humanoid beings which were lying sideways.

Both had been created naked; their large genitals were clearly visible.

Beneath the creature's legs there was a gate, a

portcullis-like affair further adorned with heads. The hundreds of tiny eyes each seemed to reflect the light with unsettling intensity.

The central creature, the largest, was coloured dark blue except for its eyes, which seemed to glow hellish red in the glow of the lamps and the intruding rays of sunshine creeping almost timidly into the transept of the church. The two monstrosities it stood upon were yellow in colour, apart from their eyes which were the same vivid red. Thick tongues had been fashioned to make it appear that they were licking their lips.

Most of the panels contained at least one representation of a child and every one, without exception, carried some letters or symbols. The words were in Latin.

Channing sat by the altar, glancing up at the window, making a note of the words, trying to make sense of them. He couldn't. The only thing that came into his mind when he looked at the window was the uncertainty of how it had come to be uncovered. And uncovered so thoroughly and expertly.

He and Cath had spoken barely ten words to each other since they'd arrived at Machecoul and found the restored window. He had taken a series of photographs of it; she had set to work trying to figure out the design, the date and possibly the creator.

The window was complex in its construction but relatively simple in its illustration. Just the four large creatures surrounded by over a dozen smaller ones and the children.

So many children.

'It's definitely fifteenth century,' Cath said, her voice cutting through the stillness, cutting through Channing's thoughts too. 'This window is perpendicular glass.' She pointed to the mullions which divided each compartment, segmenting every panel. 'There's a lot of white glass in it. It's been painted over, at least the large figure has, not fired like the smaller ones.' She tapped the glass with the end of her pen. 'The figures of the children have been made using a mosaic effect. Tiny pieces of coloured glass pieced together like a jigsaw. The rest of it is peculiar to perpendicular glass. Decorated style, S-pose, ogee arches.'

Channing raised a hand for her to be quiet.

'You're losing me, Cath,' he said, wearily.

'Sorry. It's just that we seem to be straight on at least one thing about this bloody window. Its date.'

'That's about the only thing we *are* sure of.'

'What about the letters? Can you make any sense of them?'

'They're basic Latin, no anagrams, no inversions, thank Christ. It shouldn't take too long to decipher them. It's those symbols I'm not sure about.'

In the top right hand panel there was a hand, severed at the wrist. It was ringed three times. Two panels below was a stone and, below it the word:

COGITATIO

Other words were dotted around the window, not in sentences but at random, almost like graffiti which someone had scrawled on the finished artefact. Other words that Channing had written down:

SACRIFICIUM
CULTUS
ARCANA
ARCANUS

He shrugged.

'They don't make much sense on their own,' he said. 'Thought. Sacrifice. Worship. Secrets. Hidden.' He shook his head.

'A secret,' murmured Cath. 'Hidden in the window, perhaps?' She turned to look at him.

There were more words at the foot of the window.

OPES

IMMORTALIS

Channing looked at the words again, repeating them aloud as he translated them.

'Treasure and Deathless.' He frowned.

The frown suddenly changed to a look of realization.

'Jesus Christ,' he murmured. 'A deathless treasure. A secret deathless treasure. Gilles de Rais was an alchemist. One of the things all alchemists sought, along with the secret of turning base metal into gold, was the secret of immortality. Perhaps that's what these figures and symbols concern.'

Cath was silent for long moments, her attention focused on the window.

'That still doesn't solve the biggest mystery of all, does it? How this window came to be in the condition it's in after just one night.'

Channing exhaled deeply.

'No, it doesn't. It also doesn't explain why an atheist child murderer, a black magician like de Rais would want a stained glass window put in a church in his name.'

'This word here,' Cath said, pointing at one on a panel which was just above the head of the largest creature. 'What does it mean?'

BARON

'It probably refers to de Rais' title,' said Channing. 'He was Baron of Machecoul and the estate around it.'

'Then why is it in English and not Latin?'

Her words hung on the air, drifting as lazily as the

motes of dust caught in the shafts of sunlight penetrating the gloom.

'The Latin for Baron, the title, is *princeps*, isn't it?' she said, eyes still fixed on the window.

'Yes, you're right,' Channing agreed, stroking his chin thoughtfully.

'I think I know what it is and I think I know what this window is meant to illustrate,' she told him.

He looked at her intently.

'One of the most popular images on stained-glass windows in the fifteenth century was a thing called the Jesse Tree. It was the literal representation of Christ's family tree, in glass. The figure of Jesse, founder of the House of David, would lie at the bottom and, from him, vines or branches come, each one bearing one of Christ's ancestors.' She nodded towards the window. 'I think this is some kind of parody of a Jesse Tree. If de Rais was a black magician, what better way to show his contempt for God than by having something like this on view in a church?'

'And Baron?'

'I think it's a name.'

They both stared at the window, at the name. At the creature with the blazing red eyes.

Who but someone as warped as de Rais would have chosen to personalize such an abomination? And if he did, why venerate it so?

'A monument, that's what the window is,' said Cath. 'A monument dedicated to this thing which de Rais called Baron.'

'What did it give him to make him worship it the way he did?' said Channing, his own thoughts now running rampant.

Cath stepped back.

194

She didn't speak.

She merely gazed at the face in the glass, her gaze held by those blazing red eyes.

Forty-Five

She knew he wouldn't be sleeping.

The need for silence and stealth were paramount. Their rooms were separated by just the landing. *If he heard her leaving …*

Catherine Roberts pulled her jacket more tightly around her, stood with her back to the door for a moment, then gently eased it open, moving as quietly as she could.

The inn was cloaked in silence and every movement, every sound seemed to be amplified in the stillness. She glanced across at the large grandfather clock which stood on the landing close to Channing's room, its pendulum swinging slowly back and forth.

2.16 a.m.

She headed for the stairs and descended, cursing under her breath when one of them creaked protestingly under her weight. She glanced back towards the door of Channing's room but there was no movement.

She reached the bottom of the stairs and crossed the small reception area.

The front door was locked but not bolted.

Slowly she turned the key, gritting her teeth when it refused to twist, but finally, with a resounding click, the lock opened.

Cath paused once more before opening the door and slipping out.

The chill wind hit her like an invisible fist as she stepped onto the street, ruffling her hair and making her shiver. She pulled up the collar of her jacket, easing the inn door shut behind her and then fumbling for the keys of the Peugeot as she hurried across to it. She slid behind the wheel and started the engine, not caring now if he heard the car. Even if he did he would not think it was her.

He would not suspect her.

The engine caught first time and she swung the car out of its parking space, through the village and out towards the road which would take her to the church.

As the houses slowly seemed to disappear, the countryside took over. So lush and inviting in the daylight, in the blackness of the night it seemed to crowd in on her. She flipped her headlamps on to full beam, the shafts of light cutting through the gloom, illuminating the narrow road which led out of the village.

Trees growing close to the roadside seemed to stretch skeletal fingers down as if to sweep the car up. A strong wind had risen and Cath could hear it gusting around the car as she drove. The moonless sky was like a blanket of mottled velvet.

She tried to concentrate on the road as she drove but the image of the window kept creeping into her mind.

The question still plagued her, all the more so because she hadn't even the beginnings of an answer. How had the window been uncovered? How could it possibly be in such a perfect state of preservation? As she shifted in her seat she felt something digging into her buttocks and she remembered she still had Lausard's lighter in her pocket.

It prompted another question.

When had the reporter been inside the church? What had made him leave his lighter behind?

Questions.

And no answers.

There were too many questions. Too much to take in. She turned a corner, guiding the car around a bend in the road, knowing that the church was close now.

Cath felt the hairs at the back of her neck rise.

Just the cold wind.

She told herself it was only that.

As she reached the top of the hill the church was invisible in the valley below, hidden by the darkness.

She guided the Peugeot down the narrow track which led to the valley floor, gripping the wheel as it bounced over the uneven surface.

As she drew closer to the church the headlamps picked out the outline of the building. It seemed to grow from the night itself, hewn from the umbra, carved from darkness.

Something moved close to the door.

Cath swallowed hard and slowed down, now less than thirty feet from the main door of the church.

Whatever had passed before the building appeared to be gone. She squinted into the blackness.

Movement again.

A rat scuttled away from the church and disappeared into the long grass that grew around. Cath exhaled deeply, angry with herself for being so jumpy but knowing that she had at least some cause to feel uneasy about being at this place alone in the middle of the night.

She stopped the car, taking a torch from the glove compartment. As she switched the engine off the lights died with it and the only light in the black was her torch. It seemed scarcely adequate for cutting through such stygian gloom but she scrambled out of the Peugeot and walked purposefully towards the building.

She pushed the door open, the musty smell enveloping her. Even after so many hours spent in the place the odour still made her cough but she passed quickly through the nave and on into the chancel.

To the window.

She shone her torch over it, looking once more at the details, marvelling at the skill which had gone into its construction but also feeling uneasy about the *reasons* for that creation.

She picked out the words with the torch.

ARCANA

ARCANUS

'Hidden secret,' she murmured under her breath.

Hidden in these panels, in these abominations which stared back at her in the torchlight.

Had Lausard seen something of that secret, she wondered, pulling his lighter from her pocket and closing her fist around it?

She knew that it would take a lot of work before the secret of the window was complete but she knew that the riddle must be solved.

God alone knew what it was.

Although she suspected that *God* had nothing to do with it.

Not the God *she* knew.

She pulled the notebook from her pocket, propped the torch on the altar so that it was illuminating the window, then, slowly, began to write.

As she did she was aware that her hands were shaking.

Forty-Six

BELFAST, NORTHERN IRELAND:

A curtain of cigarette smoke enveloped him as he walked in.

It hung in the air, not dissipating, merely expanding and thickening like man-made smog.

The saloon bar of 'The Standing Stones' was busy as usual. Both pool tables were occupied, men sat around in one corner playing dominos and there was a game of darts well under way. Hardly anyone looked at Doyle as he let the door bang shut and walked across to the bar.

He ordered a whiskey and plonked himself on a bar stool, his eyes studying the reflections in the mirror behind the bar.

As yet, none of the faces looked familiar. He glanced across to the booth where Billy Dolan had been sitting the day before last but it was empty. There were a couple of empty beer glasses on the table but they were quickly whisked away by a barmaid who, having collected some more for washing, returned to her post behind the bar. Doyle smiled at her as she passed him, glad to see the gesture returned. She wore a name tag on her white blouse which he read as she passed.

Siobhan.

He smiled again as she moved to the other end of the bar.

As she disappeared the landlord arrived with Doyle's drink and put it down in front of him.

'I don't want any trouble from you today, or you're out of that fucking door on your ear,' he snapped.

Doyle dug in his pocket, found some change and tossed it onto the bar.

'I don't know what you're talking about,' he said, eyeing the landlord coldly.

'I'm talking about the trouble the last time you were in here.'

'It wasn't me who started it.'

'I don't give a fuck who started it. I'm just warning you.' He stalked off to the other end of the bar to serve another customer who'd just entered. Doyle caught the man's reflection in the mirror but it wasn't the one he sought.

Billy. One fucking name wasn't much to go on if he had to trace the Irishman, Doyle thought, sipping his whiskey. He had a Christian name and a description. It might be enough to run through the RUC files, *if* the man was even in them. If he had a record of some description then there might be a way of tracing him. If not ... Doyle took another sip of his drink. It was a thin lead but it was all he had.

Georgie had come up with nothing at the hotel either. No overheard conversations, no conspiratorial whisperings amongst the staff.

Georgie.

The image of her floated into his mind for a moment. The remembrance of their passion. They had made love that morning, then she had dressed and left him alone in the room with his thoughts.

He took a long swallow of the whiskey, driving the visions from his mind.

He tapped on the bar to attract the attention of Siobhan. Siobhan with the badge on her blouse. On the left breast.

She came across to him, smiling. She was pretty. About five three, dark hair. Slim. Big-busted.

'Put another Jameson's in there, will you?' he said. 'And have one yourself.' He held out a five-pound note. She returned a moment later with the drink and his change. 'What did you have?'

'Just a lemonade. I don't drink while I'm working,' she told him.

'What about when you're *not* working?'

'Depends who I'm with.'

'How about with me?' He fixed her in his gaze. 'What time do you get off work this afternoon?'

'About three,' she said. 'Are you asking me out?' That delightful smile flickered on her lips again.

Doyle sipped his drink, regarding her over the rim of his glass.

'Three o'clock?' He nodded and smiled at her, his gaze momentarily distracted by some movement from behind him. The door opened, Doyle watched the newest customer in the mirror.

Billy Dolan had his collar up and his hands stuffed in his jacket pockets. He nodded a greeting to the landlord and made for the booth in the corner.

Doyle watched him sit down, rubbing his hands together as he waited for his drink to be brought across.

'I could meet you outside,' said Siobhan.

'Maybe another time,' Doyle told her, smiling.

Siobhan with the name tag on her blouse watched as he slid off the bar stool and walked across to the booth where Dolan sat. Her smile had been replaced by an expression of annoyance. She bustled off to the far end of the bar to serve someone else.

'Does that offer still stand?'

Dolan looked up as he heard the voice. He smiled that infectious smile as he saw Doyle standing there, glass in hand.

'What are you drinking?' Dolan wanted to know. When the landlord brought his own Guinness over he ordered a refill for Doyle.

'I wondered if you'd come in,' said the Englishman. 'I thought I was going to have to buy my own drinks.'

'I've been busy,' Dolan told him.

'Working?'

Again that infectious grin.

'You could say that. Preparing, more like.'

Dolan lifted his glass.

'Here's to the Cause.'

Doyle did likewise and they both drank.

'What about you?' Dolan asked. 'What do you do?'

Doyle told him about working at the Excelsior.

'When there's fucking Brits staying there and I have to take food up to them I sometimes spit in it first,' he lied.

Dolan grinned.

'What's the pay like there?'

'It's shit but they give me a room.'

Dolan regarded Doyle quietly for a moment and cleared his throat.

'You fancy making some extra cash, Sean?'

'Doing what?'

'A bit of driving. You *can* drive, can't you?'

Doyle nodded.

'It'd have to be on the quiet,' Dolan told him. 'Maybe just picking up the odd parcel here and there, sometimes a person. Think about it.'

Doyle said that he would.

'I've got to be going now,' Dolan said, finishing his

drink, getting to his feet. 'I'll see you, maybe.' He raised his hand in a gesture of farewell. He'd reached the door when he paused and looked back at Doyle.

'Hey, Sean. Are you a football fan?' he asked, that infectious grin back on his face. 'If you are there's a game on Tuesday night at Windsor Park. It should be quite something.' Then he was gone.

Doyle looked puzzled for a second but then swallowed what was left in his glass, got to his feet and followed Dolan out of the pub.

There was no sign of the Irishman.

Doyle looked quickly right and left and just caught sight of him turning a corner. He set off after his quarry, the .38 snug against his ankle, hidden by his boots.

He slowed down at the corner, peering around.

Dolan was about twenty yards ahead of him.

Doyle saw the blue Sierra pull up alongside him and spotted the driver motion for Dolan to get in, which he did quite willingly, walking round to get in the passenger side.

Doyle looked at the number-plate, consigning it to memory as the Sierra sped off.

'Shit,' Doyle hissed and ran down the street towards a phone box. He punched the digits quickly, waiting for the connection, waiting for the phone to be picked up. When it finally was he asked to speak to Georgie.

She was a moment or two coming to the phone.

'Georgie, listen to me,' he snapped, barely giving her time to acknowledge who he was. 'We've got to trace a car. Quick. Get in touch with the RUC, get them to run it through one of their computers. I need to know who owns it and where he lives. I'm in a call box. I can't do it from here. Use Donaldson's name when you call, tell them you're with the C.T.U. And tell them to hurry. Ring me back at this number when you've done it, right?' He gave her the number of the public phone and then the car number-plate. Then he hung up, stepped outside the box and propped himself against the wall of a house, eyes on the phone box, waiting for the ring.

Five minutes.

Ten minutes.

'Come on, for Christ's sake,' he muttered, pacing up and down outside the box.

A young woman pushing a pram rounded the corner and made for the phone box.

'It's out of order, love,' Doyle said to her, looking disappointed. 'I just tried it myself.'

The woman shrugged.

The phone rang and Doyle pushed past her into the box.

'Here, wait a minute,' she said angrily, banging on the door.

He snatched up the receiver.

'Yeah,' he snapped.

The woman was still banging on the door.

'Doyle, listen,' said Georgie. 'I checked up on the car.'

The woman outside opened the door and stuck her head in.

'I wanted to use this phone,' she said irritably.

'Look missus, just fuck off, will you?' hissed Doyle and kicked the door shut.

'Ignorant bastard,' she shouted from outside.

'What the hell's going on there?' Georgie wanted to know.

'Never mind. Just tell me about the car,' he said.

'Like I said, they checked it out. It's registered in the Republic. To a Mr David Callahan.'

Forty-Seven

BRITTANY, FRANCE:
'So, Lausard knows about the window. So what?'

Catherine Roberts spat out the words angrily, looking at Channing who was sitting on the edge of the bed, head lowered.

'He's a reporter, *isn't* he?' Channing hissed. 'The bloody story will be everywhere within a few days.'

'He hasn't been back to the church and nothing has appeared in the papers. Perhaps he didn't think it was a good enough story,' she said quietly.

His lighter was still in her handbag.

'There's no reason to think he'll be back. Besides, all we can do is get on with our work. I think we're worrying needlessly.'

'You sound very sure of that,' he snapped.

'Look, Mark, the window isn't *your* property,' she told him. 'Neither of us has any right to keep it to ourself. What were you going to do with it, anyway? Hide it? Take it home with you so only you could see it? If that's what you wanted, why did you call me out here, too? You should have kept the information to yourself.'

'I told you, I needed your help,' sighed Channing wearily.

'My only concern is that window,' she said angrily.

'The work on it is too important to stop now.'

Channing paced the floor for a moment, head bowed.

'What we should be thinking about is how the window managed to become free of the stone,' she said.

As she spoke she glanced across at her handbag, to where the lighter was hidden.

Lausard's lighter.

Stuffed in the side pocket was her notebook, filled with observations from the previous night.

They were not to be shared with Channing.

She got to her feet.

'Where are you going?' Channing wanted to know.

'To the Church.'

'We could leave it for today. I think we both need a rest. I didn't sleep much last night again …'

She cut him short.

'You stay if you want to, Mark. I'm going.'

'It's become an obsession with you,' he said, flatly. 'The window, what it means.'

She picked up her handbag and headed for the door.

'I'll see you later,' she said and walked out.

He heard her footsteps on the stairs. A moment later he saw her walk out of the front of the inn and cross to her car. She slid behind the wheel, started the engine and drove off.

Channing exhaled deeply and ran a hand through his hair, then he fumbled in his pocket for his car keys and also hurried from the inn.

He should be able to catch her before she reached the church.

Forty-Eight

BELFAST, NORTHERN IRELAND:
The roar was deafening.

Doyle glanced towards the pitch in time to see a green-shirted player drive a shot only inches beyond the right-hand post.

The crowd around him seemed to swell for a second, as if each of them had been pumped full of air. As the ball skidded away for a goal kick they seemed to deflate again.

Windsor Park football ground was three-quarters full, the International fixture between Northern Ireland and England not having sufficient pulling power to fill the ground. Nonetheless, it had attracted the largest gate for two years. Both main stands and one end of the terracing were full to capacity. For safety reasons the far end of the ground from Doyle was less than half full. It contained most of the English supporters.

He moved with relative ease amongst those on the terraces, glancing at some of their faces, but mostly content to let his eyes rove over the heaving mass.

He knew the chances of picking out either Dolan or Maguire in a place this size, amongst over 20,000 people, were minuscule. But he had a feeling that they were here somewhere. He had told Georgie it was only a gut instinct; a hunch. Or any other cliché he could think of. But Dolan's remark in the pub the previous day about the football match had set him thinking.

It was the first time the English national side had played at Windsor park for two years. There were obvious attractions to Maguire and his renegades. A large gathering of people, a proportion of them English.

Doyle had a nasty feeling of unease in the pit of his stomach.

It may just have been his imagination; the remark which Dolan had made may have been purely innocuous. Doyle doubted it.

'There's a game on Tuesday night at Windsor Park. It should be quite something.'

Doyle continued to move amongst the crowd, glancing at the pitch every so often.

A long ball had set the England strikers free and two of them were now bearing down on the Irish goal, defenders frantically scrambling back to get goal side of them.

'Break his fucking leg,' shouted an encouraging amateur coach close to Doyle.

Nice to see the spirit of sportsmanship hasn't been affected by the recent mayhem, he thought, smiling.

The player with the ball chose to chip the goalkeeper and his shot flew towards the goal before striking the crossbar and bouncing back into play. An Irish defender nodded it into touch and the crowd relaxed again momentarily as players went forward for the impending corner.

Doyle moved on, eyes scanning the crowd.

'Put it out the fucking ground.'

'Cover the near post.'

Words of encouragement and advice were bellowed from the terraces and stands as the corner was swung in.

The Irish goalkeeper met it with a punch, clearing his area, relieving the pressure.

Doyle paused long enough to light a cigarette, slipping the packet back into his inside pocket. As he did so his hand brushed the shoulder holster and the butt of the CZ-75 automatic. He jammed the cigarette in the corner of his mouth and walked on, wondering if Georgie was having any luck on the other side of the ground.

She wasn't.

She felt even more helpless than Doyle. She only had his description of Dolan to go on and she'd only seen photos of Maguire. The identities of the other renegades were unknown to both her and Doyle. She stopped close to a group of men who were standing watching the match and thought that, for all she knew, she could be watching the renegades now and not even be aware of it.

That was assuming they were even present.

She had gone along with Doyle's hunch about an incident at the match purely and simply because hunches were all they had to go on at present. But she also trusted his instincts.

As she pulled her jacket tighter around her she felt the reassuring bulk of the Sterling .357.

Ever vigilant, she moved on.

Doyle was approaching the tall iron fence which segregated Irish supporters from English.

Despite the progress that had been made in halting sectarian violence in the province over the past few months the fence was a reminder that football violence was almost as insidious an illness and would require treatment of a similarly spectacular nature. He walked up to the fence, wondering if this was what a beast of prey felt like in a zoo. Doyle wandered up and down the length of the fence, glancing at the policemen who formed a further barrier behind the railings on the other side. They were all standing facing the crowd, unable to see the game. Unable to see the Irish winger cutting inside the English full-back.

The crowd roared its encouragement as he left the back for dead then drove in a curling cross which was met by an Irish forward.

The ball sped goalward, past the outstretched fingers of the English goalkeeper, finding the top left hand corner of the net.

The ground erupted as the ball crossed the line and Doyle turned to watch the celebrations on the pitch as the green-shirted players congratulated the scorer and the English players looked at one another incredulously before one of them retrieved the ball from the back of the net and booted it angrily upfield for the re-start.

Men all over the terraces were jumping up and down, hugging each other, hurling scarves into the air. The feeling of jubilation was almost palpable.

Doyle watched indifferently, draining what was left of his tea from the cup and dropping it onto the ground, crushing it underfoot as he looked around.

The small black bag at the foot of one floodlight stanchion almost escaped his attention.

There was no one standing near it, not within twenty feet.

He moved quickly towards it, pushing past a man and his young son who were still celebrating.

The bag was sealed with masking tape wrapped around it several times so tightly that the outline of the shape within the bag was clearly visible. It was rectangular.

Even through the black plastic, Doyle could see a tiny red light winking.

He dropped to one knee close to the package. It was about twelve inches long, perhaps half that in width. From his jacket pocket he withdrew a pocket knife.

The roar of the crowd grew in intensity as Ireland launched another attack, but as far as Doyle was concerned, he may as well have been the only man in that stadium. All that mattered to him was the package.

He took the tip of the knife and, with infinite care, cut the plastic bag, opening a rent about six inches long.

A couple of people nearby shot him cursory glances but their attention was soon dragged back to the game as the Irish won another corner, the ball booted unceremoniously behind by the English centre-half.

The roar began to swell.

Doyle used the tip of the knife to ease open the package, peeling back the black bag enough to see inside.

The winger swung the corner in and it was met by the defender on the near post, who headed it clumsily across his own penalty area. An Irish midfield player running in from the left caught the dropping ball full on the volley and the ball rocketed towards the goal before slamming against the angle of the post and crossbar and flying back into play.

Another massive shout from the crowd.

Doyle could see the device now, the two blinking lights, one red, one green.

He could even smell the familiar marzipan-like odour of the plastic explosive.

It looked like there were at least two pounds of it.

211

Enough to create havoc, strapped as it was to the floodlight stanchion. If the explosion …

'Jesus Christ,' he murmured as the realization hit him.

The floodlight stanchion.

If the bomb went off the blast would be enough to bring down the towering structure. Enough to bring down over fifty tons of steel and glass onto the crowd and probably a part of the pitch. There was no timer on the bomb. Doyle had seen this kind before. It was detonated by remote control.

As he got to his feet he might have smiled, satisfied that his hunch had been right.

The bomb could only be detonated by a remote *within* one hundred yards.

Somewhere in the crowd, somewhere in the stadium, were Maguire and his renegades. They had to be.

That much pleased Doyle.

It was the knowledge that they could detonate the bomb at any second which made him feel slightly *less* than happy.

Forty-Nine

How long had it been there?

How long before it went off?

These and other questions passed through Doyle's mind as he hurried away from the bomb towards the iron railings and the cordon of police beyond it.

On the pitch the English team, searching for the equalizer, were mounting a sustained attack. Shots rained in, striking defenders or parried by the goalkeeper but the Irish couldn't seem to clear their lines. Just outside the penalty area one of the English wingers cut inside, left two men for dead and, dropping his left shoulder, flipped the ball past two more defenders.

The crowd howled for him to be stopped as he bore down on the goal.

Doyle reached the fence and bellowed something at the nearest policeman.

The man didn't even acknowledge his presence.

A desperate lunge from the Irish centre-half brought the England winger crashing to the ground.

The referee pointed to the penalty spot.

'Hey, you, listen to me,' roared Doyle, his own entreaties completely lost in the shouts of the crowd as they vented their anger on the referee.

'Listen,' he bellowed again, realizing how useless it was. 'Fuck,' he snarled and ran to the bottom of the terrace, pushing past a number of people who had moved nearer to get a better view of the spot kick which was about to be taken.

Doyle leapt at the fence, climbing it quickly and skilfully, finally swinging himself over and landing with a thud on the outer rim of the pitch.

Two policemen hurried towards him.

The kicker ran forward to take the penalty.

Doyle saw the policeman getting closer; he stood and waited.

The English forward connected firmly with the ball and sent it high into the roof of the net.

The crowd responded with a chorus of cat-calls and shouts of derision.

The two policemen reached Doyle, one of them grabbing his arm.

'Get off me, you arsehole,' he snarled. 'Listen …'

'Come on, sunshine. Out,' snapped the first man, grabbing his arm again.

Doyle again shook loose, stepping back a couple of paces.

'You can do this the hard way if you want,' the second policeman said. 'It makes no odds to us.' He reached for his baton.

'There's a bomb in there,' snarled Doyle, pointing at the enclosure from which he'd just clambered.

'Yeah, and I'm fucking Frank Sinatra. Now come on you bastard,' said the second man, the larger of the two, drawing his baton and raising it menacingly towards Doyle.

'What the hell were you doing in there anyway?' said the first policeman. 'The area there,' he motioned behind him, 'is for English supporters. Now come on.'

'Look, I won't say it again,' Doyle rasped. 'There's a bomb in that enclosure. Get the fucking people out now, as quick as you can.'

'You're a real comedian, aren't you?' said the second man, lunging at Doyle with the baton.

The Englishman side-stepped and, his hand went to the inside of his jacket.

He pulled the CZ free of its holster and pointed it at the two uniformed men.

'Now listen to me,' he snarled. 'I'm not going to say this again.' He saw other policemen approaching now, running. 'There is a bomb secured to the floodlight in there. Check it out.'

One of the men reached for his radio.

'Unit two, come in, over,' he said, struggling to

make himself heard over the sound of the crowd. 'We require assistance in sector five, armed suspect ...'

Doyle snatched the radio from him.

'Unit two,' he shouted into the set, one eye on the uniformed men. 'Check out the floodlight stanchion in sector five. Suspected bomb found there. Do you read me?'

A hiss and a crackle of static on the set.

'Suspected bomb, we'll check it, over and out,' said a metallic voice.

'Now back off,' said Doyle, the CZ still pointed at the policemen.

Three or four others had arrived now and were gathering around Doyle, trying to cut off his escape routes. Not that he had many to choose from, with his back to the perimeter fence and the pitch blocked off by at least three men.

'Put the gun down,' said the largest of the men, the baton still drawn.

'Fuck you,' said Doyle, the noise of the crowd ringing in his ears.

Some of those close to the fence could see he was carrying a gun and many had moved back, fearing the worst.

'You'll never get away,' said another man. 'Not unless you kill us all and you're not going to do that.'

'Don't count on it, shithead,' snapped the Englishman.

A radio crackled.

'Unit two reporting.'

The words were scarcely audible over the noise of the crowd.

'Unit two, come in, over,' said a sergeant to Doyle's right.

'We've found it. There *is* a bomb here.'

'Get those fucking people out of there *now*,' shouted Doyle, angrily.

Stewards, alerted by the commotion, were already unlocking the gates in the fencing.

The police began filing through onto the terraces.

Doyle swallowed hard and looked towards the floodlight.

Would they be in time?

He wondered if Maguire was watching all this now, his finger poised over the button of the detonator.

Just waiting.

After all, *he* had plenty of time.

Doyle knew that for him and the people close to the bomb, time might have run out.

Fifty

She counted at least a dozen policemen on the touchline near the single figure and, as Georgie squinted across the length of the ground, she realized that it was Doyle.

Moments later she saw more police clambering over the barrier, moving around the side of the pitch towards the area of terracing where Doyle stood. He looked as if he was directing them, standing alongside a tall sergeant.

What the hell was going on?

She had to get round there, help him if she could.

Georgie turned, accidentally bumping into two men as she did.

She looked up and apologized.

James Maguire smiled politely and stepped to one side to let her through.

Don't react. Even though you know it's him, don't react.

She moved past the renegade IRA man, taking up a position about ten feet to his right. Each time she glanced past him towards the match, she was able to look at his face.

The square features. The dark hair.

Could she be mistaken?

Maguire stood with his hands dug deep into the pockets of his overcoat, occasionally muttering something to the man next to him, a tall man in his mid-thirties with a pale complexion and short brown hair.

She remembered the photo of Maguire she'd seen back in London, in Donaldson's office.

There was no mistake, this was the man.

But what to do? Pull down on him right here and now in the crowd and risk a shooting match?

Her hand went almost unconsciously to the .357 tucked in the holster beneath her left arm, her fingers touching the butt for reassurance. Then she hooked her thumbs in the pockets of her jeans and stood still.

Watch him.

Her gaze travelled across the pitch to where the police were still flooding onto the terracing.

The game continued, despite some bemused looks from the linesman on that side. Most of the crowd didn't even seem to have noticed the commotion; shouts and roars greeted every pass from the Irish side as they mounted another attack.

Maguire nudged his companion and nodded in the direction of one of the exits. They turned and made their way slowly through the crowd.

Georgie waited a moment before following them.

There was no way of telling Doyle what was going on; she couldn't afford to let Maguire out of her sight now. She had little doubt that he and his companion were armed. If it came to a fight she was ready. The Sterling was full and she carried two speed-loaders as well.

They were drawing closer to the steps which led down to the exit.

Georgie paused at the top of the steps, glancing back at the hordes of police still flooding onto the terracing. She could see Doyle standing on the edge of the pitch looking around.

Perhaps he was looking for *her*, she mused.

With that last thought she hurried down the steps after Maguire.

Others were leaving, too, so her presence wasn't noticeable as she walked briskly along twenty feet behind the Irishman. She followed both of them out into the car park and through the rows of stationary vehicles, aware that her pursuit became more obvious with every step.

Should she try and arrest them now?

There was a massive roar from inside the stadium and Maguire turned slightly.

Georgie walked off to the right, away from him, and headed towards a car, digging in her pocket as if to find her keys.

Maguire and his companion walked on. This time she circled around in a wide arc, trying to see which car they were headed for.

There was a man behind the wheel of the blue Sierra they climbed into. A short, heavy-set, brutish individual who had not used a razor for many days.

218

Georgie moved closer to the car, her eyes narrowed to read the number plate.

There was something familiar about the car.

Something ...

She recognised the number plate as the one Doyle had given her over the phone the other day. This was the car she had traced.

She undid her jacket, ready to pull the .357.

She moved closer to the vehicle, hearing the engine start up.

If she didn't move fast they were going to get away.

To her right she spotted a man opening the door of his Cavalier.

Georgie took a few steps towards him, glancing back at the Sierra. It wasn't moving. The bloody thing was just sitting there, engine idling.

What the hell were they playing at?

She could see them through the back window.

All three were checking their watches.

Fifty-One

They would never do it in time.

Doyle was convinced of that. He watched countless uniformed men flooding onto the terracing, shepherding the spectators away from the bomb. He heard garbled messages over radios that an army bomb disposal unit was on its way. But he was sure that they would never clear the scene in time. In his mind's eye

he could see Maguire standing watching the pandemonium, finger poised over the button that would
detonate the device.

If you're going to push it, push it now, you bastard.

The crowd in that sector of the ground were moving
swiftly, co-operating with the police, bewildered by
what was happening but convinced that it was in their
own interests to evacuate the area.

Men ushered their children away; some carried their
off-spring. The evacuation was orderly, considering the
imminent danger.

Doyle wondered why nothing had been announced
over the public address system. He wondered why the
game was still going on. There could be other devices
in other parts of the ground. Why take chances?
Evacuate the whole bloody ground!

He scanned the faces of the spectators as they left,
looking pale and frightened. The exodus from this
particular part of the stadium must have been noticed
by others in the ground by now, surely. Others would
be asking questions, wondering what was happening.

Some would realize.

He saw many in the stand on the other side of the
pitch out of their seats, looking across towards the area.
For many the match itself was becoming something of a
sideshow.

He glanced back at the terracing behind him.

It was almost empty.

The police had done their work well. Doyle felt a
momentary rush of expectation. Perhaps the bomb
would not cause any loss of life.

A thin smile touched his lips.

Perhaps he'd got to the bomb before Maguire had
anticipated. Thwarted him. Doyle's smile broadened as

he heard word come over a radio that the terraces were clear and cordoned off.

'Fuck you, Maguire,' he murmured. 'Not *this* time.'

He turned to look back across at the main stand, at the spectators still gazing at the now-empty terracing.

It was then that the explosion came.

The blast was massive, ripping through the main stand, sending seats, pieces of concrete and plastic, metal and bodies flying into the air.

So enormous was the explosion that, even a full pitch width away, Doyle felt the concussion blast. Felt the wave of heat which followed the gigantic eruption.

He saw bodies flung skyward, some trailing blood like grotesque fireworks.

A searing red and white ball of flame filled the stand, momentarily blinding Doyle. It was followed by a secondary blast and reeking clouds of black smoke which rose above the scene of devastation to form a thick noxious mushroom cloud which rose into the sky, lifted on tongues of flame which leapt a full thirty feet.

Portions of the stand roof, blasted away by the fearful explosion, fell to the ground, huge sheets of twisted metal crashing down on those not already killed or maimed by the initial blast. As the thunderous roar of the detonation died away Doyle heard screams of pain and terror.

He set off across the pitch, past players who stood dumb-struck, gazing at the carnage, past others who had thrown themselves to the ground. Others were running towards the tunnel, towards the terracing. Anywhere to escape the horror.

There were bodies on the pitch, flung there by the ferocity of the discharge.

Doyle passed a man with one leg missing, torn off at

221

the hip, blood spouting madly from the stump.

Another had been decapitated by the blast, his lifeless body spread-eagled on a pitch now slicked heavily with crimson.

A hand, most of the arm still attached, lay close to the touchline. Two or three paces to the left was the body of a child, the back of the skull sheared off, the spine exposed between the shoulder blades.

Others still moved.

A man with his arm torn off above the elbow tried to drag himself away from the blistering flames. A woman ran screaming from the remnants of the stand, her hair and clothes alight.

Doyle grabbed her, singeing his hands in the process, and rolled her on the grass to extinguish the flames. She rolled onto her back, skin blackened by the incredible heat. He saw blisters actually rising on her face. Rising then bursting, spilling their sticky contents over her charred features. She coughed and smoke puffed from her mouth. As he stood up he knew she was dead.

Debris littered the ground everywhere, some of it red hot. Doyle looked up into the blazing wreckage and saw other bodies lying across seats; unable to move, they could only wait to be devoured by the flames which still leapt and danced in the cool night air and now brought with them a new stench.

The sickly sweet odour of burning flesh.

Doyle turned and saw policemen and ambulancemen dashing towards the scene of devastation. They were helping the wounded, comforting the dying. Some were lifting the dead and carrying them to the edge of the pitch.

A young boy, his face a mask of blood, stood over his

dead father, crying softly as he looked down at the eviscerated corpse. An ambulanceman tried to usher him away but the boy wouldn't go.

'Jesus Christ,' muttered Doyle through clenched teeth. He could feel the sweat on his body, could feel the heat as he stood looking into the flames which still blossomed from the stand. His ears were filled with screams and moans, his hearing still slightly impaired by the aftermath of the massive blast. He fixed his eyes on the crying child, its sobs echoing inside his head.

Doyle wished he'd been completely deafened.

He spun round to look back across the field at the section of terracing which had been cleared.

Cleared so effectively, people ushered away so efficiently from what was now, he realized, merely a decoy. The package had been placed there in order to be found.

He kicked at the ground angrily, his frustration spilling over into rage.

Behind him the stand continued to burn.

The wounded continued to moan in pain.

The child continued to cry.

Fifty-Two

The Sierra pulled away as the explosion ripped through the stand.

Georgie spun round, ducking down instinctively as she heard the thunderous roar, saw the screaming funnel of fire rocket into the air. She didn't wait to

223

watch the mournful black smoke rising like a vast shroud over the scene of devastation. She turned in time to see the blue car pulling smoothly out of its parking space. No speed, no haste. They had no reason to hurry now, their job was done. They'd be clear of the stadium before the first ambulance even arrived.

The owner of the Cavalier was still sitting behind the wheel, rear-view mirror tilted towards him as he combed his hair. That simple act, however, had also been interrupted by the explosion. All eyes in the car park had turned towards the source of the blast and now looked on in horror and awe as the flames took hold.

It seemed the only ones not looking at the aftermath of the blast were the three men in the blue Sierra and Georgie who, by now, had reached the Cavalier.

She pulled open the driver's side door with one hand, reaching for the Sterling with the other.

'What the hell are you doing?' the driver snapped angrily, but the annoyance soon faded, transformed to fear as he saw the .357 drawn from its holster.

'Get out,' snapped Georgie, pushing the weapon into his face, motioning with her head.

He didn't need telling twice.

He raised his hands in surrender and slid from behind the wheel, his bowels loose. Helpless, afraid he was going to fill his pants, he watched as Georgie got into the car, stuffed the .357 back into its holster and started the engine. She pulled away smoothly, eyes searching for the blue Sierra.

It was about thirty yards ahead of her, turning out of the main entrance to the car park. The security guards and police who had been manning the entrance were running towards the stadium, presumably thinking that their duties now lay within. The IRA men slipped out unchallenged.

Georgie followed, shifting her position in the driving seat, angry when she found that the chair was uncomfortably far from the pedals. Still, no time to stop now, she'd have to manage.

As she pulled out into traffic behind the Sierra she heard the first wail of sirens, saw the first of the emergency vehicles come screeching around a corner and hurtle towards the stadium. Red and blue lights filled her eyes but she blinked the glare away, more intent on not losing sight of her quarry.

The Sierra was approaching a set of traffic lights.

Georgie kept a reasonable distance between herself and the other car, glancing down at the Cavalier's fuel gauge, relieved to see that the needle was hovering on a mark just below full. She had no idea how long this was going to take.

What was she hoping for?

That they would lead her to their hideout?

Perhaps to the man who hired them in the first place?

Another police car went flashing past, sirens screaming.

The Sierra crossed the junction with the lights on amber.

'Shit,' hissed Georgie, knowing what she must do.

They were going to spot her sooner or later anyway.

Hold tight.

She put her foot down and the Cavalier sped through the red lights. A car coming the other way swerved, narrowly avoiding her, the driver slamming hard on his brakes, hitting his horn at the same time.

In the Sierra, the driver, the thick-set man with a heavy growth of whiskers, looked back and glimpsed the

Cavalier in the rear view mirror.

'I think we've got company,' he said quietly.

Maguire turned and looked out of the back window.

'Police?' asked Paul Maconnell, swinging the car around a corner.

'I don't know,' said Maguire, squinting through the window to get a better look at their pursuer. 'Lose them.'

Maconnell nodded and put his foot down.

The Sierra shot forward as if fired from a cannon.

Georgie knew now that they'd spotted her. At least now she knew what to do.

She stepped hard on the accelerator, the needle on the speedo nudging seventy.

Ahead of her the Sierra took a corner doing nearly seventy-five, the tyres squealing as they struggled to grip the road. The car skidded, spun then shot off once more, leaving tread marks for at least ten feet behind it. She smelt the burning rubber as she hurtled after it, the wind rushing through her open side window.

More traffic lights ahead.

Red.

Fuck it. Both cars roared straight through, Georgie forced to guide her car up on to the pavement to avoid a Metro which had stalled ahead of her. She felt the Cavalier bounce up onto the kerb, the jolt throwing her against the door, almost knocking the wind from her.

Another corner and the Sierra took it approaching eighty.

Georgie tried to coax more speed from the Cavalier, gripping the wheel tight as she wrenched it hard to guide the car around the corner. The street she came into was narrow and she saw the Sierra directly ahead.

It scraped the side of a parked car, sparks flying from the chassis. Maconnell controlled the vehicle, though, swinging it away from the parked car, allowing it to screech across a corner of the pavement. It hit the kerb and rose a couple of feet, slamming down again, skidding violently. But the Irishman regained control and drove on.

Georgie also took the short cut across the pavement, the wheels thumping the kerb so hard she thought for one terrible second she'd had a blow-out, but the Cavalier continued on and she leant forward, as if to put more pressure on the accelerator.

Ahead of her on the left was a supermarket, shoppers filling parked cars from trolleys.

The Sierra managed to swerve in time to avoid the trolley which rolled in front of it.

Georgie tried but couldn't.

The wheeled basket was catapulted into the air by the collision, twisted into scrap by the impact. It skidded off the roof and fell back into the street.

Georgie kept her foot on the gas pedal, her palms moist now on the wheel.

More sirens, behind her this time. She glanced into the rear-view mirror and saw a police car.

Maconnell saw it too.

'The fucking law,' he hissed, twisting the wheel violently as he took another corner.

'Fuck the law,' said Mick Black from the back seat. 'Who's this comedian that's chasing *us*?'

Maguire said nothing; he merely glanced again at the oncoming Cavalier. He reached into the glove compartment and took out a gleaming object.

A loud metallic click filled the car as he slammed in the magazine of the Skorpion machine pistol. Then, as quickly as he could, he slid over the passenger seat and into the back with Black.

'Slow down, Paul,' said Maguire, winding down one of the rear windows. 'Let the bastard get a bit closer.'

Maconnell nodded and did as he was instructed.

Cold air rushed into the car as Maguire wound down the window, steadying himself on the back seat.

Georgie saw the sub-machine gun a fraction of a second before it was fired.

She hit her brakes, the Cavalier skidding madly.

Maguire opened up.

The staccato rattle of automatic fire filled the evening and bright flames spewed from the barrel of the Skorpion as it spat out its deadly load. The single burst of 9mm ammunition spattered the front of the Cavalier.

Bullets screamed off the bonnet, tearing off a wing mirror. Three or four hit the windscreen.

Georgie was lucky. The fact that the Cavalier had spun to one side ensured that the high velocity slugs didn't hit directly. Two merely whined off the glass but the others shattered it. The windscreen spider-webbed. It was like looking through ice.

She eased her foot slightly on the accelerator, slowing down a little as she struck at the shattered glass, managing to punch a hole in it. Wind rushed in, blasting into her face, but she kept punching until all the windscreen seemed to fold in upon itself. Some fragments merely collapsed and were blown off the bonnet of the car as they fell outwards. Others, blown by the wind, were flung back into the car.

Georgie hissed in pain as one needle-like sliver sliced her cheek. She felt blood running down her face. The cold wind screaming in through what was left of the windscreen seemed to deaden the pain. She saw that Maguire was steadying himself for another burst of fire.

Georgie pressed her foot down as hard as she could on the accelerator and the Cavalier rapidly closed the gap on the Sierra. Closed it, cut it and ...

She slammed into the back of the fleeing vehicle, smashing one of its tail lights. Pieces of glass and plastic housing skittered away on the road. She rammed it again, the jolt throwing her back in her seat, but she gripped the wheel more tightly, watching with satisfaction as Maconnell struggled to keep control of the Sierra.

A third time she rammed it, seeing Maguire knocked off balance by the impact.

Now. Do it now.

Using one hand to steer, she reached into her jacket and pulled the .357 free, resting it against the window frame ahead of her for support. She knew there'd be one hell of a kick; she needed all the help she could get. She thumbed back the hammer, feeling the six pound pull on the trigger as she squeezed it.

The Magnum bucked in her fingers, the butt slamming into the heel of her hand, making it tingle. But she fired again. The retort was deafening, mingling with the howling wind and the scream of tyres as the Sierra skidded again.

The first bullet blasted away the remaining rear light on the fleeing car, the second punched a huge hole in the back windscreen. Glass was sent flying into the car by the explosion and she saw the two men on the back seat dive for cover.

Behind her another police car had joined the chase but Georgie was concerned only with what was ahead of her.

A car reversing out into the street.

The Sierra swerved, slamming into another car on the opposite side of the road.

Georgie hit the tail end of the reversing car so hard the Chevette turned almost one hundred and eighty degrees. A massive jolt shook the Cavalier; she grunted as the steering column struck her in the chest. She almost dropped the .357, the breath momentarily knocked from her.

Behind her the blaring of sirens was deafening.

She drove on.

Maguire was up on the back seat again, steadying the Skorpion.

He fired two quick bursts.

The first peppered the radiator of the Cavalier. The second was aimed low, bullets screeching up off the street.

Both her front tyres were shot out.

She heard the bangs, felt the car begin to slide out of control. Knew she'd never control it around the corner, which was coming at her like something on a fairground ride gone mad.

She wrestled with the wheel but lost the battle. The Cavalier hit the kerb doing sixty-five. It flipped, rose into the air, spinning, before finally crashing down on its passenger side, the door punched in. As it continued to roll Georgie gripped the wheel tight, shoulders drawn up, her head sunk low to avoid any damage to her neck as the car spun like a toy a petulant child had tossed away.

It felt as if someone had taken her by the lapels and was shaking her. She closed her eyes tightly, not wanting to see the world spinning round through the shattered windscreen.

The car finally came to a halt, flopping down on its roof, turning slightly.

She felt sick. Her head was spinning. She tasted blood in her mouth but didn't know where it came from. Perhaps she was bleeding internally. There was no pain, though. Just the nausea, waves of it washing over her. There was a ringing in her ears.

She managed to push open the driver's side door and fall out onto the pavement, her face pressed to the cool concrete.

She heard sirens.

Saw people running towards her.

Then there was only darkness.

Fifty-Three

The wound on her cheek was a superficial one; she probably wouldn't even have a scar to show for it. Georgie was more concerned with the constant pounding inside her skull. It felt as if ten men with pneumatic drills were trying to tunnel their way out.

The headache had grown steadily worse during the questioning, the fluorescents in the main interview room of Hastings Street police station adding to her discomfort. She sat forward at the desk, shielding her eyes as the barrage of questions were directed at her.

She couldn't remember how long they'd kept her there; all that she could remember was the chase, the gunfire and the crash.

The officers questioning her seemed to be in another

dimension, their questions floating towards her as if spoken by disembodied inquisitors. Georgie kept her eyes closed most of the time, irritated by the fluorescents, angered by the splitting headache.

Angered, too, by the fact that Maguire and his men had escaped.

They had brought Doyle in around eleven o'clock, and threatened to charge him with illegal possession of a firearm.

Or anything else they could think of.

Georgie had been told she was likely to be charged with a breach of the peace, causing an affray, endangering lives, reckless driving. The list seemed to go on and on until it reached attempted murder.

They had been questioned separately, then together.

When she next looked at her watch it was approaching two in the morning. She felt tired, irritable and dirty. The blood she had tasted in her mouth when the car crashed had run down from the cut on her cheek. One tooth was cracked as well, she discovered, probing it with her tongue.

The two counter-terrorists allowed their captors to question them, never replying to any of the enquiries.

It was Doyle who finally decided he'd had enough.

He gave them Donaldson's telephone number in London and waited while they rang it.

He had merely shrugged at Georgie as the RUC man went off to make the call, returning about ten minutes later with a disappointed look on his face.

They were, he told his superiors, indeed British counter-terrorists. Their identities had been confirmed from London.

Within thirty minutes they were released, their weapons restored to them.

Anxious to get the English agents away from the police station, the RUC put them in separate cars and had them driven back to the Excelsior.

On the way back Doyle asked if a figure had been put on the number of casualties at the Windsor Park blast. He was told that so far more than thirty people had been killed and four times that number injured, many critically.

Doyle asked to be dropped off about two hundred yards from the hotel. Not that it really mattered any more.

When he finally entered the foyer he found Georgie sitting, head in hands, on one of the seats close to reception. They rode the lift together to the tenth floor. She told him she was going to shower.

He told her to come along to his room in ten minutes.

Doyle's small case was packed when Georgie entered the room, dressed in just a towelling robe. She wandered across to the bed and sat down, glancing at the case and at what lay on top of the carefully folded clothes.

It was an MP5K sub-machine gun.

Despite being only eight inches in length, the sub-gun was capable of firing over 650 9mm rounds a minute in the right hands and, she concluded, they didn't come much better than Doyle.

He sat down on the bed facing her and flipped the case shut.

'The bastards tricked us,' he said. 'That fucking bomb ...' He allowed the sentence to trail off.

'Your hunch was right, though.'

'Fat lot of good it was to the poor sods who got blown up, eh?'

She nodded.

'So what now?' she wanted to know.

'They know we're after them,' he said. 'This incident tonight has blown what little cover we had anyway. There's no point in staying in Belfast. I think it's time we moved into the Republic. Fight the bastards on their home ground. Besides, I think it's time we found out who this Mr David Callahan is. I'd like to know what the IRA are doing driving around in his car.'

'Fake name?' she suggested.

'More than likely, but we've got to check it out.'

'What makes you think they'll move into the Republic?'

'They've pulled too much exposure here. They need to lie low for a while, too.' He got to his feet, walked around the bed and touched her cut cheek with the back of his hand. He smiled.

'You got too close to them. I think you scared them,' he told her.

'I would have killed them, Doyle,' she told him.

He nodded, then bent and kissed her lightly on the lips.

When he straightened up he turned away from her, looking towards the window.

'I bet Donaldson didn't appreciate being woken up at that time in the morning,' she said, smiling.

'We're lucky he verified who we were. We'd have been right up shit creek if he hadn't.' Doyle turned to face her again.

'How long will it take you to pack?' he wanted to know.

'Ten minutes.'

He nodded.

She got to her feet and made for the door, leaving Doyle to gaze out of the bedroom window, out over the

234

city. He was glad she was all right, relieved that she hadn't been injured but he didn't tell her, wouldn't tell her.

Couldn't.

Don't drop the barriers now. No need.

Keep that distance.

He sucked in a weary breath.

Ten floors below, seated in a car parked across the street from the hotel, other eyes were also watching.

But they were watching the hotel entrance, waiting for Georgie and Doyle to appear.

They didn't know how much longer they'd have to wait, they'd already been sitting there for over two hours.

They had played this waiting game before.

It was only a matter of time.

Fifty-Four

Simon Peters took one final drag on his cigarette and tossed the butt out of the window. He held the smoke in for a moment, then blew it out in a long blue stream.

The whole interior of the Ford Escort was full of smoke.

Beside him Joe Hagen puffed away at a Dunhill. In the back seat Eamonn Rice and Luke McCormick were also smoking. It was like sitting in a mobile ashtray.

They were parked on a hill overlooking Milltown cemetery. The sun was rising slowly in the morning sky, dragging itself reluctantly towards the heavens, spreading an orange glow over the countryside. A thin film of mist still hung in the air, like dry ice. As Peters stepped out of the car it swirled around his feet. The grass was slippery underfoot but he walked with assurance, breathing in the crisp morning air, clearing his lungs of cigarette smoke.

It was so peaceful up here at this time, he mused, watching the sun climb higher in the sky. He had often driven up here and sat for an hour or so, watching over the city as it woke from its slumbers. The sound of early morning birds twittering in the trees only served to reinforce the beauty of the scene. He sometimes thought that the newsmen who came to the province to report on the violence should see scenes like this, should watch the sun staining everything gold. Should hear the birds singing. But they weren't interested in the beauty of Northern Ireland. None of them. They could see no further than the troubles in the Falls Road. The bomb blasts in Londonderry. The sniping in Clonard. They saw what they wanted to see. They saw his country being crushed into the ground by years of bigotry, hatred and jealousy.

Many victims of that conflict lay below him in Milltown now. The cameras came there when there was a funeral. They came to record death with a relish Peters found obscene. And he had seen enough death during his time in the IRA to know it for the vile thing it was. But death was a necessary part of the province. Just as violence had been for the last twenty years. He had caused some of those deaths himself: soldiers, security men, civilians when necessary. But it all had a purpose. His was not the campaign of a psychopath. He had no more time for the slaughter than those he had fought against, but for Simon Peters it was a way of life.

The only way to free the country he loved.

No one had been happier than he when the Stormont peace summit had finally gathered, but the promise of an end to the bloodshed, the hope of a united Ireland had been dashed. Blown away in a hail of bullets by men who dared to call themselves members of the very organisation to which he was so proud to belong.

Those same men had been responsible for the deaths of over sixty people at Windsor Park the previous night.

Men like James Maguire.

Peters knew Maguire well; he had even worked with him on a number of jobs during the past few years. He knew some of the men he had with him, too.

Men like Billy Dolan and Mick Black.

Even the thought of them set the knot of muscles at the side of his jaw pulsing angrily.

He would not let them destroy his own dreams. He would find them before they could do so.

Find them and kill them.

Joe Hagen climbed out of the car and wandered over to join him, hands dug into the pockets of his trousers. Dew darkened his suede boots as he walked across the long grass.

He stood beside Peters, watching the sunrise and the city coming to life beneath it as if coaxed into stirring by the warm rays.

'My father used to say that the sunrise was the colour of the gold on the tricolour,' Hagen murmured reflectively. 'When people used to talk about the gold meaning the Catholics and the green meaning the Protestants he'd say it was the bit in the middle you had to worry about. The part where the two colours could never join.'

'Quite a philosopher, your old fella,' Peters nodded, smiling.

'He was that. I wish he could have lived long enough to see a United Ireland.'

'If we don't find Maguire soon then none of us will see a United Ireland, because things will go back to how they were before,' Peters said, his smile fading.

On a branch nearby a thrush chirped contentedly, then flew off, its outline a black arrowhead against the brightening sky.

'I spoke to Coogan this morning,' said Peters. 'There's at least one English agent on Maguire's tail, too. The RUC are looking for him as well. Belfast is too hot for him and his men right now. They've probably already crossed over the border.'

'Who's the British agent?' Hagen wanted to know.

'James Bond,' said Peters flatly. 'How the fuck do I know?'

'He could get in the way, Simon.'

'God help him if he does. This is *our* business, not the bloody Brits'.'

He sucked in another lungful of crisp air, turned and began walking slowly back towards the car.

'I think it's time we paid a visit to some of the families of these ... *renegades*.' He emphasized the word with contempt. 'If Maguire and his men have crossed the border, someone might know where they've gone. Someone close to them.'

'And if they won't talk?' Hagen wanted to know.

Peters smiled.

'They'll talk. I guarantee it.'

238   ·

Fifty-Five

BRITTANY, FRANCE:
They weren't reporters.

Channing knew that much from the moment the couple stepped from the car. The new arrivals were too smart to be press.

The man wore a light grey suit, immaculately pressed and tailored. He was powerfully built, his shoulders broad, his features heavy.

The woman with him was dressed in a black dress which came to just above her knees, hugging her fine figure tightly. She had a red leather jacket draped around her shoulders. The slight breeze stirred her shoulder-length brown hair as she walked.

Channing drew a hand across his forehead and sighed, eyeing the couple suspiciously as they drew nearer. The man was smiling.

'Good morning,' he said, nodding at Channing.

He returned the greeting, still running appraising eyes over the couple.

'What can I do for you?' he asked warily, expecting the answer even before it came.

'We want to see the window,' David Callahan told him. 'We've come from Ireland; we flew in last night.' He introduced himself and Laura.

'Why do you want to see it?' Channing asked.

'I have an interest in artefacts like this.' Callahan looked the other man up and down. 'Who *are* you, anyway? How come *you're* here?' There was an edge to Callahan's voice that Channing wasn't slow to notice.

'My name is Mark Channing. I'm the one who found the window,' he said.

'Good for you,' Callahan countered acidly. 'May we see it?'

'I am here trying to work. All I want is some peace and quiet.'

'That's fine by me, Mr Channing, but we have a right to see the window if we want to. You can't keep us from it.'

'Why do you want to see it?'

'You've already asked me that.' Callahan's temper was beginning to fray.

'We know something about the man who had this church built,' Laura interjected.

'We've been here before,' added Callahan. 'Probably before *you*.' He was breathing heavily and a vein in his temple throbbed angrily. 'You don't own this land, do you, Mr Channing?'

He shook his head.

'Then there is nothing you can do to stop us going inside that church and looking around. You found the window; you're not its protector, the judge of who should or shouldn't look at it.'

Channing still blocked their path to the main door but he could see the anger in Callahan's eyes, could hear it in his voice.

'We came here out of *genuine* interest,' said Callahan. 'I've made a study of Gilles de Rais. This window you've found is of concern to me and I don't intend leaving here until I've seen it. Now you can take us and show us the window, step aside and let us in or you can carry on being difficult. But I warn you, Mr

Channing, I'm not leaving here until I've seen what's inside that church.'

'Are you threatening me?'

'I'll do more than threaten you if you don't get out of the way,' snarled Callahan, taking a step forward.

'What's going on?'

All heads turned as Catherine Roberts appeared in the doorway of the church.

'They want to see the window,' Channing told her.

Cath nodded slowly.

'Come on, I'll take you through,' she said wearily.

Channing shot her an angry glance.

Callahan smiled thinly and he and Laura followed Cath into the church.

As they entered both were struck by the smell of damp and decay and Laura had to tread carefully, cautious not to trip over any of the pieces of rotting wood which littered the stone floor. Dust several inches deep rose up like puffs of smoke each time they put their feet down. It was like walking on a bed of ashes.

'I apologise for my companion,' said Cath as they moved through the nave. 'He's become a little over-protective where the window is concerned. It's important to him.'

'It's important to me, too,' Callahan told her. Then he remembered he didn't know her name. Hasty introductions were exchanged.

'What's your interest in the window, Mr Callahan?' Cath asked.

'You could say I'm a collector,' Callahan said, smiling.

Cath, puzzled, opened the door which led through to the chancel.

Shafts of sunlight which had managed to force entry

through broken slats on the far side of the chancel now struck the window, illuminating its colours so vividly it seemed to be glowing.

Callahan and Laura entered.

'Jesus Christ,' murmured Callahan, gazing in awe.

Laura stood as if mesmerized, her eyes never leaving the glass.

Callahan moved closer, reaching out to touch the panel which showed the clawed hand holding a child. The glass was cold against his fingertips.

Channing entered the chancel and looked at the two newcomers, then at Cath. He reserved the same look of distaste for all three.

'What do the words mean?' asked Callahan, pointing at the Latin legends within the glass.

'We're still working on that,' Cath told him.

'Who's paying you?' Callahan wanted to know.

'No one,' Channing said. 'This is research.'

Callahan smiled.

'It can't be comfortable working in these conditions,' he said.

'We manage,' Channing snapped.

'You don't have to *manage*. I'm offering you the chance to work at your own pace, in private, without press interference in a controlled environment. Anything you could want.'

'How?' Cath sounded intrigued.

'Work for me,' said Callahan quietly. 'It's your choice. But if you don't then someone else will, and I warn you now I want this window. And what I want I get.'

Channing smiled.

'What are you going to do? Wrap it up and put it in your suitcase?'

242

'No. I'm going to have it flown out by private plane back to my estate in Ireland.'

'You can't.'

'Are *you* going to stop me?'

'How much would you be willing to pay for the work to continue on the window?' Cath asked.

'You can't …' Channing hissed but she raised a hand to silence him.

'Fifty thousand pounds. More, if you want it,' Callahan said flatly.

'You can't buy this window and you can't buy our expertise,' Channing said.

'The window doesn't belong to you, and if you don't want to work on it that's your business. If you want to throw fifty thousand back at me that's your business, too.' He looked at Cath. 'What about you, Miss Roberts? The offer stands.'

'Make it a hundred thousand,' she said.

'Cath, for God's sake,' snarled Channing.

'Right,' Callahan agreed. 'One hundred thousand it is.' He looked at Channing. 'And you?'

'No. I won't let you take the window.' He turned and wrenched open the chancel door. 'I'd rather see it destroyed.'

They heard his footsteps as he stalked off through the nave.

Callahan looked at the window, then at Cath.

He was smiling.

Fifty-Six

Channing paced the floor of his room agitatedly, occasionally stopping to look at Cath, who stood by the window watching him.

'All Callahan's offering us is better working conditions,' said Cath softly.

'You make him sound like a factory boss.'

'Don't be so bloody ridiculous. You know what I mean. There's nothing more we can do on the window in its present position or location. Besides, I'm sick of working inside that church.'

'He has no right to take the window. It isn't his.'

'And it isn't *ours*, either,' she reminded him. 'Work with him, Mark, not against him. You want to find out the secret of the window. So does Callahan, and he's prepared to pay money to find it.'

'You told him about it, then? About the secret?'

'*He* mentioned it. After you'd gone he said something about the treasure, about some kind of secret de Rais had. Callahan's no fool, Mark.'

'So just because he happens to have read a couple of books about Gilles de Rais, you're impressed with his knowledge, eh? For that you'll allow him to take the window? For that you'll sell your talents and your skills to him to help him find the secret?'

'It's not just for *his* benefit,' she snapped. 'I want to know what that window means, what it meant to de Rais. *I* want to know and I intend to find out. You said

I was obsessed with it; well, perhaps you're right. I'm not going to stop working on it until I find out.'

'You bargained with him,' said Channing scornfully, 'like a whore doing a deal with a customer. Fifty thousand wasn't enough, so you pushed him to a hundred. A whore's bargain.'

She took two steps towards him and slapped his face hard.

Channing looked at her angrily, his cheek stinging from the blow.

'Don't ever call me that,' she hissed.

'I won't let you do it, Catherine,' rasped Channing.

He swung at her, his fist catching her across the jaw, a blow which sent her sprawling. She tasted blood in her mouth as he advanced on her.

'I won't let you take the window,' he repeated, and grabbed her by the hair, tearing a great chunk from her scalp. She screamed in pain as he ripped it free, staring at the clump for a moment before lunging at her again.

Cath tried to roll to one side, to escape him, to reach the door of the room but Channing was too fast for her. As she made a dive for the bed he grabbed her leg and pulled her back, throwing all his weight on her, pinning her down.

He fastened his hands around her throat and began to squeeze, his thumbs digging into her larynx.

She struck at him, raking his cheek with her nails, pieces of his skin coming away. Blood dripped onto her face from the deep gashes but the pressure on her throat didn't ease.

'I won't let you go,' he hissed, shaking her now, exerting more pressure, driving his thumbs deeper until she thought he must begin to crush her spinal cord.

White light danced before her eyes and she could not

245

get her breath. It felt as if someone were sucking every last drop of air from her lungs as Channing pressed down harder.

She hooked her legs around him and tried to bring her heels down hard into the small of his back. For brief moments, with Channing lying between her legs, her own limbs around him, they looked to be in some kind of murderous coital embrace, but then her legs seemed to lose their strength and slip to either side. Waves of nausea swept through her. She realized with horror that she was losing consciousness. The blood pounded in her ears. Through eyes blurred with pain and fear she saw Channing's face above her. There was spittle on his lips, his teeth gritted together.

He looked like a madman.

In her last few moments of rational thought she guessed that madness had indeed finally taken him.

She couldn't breathe. His thumbs were gouging even more deeply into her throat.

She realized with unshakeable certainty that she was going to die.

One last effort.

She forced strength into limbs she had thought incapable of movement.

Summoning every last reserve of will she managed to bring her left knee up with terrific force, driving it into his groin.

The grip on her throat weakened noticeably.

She heard Channing's strangled cry of pain and brought up her knee again, this time so hard she felt it connect with his pelvic bone.

He rolled off her, groaning and clutching his testicles.

She fell from the bed, hit the floor hard. Holding her

bruised throat with one hand, her breath coming in choked gasps, she made for the door.

She'd almost reached it when she felt the hand on her shoulder.

Channing, his face still contorted with pain and rage, grabbed her by one arm and swung her round with such force that she was catapulted across the room. Unable to stop herself she smashed into the dressing table, her head snapping forward, striking the mirror with sickening force. The glass shattered, great long shards of it spraying out around her.

She slid to the floor, blood pouring from the savage wound on her forehead.

Through a mist of semi-consciousness she saw Channing coming towards her, bending to snatch up a particularly long, rapier-sharp piece of shattered mirror. The jagged edges cut his hands but he seemed to ignore his own pain.

'You won't take the window,' he hissed, his face twisted and bloated.

He looked like something embodied in the window, Cath thought.

Something monstrous.

It was her last thought before he drove the razor-sharp length of glass into the top of her skull.

She didn't scream.

Cath merely sat bolt upright in bed, her entire body coated with perspiration.

She looked frantically around, her eyes wide, still unsure for a second if she was immersed in the nightmare. Her hand went to her throat and she felt no marks, found that she could swallow without pain. There was no blood on her face. No wounds.

'Jesus,' she murmured and swung herself, naked, out of bed, feeling the sweat dry on her skin as she crossed to the door. She stood there for a moment, the residue of the dream still seared onto her retina like the muzzle-flash of a gun. Then, quickly, she locked the door and went back to bed, but it was a long time before she slept. Instead she watched the curtains billowing in the breeze like the wings of some gigantic moth.

Across the landing Mark Channing also lay awake, only shortly having emerged from the nightmare.

The nightmare in which he had murdered Catherine Roberts.

He lay motionless for long moments, then climbed out of bed and crossed to the wardrobe where his case was. He pulled it out and rummaged about inside.

The knife was almost eight inches long, double-edged and sharp as a razor. He examined it in the gloom, feeling the edges with his thumb. The blade itself was scratched and worn from many years' use: whittling, prising rocks from the ground.

It was a useful tool in his field work. His father had presented him with it just before he'd died and Channing treasured it for that as much as for its practicality and usefulness.

He scraped the pad of one thumb across the edge a little too hard and drew blood. He wiped the crimson droplet away.

He hefted the knife once more, glancing towards the door, wishing he could see beyond it. Into Catherine Roberts' room.

He turned the knife slowly in his hand and slid it carefully back into his case.

Fifty-Seven

Number Forty Glenarvon Road was as unremarkable
and as uniformly ordinary as most of the other houses
on the Turf Lodge estate.

It was terraced, with a blue-painted front door which
was blistered and in need of redecoration. The window
frames were in a similar condition. There were slates
missing off the roof, as there were on many of the other
houses on the street.

The early morning sunrise, which had spread its
orange glow through the sky and made even the worst
areas of the city look inviting, had passed. The sun
itself had disappeared behind banks of clouds which
periodically spattered the earth with rain. The sky was
grey. The street was grey. Even the people in it looked
grey; colourless entities who led grey lives.

There was movement behind the curtains of Number
Forty.

Simon Peters watched quietly, drumming on his
knee.

'Someone's at home,' said Luke McCormick. He
flicked on the windscreen wipers every now and then to
clear the spots of rain from the glass and to give the
men an unobstructed view of the house.

There were just the two of them in the car. Hagen
and Rice were a few miles away in Ballymurphy,
checking on the whereabouts of Michael Black.

The four men were to meet up at the Divis flats in two hours' time.

Peters continued to watch the house, moving slightly in his seat every now and then. As he did he felt the weight of the Browning Hi-Power against his left side. Tucked in his belt was a Charter Arms 'Pathfinder', a .22 calibre pistol.

The use to which the IRA put .22 pistols was limited.

But the smaller calibre weapons served their purpose admirably.

After all, anything larger would mean the whole of the lower leg being blown off, and why do that when a knee-cap was sufficient?

The curtain of Number Forty moved again.

'I wonder if young Billy is home,' said Peters.

'Perhaps he is and he's seen us,' McCormick suggested.

'If he'd seen us, Luke, he wouldn't be standing there looking out of the window at us, would he, now?' Peters observed, smiling. 'He'd have legged it.'

Peters glanced down at the clock on the dashboard, checking it against his own watch.

9.26 a.m.

The door of Number Forty opened and a tall youth dressed in jeans and a denim jacket nosed his way out, looked both ways then turned back to peer into the house. He was speaking to someone.

'Is that Billy's brother?' McCormick said.

Peters shook his head.

The youth waited a moment longer then wandered out, slammed the door behind him and ran off down the street, disappearing round a corner.

Peters pushed open his door and climbed out.

'Come on,' he said quietly, and his companion

250

joined him as they moved slowly across the street from the parked car.

A woman cleaning her front step looked up and saw them. McCormick waved to her and she waved back, continuing with her task.

As they reached the door of Number Forty Peters slid one hand inside the jacket. With the other hand he knocked.

No answer.

He tried again.

There was a hasty movement behind the door and it was opened a fraction.

Maria Dolan looked out at the men, her hair tousled, her face flushed, with only a towel wrapped around her.

'Who are you?' she asked, brushing a strand of blonde hair from her forehead.

Peters ran appraising eyes over her. She was in her late teens, not particularly pretty, a little on the thin side. Her legs needed shaving, he noted, seeing the shadows on her shins. The dye was beginning to grow out of her hair and the dark roots were showing where it was parted.

'Is your brother in, Maria?' Peters asked.

'Who wants to know?'

'Is he here?' McCormick added. 'We just want to talk to him.'

She regarded both men warily, her brown eyes flicking back and forth between the two of them.

'Are you with the RUC?' she wanted to know.

Peters grinned.

'No, we're not. We're friends of Billy's. We just want to speak to him.'

'He's not here,' she said and tried to push the door shut.

Peters saw what she was doing and managed to get one foot across the threshold.

'Open up, come on. If Billy's not here we'll have to talk to you,' he said, his hand gripping the pistol in his belt.

'Fuck off,' she said, trying to shut the door again.

Peters pulled the pistol free and, keeping it hidden, aimed it at her stomach.

'Open the door, you little tart. Now.'

She obeyed instantly, allowing them both inside. McCormick closed it behind them.

The sitting room was small and untidy. There were clothes lying around on the sofa. Peters noticed a pair of knickers on the arm of a chair. In an ashtray on the small coffee table there was a condom wrapped in tissue paper.

'Been entertaining, have you, Maria?' he said, smiling and pushing the .22 back into his belt.

She pulled the towel tighter around herself, the colour drained from her face. The bravado had gone from her voice.

'Who are you?' she asked quietly.

'Like I said, we're friends of your brother.' Peters looked around the room. A painting of Mary Magdalene stared back at him from one wall, encased in its plastic frame. On another wall there was a crucifix. Over the fireplace hung a calendar showing different views of Ireland. It was a month out of date. He crossed to it and turned it to the correct month.

'Parents out, too?' he observed.

'Dad's on the early shift, Mum left about two hours ago,' she said.

'So you invited your boyfriend round?' he chuckled.

McCormick looked into the small kitchen, then left

the sitting room and Maria heard him walking about upstairs.

'You're not going to hurt me, are you?' she said softly.

Peters shook his head.

'We just want to talk to you,' he told her. 'Has anyone else been here to see you in the last few days?'

She shook her head.

McCormick returned from upstairs, looked at Peters, shook his head and went into the kitchen.

Peters picked up the jeans from the sofa and a T-shirt, threw them to Maria and turned his back.

'Get dressed,' he told her, gazing out of the small front window. She did so hurriedly. When he thought she was finished he turned to face her again. She stood quivering before him like a naughty child in front of a headmaster.

McCormick returned from the kitchen.

The carving knife he carried was over ten inches long, broad-bladed and wickedly sharp.

Maria took a step backwards towards the picture of Mary Magdalene.

'You said you weren't going to hurt me,' she blubbered, tears filling her eyes.

'We're not,' Peters reassured her, stepping closer.

He grabbed her by the arm and pulled her close to him, one hand going across her mouth to stifle the scream she tried to release. He gripped her hard, one arm bent up her back.

McCormick advanced towards her, the knife levelled.

It was as he was reaching for her that they heard the key turn in the front door.

Fifty-Eight

Frank Dolan shrugged off his jacket and closed the front door behind him without looking up.

'Mr Dolan.'

The voice made him jump and he looked up, frozen by the tableau before him.

Two men held his daughter, one of them with a knife close to her face, the other holding a gun. A gun that was pointing at *him*.

'What's going on?' Frank Dolan said, his voice a mixture of fear and outrage. How dare these men come into his house? And what were they doing to his daughter? Anger began to filter into his emotions but it was beaten down rapidly by the fear. The barrel of the .22 was unwaveringly pointed at his chest.

'Sit down,' Peters told him, moving away from Maria, leaving McCormick to hold her.

Dolan did as he was told.

He was in his late forties, his face thin and pale, the skin looking as though it had been pulled taut over his high cheek-bones. His nose had been broken in a fight many years before. Beneath thick eyebrows his eyes were wide and alert, darting to and fro around the sitting room.

'You're supposed to be at work, aren't you?' said Peters conversationally.

'The Union called an unofficial strike,' Dolan said. 'Sent us all home.' He swallowed hard. 'You know why

254

I'm here; would you mind telling me why *you* are?'

Peters smiled thinly.

'Your son, Billy. Where is he?'

'How the hell should I know? I haven't spoken to him for a couple of months now.' He glanced across at Maria who stood silently, the blade held to her throat. Her cheeks were stained with tears.

'Please let my daughter go,' he said, looking at Peters.

'We've already said we're not going to hurt her. We're not,' the IRA man reassured him. 'I just want to know about Billy.' He knelt down in front of Dolan and looked into his face. 'You know who we are?'

The older man shook his head.

'You know why we want Billy?'

Again a shake of the head.

'You know what he's done?'

'I can't be doing with your bloody guessing games, for God's sake. Just tell me who you are and what you want.' Dolan's voice was strained, the fear seeping into it.

'You follow the news, don't you?' Peters said. 'You heard about the shootings at Stormont, the murder of Reverend Pithers, the bombing at Windsor Park?' He looked into Dolan's eyes. 'Your Billy was involved in them all. Him and his friends. They used to be *our* friends.'

The realization hit Dolan like a hammer.

'IRA,' he said, flatly.

'Have you seen him lately?' Peters demanded, the warmth disappearing rapidly from his voice.

'No, I swear it. Not for a couple of months, like I said,' Dolan said.

Peters turned briefly and nodded towards McCormick.

The other IRA men took hold of a hunk of Maria's

255

hair and, in one swift movement, sliced through it, dropping the dyed mass onto the floor.

'Oh, Christ,' Dolan murmured.

Maria couldn't scream; it was as if her vocal chords were frozen. Even as McCormick carved more of her hair away she stood motionless, tears streaming down her face.

'Where's Billy?' Peters asked again, his voice low and even.

'Let her go,' Dolan protested. 'Please.'

'Where is he?'

'I don't know, I've told you.'

McCormick carved away more of Maria's hair. There was a small pile of it at his feet now.

'Do you know what he's done, that fucking son of yours?' said Peters. 'The damage he's done? Not just in human lives but in the work he's destroyed. Work that's been going on for years.'

'I don't know where he is,' Dolan wailed.

McCormick tugged hard on Maria's hair and carved away a huge hunk of it, exposing one ear, nicking it accidentally in the process.

She let out a small whimper of pain but other than that the only sound she made was a low sobbing.

'What about his friends?' Peters asked, still squatting in front of Dolan, still glaring into his eyes. 'Did you ever meet any of them?'

'No,' the older man said, tears forming in his own eyes now. 'Leave my daughter alone, please. I'm telling you the truth. Please.'

'Do the names James Maguire, Michael Black, Damien Flynn or Paul Maconnell mean anything to you?' Peters asked, calmly.

McCormick cut away more of Maria's hair.

'No,' shouted Dolan. 'I don't fucking know them. Any of them.'

Peters drew the Pathfinder but kept it low at his side.

'You've almost convinced me,' he said, thumbing back the hammer.

Dolan was so intent on seeing that no harm came to his daughter he hardly noticed the gun.

'Do you do much walking in your job, Frankie?' Peters asked.

Dolan looked puzzled.

Peters smiled.

'Because if you do you'd better learn how to use crutches,' he said.

The last word had barely left his lips when he raised the .22, pressed it against Frank Dolan's left knee and fired once.

The retort of the weapon was almost as loud as the sickening crack as Dolan's patella was shattered by the bullet. The knee splintered as the bullet tore through his leg, ripping its way from the back, severing the cruciate ligaments. Blood began to soak through Dolan's trousers as he shouted in pain and clutched at the pulverized joint, crimson running through his fingers.

As she saw her father crippled by the bullet, Maria at last found the breath to scream.

McCormick didn't try to stop her as she ran to him, her stomach somersaulting as she saw the blood running down his leg and staining the carpet.

Peters stepped back, pushing the pistol into his belt, and motioned for his companion to join him. They headed for the front door.

'When you see Billy, tell him we want to talk to him,' Peters said, as if their departure required some form of etiquette.

Dolan was groaning in agony. Maria was sobbing as she gaped at the wound.

'I'd call an ambulance,' Peters advised, opening the door.

Then they were gone.

They walked back unhurriedly to the car and climbed in.

If any of the neighbours had heard the shot or the screams, they weren't exactly rushing to the Dolans' assistance. A couple of front doors were open, their occupants peering out into the street.

'Let's get out of here,' said Peters. His companion started the car and drove off.

'Do you think he was telling the truth?' McCormick asked. 'About Billy? That he hadn't really seen him?'

Peters nodded.

'I wonder where the bastard is.'

'Ireland's not a very big country, Luke. He can't run forever. We'll find him. *And* Maguire *and* the others. Count on it.'

Fifty-Nine

BRITTANY, FRANCE:
There was no sound from inside his room.

Catherine Roberts stood on the landing and listened for movement within but there was none.

She knocked once and waited.

Perhaps he was still sleeping. Neither of them had enjoyed a good night's rest since arriving; they had both been forced to content themselves with naps here and there. Deep sleep brought the nightmares.

There was still no sound from inside.

'Mark,' she called, knocking again.

This time when he didn't answer she pushed the door and walked in.

The bed was made, the room tidy. None of Channing's personal belongings were on the dressing table. She crossed to the wardrobe and opened it.

His case was gone.

Cath frowned and moved over to the window, peering out at where the Renault should be parked below. She was not surprised to find it gone. She hurried out of the room and down the stairs to the reception area, pausing at the desk and banging the little bell.

The plump woman who owned the inn emerged from a room at the rear wiping her hands on her apron. She smiled broadly at Cath.

'Have you seen Mr Channing?' Cath asked.

She was told he had checked out that morning about an hour ago.

'Where did he go?'

The woman had no idea.

Cath hesitated a moment. Then, thanking the woman, she dashed back up the stairs. The plump woman watched her, shrugged, and disappeared into the back room.

Upstairs Cath snatched up the keys to the Peugeot and hurried back down the steps and out into the square. Opening the door she slid behind the wheel and started the engine.

Where the hell was Channing?

Why had he left without telling her?

As she drove through the village she wasn't even sure where she was going but she felt she must try the obvious place first.

She swung the Peugeot onto the road to Machecoul.

As she did, Channing's words echoed in her mind;

'I won't let you take the window. I'd rather see it destroyed.'

He sat cross-legged, staring at the window as if mesmerized.

Mark Channing had been in that position for the last thirty minutes.

Staring. Dazzled, awestruck by the designs, the colours and the sheer artistry. It seemed to hold an even more potent spell over him than when he'd first seen it.

The eyes of the creatures depicted in the window, and the eyes of those who surrounded them, millions of eyes it seemed, all met his gaze, held it and fixed him in their own unblinking stare. He looked at the words, spoke some of them aloud:

'Sacrificium. Cultus. Opes. Immortalis.'

Even though he whispered, the words still seemed to echo around him.

Finally he rose, aware of the stiffness in his joints, of the chill in the air. His breath frosted as he exhaled.

A ray of sunlight struck the window, reflecting its colours even more vividly. The red eyes of the largest creature looked like puddles of boiling blood.

Channing gripped the piece of wood in his hands. It was heavy, about four feet long and five inches thick. Solid. He gritted his teeth as he raised it above his head and advanced towards the window.

It was growing colder.

He stared into the eyes of the glass monstrosity, steadied himself and brought the lump of wood down with incredible force.

He may as well have struck stone.

The thick wood slid off, the impetus of his swing causing Channing to overbalance. He went sprawling in the dust on the floor. Even as he rose he looked at the window, his eyes wide with disbelief. He dragged himself upright, raised the wood again and struck with even greater force, yelling loudly, as if the exhortation would give him the added strength needed to shatter the glass.

The wood connected but seemed to bounce off.

Channing shook his head and struck again.

And again.

Despite the cold inside the church he felt perspiration beading on his forehead from his exertions. He beat at the window relentlessly, unceasingly, until his strength seemed to drain away.

The window remained intact.

The eyes of the largest creature still stared at him.

Were they mocking him?

He dropped the wood, picked up a piece of stone and hurled it at the glass.

It too bounced off.

Channing was panting now, his chest heaving.

He stepped towards the window and leaned close to the glass.

It was unmarked.

No scratches. No marks. Nothing.

He picked up the stone and prepared to strike again. But before he could do so, he heard a thin keening wail, building slowly in volume, deepening too, growing louder, to unbelievable proportions.

He tried to move back from the window, tried to look away.

He opened his mouth to scream but no sound would come.

His eyes bulged madly in their sockets; the blood roared in his ears, ears that were already bleeding from the deafening cacophony of sound that filled them.

And it was the source of that sound which made him shake his head in disbelief.

On the window, every creature, every severed head, every child had its mouth open. And it was from the window that the wall of sound was coming.

Channing stood motionless, the rock still held in his hand, waiting for the dream to end, waiting to be catapulted back from the nightmare.

The roaring continued, the mouths open, screaming, shouting.

He raised the stone once more then brought it down with incredible ferocity against the window.

The screams rose in pitch, joined by one other.

It was Channing's turn to scream.

Sixty

She saw the Renault parked outside the church.

As Cath guided the Peugeot along the narrow road which led to Machecoul she spotted Channing's vehicle parked on the gravel surrounding the old building. The bright sunlight reflected off the roof and windows. The car looked as though it was on fire.

As she drew closer she managed a smile; her hunch had been right. Perhaps Channing just wanted one last look at the window before he left.

Perhaps.

She brought the Peugeot to a halt and climbed out, walking briskly across to the other car. She peered through the driver's side window. His camera was lying on the passenger seat. Cath wondered how long he'd been here. She turned and headed for the door of the church, pushing it hard to gain entry.

The silence was almost palpable.

'Mark,' she called, her voice echoing off the walls.

She walked briskly through the nave towards the door that would take her through into the chancel.

To the window.

He had to be there.

She was about to open the chancel door when she noticed the smell.

Cath hesitated a second, repelled by the stench. It was a cloying, thick, pungent odour which clogged in her nostrils as surely as the dust which her footsteps had disturbed. She rested her hand on the ornate knob, feeling how cold it was.

'Mark.' This time she spoke his name, low, under her breath.

She opened the door.

The stench rushed to meet her, enveloping her, but she didn't notice it; the sight before her filled her senses.

She stood rigid in the doorway, staring into the chancel.

The window was there.

Untouched.

Channing was there, too.

She stood for interminable seconds, waiting for the nightmare to end, waiting to drag herself upright and free of this dream. But as she felt the cold surrounding her and became aware of the stench once more, she knew there was to be no release from this particular nightmare.

Mark Channing lay in the middle of the chancel, a few feet from the window.

At least, that's where his legs and torso were.

One arm, she noted with disgust, was lying close to the door.

A leg, severed just below the knee, was over by the belfry door.

The whole chancel was covered in blood; the walls, the floor. There was even some on the window.

Cath put one hand to her mouth. Her breath was coming in short gasps. Her throat felt as if someone had filled it with sand. She couldn't swallow. All she could do was stare dumbly at what remained of Channing's body.

It took her a couple of seconds to realize why it was lying at such an unearthly angle, then she gritted her teeth and moved closer.

The body looked as if it had been twisted in half at the waist, the head and upper torso turned completely around, facing backwards. There were dozens of deep lacerations on Channing's face, neck and chest. Some of the cuts on his neck were so deep that the head had been almost severed. His clothes were bloody rags; portions of his jacket and trousers had been ripped away and lay scattered around like crimson confetti with other pieces of tissue, which she realized were flaps of skin.

One eye was missing from the socket.

It hung by the optic nerve, dangling in the blood and dust on the floor. Channing's other eye was open, wide and staring. As she approached his corpse, Cath tried to look away from it, disliking the blind stare. She did notice, with renewed revulsion, that his upper eyelid was missing.

She was careful not to slip in so much blood. It stuck to the soles of her shoes, still uncongealed in many places. Had she been able to manage rational thought she might well have realized that he had not been dead that long but rational thoughts eluded her when faced with the destruction of a human body as comprehensive as this. Cath knelt down a couple of feet from him, looking more closely at the pulverized corpse, cursing that infernal eye which hung from the dripping cord of nerve like a bloodied ping-pong ball. The eye seemed to be staring at her.

She tried to ignore it, aware again of the overpowering stench.

Cath felt light-headed, the combined effects of her grisly find and the odour which seemed now to be permeating her pores. She stood up and backed away, turning at last to look at the window.

Blood had spattered across it in several places, over the figure of the child held in the large demon's hand and also across the mouth of the demon itself.

Cath exhaled deeply and shook her head.

What had happened?

Channing had been killed (that seemed a reasonably safe assumption, considering the state he was in) but by who? And why?

Questions whirled in her head, her mind spinning almost as violently as her stomach.

Callahan?

He had known Channing's reluctance to let the window leave Machecoul.

But even if it had been Callahan, why would he destroy Channing's body in such a way? Why leave it for *her* or anyone else to find?

She shook her head again, her eyes drawn to the mutilated, twisted remains of her former colleague. His appearance made her feel sick. She thought she was going to faint and made for the chancel door, leaning against it until the feeling passed. She could feel the perspiration on her forehead and back, despite the chill in the air.

As Cath stepped back she noticed that blood from the door was now on her hand. She pulled a tissue from the pocket of her jeans and scrubbed the crimson liquid away, scraping frenziedly, as if she feared she would be marked with it forever. Slowly she turned to look at Channing once more, wondering what she should do.

Call the police?

Call Callahan?

She swallowed hard, her stomach churning less violently now, her composure returning slowly. She sucked in a long, deep breath, tinged as it was with the scent of death, held it for a moment and released it slowly. Her mind began to clear.

She wished that dangling eye would stop staring at her.

She knew she had to think.

What was she going to do?

Come on, get a grip.

A thought occured to her. Struck her like a hammer blow.

What if Channing's killer was still in the church?

The thought sent her heart racing, thudding so hard against her ribs she feared it would burst. She listened for any sounds from the nave. From the belfry above her. Perhaps she should leave the church, go now, pretend she'd never been here, just get out, leave the country. Anything to be away from this place, this carnage that lay around like the work of some careless butcher.

The killer would have no need to stay around, she reasoned, her heart slowing its frantic pace a little.

What should she do?

She looked at the body once more.

Something was glinting just inside the pocket of Channing's jacket.

Cath moved towards him, trying not to inhale too deeply, attempting to minimize the vile stench.

She reached for the glinting object and pulled the car keys from his pocket, holding them tightly in her fist.

The car. Someone would find his car eventually.

She stepped back again, glancing at the window, at the slicks of blood which covered it. Pulling another tissue from her pocket she fastidiously wiped the crimson liquid from the glass where it covered the figure of the child.

What would happen to the window if Channing's murder was discovered?

The church would be closed, the window lost to her forever.

The secret would be taken.

She looked at the car keys and gripped them tightly in her hand.

The secret.

She turned back to face the window, to wipe away the blood that had covered the mouth of the largest demon.

It was gone.

Not a trace of the sticky fluid remained on the glass.

Cath stared into the blazing red eyes of the creature,

then turned back to look at Channing, his own blank eyes fixing her in that blind stare.

She felt the car keys cold against the warm flesh of her palm.

And she knew what she must do.

Sixty-One

'Channing's dead.'

Catherine Roberts didn't wait to be either formally greeted or welcomed into the hotel room of the Callahans. She told David Callahan as soon as he opened the door and stepped past him into the room. Laura was sitting on the bed dressed only in a thin robe, unconcerned that her breasts and also the dark triangle of her pubic hair were visible through the diaphanous material. She looked at Cath indifferently.

Catherine Roberts was angry. The drive from Machecoul to St. Philbert had not served to calm that fury. She had found the hotel where the Callahans were staying without any trouble, asked which room they were in and rode the lift to the appropriate floor while the concierge was still attempting to alert the guests of her presence.

Now she stood in the room, looking calm, wiping a stray hair from her forehead, but seething inside.

Callahan's attitude to her announcement further irritated her. She may as well have announced that smoking could cause lung disease for all the reaction she elicited from the man. He merely looked at her and shrugged.

'Did you hear me?' she snapped. 'I said Mark Channing is dead. Murdered.'

'How do you know he was murdered?' asked Callahan.

'Because I saw his body,' she hissed. 'Believe me, it wasn't suicide.'

Callahan offered her a drink and she accepted.

'What happened?' he wanted to know.

She told him the story as briefly as possible. She even mentioned her nightmare. When she arrived at the part about reaching the church she paused and sipped at her drink. Laura was watching her intently.

'His body was ...' Catherine struggled for the words. 'He was mutilated. Very badly.'

'How?' Laura wanted to know.

'I told you, I don't know.'

'I mean, what kind of injuries?' asked Laura quietly.

'He was cut very badly,' Cath said wearily, the recollection of the sight she'd seen making her feel queasy once again. She sipped her drink. 'I don't know how to describe it without sounding stupid.' She looked at each of them in turn. 'He'd been torn to pieces. His body was smashed, broken.' She lowered her gaze, content to look into the bottom of her glass.

'What did the police say?' Callahan asked.

'They don't know,' Cath told him. 'No one knows. No one *will* know.'

'What makes you so sure?' he wanted to know.

She downed the remainder of the drink and put down the glass a little too heavily.

'Because I took his body out of the church.' She looked at Callahan. 'I dragged it out to his car and put it in the boot. Then I drove the car into the woods nearby and covered it up. It'll be ages before anyone finds it.' She sighed. 'After that I walked back to the church and cleaned it up inside as best I could. Then I drove back to the inn, washed, changed, packed and came here.'

'You did well,' said Callahan, smiling.

'I didn't come here for bloody praise,' Cath snarled. 'I want to know if *you* killed him.'

Callahan shook his head.

'Why should I?'

'He said he was going to destroy the window,' Cath reminded him.

'Where's the window now?' Callahan asked.

'Still inside the church.'

He nodded.

'I've arranged for it to be picked up tomorrow,' he said. 'Some men will come and pick it up in a truck. Colleagues of mine will fly it back to Ireland in a private plane. I'll be there to meet it, then it'll be taken back to my estate. You can carry on your work on it there.' He smiled. 'Laura and I are flying back today. I thought you might stay on and supervize the loading. You can travel back in the plane with the window. To keep an eye on it.' He smiled that condescending grin again.

'How do we know *you* didn't kill Channing?' Laura asked. 'You've accused *us*. *You* had as much reason.'

'You didn't want the window destroyed any more than we did,' Callahan reminded her.

'I didn't kill him,' Cath snapped.

'Why did you hide his body?' Callahan enquired.

Cath swallowed hard.

'I knew that if the police were involved there was no chance of getting the window out of the church. Their enquiries would have held up my work for too long.'

Callahan smiled.

'You're as obsessed with it as I am,' he said flatly.

She had no answer.

'Who do *you* think killed him?' Laura asked.

'I don't know,' Cath told her. 'It was the *way* he was killed that was so bizarre.' She shook her head, the images coming once more into her mind. Images of the blood, of the body twisted at the waist, the severed limbs. That eye dangling, staring blindly. She put her hands to her face and exhaled deeply. Callahan smiled.

'You realize that what you did makes you an accessory?' he said.

'What the hell are you saying, Callahan?' she snapped.

'Just telling you what I'm thinking,' he answered. 'It's a good job you *are* leaving France soon. You'll be safe on my estate.'

'You make it sound as if Interpol are after me,' said Cath sardonically.

'Could someone have found out about the window?' Laura mused aloud. 'That it was going to be removed, I mean. Perhaps someone who didn't want it taken away killed Channing.'

Callahan shrugged.

'It's possible, I suppose,' he added. 'That may be true. If it is then whoever killed Channing is going to be after *us*, too.'

PART THREE

'You know you'd have gone insane if you saw what I saw.'

– Iron Maiden

'He clings firmly out of defiance to a cause which he has seen through – but he calls it "loyalty".'

– Nietzsche

Sixty-Two

DUNDALK: THE REPUBLIC OF IRELAND:
Doyle woke early, glanced at his watch and tried to sleep again, but the more he tried to relax the more impossible he found it. It was just after six a.m.

He rubbed both hands over his face and exhaled.

Georgie was asleep with her head resting on his chest. As he lay there he watched the rhythmic rise and fall of her shoulders as she breathed. He could feel the softness of her hair against his skin. For a moment he found himself stroking the silky blonde locks, but then he withdrew his hand hastily, as if he'd touched something hot. Instead, he propped both arms behind his head, supporting himself against the headboard. Only a sheet covered them; Doyle could see the outline of Georgie's body beneath the thin material. He followed it with his eyes.

It had been she who had pulled the sheet over them after their love-making the previous night.

The ferocity of their passion, the intensity of their coupling had exhausted them both. Perhaps it was their way of releasing the tension of the past few days, Doyle thought.

Or perhaps it was because there was something deeper than just physical attraction between them.

Doyle pushed the thought angrily from his mind and decided it was time he got up. He eased himself free of Georgie, slipping out of bed, trying not to disturb her.

She murmured something in her sleep but then rolled onto her stomach and was quiet again.

Doyle walked to the bathroom and filled the sink with cold water. He splashed his face, finally lowering it into the water, scooping more up over the back of his neck. He stood up, moisture coursing down his features, rivulets of water running over his torso. He regarded his reflection in the mirror, touching the scar on the left side of his face, tracing its length with one index finger. He ran a hand through his hair, dried himself and wandered back into the bedroom with just a towel wrapped around him.

He crossed to the wardrobe and took out the small case. He set it on top of the dressing table and flipped it open.

He laid the MP5K on the floor beside the bed, lifted the CZ and the .44 from their holsters and put them beside the sub-gun. Then he sat down, cross-legged, his back against the bed, looking at the weapons. Using a piece of rag he'd also taken from the case he began cleaning the .44.

He and Georgie had crossed the border into the Republic late the previous evening. They'd stopped at a small hotel on the outskirts of Dundalk, booking in under the names of Taylor and Blake, ignoring the knowing glances the proprietor gave them as he told them where their room was. Doyle had stopped him when he'd offered to carry their small cases.

They had undressed together and climbed into bed together. It had all seemed so natural, as if sex between them was part of the job. Doyle glanced down, as he cleaned the gun, at the scars which criss-crossed his body.

Emotional scars run deeper.

276

He snapped the cylinder back into the .44 and laid it on one side.

As he reached for the CZ he heard murmurings from behind him and movement. Georgie yawned and stretched, then slid across the bed and kissed Doyle's shoulder.

'Good morning,' she whispered sleepily. 'How long have you been up?'

'Not long. I tried not to disturb you.'

'You're very thoughtful,' she told him and began stroking his back with her fingertips, feeling the indentations of his scars.

Doyle, his back to her, closed his eyes tightly and finally edged away from her. Away from her touch.

He continued cleaning the automatic.

Georgie regarded him silently, then crossed her arms and rested her chin on them.

'You didn't move away from me last night,' she said.

'That was last night,' he said sharply, working the rag around the inside of the barrel.

'What are you afraid of, Sean?'

'I don't know what you're talking about.'

'Scared that the mask is going to drop?'

Doyle pulled back the slide and continued cleaning.

'You're like Dr Jekyll and Mr Hyde,' she persisted. 'Sometimes you're warm and caring, other times you're cold. It's like being with two different people.'

Doyle pressed the slide release and the metallic crack reverberated around the room.

'I thought we'd been through all this shit before,' he said.

'I had your home-spun philosophy about life and death, if that's what you mean,' she said acidly.

'What more do you want from me, Georgie?' he

asked. 'We're here to find and kill some men, not start up a big fucking romance.'

'We sleep together. Doesn't that mean anything to you? Doesn't it make us closer?'

'Do you want it to?'

She sighed.

'I don't know,' she whispered. 'I know how you feel about …'

He cut her short.

'You don't know how I feel about anything,' he told her, his tone a little too vehement.

'I'm not asking you to fall in love with me, for Christ's sake,' she said angrily. 'I just want to know what frightens you about people getting close to you? Why does it matter so much? Why won't you let anyone get close?'

'Because the closer they get the more painful it is when you lose them.'

She was silent for a moment, her eyes never leaving his broad back.

'You're always so sure you're going to lose them,' she said softly.

'Nothing's permanent. *You* should know that. Ask the families of the people killed at Windsor Park. Think about your own brother. Did you ever think it'd be *him* who got killed? No. It was always going to be some other poor sod, wasn't it? Well, death makes no exceptions, Georgie, and today or tomorrow it could be you or me they load into a fucking body bag.' He put down the CZ. 'Like the song says, *Live for today, tomorrow never comes*.' He turned to face her, kissing her lightly on the lips. 'That's the only way I can live.' He touched her cheek with his hand, feeling how smooth her skin was.

She lay there for a moment longer then swung herself out of bed, naked.

Doyle ran one hand up the inside of her thigh as she stood before him and she sucked in a quivering breath, smiling as his fingers brushed against her pubic hair.

'I'd better get dressed,' she said softly, smiling down at him.

He nodded, watching as she padded off into the bathroom.

Doyle held the CZ before him, satisfied at its condition, then reached for the sub-machine gun and began cleaning that.

From behind him he heard the sound of splashing water as Georgie washed.

He gripped the MP5K in one fist, his thoughts turning to Maguire and his men.

He squeezed the trigger of the machine pistol, the hammer slamming down on an empty chamber.

Soon.

Very soon.

He knew the time was coming.

Sixty-Three

'I don't like graveyards.'

Damien Flynn looked around him at the uneven rows of stone crosses and headstones as he picked his way carefully over the wet grass.

'Remind you that you'll end up in one yourself one day, eh, Damien?' James Maguire said, careful to step over a freshly-laid bouquet.

'I've been to too many bloody funerals,' Flynn observed, glancing over his shoulder towards the path that cut through the cemetery.

Billy Dolan was guiding the dark blue Ford van up the narrow path, its wheels crunching gravel. He saw Flynn looking at him and waved happily, his infectious grin lighting up his face. Flynn stepped on a plot, apologising quietly to its inhabitant as he did so.

The cemetery was about two miles south of the town of Navan, on the Boyne river, the resting place of so many inhabitants of that small community. It was on a slight rise; in clear weather, the ruins of Bective Abbey could be seen further to the south. However, Maguire and his men weren't on a sight-seeing trip and Flynn's preoccupation with where he put his feet prevented him taking all but the most perfunctory interest in his surroundings.

Ahead, the church was built on a slight incline, its bell-tower thrusting up towards the overcast sky, a weather vane turning gently in the breeze. To their left were more graves; much smaller plots, these. The resting places of those who chose to be cremated.

To their right was the mausoleum.

It was about twelve feet in height, its stonework weather-beaten, scarred by time. Cracks in the outer walls had been infested with moss, which filled the rents like gangrene in septic wounds. Weeds grew high up the walls, some clinging to the stonework so thickly they looked as though they would pull the edifice over. Flynn noticed the remains of a bird's nest on the top of the mausoleum.

More weeds grew thickly around the door, which was secured by a padlock. It was brand new and looked incongruous against the aging stonework.

Maguire fumbled in his jacket pocket and pulled out a key which he fitted into the padlock, turning it and snapping it loose. The chain fell away and he pushed the door, which opened with relative ease apart from a squeal of protest which came from hinges that hadn't tasted oil for many years.

A stench of neglect and damp swept out into the early morning air, making Flynn cough as he inhaled the dank odour.

Billy Dolan turned the van and reversed it up to the door of the mausoleum, then climbed out and threw the back doors open. Maguire pulled the torch from his belt and entered the ancient edifice, closely followed by Flynn. It was as black as pitch inside, the beams of the torches scarcely cutting through the tenebrous gloom. Ahead of them was a short flight of steps, slippery with mould. The walls were also stained green, and in several places the stone had been breached, allowing rain through to further erode the construction. As Maguire moved towards the steps, Flynn shone his torch around the inside of the small tomb. There were at least five coffins, each one lying on a ledge protruding from the wall. Flynn half-expected to see rats sitting up on the coffin lids but there were none. There were only one or two dusty cobwebs on the boxes, too. He seemed almost disappointed.

'Damien, come down here.'

Maguire's voice, lancing through the darkness, startled Flynn, but he regained his composure and scuttled towards the short flight of steps, using his torch as a guide. Careful not to slip on the mould he made his way down to where Maguire was standing.

He was leaning against one of half-a-dozen crates, each one about six feet by three. The wood was new;

Flynn could smell its tangy odour even through the mustiness of the tomb. A crowbar lay on top of one of the boxes and Maguire used it to prise the first one open. Inside there was a layer of straw. The IRA man pulled some of the straw away and dug his hand in, smiling as he raised his find like some kind of prize.

'Jesus,' murmured Flynn, shining his torch on his companion and the Sterling-Armalite rifle which he held.

There were more in the box.

Flynn put down his torch so that the beam was pointing at one of the other crates and used the crowbar to open the large container. Inside there was more straw. More weapons. He lifted the Armalite out of its packing and pressed it to his shoulder, squinting down the sight.

'Billy,' Maguire called, 'let's get these loaded up and get out of here.'

Flynn squeezed the trigger and heard a dull thud. He frowned.

'Wait a minute, Jim,' he said, lowering the rifle. 'Hold that torch over here.'

Maguire shone the beam in the direction of the weapon, watching as Flynn skilfully and quickly removed the top portion of the rifle and peered at it.

'What's wrong?' Maguire wanted to know.

Flynn didn't answer. He put down the partly-disassembled weapon and reached for another, cocking it and squeezing the trigger.

He heard that same dull thud.

He reached for another and another.

His reaction was the same every time.

'Fucking bastard,' he snarled, hurling the gun to one side. He looked at Maguire, his face contorted with

282

anger. 'There's no firing pins in these guns. They're bloody useless.'

Maguire was about to say something when Dolan's voice cut through the blackness.

'You'd better get up here quick,' called the younger man. 'We've got company.'

Sixty-Four

The car carrying the two Garda officers moved slowly up the gravel path towards the stationary blue van.

About twenty yards away it stopped and both men stepped out. One remained beside the car. The first, a tall, broad-shouldered man with greying hair, began walking purposefully towards the van.

Billy Dolan took a step backwards, his hands dangling at his side, the 9mm Bernadelli tight against his left side.

Not yet.

From inside the mausoleum Maguire could see the uniformed officer. He eased the Browning Hi-Power from its holster and gently worked the slide, chambering a round.

Officer Gary Farrow slowed his pace slightly when he came to the end of the gravel pathway. The big man fixed Dolan in his gaze, taking in details of his features, trying to see if there was anyone with him. He noticed the door to the mausoleum was open. Farrow also glanced at the number-plate of the van.

Behind him, at the waiting car, Officer Christopher

Page was also taking a note of the number. He moved away from the car, peering around the cemetery as his companion drew closer to the van.

'Can I ask what you're doing, sir?' Farrow enquired, his voice even.

Dolan smiled.

'I was looking for the priest,' he said gaily.

'I don't think you'll find him in there,' Farrow answered, nodding in the direction of the tomb. 'Could I have your name, please?'

From inside the vault Maguire raised the pistol and steadied himself, watching as Farrow drew closer to the van.

'What about the other one?' whispered Flynn, spotting Page standing by the car further down the pathway.

'Your name, sir, and I'd like to see your driver's licence, too,' Farrow said, moving closer to Dolan.

Maguire prepared to fire.

'Fuck you,' snarled Dolan, and plunged a hand inside his jacket, gripping the Bernadelli.

He fired twice as he pulled it free.

The first shot sliced through empty air, the second struck a gravestone, blasting a chunk of it away.

Farrow threw himself to the ground, rolling onto the gravel, trying to find cover.

'Shit,' hissed Maguire, emerging from the tomb like a vengeful resurrected corpse. He gripped the Browning tightly and squeezed off three rounds, two of which hit the Garda car. A wing mirror was torn off; another bullet holed the windscreen. Page ducked down behind the open door, scrambling to pull his own gun free.

Farrow was still rolling, trying to get to his feet, to find some cover.

Dolan fired another four rounds from the Bernadelli, the savage recoil slamming the weapon back against the heel of his hand until it felt numb. The stench of cordite filled the air.

Farrow was hit in the back, the bullet macerating one kidney, travelling upwards to shatter and bounce off a rib before lodging below one lung. He grunted in pain and felt the strength draining from him along with so much of his blood. He crawled towards a headstone as more bullets struck the ground around him, sending up geysers of earth and gravel.

Another shot struck him in the side of the face, pierced both cheeks and pulverized three of his back teeth, carrying portions of enamel away through the gaping exit wound. Blood filled his mouth, but he kept crawling.

'Kill him, for fuck's sake,' snarled Flynn, leaping into the back of the van, watching as Maguire fired a full magazine towards the car.

Bullets struck the body work, the windscreen, the tyres.

Two hit Officer Page.

One tore through his left calf, ripping away most of the muscle there, snapping his shin. As he sprawled on the ground another bullet struck him in the face, just above the chin. His bottom jaw seemed to disintegrate, portions of bone and shattered teeth falling to the ground, propelled by the gushing blood which erupted from the wound. He lay still until a third shot caught him in the chest and sent him rolling over onto his back, his sternum destroyed. Blood flooded over his lips, bubbling as he exhaled. He felt incredible pressure on his rib cage, as if someone had put heavy weights on it. When he tried to breathe the pain prevented all but the smallest of gasps. He felt unconsciousness beginning to creep over him.

The fourth bullet which hit him tore off most of the left side of his head.

'Start the fucking van,' shouted Maguire, pushing Billy towards the vehicle.

He himself hunched low to the ground and scuttled towards the headstone where Farrow was sheltering.

There was a loud retort and Maguire actually heard the bullet sing past his ear, no more than two or three feet away. Farrow fired again, his hand remarkably steady as he pumped the trigger of the .38.

Maguire hurled himself down, rolled over and, using a marble cross as support, squeezed the trigger again. The slide shot backwards to signal that the Browning was empty and Maguire dug in his jacket pocket for a fresh magazine which he slammed into the pistol butt. He wrenched back the slide and fired again.

Farrow was hit in the shoulder, the bullet shattering his collar bone. The impact flung him backwards, the revolver flying from his hand.

As he lay on his back staring at the sky he heard footsteps coming closer to him and saw Maguire looking down at him, the barrel of the Browning yawning massively.

Maguire smiled and shot Farrow in the temple.

Billy Dolan guided the van back onto the gravel path, pushing open the passenger side door for his companion to get in. As Maguire clambered into the van, he put his foot down. Gravel was sent spinning into the air as the wheels skidded on the surface, finally gaining purchase. The van sped off past the Garda car and the body of Officer Page towards the gates of the cemetery.

Dolan swung it left onto the road.

'What about the rifles?' he said, his eyes fixed on the road ahead.

'They were no fucking good,' Flynn rasped from the back.

Dolan glanced across at Maguire as if for verification.

The older man didn't speak. He merely continued thumbing 9mm shells into an empty magazine, his features set, the knot of muscles at the side of his jaw throbbing angrily.

'What are we going to do about the rifles?' Dolan persisted.

'I'll take care of it,' said Maguire quietly. 'Just drive.'

Sixty-Five

Doyle tapped impatiently on the wheel as he drove, eyes on the horse-drawn cart which blocked the road ahead of him. He thought about hitting the Datsun's horn – anything to clear the bloody cart out of the way – but decided against it. He wound down his window, one arm draped over the edge. The sun was warm against his skin and the countryside smelt fresh and clean after the light shower which had fallen just half an hour earlier.

Georgie looked across at him and caught the impatience in his expression. She smiled thinly. Doyle glanced at her and noticed her grinning.

'What's so funny?' he wanted to know.

'You,' she told him. 'You're so impatient. Life's slower out here, Doyle. This isn't London, you know.'

'If it was any slower it'd be fucking comatose,' he said, shaking his head, relieved to see that the horse and cart were turning off to the right into a field. Doyle put his foot down and accelerated past.

A sign announced that Dublin was just under twenty miles away.

'So where do we find this Mr David Callahan?' asked Doyle. 'If he's leasing cars to the IRA I think we ought to talk to him.'

'He lives on a private estate in County Cork,' Georgie announced, consulting the notes she had scribbled on a pad. 'He's lived there for the past two years. Used to live in London. Married. No kids. He employs about six staff.'

Doyle chewed his bottom lip contemplatively.

'You know there's something familiar about that name,' he said. 'Has he got any form?'

'If he has he was never convicted. He's got no criminal record of any description, as far as I could find out.'

'So what are the IRA doing driving around in his car?' Doyle mused.

'There's no reason why Callahan should be mixed up with them. The car could have been stolen; *this* David Callahan may even be a completely different person. Maguire and his men probably just used a false name when they bought it.'

'Coincidence, though, isn't it? There can't be that many David Callahans living in the Republic who own a blue Sierra.' He smiled. 'Or used to, until you shot it to pieces.'

'Just doing my job.' She chuckled.

Doyle reached across and fumbled with the dials of the radio, flicking from station to station. He found a

288

Gaelic speaking station, a pop channel, then some news.

'...*early this morning. One officer was killed in the gun battle.*'

Doyle turned up the volume.

'...*There were no witnesses to the shooting and the bodies were only discovered by a visitor to the cemetery, which has now been closed off by the Garda pending investigaton into the shootings.*'

Georgie looked across at Doyle, who was listening intently.

'*The wounded officer, whose name has not been released, was taken to hospital in Mullingar where his condition is said to be critical.*'

'Where's Mullingar?' Doyle snapped, flicking off the radio.

Georgie hesitated a moment, then reached for the map which lay on the parcel shelf. She ran her finger over it, searching for the location.

'About six miles west of where we are now,' she told him. 'Doyle, you don't even know if these shootings are anything to do with Maguire ...' Her words were cut short as Doyle quickly checked his rear-view mirror then pulled hard on the wheel, swinging the Datsun around in a U-turn.

'Two Garda officers shot,' he said. 'It's worth checking out. Especially if one of them is still alive.'

'How the hell are you going to get to him?' Georgie asked. 'By the sound of it, the poor devil is almost dead anyway. What can he tell you?'

'He can tell me who shot him,' said Doyle flatly.

Georgie shook her head.

'I thought we were supposed to be going after Callahan,' she said.

'We are.'

289

'I'm telling you, Doyle, you'll never get near the guy who was shot,' she repeated.

'I know. *I* might not be able to.' He glanced across at her. 'But *you* can.'

Sixty-Six

The flight had been smooth enough, but David Callahan had been glad to touch down all the same.

Their car had been waiting at Shannon airport and they had climbed in gratefully, relaxing in the plush seats of the Mercedes as they were driven home.

The drive took less than two hours. Laura smiled as the car finally came to a halt outside the house. She and Callahan got out, their luggage was brought into the house and the car was put in the double garage. It was as if they'd never been away, thought Laura, as she made her way up the stairs. The thought of a bath made her smile.

Callahan joined her upstairs carrying two drinks.

They kissed as they waited for the bath to fill, the sound of running water filling the bathroom.

'Do you think the window will be safe?' Laura asked, slipping out of her clothes and walking naked from the bathroom to the bedroom, where she sat in front of the dressing table and began combing her hair, finally putting it up into a bun.

'Sure it will,' Callahan said. 'It's only got to be taken from the church. It'll be picked up. I don't see why there should be any problems.'

'Do you trust that woman?'

'Why shouldn't I? She's got more to lose than us if anything happens to the window. Don't forget, she was the one who covered up a murder.'

Callahan pulled his shirt off and stepped out of his trousers. He stood naked for a moment, then pulled on a bathrobe.

'What you said about Channing's killer coming after us,' Laura said quietly. 'Do you think it *is* possible?'

Callahan could only shrug.

There was a knock on the bedroom door.

Laura called out, 'Come in,' and they both looked up to see one of the maids standing there. She smiled at them, told them she was glad they were back, asked briefly about their trip.

'Did anything exciting happen while we were gone, Trisha?' asked Laura, smiling, heading towards the bathroom to turn off the taps.

'There were some phone calls,' the maid said, brushing her long blonde hair from her face. 'I made a note of them.' She handed Callahan a pad which he scrutinised, nodding as he looked at the names.

'Thanks, Trisha,' he said.

'Someone else called,' she said. 'But he wouldn't give his name. He called four or five times while you were gone. He wanted to know where you were, but when he wouldn't give his name I didn't tell him.'

'You did the right thing,' Callahan assured her. 'What did he say? Did you recognise the voice?'

She shook her head.

'When I wouldn't tell him where you were he got a bit abusive. Mary answered the phone to him a couple of times and he was the same to her,' Trisha told him.

'When did he last call?' Callahan's face darkened.

291

'A couple of hours before you got back. He still wouldn't leave his name.'

Callahan swallowed hard as the maid continued.

'All he said was that he had something to discuss with you and that he'd be seeing you very soon. Then he hung up. If he calls again, do you want to speak to him?' she enquired.

Callahan didn't answer.

'Mr Callahan, I said if ...'

He cut her short.

'I heard you. No. If he calls again tell him I'm not back yet.'

She nodded and left.

Callahan took a sip of his drink, rolling the crystal tumbler between his hands.

'*Be seeing you very soon.*'

He would be ready.

Sixty-Seven

Doyle replaced the receiver, pushed open the door of the phone box and walked unhurriedly back towards the waiting car.

'This will never work,' said Georgie as he slid back behind the steering wheel.

'Oh ye of little faith,' he said, not taking his eyes from the hospital entrance.

There were two Garda cars parked outside the main doors, uniformed men in both.

The building itself was small, a four-storey concrete

and glass affair which looked as if it could do with some modernisation. An ambulance was parked close to the other vehicles. It was empty, as far as the two counter-terrorists could see.

'I wonder why he was shot,' said Georgie.

'That's what we've got to find out,' Doyle told her.

'And if it's nothing to do with Maguire and his men?'

He shrugged.

'Then we carry on looking. This is worth a go, Georgie. Anything is, no matter how remote. If it means getting to Maguire it's worth trying.'

Doyle reached onto the back seat and retrieved the bunch of flowers they'd bought a couple of streets away.

'Let me carry them,' she said. 'You don't look like the caring *type*.'

Doyle raised one eyebrow quizzically and handed her the flowers. They both climbed out of the Datsun and walked across the street towards the main entrance of the hospital, moving slowly, apparently oblivious to the uniformed men in the cars on either side of the short flight of steps to the main doors of the hospital. They passed unchallanged and wandered through into the reception area.

It was cool in there, the air-conditioning set a little too low. On their right, as they entered, was the hospital shop and Doyle saw a woman there buying chocolates. There were several rows of plastic chairs set next to a large picture window that looked out onto a small enclosed garden. About half a dozen people sat in the chairs, one man with his head bowed, hands clasped on his lap. Doyle nodded almost imperceptibly to Georgie, who went and sat on one of the seats. To his left there was a vending machine. A weary-looking man not much older than Doyle was feeding coins into it.

Doyle crossed to him, standing close behind him.

As the man turned from the machine, Doyle stepped closer to him.

The man couldn't help himself and spilled hot coffee on Doyle's hand.

'Christ, I'm sorry,' he said.

'Don't worry about it,' Doyle told him, wiping the hot liquid with a handkerchief. He patted the man on the shoulder. 'I shouldn't have been standing so close. I'll get you another one.'

'It's ok.'

'No, please,' Doyle insisted, already pushing coins into the machine.

The man smiled thinly and discarded the half-empty plastic cup.

'I hate hospitals,' Doyle said. 'I'm here visiting my wife. She was in a car accident. Broke a leg and an arm, shook her up badly.'

'I'm sorry about that.'

'How about you? Who are you here to see?'

'My father. He had a heart attack a couple of days ago. They moved him out of intensive care yesterday, though. He seems to be on the mend. Tough old sod.'

'My wife's mother was in intensive care here,' Doyle lied. 'I didn't like the doctor at all. Didn't seem to know what he was doing. Tyrone, I think his name was. That's not who's looking after your old fella, is it?'

The man shook his head.

'It's Doctor Collins. He's a nice guy.'

Doyle nodded and sighed theatrically.

'Well, I'd better go,' he said. 'Sorry about the coffee,' he added, shrugging, managing a smile.

The man said goodbye, finished his drink and wandered out of the hospital. Doyle watched him go then walked across to the reception desk, his face emotionless.

'Excuse me,' he said earnestly, not returning the smile the receptionist gave him. 'Doctor Collins spoke to me on the phone this morning. He told me that I could see my brother, that they'd operated on him.'

'Doctor Collins is up in intensive care at the moment, sir,' the receptionist said. 'What's your brother's name?'

'Jonathan Martin.'

The receptionist looked down at a list of names pinned to a clipboard, following the column with the end of her pen.

'There's no one here under that name, sir,' she said, puzzled.

Doyle sighed.

'Could you please check again. Doctor Collins said I could see him.'

'When was he admitted?' she wanted to know.

'Last night.'

'His name might be on another list of admissions. This one,' she tapped the clipboard with her pen, 'only covers those brought in today.'

Like Officer Gary Farrow, Doyle thought.

The receptionist got to her feet and wandered into an annexe beyond her desk. Doyle leant across the low partition and scanned the list of names.

FARROW. G. I.C. 4.

He spun round and walked away, tapping Georgie on the shoulder as he reached her.

'Fourth floor,' he said as they walked to the lifts. Doyle jabbed the call button and the lift arrived. The doors slid open, disgorging three passengers, one of them a uniformed Garda officer.

Doyle and Georgie got in and Doyle pressed 3 and 4.

The lift began to ascend.

It stopped at 3.

Doyle got out and headed for the stairs, scurrying up the stone flight, trying to time his arrival on the fourth floor with that of the lift.

He reached the landing and peered through the small window in the door, watching as Georgie emerged holding the flowers. To her right was a desk and switchboard with a nurse seated behind it. Standing close to this desk was a Garda officer. He saw Georgie approach the man. He couldn't hear what she was saying but he could see the Garda officer nodding.

Doyle slipped through the door, moving almost soundlessly, eyes still on the tableau at the end of the corridor. He saw Georgie offering the flowers to the uniformed man. There were about five doors facing him, each one closed, but they all had a small square window. He moved hurriedly from one to the other, peering in.

A woman, old, dying.

A man in an oxygen tent. Forty years old. It was hard to tell from looking at his pale skin and sunken features. Doyle moved to the next window.

The man's face was bandaged heavily, with only his eyes showing. There were intravenous drips attached to both his arms and tubes ran from his nose and mouth. Doyle could see the blip on the oscilloscope beside the bed moving in lazy waves.

He glanced down the corridor to where Georgie was still speaking with the uniformed man and the nurse, then at the door of the room.

STRICTLY NO ENTRY TO UNAUTHORISED STAFF

This had to be the one.

He slipped inside, recoiling immediately from the

antiseptic smell. The blip of the oscilloscope was audible now, as was the man's laboured breathing. Doyle noticed that he had a catheter attached to him, the bag half-full of dark fluid.

He knew he had to move quickly.

'Farrow,' he whispered.

No reaction.

'Farrow,' he said again, touching the man's shoulder this time.

The injured man's eyes flickered open for a second, closed and then opened again.

'Listen to me,' said Doyle. 'The man who shot you,' he fumbled inside his jacket, pulled out a small photo of Maguire. 'Was this him?'

The blip of the oscilloscope.

The laboured breathing.

'Was this the man who shot you?' Doyle persisted.

He heard footsteps in the corridor. Heavy footfalls.

'Was this the man?' he continued.

The blips increased in rapidity.

Farrow blinked at the image of the picture. Doyle realized that the footsteps were coming closer.

Come on, come on.

He gripped Farrow's hand.

'This man shot you, didn't he?' Doyle said. 'Squeeze my hand if he did.'

Footsteps drawing nearer. Had Georgie's ruse failed?

The blips increased in speed. Doyle shot a glance at the bouncing green dot.

'Was this the man who shot you?'

Farrow squeezed his hand once.

The door opened.

Doyle spun round, pulling the CZ from its shoulder holster.

297

The door swung. He caught sight of the Garda officer standing there, looking back down the corridor.

Doyle had time to straighten up and take a couple of steps back, ducking behind the door as it opened. He held the automatic close to him and waited.

The Garda officer entered. Doyle didn't hesitate.

He struck him hard across the back of the head with the butt of the pistol, catching the man before he could drop, easing him to the floor. Then he turned and slipped out again.

The corridor to his left and right was empty. He sprinted for the door which led to the stairs, took the steps two at a time until he reached the second floor, then sucked in a deep breath, wandered calmly towards the lifts and rode one to the ground floor.

Georgie was sitting in the Datsun when he emerged from the main entrance of the hospital.

He slid behind the wheel, started the engine and drove off.

'It *was* Maguire who shot him,' he said flatly. 'I fucking knew it was.'

'I thought they were going to catch you,' Georgie told him. 'I managed to stall him as long as I could. I said I'd heard what had happened, that my husband had been in the Garda, that the IRA had killed him and I wanted to pay my respects.'

Doyle seemed unimpressed with her story.

'Maguire must be close,' he said, his eyes narrowed. 'I can smell him.'

He drove on.

SACRIFICE

It was cold like the grave.

The chill seemed to penetrate his very bones.

His very soul.

He huddled in the centre of the room, shivering in his nakedness, his body sheathed in sweat despite the cold.

Candles were arranged in a circle around him. Their dull glow did little to cut through the darkness. When he looked around their tiny flames seemed to flicker in his wide eyes.

Gradually he stood up, his shivering diminishing. The stone floor was wet beneath his feet, the dark stains quite black in the dull glow of the candles.

He held the knife in his right hand for a moment, inspecting its razor sharp edge.

He glanced only briefly at the small bundle at his feet.

The other occupant of the room watched impassively as the tall man took the knife and rested it gently against his chest, the blade cold against his flesh. He pressed the point against his left breast then pulled it away, the pin-prick causing a tiny indentation in his skin.

The other did not move.

The tall man held the knife to his chest once more, pressing harder this time, gritting his teeth as he pushed the point with infinite slowness into his pectoral muscle. Blood began to bubble from the small cut, flowing more rapidly as the knife was drawn easily through the slippery skin. A cut about four inches long was opened up on his chest. He relaxed as he withdrew the knife, feeling the blood running warmly down his chest.

He reached for the large goblet which stood at his feet.

Lifting it, he inspected the contents.

The human eye which lay in the cup stared back at him, tendrils of nerve still attached to it.

He smiled and glanced down at the body at his feet.

The body with the left eye missing.

The tongue was also gone. That too was in the cup.

The tall man smiled and held the goblet to his chest, feeling the coldness of the gold against his hot breast. He looked down to see his blood dribbling slowly into the receptacle.

He opened another cut on his chest, slightly deeper this time, and the blood flowed much more swiftly, half-filling the goblet, running over the gouged eye and the severed tongue.

The man grunted in pain but gritted his teeth and remained standing, watching as the dark fluid rose almost to the top of the container.

He took it away from his chest, feeling his own life fluid dripping down his torso, over his belly and into his pubic hair, onto his throbbing erection. Some dribbled from the end of his penis like crimson ejaculate. He watched the droplets fall and strike the ground, splashing in the puddle of gore he stood in.

He held the goblet at arm's length, feeling the already unbearable chill deepen.

His breath frosted in the air and his heart began thudding faster against his ribs.

The other drew closer until the tall man felt his hand enveloped by another.

It was like being touched by fingers of ice.

The goblet was taken from his hands. He smiled, pleased that his token had been accepted, happy that the offering was satisfactory.

He watched as the other held the goblet, steam rising in the cold room, wisps of it floating from the hot blood in the goblet.

The other was satisfied with the offering.

The tall man smiled again.

It was a small price to pay.

Gilles de Rais was satisfied, too.

Sixty-Eight

BRITTANY, FRANCE:

Catherine Roberts yawned and rubbed her eyes. The notes looked blurred for a second, but as she blinked myopically at them they gradually swam back into focus. She looked around the hotel room, vacated by the Callahans, which she now occupied.

The ticking of her watch, lying on the dressing table beside her, sounded loud in the silence of the night. It was almost 11.48 p.m. The curtains stirred gently, blown by a cool night breeze which had also brought with it the first spots of rain. Cath looked up and watched the rain spitting against the glass for a moment.

Glass.

She reached forward and touched her reflection in the mirror on the dressing table.

Glass.

Her whole life seemed to be like a piece of glass at the moment; brittle and about to shatter if too much pressure were applied to it. She was at this place because of glass, because of the window and now she sat staring into glass, staring at the tired face reflected there. Notepads were spread all around her, scribblings about Machecoul, about Gilles de Rais. Written on a fresh sheet of paper were the words she had seen on the window.

COGITATIO – Thought
SACRIFICIUM – Sacrifice
CULTUS – Worship of the gods
ARCANA – Secrets
ARCANUS – Hidden
OPES – Treasure
IMMORTALIS – Deathless

They made as little sense to her now as they had when she'd first seen them. She tapped on her pad with the end of her pen, running her free hand through her hair.

The part about the hidden treasure was almost self-explanatory. Something in the window in Machecoul unlocked the secret to a vast fortune, of that she had no doubt. De Rais had been a remarkably wealthy man; perhaps the window held the key to where some of his vast fortune was hidden. She shook her head. He had died relatively penniless, bled dry by charlatans and con men who had promised to help him look for the *real* treasure he sought. That of eternal life.

IMMORTALIS.

'Deathless,' she said aloud.

She paused for a moment, her eyes fixed on one of the words;

CULTUS
Worship of the Gods

She chewed the end of her pen thoughtfully.

But worship of which gods? Not her god, that was for sure.

Satan?

She dropped her pen and rubbed her eyes again. Her neck was beginning to ache from constant leaning over. Her head was throbbing with the persistent strain of so much thought. She felt as if she were trapped in some kind of maze, unable to find her way out, not even sure of what she sought.

Gilles de Rais was not immortal; he had not gained immortality. He had been strangled and then ordered to be burned, after being found guilty of many crimes including murder, invocation of demons, sodomy, bestiality, conjuration and ...

Conjuration.

He had been accused of witchcraft, of summoning demons. Perhaps he had actually been successful. She almost laughed, realizing that she was clutching at straws. She reminded herself that she was supposed to be approaching her subject with a scientific mind, not relying on superstition and legend.

She thought about Mark Channing.

The vision of his mutilated body came into her mind unbidden, forcing its way into her consciousness and sticking there like a splinter in skin. Who had killed him? And why? Whoever it was had done so in a manner she could never have imagined. Channing had not been murdered so much as destroyed. Destroyed by someone extremely powerful.

'Something beyond our understanding.' She chuckled humourlessly, remembering a cliché from a hundred bad horror films. Thoughts of Channing made her shudder and she tried to push them from her mind but they persisted.

Had he found something before she arrived at the church that day? Something which would unlock the secret of the window?

She got to her feet and walked to the window. The breeze blew droplets of rain into her face and she closed her eyes, hoping that the night air might clear her head. It didn't. She felt as tired as she could ever remember feeling. A heavy, almost numbing exhaustion which had sucked her energy like some kind of invisible leech. She realized that she could work no more this night and she began to peel off her clothes, stopping for one last look at the column of words written on one of her notepads. At the words which she had copied from the window. The key? Her eyes were drawn to the one word which didn't belong.

BARON

It *had* to be a name. But whose?

Charges against Gilles de Rais included conjuration of demons ...

She pulled off her skirt and sat at the dressing table in just her panties. She felt perspiration beading on her back despite the cold breeze blowing through the window.

De Rais was an alchemist. He sought the secret of turning base metal into gold. Each alchemist had a familiar, a creature which would give him that secret.

A demon?

She remembered her own words:

'*A monument, that's what the window is.*'

ARCANA

ARCANUS

IMMORTALIS

And the name: Baron.

BARON.

'A familiar,' she whispered. She was sure of it now, BARON was a name. The name of de Rais' familiar.

That was why he had venerated it so. The window had been built in its honour. Because it had given him a treasure without equal. She sighed.

It had to be the answer.

Cath got to her feet, her eyelids feeling leaden. She crossed to the bed, slipping off her panties as she reached for the edge of the sheet.

She pulled it back.

Lying there, one eye still dangling from an empty socket, was the body of Mark Channing. Blood had soaked into the bedclothes around his remains and she could smell the stench of blood.

The head turned and smiled at her.

She screamed.

Screamed and woke up.

Cath struggled from the bed, her body covered in perspiration. She almost fell as she hurried to get out. She ran to the door, then pressed her back against it and stared at the bed.

It was empty. No mutilated corpse. No grinning head.

She swallowed hard, feeling sick. She crossed to the bathroom, snapped on the light and spun the cold tap, scooping water into her hand. She drank then wiped the remaining moisture over her face and chest, trying to slow her breathing. Her heart was hammering against her ribs. She took a couple of deep breaths and gradually felt the calmness returning. Even so, she couldn't resist a glance back at the bed to check that it was unoccupied.

There was nothing there, just sweat-sodden sheets.

She knew she wouldn't be able to sleep again that night. Pulling a bathrobe around her she sat down at the dressing table with her notes. She picked up a pen and began writing.

It was 3.36 a.m.

Laura Callahan sat bolt upright in bed, her eyes bulging, the scream still locked in her throat.

It took her a moment or two to realize where she was.

Home. Safe in bed.

In bed.

She looked across to the side where her husband usually lay, but he wasn't there. She hauled herself naked from the bed. She had to tell him about the nightmare. About how she had seen Catherine Roberts pull back the sheet to find Mark Channing's mutilated body, and how the body had been twisted in half at the waist, lacerated on every inch of skin.

As she left the bedroom she glanced at her watch.

2.36 a.m.

She wondered why the name Baron had suddenly entered her mind.

Sixty-Nine

She didn't know the men. She didn't know where Callahan had found them. She didn't really care.

Catherine Roberts watched in silence as the four men gathered around the window in the church of Machecoul. It was secured firmly inside a large packing crate, protected inside by another smaller box and wedges of padding. Each panel had been covered with transparent tape then blockd with styrofoam. The men

306

had arrived with all the equipment. They had been at the church before her that evening. They had said little as she pulled up in the Peugeot, one had watched her a little too intently as she climbed out of the car, her skirt riding up around her thighs. He had looked at her but he hadn't smiled.

She had given them their instructions about moving the window, about taking care with it. If they had been listening then they certainly gave no indication that they were. All of them had been too preoccupied with looking at the window. When the time came to begin preparing it for its journey from Machecoul, the men had worked quickly. As if they were anxious to be rid of the window, away from its presence.

Cath leant against the door of the chancel, watching the men. Her eyelids felt heavy, swollen through lack of sleep. She rubbed her face every few minutes, flexing her shoulders every so often to try and relieve the ache.

Outside the trunk which would carry the window had already arrived. The driver sat in the cab smoking, waiting for his colleagues to emerge from the church. Even from inside the church Cath could hear the steady drone of the engine.

She watched now as the four men prepared to lift the window, each one getting a grip on a corner of the crate. They were talking amongst themselves and she feared that her pleas to them to be careful were in vain. She watched as they lifted the crate.

One of them shouted something Cath didn't understand and they hurriedly lowered the crate again, stepping back away from it.

She asked what was wrong and walked across to the box.

The oldest man muttered something under his

breath and held out a hand.

On the palm was a burn about the size of a large coin. The skin was red and a blister was already forming, rising up from the mottled flesh.

Cath frowned and reached out to touch the box.

It was freezing cold, like touching a lump of ice.

The oldest man wrapped a cloth around his hand and then he and his companions began lifting again. Cath watched as they manoeuvred it towards the chancel door.

She was aware of a chill filling the room, growing in intensity.

They edged the crate through, careful not to trap their hands against the door frame in the process. Cath blinked hard and stared at the box.

There was a dark patch on one side of it, like a burn. As if some source of heat inside were being pressed against the wood. The mark was growing larger by the second.

She rubbed her eyes.

The mark was gone.

Get a grip on yourself, she thought angrily. It was only a shadow on the crate.

She waited a moment until the men had moved the crate through into the nave then she followed them out. The acrid smell filled her nostrils as she passed through the chancel door.

A smell which reminded her of scorched wood.

They loaded the crate onto the lorry without difficulty, then three of the men climbed into the back of the vehicle with the box while the fourth joined the driver up in the cab. The driver finished another cigarette, tossed the butt out of the window and prepared to start the engine.

Inside the church Cath took one final look around the chancel, shuddering as she glanced at the place where she had found Mark Channing's body. But she pushed the thought from her mind. The dust was thick on the ground except for the place where the window had stood. The silence was oppressive and Cath turned and headed out of the chancel, out of the church to the waiting truck. She checked with the driver that he had his instructions right. He would drive, she would follow in her car and, when they arrived, the crate would be loaded aboard the aircraft Callahan had chartered. The instructions were understood. The driver started the engine and pulled away. Cath watched the truck move slowly away up the narrow track towards the road then she slid behind the wheel of the Peugeot and twisted the key in the ignition.

She glanced in the rear-view mirror, catching sight of her haggard reflection. She reached into her handbag and pulled out her sunglasses, anxious not to look at her own red-rimmed eyes. She slipped on the glasses and looked at herself again.

The visage which stared back at her was that of Baron.

Reflected in the rear-view mirror was the face of the creature on the window.

In place of her own dark, shrouded eyes, the eyes of boiling blood glared back at her. The mouth was open, leering, the long tongue lolling wolfishly from the gaping maw.

Cath only just managed to stifle a scream.

As she pushed herself back in her seat she closed her eyes, feeling cold pressure at the back of her neck.

When she looked in the mirror again she saw only her own face.

What was happening to her?

Not enough sleep. When she reached Ireland she would rest. She promised herself she would sleep. It was the pressure of the past few days, the lack of rest, what had happened to Channing. There was a logical explanation to it all. She nodded and started the car, winding down her window, allowing fresh air to blow in, hoping it would clear her mind.

She glanced at the rear view mirror again and saw only her own reflection.

She frowned and reached up to touch the mirror. The breath caught in her throat.

From one side of the mirror to the other was a crack. Right across her eyeline.

Seventy

She heard the bang.

Gunshot loud, it startled her badly. The next thing she knew the car was skidding across the road.

Cath struggled to keep control of the vehicle, slamming on the brakes and finally bringing it to a halt at the roadside. She sucked in a deep breath, relieved that there had been no traffic coming in the opposite direction. She pushed open her door and walked around the car. The front offside wheel was holed, punctured by a piece of sharp stone. She stood with her hands on her hips for a moment, surveying the damage, then glanced up the road to where the lorry carrying the window had stopped. They had obviously seen what happened. Even as she watched one of the men jumped down from the cab and ran back towards her.

He offered to help her change her wheel, saying that they would wait for her, but Cath shook her head and told him that the lorry must continue. The window must reach its destination at the appointed time so that it could be loaded aboard the plane which was waiting for it. The window was the important thing, she told him. She could manage the tyre on her own. The man looked at her, then at the wheel, and nodded, running back to the waiting lorry which pulled away.

'Damn,' snarled Cath and angrily kicked at the tyre.

She watched the lorry disappear around a bend in the road. Then she walked to the boot of the car and opened it; checking the spare tyre.

There was no way now that she would reach the plane in time to travel with the window. She would have to catch a commercial flight.

A car drove past, the occupants giving her a cursory glance as she removed the jack and the spare wheel from the boot. She wondered how long it would take her to change the tyre. Perhaps she should have allowed the man to stay and help her, she thought as she pulled her hair back and tied it up, ready to begin her task.

She would ring Callahan when she reached the airport.

The plane was a Cessna 560, over forty-eight feet in length and with a wing span of fifty-two feet. It stood motionless, the pilot glancing out of his window as the lorry carrying the crate drew up alongside.

The cabin, which usually held seven passengers, had been modified, the three aft-facing seats removed to increase the capacity of the hold.

It was into this hold that the crate containing the window was carefully placed then secured by the three-man crew of the plane with the help of the men from the truck who, once the task was completed, clambered back into their vehicle and drove off.

'I thought we were supposed to have a passenger too,' said the pilot. 'A woman.' John Martin stroked his chin thoughtfully and shrugged.

'Looks like we're out of luck,' Nick Cairns said, smiling. 'Just the box.'

Martin nodded again.

'What's in it, anyway?' asked the third member of the team, a tall Scot called Gareth James.

Martin shook his head.

'I didn't even think to ask,' he said. 'But it's supposed to be valuable, whatever it is.'

Cairns raised his eyebrows quizzically. They were used to a diversity of cargo, human and otherwise. They owned the plane jointly and had done for the last year. Martin had been a civil pilot for more than five years prior to going into business with his two colleagues, both of who had been engineers. Cairns had experienced a short spell in the R.A.F. ten years before. He was the eldest of the trio.

Their business was smuggling.

The hold had been converted for that reason, to carry more contraband. They had carried most things in their time, from drugs, to clothes, to guns. People were their cargo too, if necessary. They had taken criminals to countries where they could not be traced. Flown men out of places where they'd been sprung from prison. As long as the money was right they would do the job.

The money had certainly been right for *this* job.

Martin could not think what could make the contents of one box worth £250,000 to the man who had chartered the plane, but wondering wasn't his business. Flying was.

Cairns checked the instrument panel as Martin seated himself.

The pilot glanced at his watch and stifled a yawn. They should be at the drop-off point in about three hours.

The final checks were completed and he allowed the plane to taxi for a moment, bringing it into take-off position. Then, when he was ready, the twin Pratt and Whitney engines began to roar and the Cessna sped off.

The sound of the turbo-fans grew to a crescendo as the plane finally left the ground, climbing at a rate of 3,650 feet a minute. In fifteen minutes they were at 35,000 feet. Only when he drew close to the Irish coast would he bring the plane down low enough to elude radar, enabling them to reach their drop point undetected. For now he settled back in his seat and gazed out at the clear night sky. They were promised good weather all the way, even over the Irish sea. But for a little cloud cover it was a pleasant, humid night.

Odd, then, that it should feel so cold inside the plane.

Seventy-One

COUNTY CORK, THE REPUBLIC OF IRELAND:
Doyle guided the car through the massive open gates
that led onto David Callahan's estate. He slowed
down, looking around him at the sprawling, green
land, the thickets of trees. The long driveway snaked
through the grounds for a good two miles until finally it
curved to the right and the house came into view.

'Christ,' murmured Georgie. 'Look at the size of it.'

Doyle slowed down a little more, looking with even
closer scrutiny at his surroundings. To the left he
noticed some movement: a horseman.

The man rode towards them on a large bay which he
reined in as he rode closer to the car. Doyle ran
appraising eyes over him and noticed a large bump
inside the man's coat beneath his left arm.

Probably armed.

Little wonder, too. On a place this size Callahan
would need security.

The horseman guided his mount around to Doyle's
side of the car and looked down at him. The
counter-terrorist slowed the car to a crawl.

'Can I help you?' asked the horseman.

'We're here to see Mr Callahan,' Doyle told him.

'Is he expecting you?'

'Not really. We just want to talk to him.'

'You're not from around here.'

'You're quick,' said Doyle, smiling thinly.

The man caught the sarcasm in the Englishman's voice and glared at him. Doyle held the look for a moment then pressed his foot slightly on the accelerator, revving the engine. The bay whinnied nervously and moved away, the rider struggling to keep control of the animal. Doyle pressed harder on the gas and the Datsun moved away swiftly. The horseman rode after them.

'You should sue them, Doyle,' said Georgie, shaking her head.

He looked vague.

'Your charm school,' she said flatly.

'Very funny,' he murmured without looking at her. In his wing mirror he could see the horseman riding up alongside. By now they were at the house and Doyle brought the car to a halt outside the massive building. Both he and Georgie got out.

'I'll tell him you're here,' said the horseman.

'No need. We can manage,' Doyle assured him, striding towards the front door. He rang the bell and waited, looking at the horseman who was still glaring. The door opened and Doyle found himself confronted by a pretty young woman, he guessed in her early twenties. Shoulder-length brown hair, highlighted. She wore little make-up. Doyle smiled at her.

'Good morning,' he said. 'My name is Sean Doyle and this is Georgina Willis. We're here to see Mr Callahan.'

'Do you have an appointment?' the girl asked.

'Do we need one?' Doyle asked, still smiling.

'Who are you?' she persisted.

'Is something wrong, Trisha?'

Georgie saw Laura Callahan first. Dressed in jeans and a sweatshirt, her hair freshly washed, she was inspecting the two newcomers.

315

'You want to see my husband?' Laura said.

'I don't know who they are, Mrs Callahan,' Trisha said.

'British Counter-Terrorist Unit,' Doyle said, his smile fading. 'This is official. Where is your husband, Mrs Callahan?'

'Do you have identification?' Laura wanted to know.

'No, we don't, but you'd save everyone, your husband included, a lot of trouble if you'd let us speak to him.'

'How do I know you're who you say you are?' Laura persisted. 'My husband is a very rich man. You could be anyone. You might want to kill him.'

Doyle sighed.

'If I wanted to kill him I wouldn't have rung your fucking doorbell, would I?' he snapped. 'We just want to talk to him about a couple of things, then we'll go.'

There was an uneasy silence, then Laura finally nodded. Both she and the maid stepped aside. Doyle and Georgie entered, Georgie looking around at the huge hallway.

'It's all right, Trisha,' said Laura Callahan. 'You can go back to work now. I'll take care of these people.' The maid nodded and disappeared up the stairs. Laura led them along a carpeted corridor to her right towards the sitting room. She pushed open the door and walked in.

David Callahan turned as they entered, his brow furrowing as he caught sight of Doyle and Georgie.

Introductions were swift and cursory.

'They're with the police,' said Laura.

'Not quite,' Doyle corrected her. 'Counter-Terrorist Unit.'

'Would you like a drink?' asked Callahan, smiling.

Georgie accepted an orange juice, Doyle a whiskey.

'What can I do for you?' Callahan wanted to know.

'I won't beat about the bush, Mr Callahan,' Doyle told him. 'Just under a week ago in Belfast there was an explosion. The men responsible were driving a car which was registered to you. They were members of the IRA. We wondered if you could tell us how three IRA men happened to be driving *your* car.'

'The Sierra?'

Doyle nodded.

'It was stolen a couple of weeks ago,' Callahan told them.

'Did you report it?'

Callahan shook his head.

'Why not?'

'The police around here aren't too bright, Mr Doyle.' He smiled. 'Besides, it's only a car.' Callahan looked at his watch.

'You've lived here for two years, right?' Doyle said.

'A little less than that, actually,' Callahan told him.

'And before that?'

'Here and there.'

'London, for instance?' Doyle said, a slight smile playing on his lips.

'We lived in London for a time, yes.'

'And ran some businesses there?' Doyle persisted.

'Look, if you've got something to say then say it,' snapped Callahan, looking at his watch again. 'I've got to leave soon. I haven't the time to stand around here playing games with you.'

'Where are you going?' Doyle wanted to know.

'That's none of your business.'

'Maybe not, but finding out how the IRA got hold of your car *is* my business.'

'I told you, it was stolen.'

'Yeah, and you never reported it. Bollocks.'

317

'Look, Doyle, I don't have to listen to this crap. If you've got something to say then come out and say it. If you're who you say you are then show me some bloody I.D. to prove it. If not, you and your ...' – he looked at Georgie – 'your *companion* can get out of my house. Now.'

'The Flying Squad in London questioned you about an arms deal about five years ago, didn't they?' Doyle said. 'Selling weapons to a number of terrorist organisations. The IRA included.'

'Get out of here now,' snapped Callahan.

'It's true, isn't it?' said Doyle. 'You were questioned about selling arms to the IRA?'

'Questioned, but never anything more,' Callahan told him smugly. 'It was guesswork, Doyle. New Scotland Yard wanted me, and gun-running was the only charge they thought they could make stick. But they couldn't do it. I haven't got a criminal record, as you doubtless already know. Get out now,' he snapped, walking to the door of the sitting room and opening it.

Doyle got slowly to his feet.

'We'll be back, Mr Callahan,' he said, handing the millionaire his empty glass.

'If you come back onto my estate you'll be treated as trespassers and my staff would have every right to shoot you. Now get out.'

'I'll be back,' Doyle assured him. He and Georgie headed for the front door escorted by Callahan, who opened the door for them, ushering them out.

'If you've got nothing to hide, why are you so jumpy?' Doyle wanted to know.

'Get off my land, Doyle,' Callahan snapped.

He watched as they walked to the car, climbed in and drove off. Only then did he shut the door and lean against it for a moment breathing heavily.

As he headed back towards the sitting room the phone rang.

'Stolen my arse,' snapped Doyle. 'He knew where that fucking car of his was *and* who was driving it.'

'We've got to prove that,' said Georgie.

'No problem,' Doyle told her, putting his foot down.

'We're going to have trouble getting back in, Doyle,' she said.

He didn't answer.

Doyle finally swung the car out of the huge gates which marked the exit from the estate. He spun the wheel to the left, guiding the car along the narrow road in the direction of the nearest town.

Neither of them saw the vehicle parked in the trees at the roadside behind them.

Its driver lit his roll-up and glanced at his watch.

Give them two minutes, he thought. Then follow.

Seventy-Two

He'd been forced to kill the man.

There had been no time to think, only to act. The hold had been full of weapons at the time, a batch of brand new AK-47's. The guard had insisted on searching the plane. John Martin had been given no choice. He'd drawn his pistol and shot the guard twice. The pilot had taken off immediately, grateful to escape Libyan air space without attack. But then, he reasoned,

319

there had been no one else at the air strip that day to report what had happened. The arms had been bound for a terrorist group in France. They had paid well for them and they had paid John Martin well to collect and deliver them in the same Cessna 560 in which he now cruised, glancing at his instrument panels every now and then, wondering why he should suddenly think of the incident with the Libyan guard. It had been eight months ago. Perhaps it was because the man had been the first he'd killed.

They'd been in the air for over two hours, a journey untroubled by turbulence or bad weather.

Yet there was still that chill in the cabin.

He checked the temperature and the mercury was at a steady sixty-eight degrees.

Why was it so bloody cold?

He felt like blowing on his hands. This was crazy.

'You ok?' asked Cairns from his co-pilot's seat.

Martin nodded.

'Cold,' he said flatly. 'I have been since we took off.'

'Join the club,' Cairns said, rubbing one hand over his forearm which was bristling with goose-pimples. 'Turn the heating up.'

The plane dropped like a stone.

It was as if some invisible hand had torn both of the aircraft's engines free in one clean movement. They had no power.

The plane plummeted earthward.

'Jesus Christ,' hissed Martin, struggling with the controls. He glanced at the altimeter and saw the needle spinning madly, like a coil winding down as the miles sped past and the distance between the plane and the ground lessened by the second.

The cabin door opened and James stuck his head in.

'What's going on?' he shouted, his face pale.

'We must have lost an engine,' Cairns said, his eyes darting around in search of the problem.

'No, we're still on full power,' Martin told him, struggling with the controls.

The descent stopped as suddenly as it had begun.

The Cessna levelled out again at 22,000 feet and Martin allowed it to cruise at that height for a few minutes while he and his two companions regained their composure.

'What the fuck is happening?' James wanted to know. 'Could it have been turbulence?'

'No,' Martin said flatly. 'Turbulence or any downward thermo-draft wouldn't cause us to drop *that* far *that* quickly. It was as if the power just failed completely.'

'But it didn't because the instruments were still working,' Cairns reminded him.

Martin didn't answer. He merely gazed around at the inside of the cabin, looking for any blinking warning light, some clue as to what had made the Cessna behave in such an aberrant manner. The other thing he found curious was that the plane had not gone into a dive as it should have done if power had cut out. It had dropped still in its flight position. As if suddenly released from the strings of a giant puppeteer.

'I'm taking her back up to 35,000 feet,' he announced and the Cessna began to climb steadily once more into the clear blue sky. As it levelled out again he shuddered, not so much from the chill in the cabin this time, he thought, although that was still growing.

'We'll check her out when we land,' Martin said.

The altimeter needle began to waver again.

'Look,' snapped Cairns, pointing at it.

321

The plane continued to cruise.

The altimeter continued to register that they were losing height.

The needle began to hover over 35,000 once more.

'I just can't understand what's happening,' Martin said. 'The instruments were checked before we took off, the whole bloody plane was given the once over a month ago. It doesn't make sense.'

Just like the chill in the cabin. That didn't make sense either.

'Why don't you check out the radio,' Martin said.

Cairns nodded and reached for it.

He flicked the switch to transmit. A hiss of static erupted from the radio. Cairns held it away from him as if it were some kind of venomous reptile. The static didn't abate but merely kept up its hissing rasp, filling the cabin with nerve-grating sound.

The two men looked at each other for a moment then Cairns switched the set off.

'I don't *know* what's going on,' said Martin, answering his companion's unspoken question.

'Drop her anyway,' said Cairns.

Martin nodded and the plane began to descend.

It was as he felt the first bumps of turbulence that Gareth James noticed the wisps of thin smoke rising from the hold.

'John,' he called, his eyes still fixed on the slowly rising plume. 'There's something wrong in the hold.'

'If there is it's not registering on any of the instruments,' Martin told him, checking the rows of lights and expanse of dials. 'What is it?'

'I think it's a fire,' James told him, snatching an extinguisher from the wall and advancing towards the rear of the plane.

322

As he stood over the hold he could smell the gossamer vapour as it rose.

It smelt rancid, corpulent. It wasn't the acrid smell of smoke. That much he was sure of.

Then what?

'I'm going to have a look,' he shouted back, unfastening the catch that secured the hold doorway. He put down the extinguisher and used both hands to lift the flap, feeling how cold the metal was against the flesh.

'Is it a fire?' Martin called from the cabin.

James was staring down into the hold, peering through the malodorous fumes, his eyes bulging so wide in their sockets they threatened to burst from his skull.

'Gareth,' Martin bellowed. 'Is it a fire?'

James was shaking violently, his eyes still riveted to the holds entrance and to what lay beneath.

The vapour rose around him, swirling and enveloping him like ethereal arms, closing tighter.

Seventy-Three

She fought off the tiredness, determined not to let herself drift off to sleep.

Catherine Roberts glanced down at the notes spread on the small table-top before her and peered out of the plane window. She'd been lucky to get a seat on the flight, the last seat, she'd been told. It had been in the smoking area but she could put up with that for the three hours it would take to reach Ireland, even if it did seem as if the man sitting next to her was determined to consume as many Marlboro as possible before the flight terminated. She coughed, waved a hand before her face and looked down at her notes once again.

She had no way of knowing whether the window had been loaded aboard the plane chartered by Callahan. She just hoped everything had gone smoothly. It should arrive a couple of hours before her if everything went according to plan.

She rubbed her eyes, trying to fight off the tiredness. Cath wanted to sleep, to push aside the notes and lie back in her seat and drift away into oblivion for a couple of hours, but she knew she couldn't because with sleep came dreams.

Those dreams.

Even so she felt the weariness pressing down on her like a palpable force, a parasite draining her resolve and her consciousness. She put her head back and immediately felt her eyelids growing heavier. She closed them for a moment and a wonderful feeling of release flowed over her.

She snapped her eyes open again just as quickly, wanting to sleep but not daring to.

There was a child seated in front of her, a young boy kneeling on his seat peering over at her. Cath looked at him wearily and managed a perfunctory smile. The child looked on indifferently, staring at her then looking down at the notes spread out in front of her. She tried to work, to ignore the unblinking gaze of the child.

BARON

She wrote the word in capitals and gazed at it, looking up briefly to see that the child had tired of staring at her and had slumped down in his seat once again.

324

She had no doubt that Baron was a familiar, summoned by Gilles de Rais to impart to him the secret of turning base metal into gold.

But how to carry out that summons?

SACRIFICIUM.

A sacrifice.

De Rais had murdered over two hundred children in his time. What better offering to his own particular deity than the lives of so many so young?

She rubbed her forehead with her fingers.

Did she really believe that? Did she really believe what she had written? Demons were the products of superstition and fear. She was meant to be a professional, an expert in her field. She dealt with facts, not with legends and hearsay. Horror stories had no part in her world. The idea of a demon was ridiculous and yet the window, everything that had happened so far, all seemed to point at least to a belief in such an entity. Perhaps even to its existence.

She thought about Mark Channing.

Could a human being have done to his body what was perpetrated?

But if not a human being, then who?

Had Channing somehow discovered the way to release Baron?

She sighed and sat back in her seat once more, aware that the man next to her was lighting another cigarette. More smoke began to drift across her. She closed her eyes.

There had to be a rational explanation for what was happening.

There had to be.

She felt herself dozing; she tried to wake herself up but found the effort was growing more each time.

'Baron,' she whispered as she felt sleep slipping over her.

Logical explanation ... had to be one ... Demons don't exist ...

Don't exist.

She shivered as she dozed.

She was cold.

Seventy-Four

David Callahan checked his watch as the Mercedes pulled out of the main gates of his estate. The drive should take less than two hours. The plane may even have arrived by that time. He sat back in the rear seat of the car, glancing ahead to the flat truck driven by one of his workers. Once the window was unloaded from the plane he'd chartered, it would be placed on the truck and returned to his estate.

Callahan lit a cigarette and puffed agitatedly at it. He felt uneasy. The clash with Doyle had left him feeling angry and a little edgy. The counter-terrorist was a little *too* inquisitive for Callahan's liking. Mind you, the girl with him had been nice. Attractive. Callahan took another drag and forced thoughts of Georgie from his mind. He was more concerned with other matters now.

As the Mercedes turned a bend in the road, the estate began to fade into the landscape, the house itself now hidden behind high hedges and trees.

*

'Do we follow him?' asked Georgie, as the Mercedes passed them.

'No,' said Doyle. 'We wait awhile and then we go back in.'

'I think we'd be better off talking to Callahan,' she offered.

Doyle shook his head.

'We'll get nothing out of him. Not yet. But his wife, she's a different matter.' He checked his watch. 'Not long now. Let him get clear.'

The truck pulled up beside a thickly wooded area overlooking a long flat stretch of land. Callahan's Mercedes pulled up alongside and the millionaire stepped out, sucking in the crisp night air, gazing up at the sky.

He lit a cigarette, wondering how long it would be before the plane arrived.

Behind him his two workers stood chatting idly while the Englishman drew slowly on his cigarette, holding the smoke inside for a moment before blowing it out in a bluish-grey plume. He watched the smoke slowly dissipate.

Not long now, thought Callahan. Again he looked at his watch.

She saw it.

Saw the plane.

Saw the twin-engined Cessna rocking lazily in the air as it began its descent.

Catherine Roberts stirred in her sleep aboard the Air France flight, murmured something under her breath and clenched her fists.

Somewhere in that dream she thought she heard laughter.

Laura Callahan sat at the bedroom window looking out over the grounds, which were practically invisible in the gloom. In the darkened bedroom she could see her own reflection in the glass as she stared out. But when she closed her eyes she could see something else.

She could see a small, twin-engined plane approaching a dark clearing.

She could hear its engines as it bore down on its destination.

Laura opened her eyes and found that her breath was coming in gasps. There was perspiration on her brow.

She felt frightened.

More frighened than she could ever remember.

Seventy-Five

The plane was going to crash.

As Callahan watched the Cessna come hurtling out of the night sky he was convinced of that fact.

It was going to crash.

Like some unguided missile it rolled and swooped on the air, its nose dipping violently every few moments.

As it passed overhead he could see that the undercarriage was down.

What the hell was happening?

It turned and he watched as it cut across the black canopy of night, only the landing lights on its very wingtips glowing. Apart from those twin pinpricks of red the rest of the Cessna was a floating black hulk.

Callahan frowned as he saw it level out once again, preparing to land on the flat piece of ground below him. He took the cigarette from his mouth and tossed it aside, his attention now riveted on the plane which was dropping lower by the second.

One hundred feet and it would be able to touch down.

Callahan still couldn't shake the conviction that it was going to crash.

Fifty feet.

The window.

Thirty feet.

If it should crash, the window would be destroyed.

Fifteen feet.

He tried to push the thought from his mind.

The plane hit the ground, seemed to bounce back into the air momentarily then skidded for about thirty feet, the wheels unable to gain purchase on the slippery grass. Finally, it came to a halt.

Immediately Callahan ran down the slope towards the stationary craft. His workers followed him.

He was about fifty feet from the Cessna when the pilot appeared.

In the darkness Callahan could see how pale he was. He gripped the frame of the door, hanging on with difficulty.

The millionaire slowed his pace as he drew nearer.

'What is it?'

The words came from Martin. He was pointing towards the rear of the plane. Towards the hold.

'What's in that fucking box?'

His voice was low, quivering.

'Get it off my plane now,' he gasped without waiting for the millionaire to answer. 'Quickly,' he shouted.

Callahan called for the truck. The two men hurried back up the slope and jumped into the cab. The driver guided the lorry down the slope and along the shallow valley until it was beside the Cessna.

Cairns, his face white, his eyes wide and staring, clambered down from the plane and unlocked the hold.

'Get it out of there,' Martin called breathlessly.

Callahan's men did as they were told, easing the box containing the window onto the back of the flat truck.

Cairns was already climbing back into the plane.

'Just give me the money and let us get out of here,' snarled Martin.

As Callahan passed him the briefcase full of notes the pilot's hand brushed against his own and the millionaire felt how numbingly cold the man's flesh was.

'Check it,' Callahan said.

Martin shook his head and slammed the door shut. Immediately the Cessna's engines roared into life. Callahan scurried for the bank as the aircraft turned swiftly and began building up speed, as if the crew couldn't wait to be away from this place. The aircraft rose into the air and, in a matter of seconds, had disappeared into the blackness, swallowed by the night.

Callahan touched the back of his own hand where it had brushed against Martin's flesh and shuddered as he recalled the icy feel of the other man's skin. He looked across at the flat truck and the large box now firmly secured to it.

He had the window at last.

As he walked to the waiting Mercedes he *too* felt a chill envelope him.

Seventy-Six

Doyle banged the door hard and kept banging until it was opened.

The good-looking maid he remembered as Trisha stood before him, frowning.

'We're here to see Mrs Callahan,' said Doyle, pushing past the Irish girl.

'You were told to stay away from here,' she protested as Georgie stepped over the threshold. 'I'll call the Garda.'

Doyle smiled thinly.

'I don't think your boss would appreciate it,' he said cryptically. 'Where's Mrs Callahan?'

'She's upstairs,' said Trisha, regarding them both angrily.

Doyle took the steps two at a time in his haste to reach Callahan's wife. He pushed open doors as he emerged on the landing, finally discovering Laura in the master bedroom. She was lying on the bed dressed in just a bathrobe watching the television at the foot of the bed.

'What the hell are you doing here?' she rasped as Doyle entered, followed by Georgie.

'I tried to stop them, Mrs Callahan,' Trisha interjected, her way into the room barred by Georgie.

'It's all right, Trisha,' Laura said, eyeing the counter-terrorists warily. 'I'll be fine.'

The maid paused, then closed the door. Doyle heard her footsteps as she padded down the stairs.

'You have no right coming back into this house,' said Laura.

'We have every right,' Doyle snapped. 'Your husband wasn't very co-operative. I hoped you might be a little more reasonable.'

'What do you think *I* can tell you that David couldn't?' she wanted to know.

'Couldn't or *wouldn't*?' Georgie said.

Laura got to her feet, pulling the bathrobe more tightly around her.

'I don't know why you're asking me about my husband's business,' she said. 'I don't know what he gets up to. I'm not interested.' She poured herself a drink from the cabinet.

'Selling guns to the IRA is a serious offence,' Doyle said. 'Being an accessory should get you at least ten years.'

'I don't know what you're talking about.'

'I'm talking about the shit that's been happening in Northern Ireland for the last few weeks,' he snapped. 'I'm talking about the murder of politicians at Stormont, the assassination of a clergyman, the bombing of Windsor Park football ground. Your husband was involved in all of those incidents.'

'That's rubbish,' Laura said.

'Is it? Then how come the fucking IRA were driving a car owned by your husband when those incidents happened?'

'He told you, the car was stolen.'

'Bullshit. They were driving one of his cars, using weapons he sold them.'

There was a heavy silence.

'How much did he pay Maguire to go on this fucking killing spree?' the counter-terrorist persisted.

Laura sipped her drink.

'How much?' he roared, taking a step towards her.

'I don't know anything about it,' said Laura, a flicker of fear in her voice.

'Who's he working with?' Doyle rasped. 'Come on, this is too big even for someone as rich as your old man. Who's backing him? And why?'

'Where is he now?' Georgie interjected.

Laura said, 'He's meeting a plane.'

'Who's on it?' the counter-terrorist wanted to know.

'Nothing of interest to you. A stained-glass window.'

Georgie looked puzzled.

'Fuck the stained-glass window,' snapped Doyle. 'Where are the weapons? When is he next trading with Maguire?'

'I don't know what you're talking about,' Laura shouted.

'I'm going to search this house,' Doyle told her, 'search it until I find what I want. And I don't care if I have to tear it apart in the process.'

He turned and dug both hands under the mattress of the bed. With a grunt he overturned it.

Laura shouted something he didn't hear. She took a step towards him but Georgie stepped in front of her, pulling the Sterling .357 from its holster.

Doyle overturned the TV which promptly expired in a sputter of sparks and a plume of smoke.

He grabbed the drinks cabinet and hauled it over, crystal glasses and bottles of drink crashing to the carpet, liquor spilling over and soaking into the deep pile.

'Stop it,' shouted Laura.

'Where are the guns?' Doyle responded, gripping the curtains and tugging hard. They were torn free, falling

333

to the floor with a thud.

'When is he supposed to contact Maguire again?' He swept his arm along the dressing table. Expensive perfume and ornaments were sent hurtling to the floor, delicate bottles shattering.

'I don't know what you're talking about,' Laura told him, watching helplessly as he continued to destroy the bedroom.

Finally he tore open the door and stormed out onto the landing. There was a large vase on a dresser close by. Doyle swept it to the ground, watching as it shattered.

'If I were you I'd tell him what he wants to know,' said Georgie quietly. 'Otherwise he'll get mad.'

Doyle headed down the stairs. As he reached the bottom he roared up to Georgie to join him.

'You take the West wing, I'll take the East,' he said. 'Turn everything over if you have to.'

'And what if you're wrong?' she offered.

'Just do it,' he snapped and they headed off in opposite directions.

Laura appeared at the top of the stairs.

'Stop it, you bastards,' she bellowed. 'My husband will kill you when he gets back.'

'Let him fucking try,' Doyle roared back.

'Car,' said Georgie, hearing a sound from outside. She nodded in the direction of the front door.

They both listened, heard footsteps. Running. Approaching the door fast.

What the hell was going on?

Three shots.

Doyle pressed himself back against the wall as bullets tore holes through the door, blasting the handle of the front door away. Then he heard voices outside and, as

touching skin. He could smell the odour of cordite and burnt material. To his left was Maconnell, above him Maguire and Black.

That left two more.

He heard shots from outside, heard the crash of breaking glass.

Georgie had slipped out of the house through a window in the room to which she'd retreated. Now, standing on the gravel drive outside the building, she steadied herself and fired three times from the .357. The pistol bucked in her grip as the weapon spat out its lethal load. The first bullet blasted away the offside headlamp of the car, the second missed and the third hit the radiator, staving in most of the grille as if it had been struck with a sledgehammer.

From inside the Orion Billy Dolan leant out of the driver's side and fired off a burst from an Ingram M-10. The sub-gun spattered off two dozen shots, its muzzle-flash illuminating the area in front of the house. Spent cartridge cases spewed from the weapon in a brass arc, clattering down on the gravel. He dropped the gun onto the passenger seat and reversed, the rear wheels spinning on the rough ground. Pieces of stone were sent flying into the air by the ferocity of his manoeuvre. The car shot backwards and Georgie ran after it, firing off her last two shots.

She ducked behind one of the stone pillars in front of the main door, flipped the cylinder from the Sterling and ejected the shell cases. Then, moving with practised precision, she pulled one of the quick-loaders from her pocket, jammed the slugs into the chambers and snapped the weapon closed again.

Dolan put his headlights on full, snatched up the Ingram and drove straight at her, swerving past at the last moment, raking the front of the house with fire.

Georgie squeezed herself against the pillar for cover, wincing as bullets drilled into the concrete around her. One blasted away a piece of stone only inches from her face, the dust flecks filling her eyes momentarily.

'Who the fuck is that?' roared Damien Flynn from inside the car.

Dolan didn't answer but swung the car around and drove towards the pillar again, firing as he went.

'Come on, you fucker,' he bellowed.

Georgie waited until the car had passed, then sprang out and fired at the back of the Orion. Her second shot exploded one of the rear lights.

Inside the house, Maguire knew that the only way out was through the front door and past the fucking maniac in the hall, whoever he was.

'Get her to the car,' he told Black, nodding at Laura Callahan who was firmly held by the IRA man. He had one hand over her mouth; the other held her arms. 'When I tell you to move, you move, right?'

Black nodded, thinking how far down he had to go, how long a staircase he had to descend. He suddenly seemed miles from his goal. The door yawned open invitingly but he could still hear gunfire from outside.

Maguire slammed another magazine into the Skorpion and looked at his companion.

'Set?' he muttered.

Black nodded.

'Come on,' roared Maguire and opened fire.

Doyle ducked down as a concentrated burst of fire blasted the chair behind which he was crouching to atoms. He threw himself towards the nearby door, looking round to see that Maguire, Black and their

338

captive were making for the front door. Maconnell was following, also firing.

Doyle steadied himself and fired off one round from the .44.

It struck Black in the left shin, pulverizing the bone, ripping through his calf muscle, crippling him immediately. He screamed in pain and fell, letting loose his grip on Laura, but Maguire grabbed her and hurried her through the front door.

Maconnell dragged his companion through after them, leaving a thick trail of blood from the man's shattered leg.

Dolan saw them come out and sent the Orion speeding up alongside. Flynn flung open the doors and they clambered in, Black only scrambling inside with some difficulty, yelping in pain as he banged his injured leg on the door frame. Georgie took her chance and fired off another couple of shots, one of which punched in the nearside rear window, showering those in the back with glass.

Dolan spun the wheel and the Orion spat more stones into the air.

'Go, go,' bellowed Maguire and the car hurtled off down the driveway.

Doyle dashed from the house and saw the single tail-light disappearing into the night. He was half-way to the Datsun already.

Not this time.

I've got you this time, you bastards.

He wrenched open the driver's side door and slid behind the wheel. Georgie hurled herself into the passenger's seat and was flung backwards as Doyle stepped on the accelerator. The car was catapulted forward, wheels spinning for a second before gaining purchase, then it was off, the needle on the speedometer touching sixty as Doyle pressed down harder on the accelerator.

'In the glove compartment,' he hissed and she fumbled for what he wanted.

The MP5K was only inches larger than the .357 she herself carried, but it was capable of firing over 650 rounds of 9mm ammunition a minute. Doyle cradled it across his lap, both hands locked on the wheel as he followed the fleeing Orion.

The lead vehicle hit a bump in the drive and all four wheels left the ground before it slammed back to earth, skidding violently as Dolan regained control of the wheel.

The gateway to the estate was approaching. In his haste to escape the pursuing Datsun, Dolan drove too close to the stone wall. There was a high-pitched squeal as sparks spattered from the side of the vehicle, the paint stripped off as surely as if someone had turned a blowtorch on it. Then the car turned sharply to the right onto the main road. For precious seconds it seemed as if the vehicle must turn over but Dolan kept it under control and it roared on.

In the back Laura Callahan's scream was cut short as Maguire struck her in the face with the butt of the Skorpion. She fell across Maconnell, her lip split, blood weeping from the cut.

Doyle followed, his face set in harsh lines as he struggled to control the Datsun. He took the turn too sharply, one of the wing mirrors being torn from the car as he collided with the wall, but he ignored the minor inconvenience and drove on.

Beside him, Georgie was pushing more shells into the Sterling.

Neither of them noticed the car which pulled out of the trees to their left and began following *them*.

Seventy-Eight

The road that led away from Callahan's estate was so narrow in places it barely allowed two cars to pass one another.

Doyle didn't seem to care. He floored the accelerator of the Datsun in an attempt to get up alongside the fleeing Orion.

He could see the tail light tantalisingly less than twenty yards from him. As they reached a straight stretch of road he picked up the MP5K and, steadying himself, gripped it firmly in one hand and fired off a burst. The muzzle-flash lit the night, momentarily blinding him, but he kept his foot pressed down, the needle on the speedo never dropping below seventy.

Bullets spattered the road and some drilled into the rear of the Orion.

'Laura Callahan's in there, Doyle,' Georgie reminded him.

'Fuck her,' he rasped. 'I want Maguire.'

He fired again, shouting his pleasure as the sub-gun flamed.

The back window of the Orion was peppered, the glass spider-webbing then crashing inwards onto the occupants.

Shots came from the rear of the fleeing vehicle, one of them cracking the windscreen of the Datsun.

341

Georgie fired from her own side, trying to hit a tyre, but in the dark and moving at such speed it was almost impossible. She heard one shot sing off the rear of the Orion.

As she eased herself back into the car she caught sight of the third car's headlamps in the wing mirror. She turned in her seat to see the Mazda close.

'We've got company,' she told Doyle, who checked his rear-view mirror.

'Police?' he wondered aloud, catching sight of the headlamps.

'I don't think so,' she said quietly, holding on to the seat as the Datsun ran dangerously close to the edge of the roadside ditch. She squinted through the gloom, trying to see how many people were in the car, but it was impossible; the glare from the pursuing vehicle's head-lights made it a futile cause.

Up ahead the Orion turned a corner, crashing through a wooden gate and skidding across a field.

Doyle followed without hesitation.

The Mazda followed too.

'Who the fuck are they?' he hissed, glancing once more into the rear-view mirror.

A burst of fire from up ahead interrupted his musings.

Bullets struck the front of the Datsun, two of them blasting out a headlamp. Doyle swung the car back and forth to make it a more difficult target to hit. Simultaneously he fired another burst from the MP5K, his hand numb from the prolonged and powerful recoil. The stench of cordite filled his nostrils despite the gust of cold air pouring through the side window.

'Could they be more of Maguire's men?' Georgie mused aloud, peering over her shoulder again at the oncoming car.

342

'They'd have taken us out by now,' Doyle said with an air of certainty. 'Probably have been sitting there with a fucking rocket-launcher waiting for us.' He glanced into the rear-view mirror, frowning. The Mazda didn't appear to be making any attempt to catch up with them, but was maintaining a steady distance. *Tracking it as well as following* he thought.

The cars were bumping over deep ruts in the ground now, bouncing and skidding every few yards, yet they didn't reduce their speed but roared on through the night, across the field, the occasional shot flying back and forth between the two vehicles.

There was a hedge on the far side of the field. Dolan put his foot down and sent the Orion crashing through.

Doyle followed suit.

So did the Mazda.

The road they found themselves on was wider now and Doyle saw his chance to get up alongside the Orion. He floored the accelerator, slamming into the rear of the escaping vehicle, dropping back immediately. Then he repeated the move, smashing the other tail light of the Orion, smiling to himself as he saw the vehicle skid. He drove up alongside it, twisting the wheel, slamming the Datsun into the other car.

He could actually see Billy Dolan's face, the Irishman yelling at him angrily as the two cars collided once more.

Dolan raised the Ingram and fired.

Doyle hit the brakes a fraction too late and bullets ripped into the side of the Datsun, punching holes in the bodywork. He dropped back then shot the car forward again, coming up on the other side of the Orion, bringing his own sub-gun to bear on the vehicle.

He'd fired half a dozen shots when the hammer slammed down on an empty chamber.

'Shit,' Doyle snarled, tossing the weapon to Georgie. She reloaded it, punched open the sun roof and stood on the passenger seat, her head and shoulders through the top of the car. She took aim and fired, the spent cartridge cases flying back at her, hurled by the wind. Red hot, they singed her skin and she winced.

Both side windows were blown inwards, bullets drilling across the side and roof of the Orion.

Dolan twisted the wheel and sent the vehicle crashing through another hedge into another field.

Georgie dropped back into her seat as Doyle followed, glancing once more at the ever-present Mazda behind.

Doyle felt like telling Georgie to riddle the fucking thing with bullets, just to get it off their tail, but for now his attention remained locked on the fleeing Orion.

The burst of fire which took out his windscreen was lethally accurate.

The glass was blasted inwards as surely as if a maniac with a sledgehammer had been standing on the roof of the Datsun swinging wantonly at the screen. Pieces of glass flew back at Doyle and Georgie, cutting them and causing Doyle to swerve.

Another shot caught him in the fleshy part of the shoulder.

The pain was sudden and unexpected and Doyle felt a dreadful numbness spreading rapidly through his left arm. His hand slipped from the wheel for precious seconds, long enough for him to lose control of the car. It spun round, fish-tailing suddenly. With a feeling of rage and apprehension he realized that it was going into a roll.

It spun viciously, twisting over more than a dozen times, finally ending up on its roof.

The Orion sped off into the night.

The Datsun lay still like some stricken beast, its occupants unmoving.

The Mazda pulled up a few yards behind, headlamps pointed at the upturned car. Slowly both its occupants clambered out and walked towards the Datsun, watching for any sign of movement.

Both men carried guns.

Seventy-Nine

As she stared out of the window, Catherine Roberts' reflection looked back at her, mirrored against the blackness of the night sky.

The plane moved silently through the low clouds, its engine apparently muffled by the darkness which seemed to envelope it like a velvet glove. Every so often it would judder slightly as it passed through an air pocket.

She looked down at the papers and notes spread out on the table in front of her.

In that maze of jottings and jumble of papers lay the answer to the riddle she and Channing and probably hundreds more before them had sought to find.

She had the riddle of the window solved.

Cath glanced at her watch, wondering how much longer it would take to reach Dublin. Once the plane set down she still had to reach Callahan's estate.

He had to know about the window. *Had to know everything.*

She sighed wearily and glanced out of the window again. There was nothing to see but blackness. Cath looked down at her notes, eyes flickering over the scrawled sentences and drawings. There was a page of latin, a sketch of the window with arrows drawn to point out meanings in the different panels.

Callahan would have to see these.

The child sitting in front of her peered over its seat and looked at her again. The man next to her was still smoking, wreathing both of them in a cloud of bluish fumes.

Cath tried to ignore them and concentrate on her notes. She pulled a pad from her bag and began transcribing some of the less legible sentences onto a fresh sheet of paper, aware all the time of the child's gaze upon her.

How much longer before they reached Dublin?

As if in answer to her unspoken question, the voice of the Captain suddenly filtered over the radio and told the passengers they would be landing in approximately thirty minutes.

Cath glanced at her watch.

She had to reach Callahan as quickly as possible.

The child tired of staring at her and slipped down into its seat. Cath continued writing, stopping every now and then to re-read what she'd written, wondering perhaps if there had been some mistake.

Wondering?

Could she have been wrong somewhere along the line? Wrong with her translation of the words? Wrong with her understanding of the window? Wrong, perhaps, in her reading of the stained glass? But the more she looked at the findings before her, the more she re-checked her work, the more certain she was that there had been no errors. Her findings were correct. She had found the secret, of that there was no doubt.

As she looked at her watch she realized she was not *wondering* if she'd made a mistake.

She was *hoping*.

At Dublin Airport she rented a car. The drive, she knew, was not going to be easy, her speed hampered by little knowledge of the roads and also by the need constantly to consult a map.

She felt tired, both because of the lateness of the hour and the incidents of the past week or so. She felt as if all the energy had been drained from her. She had to fight to keep her senses alert, winding down her window to allow cold air to sweep over her face.

Beside her in a briefcase on the passenger seat were her notes. Answers to questions.

Twice she had to stop and consult the map given her by the rental company, pulling into the side of the road and tracing the routes with her index finger, conscious all the time of her own slow progress. If only she could pull into one of the hotels and book a room for the night. Sleep. She could continue with her journey in the morning refreshed. But Cath knew that she could not do that. She had to keep driving, despite the crushing weariness.

She had to reach Callahan, and the window, no matter what.

He had to know.

Cath tried to coax more speed from the car.

She hoped she wasn't too late.

347

Eighty

There were pieces of bone protruding through the pulped flesh.

Mick Black looked down at the savage wound in his left leg and howled in pain again. Blood was still oozing from it, running down to stain his sock. It was matted in the hairs on his leg. On the back seat beside him, still unconscious, was Laura Callahan, her bathrobe dotted with blood. Her own and Black's.

'What the fuck was that bastard firing out of that gun?' Maconnell wondered aloud, looking down at the massive destruction Doyle's shell had wrought on his companion's leg.

Maguire didn't answer.

Black continued to moan softly, his pain intensifying.

'We've got to change cars quick,' said Maguire, glancing over his shoulder. 'If we run into any Garda we've had it.' He looked at Dolan. 'Dump this fucking thing as soon as you can. Find something else.'

The driver nodded, his youthful features sheathed in perspiration. There were flecks of blood on *his* face too from a couple of slight gashes he'd sustained when flying glass had exploded into the car.

'Who the fuck were they?' he wanted to know.

'How do I know?' Maguire said irritably. 'Probably the same ones who were after us in Belfast.'

'We've lost them twice. We might not be so lucky

the third time,' Damien Flynn offered.

'There won't *be* a third time,' snapped Maguire.

Black's teeth were gritted against the waves of agony that racked his body. He had lost a lot of blood. He felt sick. The back window was open and the cool night air washed over him, yet still he felt nausea sweeping through him in unrelenting waves.

'We've got to get him to a doctor, Jim,' said Maconnell, glancing down at Black's wound again. The other man was slumped back in his seat. Even in the darkness his features looked waxen. 'That bullet nearly took his fucking leg off.'

'We'll dump *her* first, then see to Mick,' Maguire said, nodding in the direction of Laura, sprawled unconscious across Flynn's lap. 'I want to get rid of this car.'

They passed a sign that proclaimed:

KINARDE 2 MILES.

'First car we see, we take it,' Maguire continued. The road curved around to the right, flanked on both sides by trees and hedges which looked as if they had been formed from the night itself, so dense and impenetrable were they. About two hundred yards ahead a car was parked in what passed for a lay-by.

'Kill the lights,' said Maguire and Dolan obeyed, cruising up to within ten feet of the stationary Citroen Estate. He pulled up.

The car was in darkness, with no tail lights on, no hazard warning lights. Nothing. Of the driver there was no sign.

Maguire got out of the Orion, sliding the Browning Hi-Power from its shoulder holster, keeping it low by his side as he approached the car. He moved around it, saw that the dashboard was illuminated, tried the door and found that it was open. Movement in the hedge behind him made him spin round.

The man, who Maguire took to be the driver of the car, was still doing up his flies as he emerged from his position behind the hedge. He raised his hands in an attitude of surrender, the colour draining from his face. Despite the fact that he'd just relieved himself, urine suddenly darkened the front of his trousers as he saw the automatic in Maguire's hand.

Maguire fired once.

In the silence of the countryside the sound was thunderous. The 9mm bucked in his fist as he pumped the trigger, the bullet catching the man in the face just below the right eye. The impact propelled him back through the hedge, where his body lay twitching. Maguire stood over him, watching as the last muscular spasms racked the body, then prodded the corpse with his toe and turned back towards the Orion. His companions were already scrambling from it, Maconnell supporting Black, Flynn carrying Laura bodily. Maguire watched as he laid the woman across the back seat and slid in beside her.

Black was burbling incoherently as Maconnell half-dragged, half-walked him to the waiting Citroen.

'I'll take him,' said Maguire. 'You get in the front.' Maconnell nodded and eased his companion towards Maguire who snaked one arm around Black's shoulder, supporting him. 'It'll be ok, Mick,' he said. 'We'll get that leg sorted out.'

Black nodded and groaned, afraid he was going to vomit. The pain from his leg was intolerable.

Maguire looked down at the wound and saw the portions of bone poking through the torn flesh.

'It's bad,' he said, shaking his head.

With that he pressed the Browning to the base of Black's skull and fired once.

Again the sound reverberated in the stillness, the harsh blast mingling with the wet slop of exploding brains as the roof of Black's skull was blown away, the skull resembling a volcano as it spewed blood, fragmented bone and grey matter into the air. Maguire stepped aside, allowing the body to fall into the grass at the roadside, then slipped into the back seat and slammed the door.

'There was nothing we could have done for him,' he said.

Silence greeted the remark.

The reaction was a combination of shock and acceptance. There was a cold logic to it.

Maconnell nodded thoughtfully.

'Let's get out of here, Billy,' said Maguire.

Dolan nodded and started the car, pulling out of the lay-by, leaving the two bodies where they had fallen.

Eighty-One

Doyle heard the soft footfalls drawing closer but lay still.

Next to him in the overturned Datsun, Georgie had her eyes closed. As he swivelled his eyes, he could see a thin ribbon of blood coming from beneath her hair, some of the crimson liquid dripping onto her cheek. There was a dull pain in his left shoulder where the bullet had clipped him and his neck was throbbing.

The ache was beginning to fill his skull. When he tried to draw in a deep breath it felt as if his chest was constricted but there was no pain. He concluded that he had no broken bones.

The footfalls drew nearer, muffled by the grass in the field.

Doyle reached with infinite slowness across his body, allowing his fingers to touch the butt of the .44, ensuring he could reach it if he had to.

Right, you bastard, keep coming.

He allowed the arm to rest across his chest, then lay still again.

A torch was shone into the car.

'Get them out.'

The voice was English.

He heard hands scrabbling at the doors, tugging open the buckled panels. Then he felt himself being hauled from the upturned vehicle and pulled onto wet grass, which soaked into his sweatshirt and jeans as he lay on the ground. He could smell petrol, and wondered if the Datsun's fuel tank had been ruptured in the spin.

'Is she alive?'

The same voice.

'Yes, she's just dazed.'

The second voice was English too.

Doyle smelled tobacco smoke, felt himself being pulled upright, pushed back against the car.

'Doyle.'

The sound of his own name surprised him. Startled him into opening his eyes.

'Doyle,' the man said again, shaking him slightly.

The counter-terrorist blinked myopically, exaggerating the extent of his confusion.

He didn't recognise the man who stood before him glaring into his eyes.

A hand crashed against his cheek.

'Come on, snap out of it,' the first man hissed, shaking him again.

Doyle groaned and allowed his head to drop forward onto his chest. The man gripped his chin and raised it so that he was staring into his face again.

'Where did Maguire and his men go?' the man asked.

What the fuck was going on here?

They knew Doyle's name, they knew who he was chasing.

Garda? No, the voices were English. And they were in plain clothes.

'Come on, you bastard, wake up. Talk to me.'

Doyle was slapped again.

He gazed at the man blankly, satisfied that his pretence was working.

'Where's Maguire?' the man insisted angrily.

Doyle was pushed back harder against the car, the man bringing his face closer. The smell of cigarettes was strong on his breath.

'Talk,' rasped the man.

Doyle opened his eyes wide and, for a fleeting second, the man who held him realized that the counter-terrorist was vividly conscious.

Doyle drove his head forward with terrific force, the snake-like speed catching the man unawares. There was a harsh crack as his nose was broken. Blood burst from the shattered appendage and now it was Doyle's turn to grab him. He butted him again, this time letting his body fall as he reeled from the impact, sprawling on the grass. Doyle reached for the Bulldog and pulled it from the holster, aiming it at his fallen foe. The man tried to rise but Doyle drove a foot hard into his crutch. The man doubled up in agony and lay writhing on the grass, clutching his throbbing genitals.

The counter-terrorist spun round to see that the second man was approaching him from the other side of the car. He held Georgie in front of him. Doyle could see that she was conscious but still groggy.

'Drop the gun, Doyle,' the second man said, pointing his own Beretta automatic at the younger man.

'Fuck you,' Doyle hissed, steadying himself. He raised the pistol until the barrel of the .44 was aimed at the man's head.

'Drop it or I'll kill the girl,' the man said as Doyle took a step towards him.

'So kill her,' Doyle said flatly, thumbing back the hammer.

'I mean it,' the man snarled, pressing the barrel of the Beretta against Georgie's cheek, pulling her in front of him as a shield. 'I'll shoot her.'

'Let go and drop your own gun,' Doyle told him. 'Or I'll fire. You've got three seconds.'

'You'll hit her not me,' the man said defiantly.

'Do you know what I've got in here?' Doyle said, indicating the .44. 'Glaser safety slugs. They'll put a hole in a brick wall at fifty feet. I'll shoot straight through her. And you *know* I will.'

The man swallowed hard, lowered the Beretta a fraction.

'Two seconds,' Doyle reminded him. 'Let her go.'

The man pushed Georgie away from him, dropped the Beretta and raised his hands in a gesture of surrender. Doyle walked across to him and looked into his face. Then, with one swift movement, he struck him with the butt of the pistol. The blow split his bottom lip and loosened two of his front teeth. He dropped to his knees.

'Who are you?' he demanded, the .44 pressed against the man's head.

The man raised one hand to his torn lip, seeing the blood on his fingers.

'Fuck you,' he hissed, the words emerging with a slight whistle through the gap in his teeth.

'Suit yourself. You're wasting my time.'

His finger tightened on the trigger.

Eighty-Two

'Wait.'

Doyle heard the voice but didn't turn. He kept the Bulldog pressed against the man's skull.

Georgie rubbed her head and exhaled deeply, joining her companion, looking down at the helpless figure who knelt before them in what looked like an attitude of supplication.

'I recognise him,' she said.

Doyle frowned.

'That night in Belfast, when we were followed? He's the one who followed *me*. Remember, I said I went through his pockets but there was no I.D.'

Doyle eased the hammer forward on the .44, gripped the front of the man's shirt and dragged him to his feet.

'Who the fuck *are* you?' he snarled.

Georgie turned to see that the first man was rising

painfully to his feet, one hand clutching his throbbing testicles, the other dabbing at his broken nose. She pulled the .357 from its holster, wiped blood from her eyes with the back of her hand and fixed the man in the sights.

'Stay where you are,' she told him.

'I'm getting sick of this game,' Doyle said through clenched teeth, lifting the man higher until it seemed he would propel him into the air. 'I'm going to ask once more who you are, then I'm going to blow your fucking head off.'

'Tell him,' called the first man, forced to breathe through his mouth as blood clogged his nostrils.

'We're British agents,' said the man Doyle held.

'Bullshit,' he snarled

'It's true,' the other man said. 'Donaldson and Westley sent us.'

Doyle released his grip on the man, pushing him back a few paces. If the news was a shock it didn't register on the counter-terrorist's face. His features still bore the stamp of rage.

'And you've been following us since we arrived in Belfast?' said Georgie, the revelation catching her somewhat by surprise too. 'Why didn't you contact us? Why the cloak and dagger stuff?'

'We had orders not to,' said the second man.

'This doesn't make sense,' Georgie mused aloud.

'What *were* your orders?' Doyle wanted to know.

'To tail you, keep a watch and observe until you tracked down Maguire,' the first man told him.

'And then what?'

'We were to take over.'

Doyle nodded.

'Let us do the dirty work, let us risk our fucking necks, then stroll in and take all the glory. Why?'

'Westley and Donaldson didn't trust you to bring Maguire in alive. They were frightened you'd kill him.'

'We had to get to him first anyway,' said the second man. 'There are a unit of Provisional IRA men on his tail, too. They've got orders to kill him and his men. We have to reach him before *they* do.'

'Popular bloke, isn't he?' said Doyle cryptically. He kept the gun aimed at the second man.

'You said you were supposed to "take over" once Maguire had been found,' Georgie interjected. 'What were *we* supposed to do? Just stand aside and let you bring him in? What if we hadn't co-operated?'

Neither of the men spoke.

'You had orders to kill us,' Doyle said, the words coming out as a statement rather than a question. 'Didn't you?'

Still no answer.

'Didn't you?' he roared, raising the gun so that it was level with the second man's head again.

He nodded.

'Yes. Orders from Westley. He wanted you dead. Both of you.'

'I can't say I blame him,' snarled the first man.

'So who are you? Your names?' Georgie wanted to know.

'Rivers,' said the first man.

'Todd,' the second added.

'Why?' Doyle asked. 'Why did Westley want us killed?'

Neither Rivers or Todd spoke.

Doyle raised the pistol and advanced a pace.

'He wanted to protect ...'

357

'Shut up,' Rivers bellowed, noticing the fear on his companion's face.

'To protect who?' Doyle insisted, his back still to Rivers, the Bulldog still aimed at Todd's head. 'Who, you bastard? Tell me or I swear to Christ I'll kill you.'

'Don't tell him anything,' shouted Rivers.

Doyle spun round and, in one fluid movement, raised the Charter Arms .44 and fired off one shot. It hit Rivers squarely in the chest, the thunderous retort of the pistol drowning out his shout of pained surprise as the slug exploded inside him, the impact throwing him several feet backwards. He hit the ground with a thud, blood spreading rapidly around him. His body twitched once then was still.

'Jesus,' gasped Todd as Doyle rounded on him again.

'Talk, you fucker,' he hissed. 'Tell me what you know. Everything. Who was Westley trying to protect?'

'All right, I'll tell you,' Todd said, his face now sheathed in perspiration.

Doyle motioned him towards the Mazda and glanced at Georgie.

'Are you ok to drive?' he asked her.

She nodded.

'Get in the back,' he snapped at Todd, who obeyed. Doyle clambered in beside him, the Bulldog pressed into the other man's groin. Georgie started the engine, flicking on the headlamps. They illuminated the body of Rivers.

'Where to?' she asked.

Doyle glanced at his watch.

11.22 p.m.

'Get us to a phone,' he said flatly.

Eighty-Three

Peter Todd shifted uncomfortably in the back seat of the Mazda. Every time he moved he felt the barrel of the .44 pressed harder against his groin. Doyle's stare was unwavering.

Todd had read files on the man and had spoken to others who'd worked with him. It had frightened but not altogether surprised him when the younger man had shot Rivers. He was as unpredictable as he was dangerous. What was more he seemed to enjoy what he did. Todd had guessed early on that there was no room for heroics where Doyle was concerned; with the gun probing against his testicles, he certainly didn't intend being obstructive. To hell with Donaldson and Westley. *They* weren't the ones close to a .44 calibre vasectomy.

'I told you earlier I'm sick of bloody games,' said Doyle. 'I'm going to ask you questions and I'm going to ask you once. Tell me what I want to know, got it? Otherwise you'll wish it was *you* I'd shot, not Rivers.'

'I told you I'd talk,' Todd reminded the counter-terrorist.

Doyle re-adjusted his position on the seat, wincing at the dull ache spreading from his shoulder wound.

'Why did Donaldson and Westley send you to tail us?' he began.

'I told you, they didn't want you to kill Maguire.'

'So when did you intend "*stepping in*" to take over?'

'After you'd tracked him down.' Todd swallowed hard. 'That was when we were supposed to kill you both.'

'You said that Westley was trying to protect someone. Who?'

Todd licked his lips, aware that they were dry.

'His name is David Callahan.'

Even Doyle looked surprised.

'What the hell has *he* got to do with all this?' he asked quietly.

'You know him?'

Doyle nodded.

'Callahan *was*, still is, a gun runner,' said Todd. 'Westley knew him, knew where he lived and that he was still trading. He sold guns to the IRA, among others. When the plans for the Stormont summit were first put forward he realized that he'd be losing a sizeable chunk of his income. With peace in Northern Ireland the IRA would have no need of weapons; he'd lose a lot of money.'

'What has this got to do with Westley and Donaldson?' Doyle wanted to know.

'They were in partnership with Callahan.'

'They knew he was selling arms to the IRA?' Georgie interjected.

'They supplied him with some of them to sell,' Todd told her. 'They've been in business with him for a very long time. They've been making money out of the troubles for years and they don't want it to stop. Callahan paid Maguire a million pounds and supplied him with weapons. There was supposed to be a campaign in England, too, but *you* broke that up when you raided that house in Hammersmith.'

Doyle nodded at the recollection.

'Maguire got out of hand,' Todd continued. 'He

360

exceeded his orders. That's when Westley and Donaldson called *you* in. They knew you'd be able to find him but they didn't want you getting to him in case you found out about the conspiracy, found out that they were involved.'

'Then why didn't they just leave us alone? If they were so sure we were going to kill Maguire they shouldn't have had anything to worry about.'

'Westley wanted you dead, anyway.'

Doyle smiled.

'Isn't it great to be wanted?' he said cryptically.

'Westley and Donaldson were going to say that you two had been killed in a shoot-out with Maguire and his men, after Rivers and I had shot you.' His voice dropped to a whisper.

Doyle glared at his captive.

'What was Callahan getting out of this, apart from money?' the counter-terrorist wanted to know.

'Immunity from extradition. As long as the fighting went on in Northern Ireland, as long as there was no peace settlement, it meant that diplomatic relations between Britain and Ireland were still rocky. If there'd been a settlement then criminals from the Republic would lose their protection. Callahan thought the British police were after him.'

'Why was Laura Callahan kidnapped?' Doyle said. 'That couldn't have been part of the plan.'

'It wasn't. When Westley and Donaldson saw how powerful Maguire was becoming they decided to slow him down. Callahan was supposed to sell them a batch of weapons, deliver them to a place near Bective Abbey in Meath.'

'That's where those two Garda officers were shot,' said Georgie.

'The weapons were faulty, but Maguire had already paid for them.'

'That's why Laura was taken, then?' Georgie offered. 'Revenge?'

'If it's a kidnapping, Maguire's going to have to get in touch with Callahan,' Doyle said. 'Turn the car round, head back to Callahan's place.'

'It'll be swarming with police after what happened,' she protested.

'Just do it,' Doyle snapped. 'Besides, I'd like a word with Mr Callahan when I see him.'

'No one knew they were going to snatch his wife,' Todd added.

Georgie turned the car and headed back the way they'd come.

'You said there were a bunch of Provos after Maguire, too,' Doyle remembered.

'They want him dead.'

'They're not the only ones,' the younger man said, running a hand through his hair. He spotted a phone box up ahead and told Georgie to pull in. Jabbing the gun into Todd's stomach he forced him out of the car, pushing him towards the phone box. Once inside he fumbled for change, fed it into the phone and dialled. And waited.

It rang and rang.

'Yes,' a sleepy voice finally said.

Doyle held the receiver tightly in his fist.

'Who's there?' the voice asked.

'Westley, did I wake you?' said the counter-terrorist, his face expressionless.

'Who the hell is this?'

'It's Doyle.'

Silence.

'I know everything. About you and Donaldson, about Callahan. About the conspiracy. One of your dogs told me.' He shoved the receiver into Todd's face, pressing the .44 against his head with the other hand. 'Say hello.'

'He *does* know,' Todd blurted. 'I ...'

Doyle pulled the receiver away from him.

'I just thought you'd like to know that when I've finished with Maguire I'm coming for you, you cunt.' Doyle slammed the receiver down. He shoved Todd out of the box. The agent began walking back towards the car. 'Wait,' Doyle told him. 'Is there anything else I should know?'

'I've told you everything, I swear,' Todd insisted, a note of fear in his voice.

'Everything?' Doyle repeated.

'I swear it.'

Doyle shot him twice, the massive impact of the bullets blasting holes in him large enough for a man to get two fists into. The counter-terrorist walked back to the car and slid into the passenger seat, holstering the Bulldog.

'Why did you kill him?' Georgie wanted to know. 'He told you what you wanted to know.'

Doyle dabbed at his injured shoulder and winced slightly.

'That's right,' he said. 'He had nothing more to tell me. I didn't need him any more. Come on, let's go, I want to talk to Callahan.'

'Are you going to kill *him*, too?' she wanted to know.

Doyle continued looking straight ahead.

'Eventually.'

Eighty-Four

'Drive on.'

Doyle spotted the Garda car parked at the entrance to Callahan's estate, and two uniformed men standing beside it. They glanced impassively at the Mazda as it passed, Georgie swinging it around a corner out of sight.

'Keep going,' Doyle told her.

'I told you it'd be swarming with police,' she said.

'We've still got to get inside,' he murmured, stroking his chin and glancing at the high stone wall which rimmed the estate grounds. About two hundred yards further on he told her to pull up. She stopped the car and switched off the engine.

'And if we do get in? What then?' Georgie wanted to know.

'Come on,' Doyle said, clambering out of the car. He crossed to the wall and stood beside it, locking his fingers together to form a stirrup into which Georgie put one foot. Doyle steadied himself then lifted, giving her the added momentum to reach the top of the wall. She got a grip and held on, looking down at him.

'Are the grounds clear?' he wanted to know.

Georgie looked around. It was difficult to see in the blackness. Trees grew thickly over most of the estate. They would mask their approach.

'It looks safe,' she told him. 'How the hell are you going to climb this bloody wall with an injured shoulder?'

Doyle didn't answer. He took a couple of paces back then ran at the wall, launching himself and hooking his fingers onto the stonework. He gritted his teeth and pulled himself up inch by inch until he reached the top. Georgie grabbed one of his legs to aid him in the final surge. He lay panting for a moment, massaging the wound. It had started bleeding again. Georgie pushed a handkerchief towards him and he stuffed it inside his sweatshirt, pressing it against the wound.

'The bullet went straight through,' he told her. 'It would have been worse if it'd chipped the bone.'

They sat on the wall for a moment, contemplating the drop. Perhaps twelve feet, Doyle thought.

He went first, landing well, rolling over in the damp grass, cursing when he caught his shoulder on a fallen tree stump. He straightened up and urged Georgie to join him. She too jumped and Doyle helped her to her feet, brushing a dead leaf from her hair.

'You ok?' he asked quietly.

She smiled at him and nodded.

They set off towards the house.

The driver of the lorry saw the Garda car blocking the entrance to the estate and slowed down. Behind him, the driver of the Mercedes saw his brake lights flare and followed suit.

Callahan stuck his head out of the rear window to see what was happening. He saw the Garda officer approach the lorry and talk to the driver.

'Officer,' the Englishman called. The uniformed man made his way over to the Mercedes. 'What's happening?'

'Are you Mr David Callahan?' the man asked.

The Englishman nodded.

The officer began explaining what had happened as best he could, using as much tact as he could muster. Well, he thought, how can you *delicately* tell a man that his house has been shot up and his wife kidnapped? Callahan demanded to be let through. The car blocking the way reversed and the Mercedes and truck passed onto the estate, the car speeding past the larger vehicle as Callahan urged the driver to hurry.

From the trees Georgie heard the sound of roaring engines and squinted through the gloom to see headlamps piercing the night. She nudged Doyle and pointed to the speeding car.

'I think Mr Callahan is home,' he said softly, a slight smile on his face. 'I hope he's still in the mood for entertaining.' They pressed on, close to the house now but still hidden from its approaches by the trees.

They saw the Mercedes pull up outside the main door. Callahan leapt from the vehicle and ran inside.

He slowed his pace as he passed the bullet-riddled entryway, his heart thudding hard against his ribs. In the hall there were more bullet holes. There was blood on the carpet, pieces of shattered porcelain and blasted brick. Motes of dust still swirled in the air from portions of plaster blown away from the walls and ceiling. Callahan rushed upstairs, his passage halted halfway by the appearance of a Garda sergeant. The man was broad, his hands like ham-hocks. He carried a radio in one of them.

'Where's my wife?' Callahan demanded, his face pale.

'We don't know that yet, sir,' said the sergeant, still descending.

'Who took her?'

'We don't know that, either. We spoke to your

366

servants but they didn't see much; they were too frightened. I can't say I blame them. We've got them in town now, in a hotel. They didn't want to stay here. If I were you I'd leave, too. Just for tonight. Give us time to go over the place ...'

'I'm staying,' Callahan said, interrupting the man. 'I want you and your men out of here now.'

The sergeant opened his mouth to say something but Callahan raised a hand to stop him. 'Just leave me, please,' he said wearily. The sergeant nodded reluctantly and wandered downstairs, talking into his radio. Other Garda men emerged from other rooms below and waited in the hall.

'We've been ordered to keep up a guard on the house, sir,' he called from the bottom of the stairs. 'If you need anything my men will be nearby.'

Callahan nodded and watched as they filed out, closing the bullet-riddled front door behind them. The house suddenly seemed very quiet. He gripped the banister and looked over into the hall.

At the blood stain on the carpet.

He walked into their bedroom, where some of Laura's clothes were draped over the back of a chair. Callahan picked up her blouse and held it to his face, inhaling her scent. He closed his eyes, his teeth gritted. He murmured her name and replaced the blouse gently. Crossing to the drinks cabinet in the bedroom he poured himself a large whiskey and downed it in one. The liquid burned his stomach. He sucked in a deep breath, eyes closed again, hand tightening around the glass. Suddenly, with a shout of rage and frustration, he threw the glass across the room. It hit the far wall and shattered, crystal spraying in all directions.

'Not part of the plan, was it?'

The voice startled him. He spun round to see Doyle standing in the bedroom doorway, Georgie close behind him.

Callahan could see blood on the counter-terrorist's shoulder. He took a step towards the bedside cabinet.

If he could reach the .38 in there, perhaps take them by surprise ...

'You shouldn't have double-crossed your Irish friend,' said Doyle, a smile on his lips. 'This wasn't part of the deal, was it?'

'How did you get in?' Callahan asked, edging closer to the cabinet.

'I told you we'd be back,' Doyle said flatly, glancing across at the cabinet. 'If you've got a gun in there,' he nodded towards it, 'I'd forget about trying to get hold of it.' He pulled the .44 free of its holster and pointed it at the millionaire.

Callahan shrugged and sat down on the edge of the bed, head bowed.

'How do you know?' he asked wearily.

'That's not important. What does matter is that we *do* know. Everything. Your involvement with Maguire, with Westley and Donaldson. The pay-off to the IRA. About the only thing we don't know is what time you have a shit in the mornings.'

'We were here when Maguire took your wife,' Georgie told him.

'Did they hurt her?'

'I don't know, but they seemed pretty keen on hurting *us*.'

'Help me,' Callahan said. 'Help me get her back. I'll pay you as much as you want. You know I've got money.'

Doyle shook his head.

'I don't think Maguire would be very happy to hear you trying to make a deal with us, Callahan.' He glared at the millionaire. 'Besides, not everyone can be bought.'

'So there is some morality inside you, is there, Doyle?' the millionaire said, smiling bitterly.

'I couldn't give a fuck if they slice up your old lady and send her back piece by piece. I want Maguire for my own reasons and I'm going to get him. If you want your wife back you might be able to help.'

It was then that the phone rang.

Once. Twice. Three times.

Callahan looked at it dumbly, then picked it up.

'Hello,' he said, his throat dry.

'Callahan.'

He recognised the voice immediately, jabbed a button and switched the call to speaker-phone.

James Maguire's voice filled the room.

'We have your wife, Callahan. Think about it. I'll call back in an hour.'

And he hung up.

Eighty-Five

She slowed the car down when she saw the Garda vehicles parked across the entrance to Callahan's estate. As Catherine Roberts drew closer one of the uniformed men approached the car and signalled for her to wind down the window.

He asked for some I.D.

She produced a driving licence which he pored over like a valuable antique, looking at her occasionally as if the name on the licence was suddenly going to transform itself into a photo to verify the truth of her identity. Handing the licence back he asked why she was at Callahan's place.

'I've got some business with Mr Callahan,' she said. 'He *is* expecting me.'

The officer wanted to know what kind of business.

'I work for him,' she said, glancing around furtively. *Did Callahan always have this kind of security?*

He told her she couldn't go through.

'It's important,' she insisted. 'I have to see Mr Callahan. If you let him know I'm here …'

The officer cut her short, telling her that the estate was sealed off, no one was to enter.

'Please just call him, let him know I'm here. He'll see me, I'm telling you.'

The officer looked at her for a moment, then pulled the two-way from his belt and flicked a switch. Catherine watched and listened as he contacted one of his colleagues. He gave the other man her name and waited. He told Catherine she would have to wait while the officer inside the grounds checked with Callahan himself.

Another officer wandered over and asked her to open her boot.

'What for?' she demanded.

Security check, she was informed.

Reluctantly she got out of the car and did as she was instructed, waiting impatiently as the Garda officer rummaged around inside. Satisfied that there was nothing offensive he slammed the lid down and wandered around to the front of the car.

'What now?' she said irritably. 'Do you want to check under the bonnet too?'

He did.

'For Christ's sake,' Catherine snapped. 'What's going on here? Just let me through, will you?'

Neither of the Garda officers spoke. The one at the front of the car merely stood waiting for Cath to release the bonnet. Then he began peering inside that, too, shining his torch over the engine.

'Does Mr Callahan know I'm here yet?' she asked angrily.

The officer could only shrug.

She continued to wait.

Georgie dabbed gently at the last smears of congealed blood around the wound in Doyle's shoulder and dropped the cotton wool into the sink.

He had been lucky. The bullet had passed straight through without damaging either bone or nerves. It ached, and the area around the wound stung like hell, but apart from that he had little discomfort. The hole, large enough to push the tip of an index finger into, was already beginning to close up. Georgie pressed a gauze pad to it and began bandaging, her eyes drawn again to the maze of scars on Doyle's torso. He caught sight of her looking in the mirror but said nothing.

'Do you think they'll kill her?' asked Georgie, continuing with the bandaging. 'Laura Callahan? Do you think Maguire will kill her?'

'I wouldn't doubt it,' Doyle answered. 'But not yet. If they'd wanted her dead they'd have shot her when they first broke in here. Maguire wants something, that's obvious.' The counter-terrorist glanced at his watch.

'Another twenty minutes before he rings back. *If* he keeps his word.'

Georgie finished bandaging the wound and tied a neat bow in the dressing. Doyle reached for his sweatshirt.

As he did so, Callahan walked into the bathroom. He saw the patchwork of scars on the other man's body and winced. Doyle caught his reaction in the mirror but ignored it, slipping his sweatshirt back on.

'Keep out of the way,' Callahan told them. 'There's a policeman at the door. I don't think the Garda would appreciate it if they knew you were in here.'

'What does he want?' Doyle asked.

'He says there's someone to see me. I've been expecting her.'

'Do they know that Maguire phoned here?' asked Doyle.

Callahan shook his head.

'Not yet.'

'Don't tell them.'

'They might be able to get her back,' snapped Callahan, 'which is more than you're doing.'

'Ok, tell them. But if you do, I can guarantee your wife will be dead within the hour. The Garda will go thumping all over the countryside looking for her. If Maguire thinks you notified them he'll kill her.'

'How can you be sure he won't kill her anyway?'

'I can't,' said Doyle flatly.

'Who's the woman who's come to see you?' Georgie enquired.

'She's doing some work for me,' Callahan said sharply. 'Now, like I said, keep out of the way until I tell you it's clear.'

Doyle watched as the millionaire left, then touched

his bandaged shoulder lightly, satisfied with the dressing. He looked at Georgie and smiled.

For a second she thought she saw some warmth in the gesture but it quickly faded.

She could go up to the house.

The first officer told Cath that she had been cleared. She muttered something under her breath, started the engine and drove through the gates to the estate, past the two vehicles parked on either side.

The long driveway was rutted in places and the car bumped unceremoniously over it. When she finally came within sight of the house she had time to be impressed by its size and appearance before she brought her car to a halt. There was another Garda car parked about a hundred yards to her right, the men inside watching her as she walked across to the front door of the building and knocked. She was slightly perturbed by the bullet-holes in the wood.

The door was opened a moment later by Callahan, who ushered her in.

Pleasantries were exchanged briefly, then he led her through into the sitting-room and poured them both a drink.

'I have the window here,' he said. 'It's in a room in the West Wing.' He sipped his drink. 'You can begin work on it as soon as you like.'

'I don't need to,' she said. 'I didn't come here to continue work. I came here to warn you about the window.'

Callahan frowned.

'There is a treasure connected with it,' she told him. 'But the treasure is guarded.'

Callahan looked vague.

373

'What are you talking about?' he said irritably.

'Do you remember the figure on the window, the large figure in the centre of it?'

He nodded.

'*That* is the guardian: a demon called Baron. Gilles de Rais worshipped it. That's why he had the window constructed in the first place, to honour it and to thank it for giving him the secret he wanted so badly. I worked out that the panels of the window hold that secret.'

'Do you know how to release it?' Callahan demanded.

Cath looked at him incredulously.

'This creature, this force, whatever you want to call it, would be unstoppable if it was released now.'

'What is the secret that it guards?'

'Immortality,' she said flatly.

Eighty-Six

The silence seemed interminable.

Callahan stood in the centre of the room looking towards one window while Cath stared at him. It was as if neither wanted to disturb the stillness. Finally Callahan spoke.

'Are you trying to tell me this creature can materialize?' he asked softly.

Cath nodded.

'The guardian will be released if a sacrifice is made,' she told him. 'The death of someone will release it. De

Rais used children.' She got to her feet. 'Mr Callahan, I never thought I'd say this but you must destroy that window.'

He laughed.

'Destroy it? I have no wish to destroy it.'

'If Baron *is* released, you can't hope to control him.'

'He will give the secret to whoever summons him, correct?'

'Yes, but –'

'Correct?'

'I told you, there has to be a sacrifice.'

He looked at his watch.

Maguire would be ringing in a few minutes with news about Laura.

Laura.

Callahan looked at the phone, willing it to ring.

They would kill Laura.

'Destroy that window,' Cath said forcefully.

Ring, you bastard.

'If you don't I will,' she threatened.

'You stay away from it,' snarled Callahan. 'I thought you wanted to know its secrets as much as I did.'

'I did, until I found out what they were.'

'You were obsessed with the window. Don't tell me you wouldn't want to witness the materialization of that creature; don't tell me you wouldn't want to learn from it,' he hissed. 'You've been to far more elaborate lengths than I have to protect it. You were the one who covered up a murder, not me.'

Cath glared at him.

'That was before I knew the truth,' she snarled. 'If I'd known then I'd have *helped* Channing destroy it.'

'But I told you, it *can't* be destroyed. It mustn't be.'

375

'So who are you going to kill? I told you there has to be a sacrifice.'

'*I'm* not going to kill anyone,' he said quietly.

Cath looked puzzled.

It was then that the phone rang.

Callahan looked at it for long moments, then took a step towards it.

Upstairs Doyle and Georgie looked at the phone by the bedside.

It rang. And rang.

'What the hell is he doing?' muttered Doyle.

Callahan finally picked up the receiver and pressed it to his ear.

'Yes. Who is it?' he said.

'You know fucking well who it is,' Maguire hissed. 'You've had an hour to think about it, to wonder what we're doing to her. Or what we *will* do to her. Now listen to me.'

Upstairs, Doyle carefully switched the phone to speaker. He and Georgie listened intently to the conversation, Georgie picking out not just the words that were exchanged but also the sounds in the background. She could hear a low rumbling growing steadily louder.

'I want one million pounds,' said Maguire. 'Paid within twenty-four hours. No interference from the law. I'll call you again to tell you where to leave the money.'

'I can't get hold of that sort of money in twenty-four hours,' said Callahan.

'Bollocks,' snapped Maguire. 'One million or I swear I'll cut her fucking head off myself and send it back to you.'

Callahan didn't answer.

'You shouldn't have crossed me, Callahan,' the Irishman snarled.

Georgie could here the rumbling in the background growing louder. It built to a crescendo then faded slowly away again.

'Twenty-four hours,' Maguire repeated, then slammed the phone down.

'What's going on?' asked Cath, bemused.

'The IRA have my wife,' he said quietly.

'Oh God, I'm sorry,' she said.

Callahan smiled thinly.

'It'll be all right,' he said. 'After all, sacrifices have to be made.' The smile broadened into a grin.

She understood.

'No,' Cath murmured, shaking her head. 'You can't do it.'

'For years my wife and I have searched for the ultimate thrill. The realization of that dream is here now; do you think my wife would deprive me of it?'

'You're going to let them kill her,' Cath said, her voice a low whisper.

'It seems I have no choice. I can't get a million pounds together in the time they've given me.' He looked at her for a moment. 'There's nothing I can do.'

'You're insane,' she said, her voice catching.

'Insane to want knowledge? Insane to want a secret men have dreamt about since the beginning of time? Insane to want immortality?' He shook his head. 'I'd be insane *not* to want it.' He gripped her arm. 'Now come and show me what the window means.' He smiled. 'I need to know.'

Eighty-Seven

She could see nothing. The piece of tape across her eyes ensured that.

She couldn't speak because of the rolled-up length of cloth they had stuffed into her mouth, secured by a tightly-knotted cord which cut into the soft flesh of her neck. Her lip still throbbed where it had been split.

All Laura Callahan's senses could take in was the babble of voices close by, the smell of damp and the bare boards of the floor on which she sat, some of them mildewed. She jerked as she felt something scuttle across her bound hands. In the blindness of her captivity she imagined all kinds of things, all manner of noxious creatures crawling over her skin. Spiders. Cockroaches. Ants. She wanted to scream, then to ask them to remove the tape, to loosen the bonds cutting into her wrists. But she could not ask, could not beg, could not implore because of the gag which filled her mouth. It tasted stale, like an unwashed handkerchief; she realized with revulsion that was what it probably was. The thought caused her stomach to contract, and for a second she feared she would vomit. But would they remove the gag then or leave her to drown in her own puke? She had heard them threaten her with death and had no doubt they would carry out the threat if they were not given what they wanted. She felt like crying, but her fear prevented even that release of emotion.

She heard footsteps crossing the room towards her. Heavy footfalls which echoed on the bare boards. With her eyes covered she was able to pick out sounds much more clearly, just as she had done earlier with the train when it had passed by, its low rumble shaking the room. Now the footsteps came closer and she was aware of someone close to her. She could smell cigarette-tainted breath on her.

The tape which covered her eyes was torn away with one tug. The pain was startling. Portions of her eyebrows and some of her eyelashes were ripped away with the sticky covering. Again she wanted to scream, but again the gag prevented her.

A face leered into her own, hard-featured, cold-eyed.

The man's face was impassive.

'Take a look,' he said, holding the back of her head and ensuring she could see every detail of his features. 'If your husband doesn't pay what we asked for, I'll be the one who'll kill you,' Maguire said tonelessly. 'You probably didn't know much about his business, did you? Probably didn't know he sold us a batch of duff guns, did you?'

She tried to shake her head.

'Well, because of his stupidity, you could probably die,' the Irishman continued. 'I just hope he has more compassion than he has common sense.' He released her hair and stood up, motioning for Dolan to come over across and join him. As the younger man sauntered over, that ever-present grin on his lips, Laura looked around the room. It was about twelve feet long, perhaps ten feet across. There was a sink at one end and a small two-burner stove. A kettle stood on it now, steaming. She saw another man pouring the contents of the kettle into a tea pot. She could still not make out what the place was. There was a door to her left, firmly closed. She wondered if there were more men inside. She heard another rumbling sound. It approached quickly and passed.

A train. Just like before.

'Watch her,' said Maguire and wandered down to the far end of the room.

Dolan smiled down at her, his eyes fixed on the gap in her house-coat. He could see most of her left breast. His smile broadened. He leant forward, pulling the house-coat open a little more until both her breasts were visible. Then he cupped one in his right hand, feeling the warmth of the plump orb.

'Get your fucking hands off her.'

Maguire's voice lanced across the small room.

Dolan released his grip and stepped back, his grin fading rapidly.

'What do you think this is? A game?'

'Sorry, Jim,' the younger man murmured. 'But what the hell? She'll be dead soon.' The smile started to return.

'So will you if you don't keep away from her,' Maguire said. 'Now just watch her.'

Dolan nodded.

When he looked at Laura again, she was crying.

He knew it was nearly over now.

The hunt had taken them from Belfast deep into the Republic but they had never once lost the trail of their quarry and now they were closing in.

They had heard that there were two British agents on Maguire's tail too. To hell with them. They would die too if they got in the way. This was a personal thing

380

and it always had been. Outsiders had no place in it, just as they had no place in the country.

The car moved swiftly through the darkened country lanes, its four occupants sitting silently, three of them checking weapons. Pistols, rifles and sub-machine guns. They had used stealth to track down their opponents but now the time for cunning was over. Force was the next step. Pure, unbridled, unstoppable force. Force which would see the destruction of Maguire and his men and anyone else who got in the way.

The hunt was nearly over. The killing was about to begin.

Simon Peters and the other three men in the Provisional IRA unit rode in silence. There was no feeling of excitement or anticipation, merely the knowledge that they had a job to do.

And they intended completing it, no matter who got in the way.

Eighty-Eight

The room had been specially prepared for the window.

To the rear of the house it was about thirty feet long, and half that in width. Cath wondered if, at some time, it might have been a sitting room. Every stick of furniture had been removed, the carpets taken up and the floor covered with tarpaulin. There were marks on the walls, slight discolorations where pictures and paintings had once hung.

The window itself was in the centre of the room, propped up on three large and sturdy trestles about three feet high. There was a small work bench beside it. Callahan had certainly been thorough, thought Cath, as she walked into the room, the millionaire still holding onto her arm but with less force now.

In the glow of the overhead lights the window seemed to be lit by some inner radiance, its colours more vivid than she had ever seen them. Together they walked across to it, Callahan smiling down at the artefact as if he were greeting a long lost friend.

'It's magnificent,' he said quietly, a note of awe in his voice.

Cath's eyes flickered over details here and there. The heads of the children. The figures held in the taloned hands of Baron. And Baron himself. Those glass eyes seemed to bore into her, the deep red hue still reminding her of boiling blood.

'I want to know about it,' said Callahan. 'Everything.' He walked slowly around it, glancing up at Cath. 'Everything *you* know. I want you to tell me. What do the words mean?'

'Is it really important?' she snapped. 'I told you the secret of the window. I warned you of its danger.'

'You were willing to risk that danger, otherwise you wouldn't have kept working on it,' he told her. 'And don't tell me you're not as intrigued as I am to see the materialisation of this ... demon or whatever the hell it is.' He stood by the head of Baron, the red light from the eyes shining upwards, lighting his face with a hellish crimson glow. 'You're as obsessed with finding the truth as I am.'

'Not if it involves someone dying, I'm not,' she countered.

382

'Mark Channing died; that didn't stop you working, did it? That didn't sting your morals to the point where you abandoned the project.'

She heard the scorn in his voice and knew she had no defence.

'But I told you, Callahan, if this creature, this force does materialise, then there's no way of knowing what form it will take. Or, more to the point, how powerful it will be. It could destroy you, you and anyone else it comes across.'

'I'm willing to take that chance,' he said flatly, looking down at the multi-hued panels.

'What's this?'

Doyle's voice cut across the room and Callahan looked up to see him standing in the doorway, Georgie close by him.

Callahan smiled and performed the introductions with the calm formality of a cocktail party host.

'We heard the call from Maguire,' said Doyle. 'When are you going to pay?'

'I'm not,' Callahan said.

'He'll kill her. You should know him well enough by now to realize he's not fucking about. If you don't come up with that money your wife is dead meat.'

Callahan merely shrugged.

'What the fuck is wrong with you?' snapped Doyle. 'They're going to kill her, don't you understand that?'

'You must save her,' Cath interjected.

'Shut up,' snapped Callahan.

'Why is it so important to *you*?' Doyle wanted to know.

'It's not just me,' she told him. 'If Mrs Callahan is killed then her death will release the guardian of this window.'

383

Doyle smiled thinly.

'Guardian?' he said. 'What is this shit?'

'Something you'd never understand, Doyle,' Callahan told him. 'Something beyond your grasp, beyond your intellect.'

'Fuck you. Just tell me what this window has to do with what's going on here.'

'You're used to dealing with weapons, Doyle,' Callahan said. 'We both are. Look on this window as the ultimate weapon. It contains a power, a force unlike anything created by man.'

'You've been watching too many bad horror films, Callahan. You're talking like a fucking mad doctor. I'm not interested in all this voodoo bullshit or whatever the fuck it is.'

'Then leave,' said Callahan. 'Go now.'

'You must find Mrs Callahan,' Cath said. 'Save her. If she dies …' She allowed the sentence to trail off.

'I'm getting sick of these games,' Doyle rasped. 'And I'm sick of you, Callahan. Start making sense.'

'What kind of force?' Georgie asked.

'Don't *you* start,' Doyle snapped irritably. 'I've got enough with fucking Boris Karloff here.' He nodded in Callahan's direction. 'You want her back, we'll get her back, but I can't guarantee she'll be alive.'

'She *has* to be,' snapped Cath.

'The sounds in the background when the phone calls were made,' said Georgie. 'It sounded like trains. Are there any stations near here?'

'There's a signal box,' said Doyle. 'About twelve miles East, close to the village. The IRA used to keep arms or money there. I tracked a couple of their men to it about five years ago.'

Georgie spun round, heading for the door.

384

'Stop there,' shouted Callahan.

He had pulled the .38 from his belt and now had it aimed at Georgie.

'Go,' Doyle urged her.

'I'll kill you all,' Callahan said, raising the pistol so that it was level with her head.

'The place is surrounded with Garda,' Doyle reminded him. 'One shot and they'd be in here quicker than flies round a fresh turd. You're fucked, Callahan. Give it up.'

'Take off your guns, both of you,' the millionaire said. 'Do it.' He watched as first Georgie then Doyle pulled off their holsters and laid them on the floor, the weapons still inside. 'Now move. Slowly. You too.' He motioned for Cath to follow them.

He forced them out into another narrow corridor and along towards a room further up, close to the hallway. One by one they filed in, then Callahan locked the door behind them.

The room was a study, the walls lined with books. There were just two windows, both small, both high up on the walls.

'You must get out,' Cath said. 'You must save her.'

'I'm going to kill that bastard when I get out of here,' snarled Doyle, punching the wood of the door.

'Didn't you hear what I said?' Cath shouted angrily.

'Look, we've got a job to do,' Doyle told her. 'You take care of your *demons*,' he emphasised the word with scorn. 'I'll take care of Callahan and the fucking IRA.'

'You don't understand, do you?' she said wearily.

Somewhere in the house a phone rang.

Callahan picked it up.

'Time's up,' James Maguire said. 'Here's how we want the money.'

'Fuck you, Maguire,' said Callahan.

'You really are a stupid man, aren't you? You think I won't kill her?'

'So kill her,' Callahan told him and slammed down the phone.

He smiled thinly, looking at the telephone as if waiting for it to ring again. Finally he swept it from the table, allowing it to smash on the floor.

He headed for the cellar.

Eighty-Nine

James Maguire slammed the phone down and stalked across the room to where Laura Callahan lay, still bound and gagged. He dropped to one knee, easing the Browning from its holster and pressing it against her face.

'Do you know what he said?' snarled Maguire, watched by his companions. He tore away the cord that held Laura's gag in place, allowing her to spit it out. She coughed.

'Do you know what your fucking old man said?' the IRA man snarled at her. 'He said he won't pay the ransom. He told me to kill you.'

She shook her head, tears of fear and bewilderment now filling her eyes.

'Why won't he pay?' Dolan demanded.

'How the fuck do I know?' rasped Maguire.

'Let me speak to him,' Laura implored, trying to twist her head away from the barrel of the pistol pressed tight against her neck.

'I'm sick of talking and I'm sick of your fucking husband,' Maguire snarled. 'First he fucks us up with that batch of guns and now this.'

'Kill *him*, not her,' Dolan said half-heartedly.

Maguire glared at him.

'I'm going to kill him, Billy, you can bet your life on that. But I said I'd kill her too if he didn't pay up, and that's just what I'm going to do.'

'Killing *her* won't solve anything. Let's get to Callahan now, make that bastard pay.'

Maguire smiled.

'Just because you've touched her doesn't mean you can have her, Billy,' he sneered.

'Let me speak to my husband,' Laura interjected. 'I can persuade him to pay you.'

'I don't want his fucking money now. I just want his life,' Maguire said quietly.

'If you're going to do it then get on with it, for God's sake,' shouted Damien Flynn. 'Shoot her.'

'No,' Billy Dolan interrupted. 'Leave her. It's Callahan we want.'

'You're going soft, Billy,' said Maguire, standing up. He took a pace backwards, thumbing back the hammer on the automatic.

Laura tried to scream but her throat and mouth were dry.

She could only shake her head as Maguire levelled the pistol. His finger tightened around the trigger.

'There's someone outside.'

The shout came from beyond the closed door, from Paul Maconnell.

For interminable seconds Maguire stood still, the Browning aimed at Laura's head, then he eased the hammer forward and re-holstered the gun, heading for the other door. As he reached it he turned to Dolan.

'You keep away from her,' he snapped. Then he passed through into what had once been the signalman's box. The levers which had once controlled the tracks were still there, now covered in a layer of dust and cobwebs. The huge glass front of the building offered a clear view over the flat countryside beyond. To the right there was a clump of trees. To the left the ground was flat and overgrown.

'I saw someone there,' said Maconnell, indicating the trees.

'Garda?' Maguire wanted to know.

Maconnell shook his head.

'No uniforms,' he said.

To the right another figure moved through the tall grass, appearing momentarily before disappearing once again like a spectre.

Maguire frowned.

Who the hell were they?

In the sub-cellar of the house David Callahan moved swiftly around the stacks of boxes, pulling out the weapons he required.

A Spas Automatic shotgun and some shells which he stuffed into his pocket.

An Ingram M-10 sub-machine gun. He selected half a dozen magazines to go with the weapon, each holding thirty-two rounds.

Callahan smiled to himself. He made his way back upstairs, straining under the weight of the weapons. He carried them to the top of the stairs and ensured that each one was loaded. From the landing he could cover all possible entrances to the hall. There was only one way to reach him and that was up the stairs.

He pushed cartridges into the magazines, thumbed bullets into the .38 and jammed it in his belt.

He was ready at last for the time he had known for so long was coming.

They were all in position.

The signal box was covered. There was no way out.

Simon Peters gripped the Uzi sub-machine gun tightly in his hand and glanced at his watch. Two hours before dawn. When this was over he would watch the sun rise.

Peters gave the order for his men to attack.

Ninety

Doyle took a firm grip on the bookcase and pulled, stepping aside as it crashed to the floor, spilling its contents everywhere. With help from Georgie and Cath he pushed it upright once more, so that it was close to one of the small windows in the study.

Georgie began to climb, using the shelves as rungs, until she finally reached the top and the window. Steadying herself, she kicked out at it, smashing the glass.

'Can you get through?' Doyle asked.

She knocked away some jagged shards which surrounded the frame, trying to work out if the gap was large enough for her to crawl through. She decided that it was.

'Take this,' said Doyle, pulling the .38 from the holster on his ankle. He handed it up to Georgie.

'They're hollow tips in there. They'll stop most things that get in your way.' He even managed a thin smile.

'What about you?' she asked. 'Callahan's armed.'

'I'll worry about Callahan. Just get a move on. Get to his wife,' he told her.

'My car is parked at the front of the house,' Cath told her. Georgie opened her fist, looking down at the keys to the BMW.

'If any of those bloody Garda try to stop you, shoot them,' Doyle said flatly.

He and Cath watched as Georgie gripped the side of the window-frame, wriggling through. The night air greeted her, cold on her face. There was a drop of about six feet to the ground. Looking round, she could see no signs of movement and reasoned that the room must be at the side of the house. Her problems would come when she got round to the front, but for now her only concern was to get out.

She hauled herself the last few inches, realizing that she was going to fall headfirst onto the ground. She was grateful that the house was flanked by lawns. Georgie gritted her teeth and dropped.

Even though the grass provided a relatively safe surface to land on, the impact still knocked the wind from her and she rolled over, groaning under her breath, feeling a sharp pain in one shoulder. She hauled herself upright and, pressing her back to the wall, made for the front of the house. Much to her dismay, it was brightly lit.

Two Garda cars were parked about one hundred yards from the building. She could see their occupants quite clearly.

Catherine Roberts' car was closer. Perhaps twenty yards.

A short sprint.

She gripped the keys in one hand and the .38 in the other, her eyes constantly scanning the front of the house. She watched as one of the Garda officers clambered out of his vehicle, looked around and hurried off towards a tall bush to relieve himself.

Ducking low, Georgie scuttled towards the BMW.

She reached it unseen, pushed the key into the lock and eased the door open, sliding behind the steering wheel. She put the key in the ignition and twisted it.

The engine burst into life first time and she stuck it in gear, reversing, swinging the car around so that it was facing the two Garda cars.

She stepped on the accelerator and the car shot forward, gravel flying up behind it. The BMW sped past the other two cars before their drivers could even start their engines. She saw them fading away behind her in the rear-view mirror. The needle of the speedometer touched sixty as she sped down the long driveway, not flicking on her headlamps until she saw the gates.

There were two cars parked across the exit, nose to nose.

Georgie gripped the steering wheel tighter, hunched over it and floored the accelerator.

She saw men struggling out of the cars as she bore down on them.

There was an almighty crash as she smashed through the makeshift barrier. The jolt slammed her back in her seat but she kept her foot down, only easing up as she reached the road, slamming on the brake to prevent the car hurtling into the ditch on the far side. She twisted the wheel, trying to keep the wheels on the tarmac. They screamed as they tried to retain a hold, smoke rising from the back pair. For one terrible second she thought she was going to turn over but the car held and she drove on.

No one followed.

Twelve miles to the signal box.

She pressed down on the gas again.

'I've got to destroy that window,' Catherine Roberts said.

'We've got to get out of here first,' Doyle reminded her. He glanced at her a moment. 'You really believe that shit about the window? This force, or power, whatever you call it?'

'It exists, Mr Doyle. It has done for hundreds, perhaps thousands of years.'

'Then what makes you think *you* can stop it?' he asked.

She had no answer.

Ninety-One

The first prolonged burst of fire from the Uzi blasted in the glass front of the signal box.

Shards flew into the room and bullets tore into the walls, some ricocheting wildly, screaming off the wood and concrete.

The attacker could only be seen by the blinding muzzle-flash which came from the weapon as he fired.

Maguire and Maconnell threw themselves down as the bullets shattered the windows and parted the air above them. Then Maguire, keeping low, headed for the other room, the Browning already free of its holster.

'What the fuck is happening?' snapped Damien Flynn as the staccato rattle of automatic fire filled the night.

'Someone's trying to kill us,' snarled Maguire. 'Cover that door,' he told Flynn, jabbing a finger. Flynn opened it a fraction, and immediately a hail of bullets shredded the wood, one of them catching him in the thigh. He fell to the floor clutching at the wound, relieved to see that the blood flow was relatively small. The bullet had missed his femoral artery. He cursed, recovered his own Skorpion machine-pistol and fired off several short bursts in the direction of the muzzle-flash. Spent cartridge cases flew into the air and soon the room was thick with the stench of cordite.

'Help Paul,' Maguire said, pushing Dolan towards the other room. The younger man hesitated a moment, then scuttled through to join his companion who was blasting back at the attackers with an MP5. Smoke was drifting in noxious clouds across the bullet-blasted windows.

'How many are there?' asked Dolan, forced to raise his voice to make himself heard above the incessant chatter of weapons.

Maconnell had no idea. It seemed as if there were hundreds out there. More bullets spattered the room, one catching him in the left forearm, shattering the ulna. The crack of the breaking bone was audible even above the rattle of fire. He fell back, a portion of the bone poking through the flesh. Gripping the sub-gun in one hand he stood up and fired a sustained burst, hoping to hit the one who had shot him, his anger overriding his common sense. He kept his finger tight on the trigger, the weapon bouncing in his grip as the savage recoil slammed it back against the heel of his hand. Wreathed in smoke, his face lit by the muzzle-flash, he looked like a creature from a nightmare. Then the hammer struck an empty chamber.

In that split second a bullet caught him in the right eye.

It drilled the socket empty, lifting him off his feet, smashing the sphenoid bone and erupting from the back of his head with a huge portion of pulverized cranium. Blood, brain and bone splattered the far wall as Maconnell went down, crashing into the wall, his face a bloody ruin, crimson gushing from the yawning hole where his eye had been. A dark stain spread rapidly across the front of his trousers as his bladder released its load and Dolan smelt the pungent odour of excrement. A soft spurt as the sphincter muscle gave out.

He scrabbled towards Maconnell, not attempting to touch the body. Why search for signs of life? Most of the poor fucker's head was plastered over the wall. Dolan grabbed the MP5 and slammed a fresh magazine into it, then crawled over to the shattered window, knelt up and began firing short bursts into the trees.

A dark shape moved and he fired at it, gratified to see it stumble and remain still. He fired at it again, a longer burst this time, rewarded by a cry of pain.

In the other room Maguire pulled Laura Callahan to her feet and pressed the gun to the side of her cheek, leaving a grease mark on her soft skin.

'Who are they?' he demanded. 'Are they from your husband?'

394

'I don't know,' she whimpered. 'Believe me. I swear to you, I don't know who they are.'

Maguire nodded slowly.

'You know something?' he said softly. 'I *do* believe you.'

And he shot her in the face.

Even Doyle felt it.

Inside Callahan's house it was as if the air had suddenly been charged with electricity. He felt the hairs on the back of his neck rise.

Catherine Roberts groaned and fell against the wall, one hand pressed to her head, her eyes closed.

Doyle spun round and saw her, aware that the air seemed to be cooling. He felt goose-pimples rising on his flesh. It was as if someone had sucked all the warmth from his body.

'What's wrong?' he asked Cath, snaking an arm around her waist to support her.

At first she mumbled, her eyes still closed, but then she blinked hard, as if she were emerging from a deep sleep. She looked directly at Doyle and he saw the fear flicker behind her eyes. She tried to suck in a deep breath but the chill in the room seared her throat as she inhaled.

'It's started,' she murmured.

Luke McCormick was dead. As he bent over his colleague, Simon Peters had no doubt of that fact. The other man was lying on his stomach, several large bullet holes in his back. One shot had caught him in the nape of the neck. That was the one which had killed him.

Peters scuttled across to the trees where Eamon Rice

crouched, the Uzi gripped tightly in his hands. He was peering up at the signal box, watching the occasional muzzle-flashes from inside.

'We've got to get inside,' said Peters. 'Where's Joe?'

'Round by the stairs,' said Rice, nodding towards the building.

Peters nodded.

'Give me two minutes, then open up on the window. Just keep firing. They've no way of knowing how many of us there are. It'll give Joe and myself a chance to get through that door.'

'Two minutes,' Rice repeated, checking his watch.

Peters disappeared into the darkness once again.

Georgie could hear the stutter of sub-machine guns, the crack of pistols and rifles. Their sounds carried far on the stillness of the early morning.

She tried to coax more speed from the car, praying that she wasn't too late.

As she drew closer the gunfire filled her ears more insistently.

She reached almost unconsciously to touch the butt of her .357.

The signal box was less than half a mile away now.

The gunfire continued.

Ninety-Two

The room was getting colder.

The chill was intensifying.

'We have to get out,' Cath said, her face as white as

milk. 'I must get to that window and destroy it. There has to be a way.'

Doyle glanced at the door which barred their way to freedom. He crossed to it, tugged on the handle, took a step backwards and kicked hard against the white panelled barrier. The wood creaked but held firm, even when he kicked again. And again.

He paused for a moment, perspiration beading on his forehead despite the growing cold. Then he directed his fury at the door handle itself, kicking furiously at it, cursing when it wouldn't give. There was a large glass paper-weight on the desk to his left. He snatched it up, pulled off his sweatshirt and wrapped the weight in it.

Cath winced as she saw the patchwork of scars on his torso, but Doyle did not see her look of distaste; he was more concerned with the door. He gripped the paper weight in both hands and brought it down on the handle with incredible ferocity. He maintained his hammer blows, the muscles in his arms and shoulders throbbing, the veins standing out.

'Come on, come on,' he snarled, driving the weight down with ever greater strength.

The handle started to come away from the wood.

Encouraged by his success Doyle struck again, his face set in an attitude of determination. He was oblivious to all around him as he battered away at the door.

His own frantic banging masked the sound of movement on the other side of the door.

One last blow.

The handle came free. The door opened a fraction. Doyle grinned crookedly and tossed the paperweight to one side, pulling his sweatshirt back on. He pulled open the door and dashed out.

He had to reach the room with the window, had to retrieve the .44 Bulldog.

Had to find Callahan.

Callahan was standing in the doorway of the room opposite, the Spas automatic shotgun levelled and ready.

Doyle saw it. Saw the yawning barrel.

Callahan fired once.

The discharge was massive, blasting a hole almost twelve inches across in the door as Doyle threw himself frantically to one side.

Callahan emerged from the room, working the slide, firing again.

The second shot blasted away some plaster from a wall above Doyle's head.

The counter-terrorist knew he hadn't much time. Eventually Callahan would get lucky and one of the massive blasts would strike him. He hurled himself at a door opposite and found to his relief that it was open. He crashed into it, rolling still, into the room beyond.

In the study behind him Cath pressed herself against the wall, praying that Callahan would not step in. It seemed he was more preoccupied with killing Doyle.

If she could find some way out ...

Doyle ran towards the window, leaping at the glass.

He met it as Callahan stepped inside, firing off two more blasts in quick succession.

One struck the window at the same instant as Doyle.

There was a deafening explosion of shattering glass as the counter-terrorist smashed through, pieces of the crystal cutting him as he landed heavily on the grass outside. He felt a searing pain in his left calf and realized that some of the shot from the Spas had hit him. As he stood up he saw blood on his jeans and a ragged hole in the material, but he gritted his teeth and scuttled along towards the window of the room at the rear of the house.

Where his gun lay.

Cath heard the shattering glass, heard the retorts of the shotgun and realized that Callahan must be pursuing Doyle.

She stepped out into the corridor.

Callahan moved back, swinging round to face her. For interminable seconds she froze.

Callahan was smiling.

Even when he fired.

The discharge hit her squarely in the chest, staving in her sternum, tearing through her lungs before portions of the lethal shot erupted from her back. She was lifted into the air by the impact and thrown several feet down the corridor as blood sprayed out from both entry and exit wounds. She landed heavily, dead even as she slumped against the wall, spilling her life fluid onto the carpet.

Callahan ran to her and looked down into her blank eyes. He stepped over the body and headed for the hall as he heard banging on the front door.

Someone shouted his name.

He heard the door being forced and scuttled up the stairs, picking up the Ingram, pulling back the slide to cock it. Then he stood at the foot of the stairs and waited.

The door burst inwards and two Garda officers careered into the hall.

Callahan cut them down with two bursts from the sub-gun. Outside he saw a third man turn and run back towards his car. The millionaire fired again, the weapon bucking in his hand, cartridge cases spraying from it. His burst was accurate. The Garda officer was hit in the back, pitching forward onto the gravel drive, where he lay still.

Doyle heard the shots too, but he paused for only a second before using a stone to smash his way into the room where the window lay. It was not, however, the ancient artefact which interested the counter terrorist, but the Charter Arms Bulldog that lay close to it. He snatched up the weapon, smiling as he felt its weight in his fist. He flipped open the cylinder and smiled as he saw that the chambers were full.

Glancing down at his injured leg he gritted his teeth.

'Now, Callahan,' he hissed under his breath, 'it's Party time.'

The Garda sergeant had seen his men shot down. The sight had shaken him badly but he snatched up his radio and flicked it on.

'I need reinforcements, quick,' he barked into the two-way. 'The Callahan house. Tell them to bring guns.'

Ninety-Three

Ten seconds.

Eamon Rice checked the second hand on his watch, counting off the moments, steadying himself.

Eight seconds.

He checked that he had enough spare clips of ammunition.

Six seconds.

The firing from inside the signal box had all but ceased now; there was just the odd single shot every now and then. Both sides, it seemed, were waiting.

Four seconds.

He raised himself up slightly, ready to fire.

Three.

He hoped that Hagen and Peters were in position.

Two. One.

He opened up, bullets drilling a path across the front of the signal box, blasting in yet more pieces of glass that had somehow stayed untouched.

On the other side of the box Simon Peters made a dash for the bottom of the wooden stairs which led up to the first level. He could see the shape behind the door; he swung the Uzi up and fired off a long burst. Bullets struck the door and the frame.

He heard a scream from inside, knew that the man who'd been guarding the door had been hit.

He motioned Hagen forward and the other man scuttled up the steps, pausing at the top, the MP5 levelled at the door.

Inside, James Maguire stood looking down at the body of Damien Flynn. Two bullets had penetrated his chest and the third had punched a hole in his throat, shattering his larynx. There was surprisingly little blood. Flynn lay on his back, his eyes still open, flecks of dust settling on the blank orbs. Maguire gripped his own pistol in one hand, the Skorpion machine pistol in the other. He waited.

'Come on, you bastards,' he shouted, raising his voice to make himself heard above the chatter of sub-gun fire behind him. Billy Dolan fell into the room, his face sheathed in sweat, the sub-gun empty in his hand.

'They're moving in, Jim,' he gasped.

Maguire didn't answer; he had his eyes fixed on the door.

It burst open.

There was a deafening explosion of fire as bullets from automatic weapons tore back and forth in the small room. Cartridge cases clattered onto the floor, the smell of cordite filled the air and a reeking bluish-grey haze of fumes billowed upwards as the firing continued.

Dolan was hit in the chest and shoulder.

Maguire took one in the stomach but remained upright, oblivious to the pain spreading through his lower body. Blood ran down his shirt and the front of his trousers.

As Hagen crashed through the door the bullet from a 9mm pistol hit him in the cheek, ripped through and exited on the other side, carrying several teeth with it. He went down firing, raking the inside of the signal box, putting two more shots into Dolan. One of which caved in the left side of his head.

Simon Peters was hit in the leg, his knee shattered by the impact. He fell forward, his finger still on the trigger. He saw bullets strike Maguire in the chest and upper arm, saw him stagger back as another smashed his right collar-bone. Blood was gushing from the wounds. He felt his own lung collapse as a bullet pierced it, erupting from his back with pink gobbets of lung tissue. It was as if someone had applied a very tight tourniquet to his chest. He found it difficult to breathe.

Dolan was lying on his side, twitching madly, a purple foam dribbling over his lips as more bullets hit him. He finally rolled onto his back, slops of brain spilling from the massive holes in his skull.

Maguire managed to move into the other room, trailing blood and urine behind him. He could scarcely breathe and it felt as if his upper body was on fire, but he slammed a fresh magazine into the Skorpian and waited. Framed against the blown-out windows of the signal box, his silhouette quite visible, he didn't even see Eamon Rice drawing a bead on him.

'Come on, Peters,' he gasped, waiting for his foe. 'We'll fucking go together.' He chuckled, blood spilling over his lips.

Rice opened up.

Half a dozen bullets from the burst hit Maguire, catapulting him across the room and slamming him into the far wall, where he seemed to remain standing for long moments before sliding down leaving a huge crimson smear.

The Skorpion was still in his hand.

Peters dragged himself into the other room, past the bodies of Laura Callahan and Billy Dolan. He saw Maguire lying there and nodded slowly.

Behind him Hagen coughed, his mouth hanging open slackly, blood from his punctured cheeks and shattered jaw running in a steady torrent from his mouth. Peters tried to suck in a breath and felt cold air hiss through the lung wound. He winced and clapped one hand to it, gritting his teeth against the pain, raising himself up with great difficulty. He looked down at the corpse of his adversary, then back at Laura. Peters shook his head and dug the toe of his shoe into Maguire.

'Animal,' he murmured, then closed his eyes as a wave of pain swept through him. For a second he thought he was going to collapse but the feeling passed. He turned to look at Hagen.

403

He was unconscious.

'Eamon,' Peters called, the effort making him wince. 'It's finished.'

Outside, Eamon Rice lowered the Uzi and took a step forward.

All he heard was the click of a hammer being pulled back as a gun was pressed to the back of his head.

'Drop the gun,' Georgie told him.

He did as he was told.

'Who the fuck are you?' Rice asked, puzzled that the voice was not only English but also female.

'British agent,' she told him. 'Was that Maguire and his men in there?'

'It *was*,' said Rice.

'Go on,' Georgie snapped, pushing him before her. He led the way to the stairs and ascended slowly, the agent behind him.

'Company, Simon,' he called as they reached the door.

Georgie pushed him inside and looked in at the carnage. She saw Laura Callahan immediately, her face blasted away by the close range discharge which had ended her life.

'We knew you were coming,' said Peters quietly.

'Who killed the woman?' Georgie asked.

'She was dead when we got here,' wheezed Peters. 'You wanted Maguire, didn't you?'

She nodded.

He smiled thinly, a ribbon of blood running from the corner of his mouth.

'It was none of your business.' he told her. 'Never was. We take care of our own.'

'So I see,' she said quietly.

'It's over,' Peters told her.

Georgie looked at the wounded IRA man, at the bodies.

At Laura Callahan.

Over? As she ran back to her car she had but one thought.

She had the most terrible feeling it had barely started.

Thirty of them.

All armed with AR-180 Sterling semi-automatic rifles.

Ten in each van.

The Garda men were briefed as they drew closer to David Callahan's house.

No one was to enter. No one was to leave. Several armed and dangerous suspects were believed to be inside the house. If they couldn't be taken alive they were to be shot dead.

Ninety-Four

The room looked as though it were full of smoke. Great thick bands of it swirled around the window, writhing along the ground like ethereal tendrils, poking beneath the door and reaching towards the window, stirred by the breeze that swept into the room.

Yet through that grey mist there was a radiance, a glow which seemed to build in intensity until the window itself shone. The room was dark; the glass of the window might have been sucking in the light, digesting it like some living thing then disgorging its feast in the form of brilliant-coloured hues.

The trestles that held it in place creaked and groaned, as if the weight of the window had suddenly become too much for them. The wood bowed and split, threatened to collapse.

And still the greyish-white vapour poured out of the very glass itself.

The colours grew more vivid within the heart of the cloud.

A low rumble began, growing in volume.

A chill so intense it left frost on the walls shivered through the entire house.

Then came another sound.

Like that of cracking glass.

Doyle moved from room to room, the .44 held before him, his ears and eyes alert for the slightest sound or movement.

Just step out in front of me, you fucker.

He reached the door which led through to the hallway.

Lying up against it, a gaping hole in her chest, was Catherine Roberts. Doyle gritted his teeth and looked around quickly, checking that Callahan wasn't skulking in either of the rooms to his left or right. Satisfied that it was safe he knelt beside Cath, resisting the temptation to feel for a pulse. The Spas had been lethally effective. The portions of her lungs and spine that still stuck to the wall testified to that fact.

He moved closer to the door, peering through a crack up towards the landing.

There was no sign of Callahan.

Just because you can't see him doesn't mean he's not there.

406

The counter-terrorist opened the door a fraction, his thumb on the hammer of the Bulldog, ready to cock it. With a fourteen-pound pull on the double-action trigger he couldn't risk the massive recoil, couldn't risk missing Callahan.

He might only get one chance.

Still, he comforted himself, one was all he'd need. If he hit Callahan with one of the Glaser safety slugs there was no fear of him getting up.

He edged forward a little, ducking low, seeing that he had a distance of about twenty feet to cross before he reached the door on the opposite side of the hallway.

As he looked across he saw the bodies of the two Garda officers leaking blood onto the expensive carpet.

Why the fuck had Callahan killed them, too?

Doyle shuddered involuntarily, aware of the biting cold now. He had to cross the hall, had to search the rest of the house in order to find Callahan. But the place was huge. It could take an age.

Unless he finds you first.

Doyle glanced up at the landing again and down at his own injured leg. The wound was throbbing but it didn't hamper his movement. He sucked in a deep breath and pushed the door a little more.

Come on, you can't stand here till daylight.

He ran as fast as his injured leg would allow across the hall, hurdling one of the dead Garda officers.

No shots were fired.

There was no sign of Callahan.

Doyle pushed open the door and stepped back, waiting for the blast of gunfire; it never came. The corridor beyond was in darkness. How many rooms lay hidden in that darkness he could only guess at.

Only one way to find out.

He pressed on, aware now that the cold was becoming almost unbearable.

Callahan had watched the counter-terrorist rush across the hall.

He'd had him in the sights of the HK33 the entire time. How tempting it would have been to have pulled the trigger, but a moving target was always more difficult and Doyle was a dangerous man. A head shot would have been preferable but difficult. Better to let him pass. He waited a moment, then picked up the assault rifle and began to make his way down the stairs, slowly and cautiously.

When he reached the bottom he raised the rifle to his shoulder and sighted it on the door through which Doyle had disappeared. The counter-terrorist didn't appear and Callahan moved stealthily across the hall.

He smiled to himself.

By the time Doyle found him it would be too late.

Much too late.

He also felt the numbing cold but he, unlike Doyle, welcomed it. He knew what it signified.

Ninety-Five

She guessed she was less than three miles from the house now.

Georgie kept her foot on the accelerator, her eyes fixed on the road. Another few minutes and she would be at Callahan's place again. She felt a shiver run up her spine. What would she find when she returned? She tried to push the thought from her mind, suddenly overcome with a feeling of great sadness as she thought of Laura Callahan lying back there, half her head blown away. Georgie felt a crushing weariness; there suddenly seemed to be a ridiculous futility to everything. To her mission with Doyle; to this whole business. It seemed there was only one way for it to end and that was in death.

She sucked in a deep breath, clutching the wheel more tightly, feeling the .357 in its shoulder holster against her ribs.

How many more deaths before this affair was concluded?

She swung the car round a corner and onto the road which led to the main entrance of Callahan's estate.

As she rounded the corner she saw the large black transit vans parked close to the gates. There were men clambering out of them.

She saw that they carried rifles.

For one fleeting second her thoughts turned to Doyle.

Let him be alive.

The thought passed as quickly as it had come. Her attention was re-focused on the men who climbed from the vans. There were three of them parked outside the entrance, but as she watched two drove on and into the grounds, heading for the house.

What the hell was happening in there?

She had to know.

First she had to get past the riflemen.

The leading van hurtled up the long drive towards David Callahan's house, its occupants sitting quiely in the back, automatic rifles clutched across their laps.

One or two were checking that the magazines were full, the others waited patiently until the vans came to a halt and they were ordered out. The chill night air met them like a cold wall.

It was unnaturally cold, a deep biting crispness that caused the hairs on their flesh to rise.

They were deployed in the bushes around the house, behind the cars. Anywhere that offered adequate cover.

The marksmen waited for orders.

The house was in darkness except for the porch light. It glowed feebly, the dull glow illuminating the body of their dead colleague sprawled on the gravel in front of the building.

When the time came, if necessary, they would storm the house. All they needed now was the order.

They waited.

A door up ahead.

Doyle pressed his back to the wall and moved towards it, treading as softly as he could, his eyes constantly darting to and fro in the blackness. He held the .44 in his right hand and reached for the handle with his left. He turned it and pushed. The door swung open. He ducked low and stepped across the threshold.

The kitchen.

He glanced around but there was no sign of Callahan. No sign that he'd been in here recently, either. Doyle backed out of the room, shivering now from the intense cold. He blew on his hands, transferred the Bulldog to his left hand and rubbed the palm of his right against his thigh in an effort to restore circulation. *Christ, it was cold.* He moved across the corridor to another door, paused and then pushed that one open too.

Again the room beyond was empty, but as Doyle

moved into it he glanced out of the large picture window and saw movement outside. Keeping low, he scuttled across the room towards the window and looked out.

Two Garda officers were taking up firing positions in the shelter of some trees about two hundred yards from the house.

Glancing round he saw more of them, all with rifles trained on the house.

'Shit,' he murmured under his breath and moved away from the window, edging back into the corridor, making his way back towards the hall.

He would have to search for Callahan upstairs. As he paused at the hall door he saw the risks. To ascend that staircase was to invite death. There was no cover, should Callahan be waiting at the top. If he opened fire there was nowhere to hide. And yet how else could he reach the first floor?

Doyle pushed open the door a fraction, peering up at the gloom of the landing. Even if Callahan was up there now he was invisible in the darkness.

Garda outside, Callahan inside.

This was going to be one hell of a fucking party.

Doyle edged out into the hall, not even looking at the dead Garda officers. He moved to the foot of the stairs, the Bulldog held before him in readiness. No sounds from above.

He began to ascend.

Callahan stood mesmerised, the vapour swirling around him. He held the HK-33 at his side, his attention focused on the stained-glass window, on the brilliant radiance that emanated from it. The walls of the room were thick with ice now, layers of it gathering and

411

clinging as the vapour continued to roll across the floor like fog. There was a smell which reminded Callahan of bad meat; like the cold, it was growing more intense.

He took a step towards the window, watching the tendrils of mist snaking upward towards the ceiling, watching the multi-hued effulgence swelling as if it were being pumped up, throbbing like some rainbow-coloured growth.

The crack of breaking glass was like a whiplash in the silence of the room. It made him jump; his heart thudded against his ribs.

Another crack, louder this time.

A portion of the glass seemed to fly upwards, as if from an impact beneath it. But that could not be so; the window was suspended on trestles, there was nothing beneath it. But Callahan watched the piece of glass rise into the air in slow motion, twist in the mist and fall to the ground, where it lay in small fragments.

A series of cracks. Low rumbling.

Callahan's teeth were chattering, so intense was the cold. He kept his eyes fixed on the window, eyes which were bulging not only in wonder and exhilaration but in fear.

Ninety-Six

She saw the two officers waving for her to stop.

Two of the marksmen were close by, rifles held across their chests, ready to swing them up into a firing position if necessary.

Take it easy.

A hundred yards from the main entrance Georgie slowed down. She could feel her own heart beating hard as she drew closer, could hear her own breathing, rapid and harsh.

Drive through them.

She tapped her fingers on the wheel as she guided the car nearer.

Get closer.

Fifty yards now. She had slowed to a crawl but her foot was poised over the gas pedal. It was just a matter of timing. She had to get through. Had to reach the house. The first Garda officer was still motioning for her to slow down, to stop now. Get out of the car.

Twenty yards.

The gap between the vehicles parked across the entrance was just about wide enough.

Georgie gripped the wheel tightly and glanced at the marksmen. The officer called to her to stop the car and get out.

Ten yards.

She sucked in a deep breath and held it, teeth gritted.

She pressed down hard on the accelerator and the car hurtled forward, dirt spinning up behind it. It slammed into the Garda officer, catapulting him into the air. His colleague dived to one side as she sped towards the cars which blocked the entrance to Callahan's estate. She crashed through them, the impact throwing her back in her seat. The BMW skidded but she gained control of the wheel, glancing in the rear-view mirror. She saw three of the marksmen taking aim. Seconds later bullets began to hit the car.

Georgie put her foot down as the first of them blasted off a wing mirror.

The second punched a hole through the rear windscreen, glass showering the back seat. More 7.62mm slugs tore into the fleeing vehicle, one blasting a hole in the dashboard, destroying the speedometer. Another took out part of the windscreen.

Georgie drove faster, anxious to escape the deadly salvo but it continued unabated, bullets striking the car, others ricocheting around it, blasting up small geysers of earth when they struck the ground.

She felt an incredible impact in her back, just below the right scapula. It was as if someone had struck her with a massive red-hot hammer. The contact slammed her forward against the steering wheel. For a second she let go of it, one hand clapped to the huge exit wound in her chest. The bullet had punctured a lung and shattered several ribs before blasting its way out through her right breast. Portions of flesh and slicks of blood spattered the wheel. She gasped in pain.

Another thunderous impact, this time in the small of her back.

She saw dark blood spurting onto the seat, realized that the shot had destroyed part of her liver. Georgie tasted blood in her mouth. It felt as if the lower part of her body was on fire. She gripped the wheel as tightly as she could, foot still pressed down hard on the accelerator. The house was coming into view and so too were the other Garda officers. Red-hot pain filled her body, as if someone had pumped molten metal into her veins. She found it hard to breathe now. Her eyes clouded alarmingly and she blinked hard to clear her vision.

Ahead of her were more men with rifles.

The house was coming up fast.

Blood ran from her wounds, pain filled her body.

Several shots struck the front of the car, one smashing in the radiator grille. Another blew out a headlamp. More smashed the windscreen. Georgie felt one nick her left ear, slicing off the lobe. More blood. She felt it splash her cheek.

She guided the car towards the windows of the sitting-room and clung on, cold air blasting through the remains of the windscreen keeping her conscious, although it was a battle she knew she must lose.

The harsh crack of more rifles filled the air.

She was hit again. In the shoulder. In the chest.

With a despairing wail she let go of the wheel, slumping forward as the car sped towards the house, her foot now jammed on the accelerator.

Her last thought was of Doyle.

Then the car hit the side of the house.

Georgie was flung through the remains of the windscreen, through the window of the sitting-room as the BMW simply folded up against the wall, the metal buckling and bending until the impact ignited the petrol tank. There was a thunderous blast as the car went up in a blinding white ball of flame, the heat sending a rolling blanket fully fifty feet back, making the Garda men shelter momentarily as the wreckage flamed and great clouds of black smoke belched from the ruins. They stood back and watched as the twisted chassis turned white hot beneath the searing flames.

The order came across the radios the Garda carried.

'Prepare to move in.'

Ninety-Seven

Doyle was almost at the top of the stairs when he heard the explosion.

The entire house seemed to rock under the thunderous detonation. Then, from outside, he heard shouts. Orders. He spun round, glancing up at the landing, as anxious now to discover the source of the blast as to find out where Callahan was. He turned and hurried back down the stairs, wincing when he felt pain from his injured leg. He could feel the heat from the fire the car had started. As he entered the corridor it washed over him like a wave. Ahead, one of the doors had been blown open by the explosion. Doyle slowed his pace slightly, gun held before him, then ducked low and peered around the frame into the room.

Flames from the wrecked car were still leaping in through the shattered window and the curtains were ablaze. Thick smoke filled the air.

Georgie was lying on her stomach in the centre of the room, her body twisted into a foetal position, one arm crushed beneath her. Blood had spread in a dark puddle around her.

As Doyle looked at her he could see the bullet wounds in her body and gashes in her face where she had been thrown through the window. Her blonde hair was matted with blood, plastered across her face as if she'd showered in the crimson fluid. Her eyes were closed.

'Oh Christ,' he whispered, moving slowly towards the body. He knelt beside her, touching his hand to her cheek. When he brought it away it was smeared with blood. Her eyelids were open a fraction so Doyle reached forward and gently pushed them shut. Seemingly oblivious to the fire that raged in the room he remained beside her, keeping up his vigil for a moment longer before finally retreating back into the corridor, closing the door behind him. It should contain the fire for a time.

At least until he found Callahan.

He stood with his back to the wall, staring at the door behind which Georgie lay, and felt great weariness. It was as if someone had sucked all the life from him. For the first time in his life he felt not the horror or inevitability of death but the sheer futility of it. Or perhaps it was the futility of *life* that he felt more profoundly.

And if life was futile why prolong it?

He shook himself free of the lethargy and strode down the corridor, intent again on finding Callahan.

The sound of shattering glass came from up ahead.

Doyle quickened his pace until he reached the room, the room where he knew the stained glass window was. The door was still firmly shut. He took a step back and prepared to kick it in. If Callahan was in there waiting for him then so be it.

He drove one foot against the door and it flew back on its hinges, slamming against the wall.

Doyle rushed in, the Bulldog held before him.

Callahan was in the room, but he was not alone.

'Jesus,' muttered Doyle through clenched teeth, his eyes wide with disbelief as he looked at the other occupant of the room.

The creature towered over Callahan, its red eyes burning insanely as it looked around, finally focusing on Doyle, who could only stand as if frozen to the spot, gawping at the monstrous apparition. Conflicting emotions clashed inside his mind. Bewilderment. Disbelief. Fear. Revulsion.

What the fuck was it?

Callahan still had his back to Doyle, looking up at the creature in awe. Had Doyle been able to see the millionaire's face he would have seen the smile on his lips.

'Get away from it,' Doyle shouted, his eyes riveted on the monstrosity. He raised the Bulldog and steadied himself, then squeezed off two shots.

Both struck the creature in the chest, the shells exploding and the glaser slugs opening up inside their target. A thick mixture of blood and pus spewed from the wounds but the creature only swayed slightly as the massive impacts rocked it.

'No,' roared Callahan and spun round, the HK33 levelled at Doyle.

He fired twice.

The first shot missed. The second caught the counter-terrorist in the side. It punctured his torso just above the right hip but, fortunately for him, tore through the fleshy part of his body without damaging any vital organs. The impact, however, sent him spinning, blood running from the wound. He fell to the ground, his eyes still fixed on the creature. Doyle dragged himself to his knees and aimed once more. This time at Callahan.

He fired once.

The .44 calibre shell, moving at a speed in excess of 1,500 feet a second, hit the millionaire in the back. It

418

tore easily through his shoulder blade, opening up immediately, spreading its lethal contents inside as it exploded. Doyle saw the other man lifted off his feet by the shot. He fell at the feet of the creature, which looked down at him and then at Doyle. By this time the counter-terrorist had managed to scramble to his feet and was propped up against the door frame preparing to fire again.

Callahan's body was twitching slightly. He was finished. Doyle had to kill this other fucking monstrosity.

It took a step forward and he fired.

The bullet struck it in the stomach but barely halted it. It bent down and swept Callahan up in one huge clawed hand, dangling him before it as a child might hold a doll. Then it placed its other hand on his face. Doyle saw its mouth open, saw its lips flickering as if it were speaking. Then it gently lowered Callahan to the floor where he lay still, his eyes closed.

The creature backed off towards the stained-glass window, pieces of which now lay all over the floor like glass confetti.

Doyle thumbed back the hammer of the .44 once again and fired.

This shot hit the creature squarely between the eyes and he watched with satisfaction as its face seemed to fold inward, the skull collapsing under the massive impact of the shell. The monstrosity swayed uncertainly for a moment and Doyle fired again. Again into its head. The entire skull seemed to explode, gobbets of yellow and red matter flying about the room as if someone had placed an explosive charge inside the beast's skull. Portions of bone hurtled through the air, propelled by the massive impact of the glaser slugs and also projected by the streams of foul-smelling fluid which erupted from the ruined head.

The creature stood perfectly still for long seconds then fell to the ground.

Doyle saw it falling.

Saw the ground rushing up to meet it.

Saw it hit the floor.

Saw it disappear.

As he looked on in stunned disbelief, the creature vanished. All that remained were the puddles of vomit-like discharge which had been spread around the room.

Doyle shook his head.

That wasn't possible.

He wondered if he'd blacked out momentarily.

The creature couldn't disappear. *Couldn't.*

He stood panting, propped against the wall, blood running from the wound in his side, his eyes still bulging wide, staring at the place where he had seen the creature fall. It had hit the ground beside Callahan's body. Fallen, dying, beside the man who had summoned it. Fallen ...

Callahan sat up.

Doyle shook his head.

This is fucking crazy. I'm fucking crazy.

He watched as Callahan scrambled to his feet, his flailing hands reaching for the HK33. The millionaire turned around, looking at Doyle.

As he opened his eyes, Doyle could see that they now glowed red, like those of the creature.

And he understood.

Callahan raised the HK33 and fired.

Ninety-Eight

The weapon was on automatic now. The salvo raked the walls, blasting chunks of plaster free. Doyle tried to dive to one side but he was too slow. A bullet hit him in the shoulder, shattering his left collar-bone. Another caught him in the chest, punching through his lung before exiting, carrying bloodied pink tissue with it. He was thrown back against the wall by the impact, blood spattering against the stonework. He fell to the side, dragging himself through the doorway and out into the corridor.

He tried to rise, fumbling in his pocket for more slugs, knowing his own pistol was empty. He found some and pushed them into the empty chambers as Callahan advanced.

'Immortality, Doyle,' the millionaire called. 'What greater treasure could there be than that?'

He rounded the door, his red eyes bulging as he looked down on the wounded counter-terrorist.

Doyle fired twice, upwards into Callahan's stomach.

The blasts lifted the other man off his feet, throwing him back several feet, blood jetting from the massive holes blasted in him by the Bulldog bullets.

Doyle scrambled to his feet, breath hissing through his lung wound.

He ran to the end of the corridor and out into the hall, heading for the stairs.

He was half-way up when Callahan came staggering

into view. He swung the assault rifle up to his shoulder and fired off another burst.

Doyle was hit again. In the back of the leg. In the small of the back.

Searing pain filled his body and he cried out as the bullets ripped a path through his flesh and muscle. More blood flowed from the wounds. Doyle felt pain unlike anything he'd experienced before. No. He shook his head. He had felt worse than this. He had felt agony the like of which no man should be forced to endure.

For a moment he thought he was lying on the street in Londonderry again.

Not a bomb blast this time, but several high velocity bullets had destroyed his body.

Had killed him?

He turned on the stairs, raising the .44 again.

Callahan was coming closer.

He was smiling.

Doyle didn't wipe the smile off his face. He blew it off.

One shot from the .44 caught Callahan in the face, powering through his teeth, exploding from the back of his head. Pieces of enamel were driven back into his mouth, carried through the hole in the base of his skull by the massive force of the bullet. He was lifted into the air as if jerked by invisible wire, his body flying like an unwanted puppet before he finally crashed to the ground at the foot of the stairs, smoke rising from his face, or what remained of it.

Doyle peered down at the body through eyes which were clouding over.

Callahan wasn't moving but Doyle had to check. He tried to stand but the effort made him cough, bright red blood spilling over his lips. His legs felt as though they would give way as he dragged himself upright and made his way tortuously down the steps towards the motionless body of his foe.

He kept the Bulldog trained on him the whole time, ready to fire.

Waves of pain so intense he thought they would make him black out swept over him and he had to pause, trying to draw air into lungs holed by bullets. He could feel an enormous pressure on his chest every time he tried to swallow. When he exhaled the air hissed through the torn lungs like punctured bellows.

He drew closer to Callahan.

'Move in'

The order came and the Garda men scurried towards the house, slowing down as they reached the front door.

Those at the rear and sides of the building crashed through windows in their haste to get inside.

Half a dozen of them waited outside the front door, rifles at the ready.

Doyle heard them on the porch but his attention was focused on Callahan.

The millionaire's face was a bloody ruin, his mouth still open, portions of his upper jaw blasted back into his palate.

Doyle stood over him, fighting off unconsciousness, wanting only to lie down. To rest.

To die if necessary.

Callahan grabbed his left leg and pulled him over.

Doyle felt the incredible strength in the grip, felt himself being pitched forward, hurled across the hallway as Callahan rose and turned on him.

423

He was smiling, the remains of his face twisted into a sickening mask.

The front door burst open and the first two Garda men came crashing inside. Doyle watched as they swung their weapons round, bringing them to bear on Callahan, but the millionaire was too quick for them. He cut them down with one burst of the HK33. Then, with incredible agility, he sprinted up the stairs.

Doyle could only watch as he reached the top, turning as the remaining Garda marksmen burst in.

They opened fire simultaneously.

Doyle was deafened by the massive fusillade of fire which seemed to go on for an eternity, the hallway filling with fumes as they pumped more and more bullets into Callahan. Bullets hit him in the chest, legs, stomach, face. One even blasted off his nose. The impact hurled him back against the wall with savage force, then he staggered forward again, crashed into the banister and toppled over it, his body falling the twenty or so feet to the hall where it landed with a sickening thud.

This time he did not move.

'This one's still alive,' shouted one of the Garda officers, crossing to Doyle who had rolled onto his back. 'Get an ambulance, quick.'

What's the rush? Doyle thought. He looked across to where one of the Garda was prodding Callahan's body with the toe of his boot.

Doyle opened his mouth to speak, choking on his own blood but managing to force the words out.

'He's still alive,' he croaked feebly.

The Garda officer shook his head.

'He's alive,' Doyle insisted, his entreaty dissolving into a coughing fit which sent fresh spasms of pain through him. 'Believe me, he's alive. For fuck's sake, I'm telling you, he's alive.'

There was fear in his voice now as his words grew weaker.

'Alive,' he whispered.

Blood spilled over his lips.

'Where's that ambulance?' one of the Garda shouted angrily.

It didn't seem to matter, thought Doyle.

He closed his eyes.

Ninety-Nine

Another twenty minutes and his shift would have been finished. If they'd been twenty minutes later some other poor sod would have had all the work. As it was, Paul Rafferty pulled another of the bodies from the gurney and laid it out carefully on the metal-topped slab. Another policeman.

Where the hell were they all coming from? He'd heard something on the news earlier that morning about a gun battle, but he'd never expected anything like this. He'd seen the victims of road accidents, house fires and those who had succumbed to old age or disease during his time as a morgue attendant in Kinarde hospital, but never anything like this before. No sooner had he laid out one corpse than they brought in another. They must have a bloody conveyor belt out there beyond the green double doors, he thought as he removed the clothes from the policeman, noticing the

425

savage bullet wounds in his torso as he did. All the clothes were put into separate black plastic bags and tagged with the name of the former owner. Rafferty attached the necessary identification tags to the left big toes of each of his new arrivals.

The next was a woman, a blonde woman in her late twenties, he guessed. He also guessed that in life she had been pretty but now, with her body and face disfigured by bullet wounds and lacerations, she was a travesty of her true self. There had been another woman too, older, attractive he thought in life. She had been the one with the shotgun wound in her chest.

He began undressing the blonde woman, administering a swift mental rebuke when he allowed his gaze to dwell a fraction too long on her breasts. One had been pulverized by a bullet, anyway. He pulled the green sheet over her, covering her face, then paused for a cigarette, looking over at the remaining gurneys that stood by the door. He took a couple more drags on his cigarette then wheeled the first of them over to the assigned slab and placed the body on it. He looked at the face, or at least what remained of it. He knew this man, recognised him. Rafferty nodded to himself. It was David Callahan, the Englishman who lived on the large estate not too far from Kinarde.

His body was shredded by bullets; hardly a portion of his body was unpenetrated by rounds. Again Rafferty wondered what had happened. How had so many people come to die so violently? He pulled off Callahan's clothes and dropped them into the bag he'd set aside. Then he folded the dead man's arms across his chest and pulled the sheet up over him, crossing to the last gurney and its occupant.

Behind him, he didn't notice that one of Callahan's

arms had slipped from his chest and now dangled at his side.

Rafferty pushed the last gurney over and performed his task one last time. Then he washed his hands, scrubbing the blood away, watching as it swirled around the plug-hole before disappearing.

As he turned he noticed Callahan's arm dangling.

Muttering to himself Rafferty returned to the corpse and pulled the sheet back, peering into the face for a moment. Then he gripped the arm and folded it back into position.

The fingers flexed slightly.

The temperature must be too high inside the room, he thought. It was a phenomenon that happened whenever the temperature rose above fifty degrees. Heat seeped into the dead pores and appeared to reanimate particular limbs. He remembered how, during his first week in the job, the cooling system had packed up completely. To his absolute horror, one of the corpses he'd been cleaning had sat up. Now he merely smiled and crossed to the thermostat on the wall, easing it down a few degrees.

Behind him on the slab Callahan's fingers twitched again.

Rafferty returned to the body, pressed the arm back across Callahan's chest and pulled up the sheet again.

He glanced at his watch. Where the hell was Riley? His replacement was late. Rafferty wanted to get home. He hoped to Christ that the coming night was quieter.

Behind him the bodies lay on their slabs, each covered by a green plastic sheet.

He could feel the air temperature dropping noticeably. The thermostat was starting to do its work. Rafferty smiled, pleased with his handiwork.

427

When the sheet covering David Callahan moved again he ignored it.

Maybe it needed to go down a few more degrees, he thought. Strange that just the one body should be affected, though. Rafferty shrugged and thought nothing more of it. He picked up his paper and sat down behind his desk, waiting for Riley to arrive.

Again movement. Again from Callahan.

Rafferty continued reading.

One Hundred

They were buried together, as had been specified in their wills.

In the same grave, dug twelve feet into the ground, beneath a huge oak tree in the grounds of the estate.

David and Laura Callahan were lowered into their final resting place watched by only a handful of onlookers. Two or three of their staff and the priest attended as they were placed in the hole that would house them for the rest of eternity.

After the ceremony the onlookers drifted away. They went home. The priest stood by the graveside for a moment composing himself, then he too went. The gravedigger was left alone to fill in the hole, something he did quite happily and with no haste. He had no fear of the dead. He had been in the job too long for that. Besides, what was there to fear from a dead man? He whistled happily as he refilled the hole, finally patting down the top soil before replacing the carefully cut sods. It would take a few weeks for the grass to grow back fully. By the end of the month the only evidence of the grave would be the small marble headstone that bore the names of David and Laura Callahan.

When the man had patted the sods down he stood by the grave and lit a cigarette, leaning against the tree and looking up into the sky. The sun was shining brightly, spreading its warmth over the land. Only beneath the leaves of the oak tree was it still a little cool. Eventually he moved away from the green canopy, glad to feel the sunshine on his skin. He carried his spade over to his van, put the tool in the back and slid behind the steering wheel. He swung the car out onto the long driveway.

Behind him the grave was silent.

A blackbird settled on the freshly-turned earth, snatching up a worm that had been disturbed by the gravedigger. The bird took off with its prize, soaring high into the blue sky.

The grave remained in shadow, untouched by the sun.

EPILOGUE

The Beginning

Darkness.

Darkness and pain.

He was aware of them both at the same time. He tried to sit up but his head connected with the lid of the coffin and he slumped back down again.

David Callahan sucked in a deep breath and tasted stale air.

He tried to reach up, to touch his eyes, to feel the stitches which had sewn them shut, but he could not move in the confines of the casket. He tried to open his mouth but his jaws had been wired together with the same care and attention to detail with which his eyelids had been stitched shut.

And there was the pain.

Excruciating, mind-numbing pain that filled every pore of his body. His now living body.

The secret had been his, still was his. The treasure was his, would always be his.

But he had the pain to go with it.

A pain he could not endure but knew he must endure. A pain he would know forever.

Had he been able to smile he might have done so, smiled at the supreme irony of the situation. He was immortal. He could not die. It didn't matter if the stale air inside the coffin ran out. He would not die. He could not die.

The realization grew on him gradually The understanding that he was twelve feet below earth packed so tightly he could never claw his way through, even if he managed to free himself from the coffin.

The knowledge that no matter how long or hard he screamed no one would ever hear him.

The remembrance that whoever had worked on his body in the funeral parlour had sewn his eyes and mouth shut, had filled in the bullet holes in his body with morticians' wax.

Had sucked out every drop of blood and replaced it with embalming fluid.

That was what caused the excruciating pain.

A pain he must learn to live with because live was exactly what he would continue to do.

The agony seemed to grow upon that realization.

He was immortal.

He had the secret forever.

And he had the rest of eternity to enjoy his agony.

Newport Library and Information Service

LL 23110104

Z367976